TANITH LEE

A TO Z

TANITH LEE A TO Z

Tanith Lee

First published in 2018 by Telos Publishing, 139 Whitstable Road, Canterbury, Kent CT2 8EQ, United Kingdom

Telos Publishing values feedback if you have any comments about this book please email feedback@telos.co.uk

ISBN: 978-1-84583-976-5

British Library Cataloguing in Publication Data. A catalogue record for this book is available from the British Library.

CONTENTS

All the Birds of Hell

1

Once they left the city, the driver started to talk. He went on talking during the two hour journey, almost without pause. His name was Argenty, but the dialogue was all about his wife. She suffered from what had become known as Twilight Sickness. She spent all day in their flat staring at the electric bulbs. At night she walked out into the streets and he would have to go and fetch her. She had had frostbite several times. He said she had been lovely twenty years ago, though she had always hated the cold.

Henrique Tchaikov listened. He made a few sympathetic sounds. It was as hopeless to try to communicate with the driver, Argenty, as to shut him up. Normally Argenty drove important men from the Bureau, to whom he would not be allowed to speak a word, probably not even Good-day. But Tchaikov was a minor bureaucrat. If Argenty had had a better education and more luck, he might have been where Tchaikov was.

Argenty's voice became like the landscape beyond the cindery cement blocks of the city, monotonous, inevitably irritating, depressing, useless, sad.

It was the fifteenth year of winter.

Now almost forty, Tchaikov could remember the other seasons of his childhood, even one long hot summer full of liquid colours and now-forgotten smells. By the time he was twelve years old, things were changing forever. In his twenties he saw them go, the palaces of summer, as Eynin called them in his poetry. Tchaikov had been twenty-four when he watched the last natural flower, sprung pale green out of the public lawn, die before him – as Argenty's wife was dying, in another way.

The Industrial Winter, so it was termed. The belching chimneys and the leaking stations with their cylinders of poison. The rotting hulks along the shore like deadly whales.

The doctor says she'll ruin her eyes staring at the lights all day s' Argenty droned on.

'There's a new drug, isn't there?' Tchaikov tried.

But Argenty took no notice. Probably, when alone, he talked to himself.

Beyond the car, the snowscape spread like heaps of bedclothes, some soiled and some clean. The grey ceiling of the sky bulged low.

Argenty broke off. He said, 'There's the wolf factory.'

Tchaikov turned his head.

Against the greyness-whiteness, the jagged black of the deserted factory which had been taken over by wolves was the only land mark.

'They howl often, sound like the old machinery. You hear them from the Datch'a.'

'Yes, they told me I would.'

'Look, some of them running about there.'

Tchaikov noted the black forms of the wolves, less black than the factory walls and gates, darting up and over the snow heaps, and away around the building. Although things did live out here, it was strange to see something alive.

Then they came down the slope, the chained snow-tyres grating and punching, and Tchaikov saw the mansion across the plain.

'The river came in here,' said Argenty. 'Under the floor.'

A plantation of pine trees remained about the house. Possibly they were dead, carved out only in frozen snow. The Datch'a had two domed towers, a balustraded verandi above a flight of stairs that gleamed like white glass. When the car drove up, he could see two statues at the foot of the steps that had also been kept clear of snow. They were of a stained brownish marble, a god and goddess, both naked and smiling through the brown stains that spread from their mouths.

There were electric lights on in the Datch'a, from top to bottom, three or f our floors of them in long, arched windows.

But as the car growled to a halt, Argenty gave a grunt. 'Look,' he said again. 'Look. Up there.'

They got out and stood on the snow. The cold broke round them like sheer disbelief, but they knew it by now. They stared up. As happened only very occasionally, a lacuna had opened in the low cloud. A dim pink island of sky appeared, and over it floated a dulled lemon slice, dissolving, half transparent, the sun.

Argenty and Tchaikov waited, transfixed, watching in silence. Presently the cloud folded together again and the sky, the sun, vanished.

'I can't tell her,' said Argenty. 'My wife. I can't tell her I saw the sun. Once it happened in the street. She began to scream. I had to take her to the hospital. She wasn't the only case.'

'I'm sorry,' said Tchaikov.

He had said this before, but now for the first time Argenty seemed to hear him. 'Thank you.'

Argenty insisted on carrying Tchaikov's bag to the top of the slippy, gleaming stair, then he pressed the buzzer. The door was of steel and wood, with a glass panel of octople glazing, almost opaque. Through it, in the bluish yellow light, a vast hall could just be made out, with a floor of black and white marble.

A voice spoke through the door apparatus.

'Give your name.'

'Henrique Tchaikov. Number sixteen stroke Y.'

'You're late.'

Tchaikov stood on the top step, explaining to a door. He was enigmatic. There was always a great deal of this.

'The road from Kroy was blocked by an avalanche. It had to be cleared.'

'All right. Come in. Mind the dog, she may be down there.'

'Dog,' said Argenty. He put his hand into his coat for his gun.

'It's all right,' said Tchaikov. 'They always keep a dog here.'

'Why ?' said Argenty blankly.

Tchaikov said, 'A guard dog. And for company, I suppose.'

Argenty glanced up, towards the domed towers. The walls were reinforced by black cement. The domes were tiled black, mortared by snow. After the glimpse of sun, there was again little colour in their world.

'Are they … is it up there?'

'I don't know. Perhaps.'

'Take care,' said Argenty surprisingly as the door made its unlocking noise.

Argenty was not allowed to loiter. Tchaikov watched him get back into the car, undo the dash panel and take a swig of Vodka. The car turned and drove slowly away, back across the plain.

The previous curator did not give Tchaikov his name. A tall thin man with slicked, black hair, Tchaikov knew he was known as Ouperin.

Ouperin showed Tchaikov the map of the mansion, and the pamphlet of house rules. He only mentioned one, that the solarium must not be used for more than one hour per day; it was expensive. He asked if Tchaikov had any questions, wanted to see anything. Tchaikov said it would be fine.

They met the dog in the corridor outside the ballroom, near where Ouperin located what he called his office.

She was a big dog, perhaps part Cuvahl and part Husky, muscular and well-covered, with a thick silken coat like the thick pile carpets, ebony and fawn, with white round her muzzle and on her belly and paws, and two gold eyes that merely slanted at them for a second as she galloped by.

'Dog! Here dog,' Ouperin called, but she ignored him; prancing on, with balletic shakes of her fringed fur, into the ballroom, where the crystal chandeliers hung down twenty feet on ropes of bronze. 'She only comes when she's hungry. There are plenty of steaks for her in the Cold Room. She goes out a lot,' said Ouperin. 'Her door's down in the kitchen. Electronic. Nothing else can get in.'

They visited the cold room, which was very long, and massively shelved, behind a sort of air-lock. The room was frigid; the natural weather was permitted to sustain it. The ice on high windows looked like armour.

Ouperin took two bottles of Vodka and a bunch of red grapes, frozen peerless in a wedge of ice.

They sat in his office, along from the ballroom. A fire blazed on the hearth.

'I won't say I've enjoyed it here,' said Ouperin.

'But there are advantages. There are some videos and magazines in the suite. You know what I mean. Apart from the library. If you get … hot.'

Tchaikov nodded politely.

Ouperin said, 'The first thing you'll do when I go is look at them, won't you?'

'Probably,' said Tchaikov.

'You know,' said Ouperin. 'You get bored with them. At first they remind you of the fairy story. What is it? The princess who sleeps. Then you just get bored.

Tchaikov said nothing. They drank vodka, and at seventeen hours, five o'clock, as the white world outside began to turn glowing blue, a helicopter came and landed on the plain. Ouperin took his bags and went out to the front door of the Datch'a, and the stair. 'Have some fun,' he said.

He ran sliding down the steps and up to the helicopter. He scrambled in like a boy on holiday. It rose as it had descended in a storm of displaced snow. When its noise finally faded through the sky, Tchaikov heard the wolves from the wolf factory howling over the slopes. The sky was dark blue now, navy, without a star. If ever the moon appeared, the moon was blue. The pines settled. A few black boughs showed where the helicopter's winds had scoured off the snow. They were alive. But soon the snow began to come down again, to cover them.

Tchaikov returned to the cold room. He selected a chicken and two steaks and vegetables, and took them to the old stone-floored kitchen down the narrow steps. The new kitchen was very small, a little bright cubicle inside the larger one. He put the food into the thawing cabinet, and then set the program on the cooker. The dog came in as he was doing this, and stood outside the lighted box. Once they had thawed, he put the bloody steaks down for her on a dish, and touched her ruffed head as she bent to eat. She was a beautiful dog, but wholly uninterested in him. She might be there in case of trouble, but there never would be trouble. No one stayed longer than six or eight months. The curatorship at the Datch'a was a privilege, and an endurance test.

When his meal was ready, Tchaikov carried it to the Card Room or office, and ate, with the television showing him in colour the black and white scenes of the snow and the cities. The card room fire burned on its synthetic logs, the gas cylinder faintly whistling. He drank Vodka and red wine. Sometimes, in spaces of sound, he heard the wolves. And once; looking from the ballroom, he saw the dog, lit by all the windows, trotting along the ice below the pines.

At midnight, when the television stations were shut down to conserve power, and most of the lights in the cities, although not here, would be dimmed, Tchaikov got into the manually operated elevator, and went up into the second dome, to the top floor.

He had put on again his greatcoat, his hat and gloves.

The elevator stopped at another little air-lock. Beyond, only the cold-pressure lights could burn, glacial blue. Sometimes they blinked, flickered. An angled stair led to a corridor, which was wide, and shone as if highly polished. At the end of the corridor were an annexe and the two broad high doors of glass. It was possible to look through the glass, and for a while he stood there, in the winter of the dome, staring in like a child.

It had been, and still was, a bedroom, about ten metres by eleven. His flat in the city would fit easily inside it.

The bedroom had always been white, the carpets and the silken drapes, even the tassels had been a mottled white, like milk, edged with gilt. And the bed was white. So that now, just as the snow-world outside resembled a white tumbled bed, the bed was like the tumbled snow.

The long windows were black with night, but a black silvered by ice. Ice had formed too, in the room, in long spears that hung from the ceiling, where once a sky had been painted, a sky-blue sky with rosy clouds, but they had darkened and died, so now the sky was like old grey paint with flecks of rimy plaster showing through.

The mirrors in the room had cracked from the cold and formed strange abstract patterns that seemed to mean something. Even the glass doors had cracked, and were reinforced.

From here you could not properly see the little details of the room, the meal held perfect under ice, the ruined ornaments and paintings. Nor, properly, the couple on the bed.

Tchaikov drew the electronic key from his pocket and placed it in the mechanism of the doors. It took a long time to work, the cold-current not entirely reliable. The lighting blinked again, a whole second of black. Then the doors opened and the lights steadied, and Tchaikov went through.

The carpet, full of ice crystals, crunched under his feet which left faint marks that would dissipate. His breath was smoke.

On a chest with painted panels, where the paint had scattered out, stood a white statue, about a metre high, that had broken from the cold, and an apple of rouged glass that had also broken, and somehow bled.

The pictures on the walls were done for. Here and there, a half of a face peeped out from the mossy corrosion, like the sun he had seen earlier in the cloud. Hot-house roses in a vase had turned to black coals, petrified, petals not fallen.

Their meal stood on the little mosaic table. It had been a beautiful meal, and neatly served. An amber fish, set with dark jade fruits, a salad that had blackened like the roses but kept its shape of dainty leaves and fronds. A flawless cream round, with two slivers cut from it, reminding him of the quartering of an elegant clock. The Champagne was all gone, but for the beads of palest gold left at the bottom of the two goblets rimmed with silver. The bottle of tablets was mostly full. They had taken enough only to sleep, then turned off the heating, leaving the cold to do the rest.

The Last Supper of Love, Eynin had called it, in his poem, *This Place*.

Tchaikov went over to the bed and looked down at them.

The man, Xander, wore evening dress, a tuxedo, a silk shirt with a tunic collar. On the jacket were pinned two military ribbons and a Knight's Cross. His tawny hair was sleeked back. His face was grave and very strong, a very masculine face, a very clean, calm face. His eyes, apparently, were green, but invisible behind the marble lids.

She, the woman, Tamura, was exquisite, not beautiful but immaculate, and so delicate and slender. She could have danced on air, just as Eynin said, in her sequined pumps. Her long white dress clung to a slight and nearly adolescent body with the firm full breasts of a young woman. Her brunette hair spread on the pillows with the long stream of pearls from her neck. On the middle finger of her left hand, she wore a burnished ruby the colour and size of a cherry.

Like Xander, Tamura was calm, quite serene.

It seemed they had had no second thoughts, eating their last meal, drinking their wine, perhaps making love.

Then swallowing the pills and lying back for the sleep of winter, the long cold that encased and preserved them like perfect candy in a globe of ice.

They had been here nine years. It was not so very long.

Tchaikov looked at them. After a few minutes he turned and went back across the room, and again his foot-marks temporarily disturbed the carpet. He locked the doors behind him.

In the curator's suite below, he put on the ordinary dimmed yellow lamp and read Eynin's poem again, sipping black tea, while the synthetic fire crackled at the foot of his hard bed.

We watched the summer palaces
Sail from this place,
Like liners to the sea
Of yesterday.

Tchaikov put the book aside and switched off the light and fire. The fire died quite slowly, as if real. Outside he heard the wolves howling like the old factory machinery.

Behind his closed eyelids, he saw Tamura's ruby, red as the cherries and roses in the elite florist's shops of the city. Her eyes, apparently, were dark.

Above him, as he lay on his back, the lovers slept on in their bubble of loving snow.

2

The first month was not eventful. Each day, Henrique Tchaikov made a tout of the Datch'a, noting any discrepancies, a fissure in the plaster, a chipped tile, noises in the pipes of the heating system – conscious, rather, of the fissured plaster and tiles, the thumps of the radiators, in his own apartment building. He replaced fuses and valves. In the library he noted the books which would need renovation. And took a general inventory of the stores the house had accumulated. Every curator did this. Evidently, some items were overlooked. The books, for example, the cornice in the ballroom, while lavatory tissue and oil for the generator were regularly renewed.

He used the hot tub, but only every three or four days. In the city, bathing was rationed. For the same reason he did not go into the solarium, except once a week to check the thermostat and water the extraordinary black-green plants which rose in storeys of foliage to the roof.

Most of the afternoon he sat reading in the library, or listening to the music machine. He heard for the first time, recordings of Prokofiev and Rachmaninov playing inside their own piano concertos, and Shostakovich conducting his own symphony, and Lirabez singing in a slightly flat but swarthy baritone, a cycle of his own songs.

For those who liked these things, the Datch'a provided wonderful experiences.

Tchaikov also watched films, and the recordings of historical events.

Sometimes in the mornings he slept an hour late, letting the coffee-plate prepare a sticky brew, with thick cream from the cold room.

Usually he kept in mind these treats were his only for eight months at the most, less than a year. Then he would have to go back.

The dog became more sociable, though not exactly friendly. He stroked her fur, even brushed her twice a week. He called her Bella, because she was beautiful. Probably this was not the right thing, as again, when he left, some other person would be the curator, who might not even like dogs.

Bella, the dog, each evening lay before the fire in the card room, sometimes even in the suite. But normally she would only stay an hour or two. Then she wanted to go down through the house and out by the electronic dog-door.

He began to realize that the wolf howling was often very close to the mansion. At last he saw the indigo form of a wolf on the night snow. The wolf howled on and on, until the dog went out. Then the wolf and the dog played together in the snow.

The first time he saw this, Tchaikov was assailed by a heart wringing pang of hope.

The house manual told him that the wolves had invaded the factory, and remained there, because they lived off the rats which still infested it. The rats in turn lived off the dung of the wolves. It was a disgusting but divinely inspired cycle. Bella and the wolf must have met out upon the frozen ice of the ancient river buried below the Datch'a and the pines. Although there would be females of the wolf kind for the wolf to choose from, instead he took to Bella. An individualist. Tchaikov did not see them join in the sexual act, but he accepted that they too were lovers. This seemed to symbolize the vigour still clinging in the threatened world, its basic tenacity, its *magic*. But he put such thoughts aside. Magic was illusion. Sex was only that, just like the hot magazines Ouperin, or someone, had secreted in the suite and which Tchaikov did not bother with. For him, sensuality was connected to personality. He preferred memory to invention.

Of course, occasionally he pondered Tamura and Xander, their intrinsic meaning. But never for long. And he did not go up again to look at them.

On the first day of the second month, a fax came through from the city computer, informing him a party would be arriving at midday.

He shut the dog Bella in the kitchen, and put on his suit and tie.

At sixteen hours, or four o'clock – they were late, another avalanche – the party drew up in two big buses with leviathan snow-tyres.

Tchaikov understood he was unreasonably resentful at the stupid intrusion, for which the place was intended. He wanted the Datch'a to himself. But he courteously welcomed the party, twenty-three people, who stared about the hall with wide, red-rimmed eyes, their noses running, because the heating in the buses was not very good.

They had their own guide, who led them, following Tchaikov, up the stairs to the manually operated lift. Tchaikov and the guide took them in two groups of eleven and twelve, up into the dome.

They seemed frightened on the narrow stair, and in the corridor, as though extreme cold still unsettled – startled – them. They peered through the glass doors, exactly as Tchaikov had. When he and the bossy guide ushered them through, they wandered about the bedroom. Told not to touch anything, they made tactile motions in the air over ornaments and furnishings, with their gloved hands.

One woman, seeing the lovers, Tamura, Xander, on the bed, began to cry. No one took any notice. She pulled quantities of paper handkerchiefs from her pocket; possibly she had come prepared for emotion.

Downstairs in the ballroom, the guide lectured everybody on the Datch'a. They stood glassy-eyed and blank. The significance of Tamura and Xander was elusive but overpowering. Tchaikov too did not listen. Instead he organised the coffee-plate in the card room, and brought the party coffee in relays, laced with Vodka, before its return to the city in the two draughty buses.

When they had gone, about six, Bella was whining from the kitchen. He fed her quickly, knowing she wanted to be off to her lover. He gave her that night two extra steaks, in case she should want to take them out as a gift, but she left them on the plate. Oddly, from this, he deduced she would eventually desert the Datch'a for her wolf partner. Instinctively she knew not to accustom him to extra food, and to prepare herself for future hardship. But doubtless this was fanciful. Besides, she might by now be pregnant with the wolf's children.

Bella lay before the synthetic log fire, her gold eyes burning golden-red. Her belly looked fuller than it had. It was about twenty-two hours, ten o'clock.

Tchaikov read aloud to her from the poem, *This Place*.

> '*I dreamed once, of this place,*
> '*When I was young,*
> '*But then I woke –*
> '*When I was young.*'

It was five nights since the bus party had visited. Once the dog had got up, shaken herself, and padded from the room, Tchaikov went upstairs and stepped into the elevator.

The night was extra cold, minus several more degrees on the gage, and the great bedroom had a silvery fog in it.

He could look at the couple now quite passively, as if they were only waxworks. A man and a woman who had not wanted to remain inside the sinking winter world. But was it merely that? Was their mysterious suicide cowardice – or bravura? Did they think, in dying, that they had somewhere warm to go.

The Bureau had not advanced any records on them, and probably their names were not even those they had gone by in life.

Again, he asked himself what they meant. But it did not really matter. They *were*, that was all.

In the night, about 4 am, an unearthly noise woke him from a deep sleep, where he had been dreaming of swimming in a warm sea jewelled by fish.

The sound had occurred outside, he thought, outside both the dream and the room. He got up and went to the window and looked out through the triple glazing which was all the suite provided.

The snowscape spread from the pines, along the plain, and in the distance billowed up to the higher land, and the black sky massed with the broken edges of stars. Far away to the right, where the plane was its most level and long, a black mark had appeared in the snow. It must stretch for nearly twenty metres, he thought, a jagged, ink-black crack in the terrain.

Tchaikov stared, and saw a vapour rising out of the crack, caused by the disparity between the bitter set of the air and some different temperature below.

The sound had *been* a crack. Like a gigantic piece of wood snapped suddenly in half – a bark of breakage.

But new snow was already drifting faintly down from the stars, smoothing and obscuring the black tear in the whiteness. As Tchaikov watched, it began to vanish.

Probably it was nothing. In the city apertures sometimes appeared in the top-snow of streets, where the thermolated pipes still ran beneath. Somebody had told Tchaikov there had been a river here, passing below the house. The driver had mentioned it too. Perhaps the disturbance had to do with that.

Tchaikov went back to bed, and lay for a while listening, expectant and tensed. Then he recalled that once, in his early childhood, he had heard such a crack roar out across a frozen lake in the country. Instinctively, hearing it now, he had unconsciously remembered the springs of long-ago, the waxing of the sun, the rains, the melting of the ice. But spring was forever over.

He drifted back down into sleep, numb and calm.

The next morning, as he was coming from the solarium, having switched off the sprinklers, he heard the sound of a vehicle on the plain. He went into the ballroom, and looked down at the snow, half noticing as he did so, that the curious mark of the previous night had completely disappeared. A large black car was now parked by the Datch'a's steps, near the statues. After a moment, Tchaikov recognized the car which had brought him here. Puzzled, he waited, and saw the driver, Argenty, get out, and then a smaller figure in a long coat of grey synthetic fur.

They came up the steps, Argenty pausing for the smaller figure, which was that of a woman.

After a minute the house door made a noise.

There had been no communication from the city computer, but sometimes messages were delayed. In any case, you could not leave them standing in the cold.

Tchaikov opened the door without interrogation.

Argenty shot him a quick look under his hat.

'It's all right, isn't it?'

'I expect so,' said Tchaikov.

He let them come in, and the door shut.

Argenty took off his hat, and stood almost to attention..He said, 'There aren't visitors due, are there?'

'Not that I know of.'

'I thought not. There's been another power failure. I shouldn't think anyone would be going anywhere today.'

'Apart from you.'

'Yes,' said Argenty. He turned, and looked at the woman.

She too had taken off her hat, a fake fur shako to match the coat. She had a small pale slender face, without, he thought, any make-up beyond a dusting of powder. Her eyes were dark and smoky, with long lashes of a lighter darkness. Her dark hair seemed recently washed and brushed and fell in light soft waves to her shoulders. Just under her right cheekbone had been applied a little diamante flower. She met his eyes and touched the flower with a gloved fingertip. She said quietly, 'A frostbite scar.'

'This is my wife,' said Argenty. 'Tanya.'

Then she smiled at Tchaikov, a placating smile, like a child's when it wants to show it is undeserving of punishment. She was like a child, a girl, despite the two thin lines cut under her large eyes and at either side of her soft mouth.

He remembered how Argenty had talked on and on about her, her light-deprived Twilight Sickness, her wanderings in the night and cries. She had been lovely, he said, twenty years ago. In a way she still was.

Unauthorized, they should not be here. It could cost Argenty a serious demotion. What had happened? The power failure? The electricity off in their flat, gloom, and the refrigerator failing, and Argenty saying, 'Leave all that, I'll take you somewhere nice.' As you might, to stop a miserable and frightened child crying.

Tchaikov said, 'Come into the card room. There's a fire.'

They went through with him, Argenty still stiff and formal, absolutely knowing what he had risked, but she was all smiles now, reassured.

In the warm room, Argenty removed his greatcoat, and helped her off with her fur. Tchaikov looked at them, slightly surprised. Argenty wore the uniform of his city service, with an honour ribbon pinned by the collar. While she – she wore a long, old evening gown of faded pastel crimson, which left her shoulders and arms and some of her white back and breast bare. On her left hand, under the woollen glove, was another little glove of lace. She indicated it again at once, laughed and said, 'Frostbite. I've been careless, you see.'

Tchaikov switched on the coffee-plate. He said, 'I usually have lunch in about an hour. I hope you'll join me.'

Argenty nodded politely. She began to walk about the room, inspecting the antique oil paintings and the restored damask wall covering. Argenty took out a brand of expensive cigarettes and came to Tchaikov, offering them.

Argenty murmured, very low, 'Thank you, for being so good. I can't tell you what it means to her.'

'That's all right. You may even get away with it, if the computer's out.

Argenty shrugged. 'Perhaps. What does it matter anyway?'

After the coffee, Tchaikov showed them the ballroom, then went to organize a lunch. He selected caviar and pork, the type of vegetables and little side dishes he did not, himself, bother with, fruit and biscuits, and a chocolate dessert he thought she would like. He took Vodka and two bottles of Champagne from the liquor compartment. For God's sake, they might as well enjoy the visit.

He opened up the parlour off the ballroom. It too had a chandelier dripping prisms. He turned on the fire and lit the tall white candles in the priceless candelabra. He was not supposed to do this. But against Argenty's tremendous gamble it was a small gesture.

Everything sparkled in the room. It was now only like an overcast snowy winter day in the country. Perhaps before some festival. And the lunch was like a celebration.

Argenty ate doggedly, drank quite sparingly. She ate only a little, but with interest, excitement. She sparkled up like the room, her personal lights switched on.

In the middle of the meal, the dog, Bella, padding in, her coat thick with rime and water drops. Tchaikov got up, thinking Tanya would be afraid of the dog. But Tanya only laughed with delight, and went straight to Bella, ruffling her fur, and drying her inadequately with linen napkins from the table.

As Bella stood before the fire, and the slight woman made a fuss of her, Tchaikov could see the swelling shape of the dog's belly, her extended nipples. She was definitely pregnant from the wolf. And the girl-woman bent shining over her, caressing and stroking, kissing the big animal on the savage velvet of her brow.

Argenty said, 'Tanya used to live on a farm. They had dogs, cats, horses, everything.'

Tanya said, lightly, 'I came to the city to sell stockings. Isn't that ridiculous?'

When the meal was finished, they drew the large chairs to the fireside. They sat drinking coffee and brandy, and the dog lay between them, glistening gold along her back from the fire.

Outside, the dusk of the afternoon seemed only seasonal through the openings of the heavy drapes.

They were sleepy, muttering little anecdotes of their pasts, quite divorced from their present. In the end, Tanya fell asleep, her head gracefully drooping, a lock of her hair like dark tinsel on her cheek.

'When she wakes up,' said Argenty, 'we'll be going.'

'Why don't you stay tonight?' said Tchaikov. 'Leave early in the morning. There's another bedroom in the suite. Quite a good one – I think it's for visiting VIPs. By tomorrow the power failure will be over, probably.'

'That's kind … you've been kind … but we'd better get back.'

They looked at the sleeping woman, at the sleeping dog, and the fire.

'Why did this happen?' asked Argenty. His voice was gentle and unemphatic. 'Couldn't they have seen – why did they give up all the best things, let them go – they could have – something – surely.'

Tchaikov said nothing, and Argenty fell silent.

And in the silence there came a dense low rumble. For a moment Tchaikov took it for some fluctuation of the gas jet in the fire, and then, as it grew louder, for the noise of snow dislodged and tumbling from a roof of the mansion.

But then the rumbling became very loud, running in towards them over the plain.

'What is it ?' said Argenty. He had gone pale.

'I don't know. An earth tremor, perhaps.'

The rumbling was now so vehement he had to raise his voice. On the table the silver and the glasses tinkled and rattled, something fell and broke, and on the walls the pictures trembled and swayed. The floor beneath their chairs was churning.

The dog had woken, sat up, her coat bristling and ears laid flat, a white ring showing round each eye.

Argenty and Tchaikov rose, and in her sleep the woman stretched out one hand, in its lace glove, as if to snatch hold of something.

Then came a thunder clap, a sort of ejection of sound that ripped splintering from earth and sky, hit the barrier of the house, exploded, dropped back in enormous echoing shards.

The windows grated and shook. No doubt some of the external glass had ruptured.

'Is it a bomb?' cried Argenty.

Tanya had started from sleep and the chair and he caught her in his arms. She was speechless with shock and terror; the dog was growling.

'I don't know. It's stopped now. Not a bomb, I think. There was no light flash.' Tchaikov moved to the door, 'Stay here.'

Outside, he ran across the ballroom, and to the nearer window which looked out to the plain.

What he saw made him hesitate mentally, stumble in his mind, at a loss. He could not decipher what he was looking at. It was a sight theoretically familiar enough. Yet knowing what it was, he stood immobile for several minutes, staring without comprehension at the enormous coal-black dragon which had crashed upwards through the dead ice of the frozen river, showering off panes of the marble land, like the black and white concrete blocks of a collapsed building. In the puddle of bubbling iron water, the submarine settled now, tall, motionless, less than thirty-five metres beyond the Datch'a, while clouds of stony steam rose in a tumult on the steel sky.

3

They marched steadily to the mansion, over the snow. Henrique Tchaikov watched them come, black shapes on the whiteness. Reaching the steps, they climbed them, and arrived at the door. He could see their uniforms by then, the decorations of rank and authority. They did not seem to feel the cold. They did not bother with the buzzer.

He spoke through the door apparatus.

'You must identify yourselves.'

'You'll let us in. The one who spoke then gave a key word and number. And Tchaikov opened the door.

The cold gushed in with them, in a special way.

'You're the current Bureau man,' said the commander to Tchaikov. He was about thirty-six, athletic, tanned by a solarium, his hair cut too short, not a pore in his face. Hi teeth were winter white. 'We won't give you any trouble. We've come for the couple.'

Tchaikov did not answer. His heart kicked but it was a reflex. He stood very still. He had taken Tanya and Argenty down to the kitchen, with the dog, and shut them all in.

The commander vocalized again. 'We don't need any red tape, do we? My men will go straight up. It'll only take the briefest while. The dome, right?'

Tchaikov said slowly, 'You mean Tamura and Xander.'

'Are those the names? Yes. The pair in the state bedroom. Here's the confirmation disc.'

Tchaikov accepted the disc and put it in the analyser by the door. After ten seconds an affirmative lit up, the key number, and the little message. *Comply with all conditions.*

The commander took back his disc. 'Where would we be,' he said, 'without our machines.' Then he gave an order, and the four other men ran off and up the stairs like hounds let from a leash, towards the upper floors and the elevator. Obviously they had been primed with the layout of the mansion. Tchaikov saw that two of them carried each a rolled rain-coloured thermolated bag. They would have some means of opening the upper doors.

He said, 'Why are you taking them away? Where are they going?'

The commander showed all his pristine, repulsive teeth. 'Quite a comfortable stint here, I'd say, yes? Don't worry, they won't recall you until your time's up. Messes up the files. Seven months to go. You can just relax.'

Tchaikov grasped it would be useless to question the commander further. He had had his orders, which were to remove the frozen lovers in cold-bags, take them into the submarine, go away with them, somewhere.

Tchaikov said, 'It was impressive, the way you surfaced.'

'That river,' said the commander, 'it runs deep. So far down, you know, the water still moves. We came in from the sea, thirteen kilometres. Must have given you a surprise.'

'Yes.'

'There's nothing like her,' said the commander, as though he boasted about a selected woman, or his mother. 'The X 2 M's. Ice-breakers, power-hives. Worlds in themselves. You'd be amazed. We could stay under for a hundred years. We have everything. Clean reusable air, fool-proof heating, cuisine prepared by master chefs, games rooms, weaponry. See how brown I am,' he added, dancing his narrow eyes, flirting now. 'Have you ever tasted eggs?'

'No.'

'I have one every day. And fresh meat. Salads. My little boat has everything I'll ever need.'

There was a wooden, flat sound, repeated on and on.

The commander frowned.

'It's only the dog,' Tchaikov said. 'I shut her in, below. In case she annoyed you.'

'Dog? Oh, yes. Animals don't interest me, except of course to eat.'

Tchaikov thought he heard the lift cranking up the tower, going to the dome.

The commander looked about now, and laughed at the old regal house, the old country Datch'a with its sleeping, white-candy dead.

They stood then in silence in the hall, until the other four men ran down again, carrying, not particularly cautiously, the two thermolated bags, upright and unpliable. Filled and out of the dome, the material had misted over. Tchaikov could not see Tamura or Xander in these cocoons, although he found himself staring, thinking for a second he caught the scorch of her ruby ring.

'Well done,' the commander said to him. 'All over.' It was like the dentist's in childhood. 'You can go back to all those cosy duties.' He grinned at Tchaikov. But his use of jargon was somehow unwieldy and out of date. Did they speak another tongue on the submarine? 'A nice number. Happy days.

The dog had suddenly stopped barking.

The door let the men out. Tchaikov watched them returning over the snow, towards their black dragon-whale. Already the ice was forming round the submarine's casing, but that would not be much of an inconvenience. He wondered where, they had been, how far out in jet black seas, where maybe fish still swam. When the vessel was gone, the ice would swiftly close, and tonight's fresh snowfall heal the wound it had made, as snow had healed the preface to the wound, last night.

Tamura and Xander, preserved from the submarine's warmth in some refrigerated cubicle. He did not know, could not imagine for what purpose. Although the nagging line from some book – was it a Bible? – began to twitter in his head … *And He said: Make thee an ark* –

Above, the dome was void. The great polar room with its stalactites of ice, the footsteps already smoothing from the carpet .

He descended quickly to the kitchen. He had told Argenty where the medicine cabinet was, and suggested that he dial some sedative tablets for his wife. Tchaikov was unsure what he would find.

Yet when he reached the lower floor, there was only quietness. Opening the kitchen door, he found the two of them seated urbanely at the long table.

The dog Bella had gone. But Tanya sat in her red dress, and looking up, she met Tchaikov only with her lambent eyes.

She said to him, reciting from memory from Eynin's poem that he too knew so well:

'In Hell the birds are made of fire;
'If all the birds of Hell flew to this place,
'And settled on the snow,
'Still darkness would prevail,
'And utter cold.'

'She knows it by heart,' said Argenty.
'So do I, most of it,' Tchaikov answered.
'The dog went out,' said Argenty. 'We thought we heard a wolf.'
'Yes. They've mated.'
The kitchen was bathed in vague ochre heat, only the light of the new cooking area was raw and too bright.
Tanya's eyes shone.
'You were very good, to hide us away.'
'It's all right,' he said. 'The military are short-sighted. They came for something else.'
In a while they heard the strange, sluggish hollow suction of the submarine, its motors, diving down again below the ice. The house gave now only a little shudder, and on its shelf, one ancient plate turned askew.
Tanya laughed. She lifted her dark springy hair in her hands.
Tchaikov saw that Argenty's hair, under the polishing light, was a rich dull gold.

He slept a deep leaden sleep and dreamed of the submarine. It was taller than the tallest architecture of the city, the Bureau building. It clove forward, black, ice and steam and boiling water spraying away from it, rending the land with a vicious hull-like the blade of some enormous ice-skate. In the dark sky above red and yellow burning birds wheeled to and fro, cawing and calling, striking sparks from the clouds. The birds of Hell.

When the submarine reached the Datch'a, it stopped just outside the wall of the suite,, which in the dream was made of glass. The wall shattered and fell down, and looking up the mile of iron, steel and night that was the tower of the submarine, Tchaikov noticed a tiny bluish porthole set abnormally in the side, and there they sat, the lovers, gazing down with cold, closed eyes.

Waking, he got up and made black tea on the plate. From the other bedroom of the suite, across the inner room, came no sound. When he looked out, there was no longer a light beneath their door. If they had switched off the optional lamp, perhaps they slept.

When the afternoon darkened, they had sat on with him in the kitchen, drinking a little, talking idly. There was the subtle ease of remaining; he realized before Argenty asked, that they did after all mean to stay a night at the house.

Later the dog came in again. Tchaikov fed her. She lay by the hot pipes for half an hour before going out once more.

During the interval, Tanya suddenly sang a strange old song in her light girl's voice, 'Oh my dog is such a clever dog.'

Bella listened. Her tail wagged slowly. She came to Tanya to be caressed before padding off into the star-spiked night.

They ate cold pork and bread for supper and finished the Champagne. Argenty thanked Tchaikov, shaking his hand, throwing his arm around him. The girl-woman did not kiss Tchaikov as he had half expected – hoped? – she would. She only said shyly, 'It's been a wonderful day. Better than a birthday.'

By the time he concluded his nocturnal check of the Datch'a, they had gone up, and just the lamp showed softly under the door.

But they were in full darkness now, so Tchaikov walked almost on tiptoe from the suite. He did not want to wake them if they slept. He wished her not to dream as he had, of the triumphant submarine.

Outside, the ice had superficially closed over again. Snow fell in gentle pitiless flakes.

The elevator seemed particularly sluggish. He had to work at the lever with great firmness.

Above, in the icy corridor, Tchaikov shivered, only his trousers and greatcoat on over his night-shirt. As he walked towards the glass doors, he had a sense of imminence. What was it? Was it loss?

As formerly, he hesitated, and stood at the doors, staring in through the glacial light, the glacial glass, the cracks, the fog of ice.

He experienced a moment of dislocation, pure bewilderment, just as he had with the submarine. He had previously seen the bed clothed by two forms. Now they were removed and the bed was vacant. But there were two forms on the bed. The bed was clothed.

Tchaikov opened the doors with the electronic key they had so noiselessly replaced on the chest in his room, before going up again. Of course, the key, lying there, had been obvious for what it was. Like the house map in the card room. There would have been no difficulty in deciding.

The bedroom, when he entered it now, did not strike him as so frozen. The breath of the living seemed finally to have stirred it, like the fluid of the deepest coldest pool stirred by a golden wand.

Tchaikov went across to the bed. Two bottles had fallen on the thick carpet. He looked down at the couple.

They lay hand in hand, side by side. Their faces were peaceful,, almost smiling, the eyes fast shut. Like the faces, the eyes, of Xander and Tamura. Yet these two lovers had needed to be brave. Despite the Vodka they had swallowed and the tablets from the medicine cabinet, they had had to face the cold, had had to lie down in the cold. He in his well-brushed uniform with its single honour, and she in her pale red sleeveless gown.

But there had been no struggle. They seemed to have found it very simple, very consoling, if not easy. Perhaps it had been easy, too.

Her sombre hair, his gilded hair, both smoked now by the rime. And on the diamante flower that gemmed her cheek, a single mote of crystal like a tear.

Tchaikov backed slowly and carefully away. It was possible they were not quite dead yet, still in the process of dying. He tiptoed out, not to disturb their death.

By the end of the ninth month, when the Bureau at last recalled him, the dog was long gone. He had seen her at first sometimes, out on the snow, playing with the wolf and their three pups. But the wolf was a king wolf, made her queen over the wolf pack, and in the end, she went away to the factory with them.

When he heard the howling in the still night, he thought of her. Once, the moon appeared incredibly for a quarter of an hour, sapphire blue, and the wolves' chanting rose to a crescendo. Her children would be very strong, cross-bred from an alpha male and such a well-nourished mother.

His faxed report had been acknowledged, but that was all. Tchaikov never commented upon or thought about the aspects of what had occurred, he detailed and visualized the events only in memorised images.

The night of the blue moon, which was two nights before his return to the city, and to his cramped flat with its thudding radiators, the tepid bath once a week, the rationing, the dark, he wrote in the back of the book of Eynin's poetry, on the blank page which followed the poem called *The Place*.

Here too he set out the facts sparely, as he had done for the Bureau. Under the facts he wrote a few further lines.

'I have puzzled all this time over what is their meaning, the lovers in the ice, whoever they are, whether right or wrong in their action, and even if they change, their bodies constantly taken and replaced by others. And I think their meaning is this: Love; courage, defiance – the mystery of the human spirit, still blooming, always blooming, like the last flower in the winter world.'

Black And White Sky

Not For the First – From an Idea by John Kaiine

1

Almost morning; it is early summer, not quite five o'clock. The sky has a colourless lightness, faintly golden in the east across the fields. In the woods birds sing in pale, clear sprinklings of sound.

From a copse one magpie rises. It flies straight upward.

There is a slight visual softness to all distances, perhaps mist, or haze. The air is fresh, but not unwarm.

A second magpie rises, this time not from the copse.

The golden edge of the sky intensifies, begins to dazzle. The sun is nearly free of the horizon.

A third magpie rises.

A fourth magpie rises.

The bird-chorus redoubles, eagerly encouraging the dawn. From the farm over towards the main road, some heavy vehicle or machinery rumbles.

A fifth magpie rises.

The sun rises.

A sixth magpie rises.

The sky floods with shell pink and golden lacquer.

A seventh magpie rises …

It was the day when Alice came to clean Cigarette Cottage. Of course, that was not the cottage's proper name. After it was built in the 1930's, someone pastorally-minded had christened the place *Woodbine Cottage*. And following various renovations, and the removal of the name-plate above the door, 'Woodbine' still stuck. But George Anderton, moving in during 2003, coined his own private version of the name, in memory of those cigarettes he could recall his grandmother puffing at, in the days when smoking was a pleasant habit rather than a capital offence. George himself had smoked, but no longer did so. He had never really been that serious a smoker. But, although having successfully given it up some twenty years before, he still occasionally missed them. The act perhaps, more than any hit.

'I've counted twenty-four magpies just as I was walking along the lane from the Duck,' said Alice, as she put down her bag and accepted a mug of coffee. 'What do you think of that?'

'Triple hell,' said George, idly.

Alice laughed. She was only about forty, and very attractive. She made no secret of the fact she found George, a man more than ten years older, attractive too. But she was happily married and so would, hopefully, never impinge on George's solitary country life. He had given up London rather as he gave up smoking, missed the act, *or idea of it*, but not constantly. Women he had *not* given up. But there had been plenty – too many, he supposed – in his previous life. To be truly alone at last was restful.

Once a fortnight Alice came in, to dust, hoover and bleach the bathroom and the cooker. Now and then she cleaned the windows unasked. She charged the going rate, damaged nothing, did not get on his nerves, and was out of the house in never more than three hours.

'Triple hell – why's that?'

'The old rhyme,' said George. 'One for sorrow, two for joy, that stuff. There are several versions. The ones I know all end at nine magpies. And one of them finishes "Seven's for Heaven, and Eight's for Hell". So: three times eight equals twenty-four – triple hell.'

'And what's nine?'

'The Devil.'

'Oh, you,' she said, beaming at him and liberating the dusters.

He was a writer; novels, and even some stage plays put on at the Isyric and the Royal Court. Now all he seemed to turn out were short stories, but his reputation, if not major, was not quite nonexistent. To Alice, he thought, he was a curiosity maybe a sort of catch in the cleaning market. The rest of her clients were more usual, weekenders or locals with enough money, plus of course the Duck pub up the lane.

When he went upstairs to his workroom, (his study, Alice called it) he glanced from the window. Downstairs by now the trees in the small front garden, and the woods to the back, were thickly leafed, obscuring much of the sky. From the cottage's upper story however, he could see out across the shorter trees to the fields, as far as the farm. So he noticed a magpie fly up at once. And then, about half a minute later, another. And *then*, approximately equally spaced, several more. They rose singly, each from a different area, from behind the ring of trees on the fields' edge, from the fields themselves, from over the farm, out where the main road to Stantham cut ugly through the curve of the landscape.

Downstairs Alice was gently clinking something. George stood at the window and watched the magpies rising, he thought at first everyone from a different spot, yet now and then another one would go up later from the same spot. There seemed always a similar interval, though he did not bother to check it exactly. It was curious. He wondered briefly what had caused it, so many of them, and so regular in rising. But then he told himself to stop prevaricating and go back to the computer. Most writers used almost anything, he knew but too well, to absent themselves from work.

It is midday. The church clock in the village a mile off chimes out twelve. The light is very bright now, metallic and clear. It shines on the hills that rim the distance, and sparks up the windows of the cottage. A woman has cycled away about an hour before. The man is working diligently in the room on the upper story, drinking his fourth mug of coffee now. He is on a roll with the story he writes, does not wish yet to stop for lunch.

A sluggish car lurches along the lane, heading for the pub. Bees buzz, and a few grasshoppers creak in the hedge. A grey squirrel performs acrobatics in the garden trees, then bounds overland for the wood.

A magpie rises.

It is now the most recent example of hundreds. The man in the cottage might have seen, if he had been looking.

It flies straight upwards, straight up into the blare of the zenith sun. Light digests it. It has vanished.

Smaller birds flutter about their business, wood pigeons finches, a robin, a blackbird. Some are already teaching their young to fly. They quarter the lower air, flit past the oak trees and the now-wild apple that cast its last blossom only a week before. None of these birds heads directly upward. Not even the crow which abruptly wings over, cawing harshly, black as computer ink.

A magpie rises. Half a minute or thereabouts ticks a way.

A magpie rises.

Soon after six pm, George Anderton backed up the day's work, checked for emails – none – and switched off the computer.

Downstairs, lingering over a drink, he made a swift mental foray into the fridge, and promptly decided to visit the Duck for dinner.

At seven he opened the door of Cigarette Cottage, and stood, gazing through the trees into the glowing upper sky. It was blue, and feathered only by faint eddies of cloud, that seemed to foretell a fine tomorrow. The sun was westering towards the hills, visible in gaps, molten yet filmy. At least another hour before it set. This place. He had never regretted coming here. The lack of unnecessary human noise, beyond the intermittent legitimate agricultural sounds from the farm, the birdsong, the notes of various wildlife, the *silences*. Absorbed, he filled his ears with blackbird music, filled his eyes with the light. He had forgotten the magpies.

Then one rose, straight up, from the copse across the lane. Straight up and into the heart of the westered light, vanishing, as if dissolved.

George was startled. He returned to himself, refocused his eyes, and waited.

Another magpie rose. This one was further over towards the hills, framed in a gap, a small pinpoint of darkness. Perhaps it was not a magpie.

He looked at the hands of his watch, counted off the seconds – lifted his eyes ... *I will lift up mine eyes unto the hills* – nothing. No magpie had risen. Crazy, why would it?

Behind him. George turned round, moving almost too fast for himself. He saw this next magpie already high above, in the last moment before the light devoured it.

Had they gone on rising, *continuing* to rise, all day?

Why? Where were they going? To the top of the sky?

In the Duck the usual evening crowd was sitting over its drinks. George Anderton had lived here long enough by now that two or three regulars greeted him. In the dining room beyond the front bar, a handful of summer visitors sat, lightly tanned and animated. George scanned them cautiously. (He had once been trapped here by a maddish youngish woman who was a fan of his work, and had apparently previously met him in London at a book signing. Her recalled London intentions were not strictly literary, but he was then involved elsewhere. Besides she was hardly his type, whatever that really meant. Age had not improved her, or her intentions, or his inclinations. It had been difficult to shake her off without being rude. He had finally only managed to by *telling* her he did not want to be rude, which did the trick. Tonight there was no visitor who appeared to recognize him, or care about him in any way.

George went to the bar and ordered his meal and a bottle of Bex.

'What do you think it is, then?' Colly asked him, as he rattled a bottle from the fridge.

'What's that?' George felt curiously oppressed. He knew already what *that* would be. He was correct.

'Them barmy birds.'

'Which birds?' My God. George realized he was pretending he had not noticed. Why on earth?

But Colly, handing him a glass, explained, 'Bloody magpies. Going up like rockets all the time.'

'Are they?'

'I s'pose you ain't seen it, mate,' said Colly, who like George hailed from London, and had kept his accent with him though in situ here for more than eighteen years.

'Well, I've seen some flying over. But so what?'

'Here,' said Colly to Amethyst, as she came from the kitchen with two plates, 'old George ain't bloody seen them magpies going up all day. One every thirty-seven seconds Arnold reckons.'

'It's true,' said Amethyst, widening her eyes at George through the pleasant steam of one meat and one vegetarian lasagne.

From along the bar a couple of the other men joined in. They told George, and the room in general, how Arnold Weller had timed the darn things. Between thirty-two and thirty-eight seconds. He had counted them for a whole half hour. Over forty- three magpies, though old Arny had lost count, he thought, by a little – not much – forty or forty-three or even forty-eight. Near enough. And still flying up, one by one. One after another, And all of them from different places, or from the places no other bird was then rising from.

An elderly voice spoke from the corner, under the oil painting of *Ducks in Flight*. 'Was on the one o'clock news. I heard it. *5:00 pm* an' all. They made a joke about it. Then someone else came in – some politician. Said he saw 'em too, in Sussex or whatever, that morning, and coming into London all the way.'

'Reports all over the country,' someone else said.

George turned to Amethyst. 'No, thanks. No fries. Just the steak and salad.'

'You're, like, clever,' said Amethyst. She was in her early twenties, bright, respectful, a non-reader who unusually and wrongly seemed to believe writing a novel or play was the act of a wise, well-educated person. 'What do you think's causing it?'

'I don't know.'

'But it's – like it's *weird*, isn't it?'

'Is it? Maybe not.'

'Maybe it's global warming,' said one of the dining room visitors, moving in to ask where the gents was. Once told, he added, amused, over one shoulder, 'Jude says she saw them from the car when we were driving down. I didn't notice. But Jude's gimlet eye picked them out Okay.'

'What's a gimlet eye?' Amethyst asked George over the two cooling dinners.

'God knows,' he said. 'I used to know. Can't remember. Old age,' he added, smiling.

'You're not, like, *old*,' Amethyst insisted so vehemently and staring in his eyes with her wide, and certainly un-gimlet-like ones, he felt a hint of random desire. But it passed. It was food he lusted after, he decided, as he walked through into the pub garden.

Dusk was coming now, gradual and inevitable. A moth flew towards him as if in greeting, then on into the lighted pub.

Night falls.

From the farm the lights blaze out, and along the main road the headlamps of the occasional truck, or group of fast cars, spangle up the cats eyes like broken glass. A badger crosses, pausing to snuff at the tainted tarmac. A lucky badger, meandering sluggish yet unscathed, in a lacuna of traffic, to the farther side.

A frog croaks from a hidden pool. The night wind stirs softly and brushes through the leaves and grasses.

A magpie rises, blanking out, in passing, the stars, which then reappear.

The moon, almost full, will rise later. It will show far better than the stars the rising magpies, thirty or forty or fifty, that passage upward during every half hour within the radius of visibility.

The Duck burns like a golden lantern in the darkness. It is almost 11 pm. A couple of vehicles glide down the lane, then away to the side-roads that lie north and west of the main one.

Later the more dedicated drinkers emerge, taking various paths homeward. Two cross the fields, a young man and a girl, pausing to kiss among the new-beginning crops, like lovers from Hardy. Behind and sometimes before them, unseen, unnoted, magpies rise one by one, straight up into the stars.

The man who is a writer, and has sat in the pub garden until utter darkness beyond the lights closed up the sky, who afterwards had a vodka at the bar, listening with the publican and a few others to the ten o'clock news, the comments and views of a celebrity, a twitcher, and an eminent ornithologist, leaves the Duck, and himself goes back along the lane. In the doorway of the cottage he stands a moment again, studying the skyscape. Indoors, upstairs, he watches too a while at the workroom window. But he can no longer be certain they are rising. If they are, then not near enough for the lights of his house to catch the white pattern on their wings.

They are like ancient Egyptian birds, he thinks, magpies. Their markings seem primal and elder as the spectacle designs about the eyes of certain snakes.

In the deep hollow of the night, dreamless, he wakes. He hears the eruption of wings leaping at heaven from the roof above his head. Then he gets up and crosses through again into his workroom. Against the yellow three-quarter face of the hot moon he sees another magpie rise. Another magpie, more southerly, side lit, half a minute, or thirty-six seconds after it. In other areas that the moon can find, presently another. Another. Another.

Back in bed he switches on the radio for the World Service. But all the BBC will give him now is war, famine and disease; misery, and a tiny bit of the tune called Lily Bolero.

He turns it off and falls asleep again, and dreams the young girl from the pub is stalking him as the maddish woman had tried to do. Nevertheless he lets the pub girl in. Then just inside the doorway, she turns into his cleaning woman. Before the dream can become properly erotic, unfortunately – or perhaps actually fortunately – it fades away from him. He does not wake until the alarm clock sounds at seven am.

2

George Anderton no longer bothered regularly to read newspapers. Any allure they ever had for him had melted away in his forties. Two days after he saw the first magpie ascending from his window, two nights after hearing the other magpie clattering up, as if suddenly evolved from the very slates of the cottage roof, he walked to the village. Orthurst had its point-topped Saxon church and ancient yews, the scatter of shops and now-defunct post office, the bus-stop for Stantham Cross, and the other pub, the Cart and Plough, and some two hundred or so cottages, several dating way back. There was also the unfinished new estate, virtually builder-abandoned, that no one had wanted here, and was called the Lavvy.

At *Rosie's*, now owned and operated by Pam, he bought some butter, lettuce, pears and bacon, the *Independent* and *Guardian*, and the local *Stantham Spotter*.

'It gives me the creeps,' said Pam. She was a nice, comfy old thing of thirty-going on sixty five. 'My gran used to tell me they were unlucky. Ill-omened birds. If you saw one you had to say, "Good-morrow, Master Magpie." Or even "Good-Morrow, *Lord* Magpie." Then it might be all right. But I tried not to see them, when I was a child. Once one flew right at me on my bike, when I was only seven, and five minutes after I fell off in a ditch. Broke my little finger. Look. It never came back straight. Doesn't bend like it should, neither.'

'Poor you,' he said. He refrained from saying gran's scare tactics had freaked Pam out enough that she had been bound to fall off the bike, after a close meeting with a magpie.

'Can't avoid seeing the blessed things now, can I? Nobody can. And the telly news goes on and on about them. They're everywhere. Going up. Did you hear about the plane at Heathrow last night? Yes, of course you did.'

But he had not heard, slept solidly last night and through the alarm, missed the news this morning, had only just now seen the Heathrow report, a secondary headline on the *Guardian*'s front page.

It seemed, rather than inhaling a flock of the birds – what usually happened – the Boeing had been struck repeatedly by magpies, rising as if blind and insane, directly in its path, therefore hitting or being hit by fuselage, wings, and next the undercarriage, as the plane descended. The pilot had lost his nerve, many of the passengers too. The co-pilot brought the plane in, but the landing was a bad one, the touchdown heavy, the Boeing slewing across the runway. Three people had died, and seventy were injured, five seriously.

Disliking his own pragmatism, George considered it could have been far worse.

'On *TV Breakfast* they said, in Scotland,' went on Pam, unhappy and excitable at once, 'one plane there ditched in a loch.' She pronounced this 'lock', but he nodded. She expanded, 'But at Manchester they've grounded them all. They're going to ground all of them, unless they can shoot them out of the sky.' He refrained, now, from asking if she meant the birds or the planes. 'No one can get home, then, except by sea. And they've closed the Chunnel, too. It's on page two in the *Mail* – a train struck so many birds on the approach it had to stop – the wheels and the windows were all … she hesitated, grimaced. 'Black and red.'

He had, by then, seen the headline glaring on the *Mail*. WINGED DEATH RISES FROM THE TRACKS. A picture of the stalled train, surrounded by firemen and railway workers, was accompanied by a caption which began: *They seemed to come up out of holes under the line, said driver Ken Rains.*

Pam, shocking him slightly, abruptly started to cry.

He had the urge to put an arm around her, tell her everything would be fine and would get sorted out. But he was unsure he himself believed this, going on the general everyday mess. And anyway, he had found out in the not-so-distant past where such gestures might land him.

'Don't worry, Pam,' he temporized.

She said, 'No, it isn't that. I don't know what it is. My age, I expect.'

Poor Pam, he thought again, but did not say it. To be gallant might also be misunderstood. He left the shop having bought the *Mail* as well, the price of an extra paper to appease her. Not much of a consolation.

All the way back, now downhill to the fields and woods, he could watch the magpies rising on all sides, and behind him should he turn round, and off towards the hills those specks which, now, he was sure were magpies too. On his way to the village, going uphill, a single magpie had sprung directly from a bush at the side of the path. And later another from about three metres ahead of him. They might, these two, indeed have been engendered out of holes in the ground. Out of holes in reality. One minute non-existent, and then – *existing.*

It was overcast today. The patch of fine weather had disintegrated. Well, this was England. High up, cloud had settled, like a pale grey duvet. And the silence. How silent it seemed. Not even the magpies made a sound, beyond the abrupt clapping of their wings, when near enough. That signature rattling chatter of theirs was oddly always absent. There was a fitful, warmish wind. It carried a smell from the farm, he thought, not strong or really unpleasant; animal. Somehow depressing.

It's my age, I expect, George told himself with.dry mimicry. He had stuck too on the bloody story.

'Eyewitnesses are mistaken. It is *entirely impossible* that the huge number of birds people are *claiming* to have seen could even be *found* in the *whole* of the British Isles.'

An argument broke out at once between the four guests in the studio. The presenter tried to quieten them in vain.

George switched to another channel. A soap filled the eye and air with over-exaggerated drama that, beside the theatre of the swarming magpies, seemed ludicrous, laughable, and redundant.

The sun was low over the hills.

It had emerged from the duvet of cloud into a swollen vividity, murky orange, more like that of a wintry dawn.

The fall moon had not been visible last night.

When the microwave disgorged the frozen pasty, presumably cooked, he started to eat it.

The next news told him, and showed him, men and women interminably shooting at rising magpies. Some birds fell at once. Some fluttered and spiralled away, mutilated and dying. Some, entirely missed, rose on into the overcast of the TV-recorded afternoon.

On the first channel they were still shouting, red in the face under their make-up tans. The presenter, unable to control the verbal fracas, shrugged wryly.

The phone sounded in the front room. George wiped his hands and went to answer it.

'Hi, George, darling. Have you seen the news?'

'Yes.' It was Lydia, an actress who had appeared in one of his plays. They had slept together at the time. Lydia was his own age, but beautiful in a way not often seen. He had always liked her voice very much. He found he accordingly tended, during her phone calls, to hear her voice rather than what she said.

'Ah – what, Lydia?'

'Yes, it's an awful line, isn't it? I've heard half the lines are down.'

'How do you mean?' He thought once more he knew. Once more, he did.

'They fly right into them. Poor old birds, all tangled. Then the lines come off those pole things. It's as if they can't see. Or only see one thing – the upper sky. Do you have it there, Georgie?'

'Everyone has it everywhere,' he said, 'it seems. At least, in Britain.'

'Sean told me it just *stops* at the sea.'

'What exactly stops at the sea?'

'The – what did he say they called it? – oh, I can't remember. But it's dire, isn't it?'

'I suppose it is.'

'*The RSPB*,' someone else said loudly. But it was the television in the other room. The sound for some reason had revved right up, then sunk away.

'… and I just sit at the window and watch them. It's quite hypnotic. They just go up, straight up, and disappear in the clouds. I wonder why?'

'Yes, I think everyone wonders that.'

'I don't think I've ever seen a magpie in central London before. Not here.'

'No.'

'Everything else. Sparrows, gulls, pigeons – and pelicans and swans in the park. But magpies … None of the other birds are doing it, are they?'

He thought they were not. Then again, he had been noticing, or imagining, the other birds were rather quieter. There was less singing, less of the territorial tweets and cries. The dawn chorus – did that still happen? It was too early in the season for all birdsong to taper off. As for the magpies themselves, they made no sound, as he had been aware for a while. Aside from the flurry of their wings as they rose.

Through the window, in the small front garden, a magpie *evolved* from the rogue apple tree. It lifted straight up into the half-tone upper sky. He could have sworn it had not been there a second before.

'Lydia, are you still –'

'Hello?' she said. 'Hello, darling? Oh bugger. I can't hear you. Just a sizzle sort of thing. Never mind. If you can hear *me*, come up to town soon, won't you? We can go to dinner at the Royal.'

The light in the other room flickered.

George heard the TV again. The new voice, a woman's, was telling someone that the lower, or upper, stratosphere – he did not take it in – was full of birds, floating, only that, like a fleet at anchor. Up draughts or thermals carrying and supporting it, or them; hundreds, thousands. But when he went back into the room, the pasty, which going by the commandment on its label under no circumstances must anyone re-heat, had congealed to a cold, gooey fudge, and the screen was blank. Only the woman's impersonal and rather annoying voice talking of helicopter gunships, or ground-to-air missiles. Another programme then, about Afghanistan, or Pakistan.

George turned off the TV. *Not with a bang*, he thought, as if an alien authoritarian voice was speaking also in his head.

Not with a bang, but with a feather.

During the night the battery-powered radio, which he had left on woke him with a blast of between-items noise, some sort of militant jangle now representing the World Service, and obviously designed violently to awaken any insomniac who had managed to fall asleep. So he heard that an Italian plane, approaching Bournemouth airport, had found itself unable to land due to the maelstrom of birds. Having circled for some time, all the while with birds smashing into it, it headed back out to sea. An adjacent bulletin announced the plane had gone down in the water, not a mile out. All passengers and crew were feared dead. On the heels of this, came reports that European and US airlines were refusing to let their craft attempt landing anywhere on British soil, until the avian crisis was resolved. Countless Britons would be stranded. Perhaps they were glad? It seemed the Bird-Blanket, as one commentator called it, was limited to the British Island, (also a recent coining) involving only England, Wales and Scotland. The radio then, despite having new batteries, began to fail. He switched it off. That the failure had nothing to do with batteries he understood perfectly.

Morning, noon, evening, night. Time has passed, is passing. Passes. Above the sky, they are to be visualised, the fleets, massed close and massing ever more closely, as more and more of the components rise up to fill them, pack them tight. A black and white expanded and expanding cumulous.

Spy planes have taken photographs. By now the phenomenon is visible from space. Satellites relay batches of curious pictures.

Fighter craft have also risen. They have blasted out gaps in the living, quasi-suspended, fluttering cloud-ceiling. There has been speculation as to what, precisely, keeps the bird cloud in place. Some oblique abnormal thermal, perhaps, some unforetold up draught, maybe created even by the birds' own upward flight. Or else it is all some new facet of pollution, global warming, some scientific experiment that has – of course – misfired, gone wrong … human worthlessness and wickedness in general.

As for the aerial fighters, frequently their planes ingest the half-destroyed bodies of their composite black and white target. Then the planes fall too, like the dead and dying burning birds. Aerial activity is cancelled. And in any event, the endless streams of magpies continue to rise, one bird it has been estimated roughly every half or three quarter minute. During an hour, a hundred, sometimes one hundred and sixty birds are reckoned to be lifting from every square mile of land. If that is at all conceivable, likely, possible. Eyewitness statements, even those of trained observers, vary precariously.

Beaters plunge for a while through fields, woods, gardens, along hillsides, over moors, by river banks, and guns blast like a never-ending soundtrack of war. In towns and cities, citizens are summarily ordered off the streets, while rapacious bird-dogs and their handlers seek, and always find, their quarry But for all the birds slaughtered, quick and clean, misjudged and horribly, for all the carnage and the debris and the stink, the pity of it all – poor things, poor things – new birds rise, and keep on rising. Fifty, a hundred, two hundred, to a square mile. They seem to burst from the concrete skin of the streets, the stony ground the trunks of trees and walls of buildings, out of the impervious world itself, self-perpetuating, in eradicable, inexhaustible.

Feathers lightly, omnipresently, carpet the earth. Feathers are caught in trees, lie along windowsills, drift into offices, houses, shops, stations, subways, alleys and avenues, caves and churches, libraries and reservoirs. Along the side-roads, high streets and motorways the feathers drift, black and white, (and red with recent blood) several scorched and many broken. Cars and other vehicles lie tumbled along these thoroughfares too. Broken, some of them also, from multitudinous collisions with the bodies of rising birds which – all dead now and decaying – are plastered against their sides, stuck in their mechanical entrails and between the teeth of their wheels. Feathers drop from the air as well, a thin drizzle of feathers, an *autumn* of feathers, always falling. Black as ink, white as snow often sheened mysteriously, mystically blue. Down from the sky that, darkened over now, and made tomb-like after each invisible day's end, reveals no sun, no moon, no single star. The magpie cloud, the blanket, an opaque dome, shuts everything out. Day is dusk, night an upside-down abyss. No more golden mornings, no more ruby settings of the sun.

Sometimes a feeble rain falls too. It is very warm and has a filthy taste, smelling of chickens and giving off a strange, sooty, chemical undertone.

There have been great rushings to and fro on the land, naturally. Flurries of anger and protest, crime and hoarding, as well as the useless bird-war. Then came escapings – towards the nearest coast, where the blanket, the dome, stops, and the fearful ceiling uncannily comes undone. But the road-long deserted ruins of cars and campers, buses and bikes, provide evidence of how few made it there. Or if they did, they will have managed it by other means.

To the majority left inside the trap of Britain, unable to reach any coast, the idea of that exit point is by now nearly a myth. Can it be true that the coast, *any* coast – is clear?

It is true. All coasts are clear, as glass. Just past the beaches or shingle or stones or rocks or cliffs, the river-mouths, estuaries, bays and sandbanks, the dunes, the spits, the coves – there, where the surf or the big rollers begin; at Eastbourne, Great Yarmouth, Whitby, Berwick-upon-Tweed, at Helmsdale and Melvaig, Aberystwyth, Weston-Super-Mare, and Plymouth – *there* – for *there* IT finishes. To look up, *there*, standing by the fringes of the water, is to see suddenly the calmness or disturbance of actual sky, clouds, real weather, light; for *there* even the night is brilliant again with its stars and moon, with summer lightning, with *distance*. Open heavens. Open, *open*. And gulls fly over, in a graceful, ordinary way.

And beyond, out across the shining sky-lit sea, the islands. All of them are quite unclosed – the Orkneys, the Hebrides, Wight and Man stand sheer, like miraculous ghosts, like platinum pebbles on a horizon of pure glow, and the hem of Ireland, that too, and the longer strand of France: these are banks of deep blue smoke under a halo of sun-or-moonshine.

What then of the ones who managed an escape, who sped away from Britain's edges, in the racing ferries, fishing boats, speedboats and yachts? Did they, having reached the shining other shores, glance back? Surely they did, surely they still do, for out of Britain now no television picture comes, no telephone call, no email, no *text*. Britain, robbed of her masts of communication, of a sky through which signals can flow, has grown silent and primitive, secretive and supernatural, as in the ages of darkness. Nor is she to be penetrated, her airways shut, her roads and railway-lines negotiable only on foot, and that with vast difficulty.

And this shutness, this secret, is all that can be seen of her through the satellite cameras, telescopes, and other lenses trained on her, with flat and weary persistence. Not even the straining periscopes of nuclear subs, drawn in from the Atlantic to patrol her shores like voiceless wolves, can determine anything much, beyond her emptied coastline, her immobile interiors veiled by cobwebs of shadow. She is a darkling plain.

Except where, now and then, something surfaces through the dimness, like a fleck of flint in dirty water, a tiny black bubble in poisoned lemonade: a magpie rising, flying straight up. And then another. And then. And then.

3

The pub looked different by now. And, it went without saying, the pub *was* different. In the first weeks the soldiers, initially in multifarious vehicles, then on foot, brought oil, matches, lamps and candles, besides gas canisters to swell the store at the Duck. Out here, in the 'heart of the country', only electricity had formerly been available, and the series of chefs at the Duck always preferred, apparently, to cook with gas. Lucky. Electricity now, along with the phone, the TV and the radio, the computer and the World Wide Web, had all become things of the past, a *recent* past, but one which already seemed to have existed some centuries ago. Tap water was gone too. Reservoirs were polluted with incredible amounts of feathers, even by dilute disseminated bird crap, which had descended into them. For while the magpies had, and did, ascend, their innumerable castoffs, sometimes including their slaughtered bodies, fell down.

In certain parts of the woodland you came into a stretch where branches were thickly coated in feathers instead of leaves. But the leaves were dying anyway. The woods, the copses, even the fields, deceived by the constipated yet oddly defecating sky, believed winter had suddenly returned. Half the trees were bare, the rest shedding their parched, rusted foliage. The grass was also turning brown. Not much hope of grain or cereal, no promise of fruit; nothing really it seemed could grow.

But for now, some fresh foods persisted. Though the fridges and freezers had long since surrendered, they did not eat too badly at the Duck. Fresh meat – rabbit, chicken, beef and mutton. (They had been lucky there too, those nearer the big cities had had their flocks and herds sequestered by the army early on, before all transportation was understood to be impractical.) Fish, or ordinary low-flying birds, might be contaminated, and were off the menu, however. Tomatoes, salad, even potatoes, all these from hot-houses run off generators, were available. And certain canned, dry, or otherwise less perishable goods, brought from Stantham, currently a two day trek, aside obviously from any extra time given to bargaining with, fighting off, or else eluding the Stantham locals.

They had boiled the water and put it through filters. Now everyone drank bottled. Alcohol, thank God, George Anderton thought, came with its own indiginous preservatives and antiseptics. He had even relearned a liking for warm beer.

Tonight he was sharing a long table with three of the refugee families now living at the 'Lavvy', the unfinished estate at Orthurst. They had been en route for the coast when their cars, spattered with birds, gave up the struggle. Some of the estate houses were not in too bad condition, floored, roofed and insulated, with closable front doors and glazed windows. Their lack of electricity and plumbing hardly mattered either, of course. No one had any.

The refugees were all right, causing little trouble, only grateful not to be cast out. They had already lost their homes. And there had been draconian rationing in London, and elsewhere, and plans for some type of peculiar military call-up of the young, that seemed to have no purpose. They took to Orthurst as the drowning take to solid land. And each communal evening, the Cart and Plough, like the Duck, did stunning business – if anyone had charged, or paid.

Over by the bar, Amethyst was laughing with one of the two soldiers who had stayed behind, when the rest were force-marched back to Stantham barracks. The young man leant forward and kissed her. An entirely normal scene, it took on instantly a look of utter abnormality.

'What worries me,' said Jeremy, from London-and-the-Lavvy, 'is the nuclear power stations. How are *they* coping with this? Have they shut down, or are they just…'

'… leaking radiation,' concluded Liz from Chatham-and-the-Lavvy.

'I'll tell you one thing,' said Dave, Liz's partner, 'they'll have taken bloody good care of the oil-rigs off Scotland. Sea's supposed to be clear there, innit? You can bet they've got those rigs well protected.'

'Who'd you mean?' asked Jeremy. 'The so-called government? They'll have scarpered straight down their bleeding bunkers. And they couldn't run anything anyhow. Couldn't run a piss-up in a toilet.'

A trio of children watched, wide-eyed. The eldest was only seven, and Sharron of Reigate-and-the-Lavvy quickly diverted their attention back to the pandas on the special kids' napkins Colly had produced.

'What I miss,' said Sharron's boyfriend – Rob, George thought he was called – 'is the sport. All had to be stopped, didn't it? Motor racing, rugby – even golf!'

Jeremy said in a light, grieving voice, 'And that match – Arsenal versus Brighton – that would have been a cracker.'

Jim was plodding by to the bar. 'Want another, anybody?'

They did.

It was handy, George thought, the way these people talked about this, regularly skimming their terrors, yet also distracting each other, with the pandas of political complaint, food and drink and company.

He was glad too, that the smell of oil and kerosene, and the candles, some of which were scented, the smell even of people now less washed and over-deodorized in compensation, helped mask the insidious presence of that metallic chicken stench, that dropped with all else from the sky. But probably too they were all becoming used to it. Soon they would not even notice.

Outside it was a jet black abyssal night, the only kind, finally. But the pub basked in its pre-electric flame-lit radiance. This was how faces, forms, suddenly moving hands and glasses might have looked in paintings from the Renaissance. Similar at least, he corrected himself, for constructed light was bound to have altered, somehow. You knew, even in the Victorian era, no oil-lamp had cast quite this sort of illumination, or shadow. Everything changed.

And the pub's noise, chatter and clatter, and sometimes a sing-song – were also like that. They stood to replace the not notes of mobiles, recorded music, radio – and still didn't make an elder noise but a modern one, anxiously filling up the void. Beyond which void loomed the agglomeration of silence the magpies had created. The magpies, that themselves no longer chattered or called, that made no sound. How silent then must be the upper skies where they clung or hung. Dumb and deaf, all questions futile, all answers obsolete.

As Jim put the new bottles on the table, George saw Alice come in out of the dark. She paused a moment to speak to Amethyst, who nodded, while her soldier turned aside to light a roll-up; no one seemed likely to object to it now.

George could see Alice, too, had changed. She had lost weight, become oddly fragile and attenuated, her hair seeming blown about. There was a bruise on her left cheekbone. She put her hand to it absently. Amethyst was pouring Alice a glass of wine. No doubt one of the birds had struck her. In the last weeks that had begun to happen. Before, the birds had seemed, when rushing upward from the ground, or wherever it was they burst from, to strike only inanimate objects. But recently several people had some tale of a magpie springing abruptly past them inches away, the slap of a wing, long scratch of a claw, minor concussion of round body and hollow bones. Old Tim claimed to have seen one bird dash straight upward through the body of a cow that had been grazing on a slope behind the farm. She had not seemed hurt, just frightened. But later a bruised and reddened area had appeared along her ribs. They had decided it best to slaughter her quickly, and then remove the perhaps-contaminated meat when preparing her for eating. But Tim had always romanced, embellished facts. Even something like the thing which now went on might seem worth enhancing, to old Tim.

Alice raised the glass and drank. Her eyes connected with George's. She seemed about twenty, he thought. An infallibly revealing illusion. She smiled a nervous little smile, as if she had never seen him before. But George smiled broadly back, and beckoned, getting to his feet, and Jeremy obligingly shoved himself and family, and their chairs, along the table to make room.

'Oh,' said Alice, very low, 'I didn't mean to –'

'You're not. It's nice to see you, Alice.'

'I'm so sorry I haven't been up to the cottage –'

'Well. Cleaning the house doesn't seem so important, frankly, do you think?'

'I suppose. I don't know. Todd –' Todd was her husband, 'always wants everything clean. Or until …' Alice stopped. She drained her glass. She glanced at George under her lashes. Their unexpected meeting had become a liaison of two spies, but what was the espionage Alice had in mind?

'It's fine, Alice.'

Jeremy leaned over and refilled her glass. It was the same red wine, or near enough, and everything was free. She thanked Jeremy, but he had already turned tactfully away, leaving the spies to their clandestine conversation in code.

'How are you?' George asked.

This was a fatal, leading question, and he knew it.

She did not answer.

Then she softly said, 'It's awful, isn't it?'

'Yes, Alice. It's awful.'

'I'm – scared,' she said.

He saw the oldest child take note, and an expression of fear creep into his face. George smiled broadly again. He said to her, 'Why don't we go back to the cottage? Talk there. I can walk you home later. I've even got some spare food.'

She too had noticed the child. She brightened, falsely but giving quite an actorly performance. 'That would be – yes, let's do that. Why not?'

As they were going out of the door, Colly appeared and handed George another bottle of wine. 'Last of the best Merlot. Go on. Have a treat. You know, I knew a feller once, he always wanted a pub. Then he comes into some dosh, buys the pub, gets it done up, cracking, ace cook, full cellar, top class guestrooms. What d'you think he does then?' George and Alice waited between light and night. A sing-song had started, *Oliver's Army* by Elvis Costello. Behind the bar Amethyst was snogging the soldier. 'He locks everyone out, and keeps the place to himself, just for him, I mean. Nobody else let in, ever. The Bugle it's called. Up Camden way. What do you think of *that*?'

'This mark on my face – it isn't anything to do with the birds. He hit me. Todd. He hit me.'

'Christ. When was this?'

'This morning. He just – did it.'

'Had it happened before?'

'No. Not … not really.'

'Where is he now?'

'With Pam Boys. You know, from the shop.'

They stood still in the lane, in the dark, among the alopecia of the trees, balancing on spent feathers. No car would try to drive through, not anymore, and footsteps would be clearly audible. He had turned the torch off, because its batteries were running low. He had had a solar-powered torch too, but it went without saying it was unrechargable.

He had an urge to touch her, hold her, comfort. But George grasped very well this was not gallantry or outrage – despite the fact that the image of her bastard husband hitting her incensed him. No, it was desire, lust. But then. What else was left? It puzzled George too, the manner in which, above all else, carnality survived, just as biological hunger and thirst, and an extraneous liking for the taste and effect of alcohol. Oh God. The Last bloody Days of Pompeii. Eat, drink and be merry before the volcano exploded, or the circus lions came to tear you limb from limb. Just as in the old B movies. But also, be fair, here at least, where some quiet remained, courtesy and camaraderie also persisted, a sort of familial gentleness. Be gentle then.

'I'm so sorry, Alice.'

She came into his arms, there in the near-blind blackness of the lane. She was beautiful, smooth and pliant, and her hair curiously rough and savage. Her mouth was as appetizing as he had believed it would be. When they drew apart, she shuddered. 'Can we get inside the house – I don't like being out here, in the dark.'

He switched the torch back on.

Not until they reached the gate of Cigarette Cottage did it occur to him he had not heard, nor even in the ray of the torch *seen*, a single magpie. By some fluke they had somehow missed the ones that must have gone on rising all about, as they continually rose, as he had even seen them rising at six this evening. What power sex had, sex, (not love) that drove out fear.

During the night he went to get a bottle of water downstairs, and stood at the window looking out into the front garden. Three foxes grouped there, limned by the light of the candle. All males, he thought, young, healthy enough, but huddled on the wild lawn and staring in at him, exactly as he stared out at them. It was as if they wanted something from him. He wished he could offer something. But maybe what they asked for was what everyone wanted: an answer. Their eyes flamed, all surface, luminous in a spiritless way that made him think of rabies posters from the '70's – or of demons.

Animals had been behaving oddly for days. You did not notice, then an especially unnatural event made you see, and so recall other incidents. He had first become aware of it with a cluster of robins, nine or ten, then almost twenty of them, a flock almost like that of starlings, flying round and round the copse, before dazzling off through the dirty dreary day-twilight towards the farm. Robins were generally solitary, just as foxes were, out of the mating season. But there had been the cats, too. Each screamed and cried and ran towards you, or from you, still calling. One he had met in the lane. It had a magpie feather in its mouth. The cat hurried up and down, up and down, not dropping the feather, not chewing it, growling low in its throat. Some animals had simply vanished. Consensus opinion had it they were hibernating, misled as were the trees. That – or they had got wise to the idea they also might be shot for food. The absence of all grey squirrel activity, squirrels who even in a real midwinter were often about, was telling enough. He had not seen or heard any frogs, or pigeons, nor heard a single dog bark or howl for weeks, either. There were no insects. Even the clothes moths had gone away.

George turned from the foxes, collected the water, and went back upstairs.

Alice sat up in the bed, no longer sobbing. She had wept after they first made love. Then fallen suddenly asleep against him. Later she woke, and told him she had always wanted him, had fantasies about him. 'But you're better.' So there had been more sex, rich, brain-flooding orgasm. And then she had begun to sob again, could not stop. She said, 'It isn't about *him*. Sod him. He can fuck off. It's the rest. It – reminds me of that Hitchcock film –'

'From the story by Daphne du Maurier?'

'Was it?'

George did not say that the short story had been far bleaker and more terrible than the film. 'But those birds attacked, didn't they,' he reminded her instead. 'Our magpies – they just fly upward.'

'Oh,' Alice whispered, 'what's going to happen?'

She knew he could not tell her, beyond the obvious, which was bad enough. He said, 'It'll be all right, Alice.'

'Will it?'

'Yes.'

And then she had calmed, knowing, he supposed, (as he did) that either it would or it would not. Out of their hands. Better off also therefore out of their minds.

Now they drank the water.

'Can I stay?' she said, like a child.

'Please do stay.'

'I can leave once it gets – once it's lighter. I don't want you to feel – I know you like to be alone.'

'How do you know that?' he inquired, playfully.

'So you can write.'

'That,' he said. He visualized the unfinished story trapped there on the computer screen, now lost in space. Backing up had hardly mattered when the whole bloody lot went. He could have foretold, and printed it. But then, why write stories while Rome burned.

'Do you remember the PM talking, just before Radio 4 went off the air?' she surprised him by saying.

'I didn't listen. He gets – got on my tits, frankly.'

'But that night he was so good, he was … It brought out the best in him.'

They laughed, bitterly. Then lay down to sleep, back to back. How long since he had felt that sumptuous comfort, female flesh against his? And for how much longer? Till the muffled sun rose behind the black and white sky? Until the food and bottled water were all gone? Tears ran also from his eyes. He cried then quietly, not to wake her. The pillow soaked them up, his tears, as eternity soaked up all such flimsy things, weeping, blood, the shells of beasts and men.

In sleep he felt rather than heard a vague amorphous rumbling. Thunder? Some storm created by the choking of the stratos – or a phantom train perhaps, once more enabled to run all those miles off in Stantham. Asleep, he did not care. He was dreaming of Lydia, faithless after all as Alice, (or Todd) Lydia in that hotel in Paris, thirteen years ago.

In the moments before daybreak, or what now passed for it, George's dreams altered into a perfectly coherent recollection of researching magpie legends, which he had done about nine days before. The book was an old one, something he had picked up in London in the '90's. A writer never knew, he had always maintained, what might or not ultimately be useful.

Birds of Ill Omen and Evil Luck. This had been the heading. But at the end of the section came a concluding paragraph, with the sub-heading: *Exonerating the Magpie.*

'The Magpie is often badly thought of, as reputedly it refused to don full (black) mourning at the death of Christ. However this would seem to be a misunderstanding of the story.

'In an older version, the Magpie donned *half* mourning; it is true, to show respect for Christ's suffering and death. But the bird's snow-white feathers were intended to indicate that life continues *after* death, and that indeed Christ *Himself* would rise physically from His tomb. Why else does the Magpie remain with the Zodiac sign of Virgo, the Virgin, which connects directly with the Virgin Mary, the Mother of Christ? At least, apparently, Jesus and Mary were sure that the Magpie was both innocent of all blame, and a witness to the Great Truth. And for that reason the Virgin herself added to his elegant attire the extraordinary sheen of blue, (Mary's own sacred colour), which is to be seen most evidently on his wings.'

Almost morning, technically; it is about twenty minutes short of five o'clock. The sky has a colourless darkness, but is strangely faded at a point near the zenith. Gradually this thinning of an upper canopy begins to fill with muffled, dulled, but undeniable light.

In the woods birds do not sing. Then a shrill chorus, not song but warning, surges up, fragments, and ends.

From the copse across the lane no bird rises. No magpie rises. All about nothing stirs. Silence is concrete, now. Stone.

To scan from horizon to horizon is to fail to detect any movement. Not an animal slinks or runs along the earth, let alone takes wing in the lower element of the sky.

No magpie rises.

No magpie rises.

Since eight pm yesterday evening, as surprisingly only a very few have noted, nowhere on the landmass of Britain has a single magpie risen, to fly straight upward. Or in any direction.

Above, just east of the zenith, the hole, for so it is, continues dully to grow lighter. Perhaps too it perceptibly widens, just a very little.

Then, to the north, another dim vague thinning seems to be taking place, another occult lightening appears to be wearing through.

Over the fields, miles up it seems, and in some other dimension, a loud indescribable crack bellows through the air. A splintering line, scribbled in silvery radioactive ink, careers across the masked dawn-dusk of the heavens.

A kind of storm, cloud shift and whirlwind, discourages darkness. The episodes of lights brilliantly flash now, knifelike. Then, the sky – is falling.

It is falling everywhere. Far off, near, immediately overhead.

It falls in masonry blocks which, as they descend, drop all apart in chunks and waterfalls and tidal waves, and is blundering and spinning downward. Bodies. The corpses of dead birds.

A million million, a trillion trillion. Lifeless and almost weightless yet, in this unthinkable and unavoidable mass, a weight of unguessable and incorrigible proportions.

The air resounds to a type of steely scream. Whether voiced or only a by-product of the avian deluge, it swamps and pierces all and everything.

Death begins to slam against the earth.

The prelude impacts are awesome enough.

Before vision becomes only a mosaic, like scenes from an ancient and damaged film, it is feasible to see whole boughs snapped off from trees, on buildings a slide and tumble of slates and chimneys and TV aerials, satellite dishes, shattering and scattered – smashing with the white-black downpour of death to the ground below.

From the church in the village the clock is silent as its automatic hands approach ten to five, yet the bell in the tower, if barely audible, clangs dolefully. Part of the church roof has been riven open and, cascading by, the dead are striking the bell.

But now the next phase of impact is arriving. To this the prelude was nothing. In the woods the young trees reel, are toppling. Hedgerows and fences crumple and disappear. From the little pool huge gouts of water are displaced – who would have thought it could hold so much?

Whole roofs buckle now. Joists give way. Windows collapse. In the village street shop-fronts disintegrate one after the other as if bombed. The pavement and road are piled high, the gardens. At the half-built estate *all* the building is coming undone. Something is on fire at the farm, smoke curdling upwards, but blotted away almost at once as the rain of the dead pours on – the main road is hidden. Even the stranded cars are covered over. Fields, tracks, hills, landscape – all now under this thick white-black snow …

Through the cacophony of *rushing*, the whine and shrill of the great lost scream, no individual sound is to be deciphered.

The cottage on the lane is piled high, high as its roof, as if with discoloured sandbags. The pub is only a mound, a sort of heap of unclean washing, featureless and silent, a mashed tree lying against it.

The magpies fall. The ultimate gush of the volcano.

They drop and strike and crush and break and are broken. They cover and they bury everything. They load the world like bandaging, like grave-wrappings. And still they are falling. The heads of distant oak trees – drowned. Eradicated.

And the stench, the thunder that seems never likely to end, tempest, tsunami, eruption. Poor things. Poor things.

It is five am. The church clock does not chime, even if anyone could hear it.

High, high above the fall, from the widening, shining chasms in the darkness, light foams clear as clean water. And in the east the sun has risen, is visibly rising, like the pitiless eye of Man Himself.

Cain

He was born seven minutes before me, and lived for two. By the time I had begun to breathe, he was dead. We were identical, so alike that if he'd lived, no one could have told us apart. Miranda revealed all this many years later, one night when she was unusually, spectacularly drunk. But by then, of course, I knew him well.

One of my earliest memories is that I thought my name was Hill Town. Actually it's Hilton, like the old hotels. I can remember asking my mother why I had this name, and had we lived on a hill. She laughed and dismissed me; I was still at the entertaining but relatively unobtrusive stage. The Girl – always there was a Girl to look after me – took me away, down to the edge of the blue creaming sea.

'Look, fishes,' said the Girl. And we watched dolphin, which sometimes came in so near the shore, leaping like grey silk balloons from the water.

The sea house was a large one, with white columns. In the garden were palms and enormous orange trees. But at other times we were in the city. I was taught at home by a succession of tutors. My remote father didn't believe in my mixing in the rough and tumble of real life before I had to. I was, needless to say, a lonely child. The Girls were pretty and mostly tried, I think, to be kind. But in a way they resented me, this dark cute little kid who was swathed in so much money, when they and theirs had had to struggle. Always a problem with servants, I suppose, however well-treated or well-paid. And frankly, I'd imagine the Girls weren't that well-treated-or-paid. My father gave some of them special attentions, and then they left. I recall my mother, white as marshmallow, shouting in a lofty room, 'Since the baby, you don't want me, do you?'

'Oh, Miranda,' said my father, solid as granite to her sweet wobbling softness, 'you're so impossibly self-centered. Why does it have to be you? Couldn't I just fancy a change?'

I remember too Miranda's tall morning glasses of fruit juice and gin, which, as the day went on, altered to glasses of pure gin, with only an orange or lemon slice swimming there like a fish.

As the years passed, her marshmallow softness became spread on her more lavishly. But she was a beautiful woman, even large, a fat, white, pampered seal, with yearning coal-dark eyes. Do you sense I loved her? I don't know. I simply watched her. She was a glamorous being hung with jewels and glasses of alcohol who normally inhabited the same buildings with me.

As I grew older she became more interested in me. Once she saw I was a male, that is, not simply a boy child. She would rub me down with a towel when I came out of the sea or the pool. She would brush my hair, take my face between her hands and stare into my eyes. She called me her 'handsome hound'. 'So streamlined and slender,' she would say. 'And such lovely heartless eyes.' At first I think I didn't dislike this. Then it embarrassed me. I can't recollect quite when my self-consciousness began. Around puberty I would think. There was nothing sexual in her actions, though sensual perhaps. But fondling had for me an amorous quality from the very first.

I said I was a lonely child, but that was in the day. I knew instinctively that my questions and conversations bored everyone. What to me was so new and odd was to them merely routine, beyond discussion. Yet also by day I was generally in the company of adults, my mother, sometimes my father, the tutors, the Girls. At night, bathed and combed and put to bed in silk pyjamas, the mosquito net drawn like a film of mist about the bed, the window showing in its long frame the indigo star-daubed vista of sea sky, or the light-hives of a city without other stars – at night, I was alone. More alone than most. My father frowned on any toys that were not instructional, in some way intellectual. I was taught chess at seven. And so no furry floppy companion shared my bed from the age of five. I'd cried when they took my bear and rabbit away. My father explained I was too old for them, and that in the children's' home to which they went, they were needed far more. He had always this habit, of abruptly seeing necessary benefits for others when he wanted to deprive his own family of something. (For example, the three Girls who were sent away would thereby lose their essential wages, bringing their kin to poverty – how was it my mother was oblivious of this? But she had obstinately continued oblivious.) However my own horror was mitigated by the knowledge my friends would be loved and housed.

I think six months elapsed before I replaced them.

How did it start? I had, when alone, talked to myself all that while, because I didn't interrupt myself, or criticize – or very little, something had come off on me from the adult world – and because I found my own voice not repellent or annoying as, very evidently, now and then others did. Somewhere in the pre-slumbering dark, lit by the blue sea window or the honeycomb of city lights, my talk began to be not to myself, but to another.

Children generally fall asleep quickly. Some nights I spoke for ten or fifteen minutes, on some for one or two. The sense that I was listened to was very definite. And presently also the sense that this was a secret thing, which should be mentioned to no one else. But then, I wasn't a confessing child, had never been encouraged to be. *Tell mother, your father wants to know*, these were the phrases attendant on transgression, not invitations to confide.

Even had I confided, of course, my nocturnal chats, though doubtless disapproved, would have been safely enough categorized. I had, like so many lonely infants, an Imaginary Friend.

The Girl had slapped me during my bath. It was a hard slap, across my legs. I'd been splashing a lot, I don't know why, I was never a very boisterous child. The point was, which I didn't then – I was eight – understand, she had on a gold lame dress. She had fallen in love with my father and wanted to catch his eye, and to do this, pretending it was for some date she had after my bath, she had had to dress up first – he only came into my room for a few minutes before dinner. Inevitably, I'd splashed the dress. There was a wet patch on the inferior lame, over her breast which she'd wanted to sparkle. It looked like the map of Italy.

The slap hurt quite badly, perhaps because I was wet. She looked at its reddening formation on my thighs in terror. She said she was sorry, so sorry, but her boyfriend was so particular – 'If senor ask,' she said, 'tell you slipped, yes?'

'Yes, all right.'

'You are good little boy.'

In fact my father never noticed, either the red slap and the map of Italy, or her gaudy clothing.

When they were all gone, I lay in bed, and rubbed my thighs where the sting had been. I told my Imaginary friend what had happened. And it was then, then for the very first, I felt him. Because he touched me. He touched the slap. He caressed it, as soothingly as a mother, over and over stroking me, until I tingled. In the end, consoled, curiously excited, yet calm, I fell asleep, and as I did, I felt his arms holding me.

Why didn't I marvel at this? Why wasn't I alarmed? Everything is strange to a child. Very little makes any sense. Why is the sky blue? Why must I eat now when I'm not hungry, and not *now*, when I am? Why are you angry with me simply because I'm here? None of these inquiries, mostly unvoiced, get proper answers.

And this – this was very nice. It was comforting, and I'd had no comfort at all. Even falling down among the sand on the beach, cutting my knee on a shell, a great fuss, painful antiseptic, a stitch put in by a scowling doctor – but no *comfort*. Be a brave boy.

Yes, this was nice. And half waking once the sense he was still there. Not seen, but warmly touching. Holding me, coiled about me, and I about him the way I had seen cats asleep on sunny walls.

Every night after that, he stroked me, and leading my hands, led me to stroke him. He felt just like myself. Smooth and thin, almost snake-like, sleek. His hair was exactly the same longish length as mine, and smelled like mine, as his body did, of expensive soap and some childish cologne, of shampoo and sea and salt. Of flesh too, of the warmth of hidden valves, extrusions and crevices, with their tang of meat and spice.

I don't remember when he kissed me first. It was a gentle brushing thing. I think I must have been ten or so. His closed mouth had a whisper-scent of toothpaste, just like my own.

I'd call him by a name – I haven't said, have I, I left off using it later – which was a makeshift of my own, a childish anagram, *Holtni.* (Hold Me?) But even then I never used this name to him, only when I thought about him by day, which now often I did.

I'll tell Holtni about this big car I saw. I'll tell Holtni Momma was sick and had to lie down. Or, *Holtni will cuddle me,* because I hadn't done my mathematics very well, and my tutor shouted, saying I was a brainless little rich boy, as if *rich* were an obscenity, as of course it was.

But I recall the next events, when everything changed, perfectly well.

Puberty had commenced, but I didn't know. No one had really warned me. There had been a book, which had diagrams, telling, it seemed – I was bored and didn't try hard with it, there were so many dull books they made me read – only things I knew. That I had a penis, and two nipples, all three of which, like soldiers, might suddenly stand to attention. This was funny. I waited, but they didn't. Probably all a mistake, just the same as the idea I would be good at sport, while, aside from swimming, I could do nothing sporting at all. One of the tutors had attempted to give me a sex lesson, but for his own ends, I would guess, judging from his overnight dismissal, something to do with the younger gardener.

I was twelve. I was in my mother's room. Sometimes I went there when she was absent. I had liked to feel her dresses and sniff them, to pry into cupboards, drawers. I found curious things. A box like a shell with a rubber thing in it like something out of the sea – appropriate enough, given the box. And once a carton of things like large cigarettes, but these were, once extracted, too white, and ultimately bendy, and I couldn't see how you would light them. Luckily. I never confided anything about these discoveries either. The notion of her pre-adolescent son routing among her diaphragm and tampons would have sent Miranda hysterical.

Her jewels intrigued me, too. As a child I loved to see her in them. She was for a second, like something from the Arabian nights, (doubtless the expurgated version), leaning to kiss me good night smelling of *Les Yeux du Noir,* her neck and ears lambent with cool, flashing emeralds, inflamed rubies or the gold cross set with three diamonds between her breasts. The jewel boxes were sometimes locked, but she was forgetful. It was not until I was fifteen I learned these were all copies. The real gems were worn only once or twice a year.

One can say I had a sexual craving that stemmed from my mother, from her attributes – garments, ornaments – more than her body, her *self*.

This must be so, because that day in her room I was moved to strip, and look at myself in her pier-glass, where I could see all of me.

My theory then for doing it was that my own mirrors were either not full-length, or in difficult places. My body seemed to me much larger and broader, and I wanted an overview.

Whatever, my clothes came off and I stepped naked to her glass, standing there on the deep carpet in the shining sunlight of the sea house. And here I was, Hilton.

I knew I was handsome. People remarked on it and I had come to recognize what they pointed out. The large dark eyes and long lashes, the thin straight nose, the thick straight brows and thick straight hair. A long and narrow physique, long-legged, the shoulders widening. Clear skin mildly tanned from the days at the beach, only the whiter band about my loins, where in a black thicket, the snake lay like a little velvet trunk. As I looked I thought, Holtni's like me, so he too looks just like this. Even though I've never seen him. I'll tell him how I've looked at me. I'll ask him.

As I said it, a blush went up my face, dark red. And my entire body quickened. I felt a wonderful, shameful, underneath pressure. My blood was full of spangles and darts, and up it rose, that velvet trunk, thickening and pushing, straight up as the diagram in the awful book had foretold.

I put my hand on it in astonishment, and a shudder of the darkest most intense feeling went through me. I shut my eyes, and played with myself, opened them and stopped. I could feel something building in me, from the base of my spine to the crown of my head, the soles of my feet. It scared me. It was like running along a corridor, and knowing at the end there must come an opening and a colossal leap – but into what?

I turned my back on my image that was also the image of Holtni-Hold Me. I put on my clothes, forcing my deflating erection inside like a naughty animal.

Then I went for a long walk along the beach, drank a Coke at a cafe I was forbidden, watched other boys, the kind I'd never met, throwing a ball in the paint-blue water.

Very carefully, I didn't think one thought about bed, night time, anything like that.

In any case, there was a dinner party that evening, and I was expected to be there for the first part of it. My father utterly indifferent to me as a person, liked to show me off as a valuable possession. I was well-trained, polite, if not witty or skilful, at least graceful in my reticence. I said very little but listened attentively. Guests tended to exclaim I was a model son.

The evening passed. Miranda wore a green Lavinché gown, and got as ever enormously drunk, showing not too many signs of it, she and her body being so accustomed to the state of drunkenness. My father moved among his friends and business acquaintances. Two daughters of some politician, thirteen and fifteen, seemed both quite interested in me. Flattered and uneasy, I sat between them at dinner, eating decorously the iced soup, and squab, the skulls of white meringues. One girl, the fifteen-year-old, told me quietly I was beautiful enough to kiss. If I could find an excuse to leave the party and come on to the balcony, where night-blooming jasmin made a canopy, she'd show me how.

I didn't want to go, and therefore felt I must. My father had always insisted I behave impeccably to his guests.

Outside, the night was full of perfumes and murmurs, the sea, distant music from the little orchestra, laughter and talk.

The girl drew me in under the jasmin. She was one inch taller than I, but this was no problem. She pressed her lipsticked mouth to mine, and slid her tongue among my teeth. Presently we clung together; I, because she clung to me.

At last she drew back. 'Not bad. You're a wicked boy. You've been with a woman, I bet.'

I said nothing. I had gathered, from literature alone, that to go with a woman was my destiny and function, a cause for congratulation, as with successful school-work.

She re-applied her lipstick, pinched my bottom, and went back in to the party.

Soon after, at about eleven, it was suggested to me surreptitiously by the current Girl, that I should go to bed.

As I climbed the stairs, nothing about the politician's daughter stayed with me. Although I knew the rising of my flesh was directly connected with what she had done and said. I had *felt* no connection as it occurred. I had not come erect, and indeed, had known enough to ease back from her, as if to stop her feeling what in fact had not happened.

Even so, I was now disturbed. For in my bed waited my intimate companion.

By now, I'd decided my own powers of the imagination had made him seem so real for me. Beginning to reason, having been made to do it by my various teachers, I'd awarded him at last the license of My Fantasy. That I was homosexual, oddly, did not occur to me. Until this particular night, I hadn't once equated his caresses and my own with anything other than true companionship.

In my bedroom, however, I began to know differently.

No sooner was the door shut, than my penis started to move independently. I'd already bathed before the dinner. Now I went into the shower and ran it chill. But this did nothing save to tone me up, and so excite me more.

I climbed into bed naked, in the dark, trembling with a terror old as life, already hot again, my lips parted.

He met me at once, my Imaginary Friend, My Fantasy, Hold Me. He coiled his arms about me and dragged me down, fierce as a lion, his nails scraping and ploughing my shoulders and my lower back. He rubbed himself against me, and I found we duelled, for he, invisible as night, tangible as flesh, was as erect as I. But he knew things that I did not. He was tickling at my balls, running a finger up and down my spine, kissing me, not as the sticky lipstick girl did, but sucking my tongue and breathe right out of me. He exquisitely tortured my penis to a raging volcano, until I thought I'd choke and lose consciousness, but instead finally I came, exploding in his phantom hand, a shower of silver needles, a gush of syrup and wine.

No sooner did it happen than I began to cry. Then getting up, I ran to the bathroom and puked out all the exotic dinner.

When I returned I expected him to be there, to comfort me as in the past. But now, for the very first, my friend was gone.

He returned. I'm sure you worked that out. He was there the next night, and the next. Initially I tried to find excuses not to go to bed. I'd sit reading in the rocker by the window. Or I'd watch my TV. Sometimes, seeing the light on, or hearing the television at one o'clock, the Girl would knock and come in, dressed in her skimpy kimono. 'Bad boy – you go to sleep now. What will senor say if I tell?'

So in the end I had to sit there in the dark. And once, when she knocked and opened the door, had to pretend I'd been visiting the bathroom.

I took to locking my door. When she knocked then, and rattled, which once or twice she did, I didn't answer. In the morning she chided me, and I said, 'Yes, you woke me up. Father isn't going to like that, is he?'

In any case, whatever I did, unless I slept all night in the chair, I must eventually go to bed. And then, after a few moments, or even immediately, My Fantasy would catch hold of me. He was only sometimes insidious. Usually he overwhelmed me at once, his arms round me, his hands on me, his tongue at my lips. But I was ready anyway. I'd sat in the chair for two hours, nursing my engorgement. Sometimes within a minute of his irresistible strokes, I erupted, whimpering into his unseen yet smothering body. Two or three times, he surprised me, was not there. Then I would thrash about, my face a furnace, the bursting sausage of desire twitching in my own unpractised grip. And then he would steal over me, shivering fingers along my buttocks, under my ear. He would draw me against his body, massaging my belly, licking my neck, his other hand riding me forward over the edge into the scarlet abyss of orgasm.

I stopped resisting. I simply got into bed without delay and put out the light, and myself up, gasping with uncontrollable eagerness.

Once he had had me, I slept. He let me, holding me close. I never ran away again, and he never again deserted me. Now and then, generally between three and four in the morning, the window lightening like a pearl, he would wake me … that is, I thought, I would wake myself, stiff again, and sometimes then he would take me in his mouth. The bliss of this caused me the first time to scream. Nobody arrived to investigate. I would have said it was a nightmare. I knew, switching on a lamp, they would see no one but me, my nudity safe under the wet sheet and through the mist of the net.

Not until I was almost fifteen did he ease me on to my stomach, and with glorious, melting intrusions, culminating in cannon thrusts, bugger me. I thought I would die of that. I bit my pillows, my saliva mingling with tears and sweat. That orgasm was like death, and in the morning I expected to be crippled, disfigured, but everything was apparently the same, save for one tiny drop of blood, my virginity, that I blamed on a bite.

You would probably ask me if I truly still thought by now I did all this myself, merely through an overactive imagination, and some unlikely contortions of my own body. What can I say? I'd given up. Reason had never been much use in my life. The rules of my daytime world were set, irksome, and unimportant. I longed for and expected nothing. And, by then, I had read of the incubus, the male demon that fastens on the hapless sleeper, drawing out their life. I had the attentions of an incubus, then. The fashionable pious religion my parents had once tried to introduce, left me unmoved and I doubted all the messages of the Church. Anyway, they were wrong. I felt no weakness. And he was my friend of long-standing. He asked nothing, only my random caresses, my blind pleasure. And the *pleasure* – it was so incredible, it was now my drug. As easy to wean Miranda from her tumblers of gin.

In fact; Miranda was easier. A few days after my fifteenth birthday, following a particularly brilliant public fiasco in an opulent shop of the city, Miranda collapsed. Soon she was in a detoxification clinic, the alcohol all sucked out of her, having to face reality head-on and alone.

She looked, no pun intended, like a mummy, when I saw her a month later. She'd lost too much weight too quickly. Without drink she had no appetite, as she told me, and in detail, constant stomach cramps, flatulence, sensations of asphyxia, headaches, joint pains, nausea, and spots in her vision. The doctors insisted all this was doing her good, but, she petulantly and pathetically mumbled, weeping strength- less tears, she felt so ill.

What could I do? My father looked at her grim-faced, told her she was paying the price for her foolishness, then took me away. A month after that she was returned to us, walking with a stick on shaking white pumps, in an awful bright cheerful mauve dress that made her look ninety.

She began after this to take an interest in charity work. Someone, perhaps a priest, had told her to have more care of others than herself, and that this would help her. Possibly it did. She ate little, but constantly drank juices, sodas, bottled water. Sometimes she would binge on chocolate, but this brought on agonizing migraines. She'd never smoked, talked about taking it up. My father warned her he detested nicotine on the hands and breath of women. Which must have been a lie, because his latest mistress, the daughter of a tobacco magnate, smoked thirty to fifty cigarettes a day.

Miranda kept away from strong drink for five years. I don't know how she managed this feat. Every day she seemed thinner and more brittle. She had developed, despite the thinness, a large stomach, a light cough, and some strange type, of eczema, always hidden in bandages that now and then showed under her sleeves. None of these ailments ever responded to any treatment. She did more and more charity work, then less and less. Sometimes she'd say, 'Thank God I gave up drinking. I'm so much better now.' The doctors seemed to have taught her to repeat this, like a magical mantra. But it didn't work.

Meanwhile, I was brought steadily into my father's world, dinners, concerts, receptions. He seemed to want me to make up my mind what I wished to do. But I wished to do nothing in particular. In a curious rush, I can't describe it any other way, and can't linger over it, all at once I was twenty. He made a decision for me. I was to go into junior partnership in the firm of some friend. It had to do with travel and imports – I couldn't have cared less. But as always my facade of polite attention, my good looks, my apparently superior education – this last a complete myth, for I'd learnt practically nothing, and had no application of ambition – saw me well-received in the spurious job. It was all right, in its way. The pretty secretaries ogled me, and a couple of men. But I was suitably aloof. There was nothing unprepossessing in the work, which consisted actually *of* nothing. And, I had my nights to look forward to, as I'd greedily looked forward to them now for years.

Soon I was sent on a series of missions to wine and dine eminent clients. This, evidently, I was excellent at.

Returning from one of these jaunts, rather drunk, ironically, I found the city house in turmoil. Miranda had been taken seriously ill and rushed to hospital.

She was in a large white room, surrounded by banks of flowers, and bulbous, undersea-looking tubs of oxygen. She sat bolt upright on her pillows, and she was smiling as I hadn't seen her smile for five years. The cause was obvious. On the bedside table stood two magnum bottles of the most expensive and cloudy gin. She'd bribed one of the nurses, and the times being what they were, the nurse had obliged.

No one else was there.

'Hallo, Handsome,' she said to me. 'Pull up a chair. Have a drink.'

'I've been drinking all evening. Should you –'

'It doesn't matter now,' she said. 'I'm going to die in a couple of weeks.'

I was, despite everything, despite my own utter self- centred callousness, shocked. At fifteen, when she was in the clinic, I can't recall being very concerned. I thought her collapse was a plea for my father's notice. But to die to get it would be, even for Miranda, a bit extreme.

'Surely that's not so.'

'It is so. Have this.' She passed me another tooth-glass of the gin. It was sweet and poisonous. I almost gagged, but got some down. 'You're pale, Hilton. Does that mean you care?'

'Of course I care.'

'I'm your mother …' she said. 'Well. There we are. I've got something else in there now. As big as a melon, he said. Did he? Was it a peach? Something appetizing. Absolutely no symptoms, except all the other foul things I've had for years. I just thought it was that. One more pain to put up with. Do you know, he said my liver was quite good. My kidneys too. It's this that's going to do it. So. Here's to *Life*!'

I wanted, being me, to run away at once. But how could I? My father was untraceably with one of his women. And no one else bothered to come, or she hadn't wanted them. The flowers were all they could manage, a call to a top-class late florist. They'd do the same for her funeral.

She was very, very drunk. The alcohol, after the space of abstinence, had hit her like a tidal wave. Maybe she'd also been given morphine. She looked happy almost radiant, her thin face flushed and her eyes limpid with the gin. She didn't seem afraid.

'I want to tell you something, Hilton,' she said. 'Your father'd never speak about it. I had no one to tell – except I had a counsellor, but he kept insisting to me what I felt: "Now, Senora, you feel *this*, don't you." Or, "you must experience the hurt, it mustn't go in but come out." And I said, "But I don't feel hurt. I feel dirty. There's been a murder inside me." "Dirty," he said, "Murder?" As if I'd confused him. And when I tried to explain, I couldn't get to it, and he corrected me, "No, no, it was *hurt* I felt." And then later I thought, So what? I've got a child. I managed that.'

'Mother, I'm sorry. I don't understand.'

That was when she told me.

She did so in vast, almost technical detail. How the labour pains began when she was in the bath, and she had to be lifted out. And then the private plane, the flight to the hospital, and how she'd given birth, and then given birth again.

'They hadn't known, Hilton. It wasn't the way it is now. And – this is a primitive place, Hilton. *Two* babies. Two little sons. You – and – and him.'

I was the second of a pair of twins. Younger by seven minutes. Even as she was screaming and ejecting me, they were slapping him and trying to keep him alive.

'But they couldn't, Hilton. He just folded up like a grey flower and died. There was no proper reason. They said, I should just never have had two babies. One had overcome the other. One was too weak, the other too strong.' She drank more gin. She said, 'You were so like each other to look at. Identical. No one could have told you apart, except *you* were alive. And if he'd lived … I used to think you would have played jokes on all of us. You know, the way it is in Shakespeare,' (she pronounced it, drunk, *Shazpure*. For some reason. I remember that very well. Shazpure). 'He'd pretend to be you, and you'd pretend to be him, and be somewhere else. Or you'd play terrible games with girls. And you'd be inseparable.'

We are, mother, I thought. I drank all the gin in the glass, retched uncontrollably, got a grip. I said, 'Why didn't you tell me before?'

'What was the point? I mean. What was the point?'

She leant back, and her face drooped. 'I think I'll have a little sleep, Hilton. Be a good boy and run along.'

'Your father'll be here in half an hour,' the nurse said.

Her glass fell from her hand but it didn't matter, it was empty. She snored softly, and I thought of the cancer in her womb, where we had been, he and I, and I'd crushed the life out of him.

When I stood up, the room spun, and I went into her bathroom and splashed cold water on my face. The nurse, I could tell, seeing me come out, thought the drops were tears.

That night I didn't go to bed. I went to a nightclub and drank, and smoked dope. In the morning I was so sick I didn't notice, and fell asleep on the bathroom floor.

It was always in a bed when he had me. Always there. Why? Did he only remember the labour-ward bed, or was the coffin, the little tiny white coffin he must have had, like a bed? And night time. Darkness.

I kept out of bed, all beds, even a hammock. Slept in chairs, mostly at the hospital, surrounded by harsh lights and muttering people. She went quicker than they said, as if she ran away. She died after three days.

In the mêlée of the next two weeks, the calls, the letters, the servants running to and fro, the ghastly arrangements for a death, it was simple to evade. Even to stop thinking.

The funeral was a classy affair. My father wore his blackest and threw a rose into her grave. He abstained from his mistress for a week. God knows why. She certainly didn't, and called him twice, pretending to the servant she was a 'friend of the senora's'.

In the end, I went and lay on my bed. It was afternoon, and I felt safe. I'd wake again before the darkness came. But I didn't wake, not until the city window of my adult bedroom was patched by black sky and bee-gold lights, and then he was there, beside me.

'I didn't know,' I said. 'You know I didn't know.' Talking to him, as I always had when a child. I'd talked to him far less in recent years, only gasps and demands, begging him to do more. 'Do you hate me? This isn't hate, is it?'

He put his long formed finger inside me, and moved there. My back arched at once, well taught. His weight was on me and he tongued my nipples while the other hand cupped my genitals and I swelled. His breath burned my chest, my face. He probed my mouth hungrily. I couldn't speak. The mounting sensation, the unavoidable, was rushing up my spine. On my side, his hand rubbing me even as he edged, twitched, became enormous inside my body.

'Wait – was it my fault – *wait* -'

But he wouldn't wait. Now he clove me in long pounding drumbeats and his fingers skidded on the engine of my seed. The world was going to blow up and I couldn't stop. I gripped the bed and spasmed, my bowl, my belly, my penis, my lungs. I heard my howl, half disembodied. I thought the rollers of it would never stop.

He's killing me, I thought, even as I bucked and grunted in ecstasy. Killing me, as I killed him.

I felt empty when it was over. I lay half off the bed. His weight, his body, were gone. 'Don't go. Listen to me. Can you hear me? Do you hear? What are you? *What*? Are you – the one she said -'

But there was nothing in the dark.

He woke me between three and four, tickling the entrance to my body. I had lain awake petrified for three hours, slept for one. Now I tried to fight him off. He paid no attention. He took me in his mouth and all my fear and rage slipped from me as constellations shot through that tiny orifice which knows so much.

And then he was gone once more. He wouldn't stay – to listen. Probably he had never heard me, was deaf and dumb. He was dead, after all. He only wanted to do this.

Did it matter? Christ, I'd come to like it so, to rely on it. In all my idiotic life, this was all that was of any real use. It asked nothing but my delight. A lovely present for me at the end of every oh-so-trying day.

And it hadn't hurt me. My last medical showed me fit and strong, as they always did.

What then – was it revenge – what was it? A demon, a ghost – should I attempt an exorcism?

I slept, exhausted. I think I felt him in the dark, holding me. Maybe I only dreamed it.

Months followed. I did my nothing work. I slept rather a lot in chairs. I wondered if a hotel room would free me. In the past he'd come to me in the houses of my – our – father. *What was his name?* They must have had him posthumously christened or blessed.

I began to feel I might be going mad, and my couth, controlled exterior only proved this all the more to me. No one could get inside me, (but for my sodomous ghost-lover). I was a dummy from a shop window. Hollow within.

(Now and then I went into my bed. There he always found me. I dreaded it, *wanted* it. I had, after all, nothing else of any interest).

I had more sense than to confront my father on the matter of my dead twin. But I went finally to the priest who had, haphazardly, received Miranda.

He tried at first to be kind to me, but I, logically was suspicious. Did he see me as reconverting back into the Faith?

I said, 'My mother told me, just before her death, that when I was born –'

'Yes?' he said. His face was bland.

'That there was another child, which died, after only two minutes.'

'She told you this.'

'Yes. I think she felt guilty, for some reason.'

'She'd used contraception in the past,' said the priest. 'It weighs heavily on some women, to break the commandments of the Church.'

I growled at him, but not outwardly. I said, 'Was he named?'

'My dear son, I don't know. You seem troubled –' How could he see what no other could? – 'Why not tell me the real root of your problem.'

I intended to get up and walk out. The slums of the city seethed with diseased and ruined girls who did not break the Church's commandments, and filled the world with unwanted, ill-treated brats.

But I heard myself blurt – 'I dream about it. About him. He won't leave me alone. Since I was a child –'

What on earth was wrong with me? I hadn't minded, had I, until just now? Until she let me know, twenty years too late, that I was preyed on by an undead brother.

Then I saw my panic, clear as a picture rising up in developing fluid. I saw how everything had changed.

The priest rose as I, belatedly, did. He put a restraining hand on my arm.

'Hilton, my son. I have something to say. God made us, and we have duties to God. To ignore them is unwise.'

'What -'

'Please listen a moment. You're of an age, my son, when I'd expect you either to have sought the priesthood – or a woman.'

I stood there and gaped at him. I was cold with horror at what I'd suddenly seen to be my existence. That nothing mattered save my nights in the arms of death. To be sucked off and wanked and buggered by death. Disgust – *despair* – both, doubtless, sins.

Then, out of synch, I heard what he'd said.

'You mean I should be involved with a woman.'

'With your father's consent, of course. And with the idea of a true union, a marriage. At your age, what could be more natural? Let me assure you, Hilton, it will get rid of any such nightmares as you've described.'

I almost laughed. I stopped myself. I *hadn't* described them. In ancient times I'd have gone to him, confessed all, been laid out naked before an altar, and flogged to get the devil out of me. Now, this.

Into his hand I put the money I'd brought, (for the orphans), and went away. My head was buzzing. I had an incoherent memory of that lipstick-girl on the balcony, and of the Girls my father had seduced.

Was it so simple? Was it even possible now? I'd never felt anything for a woman. But then, I'd felt nothing for a man, for any human thing, save myself. And him.

The evening was gathering in golden polluted clouds on the city. I stood on the steps of the church, staring at the lines of hooting traffic, the flying birds, the glassy towers that touched the sky.

I was frightened, wasn't I? Even ecstasy had become fearful to me. I was in thrall to an incestuous ghost. And going to a priest, had I been given a solution?

Standing there, I felt helpless. And I laughed out loud at the hopeless mathematical equation which, as always, I couldn't solve at all.

Two days later, I saw Meraida. Her name has a structure like my mother's, but I only became aware of that much later. I'd left my smart office, ignoring the fact of my errand-boy assistant, and gone out personally for aspirin. Then walked into a cafe to swallow them with coffee.

She was sitting at a table, alone. She wore a white short sleeveless dress that revealed a flawless, almost Martian, tan. Her hair was blue-black and gleamed like silk, falling to her waist, but so thick it was combed straight back without a parting. When she leaned forward to drink her cordial through a straw, I saw the honey tops of her breasts. Maybe I was looking for it, but I had a reaction. Very slight, but definite. I put down my cup and imagined cupping instead one of those full high girl breasts, naked in my hand. The response was immediate. It was as if I'd only been holding it back all these years, the way the celibate is supposed to.

Presently I got up, went over, and sat down at her table. She looked up without affront or dismay. I was used to women gazing at me. She had a triangular, small-boned face, slanting eyes of a hazel that matched her tan. She'd used no make-up, needed none, only a crimson lip gloss that looked as if she'd wet her mouth with strawberries.

'You're wonderful,' I said. I'd never bothered to learn any technique for women. What they wanted, after all, seemed fairly obvious.

She blinked. Her lashes were black and silky as little wings. 'So are you.'

'That's a very good start,' I said. 'Can I buy you a drink?'

'Yes, all right. I like these.'

We sat and talked all afternoon. (Mostly about her, I made sure of that). She was an art student, but she didn't mind missing her classes for me. I let her know, without quite saying, the walk of life I came from. She could see for herself the suit and shirt and shoes and watch, the Escurier gold ring. I had money all over me. But I think she'd have settled for me anyway, if I'd come in off a road-gang.

I could tell she thought we'd go somewhere almost at once, and she was willing. Young women are now so free. But naturally that wasn't what I required. So we walked in the public gardens, and sat by the fountain. About five, I called in to my partners, and stressed I was laid low by a migraine. Then I took Meraida for drinks and an early dinner.

She ate a lot, but very nicely, and drank a reasonable amount. I told her she should have topaz and amber in her ears, to match her eyes, and she laughed and said she'd never had a man talk to her the way I did, I was too accomplished, and she ought to go at once. So then I took her hand and said I was falling in love with her.

For a moment she looked quite frightened, and then her face turned into a child's at birthday time. She couldn't believe her luck. This handsome, if slightly unbalanced, rich young man, besotted with her as no doubt others more humble had been, trustingly telling her so.

'But you don't know me,' she said.

'I've always known you,' I said. (Dialogue is easy, if one keeps one's head and has read a few novels.)

'No, but I mean. I mean, my father's a truck-driver.'

'So what?' All the better. In this city, he'd consent quicker to almost anything.

'You seem so serious about this.'

'I am.'

'If we make love,' she observed, sceptical, 'then you'll cool off.'

'You don't understand. I think I want to spend my life with you.'

'There's no need to lie.'

'I'm not lying, Meraida.' And I almost wasn't.

When we left the restaurant, again she expected I would take her at once to a hotel. But I stood her on a darkened avenue, and put my hand behind her head and felt her silky hair and kissed her slowly, the way he had taught me. And again, that shivering burning upsurge. But I let her go.

'Don't you want –'

'Not yet. You see, I'm sure. But how could you be? We'll wait a little. Get to know each other better.'

She was so disappointed she glared at me, then smoothed her face. 'I think you're playing a game.'

'I'll call you tomorrow at eight, before you leave for college.'

She shrugged, trying to be brave. 'I won't expect it. It was a lovely evening.'

I caught her to me again, swept her literally off her feet, and kissed her, tasting wine and brandy and her own clean mouth. Of course, she let me touch her breasts, fleetingly. Unlike the politician's daughter, Meraida could feel me hard as a stone, pressing into her belly.

She refused a taxi, and I could sense her looking back at me as we walked away from each other. I did not look back.

In the morning, at eight, I called her. She picked up the receiver after half a second. She was breathless. 'Is it you, Hilton?'

For a week I courted her. I myself wanted to be sure, and I wanted her to be desperate. By the second outing, under the night-black trees of the gardens, I had my hand inside her low-cut black dress. My urgency reassured me, as did hers. He had taught me such a great deal, that she writhed and nearly reached a climax in my arms. She begged me, almost tearful, Couldn't we go somewhere? But I denied her. Not yet. Oh no.

It was more than cunning. (And cowardice too, let's not forget that; I was, with human beings, a virgin.) I'd thought long and searchingly about some luxurious hotel. Champagne, orchids, possessing Meraida on a milk-white bed, her screams piercing the golden chandelier fitment in the ceiling. I'd thought about it as I shifted in the upright chair, the armchair, striving for a little sleep. For I never now used my bed. (And imagined him invisibly coiled there, imagined what he'd do to me if he got hold of me, until, once or twice, between the memory of my ghost-brother and the new fantasies of a living girl, I haphazardly came anyway). I'd decided, the hotel test wasn't a fair one. It was true, he might not be able to attempt me in some other place … or he might. But in the family houses, the city house, the pillared house by the sea, there he was certain, and there he must be driven off by my woman's presence.

What he would do, what would occur, I had no idea. But he had never been with me when others were. And he had never had any competition, saving that one time on the balcony when I was twelve, which hadn't counted.

My father was going to New York. He would be gone a month. I'd take Meraida to the sea house. She'd love it. We'd swim and eat exotic meals. In the afternoons we'd walk the hills and the town or lie on the beach. At night – *only at night* – we'd go into my bedroom, spread ourselves out on my bed, and commence the athletics of desire.

Obviously, once I'd told her we were going there, once she'd said yes – it took her three seconds, this time – I began to suffer a little gnawing worry. I was totally inexperienced with women, and no amount of antics elsewhere, or even those clever novels, could teach me everything. I was partly afraid of proving myself to be a fool. But then she was so primed, so willing, she'd do half the work for me. My body was fine, I was fit. She wanted me, and I, to my continued, amazed, smug reassurance, wanted *her*.

It might happen she'd pall, or we'd tire of each other, or she might fret for the marriage I'd never be allowed to offer. But then I could wave, or buy her off. My father, the veteran, would know exactly how to handle it. Conversely, if I wanted to be safe from *him*, I would continue with Meraida until another, better, proposition came my way. And maybe, seeing how gorgeous she was, this would last forever. Some women didn't mind the role of mistress, especially not when cared for. It wasn't that I loved her. And yet I felt, if she were to save me, I might come to. I wanted to be saved. I was afraid of him, by now. Afraid of all the feverish joys I'd had with him. It wasn't I believed in the soul, or in hell, or divine punishment – nothing like that. It seemed to me he'd taken something from me, not only normal *live* sex, but a normal life of any kind. God knew what I might have been if I hadn't been possessed by my dead and deathly twin. He'd had no life, he'd pushed and pulled me away from my own. In the chairs now I had nightmares. He was looming over me, seen in dream as never before, a grey mass like a colossal amoeba. He was poking bits of himself into every crack and hole, and laughing in a soundless, seething way as I submerged, not in ecstasy, but drowning.

It was filthy, what had been. It wasn't what I should have had. Who was I? What had I lost – Only Meraida and her body could reveal the state of my potential for rescue or abandonment.

And it might be, it might be, despite everything – I might not be able – From this concluding possibility I recoiled in an icy sweat. And every sexual spasm that took me unawares I cursed, because I needed to save up my ardour. I needed to be bursting with it, like a ripe gourd.

The sky was a hot velvety blue as we were driven to the coast. She liked the chauffeur, the car, the picnic hamper and the wine. She liked the changing landscape as the city fell away, and talked about wanting to paint it, with that one white cloud there, just posing on that stand of eucalyptus …

Inevitably too the house impressed her. We had a ritual tea on the terrace overlooking the palms and orange trees of the garden. It still surprised me slightly, all she could eat. I made up the balance by picking at the food. I was well and truly nervous by now. I needed a drink, but must watch that too.

We walked on the beach in the evening rosiness, and the glassy pink sea came in and laved her bare feet. She laughed and skipped like a child. But I, looking at her beauty in the gold-brown dress I'd bought her, felt old as her grandfather. What lay in store for me?

The painted dining room set her off again, and dinner – she still eating heartily, I still leaving almost everything, reaching for the wine and cognac, tasting, putting them carefully aside – passed in a sort of whirl of fuss and excitement.

It came to me finally she too might be a little nervous. After all, I'd built it up so, kept her frustrated, all on edge. And I might, for all she knew, have strange tastes. Well I had, hadn't I?

I showered in one of the guest bathrooms while she lay in a tub of bubbles en suite to my bedroom. I looked at myself in the mirror, and saw only what I knew. Most heterosexual women would like me. There was nothing I needed to hide – physically –

Trembling with sudden fear, I sat down on the chair, and took a swig from the whisky bottle I'd brought in. Not too big a swig, caution, for God's sake. So much rested on this. Everything rested on it.

When I went into the bedroom, she was lying on my bed. I think some magazine or book, (shades of myself), had told her to arrange herself in a provocative way. She wore a semi-black transparent slip reaching to her ankles, yet slit along one thigh. It had wired-up lace cups that lifted and nearly spilled her breasts. Her hair spread everywhere. She smelled of roses and cinnamon, and through the black silk and lace, I could see the blacker nest of her centre.

The surge came. I rose, as they say, to the occasion. The relief of it almost made me yell aloud. Instead, I told her she was lovely, and crossed the floor quickly, dropping my robe as I did so. It seemed I was to be saved.

An hour later, after she had gone away into the bathroom and come back, I think after crying a little, she said, 'Is it something – have I done anything –?' She was very young. Younger even than I was, in many ways by a thousand years.

'No, I'm sorry. It's my bloody fault. I must have drunk too much at dinner. Or I'm tired.'

We sat at either end of my bed, mulling these inanities over.

Because, of course, you guessed, didn't you, despite my flood of arousal, once in contact with her, once called upon to perform the supreme conjunction, my confidence and will left me, my tower fell. Flaccid and humiliated I rolled around with her for twenty, forty minutes, allowing her to try to stimulate me back to size, kissing her with an increasingly dry unwilling mouth. Until at last we fell apart, worn out by the hopelessness of it.

No, it wasn't nerves or booze. It was initially the bed, you see. This was so obvious, and I'd never thought – the bed, the very bed where I had to have her, in order to dismiss my haunting. In that bed, in my bed, my body came alert *only for him*. For the feeling of his hands and his fleshly surfaces, that were identical to my own. I mean, *identical*. He'd taught me impeccably. I was trained. No other man, let alone a woman, could enact what I needed. And Meraida was – useless.

By the time I let her go, and she me, both of us sweating, pale, sickened, I wanted only to throw myself, or her, from the window. But it wasn't her fault.

Even without the bed – safe from the ultimate performance, in a park, on an avenue, I'd been able to deceive us both. Oh, I might say I'd try to take her on the floor, against a wall, *tomorrow morning* – but even there and then, even in the much mooted hotel – it would eventually come down to this. Even without the bed. For *he* – he was my bed – and I was his. And without that, only so far could I go.

She and no one – but he – was my twin. She and no one – but he – was the ghost of my brother. My incubus. Death. Darkness.

In the end, we put out the lights, and she had modestly drawn the curtains and the window was black, the room black, as pitch. We stretched out, not touching, and she fell asleep before I did. It was a big bed.

I thought, at least she would keep him away for this one night. But I knew then it wasn't true, andI lay sodden and still, waiting, until I felt him put his first light finger on my spine.

Then everything came back. Everything I'd tried to build with her. I resisted. I resisted for my very life. But of course it was as useless to fight him as it had been to attempt anyone *but* him.

His hands were on all of me, as it seemed at once. Under my ears, my armpits, my groin. Stroking at my balls, and coaxing my penis, licking my lips, teasing my nipples, unbearably tickling at every sensitive juncture and plain, invading me, filling me up. I'd never gone without him so long – and also I had never known him so powerful, so devastating, and he bent my back like a bow, rocking me towards oblivion. As the cosmos disintegrated in my brain and stifled my own screaming with my fists, I vaguely heard Meraida, four feet away, whimpering shrilly in her sleep.

In the morning, when I woke, dazed, debilitated as if after some fit, I heard her singing in the shower. Dismal, I lay planning how to evict her from my life. At least she was in a happy mood, absurdly had 'got over it'. Maybe she expected me to be better now and that we should try again, and I'd have to be angry, make up some crime or theatrical idiocy or illness, in order to shunt her off. I was dreading it.

But when she came in, she simply stood, naked and very, very pretty, glowing in the muffled curtained morning sunlight.

I heard her say to me then, that which I heard after, several times, (several times, before I truly learned and ended all such times, and went back alone into the dark), from the old and the young, the ugly and the sublime, from a couple more women, and from a few men, too:

'Oh, Hilton. It was so amazing. I was half asleep – but what you did to me – I never knew it could be – like *that*. And the things you did. My God, oh my God. I couldn't even see you in the dark, but you felt so *good*. Oh God, Hilton, I never came like that before. Never. Oh God, Hilton, you're the most wonderful lover in all the world.'

The Devil's Rose

O Rose thou art sick.
The invisible worm,
That flies in the night
In the howling storm:

Has found out thy bed
Of crimson joy:
And his dark secret love
Does thy life destroy.

William Blake

Because of a snowdrift on the line, the train pulled to an unscheduled stop at the little town of L—. Presently we passengers had debarked, and stood stamping and chafing our hands about the stove in the station house. It was nearly midnight, but the stationmaster's charitable housekeeper came almost at once with steaming coffee and a bottle of spirits. A boy was also roused and sent running, apparently to wake all of the town on our behalf for lodgings. We should not be able to go on for three or four days, even that depending on whether or not fresh snow was to come down. Since we had entered the great pine forests outside Archaroy, we had been seeing wolves. They were thick on the ground that winter, and in the little villages and towns, we were to hear, not a carriage or sledge could go out but it would have wolf packs running after it for mile on mile, until the lights of human habitation came again in sight.

'What a prospect!' exclaimed the estate manager who had shared my compartment from Archaroy. 'Besieged in the back of beyond by weather and wolves. Do you think, Mhikal Mhikalson, we shall ever get out?'

I said that we might, in the spring, perhaps, if not this year's, then next. But in fact, being my own creature, such unprecedented quirks of venture as this one neither dismayed nor displeased me. I had no family either behind or at journey's end to be impatient or in fear for me. My friends were used to my eccentricities and would look for me to arrive only when I did so. Additionally, in this instance, my destination was not one I hankered for. The manager, however, who had business dealings up ahead, was turning fractious. On the pretence of the errand for lodgings, I walked out of that hot room and went into the town of L—, to see what, as the isolated clocks of midnight struck, it might offer me.

It was a truly provincial backwater, such as you would expect, although the streets were mostly lit, and efforts had been made to clear the snow. There was an old marketplace with a bell tower, and close by some public gardens with tall locked gates. The houses of the prosperous ascended a hill, and those of the not so prosperous slunk down it. Some boulevards with shops all shut finished the prospect.

On a rise behind the rest was an old stuccoed house which I noticed for something Italianate in its outline, but mostly through one unprovincial lemon-yellow window burning brightly there. What poet or scholar worked late in that room when the entire town slept? Something in me, which would have done the same if so placed, sent a salutation up to him.

After looking at the house, I made my way – perversely? – downhill, observing the degeneration of all the premises. The lower town fell into what might once have been the bed of some primeval river, which had carved out a bottom for itself before sinking away into the past. Over the area, the narrow streets sprawled and intertwined; it would be easy to be lost there, but for the constant marker of the hill hanging always above.

Needless to say, the snow had here been churned and frozen in mud heaps, and the going was heavy. I was growing jaded, when, between some boarded stables and a parade of the poorest houses, I discovered an ancient church. It was of the kind you sometimes see even in the cities, crammed between newer buildings that seem to want to press the life from it and close together in its default. A hooded well stood on the snow and the cobbles near the church door which, as may still happen in the provinces, was unlocked.

The church intrigued me, perhaps only as the house had done with its window, for I sensed some life going on there. It was not an area for the wise to loiter; who knew what rough or other might not come from his hovel to demand money, or try by force to take it. Nevertheless something kept me there, and I was on the point of going nearer, when lo and behold the massive church door parted a crack. Out into the moonlight, which was now laving snow and town alike, slipped the slender, unmistakable form of a woman. It was the season when men go about garbed like bears, and she too was of course wrapped against the cold, her head mantled with a dark shawl. I recognized in her at once, even so, the thing I had sensed, the meaning of the church's 'life,' or at least a portion of it. I wondered what she would do, confronted by a stranger. In these small towns mostly anyone of any consequence knows all the others. If an alien, and a man, accosted her, what then? Yet had she not put herself, alone and after midnight, into the perfect position for such an overture?

'Excuse me, young woman,' I said, as she came along the slope.

She started, quite violently. It was so very lustrous, the moon inflaming the snow, that to tell a shadow from shadows was not easy. Perhaps I had seemed to step from thin air itself.

She was so apparently startled I wondered if there were a chance I should now take her arm to steady her, tilting our faces to the moon as I did so, that she might see me, and I her. But she had already composed herself.

'What is it?' she said in a low and urgent voice.

'The hour is very late. I wondered if you were in some difficulty. Might I assist you?'

'No, no,' she muttered. Rather than reveal herself, she snatched her shawl about her face with her gloved hands.

'I am a stranger to your town,' I said. 'Forgive my impetuosity in speaking to you.'

'How are you here?' she said. She stood like a child who is being verbally chastised by the schoolmaster, longing to break free into the yard where the other children are.

'How else but the train? We are snowbound, it appears.'

But who would be those other children, her companions, from whom I kept her?

Just then, far away over the edge of the town as if over a high cliff out at sea, I heard the howling of a wolf. The hair rose on my neck as it always does at the sound. The cry was too apt; it came too nicely on my cue.

But at that moment she turned up her face, as if straining to listen, and I saw her features, and her eyes.

Although the shawl hid everything but a trace of her hair, I judged it to be very dark. And her face was very white, and her eyes were so pale in that pale face they were like glass on the snow. Her mouth, in the shadow-shining moonlight, seemed dark also, damson-coloured, but the lips beautifully shaped. It was not a beautiful face, but rather an almost classical one.

'Is it safe for you to go about like this, in such weather?' I said. 'Have you never heard of starving wolves running into the streets?'

'It has been known,' she said. Her eyes, now they had met mine, did not leave me.

'Let me,' I said, 'escort you wherever you are going.'

'Up there,' she said, 'to the Italian House. But you are a stranger –'

'No, I have seen the very house. With a light burning.'

'For me,' she said, 'my beacon.'

'Will you take my arm?' I said. 'Where the snow has been left lying the way is slippery.'

She came with a swift half-furtive step, and put her black silk paw into my arm. She leaned close to me as we began to walk.

I would have liked to ask her at once what she had been doing, there in the old church, to give such intensity to the night. Even the lamp in her room – the room of the beacon – had blazed with it. But I did not feel it was the time yet, to ask her that. In fact we said very little, but walked together familiarly up through the town. She assured me it was not a vast distance. I said I was sorry. She did not then flirt with me, or move away. She shivered, and when I drew her hand more securely into my arm, against me, she murmured obliquely, 'It is so easy to misinterpret kindness.'

'Mine in going with you, or your own in permitting me to do so?'

Then she did not answer, and we went on again in silence. All the way, we passed not a soul, but once heard a dog snarling behind a gate after wolves or the moon. Soon enough we came onto the part of the rise which ended in her house. The high walls along the street provided cover for our approach. The light still burned before us, now a huge tawdry topaz. It looked warm, but not inviting. A blind masked that upper room from curious eyes attracted to its glow.

At the foot of some steps she detached herself from me. Feeling the cold after the warmth of me, she put her hands up to her face again. Her pale eyes were steady with their question.

'As I told you, I am marooned here a day or so. May I call on you tomorrow?'

'My parents are dead. I live with my aunt. My father's sister, she is old … Do please call, if you wish. But –' She left a long pause, to see if I could read her thoughts. I could.

'You do not wish me to say I met you at midnight by the church.'

'No, I do not.'

She had given me by then her family name. I said, 'As it happens, Miss Lindensouth, I know some distant relations of yours, some Lindensouths, in Archaroy. Or, at any rate, I believe they may be related to you and your aunt. It will give me an excuse to look her up.'

This was a lie. If she guessed, she did not seem alarmed. Her face was without an expression of any sort. She lowered her eyes and left me suddenly, running up the icy stair with a carelessness that saved her rather than put her in the way of an accident.

I waited, briefly, across the street, to see what would happen with the light, or even if her silhouette might pass across it. But the lamp might have shone in another world mysteriously penetrating this one. Nothing disturbed it, and it did not go out.

When I reached the station house I found the party had gone off to the inn I had seen on my perambulations. Accordingly, I took myself there.

At about six o'clock in the morning the town of L— began to come to life. By ten o'clock, when I returned to the church, the lower streets were seething. On every corner were the expected braziers of smoking red charcoal; lamps burned now in countless windows against the leaden light of morning.

Having negotiated the slop collectors, the carts of cabbage, and the carriage horses of some local charioteer, I gained the appropriate street, and found this scene was also changed. The well was a gossiping spot for women, who stood there in their scarves and fur hats arguing the price of butter. A wood seller was delivering farther down, and children played in the snow with little cold-bitten faces, grimly intent on their miserable game.

The church itself was active. The door stood open, and two women in black veils came out. It was plainly an hour also for business, here.

I went forward diffidently, prepared to depart again at once, but on entering the church, found it was after all now empty.

It was like the inside of a hollowed boulder, carved bare, with the half egg shell of the dome rising above. The shrine looked decently furnished, you could say no more for it. Everything that was anything was plate. A few icons were on the screen below. I paused to glance at them; they were Byzantine in influence, but rather crude, not a form I am much drawn to.

As I was turning away, a man approached me. I had not seen him either present or entering, but probably he had slipped out from some inner place. He was about forty and had the scholars' look, a high broad forehead gaining ground, and a ledge of brows and gold-rimmed spectacles beneath.

'You are one of our trapped travellers!' he cried.

My heart sank. 'Just so.'

He gave me a name and a gloved hand. I took, and relinquished, both.

'You are interested in churches?' His manner was quietly eager.

With caution I replied, 'There is something I am a little curious about –'

'Ah,' he broke in immediately, 'that will be the famous window, I think.'

What could I say?

'Indeed.'

'Come, I will show you.'

He took me into a side arm of the church, where it was very dark. Some candles burned, but then I saw shards of red, green, and mauve thrown on the plastered wall.

My scholar brought me to his prize, and directed me where to look, and unless I had been blind, I could not have missed it.

The window, small and round-headed, was like an afterthought, or perhaps (as he presently informed me) it might belong to an earlier chapel, being then the oldest thing there.

The glass itself was very old, and gave a rich heavy light. Its subject was the Garden of Eden, its colour mostly of emerald, blue, and purple. Distantly the white figures of the sinners stood beneath their green apple tree, the fatal fruit in hand. They were about to eat, and God about to say to them, like every injured parent, I gave you everything! Why could you not remain as children forever? Why is it necessary that you grow up? His coming storm was indicated by the darkling sapphires of the shadows, the thunder wing of purple on the grass. But in the foreground was a rose tree, and among the wine-coloured flowers, the serpent coiled itself, its commission seen to.

'Most unusual, such a treatment,' said the scholar.

How was it that I knew so well that she, my Miss Lindensouth, had been frozen before this window, had come out from its contemplation as if her pale skin were steeped in the transparent dyes.

'Yes?'

He quoted a supposed date of the twelfth century.

'And of course it had a name, a window like this. Probably you know it? No? Well, it has been called "Satan's Rose Bush", in church records even, for two hundred years. Or they say simply, secretively, "The Devil's Rose". And there are all sorts of stories, to do with curses and wonders and the rest of it. The best known is the story of the "Girl Who Danced". You will know that one.'

'I am afraid not.'

'How splendid. Now I have all the pleasure of telling you. You see, supposedly, if you look long enough and hard enough at the glass, here, by the rose tree, you find another figure in the window. It is one of those freak things, the way in which angles and colours go together randomly forms another shape – or perhaps the maker of the window intended it to happen. The figure is of a dark man, Satan himself, naturally, who took a serpent's appearance to seduce Eve to wrongdoing. I must say I have looked diligently at the window quite often, but I have never been able to make it out. I am assured it is there, however. The last priest himself could see it, and even attempted to describe it for me on the glass – but it was no good. My eyes, perhaps … You try yourself. See, it is here and here, alongside the roses.'

Staring where he showed me, I, like the scholar, could make out nothing. I knew of course that this had not been the case with the girl.

'And the story?'

'A hundred years ago, the tale has it, one of the great landowning families had one young fair daughter. She was noted as wonderfully vivacious, and how she loved to dance all night at all the balls in the area – for in those days, you understand, sleepy L was quite a thriving, bustling town. Well, it would seem she visited the church and saw the window, and saw the figure of Satan. She found him handsome, and, in the way of some young girls she – I do hope you are broad-minded – she fell in love with him, with the Devil himself. And she made some vow, something adolescent and messy, with blood and such things. She invited him to come in that form and claim her for a dance. And when the next ball was held, about one in the morning, a great silence fell on the house. The orchestra musicians found their hands would not move, the dancers found their feet likewise seemed turned to stone. Then the doors blew open in a gust of wind. Every light in every chandelier went out – and yet there was plenty of light, even so, to see by: it was the light of

Hell, shining into the ballroom. Then a dark figure, a tall dark man, entered the room. He had come as she requested, to claim his dance. It seems he brought his own orchestra with him. They were masked, everyone of them, but sitting down by the dance floor they struck up such a waltz that no one who heard it could resist its rhythm – and yet not one in the room could move! Then he came to the landowner's daughter and bowed and asked her for the honour of partnering her. And she alone of all the company was freed from the spell. She glided into his arms. He drew her away. They turned and whirled like a thing of fire, while all the rest of the room danced in their bones to the music, unable to dance in any other way, until all their shoes, and the white dresses of the women, and the fine evening clothes of the gentlemen, were dappled inside with their blood! How gruesome!' the scholar cried. He beamed on me. 'But presently the Devil dashed his partner away through the floor. They vanished, and the demon musicians vanished, although no other there was able to regain motion until the cocks crowed. As for the girl, they found her skin – her *skin* mark you, solely that – some days later on a *hill*. It had been danced right off her skeleton. But on her face, such as there was of it, was fixed a grin of agonized joy.'

He paused, grasping his hands together. He said presently, 'You see, in my modest way, I employ these old stories. I am something of a writer.' As if that excused him.

But I too was smiling. I was thinking of the girl, but not the girl in the story. Miss Lindensouth's strangeness and her youth, the way we had met, and the hold I had instantly obtained.

'It is a fact, young girls do sometimes,' he said, 'embrace such morbid fantasies – the love of death, or the Dark Angel, the Devil. Myself, I have penned a vampire fiction on this theme –'

I looked at the window again, along the rose tree. Nothing was there, except a slight reflection, thrown from the candles, of my own height and dark clothing and hair. These were out of scale and therefore did not fit.

The scholar offered me a glass of tea, but I explained to him I was already late for one. I told him where, to see if this might mean anything to him. But he was living in the past. He bade me a cheery regretful farewell.

I rang the bell of the Italian House, and soon enough a maidservant ushered me in. The rooms inside were no longer remotely Italianate. They had been choked up with things, furniture, and tables of photographs of staring statue-people, bowls of petals, pianos with shut lids. The entire house-lid seemed shut. It smelled aromatically, in the crumbling way an old book does.

The aunt received me presently in an upper parlour.

'Madam Lindensouth. How very kind of you. I bring you greetings from

Archaroy, but the snow acted as Providence.'

She was a stern, thin woman with a distinct look to her of the niece, the same long black brows, but these pale eyes were watery and short-sighted. She had frequent recourse to pince-nez. Her gown was proper, old-fashioned, and of good material. She wore lace mittens, too.

'And you are a Mr Mhikalson. But we have not met.'

'Until this moment.'

I approached, raised a mitten, and bowed over it. Which made me remember the Devil in the story. I smiled, but had concealed it by the time I lifted my head. She was gratified; she made no bones about that. She offered me a chair and rang for the samovar. I told her of her invented cousins in the city, concocting anecdotes, waiting for her to say, perhaps sharply, 'But I have never heard of these people.' To which I must reply, 'But how odd, for they seem to have heard of you, Madam Lindensouth, and of your niece.' Thereby introducing a careful error which would then make all well, confirming we were at cross-purposes, these Lindensouths were not her Lindensouths. And getting us, besides, to the notion of a niece.

I wondered, too, how long it would be before that niece contrived to make an entrance. Had she not been listening on an upper landing for the twangle of the bell? Or had she given me up? I had not specified, a time, but had come late for so eager a visitor.

Then the tea arrived, which Madam served up country fashion, very black, with a raspberry preserve. As we were drinking it, she still had not fathomed the cousins in Archaroy. She had simply accepted them, and we had begun to steer our conversation out upon the state of the weather, a proposed wolf hunt, literature, and the world in general.

Suddenly, however, the aunt lifted her head.

'Now that must be Mardya coming down. My niece, Mr Mhikalson. You must meet her, she will want to question you about the city,'

I felt a wave of relief – and of interest, having learned at last the phantom's familiar name.

I wondered how I should feel when she came in, but inevitably she had not the same personality *en famille* as she had had outside in the wolf-throated snow-night. Just then she had come from her trance before the window of the rose-snake. But now she had had all night to think of me, all morning pondering if I should come back.

She stole into the room. Nothing like her surefooted tread, both mercurial and wanton, of the night. She bore her hands folded on her waist before her, pearl drops in her nacre ears, her eyes fixed only on the aunt.

'Here is a gentleman from Archaroy,' announced Madam. I did not correct her.

The girl Mardya dashed me off a glance. It hung scintillating in the overheated air after her eyes had once more fallen. It said, *You? You are here?*

You are real?

'He has friends, Mardya, who claim to be related to us. It must be the fur connection, or perhaps the diamond connection.' They were suspected of being in trade, that was it – but since she did not inquire it of me, I did not hazard. Traders, evidently, she did not pretend either to know or not to know. 'Well, Mardya,' she said.

Mardya inclined her head. Her hair was piled upon it, black and silken, not wholly tidy, and so revealing it was none of it false. Her cheeks were flushing now, paling again to a perfect paper-white. The earrings blinked. She was acting shy in the presence of her kin.

'Your aunt has kindly warned me,' I said, 'that you will want to know about the city. I must tell you at once, I am a frequenter of libraries. I read and do very little else.' Behold, Madam, I am not in trade, but a beast of leisure and books.

Mardya, not speaking, stole on toward us. Taking the aunt's glass, she refilled it at the bubbling tea pitcher.

'But no doubt you ladies spend a great deal of time with books,' I said. 'The town is very quiet. Or is that only the disaster of winter?'

'Winter or summer. Such summers we have,' said the aunt. 'The heat is intolerable. My brother had a lodge up in the hills, but we have had to get rid of it. It is no use to *us*. It was a man's place. My niece, as you say, is something of a reader. And we have our sewing and our music.'

'And do you, Miss Lindensouth,' I said briskly, 'never dance?'

She had given back the glass of tea, or I think she would have dropped it. Her whole slender shape locked rigid. Her white eyelids nailed down on her cheeks quivered and would not stop.

'I do not – I do not dance,' she said – the first thing she *had* said in this presence.

'But I heard such a strange little story today,' I began to the aunt amiably. 'A man I met this morning, an authority on your local legends –'

'Will you not have another glass of tea?' said Mardya.

'No, thank you, Miss Lindensouth. But I was saying, the story has to do with a certain window –'

'Do have another glass,' said Mardya.

Her voice was hard with wrath, and her eyes were on me, full of tears. She expected betrayal. To have wounded her so easily gave me the anticipated little thrill. She was so vulnerable, one must protect her. She must be put behind the iron shield, defended.

'No, thank you so much. In fact I must tear myself away and leave you, Madam Lindensouth, in peace.' I rose. 'Except – I wonder if I might ask a great favour of you, Madam? Might I borrow your niece for half an hour?' The long brows went up, she adjusted the pince-nez. I smiled and said, 'My sister has imposed the most wretched duty. I was to buy her a pair of gloves, and forgot in my haste of leaving. Now I shall arrive late besides, and probably will never be forgiven. But it occurred to me Miss Lindensouth, who has just those sort of hands, I see, that my sister has, might advise me. She might even do me the kindness of trying on the gloves, selecting a colour. I find this sort of task most embarrassing. I have no idea of what to look for. Which, if I am honest, is why I forgot the transaction in the first place.'

The aunt laughed, superior upon the failings of the fumbling male.

'Yes, go along with Mr Mhikalson, Mardya, and assist him with these troublesome gloves. You may place my own order while you are doing so.'

I bowed to her mitten once more. She sighed, and I caught the faint acidity of medicine on her breath.

'Perhaps, since you must remain here, you will dine with us tonight?' she said, with the grudging air that did not mask a lively curiosity she had begun to have about me.

'Why, Madam Lindensouth – to be sure of that I will go personally to shovel more snow onto the line.'

She laughed heartily, and bade me get along. Her eyes of watery steel said, If I had been younger. And mine: Indeed, Madam, there can be no doubt. But I am too respectful now, and besides maybe I am in search of a wife, and you see what a fine coat this is, do you? But nevertheless, I know where the fount is, the Sybil. We understand one another in the way no man finds it possible to understand or to be understood by any woman under forty, and surely you are not much more?

Down in the street, Mardya Lindensouth spoke to me in a strange cold hot voice.

'I trust you rested well.'

'No. I could only lie there and think of seeing you again. I have thought of nothing else since our meeting.'

'But something delayed you.'

'Strategy. You saw how I have managed it. I am to dine.'

She would not take my arm.

'There are no gloves,' I said, 'I have no sisters.' I said, 'Run her errand later. Where can we go?'

And all at once, in an arch in one of the old walls of the street, she was leaning her spine to a door, her hands on my breast. It was a daring situation, hidden, unfrequented, yet anyone might look from an upper floor, or come by and see.

I leaned against her until her back pressed the backs of my hands into the damp wood. She was, though I could only speculate how, no stranger to kisses. Presently, engorged and breathless, we pulled apart, and went on down the street. This time she took my arm.

We went to a patisserie along one of the boulevards. To my dismay, at one point, I saw three of my fellow travellers from the train, the estate manager among them, going by the window, hesitating at the door – and thank heaven passing on.

She did not eat anything, only sipped the scalding beverage, which was not so flavoursome as the samovar of Madam.

'I dreamed of you,' she said, 'all night. I was burning. I thought I should run out into the snow to get cool. But I should freeze there. You would come and find me and warm me in your arms. But you would never come back. I knew you at once.'

'Who am I?'

'Hush. I do not want to say your name.'

'Mardya, tell me about the church.'

'You know everything about me.'

'The window, Mardya.'

'Not here …'

'No one can hear, you whisper so softly, and your warm breath brushes my cheek. Tell me about the window.'

'It was quite sudden,' she said. Artless, she added, 'Two years ago, when I was fourteen.'

'Well?'

'I saw it. The same way the girl does in the story. At first, I tried not to think of it. But I began to dream – how can I tell you those dreams? – they were so terrible. I thought my heart must stop, I should die – I longed for them and I feared them.'

'Pleasure.'

'Such – such pleasure. I tried not to know. But it has been all I could think of. There is nothing here – in the town. I see no one. No one comes to her house but her friends, the Inspector of Works, the banker – everyone is old, and I am old too when I sit with them. I become like them. My hands get so stiff and my neck and my eyes ache and ache. I have nothing to live for. But now, you are here.'

'Yes, I am here.' I put my foot gently against hers under the tasselled tablecloth. Our knees almost touched, the fabric of her dress stirred against me. Her cheeks were inflamed now. All about us, human things went on with their chocolate, their tea and cake and sugar.

'Tonight she will have those two or three friends to dine with you. We will dine on chicken bones and aspic tarts. We have no money.'

'Mardya, be quiet.'

'I must tell you –'

'What? How to remain behind in the house after the others have left?'

She caught her breath.

I said, 'I remember the lamp burning and how you go about improperly at night, and I would imagine you have fooled her, she never knows. So you are clever in such matters. Shall I hide in some cupboard?'

'Not now. How can I speak of it? I shall faint.'

'If you do that, we shall attract attention.'

'Secretly then. When the darkness comes. In darkness.'

'One candle, perhaps. You must let me look at you. I want to see all your whiteness.'

'Hush,' she said again. Her eyes swam, her hands pressed on the glass of tea as if to splinter it. 'I have never –' she said.

'I know.'

'You will – care for me?'

'You will see how I will care for you.'

Neither of us could breathe particularly well. We burned with fever, our feet pressing and our hands grasping utensils of the tea table as if to save them in a storm. But she shook so that her earrings flashed, and she could hardly hold the tea glass anymore. I took it from her, and found it difficult in turn to let go of.

Presently, I settled our account, and we left the shop and went to another, where she ordered needles for her aunt.

I escorted her up through the town, the second time, past the smoking braziers and the lamplit nothingness of other people and other things. On the rise, in the same snow-bounded stone archway, I thrust her back and crushed her to me. Her hands clutched my coat, she struggled to hold me as if drowning. We parted, and went separate ways, to scheme and wait like wolves for the night.

The dinner party – for such it was to be – was to be also all I had predicted from the picture Mardya had painted.

The Inspector of Works was there, a blown man with an overblown face, and his wife, a stubborn mouse of a woman much given to a sniff, an old maid in wife's clothing. The elderly unmarried banker had also come, perhaps an ancient flame of Madam's. But we animals were of a proper number and gender, and progressed two by two.

Madam Lindensouth came to dinner in a worn black velvet gown and carbuncle locket. When Mardya entered there was some life stirred up, even in the banker. She had on a dress the colour of pale fire, between soft red and softer gold, with her white throat and arms exposed. Madam did not bat an eyelash, so clearly she had not been above suggesting a choice of finery. Mardya was self-conscious, radiant. She flirted with the banker and the Inspector in a way, patently, they had never before experienced, the delicious clumsy coquettishness of an innocent and charming young girl. Only with me was she very cool and restrained. Yet as we came to the table, she did remark, 'Oh, Mr Mhikalson, I have been worrying about it. Those gloves in that particular shade of fawn. Are you quite sure that your sister will be content?'

Her daring pleased me. I said, unruffled, 'I thought they were more of a yellow tone. The very thing. But then, I told you, I have no judgment in such matters.'

All this required an explanation, that Miss Lindensouth had been in the town with me buying handwear for my relative. A knowing look passed between the banker and the Inspector's mouse.

Presumably not one of them had heard the latest news of my train. There had been a message at the inn on my return there. The line was expected after all to be clear by four the next morning. The train would depart one hour after, at five o'clock. Of course, I might be prepared to miss it. They might assume I would have no more pressing engagement than a wooing, now I was so evidently embarked.

All through the desiccated dinner, my fellow guests tried to wring from me, on Madam's behalf, the story of my life, my connections, my prospects. I remained cordially reticent, but here and there let fall a word for myself. I am a good liar, inventive and consistent, and quite enjoyed this part of the proceedings. As for the meal, it was a terrible event. There was not a drop of moisture in any of it, and the wine, though wet, was fit only for just such a table, and in short supply besides.

After we had dined, the ladies permitted the men to smoke, by withdrawing.

The banker lit up and coughed prodigiously.

'These winters,' said he, 'will be my death.'

To me he added, 'How I yearn for the city. I have not been in Archaroy, let alone anywhere else, since my thirty-fifth year. Is that not a fearsome admission? Finance has been my life. I still dabble. If you were to be seeking any advice, Mr Mhikalson –'

The Inspector broke in with a merry, 'Never trust this rogue. He is still in half the deals and plots of the town. But I must say, if you were thinking of remaining a week or so, there are some horses I think you should look at, with an eye to the summer. My cousin Osseb is quite an authority. Did you know it is possible to hunt wolf here all the year round? Well, there you are. Of course, Madam Lindensouth's brother, the father of Miss, had a lodge in the forest. But that was sold.'

'But you are not to think,' put in the banker, giving him an admonishing glance, 'that the family fortune here is on the decline. Not a bit of it. I will say, my dear friend Madam is something on the careful side, but there is quite an amount stashed away …'

'Tut tut,' said the Inspector. 'Can the ladies have no secrets?'

Finally we had smoked sufficiently, and went into the next room, where Madam regaled us all with some music from the piano, which, startled to find its lid had been raised, uttered a great many wrong notes.

Mardya would not play. She said that she had a chilblain on her finger. This evoked three remedies given at once by the mouse, the banker, and the Inspector. In each case, suffering the chilblain would have been preferable.

A card game then ensued, out of which Mardya pardoned herself, and I was left also to my own devices, being besides pushed to them by smiles and nods. I joined the girl by the piano, where she was searching among the sheet music for an old tune her father had been used to play.

'Come now,' I said, speaking low, 'how is it to be managed?'

'Impossible,' she said.

'Think of our stop on the hill.'

She blushed deeply, but continued to leaf through the music.

'I am afraid.'

'No. You are not afraid.'

'The ace!' cried the banker. He added to us, over his shoulder, not having heard a word, 'Now, now.'

'Think of the apple tree,' I said to her. 'Think of the rose.'

Her hands fluttered, some of the music spilled. Her pulse raced in her throat so swiftly it looked dangerous. We bent to retrieve the music.

'Leave before the others.' She spoke crisply now though scarcely above a whisper. 'I will go down and open the door. Return almost at once and go into the side parlour below. The blinds are down, there is a large table with a lamp on it that is never lit. You must be patient then. Wait until the house is quiet. Wait until the clock in the hallway strikes eleven.'

'Where is your room?'

She told me. She was shivering, from desire or fear, or both.

We had regained the music and arranged it together by the piano.

'There is the song my father used to play,' she said. But she did not play it.

It was almost thirty minutes past nine, and I suspected the festivity would be curtailed sharp at ten o'clock. After the banker had told us again to 'Now, now,' and the maidservant had brought in the trusty samovar and some opaque sherry, the card game lapsed. It was a quarter to ten.

'Madam Lindensouth,' I said, 'I must return at once to the inn. I had not realized how late it has grown. There are some arrangements I shall need to make.' I left a studied pause. She would deduce I meant to give up my seat on the train. 'Thank you for your kindness and hospitality.'

'If it chances you are still here tomorrow,' she said. (The banker and the Inspector laughed, and the mouse primly sniffled.) 'We take luncheon at three o'clock. I hope you will feel able to join us.'

At the concept of another meal of sawdust and pasted aspics I almost laughed myself. Something in her eyes checked me. In holding out to me the branch of unity with her niece, a girl therefore about to taste the chance

Madam had missed, there was a sudden ragged edge to her, a malevolence, which showed in a darkening of her pallid eyes, the iron smile with which she strove to underpin propriety. It was clear from this that a callous and unkind method would have sustained her treatment of Mardya from the beginning. She had never been a friend to her and never would be. Small wonder the savage innocent turned to shadows for her *fata morgana* of release and love. It even seemed probable in those moments that the aunt had known all along of midnight excursions to a church on the lower streets, of a flirtation with grisly legends and unsafety. Did the woman know even that this was where Mardya had met me? Did she know what plan we had ('Now, now') to meet in the night on the shores of lust, under her very roof? Yes, for a moment I beheld before me a co-conspirator.

When I took her hand, she said, 'Why, your hands are cold tonight, Mr Mhikalson. You must have a care of yourself.'

I uttered my farewells, got down through the house, and was shown out into the darkness and the snow.

I went down the steps, and waited where I had done so the first night, across the way, taking no particular pains over concealment.

That light was not burning in the upper – her – room.

The window was sightless, eyeless, and waiting, too. Before midnight, I should have seen the inside of that room, should have touched its objects and ornaments, invaded the air with my breath and will, my personality, perhaps a stifled cry, the heat of my sweat. I should have possessed that room, before the morning came. I did not need to see its light, now.

After about six or seven minutes, I went back. If I met anyone on the steps or in the doorway, I should say I had lost something and returned hoping it was in the house. But I met no one.

The front door was ajar, and I passed through silently, shutting it again. A muffled bickering came from above, from the dinner party.

The side parlour was as she had described, to the right of the hall, remote from the stair. It was in blackness, the table dimly shining like a pool of black water, and the unlit lamp upon it reflected vaguely, and here and there some glistening surface. I went through and seated myself on an upright chair against the wall, facing the doorway. Naturally I was quite concealed, by night, by the shapes of the furniture, best of all by being where of course I could not reasonably be.

Like the audience in the darkened theatre, then, I stayed. And down the dully lighted stair they passed in due course to the hall, the banker, and the Inspector and his mouse-wife. The maid arrived with hats and sticks, and Madam waved them off from the vantage of the staircase, not descending.

All sound died away then, gradually, above. And lastly the maid came drifting along across the open door, like a ghost, to take away the final guttering lamp. Partly I was amazed she did not catch the flash of my eyes from the black interior, the eyes of the wolf in the thicket. But she did not. No one came to bother me, to make me say how I had left behind a glove, or a cigarette case, or had felt faint suddenly in the cold, and come back to find the door was open – and sat here to wait for the maid and fallen asleep. No, none of that was necessary.

At last, the clock chimed in the hall, eleven times.

Rising from my seat, I stretched myself. I walked softly from concealment to the foot of the staircase. Hardly a noise anywhere. Only the ticking of the clock, the sighing of the house itself. Beyond its carapace, snow-silence on the town of L— , and far away, so quiet were all things now, the tinny *tink-tink* of another clock finding the hour of eleven on a slightly different plane of time than that of the Italian House.

I started to go up the stairs. The treads were dumb. I climbed them all, passing the avenues of passages, and came to a landing and a heavy curtain with a mothball fringe. And then, in an utter darkness, without even the starlit snow-light of the windows, her door, also standing ready for me, ajar.

I closed it with care behind me. The room was illumined only by the aqueous snow sheen on the blind. This made a translucent mark, like ice, in turn upon the opposite wall, and between was a floating unreality, with a core of paleness.

'Ssh,' she whispered, though I had not made a sound.

I went toward her and found her by the whiteness of her nightgown on the bed. The room was all bed. It could have no other objects or adornment.

Her hands were on my face, her arms were about my neck.

'Where is the candle?' I said. 'Let me see you, Mardya.'

'No,' she pleaded. 'Not yet …'

My vision was, anyway, full-fed on the dark. I was beginning to see her very well.

The little buttons of her nightgown irritated my fingers, to fiddle with them almost made me sick. I lifted my face from her burning face, kissing her eyes, her lips. I pulled the nightgown up in a single movement and laid her bare in the winter water of the light, the slender girlish legs folded to a shadow at the groin, the pearl of the belly, the small waist with its trinket of starlight, and the rib cage with the two cupped breasts above it, and the nipples just hiding still in the frills of the nightgown – she was laughing noiselessly and half afraid, shuddering, pushing the heavy folds from her chin, letting them lie across her shoulders and throat as I bent to her. My hands were full of her body and my mouth full of her taste. The mass of black hair stained across the pillows, shawled over her face, got into my mouth.

I threw off my coat, what I could be rid of quickly. Her skin, where it came against my skin, was cool, though her lips, ears, and forehead blazed, and the pits of her arms were also full of heat, and her hands, their hotness stopping mysteriously at the wrists. She was already dewy when my fingers sought between the fleshy folds of the rose. 'No,' she said. She rubbed herself against me, arching her back, shaken through every inch of her. 'No – no –'

'This will hurt you.'

'Hurt me,' she said, 'I am yours. I belong to you.'

So I broke into her, and she whined and lay for a moment like a rabbit wounded in a trap under my convulsive thrusts no longer to be considered, but at the last moment, she too thrust herself up against me, crucified, with a long silent scream, a whistling of outdrawn breath, and I felt the cataclysm shake her to pieces as I was dying on her breast.

'I knew you would come to me,' she murmured. 'I knew it must happen. I called out to you and you heard me. Across miles of night and snow and stone.

'Sometimes,' she said, 'I have seen you in a dream. Never clearly. But your eyes and your hair.

'Are you the one?' she said. 'Are you my love? For always?'

'Always,' I said, 'how else?'

'And my death,' she said. 'Love is death. Kill me again,' she said, but not in any mannered way, though it might have been some line from some modern stage drama.

So presently, leaning over her, I 'killed' her again. This time I even pinned her arms to the bed in an enactment of violence and force. Her face in ecstasy was a mask of fire, a rose mask.

Afterward her eyes were hollow, like those of a street whore starving in the cold.

When I began to put on my clothes, she said, 'Where are you going?'

'It will be best, I think. We might fall asleep. How would it look if the girl came in and found me here, in the frank morning light?'

'But you will come back tomorrow?'

'Your aunt has invited me to luncheon.'

'You will be here? Will you be late?'

'Of course I shall be here, of course not late.'

I kissed her, for the last time, with tenderness, seemliness. It was all spent now. I could afford to be respectful.

As I reached to open the door, she was lying like a creature of the sea stranded upon a beach. Her delicate legs might have been the slim bipart tail of a mergirl, and the tangle of nightgown and hair only the seaweed she had brought with her to remind her of the deep.

I went down again through the house with the same lack of difficulty, and as well, for I could have no decent story to explain my presence now.

As I let myself out of the front door, and descended the steps, the air cut coldly in the icy deserts before dawn. It was almost four o'clock, but I had seen to my luggage beforehand. I need only go along to the station and there wait for the train which, because the allotted hour was now both extempore and ungodly, would doubtless leave on time.

Two doctors attended me at the point of my destination, one the man I had arranged, a month previously, to see, the other a colleague of his, a specialist in the field. Both frowned upon me, the non-specialist with the more compassion.

'From what you have said, I think you are not unaware of your condition.'

'I had hoped to be proved wrong.'

'I am afraid you are not wrong. The disease is in its primary phase. We will begin treatment at once. It is not very pleasant, as you understand, but the alternative less so. It will also take some time.'

'And I believe,' said the less sympathetic frowner, 'you comprehend you can never be perfectly sanguine. There is, as such, no cure. I can promise to save your life, you have come to us in time. But marriage will be out of the question.'

'Did I give you to suppose I intended marriage?'

'All relations,' said this man, 'are out of the question. This is what I am saying to you. The organisms of syphilis are readily transferable. You must abstain. Entirely. This is not what you, a young man, would wish to hear. But neither, I am sure, would you wish to inflict a terrible disease of this nature, involving deformity, insanity, and certain death where undiagnosed, on any woman for whom you cared. Indeed, I trust, upon any woman.' He glared on me so long I felt obliged to congratulate his judgment.

The treatment began soon after in a narrow white room. It was, as they advised, unpleasant. The mercury, pumped through me like vitriol, induced me to scream, and after several repetitions I raved. One does not dwell on such matters. I bore it, and waited to escape the cage.

The ulcerous chancre, the nodulous sore, long-healed, which had first alerted me in Archaroy, has a name in the parlance of the streets. They call it there the Devil's Rose.

And in that way, Satan comes out of his window, unseen, and passes through the streets. All the lights go out as he dances with the girl who vowed herself to him. And in the morning they find her skin upon the hillside.

She died insane, I heard as much some years later in another city, from the lips of those who did not know I might have an interest.

The condition was never diagnosed. Probably she had never even been told of such things. They thought she had pinned and grown sick and gone mad through a failed love affair, some stranger who entered her life, and also left it, by train.

She had always been of a morbid turn, Mardya Lindensouth, obsessed by dark fancies, bad things. Unrequited love had sent her to perdition. She was unrecognizable by the hour of her death. She died howling, her limbs twisted out of shape, her features decayed, a wretched travesty of human life.

Yes, that was what dreams of love had done for her, my little Mardya. Though in the streets they call it the Devil's Rose.

95

The Eye in the Heart

From an Idea by John Kaiine

The last place I saw was Venice. He said he wanted it to be somewhere special – and it was. The memories are so perfect, and whenever I want, I can take them out of the cupboards of my mind and look at them. The malachite green canals, the greenish blue of the Italian skies, the gleaming domes, the white pigeons. And my husband, standing brown and smiling, his eyes full of pride in me, and love – and, yes, sexual love as well. How thoughtful he was. They were a magical two weeks.

Our holiday was marred only by one brief episode. I don't know why I think of it, but sometimes I do. To belong to our Sect of course sets us apart. All persons of deep convictions experience these odd occasional slights. One mustn't dwell on them or feel bitterness, because bitterness does no one any good.

But there. She was a young woman in a white dress, tanned, and apparently happy, as we were. Impulsively I went up to her, and asked if she would take a photo of us, my husband and I. I could imagine him, in the future, looking at it fondly, remembering our delight and oneness. But the girl edged away a little. Firmly she said 'No.' And then, blushing and frowning, to cover her bluntness, 'I'm no good with cameras. Excuse me.' Then she hurried off.

My husband, seeing I was slightly upset, at once found a man, who was much more amenable, and took the shot of us, which I've seen. It's a nice photograph. Perhaps the girl was only truthful and didn't want to let us down. Yet, I think she had realized we were people of a sect, our particular Sect, and our beliefs offended her. And somehow, now, I sometimes see her face, with my mind's eye, its blush, its frown, the sort of – terror – in it. So, using my special computer, I'm trying to explain.

There was one other thing about Venice, and other places we went through. I did feel so sorry for the older women, the married ones. I noticed especially, their eyes were so dull and heavy and troubled. But I haven't been much outside our Town, and so I'm used to our own married women, whose eyes are always clear and sparkling.

When I was a child, a lot of girls, including me, used to pretend to be married. My mother sometimes told me off for using so many of her scarves, and losing them in the woods. That was before we started Domestic Classes. Then, of course we had to practice properly. There were a few accidents, the worst one when a girl fell down the school steps and broke her ankle. Otherwise we laughed so much. But soon you get very proficient. I was, well, I'm boasting but it's a fact, one of the best. And it's stood me in good stead. Later, once they've allocated your house in Town, for a month before you marry, you have individual training. My husband told me I was an absolute star, but then I showed off to him. I demonstrated what I could do. We sneaked in the house alone, when we weren't supposed to, you see. I think quite a few people guessed, actually. His smile didn't help, it was so broad afterwards you could count all his white teeth.

The only thing I never had quite right was the cooker – I'm still working on that, but the splash-screen gets pretty dirty. Just so you know, I'm not saying I'm faultless at anything – heaven forbid.

Some people, I've heard, sometimes ask why. I mean, why we do this.

It's so obvious that it's quite hard to explain. It's that thing about bitterness again. Bitterness, and being hurt – worrying over what you can't do anything about – and then hurting others, *worrying* others, making a mess, and then – you're left with nothing.

We marry for life. Marriage is sacred. And everyone wants to be happy.

My mother had the bluest eyes. I used to stare and stare at them, so clear and darting as she spoke to me. Aquamarines. I can still see them, though she died last year. It was a sad time. Dad may marry again, though. He's still strong and young-sounding. I take flowers to her grave, and once I tripped, and this young girl, about twelve, ran over and helped me up. I could almost hear Mom laughing. *And you such a star!* She was sweet, my mother, but she was very down-to-earth, too.

I can recall quite well what she said to me, when I was about five, and she explained. So maybe I should just use her explanation, instead of trying to find the words myself.

'Women are so sensitive, darling. They have to be. They have to be aware what a man wants, what their children want. They have antennae all over them, *whiskers* of *feeling*. And unfortunately that has a down side. It means they get hurt so easily. And then they doubt. And soon they just can't believe. She'll say to her husband, 'You don't love me anymore. I can see it in your face. 'Maybe he's just tired – or maybe his *love* is tired. But she'll read something so awful into it. And then she'll nag and rave on, and drive him crazy. And in the end he won't be able to stand it. He'll slap her – or worse, he'll leave her. And what good will that do her? And men, you see, honey, sometimes they do little things ... little things it's better for a wife not to know. It's much nicer if she needn't worry about if she can forgive him. Do you remember that silly song, *Lipstick on your Collar*? Well, the women here in Town don't ever have to bother about that. Most of all, the thing they always see, with the eye of the heart, is how he looked at them last. All that wanting and care, that love. And when he tells you he loves you, why, he does. Oh darling, we're so lucky.'

When we came back from Venice, I went straight into our hospital. I had the loveliest doctor. He was the kindest man. He assured me, there isn't a single scar, and he let me feel, so I know.

'You're pretty as a picture,' he said. He even flirted, and I must have looked nothing at all after the op. 'You're eyes are green as grapes, Missy. I could look and look at those green eyes. I could eat them up.'

My husband bought them for me. Dad would have, but he just insisted. They are truly beautiful, I cried out when I saw them, in their velvet box. We displayed them with the wedding presents. I'm sorry to say I think there was a bit of jealousy here and there. Well, I'm sorry to say I enjoyed it, too.

And now we live so happily – all but for the cooker. Never mind I've got years and years to master that.

In my mind, I can see my husband as clear as a painting, and the love and wanting in his face. And when he kisses me, that's what I see, that's what I'll always see.

Oh, I know there are people out there, deluded people who perhaps even mean well, who try and try to get us stopped or hounded out of the state, but if only I could tell them how wrong they are. Though I'm blind now, *because* I'm blind, like every married woman in Town, I know I need never be afraid.

It was my twenty-first birthday last week, and my husband was a little bit late – only an hour or so. And I might well have started to worry, searching his face, trying to trap him in some lie … But no, he wasn't lying about all that at the office. I only have to remember his face, the way he looked in Venice. And I take his hand, and his lips are warm.

After all, as my mother said, 'What the eye doesn't see, the heart doesn't grieve over.'

And I've some wonderful news to give him when he gets back tonight. I'll wait up, even until three or four in the morning. I'm *pregnant*.

I wonder if it will be a girl?

Flowers for Faces, Thorns For Feet

In a village near the roof of the world, held fast by mountains whose tops were swords of snow, lived two young women. One morning the younger woman came to the elder.

'Annasin,' said the younger woman, 'I'm here to warn you.'

'Warn me of what?'

'They say the snow has gone from the pass, and a man is coming.'

'What man? What should I care? Do you think I want a husband?'

'No, he's a finder of witches.'

Then the elder woman, who was all of three and twenty, sat down on her stool. She said, 'I am not a witch.'

'Are you not? Others say differently. And besides I have been everywhere in the village, telling this thing, and many women I told have gone white and said, *I'm not a witch.*'

Annasin said, 'Mariset, go away. This is all nonsense.'

Mariset nodded, and she left the house.

Annasin sat on her stool, and she thought. She thought of the winter when she had made the fire burn by snapping her fingers. She thought of the summer nights when she had danced on the high meadows, and later how she had floated, as it seemed, up to the moon. And she had cured some of toothache and coughing. And one man, who had put his hands on her in the wood, she had made double over with a pain in his belly.

Annasin put biscuits to bake in the oven, but her heart was heavy and beat like lead. An hour later into her house through the open door, walked a slim grey cat pale as first morning.

'Come with me, Annasin,' said the cat, 'come with me you must.' It spoke in the human tongue, and as she heard it, Annasin felt herself shrink down and then she was on four feet on the floor, with her pointed ears up on her head, her tail in the flour, and the smell of burning biscuits in her dark grey nose.

'A pail of water on you, Mariset,' said Annasin.

'Come away,' said Mariset.

And together they trotted out of the house door and along the street.

None paid them any heed, two cats. They ran behind the wood stores and under the shadows of goat pens, and even the goats, with their yellow eyes no yellower now than the eyes of Annasin and Mariset, did not try to stop them.

Annasin and Mariset reached the hill above the village. They ran up the hill, and up another hill, through the wood of pines, until they were in the high pastures, where, in summer, the goats were brought to feed. Little grass was there as yet, and all about the sworded mountains rose, and then the sky.

'Let us go to the waterfall,' said Mariset.

So they ran on up the wet turf sides of the hills, to the feet of the mountains, where a white gush of water sprang. And behind the waterfall, in a cave of blue flowers, they sat on the mossy stone, the two grey cats.

'Now we're lost,' said Annasin.

Mariset answered, 'Now we are safe.'

But Annasin remembered very well how she had left her own young body sitting in her house before the oven, and she knew Mariset had left her own, younger body, in her own house near the church.

'What will they think of us?' said Annasin.

'They will say our souls have gone out of us,' said Mariset, 'and they will leave us alone.'

'I don't believe so.'

Mariset washed her paws. Then she rolled on her back in the flowers. 'There are worse fates than being a cat.'

Annasin agreed. 'To be dead, for one.'

'Who knows,' said a voice, 'if to be dead is worse than to be living.'

And there before the cave stood a third cat. He was a male, and they were well able to see this, his balls in a sheath of smooth black fur, firm as walnuts, for he showed them, courteously, first. Then, letting down his black silk tail, he turned about and coming up, touched both their noses with his own, politely. He was black all over, even his tongue, all black but for one spot of bright yellow, like a primrose, between his jet black eyes.

'Now,' said the male cat, 'we will speak in the cats' speech.'

'I regret, sir, we don't know it,' said Mariset.

'We are not true cats.'

'Oh, then it is time you learned,' said the male cat, 'for you seem true enough to me. First,' he added, 'I will tell you my name. I am called Arrow.'

Annasin and Mariset glanced at each other from their primrose eyes. It was a fact, the cat had spoken in another language, but both women understood it perfectly and at once.

And trying this language out, both found they could speak it pretty well.

'Arrow is a fine name,' said Mariset. 'But who called you that?'

'I myself, for I had another name, once. I named myself for the straightness of my fall.'

'Your fall,' said Annasin. 'Did you fall from somewhere?'

The black cat looked at her quizzically. 'Indeed I did. And need I tell you where?'

Mariset gave a nervous chirrup and Annasin searched for a non-existent flea. Both grasped they were in conversation with a fallen angel.

Arrow though, was all at ease, and lay down among the flowers. He said mildly, 'It was a great argument over one small thing. Can you guess?'

'You would be king,' said Mariset riskily.

The black cat laughed, as a cat does. He said, 'Why should I, or any of us, want that? The king must do all. We were happy enough. No, it was this way. You see, we had beheld them in the garden, the woman and the man. And we said amongst ourselves, Look, *he* has created them unequal. The man is almost but not quite as wise as the woman. That is surely unfair. So then we spoke to *him*, for in those days he was very approachable. He seemed surprised and told us we were wrong, for it had been *his* plan to have them, the woman and the man, the other way about – she less than he. And our prince – you will know his name – he laughed, he laughed until he fainted. How handsome he looked, lying at the feet of – *him*, his golden hair and wings spread out. Then I fear *he* became angry. *He* cast us out. We fell. But then, we had jumped first from those crystal casements.'

Annasin washed behind her ear. She did not venture a comment. But Mariset, the younger, ran out and began to play with Arrow, who was a fallen angel. They rolled and kicked, biting and cuffing and laughing in shrill meows.

Annasin said eventually, 'We're true witches then.'

'And almost true cats,' said Arrow, leaping on a stone before Mariset could nip his tail. 'But cats too are not always well thought of. They have pretty faces like the flowers, but sharp teeth in their mouths, and sharp claws in their feet, quicker than, but extremely like, thorns.'

'Our two bodies,' said Annasin, 'are sitting in our houses.'

'Perhaps no one will find them,' said Mariset.

Then they ran to the stream that broke below from the waterfall, and here they fished and caught their supper. They ate it raw, of course, and never had fish tasted so delicious, cold and sweet from the mountain stream.

When they were done, they walked back down the hills, and in the dusk below they saw the village, its flat red lights burning and smoke on most of its chimneys. A pair of horses were by the hospitable house, where travellers stayed, and in that window stood a bright lamp.

'He has come, that witch-finder,' said Annasin.

'It's good we are cats,' said Mariset.

'I will tell you one story,' said Arrow. And he did.

The First Story – The Hearth Cat

There was a woman who had never seen a beautiful thing in her life, except perhaps the sky, and she had little time to look at that. Since her birth she had lived in a bleak barren land, and at thirteen she was wed to a cruel oaf, who treated her like his slave and often beat her. She went in terror of him. He for his part hated her and everything, but to eat and sleep and drink. It is a fact, he did not even lie with his wife after the first few times he had her in his bed: he was too lazy. But she was glad enough to be left alone that way, and slept on the floor, on the bare boards beside his couch, with her head on a bundle of straw and an old blanket to pull over her.

There came a winter then that was terrible, like a long breath from the hells of ice. In that region the snow fell thick and froze like glass. Upon the ugly house of the man it fell too, and covered it up so it was like a lump of dirty sugar. Each morning the woman would make her difficult way to the well, and break the ice with a stick. All day she would tend the fire on the hearth. In summer she had gone often to the market and brought back, on her shoulders, a sack of logs, for there were no trees nearby. And now she fed the logs to the winter fire so that the man could sit in his chair in comfort. And on the fire she cooked his food, and mulled, with a hot iron, the ale for him to drink. But she drank the cold water from the icy well, and ate the scraps he left. Through the rest of the day the woman went about her tasks, cleaning the house and scouring the pots and washing out the clothes, but these two last things she did in the outhouse, in the bitter cold, for he did not like her to disturb him.

In the evening, which came quickly from the low grey sky, she lit the lamp for him and prepared his supper. Then he would climb the stair to his bed, and if she had not angered him at all that day he would not strike her. But often he did strike her, and sometimes her red blood fell on the floor of the house.

Once he had gone to bed, the woman would sit alone by the dying fire, for she was not allowed to keep it alight after the man had retired. Nevertheless, she would look into the golden embers, and sometimes she would dream a little, but not really of any proper thing, for she had never been told of, or seen, anything worthy of a dream. And though the embers themselves were in their way beautiful, they meant to her the coming of the cold night, and her hard sleep on the bare boards above, and the thankless tomorrow.

One morning in that winter, the woman woke as she always did at the first chill light of dawn. She got up stiff and sore from her wretched nest, and the man stirred in his furs and sheets and said, 'Not so much noise, you *cursed* cow.'

Then she crept down, and going to the hearth, she laid the logs and lit them from the tinder-box, and when she had done that she warmed herself for a few hasty minutes. When she opened the house door, there the winter lay before her as always, as if now the summer had died and would never return. Blank as death that white plate of the land stretched away to meet at last with the low white sky. The woman took her pail and stepped out, and the cold struck her as the man did, sudden and vicious, and she stood alone with her misery in the middle of that wilderness, and in that moment a finger of cold sun pierced from the cloud. The woman saw that something moved on the face of the dead world beside herself.

Amazed, she stared, and presently she saw it was a cat. Now, she had never seen one, she had only heard of them, but not, she thought, of one like this. For it was a cat the colour of an orange, sleek as silk, and in its head it had two amber jewels for eyes. And seeing her, standing in her rags at the door, the orange cat ran to her, and as it came it made a sweet and musical noise.

The woman's empty heart filled at once. She bent and touched the cat. It felt better than silk, and it was warm as a pie.

'Oh my beauty,' said the woman.

But just then she heard the loud steps of the man coming down through the house, and in a moment more, he was in the house door behind her.

'What are you idling at, you pig?' he said, and clapped her about the head. 'Go fetch the water. Where is my brew? What do I keep you for, you bitch?'

At which he saw the cat that burned so brightly in the white snow, like a piece of the summer sun.

'And what filthy thing is that? Eh, you mare, have you been keeping a darling cat all this while? Giving it too my food?' And he awarded the woman a push that knocked her down, and at the cat he aimed a great kick, but the cat was off like a flame over the snow. Then the man picked up a stone by the house door and flung it, but it missed the cat, who was gone around the outhouse, from sight. 'Learn this,' said the man, 'I'll catch that thing and skin it. It shall make me a collar.' And so saying he went back into the house, for it was cold work, raining blows in the doorway.

The woman had never thought to weep, but now, as she stumbled to the well, she did, and the tears froze on her face. She thought, what would the cat do, out in the bitter cold? But then she reached the well and broke the ice and hurried back to make food for the man.

All day, the woman thought of the cat. She thought of it in astonishment, and in fear, for how could it survive in the markerless snow? And when she went to scour the pots, she left open the door of the outhouse, in case the cat might come and shelter there, but she did not see it.

As for the man, he said no more about the cat, but he had taken down his slingshot, and his knife, and he sharpened the blade till the blue sparks flew. As the day slackened from its grey to its dark, he got up even and went to the door, but he did not venture out. The snow was so hard, there were no footsteps in it, not even the woman's from her trudges to and fro, let alone the cat's light paws.

The woman mulled the ale and brought it to the man, who drank and drank again, and then he went to his chair, and she thought, Perhaps he will forget.

But she did not forget, she wondered how the cat would be faring.

When he had eaten his evening meal, the man took himself up to bed. As he passed the woman, he smote her, so a ribbon of blood came from her lip. He said, 'That's for your bloody worthlessness.'

She listened to his steps ascend, and huddling by the perishing of the fire, she gnawed some crusts and rinds. But near his chair he had left the slingshot and the knife.

Presently the fire sank and there was only a smudge of red upon the hearth. The woman rose and went to the house door, and quiet as a whisper, she opened it. She had no lamp, for she was not allowed one, but there was a glimpse of watery moonlight over the land. Above, she heard the man snoring.

She looked at the waste, and there, like a wish, by the outhouse wall, she saw a colour shining in the snow like a golden coin.

She thought this: I will bring the cat into the house and warm it for one night. Then, before he wakes, I will take the cat away. I will take it to the place where the road starts to the market, and perhaps someone will chance on it, and give it a home. But at least he will never go so far to catch it.

Then the woman went out into the snow and she walked to where the cat lay curled up by the wall. When she bent and touched it, it felt cold now, and so she raised it in her arms. The cat opened its amber eyes and looked at her. 'How beautiful you are,' she said. 'I have never seen one like you.' And she carried the orange cat back to the house, and took it inside.

Upstairs the man still snored, and grunted in his turgid sleep, and the woman noiselessly took a little broth from the cauldron over the cooling fire, and this she gave the cat, though it was the man's food. The cat watched her. And then it licked up the broth. At last it made a wonderful low noise, but the woman put her finger to her lips, and the cat fell silent.

'You are so cold,' she murmured. 'Look there, the fire is all out, but the cinders are warm. I will put you there in the hearth till morning.'

And she put the cat into the warm dust of the fire.

It did not struggle, and feeling the heat it snuggled itself in and curled itself round, and closing the suns of its eyes, it slept.

Then the woman crept upstairs, and she lay on her straw pillow, wide awake, for the first hint of dawn, so she could hasten the cat away before the man should think to get up. Wide awake she lay, tense as a stick, and then she heard a loud creaking. A wind had sprung up like a ghost over the snow, and it was blowing the outhouse door, which she had forgotten to shut. Over and over the door complained until at last the man shifted in his bed.

'There is the door outside,' he said, 'go and close it, you damnable bitch. In the morning you shall have a beating.'

So the woman got up again, and went down. In the room below all light had failed, and on the hearth was nothing but a shadow. She hurried to the house door and slipped out, for she must stop that other door from making it noise, before he in his turn descended.

Over the hard white earth she ran. And coming to the outhouse, she secured it. And then from the veil on the moon she heard a voice call to her, from out of the night itself, from over the hills, from out of the ground.

Stand in the snow like a stone
Until your trouble is gone.

The woman was afraid, and she tried at once to fly. But it was as if iron hands held her feet rooted to the spot and there she must stand, her teeth chattering from the frigid night, and in the house she saw a light spring up, and she cried aloud in terror, for she thought he had come down and lit the lamp and he would find the cat upon the hearth.

But it was not the man. Oh no.

On the house hearth, the fire had burned up again. The old cold cinders had come alight. Or so it seemed. For on the hearth a bright fire was sparkling, yellow-red, like a hectic sunrise. But the shape of the fire was this way: it had a sleek body and four legs, and a face like a heart with two pointed ears, and a tail like a blazing stem.

And off from the hearth the fire stepped, dainty as a maiden in a golden dress. But it was a cat, a cat made all of fire.

Into the lower room of the house it moved, and there, at the touch of it, the floor burst into flame. And reaching with one paw, it rapped the man's chair, and the chair became a burning bush.

Then lightly up the stair darted the cat of fire, and the stair lit bright behind it. While above the man coughed on the smoulder, and roused himself, and called out, 'What are you doing, you cow? Haven't I said, you are never to light the fire save for me?'

And the fire cat answered, 'Oh, but it is for you,' yet it spoke in the cat tongue, and the man did not understand.

Even so, how light his house had grown, the bitch must have kindled all the three lamps, and so he sat up in bed and he readied his fist, and just then, in through the door danced the cat of fire, and all the room went up like a flowering tree of gold.

'God – God save me!' cried the man. But God is sometimes off on business, as so many know to their sorrow.

The fire ate through the bed and through the flesh of the man. First his feet burnt, and then his legs. Then his body was a bonfire, and black smoke came from his nostrils, and from his eyes tears of flame. He burst like a bad fruit, and the house fell down, and the white snow dropped sizzling into the core of it, so a cloud went into the sky and put out the moon.

All this the woman had watched and she sobbed and screamed, thinking only of the poor cat she had left in the cinders to be warm, and that she had killed the only thing she loved.

However, when the last timber of the house had settled out through a hole in the ruin walked a golden fire, and it had the shape of a cat. At this the woman's feet were free, and she ran to meet the cat, and leaning down, she held its fiery fur to her heart until she was warm all over.

Then this pair, the woman and the orange cat, walked away across the plain of snow, and the footsteps of each were deep and black, one by one for the woman, and two by two for the cat, and smoke rose from the footsteps, and rose from them, up and up, long after the cat and the woman were gone.

The night had come, and the three cats on the hill had settled on the bare earth. Above, the stars were like the eyes of black mother cats, who watched over them.

'Why did you tell us this story?' asked Annasin.

'To show that cats are not always what they seem,' said Arrow.

Mariset said, 'But this we know. We of *all* cats.'

'Then,' said Arrow, 'to show that one does not always know the heart's desire.'

They slept awhile, but the moon came up. The night was now all lit like a ballroom, but in the village the lamps were out and every head on its pillow. Just so had Annasin and Mariset slept, some nights of the year.

'No others have joined us here,' said Mariset. 'I would have said that in our village, there were at least three others who were witches.'

'Or they told that they were,' said Annasin. And she thought of the crone Margotta, who put spells on the goats and sent the milk sour, or so she said. And of the girls Vebya and Chekta, who claimed that they could fly. But Annasin, as she drifted past the moon on summer nights, had sometimes glimpsed Mariset, but never Vebya or Chekta. Though the sour milk she had tasted, and she thought Margotta had thrown something in it.

Arrow got up, and so did Annasin and Mariset, the grey cats. They played together under the moon, and ran to chase moths in the vast pine wood, which glittered with moonlight as if hung with silver and diamonds. All night they played and chased, and in the last patches of the white snow they left the prints of their flowery feet that had thorns in them.

When the pink dawn came, they watched it. Then they drank from a pool, all three, and how Arrow's black tongue lapped. They slept in an ancient burrow, breast to back. And Annasin lusted after Arrow, and was ashamed, but somewhere in the drowse of day, he mounted her, she felt him, and her whole body seethed with joy. At length, and it seemed long enough to her, he left her, and then came a sear of pain. She turned and struck him in the face. He bowed and went to spray the ferns outside the burrow.

'Thorns,' said Annasin. 'Not only in the feet.'

'*He* planned the world,' said Arrow. 'It's a wondrous deed, and we could never have done it. Alas, in the rush to get things done, *he* left certain acts untested and particular elements unkind. *He* did not mean to harm. *He* never does. You must not blame *him*.'

In the afternoon, the wood was warm. They rose all three and groomed each other tail-tip to nose-end. Then they hunted mercilessly and did terrible things, which were not their fault, nor God's, simply a flaw in the too-hasty planning of a great genius. They ate well, and the sun descended like a flaming eye.

During the sunset, there was a commotion from the village. Then Annasin and Mariset ran to see, from the vantage of the nearer hill, and Arrow sat behind them.

A tall old man was in the street. He was swarthy and dark and clad in rusty black. In his hand was a cross that shone as the wood had done by night, so they knew that it was silver. From the houses strong men were roughly dragging out some women. Old Margotta came, cursing and spitting in her stenchful garments, and next white Vebya, and brown Chekta, sobbing. Then there strode up the wood-cutter, from the house of Annasin, and over his shoulder he bore the limp form that Annasin recognized to be her own human body, its long hair down his back.

'See, she's bewitched,' said the wood-cutter.

But the grim old man, the witch-finder, he said, 'No, in the witch-trance. Her soul is off at some mischief. Flying over the chimneys on a stick, or sucking the blood from lambs and children.'

'Old fool,' said Mariset. But she had eaten a whole mouse, she could hardly pass judgement.

Annasin said, 'I am in jeopardy. I'd best go back.'

Just then, there were fresh cries, and the door of Mariset's house by the church was beaten in. Out they dragged her charming body, by its very hair, and Mariset wailed.

'What shall I do?'

Into the hospitable house, which already blazed with lamps, as if the coming night were dark, the five witches, real and false, waking or unconscious, were hauled, and the door slammed.

Silence came to the hill, until an owl with a cat's eyes went sailing overhead.

They looked up at the owl, Arrow and his ladies.

Then Arrow said, 'I will tell you a second story.'

'There's no time for tales,' declared Mariset in a pitiful mew.

'There is always time,' said Arrow, 'for time only exists by the grace of him.'

The Second Story – The Sea Cat

The ship of the thieves was painted black, and it had for a figurehead a wooden man with upraised sword, and in his other grasp, a severed hand. They sailed about, the company, and reckoned they were fair enough. For when they came on another ship they robbed it, but only killed those who resisted them or tried to hide away their goods.

They had besides, these thieves, a sort of lucky thing, or scapegoat. The mate, who liked to carve, had made it from a piece of driftwood, and it was a very rough and graceless wooden cat, with one eye big and round and the other long and narrow. When they had had fortune, the thieves would spill drink on this lucky cat, and when matters had not gone well, they would stick nails in it, kick it, and spit in its face. They called it a name which meant Ratter.

It happened that they had extreme luck for a whole month, and robbed four ships and got away with many excellent prizes, bolts of velvet and necklaces of pearls, and some casks of wine, which they liked a great deal. And one evening, when the sun had just gone down, they saw a storm go by them on the horizon like a moving cliff of wind.

So then they anointed Ratter and sat down to eat.

As they were doing this there came a great shouting from the watch above.

The captain of the thieves ran to discover what went on, and most of his men with him, and looking out from the rail, they beheld something floating on the cradle of the black night sea.

'It's a barrel of rum,' cried one. But another said 'No, for it cries. It's a baby.'

Over the sea it came, the floating, crying thing. And the moon began to rise in the east.

Now, they were miles from land, and nothing anywhere in sight. Not an island, not a sail, or anything that they knew of. But there on the water drifted, never going down, shape like a bluish flower. And raising its head it meowed to them. It was a cat.

'How does it stay up there?' said one of the thieves And another said, 'It must swim.' The captain said, 'Make haste and draw it up. It's lucky, and bad luck to leave it there. But don't say its name.'

So they cast a net and caught the blue cat, and brought it up into the ship. There on the deck it shook itself, and was quite dry. A pretty cat, and small, with a pointed face and wide eyes.

'Call it Rum,' said the captain, 'for that was what we thought it to be at first.'

Then they gave Rum a dish of fish, and Rum sat purring under the masts, and looked at them gently, and washed behind her ears.

'See, she's calling a soft wind,' said one of the thieves, and sure enough this benign wind came, and blew them on where they wished to go.

When they had dined, the thieves sought their bunks, and only the captain and the mate stayed dicing in the cabin where Ratter stood in the corner. Soon enough Rum came in, and purred, then curled to sleep on the captain's bunk.

'Look,' said the mate, 'how the lamp seems to make Ratter's eyes move about. He's jealous of Rum.'

The captain laughed, and just then there began to be shouting again, up on the deck. The captain and the mate went to see, and so they found the thief, who had relieved the watch, standing bellowing, and the thief who had kept the watch lay dead beside the wheel, not a breath in him, not a mark upon him.

'Men die,' said the captain. 'One less is one less to share with. Throw him over the side.'

So they did, and leaving the new watch at his post, rolling his eyes, the captain and the mate went to their rest. Rum was gone, like a virtuous cat, to patrol the deck, and over the ship the cool moon stared. Like a lullaby, slowly rocked the vessel.

At sunrise, there came another loud shouting. Now several turned out. And going up to the wheel, they saw the third new watch had found the second dead, as the second had found the first. And he too lay there, like a log, and not a mark on him.

'Now something goes on here,' said the captain. And he set three men to watch and keep the wheel, and had the other one, the second corpse, thrown over the side. Then he went to breakfast, and he and the mate kicked Ratter, and slung some dregs of wine into his face. But they ate well, and sat long, counting the money from the last of the robberies, and seeing how it would go further now.

And once or twice there was shouting up on deck, but often the thieves shouted at each other, for they drank by night and were quarrelsome all day until they drank again.

At noon, a man came to the captain, and he was very pale. 'Curses on Ratter,' said the pale thief, 'I have gone the length of the ship, and every man on her, but I and you, is lying dead, and no mark on him at all.'

Just then, through the door walked Rum, and sat to wash herself at the paws of Ratter. The captain looked at this, and he said, 'Rum has not been good luck to us, after all.' And the mate said, 'She must go over.' At this Rum gazed at him with her pretty round eyes, and the mate said, 'But I have no heart to do it.' Though he had sliced the throats of fifty men.

Besides the captain said, 'What can Rum do? No more than Ratter can, who's a block of wood. This is some pestilence. Let's drink wine, for that is a fine medicine.'

So the three of them, the captain, the mate, and the last sailor-thief, drank cups of wine, and then they went up and looked at all the dead men on the ship.

Some lay at their work, where they had been scrubbing or mending sail. One lay up in the look-out even, head tilted back as if at his ease. The wheel had moved a little from the course, but this they tended to. The captain said, 'They must all go in the sea or they will stink.' Accordingly they took each of the men and cast him from the side and the water received him kindly in her long blue arms. 'Now,' said the captain, 'we'll make course for the nearest port. Think how rich we will be, the three of us.' And he sent the last sailor to trim the sails, and himself took hold of the wheel.

The captain stood then at the wheel of his ship through the heart of the afternoon, and now and then he quenched his thirst by means of the cask of wine at his side. Once or twice he saw the bluish shape of pretty Rum go up and down, though he paid not much heed. But then in the end, he heard no sounds from the ship, but for the voice of her timbers and the murmur of the sails above. So he shouted for the mate, and next for the other thief, the last sailor left. None answered.

As the sun went over, and the sky deepened, and the calm smooth wind blew on, taking them to port, the captain tied the wheel where he would have it, and drew his knife, and went to see.

He found the last sailor lying amidships, dead as a nail, and a smile on his face and no mark. And the mate the captain found lying against the money chest, with some coins in his hands, and smiling, and unmarked.

Then the captain went to Ratter, and he spat on Ratter and then he gave Ratter some wine. 'I shall be,' said the captain, 'the richest man since the old days. If I live.'

But the captain did not live, for as the sun went down, pretty Rum came softly to the cabin, and looked at the captain. And the captain gazed into her shining eyes, and never, it seemed to him, had he beheld so deep and sweet a sea. And on the sea he sailed, lost in the calm air, and Rum purred, and it was a song better tahn sirens make, or the mermaids who lure men to their deaths. So the captain lay back on his bunk, in a dream, and Rum came gently up his body, and lay on the captain's face. So as he dreamed he was suffocated, and died in the same way as all the others.

When the captain was quite dead, not a mark on him, Rum jumped down and washed herself, and the wind dropped and the ship stood still on the ocean.

Rum gazed about with her bright eyes, and saw wooden Ratter looking at her.

Ratter said, in the tongue of cats, 'Now you will go back into the sea, and wait for the next one.'

'Just so,' said Rum politely.

'Take me with you,' said Ratter.

'Alas,' said Rum, 'regretfully, you can be of no use to me. I am very sorry.'

'There you are wrong,' said Ratter. 'Only grant me the power to move, and I'll show you what I can do.'

Then Rum flicked Ratter with her silken tail, and Ratter came alive, all wooden, and rough with splinters, with, sticking out of him, all the nails that the thieves had stuck in him, and stained on him the marks of their kicks and cups.

But Ratter stalked, like an old worn chair, down the length of the ship. And reaching the bow, he slipped over. Rum sat by the rail and watched.

To the wooden figurehead, with the sword and severed hand, Ratter went, and climbed upon its face. And there Ratter curled up, as Rum had done upon the faces of the thieves. And presently the sword dropped from the wooden grip of the figurehead, and next the severed hand dropped. And then the figurehead began to buckle and to bend. As Ratter sprang away, the figurehead fell over into the sea, and after this, the ship groaned, and she broke apart as if on a rock, and soon she went down.

Ratter said to Rum as they floated in the sea, 'You can kill men. I can kill ships.'

Rum said, 'Then, come with me, brother.'

Mariset sighed, and said, 'Why tell us this story?'

'So you may notice,' said Arrow, 'that men also fear cats.'

'If it was true, your tale,' said Annasin, 'they have some cause.'

'Perhaps they do.'

In the village below the lights still burned, though it was late. Noises came dim and fearful from the house of hospitality, and once or twice, even over Arrow's melodious meowing, they had heard the renting of the witch-finder, though not his words. And later, screams.

'How sweet it is,' said Mariset, 'here in the hills.'

'How safe it is,' said Annasin. 'But I keep thinking, what have they done to me, down there.'

Mariset said, quietly, 'I have never had a lover.'

Annasin said, 'You don't want one, they are clods.'

But then she remembered Arrow and his velvet, and the thorn of pain after the tumult of desire.

And Mariset had stood up, and she rubbed her face against Arrow's face.

Annasin curled herself into a ball of fur, and closed her eyes and slept calmly, until she heard Mariset screech and the sound of Arrow jumping backwards through a briar thicket in order to escape her claws. Then Annasin got up and went to Mariset and washed her, and they laughed, and Arrow pranced about, spraying the bushes, the moon in his eyes.

'Is it a fact now we have slept with the Devil?'

'Who knows?' said Annasin. 'Who cares?'

Then all three played again on the hill, but at last the moon set, and then the night was darker. They drank at the pool, and Annasin said, 'I don't mean to be abrupt, but I must go back to the village. I must go back into my shape of a woman. Perhaps I'm a fool to do it.'

Mariset said, 'I was fair of face, I had shining hair. But I haven't the courage to go back at all. I'd rather stay here on the hills. How cold the mountains look against the stars! I release you from my spell, Annasin, so you can go back into yourself. You yourself know well enough how to get out again.'

Annasin picked down the hill like a sleek grey shadow. She stole in among the byres and huts, and never a dog barked. She came into the village street, and there her house was, black as a hole, and all the other houses lit with their lamps.

She ran four-foot to the hospitality house, and outside the horses standing tethered whinnied and widened their eyes. So Annasin loosed herself, and her cat form melted away. One moment she was in the air, and then inside her skin, and inside the house.

The light was dull and low, a sort of brown, and she lay among a heap of groaning, whimpering women, and she hurt.

She realized they had been sticking pins in her and touching her with hot irons, to try to rouse her. Her body was scraped over, in and out of her clothes. Besides she had been tied, by a strong rope and too tight, to a hook in the wall that was meant for meat. And all those other women had been done up similarly.

'Look,' hissed a voice. It was Vebya, who bled from her temple and her wrists and feet. 'Annasin is awake. Oh Annasin – save us. Call a demon to set us free.'

'That I can't,' said Annasin, 'I'm no witch.'

'Yes you are,' cried Vebya. 'For I saw you float over the meadow.'

'Yes you are,' said Chekta, who had been whipped, her dress and her back all ribbons, 'you light fires by a word. I spied on you.'

'There is a limit, to what I can do,' said Annasin.

And nearby, filthy Margotta hawked and spat. Her fingers were broken on her right hand. She said, 'I've call the lords of Hell, but they won't come, the traitors. Forty years I've served them all. And the Devil has had me in my own kitchen. I told it all, to stop the hammer. And I have been loyal, but where is he now, the demon who filled me?'

Then there was a rush of movement, a chair thrust back, and out from the brown light stormed the shadow of the witch-finder. His evil tortured face loomed over Annasin, yellow from the candle that he held. He lifted high the silver cross, and Annasin bowed to it, at which he snatched it back.

'Do you mock God, you bitch?' he yelled.

Annasin said nothing.

The witch-finder spat as old Margotta had, but into the sinking fire. He said, 'Speak up, now, witch, since you have woken. Where have you been on your broomstick or your nightmare horse? Who have you poisoned? Has the Devil had you?'

Annasin compressed her lips. She said, 'You would do better in the church, father, praying for nicer health.'

'Rein yourself in, woman. Don't try to put your curse on me. I am safe in the arm of God.'

'You will die in seven months,' said Annasin. And she could have bitten out her tongue. What had possessed her? But it was true, for she saw his skull through his head like a stone in the soup.

The witch-finder struck her hard in the belly, and Annasin fell back. She fell against Mariset's vacant body, and Vebya shrilled, 'Make her tell where the other witch is. Make her tell of Mariset.'

But Annasin could not speak, and the witch-finder now was not concerned any more with confession.

'Tomorrow you will burn, all five of you. Burn and go down to Hell where you belong, and the devil awaits you with his forks and knives.'

Then the old man went back to his chair and poured more spirit into his mug.

The injured women moaned and muttered and grew still.

Annasin thought of how they would burn her as a witch. Her heart broke. There was nothing she could do, nor anything for the others, nor anything for Mariset. Each must save herself as she could, if she could.

And through the cracks in the door and window came the scent of night, over the stink of blood and useless pain and fear and human flesh.

When she had got up the hill again in her slim grey fur, Annasin found Mariset and Arrow at the stream, splashing starlit ripples with their paws.

Mariset ran to her, and Mariset asked, and Annasin told her, bit by bit, unwilling, but holding nothing back.

Cats cry. Of course not with tears. Mariset and Annasin wept by the stream and then they went to Arrow and he curled against them, and they laid their heads on his taut male belly as if for the milk of their mothers.

'I will tell you now a third story,' said Arrow, as the stars wheeled slowly overhead.

The Third Story – The Tower Cat

When people heard the sound, echoing over the long fringed grain fields, and up to the bony hills beyond, they would say, 'The ravens are noisy today,' or they would say, 'Listen, it's thunder.' Or they would say nothing. But in secret they had a name for it, that sound: the *grinding*, they called it.

What was ground? It was like bricks, like stones, mashed over and over. Like little stuff worked down to littler stuff. Yet it was never done.

What then did they suppose made the *grinding*? A church lay on the plain, and in the church was a priest. He was a fat man, tall and black-maned, and he ruled the land about like, a king. Every holy day his church was full; none dared stay away. And he preached harshly. There was no kindness in him. He told them of their vileness and how they would be made to pay for it by a God who, in his mouth, became like a ravening dragon. Then, he would pass a silver bowl among them and they would each put in a gift, all they could afford and more. And at other times he would visit them, the priest, their huts and houses, their farms, the mills and the inns. And whatever he asked for he was given, food and drink, keepsakes, wine and cloth. Even gold rings he was given off their fingers if they had gold rings and now and then he would take a fancy for a girl, and then she must go to him. They hid their sisters, wives and daughters where they could, but it was not always possible. He was a hungry man, their priest.

He was more than that, for sure. How else did he so terrify them? He was a magician.

Some nights, from the top of the church tower, that was high, and rimmed like a castle, cold lights reeled off into the sky. And those that had to pass that church by midnight, did so by going off the road, walking away over the fields, so a new track was worn there.

From the tower too, from its top, came that sound they called, in secret, the *grinding*. They did not know what it might be and did not care to know. 'The owls,' they said. 'A storm,' they said, and pulled the blankets over their heads. Some prayed he would die, but bad things happened to those that prayed in this way. One had an axe fall on his foot, and the blade severed it, and he was a cripple. One met something on the hill at dusk, and he went mad; they had to chain him. 'God bless the good priest,' they said.

There was a girl the priest had seen when she was only ten, but he waited, he did not like them so young as that. Her father and her mother hid her away, it was true, but then her hair shone like copper in the sun, and he remembered it, the priest, as he rode by the farm.

'What is that which glimmers?' said the priest.

'It's the old pan on the kitchen wall.'

'No, never any pan. Answer me again.'

'The sun catching on the window.'

'Answer again.'

'My daughter's hair.'

'Send her,' said the priest, 'to me. Let her come just after sundown. She will be thirteen now.'

The mother spat in the dust, but she said, 'Excuse me, holy father. I have a bad taste in my mouth from eating unripe fruit.'

And the father said, 'I will set her on the road to you. '

And, what use to hesitate, on the road they set her, their copper-haired girl, when the sun was burning low as a candle and the shadows reaped the fields.

She walked all the way, although the tears dropped shining from her eyes. Like gold her tears were as the sun declined, but when it was down, like silver. And in the moonlight, glass.

Then she stood by the church door, and the priest called to her to come in.

He had his will of her under the altar, and she knew better than to complain. When he was done her tears were spent. She sat against the side of God's table, and she heard above her, softly, the *grinding*.

'Shall I tell you,' he said, the priest, 'What it is makes that noise?'

The girl said, 'The old church stones rub together.'

'No,' said the priest. 'Come up and see.'

It was his whim, and she could not resist, so in great pain, for he had forced her, she climbed up the winding stair of the church tower, and came at last out on to the roof.

Open it was, that roof, to the high sky, and the moon shone down on it. There was the strangest sight. At the centre of the roof, all about which stood up huge gargoyles of grey granite, there was a pattern marked on the slates.

And in the middle of this, was a grind-stone, a huge stone wheel. And tied to the wheel was a small creature, which walked round and round, and the wheel ground something small and smaller and smallest, but it was never done.

'It's a cat,' said the priest. 'Do you see?'

The girl said that she did. And it was. The creature tied to the wheel that went round and round and never stopped. It was a tabby cat, thin and silent, like some everyday mouser of the farms, and its eyes were cold as the stars.

'I will tell you the truth,' said the priest, 'for tonight I'm fearful, miss, you will die. Out on the bony hill. A shame.'

The girl said, 'I don't care.'

'Perhaps you will,' said the priest, 'for I have given you to a demon. But, even so, you too shall have something. A little knowledge. Understand then that this ordinary cat, a common tom I found upon my travels years ago, has inside it the great magic all cats possess. And I can let such magic out. I secured tom to my magic grind-stone. The wheel goes round, and grinds away anything that is against me. No illness no ill-will, no mishap may come near. Old age is crunched, bad luck is squashed of juice. And all this my dear cat does for me.'

'Can it never rest?' said the girl, for she had a sweet heart.

'No, it never rests. Never feeds. It has no life but as my thing. And now, you may go, and meet the demon. Greet him for me.'

The copper-haired girl went down the stair, and out through the church and away into the dark fields which the moon had sliced with silver. She walked straight up to the bony hills. She did not hang back, not she.

But when she felt the rough grass under her feet, a sickly fire was there, in the distance, and she knew when she met with it, she would die. Then she paused. She turned and looked back at the church. And she said this:

Pussy cat, pussy cat, turning his wheel,
Either the world or the wheel must stand still.
Pussy cat, pussy, by power of my will,
The world, or the wheel, for I die on the hill.

And then she laughed and ran towards the sickly flame, and nothing was seen of her again.

But the priest ate roast meat and grapes, and drank wine, and slept deep in his soft bed. And all the while the *grinding* went quietly on, on the tower above.

What of the cat then? Well, he had, of course, bewitched it. He had brought out the magic of which it was made, that is old as the earth. And as it walked round and round, under the circling sun and the moon and the arrow-tips of the stars, it had nothing in its head, not a memory or a want. But then, that night, as the priest slept, a shooting star sped down the black sky, like a falling soul. And the cat looked up. In that moment it became a cat. It stood on its hind legs and it clawed at the air, at the curtains of the magical air that hung there about the wheel, it clawed and rent, and so it called, in the way of cats, a storm.

Dim were the first flashes of the tempest, smooth as blue blushes on the cheek of night. And faint the thunder. But then the storm rolled in.

Around the tower, the highest thing upon the plain, the storm glanced and battered, and the wind rocked. Rain sprang like swords. The priest turned, careless, in his sleep. But all about, in the houses and the huts, in the mills and inns, they were afraid.

For it was a storm like an animal that beat in the sky, maybe even something like the horrible God the priest ranted of, wicked and unreasonable and full of jealousy and wrath.

The cat walked on about its eternal stroll, pulling the grinding wheel, but its head was lifted into the rain it had raised, and its fur was soaked through, black now as soot. It was wet as an eel.

Then lightning hurled from the sky, and it struck the tower a crack like a whip. Stark blue, the fire, and it broke on the gargoyles, one by one. Now there burned up a thing like a bear with the tail of a snake, and now a thing like a man with the mask of a weasel. But then the lightning-strike burst full on an upright shape of stone, lean and winged, and it had the head of a cat.

The thunder bowled away down the sky like a great soft ball. The flickers of the lightning paled and stilled. The rain ebbed.

Smooth now, the night. But up there, on the church tower, the cat walked on and on, round and round, half-drowned, with its eyes blue as sapphire.

It had ground a deal of badness that day, for the sound had grown low, the sound of the *grinding*.

Yet then there came another grinding sound. It was the note of a stone arm that ended in a granite paw, stretching out. And next, another. And then a patter like pebbles skimming down into a pool, that was the rain-wet wings of the cat-gargoyle, all the flinty feathers shaken out.

It stepped from its plinth, the gargoyle, and its cat face moved, and it spoke, while it looked down upon the priest's magical cat. 'Will you be here?' it said. 'Or will you come with me?'

'What are you?' said the cat, in the language of cats, which the gargoyle itself had impeccably spoken.

'I,' said the gargoyle, 'am an angel of your kind.'

'How beautiful you are,' said the tabby cat.

'I was about to say the same.'

Then the angel bent and bit through the tether with strong stone teeth, and taking the cat in its arms, the angel rose into the sky, up, up, where the stars were, and beyond. Do not doubt there is a heaven for their kind. There is always a heaven.

Yet in his sleep, the priest did not even turn, he felt no trouble, had no warning. Nor had the world stopped spinning. It was only his wheel.

However. When he woke, it came to him at once that some awful thing had happened. He did not hear the *sound*, that sound familiar to him as his own breathing. The sound of the *grinding*.

It occurred to him that perhaps no bad thing was near, and so the wheel had nothing to work on – but always the wheel worked. So he rose and dressed himself, and went up the stairs of his defiled church, and when he reached the roof, he saw.

The cat was gone, and the wheel was still. And a crowd stood waiting beyond.

Old age was there, with his broken teeth and hoary head, and smiling, and bad luck with his claws, and disease with his pinchers and needles, and at the back of them all, a shadowy thing that had no face.

The priest screamed. He ran down from his tower, and on the way he fell, and his leg was shattered. He lay then in the hollow of the church, howling.

As he did so, out on his body broke sores and pustules, he sweated and turned green with fevers, snot ran from his nose and blood from his lips. His black hair shrivelled and dropped out. Lines were drawn in his face as if a plough had riven there. The seeds of death were planted, and presently death came down.

Death stood above the priest all morning, as he shrieked and spewed and tried to crawl and could not, and the sunlight dappled over the floor.

At last the sun stood high above the tower, and then death touched the priest. And the priest arched backwards until his body was a bow, and he snapped in the middle. From his belly and his genitals ran serpents, and out of his eyes long worms that could not see. Then he melted and was a filth on the floor. But the sun dried it.

On holy days thereafter the church was unfilled. Rumour had gone round. Three seasons passed before any came to see, and by then there was no sign, but for a dry black stain under the altar.

They shut the church and planted trees about it, to overwhelm it and pull down the stones, which in the end they did, but that was long after, when the priest had been forgotten, and the sound of the *grinding*, too.

It was the dawn in the sky, so soft and yellow, and Annasin and Mariset looked up into the face of Arrow, their lord.

'And why *this* story?' asked Annasin.

'To show,' he said, 'that vengeance is usually possible as is escape.'

The clouds were golden, and curly as fleece. How mild and ready for the spring that high land near the world's top. Even the mountains glowed, and the waterfall was like a jewel.

But they washed themselves, and then they went down, down to the place on the hill where the village was to be seen.

Already the villagers were busy. They were building up, on the open space before the church, a huge pile of wood and sticks, old broken furniture, and posts torn from the walls of byres and pens. It was the pyre for the witches the witch-finder had found.

They worked with a will. The women, some of them, were singing. Happy songs. And the children danced about squeaking, 'burn the witch! Burn her to a stitch!'

There was a man Annasin had cured of a chest-rot, heaving in long planks of dry wood. And there the woman who Mariset had blessed with a baby. But there too were the women whose husbands Vebya and Chekta had lain with, and there the man whose goats had given sour milk, and there the one who said Margotta had made him cut off his big toe with the scythe.

Yes, they worked with a will, and before the sun was very high, all was prepared.

Then the witch-finder came from the hospitality house, and on the wind blew his smell of liquor. He held in one hand his silver cross, and in the other a black book.

The witches were brought after.

Vebya and Chekta screamed and soiled themselves, Margotta cackled curses. Mariset and Annasin were like the dead already, their two young bodies limp as the rope that trailed from their ankles. All were tied among the posts of the pyre.

Only Vebya went on screaming for reprieve. Poor thing, she had never learned.

The witch-finder spoke some words, but the wind broke them and carried them about. A jumble came up the hill. *God* said the witch-finder, over and over. As if God was a name that might be forgotten and must therefore be repeated frequently.

It was the witch-finder who lit the pyre. He did it with a torch one of the men had made. The witch-finder walked all about the heap of wood and women, and put the red flower in here, and here, and finally threw the flower down on the feet of Mariset, who lay on her shining hair.

Mariset could not bear it. She saw her flesh evaporate, and she ran away, away into the wood, screeching. But Annasin stayed, and carefully beheld her human body consumed, its petals falling, its bones clothed only in smoke.

The cries and shrieks of the three waking women were terrible. Annasin prayed they would soon die and find peace. At last, bitterly she said to Arrow, 'Can you do nothing?'

The black cat answered: 'Alas. We have some power over *him*, for *he* is reasonable. But none over men.'

At last the noises were stopped. At last the pyre fell in.

Some of the villagers took bones from it for good luck. The witch-finder went back to the hospitality house. He seemed shrunken and very tired, as if he had lost hope.

Annasin and Arrow ran to find Mariset. They discovered her easily, wailing under a pine tree.

They licked her and kissed her until she lay down. They slept all three in a ray of sunlight, while the birds flew overhead.

In the late afternoon, Arrow went hunting alone, and brought back for them three of these birds. It was a wicked dance they had with them. But no one's fault, and in the end they fed. Poor world, it had never learned.

The sun sank in fire, but the fire did not crackle or shriek.

'We are cats now till the end of our days,' said Annasin.

Mariset replied, 'I have never been anything else. But am I still a witch?'

'We will have to see.'

Arrow laughed.

'And if you are,' he said, 'what, with your witch power, will you do to the village that burned you?'

Annasin and Mariset gazed into each others' primrose eyes, and then at the third primrose eye on Arrow's forehead, between the two black ones.

'I will tell you,' said Arrow, 'the fourth story, and the last.'

'Why?' said Annasin and Mariset.

'To help you to decide your vengeance.'

The Fourth Story – The Tomb Cat

In the midst of a desert, a green river ran, and on its banks cities and towns of marble had bloomed like lilies.

But beyond the river, the desert stretched mysterious and ungenerous, and out of it came many tales. Statues rose there that touched the sky. Wells sank there into the underworld. Strange beasts existed, winged lions, and dragons, and curious magicians lived among the rocks. From the desert presently there travelled the story of a tomb. It lay at the base of a mountain whose shape was like that of a giant's head. And in the tomb were heaped incredible riches room after room of them. But at the centre of the tomb stood, in great magnificence, a vacant couch. Though readied as if for a king, none slept there. The tomb was empty.

Certain lords and nobles of the cities began to covet the tomb, its wealth and glory, which would go with them into history, and also into another life beyond death.

They sent, to find the place, their captains and warriors. But none returned.

There was a princess in a town of tall gates. She was old and wicked in her ways, but she too, knowing that soon enough her time would come to die, wanted to secure for herself the mystic tomb in the desert, for her mages had assured her it existed. 'But,' they said, 'there is some guardian who bars the way. For this reason no man returns from there.'

'Men,' said the princess, 'are expendable.' And she summoned the first of her three most powerful and accomplished knights.

This first waited before her. He was young and strong; he bore the scars of many battles and the marks of much favour. She thought, since he was young and strong, it would serve him right if he perished. She commanded him to get for her the tomb, warning him only that there would be a guardian, and doubtless he would have to fight with it. At this the warrior grinned, showing his strong young teeth. The old woman laughed, showing her elderly and carious ones. Pitiless, she sent him out.

The first warrior rode from the town, where girls threw flowers to him, and came into the desert, where only the hot wind blew and whistled down the dunes of white sand.

He set his course, as the mages had prescribed, by the sun and by the moon, when it appeared. He did not listen to the voices that called in the wind, or to its songs, he drank sparingly from the water and the wine he had brought, and on the fifth day, as the light was going out, he reached the appointed spot.

Against a lavender sky, there bulked up the yellow mountain that was in the shape of a giant's head. And at the foot of it, a silver fountain broke from the rock, and poured into a gleaming pool. But no trees, no plants of any sort grew by the pool, and behind it was a round dark opening in the rock. A pillar defined either side of this, each with a plume of stone for its top. But inside the darkness there was nothing to be seen.

The first warrior dismounted and led his horse to drink from the pool, but it would not. Looking down, the man saw his reflection in the water, but it was no longer himself, it was a skull.

'I have known magic,' said the first warrior. 'I'm not afraid of it. Nor of darkness.'

Then he lit a torch and went straight forward into the cave between the pillars.

To begin with the way was narrow, though on either side the walls were carved, with flowers and stems, weapons of war, and animals, and even the phases of the moon. At last the corridor widened out and the first warrior, holding high the torch, discerned he was in a chamber made all of pink marble, and in the walls now were set scrolls of gold and emeralds and amethysts of vast size. In the middle of this chamber, which was otherwise empty, stood a marble trunk with a flat top, and on this rested a face made of gold.

'What is it,' said this face, parting its golden lips with strange ease, 'that you want?'

'To claim this tomb for the princess, my mistress.'

'Go back to her and tell her,' said the face, 'the tomb is not made ready for her.'

'She is a great lady,' said the first warrior. 'She is rich as three kings, knows sorcery, and will soon die.'

'Yet the tomb is not for her. Go back.'

'Never,' said the first warrior.

The face said, 'Ascend into the second room.'

So the first warrior walked by, his sword drawn now, and the torch upheld, and crossed the threshold of the room of pink marble, and came into a room of black marble. Against the walls rose enormous boxes and urns of gold, and they were piled over with jewels that flashed rosy and blue and green and purple. On a trunk of silver sat only this: a pure white cat, that washed itself quietly.

But then the cat spoke to the first warrior, and not in the language of cats, but in the tongue of men.

'Go back,' said the cat, 'or you must fight with me.'

The first warrior laughed. And then the cat laughed too. It jumped down light as a feather, and when its four feet touched the ground, it swelled. It grew to the size of a dog, and then to the size of a lion. It glowed in the torch fire, and its eyes were palest green.

'Still I will fight you,' said the first warrior.

'Look about you. See those that have fought me.'

The first warrior turned. He noticed that among the urns and boxes of gold were rolled ivory sticks and rounded pitted ivory balls, and these were the bones and skulls of men. But the first warrior knew that he was too young to die. He threw away the torch and raised the sword.

Then the white cat leapt straight at him, and it was not like muscle or skin or fur, but like the thunderbolt.

The young man's spine broke, splintered at the impact, and as he fell the claws of steel put out his life.

When the first warrior did not return, the old princess had his family thrown into the streets without recompense. She was amused to think of his youth and valour lost, but angry too. She had not got what she really wanted. So then she sent for the second warrior.

He too was strong, though not so young as the first.

His scars were more various, and he wore jewels that he had won. She sent him out with only a wry brown grimace. And in the streets, children pointed and stared in awe, but in the desert only the wind blew and he took no notice of either.

Five days he journeyed. And on the fifth day, at sunset, when the sky was vermilion, he came upon the mountain like a giant's head.

At the pool, the horse would not drink, and glancing in, the second warrior saw reflected nothing at all, and took this for a trick of the light.

He entered the tomb fearlessly with his torch, passed through the corridor and into the pink marble chamber, and there spoke with the golden face, defied it, and went up the sloping floor into the second room of black marble, and there the urns and boxes and bones were, and he saw the bones at once, and then a white cat washing itself on a trunk of silver.

He ran to the cat and swung his sword to cut off its head. But the cat sprang down, and next it was as big as a dog, and then big as a lion, and it spat in his eyes and he was blinded, the second warrior. And as he fell, its paw, like an axe, crushed in his chest.

When the second warrior did not return, the old princess walled up his family to starve to death. Then she summoned her third warrior.

This man was no longer young; he was aging, yet not so old as herself. He had scars for sure, but no jewels or honours. He had sold these to maintain himself, since for years the princess had given him no wages.

'What do you think?' she said to him.

'That, madam, you will not get this tomb,' said the third warrior.

The princess's hard eyes flashed with venom. It had been said her bite could kill. 'You are a coward and afraid to chance yourself for me.'

'I will go,' he said. 'I have no family for you to murder or abuse. I have no special wish to die, but then no special wish to live. Why not?'

In the town of tall gates, no one noticed the old knight as he walked along, for his horse had long ago been sold. He left the streets, and in the desert, he heeded the voices of the wind. He heard women weeping for lost love and pitied them. He heard men shouting in anger and would have calmed them if he could. He walked for thirteen days among the sands, and all his meagre food and water were gone.

In the dawn of the fourteenth day, he saw the mountain like a giant's head, but gazing at it, it seemed to him it was more like the head of an old woman with a wicked mouth.

Going to the fountain, he drank gratefully, and the water was sweet as wine.

Then the third warrior drew his sword. It was ancient and cut and battered, dull, but on the hilt was a figure in iron, an iron cat. And this he kissed for luck, then put the sword back into its sheath.

In darkness he walked into the tomb-cave, and darkness took him in, and after a while, he began to see in some uncanny way, as if it was allowed him. So he beheld the carved walls, and the walls of the pink chamber strewn with jewels, and then the face of gold, which said to him, 'What is it that you want?'

'There is an old bitch,' said the third warrior, 'wants this tomb to lie in for her comfort in death. But for myself, I'm only curious.'

'Ascend,' said the golden face, 'into the second room.'

So the third warrior, the old knight, walked into the chamber of black marble. He glimpsed the jewels and gold and bones, but then he saw the white cat washing itself on the silver trunk.

'My respects to you, sweetheart,' said the third warrior. 'May I come close and stroke your fur? For I've heard of a thing called snow, but never till now have I seen it.'

'Approach,' said the cat, in the tongue of men.

The third warrior did so, and he stroked the cat over and over, head to tail, many times. And the cat looked at him with pale green eyes, and purred.

'Never in my life,' said the third warrior, 'did I meet one who made me so welcome.'

'Never in my life, my life as here it is,' said the cat, 'did I meet one who was worth a welcome.'

'That is a shame,' said the third warrior. 'May I serve you in any way?'

'No, for I have, like yourself, my task. I keep the tomb for one who will come. However, you may serve yourself. Take anything you wish from this place, any gem or trinket.'

'Give me instead,' said the. third warrior, 'one of those snow-white quills which sprout from your face.'

Then the cat shook itself, and a long white whisker fell into the knight's hand. It grew then, and was the length of a palm branch, and from its end sprang buds and flowers of emerald and diamond.

The third warrior said, 'God bless you, white cat.'

The white cat bowed, and the third warrior left the tomb in the desert. For thirteen days he walked over the sands, and on the fourteenth, he walked into the town and went to the palace of the princess.

She shrieked when she heard the knight had returned.

She ran to him without her wig, bald as an egg.

'Is it mine?'

'No, madam. It is not.'

The princess's face shrivelled horribly, as if she had aged yet another ten years. 'What is there, then?' she screamed.

'A cat is there which purrs,' said the knight.

Then the princess jumped up to kill him with her bare hands, and it was too much for her, for usually she allowed others to work her deeds of violence. She fell dead on the floor, and the third warrior left the palace, and lived the rest of his life a wealthy man beside the river.

But one morning it chanced the knight saw a poor beggar, a leper boy, wandering in the street, and he went out to feed him. But the boy paid no heed, and strayed on. Then some of the towns-people came to stone the boy, because he was a leper, and a beggar, and innocent. The old knight drove them off. He walked behind the boy to the tall gates of the town, and allowed no one to hurt him. But here the boy went out into the desert, and it seemed to the knight he must be let go, the desert now would care for him.

It did so. From the sky ravens flew, and fed the boy small pieces of honey. And from the rocks small streams of milk ran.

The wind sang to the boy, and urged him gently on, and the moon and the sun guided him.

After fifteen days he reached the mountain that was shaped like a giant's head, and he paused only to look into the pool, but what he saw he did not understand. The sunlight led him forward into the shadow of the tomb.

In the carved corridor, the carvings touched the boy softly. They drew away his rags, laved him with water and ointments. In the chamber of pink marble the golden face smiled in silence and closed its eyes.

The boy paid no attention to the jewellery walls, and in the chamber of black marble, when he entered this in turn, no attention to anything at all, but for the white cat, which rubbed against him.

''Everything is prepared for you,' said the cat, in a tongue that perhaps was the tongue of men. 'Come with me now. '

The cat led the beggar boy into a third inner room. It was of green jade, set with beryls and rubies, and in the middle of it stood a beautiful bed of ebony formed like a lion.

'Lie down, dear child, for soon you will sleep,' said the cat. 'Here you will be safe. And I shall guard you as I have guarded your bed all this while, against your arrival.'

So the boy lay on the bed, which was the couch of the tomb, and the cat lay down at his side.

'Once,' said the cat, 'there was a young god, the son of God, and he was so perfect that many loved him, and many more feared him. And so in the end, because every word he said was too marvellous to be borne, they took him and scourged him and killed him, so that he expired in agony, mocked and reviled, on a far off hill. Yet he died forgiving them. He had promised, this god that after death he would return, return in the flesh, out of the tomb, to prove death had no power. So it was, he descended first into all the hells, and there the demons kneeled to him, for they loved him even better than his father. And then he rose again into the flesh, and he woke in his tomb, and the door of it had been opened ready for him to leave, and go back into the world of men, and show himself whole. But he lay exhausted in the twilight of that place. He said, I asked before that I might not drain this wine of death, but I did drain it. Now, spare me this last labour in the flesh. I am so tired. Surely I have done enough?'

The boy smiled as he lay upon the lion, and the cat smiled, as they do. The white cat said, 'As the young god thought this, it happened that a cat stole in at the open door of his tomb. It had no fear, for the cat is always curious, and seeing the radiance of the young god's soul through his flesh, the cat jumped lightly up on him, and stood there, staring in his face. Then the god thought, seeing the cat's face like a flower, *There is still beauty in the world.* But the cat, curious, flicked her tail, and the tail brushed the young god on the lips. He thought, *There is still softness in the world.* And the cat, for cats will, went close and began to lick and groom the young god's hair, which had been torn and smudged by dust and blood. Feeling this motherly washing, the young god thought, *There is still tenderness in the world.* But then the cat, not considering, trod on his neck, with one of her claws that were like thorns. He knew too this touch. He said aloud, *And there is still pain in the world. I must return.* So he rose then, and went out into the garden beyond the tomb.'

The boy smiled, and as he smiled he died in fearless serenity, with the cat lying at his side.

A storm beat over the desert. The sky was black as night. Rocks fell and closed the mouth of the tomb in the mountain, and for the shape of the mountain now, it was not like anything at all, formless, wild and silent.

But in the pool before the tomb was the reflection left behind by the beggar boy, a face like gold and crowned with roses that had no thorns. Until the darkness passed, and the reflection faded, and only water was there, clear water.

The last story had taken a great while to be told. Days perhaps, and nights. Maybe half a year. But when it had ended, the night had come and gone, the stars were closing their eyes, the east was lined with crimson.

'Not fair,' said Mariset, 'you are not fair to us.'

'It was after all a gentle story,' said Annasin, 'mostly.'

'But have you decided on what shall be done to the village?' asked Arrow.

Mariset yawned. 'Let the sky drop on them,' she said.

And Annasin said, 'Let them burn like us.'

Then both laughed. Arrow said, 'Perhaps it would be much funnier to have such power over them that you could make them glad.'

'Do you hate God?' inquired Mariset boldly.

'I presume to love *him*,' said Arrow, blushing cat-like even through his black fur. 'It is, I agree, a great impertinence.'

'Then the tales of your kind are not true.'

'Few tales are entirely true.'

'But you love another better,' said Annasin, slyly.

Arrow said, 'Young people are always the same. They cleave together. Sons of fathers … Do you see?'

'But you said that he – '

'Perhaps I did not speak of *him*, in the tomb,' said Arrow, washing his tail. 'Did I name him? No. Well then.'

They played with sunbeams in the wood. Then they magicked up some mice that were not real but which behaved as if real, and which, being greedily devoured, tasted real, and filled their bellies.

Then they magicked a stream from a rock, drank from it and put it away again.

They went down, to look at the village.

It went on as it always had. Goats milked and children slapped. Women cooked and gossiped, and men gossiped and mended things. Even the houses of Mariset and Annasin had smoke coming from the chimneys.

'This is my vengeance,' said Mariset. 'Let blue flowers fall on them.'

At once a rain of blue flowers, thick as snow, drifted down upon the village, covering the roofs, powdering the street; catching in the women's' hair.

The villagers shouted and screamed. The words came up vaguely to the hill: 'God save us, the sky is falling!'

And they were flinging themselves on their knees,, crying and praying.

Annasin said, 'Golden flowers then. How can they mistake those?'

The golden flowers fell.

The villagers roared in panic, scrambled up and fled into their houses. 'The air is full of fire!'

Quietness arrived, and the rain of flowers had stopped. They lay lovely and scented on the street and roofs. None came to pick them up.

'It is often hard,' said Arrow, 'to do good to those that hate you.'

And then they rose up in the air, the three cats, into the air where the flowers had been, they rose up and they flew away, and who knows where they went?

God And The Pig

God said to the pig, 'You are here on the high place. Did you want to speak to Me?'

'Probably,' said the pig. 'But doesn't everyone?'

'Of course,' said God. 'And any of them can.'

'But You,' said the pig, 'don't answer.'

'I try,' said God.

'That's a start, I suppose,' said the pig.

'I mean,' said God, patiently, 'that I am not always heard, or understood.'

'It's never Your fault,' said the pig.

'No,' said God, 'it never is.'

There is a sound behind a voice, when something of perfect and unassailable honesty is spoken. The pig detected this, like a strain of music. The pig lowered his head, and snuffed at a hundred-year-old plastic-paper chocolate wrapper. The chocolate, which had been mostly chemical, had left a fragrance. The pig breathed it in, and considered the honest words of God.

'Well,' said the pig, 'here we are.'

'I am afraid so.'

The pig sat. He was big and glossy, a smoky grey with a pink undergleam, like that of some fabulous pearl.

His small clever eyes rested on the dull polluted sky, about which brave pigeons nobly flew, pretending that the world had not been soiled. It was very hot, and a hot wind blew. Below, the mountain went down to the ground, rusty, and thick with trees, whose leaves had long since fallen in the summer gales. Beyond was chaos. The pig regarded it in turn.

'Shall I tell You my story?' asked the pig, 'or do You already know it?'

'I know every story,' said God. 'However, I am always pleased to hear such a story told by the participant. Each views their story in a different way, and so it becomes a different story.'

'Then,' said the pig, 'You know I am Pig?'

'Yes,' said God.

'That is, I am the core of all Pigness. The utter essential essence of Pigness formed me. And sent me here.'

'Yes.'

'I too,' said the pig modestly, 'am a god.'

'Yes,' said God, for the third time.

'You don't dispute this?'

'Why should I?'

'I thought You were jealous,' said the pig.

'Come now,' said God, with a sort of sad laughter in His voice, 'how can God be jealous?'

'I see,' said the pig. 'Men credit You with their vices as well as their virtues.'

The pig heard God smile, a little.

The pig ate the chocolate wrapper. He was hungry. Across the bumpy concrete top of the high place there was nothing else.

'If I asked You for acorns, the sort that came from the oak trees in ancient Greece, would You give them to me?' asked the pig.

'I should want to,' said God.

'But nothing would happen.'

'It might. It depends.'

'On what?' asked the pig.

'On you.'

'I want them,' said the pig.

There was a long pause, during which no change occurred, except that, far below, about a mile away, there was the screech of bald car tyres, and that too faded.

'I am sorry,' said God.

'The Cathars,' said the pig, 'expressed the belief that the Devil had made the world, and that You were powerless.'

'I have heard of this,' said God.

'Is it true?'

'No.'

The pig said, 'Then You are responsible.'

'In a way.'

The pig raised his snout. He caught the smell of burning. Even that had metamorphosed. Burning had once been wood and food. Now it was rubber and synthetic things. Later rain would fall and put it out, but the rain would have the odour of synthetics, too, and might be black.

'I have been a warrior,' said the pig. 'I've rushed before armies. I've ridden the storm clouds. I've hunted down my enemies with blood-red eyes. I've been sacrificed and portioned. I've been experimented upon, bred for parts, left out in the wilderness. I assisted the great composer Mozart, when he was a child. I can see the wind. I can see *You* –'

'I know,' said God. 'Describe Me,'

'You are aware,' said the pig, 'that You are indescribable.'

'I apologize,' said God. 'So many have tried. I always find it interesting.'

'Listen,' said the pig, 'I'll tell You my story. My version of it. When I was born, they didn't know me. My mother ate the rest and died, and I got out through a hole in the shed. A woman found me on the road. A young woman; she was only eighteen. She carried me in her arms. We've been together for ten years. That's a long time, isn't it?'

'A very long time,' said God. 'Have you ever thought, how long a second is?'

The pig chewed at a piece of yellow grass that had sprung through the concrete. The grass tasted bitter. 'I've seen men come and go with her,' said the pig, 'I've seen her struggle to survive. It's a treacherous and horrible world now.'

'It always was,' said God.

'Once,' said the pig, 'they were sustained by their belief in You.'

'Yes, that was the most dreadful thing,' God answered. He sighed. Somewhere far above, amid or beneath, among the damaged threads of ozone and pollution, incense moved, and was gone.

'She loved me,' said the pig.

God said, softly, 'Love has remained.'

'I noticed that,' said the pig, arrested for a moment. 'Love's never quite died out. But then, it's a biological urge, isn't it, and a desperate if hopeless desire for security.'

'Do you think so? said God.

'You tell me,' said the pig.

God said, 'In fact, it operates the other way around. Biological needs spring from love. They are the expression of an emotion so genuine, inherent and enormous, that excuses must be quickly found for it.' (The pig noted with amusement or pleasure that God did not feel He had always to be strictly grammatical.) 'The urge for security is the expression of wasted, or as yet unfounded, love. Or the sore missing of the state of love.'

'Love others as yourself,' said the pig.

'Much more,' said God, rather quickly.

'Vanity,' said the pig, getting up and sitting down again, inspired by debate, 'self-*love*, self-pity. Tut. Tsk.'

'Love of self is most important and natural. It is so often denied. The self is the first, like the mother. Without yourself, where would you be? And you must pity also yourself. How else should you pity others?'

'Did you tell them?' demanded the pig slightly irritable suddenly, for he had sat in something sticky.

'I told them everything. In any case, they knew everything.'

'What happened?' asked the pig.

God said, 'Let Me hear the rest of your own story first.'

'Soon told. I've lived with this woman for ten years. She slept with her head on my side. In winter we kept each other warm. Then, she fell in with another group. They're hungry. We're always hungry. Most of the hypermarkets are empty now. You know, obviously. Once there was anarchy, looting was a commonplace. It's how we live. And what am I? Bacon, pork, ham. I could smell her hunger, like a fire.

'She'd look at me. I'm food. Oh, you see, I know she's eaten pig. They like pig. It tastes like human flesh. They all want to eat each other. Gobble each other up.'

'So,' said God, 'you ran up here.'

'I trotted,' said the pig, with dignity. 'The last high-rise that hadn't fallen. All those little rooms crammed with rubbish. The old sofas and newspapers. It's pathetic. I mean, pathos. And up here, the roof. Trees have grown right through the concrete. It's a mountain now. And on a clear day, you can see the ocean. You note, I didn't say, *see* the *sea*.'

'Yes, I noted.'

'Unfortunately,' said the pig, 'there never are any clear days now. By night, you can just see a full moon. It's red. And the sun's red, if you see it. And the sea itself,' said the pig, mislaying its syntax, or not caring, 'the sea is brown as gravy. Brown as gravy to pour on roast pork.'

God said, quietly, 'I sense that you tell Me all this for a reason.'

'I am Pig,' said the pig. 'Do I have to die for my race the way You made *Him* die.'

'*Who*?' asked God.

'You know,' said the pig.

God seemed to ponder, deeply, and then he said, 'Ah, yes. That was very different.'

'Because you consider that I'm only a pig.'

God laughed. It was one of the best sounds the pig had ever heard, and being Pig, he recognized elements of great symphonies and concertos and songs, but only for a moment, for the laugh did not last long. 'A sacrifice is only effective,' said God, 'where it is relevant.'

The pig wiped his haunches and one leg on a stand of dark weeds by the wall. He glanced over at the broken remains of roads and houses. The haze of pollution did not allow him to see for much distance. But in any case, it was all similar.

'Why did you let *this* happen?' asked the pig.

'Animals do not normally question Me,' said God, 'but then, of course, you are Pig. I have had conversations with Cat and Dog, with Horse and Bird and Rat, and certain others.'

'Can You excuse Yourself?' demanded the pig, boldly. He felt his power, the shields and chariots, the thunder, and the stars. But only for an instant. He had been made flesh.

'This is not,' said God, 'an excuse. It is an explanation. Long ago,' said God, 'they were children playing in the gardens of joy. Every day was golden. They loved Me and I loved them. I taught them all there was to know, and they learnt it all. But children grow up. They came of age. They wanted independence, and when I tried to reason with them concerning the dangers, they grew very angry. They wanted to leave home, to move away, to begin on their own. They knew everything. They did not need Me, or so they said. In the end, I had to let them go. They made Me promise that I would not interfere. Whatever happened, I must do nothing. They would make their own mistakes. They could look after themselves. Sometimes they would come to visit Me, but as a friend more than a father. I must never again say to them, Why not do this? I must never again pick them up when they fell; or sing them to sleep. If they hurt themselves, they would find ways to care for each other. They would not miss Me, although they would write. Then they made the world. They were so proud.'

The pig was silent. At last he said, 'You promised them *that*? That You wouldn't interfere – didn't You warn them?'

'Yes. You know,' said God, 'what children are. Especially clever children who have grown up.'

'But can't You –' said the pig, '– break Your promise?'

God said, 'Sometimes, when they are able to absolve Me, yes I can break My promise. Sometimes. In the dead of night. But they begged Me. They begged Me not to. Can you imagine how terrible it is, to see them fall, and to hold off My hands? But I must. In their own way they were wise. I honour them. When they are fully grown, we can talk again.'

'But they've forgotten,' said the pig. 'They blame You. They invent laws You are supposed to have made and lies You've told.'

God said, as the pig had heard human beings say, casually, in great pain and sorrow, 'Never mind.' After all, they had not forgotten everything.'

At the edge of the high place, the roof of the ruined tower block, the pig heard a step. When he heard it, he could not recall that he was Pig.

He looked and saw, coming towards him, the young woman with whom he had lived for ten years. Her fair dirty hair was rough and wild, and her face red from climbing all the broken stairs of the building, among the roots of leafless trees. She stared at him, and her eyes turned hot with relief.

Now, he thought, what is that in her hand – a cleaver?

She ran towards him, dropped her burden, and kneeled down. She threw her arms about his neck.

'Piggy. Here you are. Why are you up here? Silly pig. Were you hungry?'

Her inner voice said to him, Oh, I love you. Why did you leave me? How can I face this world without you? Yes, I've eaten your kind, and my own. But you I love. I love the ones I ate, too. We made the world, we fools, and got it all wrong. One day, when we know better – one day.

She kissed his cheek, and showed him what she had brought. It was a battered bucket of ripe rosy apples, slightly bruised, gathered somewhere among the nettles and wrecks of a savage urban orchard. They shared the fruit, the apples of innocence.

The pig listened as he munched. There was the sound of flies and rats in the tower, but that was all. God had withdrawn, lonely and philosophical, to wait.

The Hill

Long ago, when I was about fifteen years of age, I looked out at the familiar sea, and saw that on the horizon, and without warning, it had grown into a tall and rounded hill. I mean that I saw a hill, made of the deep milky blue summer sea, standing up, far out and *motionless*, from the rest of the water. I stopped in astonishment. Part of my surprise was caused by the fact that no one else among the many people on the cliff path seemed to see what I did. This impossible, wondrous, terrifying thing. For if the liquid ocean could form a solid hill, surely the fabric of the world, and everything else we believe in, came into question. I confess too, I had at that time no doubts either about my eyesight, or my sanity.

1: Chazen's Beasts

I am an independent woman. Daughter of a handsome, feckless father, a pretty foolish mother, I grew up into a plain intelligent adult. I make no bones about the intelligence, despite its limits. I have nothing else to boast of. My person is quite tall, neat and inclined to be thin. While at the age of 22, my hair had already begun to grey. Several have asked me why this happened so early; had I received a some severe shock? I had to shock them by replying I had not. For, at that time, I hadn't.

I live alone, but not always in my own apartment, three rooms at the top of a large old house near London. At other times I live in the houses of my employers. I am a librarian. My task is to sort and regulate the libraries of others far less able, and normally far more wealthy than Miss Alice June Constable: myself.

The invitation to Northerham House, which I had been expecting some while, finally arrived on a late summer morning.

Used to such trips I was packed and on the train in less than five hours, reaching my destination at six o'clock that evening.

A warm strong wind was blowing as I walked up the lane. The trees shook their huge, tired green leaves, and through the rocking boughs I glimpsed the village of Northerham – which locals pronounce *North'rum* – below. It appeared the usual pastoral place, small houses with gardens, an inn, a pub, and a Saxon church with rambling graveyard.

The house of my employer stood off the lane, at the end of a short, curving, heavily tree-hung drive. This was no mansion either, but a pleasant two-storey building with an arch over the front door, and recently cut lawns. To the back extended long gardens ultimately swathed in woods. There was a scent of wallflowers, and zoos. I'd been told, in a letter from the master of the house, Professor Chazen, that by the time I arrived he would be away again on his travels. The housekeeper was off too. Only a manservant, a Mr Swange, and a maid of all work, (Doris) were in residence. Aside that was from the professor's collection of exotic beasts. All of these lived, I had been assured, among the back premises, sheds, enclosures and pens. Chazen travelled widely, and tended to bring back curios, often of the animal kind. I can recall I had thought that his library should prove very interesting, and looked forward to reading some of the material I was to catalogue.

My knocks on the front door got no reply. I therefore went round to the back by the gravel path.

A kitchen garden cordoned off the kitchen. Washing flapped vigorously on a line and two or three hens strutted about. The kitchen door was open, but no one in sight.

I peered over the hedge, and so came face to face as it were with the first of the animal pens about ten yards away. Eight or nine cat creatures – large for a domestic cat certainly but smaller than most of the wild variety – were prowling or snoozing in the wire-fronted box. This container was some sixteen feet by six feet high. It's true I have never left England, but I have seen many collections and read thousands of books, and never had I seen or heard of anything quite like these cats. They were a dirtyish white in colour, their fur or pelt tufted, and streaked with faint brown mottles. Their eyes glowed a pale, embered blue.

As I stared, I heard a woman's step on the gravel.

'Oh, Miss – did you knock? I never heard you –'

Doris the maid was all apologies. She led me inside and presently we were sharing the teapot at the scrubbed table. (I have never thought it necessary to keep servants at a 'correct' distance. One can learn a lot from them, and in any case I am, after all, a sort of intermittent servant myself. Besides, where needful, I can usually assert my authority.)

'Then shall I show you the animals, Miss?' inquired Doris after I had mentioned them, some quarter of an hour later.

I was curious. Also I disapproved of the cage which held the tufted cats. I asked her if all the cages were as restricted.

'Oh no, Miss. Some are very enormous. But the cats are let out at night in summer, and in winter they're moved with the others to warmer pens in the sheds.'

'Let *out*?'

'Well, there's half a mile of woods at the end of the gardens that Professor

Chazen owns with the house. They're fenced and netted right over, with small places left to let birds and mice and suchlike in and out. His cats are noctual really – they prefer night time. You may hear a bit of squawking down along the woods after dark. Take no notice, Miss.'

'Noctual' having been explained, (nocturnal), I envisioned nights pierced by weird cries, as small English rodents and fowls were rent by Chazen's felines. But I sleep well. Probably it was no worse dying like that than by the fangs of a fox, or some neighbouring tabby.

'What other beasts are there?' I asked her, as she conducted me through the hedge by the gate.

'All sorts. There's them –' (the cats) '– and some badgery things, sort of bears I think he says – and ratty things – ugh!' (a shudder, though I noticed it was more ritual than impassioned) 'snakes – great big beetles, all hairy – lizards – the professor says they're very intelligent.'

The cats growled as we passed them, lazy and bored. They had a meaty smell, and looked healthy. Their blue eyes were neither friendly or disarming, but Doris clucked at them. Favourites? A sort of netted tunnel, at present closed off dark from the cage, ran to the dark green woods that frothed up beyond the lawn, shrubs and sheds. I had been wondering how the 'letting-out' was managed.

Under the shade of oak and apple trees, we skirted other imprisoned animals, some of these, as she'd told me, in huge enclosures. I recognized none of the species. The snakes meanwhile were invisible, and the beetles shut in a large long shed to the side. I kept up my questions, now as to where the menagerie came from. 'Oh all sorts of countries,' exclaimed Doris. 'Africa – the Indies – America even. And some of them are trained, he says, to do clever things –' but when she said this her face fell suddenly. I considered why. Perhaps she did not like the idea of performing animals.

I began to see the netting running right over the woods, a roof and walls, glinting as the sun sank behind us on the orchards and fields of Kent. Birds were calling and singing in the trees, impervious or stoical about the cat-tunnel leading to their sanctuary.

Our shadows long before us, Doris pointed out the padlocked gate reserved for human entry. I saw too scattered bronze feathers and a stripe of red – which I took for the remains of a slain pheasant – just inside the man-made boundary.

'Blett has charge of maintaining the netting,' said Doris. 'Or he's supposed to. He's off on his honeymoon. Too taken up with it, if you ask me. He got sacked – nearly got himself sacked. It was just the day the professor left. There was a great hole in the fencing Blett'd missed. The professor didn't half take on. In a right two-and-six he was,' (surprising me by her Cockney rhyming slang: two-and-six: fix). 'Blett said to me the animals get restless and tear holes, trying to get out. He said things *frighten* them. I ask you, what things, *here* … not like the jungle is it? But you should hear how they go on sometimes.'

'The animals?'

'No, people in the village.'

'Do they?'

'Really silly I calls it. So does my gentleman friend.' She blushed and looked slyly at me, I, the elderly spinster. I smiled. Doris added, 'It's the old ones mostly. Professor Chazen, well he doesn't go to church, doesn't believe in God, you see. And then all this stuff he's collected in the house, and the garden – The villagers like to say the professor's tempting the Devil himself.'

'Do you believe in the Devil?' I asked Doris. I am a modern-minded old maid, so thought I had better let her know it.

A grim pause resulted.

'Yes,' she said at last, fearfully.

I was then sorry, and chided myself.

And so found we had stopped, and stood staring at a decidedly gigantic pen.

'What's in here?'

'That's the lizards.'

Roused maybe by a sympathetic awareness of her words, one of these just then emerged from a sort of bothy of twigs and stones. It straddled a piece of floor, and turned its reptilian head sidelong, to see us through a swivelling, sidelong eye. It was itself very big, the size of a small spaniel, with grey scales that seemed highly polished, gleaming in the last sunlight, and purplish claws reminiscent of those of a fowl. A spiny crest, which had been lowered, now rose high. Magnified by a power of about six, one could imagine it tramping the prehistoric plains.

I preferred the lizard greatly to the furry cat-beasts. It looked soulless, dull, intemperate and not pretty. You could mistake it for nothing that it was not.

'And these? Are they African?'

'I can't remember, Miss.' And then, 'Oh! I must run – I left my cake in the oven –'

My first days at Northerham began as have a score of other employments.

The library was large and impressive in structure and layout; a total muddle with regard to contents. Many of the tall book-stacks reared quite empty, apart from dust – one needed a ladder to ascend. Such an item had been ordered from London, it seemed, but not yet arrived. Crates massed in awkward places, savagely undone, their edges all bent nails and splinters. Some wonderful books might lie inside, unsorted and liable to be torn if not removed with extreme care.

I set to work as I always do, devising first the best system, only then unpacking. A huge old mahogany table provided help with this. In the late morning I'd lay out some appealing tome, and after lunch read for an hour at least. I am a fast reader. Little escapes me that way. And I wasn't unhappy otherwise. My room was kept clean and orderly, its bed comfortable. There was a small private bathroom next door. The view looked off down the back garden to the wood, over the pens and netting, from which, as was inevitable, uncanny warbles and squeaks would frequently sound after dark. Meals were prepared by Doris, a very good – if rather eccentric – cook. I had met Mr Swange the first evening, when he attended the bringing in of my dinner to the dining room. Unlike rose-and-cream Doris, he was a skulking iron man with a bleak expression. As so often with menservants I've met, he treated me to a polite condescension amounting to insolence. I have generally found it useless to waste time on that. Aside from exchanging a few acid civilities, we had little to do with each other.

One of Swange's tasks was, however, to inspect the outside of the pens at sunset, and let out the corracats, as it transpired they were called.

That Swange did not like either the task or the cats was plain enough. But I became used to seeing his angular figure stalking over the back lawn as I tidied myself in my room before dinner. Sometimes he was softly cursing in the way only an aristocrat or a criminal is allowed to. My hearing is good, but I had heard all such words before, and now and then in other tongues. It meant nothing to me except that the flit of his electric torch returning was as regular as seven o'clock.

On Saturday Doris, with whom I'd kept up the teatime chat in the kitchen, asked if next day I'd be going to church. I said I would not, though would visit the church some other time, as historically it might interest me. Doris seemed sorry I wasn't a church-goer in the theosophic sense. (Just like the professor.) It seemed Swange didn't attend either, Doris told me crisply. He preferred the new hotel at Hodcieux (pronounced locally as *Hoed-Say*) where probably he sometimes met his fancy woman, ten years his senior.

If Doris was offended by her present position in a house of atheists, she had managed herself. She stayed pleasant and obliging to me, and from what I saw, timidly flirtatious with Mr Swange. Perhaps she respected too the shape of a pistol I had noted in his jacket when he went out to check the pens and release the corracats. We all retain means to protect ourselves, if wise. I took no offence at his gun.

As to the house, it was curiously rambling and shadowy for its size. Certain bigger rooms had been partitioned to make two or even three chambers out of one. Some of these lacked windows. Stairs went up and down, twining behind the rooms in obscure ways, to which, fairly quickly, I became accustomed. But it was something of a maze, if a tiny example.

Everywhere one came on statuettes and fetishes from foreign climes. The majority of these were exceptionally horrible to look at, leering with pointed teeth often daubed with painted blood, garlanded by carven heads, (severed, obviously) and clutching in their claws clubs and other more spiky weapons. Doris, whom I had met now and then cleaning the rooms, refused to touch these icons. 'They're not to be disturbed, he –' (she would mean the professor) '–says. And I – well, I wouldn't *care* to touch them, Miss A.'

'Why ever not? Are they so valuable?'

'He says,' said she, 'they can – invogle things. *Bring* things on – bad wishes, curses.'

I queried inwardly what her '*invogle*' meant – *invoke*? 'But they're made of wood or stone,' I suggested.

She said then something else I was later to recall. 'People – witches – heathen priests – can call up spirits, Professor Chazen told me. Oh, he's often given me such a turn with his tales of those places – my blood ran cold. And such bad dreams I had. He said he'd seen as much, in the dark jungles … they use wooden images – even animals – as a – what did he say? – a focus – can that be right? Focus … and they can summon the *dead*.'

I refrained now from saying anything. This litany of necrotic return seemed significant to Doris, a kind of valued other-side-of-the-coin to her religious belief. I have noted similar fancies among pious persons before.

It was the next Thursday evening, about seven-thirty, as I was going down to drink a glass of sherry before dinner, that I heard the crabby voice of Swange complaining to Doris in the main hall below.

I stopped on the stairs to listen. I make no excuse for such a habit. Sometimes it's proved a sensible precaution .

'Those damn beasts are acting oddly,' I had heard Swange say.

'Oh, but – they're all so queer. You know he always says –' (again, I could assume, I thought, she referred to Chazen) '– some of them have odd ways. You'd only have to look at them twice to know it. And they often act up, don't they?'

'It's worse than usual, tonight. Plenty of them are scratch-scratching away at that netting. As for those cats – they've having a fight fit for the *Dog and Pullet* at turn-out time –' At which I heard Doris giggle.

Nevertheless, 'Maybe it's just,' she said, 'the heat.'

'They're from blinking *Africa*, Dorry.'

So he called her 'Dorry', did he?

She said softly, I only just caught it, 'Don't take on so. It won't be for much longer, will it, de –'

She broke off as *he* hissed: 'Keep it down. That old bat'll be about in a minute.'

On her cue, the old bat gave a subdued cough, measured out to sound as if she were slightly further off up the stair than she was, and resumed her passage down to prove him right.

After dinner, I allowed myself half an hour of Mozart on the rather fine, if out-of-tune, piano. Then I decided on a brief stroll around the grounds at the back. I'd done this once or twice before to get some air, while it was cooler. No one made any comment. Of course, I wanted to see if Chazen's beasts were as restive as Swange had said.

Nothing however seemed much altered, at least to me.

The corracats had already sprinted off along their tunnel into the fenced woodland. (in their vacant daytime cage, a few clumps of fur added evidence to Swange's account of a fight. But animals often fight, especially when cooped up.) Other animals were out of sight in the sleeping quarters of their pens. Nocturnals paced along the perimeters, but their sentry-go activity was also quite normal, or so I thought. Only the badger-bears, whose name I hadn't learned, seemed at all apparently disturbed. On previous walks here I had seen them lying down, grooming or playing. Tonight all three were up in the pair of trees that grew inside their pen. Blett was supposed, I had gathered, also to trim such enclosed trees down and back from the wire, both here and in the wood. He had signally failed in this. The bears had climbed as high up as they could get indeed, to where the boughs strained against the netting roof that sealed them in. Two of the animals were cuddled together. The third, alone in the second tree, gave the clear impression of their watchman. It uttered a soft, brittle chittering as I went by. And six pale narrow eyes, catching the glim of a rising half moon, observed me with intense uneasy indifference.

I reached the edge of the caged woods, and glanced at the avenues inside. But the woodland was black, and the trace of starlight here and there gave only misleading information – mirages of water, a huge black clump that might be anything, and seemed slightly to move in the windless atmosphere. Of the cats there was no sign. They would be far off down among the trees, no doubt, as distant from the habitat of man as they could get.

I turned from the wood, and looked at the lizard enclosure. This was in the same blackness, just a trickle of starlight on a stone, a leaf – seeming to be other things – a gem, an *eye*. On other evenings, I had seen four or five of the creatures moving about. Now, despite the illusions, none was visible. They must be asleep, or hiding, in their bothy.

Returning to the house, whose curtained lampshine fell dimly on the lawn, I was struck by a peculiar something about the night.

I couldn't at first have said what it was. Certainly, as I have remarked, the evening was hot and airless. That brisk wind combing the trees on my arrival had perished days ago.

Eventually I stopped still once more. I listened. There was not a sound.

Those who live in towns and cities always suppose the countryside to be quiet. In the mechanical way it probably is, aside from the chug of a tractor or the chuffing of a periodic train. But by day *and* night a constant barrage of *natural* noises goes on. Birds flute or shrill alarms. Unseen animal movements cause rustlings and bustle. Frogs croak from ponds, insects buzz, and crickets whirr. After sunset, the volume seems increased. Dogs bark to each other from the hamlets, farms and villages, mice and rabbits squeal, foxes offer eerie banshee screams, owls and night-jars sew up any silent seams of darkness with the stitches of their peculiar music.

Tonight, there was nothing. The motionless, empty air was heavy, and *charged,* as if before a storm. Yet the sky was very clear, deep blue with stars and lifting moonlight.

Back in the house I made myself tea. Bidding Doris goodnight, I went back to the library. I worked and read for another hour, then (retreated to bed.

I am not unduly fanciful. Nor am I quite insensitive.

About three in the morning, according to my clock at the bedside, I woke; without a start, but fully and totally. It was as if I had not been asleep at all, so absolute was my awareness of myself and everything about me. None of the usual brief cloudiness of sleep remained. Nor had I been dreaming. My eyes had opened on the nearer of the two windows of my room.

I tend to leave my bedroom casement ajar and the curtains undrawn, when there is the privacy for it. Here I had done so. Framed between the drapes lay the sky. The moon had gone over, but the night still was not at all dark, far less so than the bedroom. I saw very clearly. Nothing was there, looking in at the window.

And yet, along with the unusual sudden waking clarity of my brain, was a sort of definite knowledge that, a second or so before I opened my eyes – *something had been.*

2: Rising Up

Now and then in my later life, or rather this later middle part of life I now occupy, odd things have come my way. To say I'm always unnured to such amazements would be to lie. But generally I take a (perhaps foolish) interest in them.

After the window incident, decidedly I grew more alert. (Nor did I doubt some visitor had been there. A daylight inspection from said window showed the damaged creeper outside, which bore witness to something quite hefty having *dragged* itself up the brickwork, and then slithered back.)

When I went down to breakfast that morning, Doris was in that mood she had referred to before as a two-and-six.

'Excuse me, Miss A. It's them – those cats again. Poor Mr Swange went to get them back in their pen – as a rule they're already in the tunnel, and soon as they seen him they rush down like anything – it's when he feeds them, you see. Only today they wouldn't budge. Ran about along the edge of the net, and then straight back in the woods. He says they might have the rabbis –'

'The rabb – do you mean *rabies*, Doris?'

'That illness where they froth pink at the mouth, Miss A.'

'Doris, that would be very serious. Has he – have you – had contact with them?'

'Oh, we weren't bitten, Miss. And Mr Swange *never* goes into the woods without the professor going with him.'

I knew that with rabies, a bite wasn't necessary to cause fatal infection. Infected dogs have frequently licked a human hand before the madness became apparent in them. This hand having one small open cut, the poisonous saliva does its work. Even if not going into the woods, Swange *had* entered the cats' tunnel. A smear of fresh spit on the net –

It seemed best not to frighten Doris worse. She was already in her two-and-six.

'I'm sure it isn't rabies, Doris. How long have the animals been here, it's quite some time, isn't it?'

'About eight months for the cats, Miss A.'

'Then rabies is most unlikely. Symptoms present themselves inside a few days, or weeks at the most.'

Swange didn't appear. Doris seemed upset. When she produced her basket and got ready to walk down to the village I offered to go with her. I could do, I said, with the exercise.

She cheered up on the way. Between the fields and hedgerows she chattered about her family, even adding that her 'friend' and she planned one day to open a pub or hotel, and be 'independent'.

I left her in the village street to do her shopping for the house, and took myself over to the church. It was the typical Saxon model, its tower pointed and thatched. But outside I noticed the graveyard was excessively neglected. The old stones, romantic enough in high grass, weeds, moss and ivy, leaned, here and there the stagnant earth actually overturned. In some spots the tilting of the slabs had become precarious, and fallen urns massed in the grass like skulls.

Then I rounded a corner. Between two massive old yew trees another little scene was going on.

From his dress, I recognized the vicar at once. He, and a group of men more roughly clad, were frowning and peering at a solid patch of chaos.

The yews were, from my point of view, quite concealing. In their shade I paused.

'This is too dreadful,' said the vicar.

'Yes, sir. An' it's the same business as yesterday, sir, so it is. Plain as my nose.'

'Truly, Robert. But yesterday was never so bad as this.'

'Well; sir, I blame that bas – I blame that feller Blett.'

The other men rumbled. It seemed they did too.

Without doubt, someone appeared to have acted the vandal here. Worked on in a coarse, uneven circle, the old graves were riven, and in places whole slabs had been heaved upward, like unnerving trap doors. The smell of antique, hot moist earth and wetly-dried death filtered through the summer air.

I considered the name, Blett. He was the man who maintained Professor Chazen's animal pens.

'But to do such a sacrilegious thing – why would *Blett* do this, in the very graveyard he cared for less than two weeks ago?'

'We seen how he cared for it. If he scythed the grass five times this year, I'm the Prince of Wales.'

'I find it hard to think so ill of him.' The vicar was an elderly little man of twenty seven or eight. He plainly wanted to practice Christ's marvellous and ordinarily impossible teaching to love all men as himself. The difficulty, one could see, was constantly painful, but manfully he stayed at it. Believe or disbelieve as one may, the courage of such fragile warriors deserves to be saluted.

'Well, sir,' someone patiently said, 'Blett never did much about the yard here. And if he's had one sober day since I known him I'd doubt. And when he gets got the sack –'

'A rank drunkard he is,' vowed one of the others.

'And a – well, he's a bad 'un –'

'See, Vicar, he comes back after the sacking, and he spoils the graves – that were yesterday. Then last night he gets another skinful and back he comes and does worse. Allays bin a revengeful bas – a revengeful feller, Blett.'

Doris had told me Blett was off on his honeymoon.

Had she lied to spare me the more sordid details? I sensed Chazen too must have sacked the revengeful feller.

'Don't fret, sir,' the men were now reassuring the vicar, like several kind fathers with a worried little boy. 'We'll see to it. Make it proper. Then you come and bless the place over. That'll make all fine.'

As they dispersed, I slunk away. Sunday fell the day after tomorrow. I hoped everything would be tidy in time for Doris's next church attendance. Though I doubted village gossip would spare her the news of a disturbance of graves.

She looked decidedly wan at lunch but volunteered nothing, so I too pretended ignorance.

During the afternoon, just as I had set a tenement of un-crated books on the mahogany sorting table, a loud crash resounded below in the core of the house, followed at once by Doris's scream.

I descended swiftly to the ground floor and found her in a gloomy, seldom-used old drawing-room. Partitioned off from another bigger room, it had only one window, facing towards the back lawn, draped either side by thick brocade curtains. Dusty yellow afternoon rayed in., showing the clustering mammoths of dark furniture, and Doris with both hands still clamped to her mouth. Her broom leaned on a chair and on the floor lay her dusters and can of polish. With one more thing.

'It fell; Miss – it just rocked and fell.'

An example of the hideous fetish statues was in pieces on the wooden floor beyond the carpet. To my mind on its breakage involved no great aesthetic loss. The head had sprawled away intact under a sideboard, where it grinned its naked, 'blood'-splotched fangs.

'I swear, Miss A – I never touched it. I never *do* touch the horrible things – I was over there, polishing that cabinet. And there's this scraping and scratching, and I looks round – and there it goes! Oh Miss!'

In countries prone to major, or minor, earth tremors, this would be a commonplace. But earthquakes are rare, if not unheard of, in Kent.

'Never mind it, Doris. Of course it wasn't your fault.' I'd noticed the single window had been opened wide, perhaps to air the mustiness of the room, for there was a quite nasty smell, dirty and distracting. The windowsill had been scored with a little mark. I went over and saw something had scratched the sill. This had a very recent look, but that might be deceiving. Doris screamed again.

'*There! There!*'

I glared back, and under the sideboard beheld the fetish's grinning head rattling from side to side, its fangs seeming to gnash in a flutter of something white –

'Doris, stay completely still – and silent!'

At my command she froze.

Moving forward I seized her broom and thrust its bristled end directly in under the sideboard.

Something squalled and rolled out, kicking and spitting.

It was not the severed wooden head, but one of the corracats, as I had already deduced from the flutter of its tail.

With a few more irresistible shoves, I broomed the creature back across the room and up against the wall beneath the window, the window through which it must have entered. As I did so I also ripped the nearer curtain from its rings. The heavy brocade plunged down across the cat, and in a series of moments of clawing, rolling and wailing, it had thoroughly enmeshed itself beyond all hope of voluntary exit.

'Fetch Swange!' I shouted, guarding my well-wrapped trophy with the broom.

Doris ran out and was back with him inside five minutes.

In spite of his aversion, as I'd trusted Swange knew, or had been instructed how to cope. He had on thick gauntlets, and soon bundled the shrieking corracat outside and into its pen by the kitchen garden.

There it cowered alone, since the rest of its kind still ran free in the wood. Swange had found meanwhile, he said, another wide open place in the woodland fencing. He set to mending the hole, cursing Blett.

'That's how kitty will have got out,' said Doris, explaining needlessly. 'And I reckon that Blett done it before he left, to get back at us ... to be truthful,' she went on, hanging her head at the grave error of an earlier lie, 'Blett isn't on honeymoon – who'd have him? – No, the professor sacked him good and proper, like he said he would to Mr Swange. Oh, I heard the professor shouting, right down in the woods – Blett and the professor were in the wood, you see. It was just after the trap came to take the professor's bags to the train – Anyway, Blett must have slung his hook, as they say. Then come back later and mucked with the fences. And the professor was in such a rage. He went off without a word. But, well –' having raised her head she lowered her eyes. I had a sudden distinct impression she neither liked nor trusted Chazen, perhaps even feared him. She added softly, 'I didn't want to burden you, Miss, with all that tale when you'd just arrived. I thought you might think bad of us all and leave.'

I smiled and told her I understood.

However, in a while I too went up to inspect the damaged barrier around the wood. Indeed it had been mutilated but if from the outside, indicating an aggressor no longer in possession of a key to the gate, I was unsure. I pondered if Swange, or Doris, had been at all perturbed by the strange tracking leading both inside the wire and out to the scene of the crime. It was a cumbersome and dragging course Blett had made – perhaps due to more than usual drunkenness. Torn leaves and smashed shrubs described it. Yet also, surely, it was too *low* a path for a man to create – though unnecessarily wide for the progress of any animal I had seen here. Had he been crawling all the way on his knees?

Doris said nothing on this. Nor did she question why the escaped cat had come into the house. Maybe she put it down to mischief. But it seemed to me that a wild creature would prefer the wild, if it could have it. Only very great eagerness, or fright, would drive it into a human habitation.

Whatever the cause, for our various reasons, we three persons Doris, Swange and I, now seemed to generate a muted tension.

As the evening drew on, Doris was exceptionally quiet at her work. Swange had vanished, but later, as always, I noted his torch flitting back housewards through the seven o'clock dark.

He had checked the pens presumably, but not allowed the one recaptured corracat its routine nightly access to the wood. Presently it began to give off rapid short screeches. These went on and on. The sound was like that of a violin rasped by the bow of a madman. Inevitably, others among the animal prisoners soon added an intermittent chorus.

As I went down, once more I heard Doris speaking very low to Swange.

'Couldn't you let it out, Sidney? The fence is all mended now.'

But apparently Sydney, (were they so intimate?) could not. For the frantic cries went on, and only ceased, one and all, about eleven-thirty that night.

What woke me on this occasion was a noise at least as old as the Dark Ages; in other forms much older. It was the ominous clanging of a church bell – since Christian times a tocsin, the signal of invasion, or some worse calamity.

I'm not entirely unused to emergencies. I sprang up and put on my walking boots and buttoned my coat, which carried some extra protection, over my nightgown. Downstairs I found the lights all on, Doris huddling in her nightclothes and Swange fully dressed. From the smell of whisky I had the feeling he might not anyway have gone to bed.

'It's in the village,' he loftily told me, 'that bell.'

'Yes of course. The church. Hadn't we better go and see?'

'That isn't part of my work,' he replied.

'Someone may need assistance.'

'I'm not a village man. They can look after themselves.'

I shrugged. 'Well, Swange, you can let me out, if you will. I intend to find out what's happened.'

Swange swore, not very foully. Doris caught his arm. 'Mr Swange.' You can't let Miss A go on her own –'

'Of course he can. I'm quite well able to look after myself. Open the front door at once, man.'

With an iron fist for a face, he obeyed me, and slammed the door shut again as soon as I was on the drive.

The bell was yet ringing for all it was worth, much louder and more alarming in the open air and under the hanging swags of black moonless foliage. I set off down the drive and along the lane at a brisk trot. It was generally a dawdle of twenty minutes, but I covered the ground in ten.

There were plenty of lights on in the village too, and in the church. People stood out on the street along the graveyard wall, or leaned from cottage windows. I noted the pub had opened up again too, and was now serving drinks at three-twenty-five in the morning. In just over an hour the sun would rise.

As I entered the main street, the clangour of the bell suddenly ended.

The whole landscape now rang with silence. Everyone ceased to move, myself included. While from the church tower came a faint shout. The crowd repeated the message to itself and so to me. 'They've got 'un – it's Jim Hardy, is it? What's he at? Has he gone off his onion –?'

Presently two men and the little vicar, all in dressing-gowns, appeared in the church door, supporting another man of sturdy middle years. He was dressed for the day in labourer's clothes, but all awry, his hair over his face and his coat trailing half off. As they tried to bring him out of the door, he started to roar. It seemed he would fight them all rather than leave the church. But then abruptly his legs gave. He stopped roaring, and they partly carried him up the path between the graves, to the gate in the wall, and so through groups of people to the welcoming pub.

I stood decorously with a bundle of women outside. We looked in on the lighted saloon bar. Everything that was said in there we all heard clearly enough.

After the second brandy, the man called Hardy responded to the oft-asked question 'What were up with you, Jim, ringing the bell like that?'

'I see it,' he said. 'Plain as I see you.'

'See *what*, Jim?'

'Like it says,' said Jim Hardy, 'in the Bible. The graves giving them up, and the dead a-walking.'

It seemed Jim was a decent, hard-working labourer, who could turn his hand to various tasks, and he had been promised three days employment, with board, at a farm by Low Cob, a hamlet some thirteen miles from Northerham. There was only a single car in the village, this not owned by Jim, naturally. The cart-ride he had hoped for fell through. As he was expected in Cob by five-thirty that morning he had therefore had to set out on foot in the middle hours of the night.

His road took him through the village about 2 am. The moon was sinking as he paused by the graveyard wall to light his pipe.

'That was when I seen 'em.'

Unlike many older rural people, Jim Hardy was not unduly superstitious about graves. At first, he said, he thought what he was seeing was foxes or badgers, playing about there under the trees and among the tall, uncut grass. There seemed quite a few of them, a whole family, he thought, and he was asking himself what the local hunt would make of running any of them to earth on sacred ground, when something in the whole movement and method of the animals struck him as quite odd. 'They were seeming,' he said, shuddering, 'to be slinking along slow, all of 'em, on their bellies. And in a kind of – like – a circle.'

So then he'd got the notion it was men in the churchyard – after all, weren't these uncertain forms too big-looking for foxes? And carrying on like that –

they must be up to no good. There were solid silver candle-sconces in the church that were said to date back to the days of King Henry V. Though locked in a cupboard in the vestry, the church door itself was always left undone.

Jim Hardy was perfectly brave on this score. He put down his bag of work tools and selected a fine strong hammer. This in hand, he slipped through the gate, and crept by the trees and the leaning stones towards the spot where the robbers were cavorting in their peculiar, lurching circle.

He took his stand where I had, between those two vast yew trees, safe from detection as he thought in their coal-black shadow.

And then one last shaft of the sinking moon struck helpfully between the graves. And he saw.

At first – as one might not – he didn't believe his eyes. 'Was like a dream,' he said, 'like some joke som'un played on me.'

But he found he couldn't move. His limbs had changed to lead, and his eyes frozen in a stare, unable to turn away. He went cold too, he told us all, as if winter snow came down on the summer land.

'They was circling, right enough, going around and around. Like *worms* they was, great, huge worms, crawling on their bellies, but their necks and heads raised up – and their *chests* raised up clear of the ground – like snakes I see in a book – and their hollow eyes – they looked at me, they looked and the eyes shone! There was white fire in them eyes, though they was all dead hollow sockets, and the broken ribs showed through their chest-cases and the round bone showed through the scalp of their heads like old yeller felt caps.'

His perverse acuity of description held us riveted. But having said all this, Jim Hardy lapsed. He began to shake, to stamp his feet, and to pull at something invisible in the air – I came to realize he was enacting his breaking loose from paralysis, his flight into the unlocked church, his climb up the tower, and his ringing of the harsh old bell.

From the scatter of his now gasping words, we made out that from the window above, before starting to ring, he had also seen the circle of corpses, still with heads and upper torsos raised, (ribs starting through the flesh as if through unmended waistcoats) the arms and legs dragging *boneless* behind them, the glint of white hell-fire in the cores of dead eye-sockets, but each and all slithering round and round atop the wreckage of their undone graves, aimless or determined, he could not know which, in this ritual of their living resurrection.

The pub had become very still.

Finally the vicar, meaning well, put his slender hand gently on Jim's shoulder. Then Jim grew totally dumb. He sat rigid, only his head tilted back on the chair, his eyes fixed unblinking, locked again in the frozen stare he had described. He was very white, and his hands were very cold I should think, as if from the summer snow he had mentioned.

He would, or could, say no more. He would not move either, though they coaxed him.

Then the doctor arrived. Sent for long since, he'd been delayed by delivering a baby to the policeman's wife – which was why, of course, the policeman too had arrived with the doctor. Unfairly the doctor berated the men in the pub, saying that giving brandy had not been a sensible idea in a case of such extreme shock. The doctor informed us all too that corpses pushing out of their tombs and slithering in the churchyard by '*walking*' on their chests was all *tosh*. 'Did any of the rest of you see anything like that? *No?* And does it anyway seem like the Last Day to you? Is the moon turned red as blood?' The policeman was more civilized, pleased perhaps at the healthy son with which his wife had presented him. He led the party of muttering men to inspect the ruin of the graves. Their torchlight – not electric but lit on sticks from a kitchen range – soon began to fade with the coming of dawn.

I myself went down and took a surreptitious look at the site of Jim Hardy's horror. It was the exact place, obviously, the vicar and the men had been troubled at yesterday. And there could be no doubt now, doctor or no, that the graves were fully upheaved, headstones and slabs flung headlong. The soil and other debris which had also come up, including, doubtless, pieces of bone, had poured off everywhere. The ground richly stank, the terrible odour of ancient mortal decay, and one man had turned away to vomit.

Nevertheless, no one else had seen what Jim Hardy claimed to have done.

I noted however, elsewhere in the churchyard, runnels where the grass was mashed and flattened, the ivy torn in trails, and on the old dark roots, or even in some cases quite far up the trunks over my head, were peeled green wounds. Very likely, Jim rushing in his panic, and now the nervous searchers, had caused this further damage.

3: The Apocalypse

They were tender to Jim Hardy, but the hard-tongued doctor whisked him off to the hospital.

Later the policeman, augmented by two more senior others from Hodcieux, interviewed the village, and subsequently the three of us at the house.

I have no clue what Swange said, or Doris, (though I suspect it was very little.) I merely told the truth, which is usually the easiest way, where one can.

The village man nodded when I said I too had afterwards gone to look at the broken graves, and seen how the grass and ivy were disturbed. One of the senior officers, he who had already demanded why I had gone to the village at all in the middle of the night – my answer, 'to see what was wrong', made him snort – now commented sternly that for so curious and prying a woman, I appeared unmoved. I replied that in my work, curiosity is not a fault, but that also I had learned some self-control.

(Doris told me after, with a strange momentary pride in me, that she had heard the village policeman remark to the less favourable other that I was, 'The best type of Englishwoman.' I had gone fearlessly to the village in order to help, and confronted by horror had not lost my nerve. With the aid of such 'handmaidens, young or old' the Empire had been forged. This amused me rather. My ancestry is mixed, and certainly I do not regard myself as particularly British, let alone English.)

The police departed and we were left alone.

The scalding day passed uncomfortably. The animals of Chazen's menagerie seemed all of them unsettled. The cats in the wood were shrilling, the other cat, for which at last the tunnel had been unlocked in daylight, skulked and now refused to leave the pen for the trees. Neither would the small bears come down from their high perches, even when tempted with food. The beetles, rats and snakes kept intransigently to inner refuges of the cages from which they could not be seen. Various other species, including the lizards, appeared to have dug pits in the earth of their pens and hidden. Swange was in a stiff, cold rage. One could see it from his stalking about the lawns. He was like a guardian forced to take charge of unruly children he disliked. Later he too disappeared, as he so often did. Doris, when I met her, was pale and anxious.

By now I had abandoned my efforts on the library. Instead I'd searched among the crates of books; attempting to find anything that would throw light on those travels the professor had previously made, and so on the collections of curios; and animals, thereby accumulated.

I did locate certain texts relating at least to some of these. The corracats; for example, hailed from South Africa; where they were known to live in prides. Hunters and carrion-eaters both; sometimes they would climb trees, and in the heart of certain jungles, they were said to be the servants of a particular god, who, taking cat-shape, troubled the afterlife of men. The snakes meanwhile were allegedly capable of swallowing whole cows, which I doubted, judging not by their size alone, but from the formation of their jaws. The beetles were especially treasured. Asian in origin, they had evolved a means of attaching gems to their hairy carapaces, sealing emeralds and rubies in; but why or how was not properly explained. Nor had I spotted any jewels cemented on Chazen's beetles. I could find nothing written about the badger-bears, or on any other beast, apart from the lizards. There was a slim pamphlet devoted to them, slipped between the pages of another book. It seemed they could be discovered in Indonesia. Select temples maintained them as pets, and their intelligence put them under the jurisdiction of yet another god or goddess, (according to the author, rather a cruel one) in whose honour they would perform funeral rites, including, of all things, 'morbidly clowning, to inspire and agitate the dead.'

Aside from this book, I picked up another small volume, its title being: *Raising the Dead: Ceremonies of An Elder World.*

On these pages I found engravings which depicted several of the nightmarish fetishes and icons physically represented in Chazen's house. The 'instructions', if so they may be termed, were by stages stupid, insane, risible and disgusting. On the last page of the delicious tome I came across a scrawl I recognized. It was Chazen's own handwriting, familiar to me from our earlier exchange of letters. It said only this: *The eternal and unalterable secret of animation, or re-animation, is the presence of life – how can it be any other thing than that?*

By evening, every single animal in the garden-menagerie had escaped.

Immersed in my studies, I'd ceased to hear either birdsong or wailing from the back premises of the house. Nor that both had ended. The first I knew of any break-out was the very different noise of Swange shouting and swearing in the hall below. (Those who contend only women become hysterical are in error. Neither female nor male necessarily needs internal possession of a womb to lose their *head*.)

I decided to go down when Doris's high frightened voice joined his.

'What's the matter?'

'Miss A – Oh Miss –'

'Don't start telling *that* old hen,' bellowed Swange. 'What can *she* do? She's a meddler. She'll only make the whole mess worse.' Swange was not himself. High-coloured and ranting, at his wits' end.

And it was *my* fault? I descended the last stair and trod squarely on his foot. (A slap in the face is seldom essential.) He blundered back, then in again, so I detected a past history of unfortunate developments. He collected himself just in time.

'I do beg your pardon, Mr Swange,' I said. 'A misstep. At my age … my balance, you know. But whatever is wrong?'

He gaped, then replaced his iron mask. It was Doris who told me.

'They've all got out, Miss. All those animals. They must've been that scared – you could see they were – all bristly and hiding – and digging – Even the little cat in the pen, he's gone too – Oh! What shall we do?'

I asked if any were very dangerous? Could they be inveigled to return? What precisely had so alarmed them?

Doris twittered and Swange interruptively boomed, 'None that dangerous, except to ducks and chickens. But they're valuable to *him*. And no, we can't lure them back – haven't I been trying? As for what they're scared of –' here he broke off. The hot metal of his face cooled to pallor. 'That business in the village. What was *that*?'

'I don't know, Mr Swange. Something certainly. But there have been incidents of grave-robbery before here and there –'

'Oh spare me silly women! It's never that. I went and took a look myself. I spoke to some of the blokes. The graves are *empty*. No one took them, but those corpses are out and away. It's against God.'

I was quite startled to find Swange after all superstitious and at least an affiliate believer.

'Yes, I imagine God might take a poor view of such a spiritually distasteful resurrection. But what do *you* believe has happened?'

'It's Chazen. He's a bloody devil. We've meant to get away from here this twelve month. Me and her – Doris. Saving up. The old girl at the hotel – I put it about here I'm her fancy man. But it isn't that. I've known her for years. She needs some persuasion, but I'm going to buy the place, then Dorry and me can be independent.' (So Swange was indeed, incredibly, Doris's 'gentleman friend') But Swange plunged on. 'Him, with all his so-called learning and his funny ways, and all this mumbo-jumbo – *fascinates* Chazen it does, the rotten fool. The Devil himself'll carry him off, mark my words.'

'So you believe the professor is responsible –'

'I *know* the bastard is. *Know* it. We have to get away – like those animals of his – cleverer than us, eh? I'd even bet Chazen might be around the place, somewhere, watching to see how it all goes. Easy enough to get his stuff put on the train and stay behind. He's at the back of this unholy filth.' He gave an angry laugh, then swallowed it. Approvingly I saw he had done that because Doris had started to cry.

Beyond the windows, a thick brassy dusk was quickly coming down. No bird sang or flew over the trees. From the narrow window at the back, I could see the edge of the cats' deserted pen, the netting wrenched up. And night was on its way.

'Is this the real reason why Blett left Chazen's employment?' I inquired, keeping my back turned to Swange and Doris, who were clinging together in the gloaming.

'Him, that soaker? He *helped* Chazen. Blett was loony.'

'Helped him in what way?'

'You don't want to know, Miss Constable.'

'I do.'

'Every single one of those animals and insects – they're all to do with heathen death rites – raising the dead. And Chazen and Blett, they'd do the rituals in the woods, and now and then they'd kill one of the animals – a rat, a lizard, a bear, a cat. Meant to make the jungle magic happen. Stir it all up, after dark –'

'Ritual sacrifices.'

Swange only swore, vividly now. Doris's sobs became loud.

I waited, then turned and said calmly, 'What shall we do then, Mr

Swange?'

He gave me a look, but in the end, in the gathering dimness, I was only a fragile aging woman, the weaker sex, deferential at last, needing his protection. To his credit, he gave it.

'That's all right, Miss Constable. We'll be safe enough till morning if we keep inside. But we'll fasten all the doors and windows. Better start now.'

I began this narrative with a reminiscence – about the day when I was barely out of childhood; the day I saw the static hill that had grown out of the fluid of the sea.

Probably it is quite apparent that, not doubting my sight or my sanity, (at fifteen years it is sometimes easier not to) I was afraid. The phenomenon of the hill, to me, indicated a rent in the fabric of the organized world.

No one was with me. I've said, my father was feckless (and liked alcohol more than it cared for him) and my mother a ninny. I was alone, and the holiday people on the cliff, passing to and fro, evidently hadn't perceived anything out of the ordinary.

I began to cry – by which I mean water ran uncontrollably out of my eyes – tears, I presume, though in fact it was not like crying at all. Perhaps it was only a flag run up reading *Help! Help!*

Eventually an elderly couple, a man and lady, halted by me.

When I look back, I grasp that undoubtedly they were only a handful of years older than I am now. Not elderly then, in the precise sense, though his hair at least was grey. But generous they were. And wise.

Neither said to me demandingly, *What is it, girl?* Or worse, floodingly, *Oh dear, dear child, whatever is wrong?*

The gentleman bowed and lifted his hat. He said, 'May my wife and I be of service, young lady?'

And when I turned my streaming eyes on them, she solemnly said, 'My husband is always to be trusted.'

What a wonder! A sober yet gallant male, a level-headed female who utterly approved of him. Oh, yes, others might have been suspicious. But I was not, nor had I need to be. They were as genuine as new-minted gold.

I wiped my eyes and they cleared. I said, 'Look there, out at sea – that hill! It has never been there before. How *can* it be there?'

They turned and stared, as I did then, out across the blue plains of the Atlantic ocean, to the sea-blue hill rising steeply up from it.

'Upon my word,' said he, 'what a thing. What do you think –?' to his wife – 'Is it some island?'

'But the young lady would know if it was an island. She has told us. It was never there, before.'

That they too saw it, *perused* it, discussed it, this extended to me great reassurance.

While – for the first time in my life – I found myself no longer alone. I had finally successfully communicated with two other sentient and thinking things. I am well aware those moments on the cliff secured in me forever a hopeful *liking* for strangers, and a wish toward independence and – perhaps – the desire to grow up – not into some bloom of womanhood, but straight into my middle years. It's possible, I suppose, even my hair turned grey at such an early age because of this desire, rather than because of some shock or failing.

On the cliff then we three watched the mystery of the hill. And so shortly thereafter, the three of us also observed how it started to bulge, to topple, and to change –

At midnight, it began.

The doors and windows of Northerham House had been locked and bolted. Had there been bars, such as a mediaeval castle or manor boasted, they would have been lowered into their slots. Swange oversaw all. That is, he followed me about, at least, to be sure the silly old maid had got things right. She had. Mr Swange had no notion, perhaps luckily, of the number of times she had been called upon for accuracy.

Presumably he knew Doris had also fulfilled her duty. I imagine that she had.

That evening she catered for our communal meal – pretence at separation was now extraneous. We ate cold meat, pickles, hot potatoes, cheese and biscuits, with a fine claret I think Swange had liberated from the cellar, caring not much by now for his 'Master' Chazen's possessions.

Night itself descended with slight incident. But it was very overcast and black, starless, moonless and stormy, yet no thunder sounded, no lightning irritated the sky. Swange. had decided every electric lamp in the house should be switched on, and this was seen to. To me then it seemed we had made of the house a livid fiery beacon. Nevertheless, all approaches – front and back – the empty sheds and enclosures, woods both fenced and adjacent to the property, the lane which led up to the drive and the drive itself, were blankly illumined by a cold, flat yellow.

Swange refused Doris's request to close the curtains.

'We must *see*,' he said.

He meant *see what draws near*. He had become a sergeant in an ancient fort.

After our amalgamated meal, I went upstairs and, so far as I could, readied myself.

How should any of us know what might be abroad? A thrill of dismay went through me at the memory of the village, probably unprepared – yet even so it was by now far too late to venture into the dark. For the dark surrounded us, and we were only this small lighthouse perched on a rock.

Having gone up, I gazed from the library. From here I could see the tree-hung drive, and the curve of the lane beyond which led into Northerham.

No warning church bell sounded.

Hours were shed like heavy leaves, from a tree that did not mind whether spring would follow autumn and winter. Who, in like circumstance, has never felt the awful indifference of natural things? *They* know but too well they must first go down into the abyss. But we, the animals abroad on the world's face, accept nothing, and so struggle.

At five minutes to midnight I heard the large, always belated, library clock strike the quarter hour behind me among the book-stacks. Perhaps despite myself I had been dozing a little, seated there at the window. For sure, it seemed to me that all at once everything had altered.

I got up, walked about, and looked once more from the window.

Nothing anywhere moved, not even the massed clouds above.

But again I became aware of that dense tremble of silence I had noted before. The room, the whole house, was smothered by it. It occurred to me that this silence was in fact not *merely* an absence of all sound. Human things have sharper faculties than they credit. There is nothing particularly supernatural in this, save in the most literal sense – for they are primal instincts that long ago moved in us freely, and doubtless many times saved the lives of our remotest ancestors. Now and then such talents surface again. This *silence* then was my own animal faculty, which told me unerringly the moment of terror was upon us.

I concentrated my gaze along the drive. In all that motionless light and dark of shadows and electric beams, after all – *movement*. The leaves and boughs there, low-hanging to the path, were dipping, shaking. Something approached.

A twig snapped like a pistol shot. The sound seemed to splinter the night.

Out on to the drive the creature emerged. It pushed forward, in a jerky slithering. Unmistakable; it was just as Jim Hardy had recounted: a dead thing once living and mortal. Both sets of its limbs dragged bonelessly alongside and behind it, but it *walked* forward on its chest, which arched up from the driveway, so displaying the broken ribs of the body cavity among the quivering flags of mummified, cloth-like skin. Some rags of hair too fluttered over its skull and down its back. Maybe, when formerly alive, it had been female. The head and neck reared craning upwards, turning a little, stiffly, as if it glanced constantly and carefully from left to right. And in the brood light of the house, the hollow black caves of its eyes flashed with a cold white sparkle.

Undeniably, it seemed to have the definite purpose of *reaching* the house. But as it drew very near, suddenly it swung itself, with a ghastly, ungainly, almost-grace, away. Like any familiar or tradesman, it rounded the corner, apparently going round toward the kitchen door.

By then another of them had crawled out on to the drive, proceeding exactly as had the first of its kind. To judge by the no-continuous jostle of the lower boughs and bushes in the lane, there were many more close behind.

At this moment Doris shrieked, not once, but three times, very loudly and very near. Running out, I found her on the landing, standing there rigid, and Swange not five feet away from her. They must have retreated here from the ground floor. Now they were staring in petrified horror down the staircase, at something I could not yet see.

My eyes flew to the main door. It had stayed fast shut, as had all windows. Had the creatures then discovered some way in at the back? Was one of them already below in the hall?

Brushing by Doris, I went to the head of the staircase. And looked straight down into the face of death.

If there had been any doubt – I had had none – denial would no longer be possible. The thing which now came sliding, awkward and inexorable, with a quietly scraping thumping drumbeat up the broad stairs – was dead as any corpse could be. And if it was not as ancient and decayed as the others I'd witnessed outside, this one had been made dilapidated in other ways. Whole chunks had been wrenched from it, and certainly its eyes had been gouged out, for the pits were fairly fresh and still a little sticky with blood. Inside them nevertheless some kind of eyelight glared up at me, glittering. On the front of the head there clung a dense mane of blackish hair, though this was knotted and twisted too with blood, and with soil, and decorated with chips of what must be bone. Unlike the other corpses too, it wore clothing, or the remnants, modern enough, even to the stained and frayed silk tie still knotted round its torn throat. Beside all that, it was sufficiently fresh it ripely stank. It had the rich dirty meaty smell I had in error previously thought belonged only to the corracat in the drawing-room.

The corpse was by now about halfway up the stair. It showed no wish to halt its advance. And as each step was attempted and achieved, a sinister scratching sounded.

'No, Sidney,' quavered Doris in a tiny whisper behind me. 'Can't you see – it's *him*!'

Him? I turned to her for a split second. '*Who* is it Doris?'

'The professor –' she whispered before stepping back and dropping on the landing in a dead faint.

This was when Swange fired his handgun.

I spun about again to watch a vase shatter in the hall below. He had missed. Besides – if the creature were already dead, what use was there in firing at it?

And yet – do the dead walk? Do hills form from the sea? I can't say decidedly, but I will suggest, not very often.

My own little pistol was already in my hand, small and dainty as a toy, quite suitable for a silly old maid.

I raised my arm, aiming for the space between the dead man's eyes, judged the swinging of the head, and fired point blank.

The thing on the staircase leaped. Affronted it that reared right up, so that first it balanced on its knees and then swiftly rose to its feet – after which it tumbled slowly over backward and plummeted down to the foot of the stairs. There it writhed once, oddly as if trying to become comfortable. After that it grew immobile, and stayed so.

Swange and I also stayed where we were a while, each one of us with our smoking gun. Doris lay motionless on the carpet behind us.

Silence had come again. It was unlike the silence I had twice been aware of. This was simply the absence of any noise.

Swange spoke very low.

'He was in the house. All the time. He came out of the old drawing-room, from behind the dresser. Doris smelled a smell in there. We thought a rat had died in the wall. But he just came out. I said to him, Are you all right Professor Chazen? Stupid bloody thing to say. His head like that, and crawling – he was dead, wasn't he. Doris ran straight up here, and I can tell you, I came after her. They were all round the house by then. They still are –'

I started to go down.

'*Don't!*' cried Swange.

'It's all right, Mr Swange. I just need to see – ah, yes,' I said, reaching the stairfoot, standing over the corpse of my previously unmet employer, and finding what I *thought* I had in the moment he fell.

Unpleasant shrieks were beginning outside, and growls, thuds and grunting. Something slammed against the door and Swange gave a yell. But I could already make out what took place through the nearest window. 'Come and look, Mr Swange. We have some most unlikely allies.'

He bounded down, and together we watched from the security behind the glass, as three corracats scrambled among the two last corpses to have reached the drive. The cats were tearing them in pieces, and as they did this, like a macabre conjuring trick, we beheld what lay behind the facade of each of the slithering undead.

Swange spoke his most blistering oath to date.

'When the corpse of the professor reared up and fell, I could see its claws,' I said mildly, 'poking through the chest, and another set from the lower torso. That was how they could move. They'd eaten their way in, tunnelled through each corpse. Their heads were pushed up into the skull cavity. It must have been like donning a helmet, once the hindrance of any brains were either eaten or discarded.'

Swange made a stifled sound.

I said, 'As for seeing out, no doubt they could spy well enough from each side through chinks in the skull. And what glittered so brightly through the eye-holes of the dead when catching any light, was not an eye at all, in fact only their *scales*.'

Outside now the five cats were very busy, ripping away the dry old flesh to come at those same shining scales, and so to the more succulent living lizard flesh beneath. A further two cats burst from around the side of the house, involved in a vicious tug-of-war over a single dead lizard already pulled from its cadaver. Similar hunting screams came now from every direction. It seemed the cats meant to complete their hunt on all sides of the house.

Doris called feebly from above, 'Sidney, Sidney –'

I went up at once and helped her to rise.

'Did Sidney shoot it?' she whimpered, pointing at Chazen's body in the hall. Though dim with faintness, her eyes strayed to my own pistol. 'Or was it you, Miss?'

I told her firmly, 'I'm afraid I shot the vase, Doris. But Mr Swange luckily has a steady hand. He killed the thing with one shot.'

Below, Swange gave me a scowl. Then winked. 'You're too hard on yourself, Miss A. You were just rattled, that was all, and no wonder. At any other time I'm sure you could shoot like a regular trooper.'

No newspaper carried this story. It was, I assume, kept quiet for fear the grisly facts cause more upset than interest.

The police of course were for some days ever-present. After them came people to do with collecting and reinstating the disturbed remains – what survived of them. The graveyard was tidied and re-sanctified to holy ground.

The rest of Chazen's animals were rounded up and removed to a well-run zoo – aside from a pair of corracats and one snake, which eluded the searchers, and perhaps still roam the Kentish fields and woods, stealing the odd chicken or sheep. Even given the reputation of the snakes, probably no cows go missing.

Despite the bullet I had fired into the dead professor's head, experts soon enough discovered he had been killed by a savage blow to the *back* of the cranium, delivered some days earlier, and administered by a torn-up stake from the fence. Blett was the inevitable suspect. Inside a week he had been traced to a lodging house in Plymouth, and on apprehension, confessed. He had murdered Chazen in a fit of drunken wrath, fed up, he said, with Chazen's constant complaints about poor upkeep of the ground. Seeing what he had done, Blett had hastily dug a grave and tipped Chazen in. But this bodge was no match either for the heat or Chazen's cats. Unrealising, Blett had bolted with drunk optimism for the coast. He had also been drunk enough, prior to the argument and homicide, deliberately to have damaged every cage and shed, in what he afterwards termed 'cunning ways' not immediately obvious. He intended all the precious collected animals the professor used for study, (or slaughter during trials of black magic) to escape. Swange's lack of interest in the menagerie, and frequent trips to Hodcieux and the hotel, had also no doubt aided the sabotage, which went mainly undetected. Blett's subsequent fate was the usual miserable one prescribed in such circumstances. He hanged.

As for the rest, while Chazen's servants had thought he caught the train – which even Swange had ultimately doubted – the professor's body lying summer-rotting in his wood enticed the corracats to devour parts of him. For that reason they refused to return into the pen, while one which had got out through one of Blett's holes in the wood-fencing, followed Chazen's corpse into the house, once it was transported there. Mostly the *freshness* of Chazen's death had stirred up the great lizards to their original function.

For these animals had really taken a role in mystic funereal rites of certain temples. The professor had never learned, beyond foolish guesswork, what this role was. But it was one of the temples' deeper mysteries.

Only some years after did I come across a volume on the sacred death practices of eastern Asia, which, in half a page, enlightened me as to why the lizards acted as they had. They were, it seemed, trained to enter the corpses of the dead, scouring out as they did so any impeding bodily matter. Then, once in full possession of a body, they would make the cadaver 'dance'. This dance then was the appalling reared-up slither-crawl Jim Hardy, Doris, Swange and I had seen at first hand. To the initiates of the temples, however, it was neither a horrific nor a profane act. Let alone the 'morbid clowning' Chazen's own ignorant book claimed it to be. By showing the unopposed animal possession of every corpse, otherwise empty and lacking any motive power of its own, the 'dance' displayed that the human spirit had gone far away to a place of joy and safety, where its happiness was so sure, it no longer cared what became of the cast-off flesh.

Able to get out the lizards had quickly located Chazen's body. One served him as it had been trained to do, finally conveying its ceremonial corpse into the privacy and dark of the drawing-room, through a wide open window. (It had previously tried entry via a smaller casement without success – that of my bedroom.) The other lizards, now all questing to fulfil their purpose, found the graveyard. Perhaps a keen sense of smell assisted them and their formerly honourable task was soon accomplished. Why did all of them return to the house? It was no doubt part of the rite to seek their temple. The house by now stood for this temple. Alas for them. None of them survived the onslaught of the corracats – nor my single pistol shot.

Ironically, no one was abroad that night in the village. The concluding journey of the lizards, in their pantomime costumes of death, went unseen. Jim Hardy therefore remains the sole village witness, and once released from hospital, *free of charge,* drank for a month on the story.

Doris and Swange are by this time long married, and thrive in their hotel at

Hodcieux, which the locals pronounce Hoed-Say. I receive a postcard every year. And so have learned there are now also three little Swanges too, and one little Doris.

Chazen's house has become, I gather, a select school for young ladies. The books from the library were sold for a small fortune. I can't think why. Though decent enough, they were scarcely the best of their type I have catalogued.

And so. The hill.

The hill in the ocean became for me my credo, just as the two kind strangers who watched with me the hill's metamorphosis, channelled my unhappy youth quickly into a satisfactory, premature middle-age.

I've said, we saw the impossible hill begin to bulge and topple. And then it sank sidelong – and floated with a slow swiftness, away over the horizon. Other hills very like it soon followed after. They were all the same blue as the sea, and drifted now in a lifting wind, like a fleet of ships. They were clouds.

Yes. My hill, so solid and static and inexplicable, had been a cloud, placed strangely by a freak of calm weather, darker than the upper sky and matching the colour of the water, seeming therefore to be *made* of the water, upright and uncanny. A rent in the world that threatened to reveal the surrounding abysm of chaos.

We laughed, the couple and I. Less with relief than with wonder at the trick a string of coincidences of the elements had played. The gentleman thanked me too, for giving him an interesting tale to tell that night at dinner in their boarding-house. We parted, never to meet again.

A cloud. It isn't, however, that I believe that chaos does *not* lie on all sides of us. Evidently it does, and well we know it, in our innermost hearts. But it is the *fear* of the chance of *stumbling* on that chaos that makes us start at shadows. The dead at Northerham were animated by a purely physical possession. The hill in the sea was built from a cloud the wind left to lie just long enough to deceive.

If I have any hope for anything, I trust we are eternally protected from the naked view of chaos – while in this world. And if at last we must confront it, we shall then be in some other greater form, well able to contend with blasting light or shattering darkness. Like the souls of the dead who never care what is done with their cast-off flesh.

In the City of the Dead

We entered the city in the hour after the first sunset. It was twilight. Thick bluish dusk, like smoke, rose from the ground. Out of this, the cliffs of buildings towered to touch the luminous sky, that was, and would stay, too bright for any but the fiercest stars to show.

Night could never come here. Here, night was done with.

'Don't be so awed by this,' said Hassent.

I looked at him. 'No?'

'No. It's an old city, partly destroyed by aerial action, partly ruinous. And after sun fall it lies between two suns, the second and smaller of which will rise in three hours. That's all. The facts.'

'Really.'

He smiled. Oddly, in the half-dark, his own darkness was paler. 'Well, what would *you* say then, Aira?'

'There weren't always two suns.'

'True. And?'

'Once there used to be night. 'But now there isn't, only twilight. Just perfect for scum like us to burgle in.'

Why did we have this discussion? To pass the time, probably, while we rested on the terrace-wall after the appalling climb up from the valley below. We had used ropes, of course, and each of us was agile as a monkey, but it still took along while and was peril-fraught enough to satisfy even Hassent's irritating taste for dangerous, arduous exercise.

From the terrace, we could look down straight through into the City. A vista was carved for miles by a wide boulevard like the bed of a precisely ruled river. The strange smooth buildings, rising either side, with their pointed windows that had the shape of fingers, ended frequently in shattered tops, where the bombardment had hit them all those years ago. And obviously, there was nobody anymore to light a lamp. From the valley, if one was unaware, the City could pass for another feature of the surrounding mountains. It had done so often, our Source had assured us. You had to know, and have a map. And then there was the climb. But Hassent and I were used to climbs. Up the sheer towers of ancient palaces, along the sloping insides of charming sewage systems … We were thieves. The climbing, like the robbery, was part of our job.

But the second sun filled me with concern. It lay now, just under the horizon, throwing upward a preview of light the way the first sun, the real sun, does at dawn. The second sun was *not* real. It had been made and raised and set to circle the City by magic. They – the ones who once lived here – had called it the Great Lantern. Now these magicians were gone, bombed out of residence by some of their numerous enemies from across the mountain range. But the second sun, the Great Lantern, that remained, and went on rising (in the *north), so* here, there could never be night. And – what *else* remained?

I had said something like this to him, back in the desert, when we were at the last halt, and sold off the riding yurts. We had a night (yes, because there *was* night, out there) on the town, he with a pretty female pay-me, and I with a handsome male pay-me. We had also drunk the wine-wells dry. And in the intimacy post received pleasure and alcohol, I had let slip to Hassent my doubt about the magics of this place – whether they were truly finished. But Hassent had only said, 'All gone. All that's left in the City is treasure beyond the dreams of insanity. That's why we're going. And it's a bit late to coward out. We've spent all our money.'

Now, on the terrace, he said, businesslike, 'Let's make a move, shall we?'

So we hitched the ropes again and swung off over the inside drop, to where a flight of broken steps hung in the dusk.

To descend was to go down into the gathered dark. The other way, the glowing green-blue sky watched us indifferently. I looked it in the eye, coiled up my rope, and followed Hassent down the stair.

When I was a child in Sheemelay, the masters who taught me theft had also taught me quite a lot of superstition. Tie always the left boot up *after* the right boot; lick your finger and touch the stone of your marked building, to placate it with a bit of yourself. (Blood was better, but then you had to be careful.) Over the years, especially once I partnered up with Hassent, I had stopped, or tried to stop, some of this. Hassent had absolutely no time for it. He is a pragmatist. 'You take,' he was fond of saying, ''till it takes *you.*' But old habits die hard.

The lower levels of the City, as we got down into them, seemed buried, as if in a cellar. The effect was heightened by all the upper streets which rose above, and sometimes forded the lower in the form of bridges. Several of those had been smashed by bombs. The surviving masonry stuck out, and in the unending dusk seemed to have weird shapes, like the staring heads of huge beasts with open jaws –

I said nothing about this fancy to Hassent. Five years of his company had enabled me to imagine what he would say back.

There were gardens in the City. Some must have been there to begin with, parks with curious tapering pines and thin stone statues. But the gardens had overgrown themselves and spread, and elsewhere groves of weeds, bushes, and trees had sometimes seeded in the walls and avenues. Even so, the City, beyond certain areas of rubble, drifts of dust, old leaves, the ground-down shale of fallen marble, was *tidy*, spacious, and uncluttered.

After a while, we paused again under an archway, to consult the map.

Beyond lay a vast plaza. It was closely and immaculately paved except in one spot far across, where bomb damage had caused two or three buildings to collapse. A fountain stood at the square's centre, pristine. As we lurked, peering over the map by the light of Hassent's glow-worm torch, a snake hissed loudly from the square and a prickle of new stars shot off from the fountain into the air.

'It's fine, Aira. Calm down.'

'But –'

'Some of their gadgets still work here. We know that, we've been *told* that.'

'I thought it was an exaggeration.'

'Their second sun still works so why not a mere fountain?'

'Yes, I see.' Did I? I watched the water-jet playing up its spangles at the sky. Was there enough green light even so for it to glitter quite so eloquently?

'Now,' said Hassent, 'let's get our bearings. We came in over South Wall. Sun Two will rise up there, in the mountains, when it does. That's north, then. And this plaza, I believe, is *this* one on the map, with the building they call the Oratorium – look, you see? – that skinny tower with its hat off – so now we go *that* way.'

It was tepid, but not cold. Yet sometimes little breezes blew, and they varied, some much colder than the cool, some much warmer than tepid. Different atmospheres still existed here.

We walked out finally through the plaza's centre, to avoid the fallen buildings. I gazed once more at the fountain. The jet emerged from the mouth of a figure cast from some glassy, half-transparent material. It was not human, nor quite anything else. I could not make out what it was, really, although somehow *it was* disturbing. But Hassent was already about a hundred strides away, so I left the fountain and went on. At the square's furthest edge, I glanced back. And the water had sunk again, vanished. We must have trodden on some hidden lever under the paving that started it off, perhaps on another one this side to shut it down again.

If there were hidden levers for that, there might be some for less amusing things. I caught him up and told him my idea. He smiled. He said, 'It's all right, Aira. I remembered to tie my *left boot last.*'

Probably we walked for an hour more. I can judge time as a rule, even on this journey to the City after I lost my timepiece playing Blackcard in Kulbin. But I do it by the sun, or the moon, I suppose, or the infinitesimal slinking of the stars – and here that would not be possible.

To reach the place we were aiming for, we had to trek ever deeper down, down into those buried cellars of the lowest streets. Even if night had been extinguished here, the way still got steadily darker.

I noticed he failed to light anything stronger than the torch.

We stopped at last, and had a swig of water laced with ginger-root spirit.

'There it is,' he said.

I nodded, cautiously.

The building was low and long, and long again – there seemed to be acres of it. The Thesaury of the City. The bombs had never reached it, even all the way down here, where, *if* they fell, as we had already seen, they had always caused maximum destruction. I thought of the war-balloons gliding over, the deadly copper wires strung out, and the impacted electric charges descending – lovely as fireworks – each an induced lightning-strike. Once, I had had the dubious delight, in the course of my job as a thief, of pretending to be a server at an orgy arranged for some military general. I recall his holding forth on the efficiency of these bombs, invented a century before by the alchientist Xos. They have been used in many spots, always to enormous effect. Now, outside the treasure house of the City, I considered the City's own general survival. All told, it had withstood the onslaught unusually well. And yet – it was empty. None of the stories explained that. Of course, perhaps the living citizens had simply fled or been captured. I wondered too, why the clever aerialist bombardiers had not put out the second sun, while they were at it. Conceivably those electric bombs just could not fly *upward*?

'Are you ready?' Hassent inquired.

I jumped, '… not quite.'

'Come on, Aira. Stop looking like a curd-sick yurt. You're not usually as bad as this.'

Normally I would have snapped back with something. I did not.

This low, the faintest glimmer of dusk was still floating like clouds between the pillars and the finger-shaped door-mouths of the building we had come here to enter. I saw ghosts. It was a trick of the eyes. But even so. They fluttered, in and out, up and down. Poor things, were they thinking they were still alive, and wondering why the City was unlit and full of holes? Had they forgotten?

According to the Source (that man Hassent and I had eventually, after months of scheming and bribes, got to meet in Kulbin), this treasury was the one which held the greatest amount of treasure. There were zi-rubies the size of a two-year-old child, electris in bundled rods seven feet in length, emerald and qualium, and Plum-Breath, the fireless smoke-conducting purple jade. Elsewhere in the City lay other caches, but nothing like this one. Nothing but this one was worth bothering with, if you had actually managed to reach the City, scale the walls, get in. Why then, I had murmured all those miles and days ago, had no one else, the Source himself for example, ever gone there? He replied that quite a few had gone there, and returned richer than a thousand kings. But they could only carry so much down the mountains and the walls. And as there was such a lot, still plenty of it was left. As for himself, he thanked me for my compliment, but he was too old for such a jaunt. We had cut him in, of course. We left the usual pledge – a vital piece each of our entry-exit ribbons, issued by the Royal Kronarchery. The Source seemed frantically keen that we succeed. His map was of the best.

'Hassent – did anyone say there was – *anything* – here?'

'Not apart from mounds of treasure. You heard it all the same as I did.'

'But the Great Lantern is still operating. And that fountain –'

'Oh for the love of life, Aira! Forget the bloody fountain. Let's get on.' Just then, something cried in the City.

It sounded a long way off, and yet, partly due to the amphitheatre effect of this lower depth, it was *all-present*, everywhere around us. The cry was soulless, savage, yet desolate beyond description. We both stood, paralysed in the ringing pulse of it. And then it was over, and only memory replayed it on and on inside the ear.

'There are no animals here,' I said. I spoke incredibly softly – not quite a whisper. 'Everyone says, no animals, no birds, come into the City. Not even mountain wolves or lilynx. Not even eagles set down on the highest roofs – or even fly over –'

'I saw crows flying about, when we were coming up from the valley – something at least, down inside the wall, flying over, black – or maybe not. But anyway, you've said it. This thing is outside the City. Up in the mountains. Crags echo. We just heard it.' Hassent also was speaking very, very low. If his darkness had paled, in the dim-out I would never see.

'*Outside*? You're joking. It's *inside*. With us. What was it?'

I was not asking Hassent. But anyway he said, 'Some mechanism, could be. It didn't sound animal really, did it, let alone human. Machinery, like the foun –'

Whatever *it* was, it chose that moment to cry again.

Hassent's words and voice were obliterated. *Thought* was obliterated. Only *feeling* responded to the fearful sound.

It was unbearable. Heartless – yet it was filled by a terrible agony – wounded and agonized yet it was raw with malevolence beyond expression. I mean, *my* expression. The thing which cried expressed it only too well.

In the second aftermath, he and I stood like a couple more statues. Then Hassent shook himself.

'Listen, Aira. Whatever it is, and it might just be *nothing*, it's miles off. Trust me, I'm good at judging sounds, you know that. So our very best course –'

Before he had finished I had taken the hint. And we were running, both of us, light and terrifically fast, toward the shelter of the treasure-house.

Here is a confession.

When things get serious, I always find myself glimpsing back, with bittersweet nostalgia, to my childhood – which was only ten years ago, mostly, if I count adultness from when I was fifteen. In those minutes as we ran inside the dusk within that City canyon, and threw ourselves headlong up the pillars, and next at the low balcony rail of a tall window there flashed through my mind quick images of my days in the Thieves' School of Sheemelay. I saw the teachers, the fellow pupils – even the thick green quarrel trees in the courtyards. Although, as with all such institutions, the school was reckoned to be a secret, everyone knew. The town was proud of it. They also took a cut from the proceeds of the more profitable First Steals. A trained thief anyway never robs on his own turf – so the better school a town has, the safer its townizens.

But, from thinking like this, I knew how afraid I was now. The last occasion I became so nostalgic was the day in Yot, when I was nearly hanged …

The window behind the railing had a kind of glass in it. It was the type of glass that is melded all through to metal, opaque and shining like tarnished platinum. We could see nothing the other side of it either, in the non-light. But Hassent produced his glass-biter, and scored in swiftly, so a pane dropped away. We crashed through after, into the dark behind the dark.

All this while, there had been no other noise from the City. By which I mean, no other cry.

Once inside the Thesaury, Hassent and I froze again. We stood there, listening to the hoofbeats of our hearts, hoping that was all we would have to hear. It was.

Nothing in the world now made a sound.

Maybe three minutes passed. Then he spoke.

'It's as black as night in here even if there isn't any night. I'm going to chance the sparkle.'

'Hassent – that's going to be *bright*. What if –'

'What if what?'

'If something out there sees.'

Hassent said, sensibly, 'Fine. But how else do we find our way anywhere?'

'Use the glow-worms.'

'Not in here. Here's too big. And you know there might be guardians – and catches.'

This was definite. Even if there were nothing supernatural, there would surely be the sorts of pits and snares all cities, if possessed of fabulous wealth, tend to leave lying about, the way the ordinary householder leaves mousetraps.

'The sparkle,' I said, 'might activate just that.'

'A light-reactive catch?'

'They were magicians, remember.'

'Yes, but most of that has decayed. I mean, if it hadn't, we'd have been stumbling over it everywhere already.' And then, having consulted me and ignored my opinion, Hassent switched on his sparkle. It sat up on his left shoulder like a tiny obedient moon, casting out its bluish clarity. 'Going to chance yours, then?' he queried.

I thought that was unnecessary, for all about us a wide hall had become visible end to end in the single sparkle's rays.

'This is one of the outer Arrival Rooms,' I said. 'I remember from what we were told.'

'Where they took the tribute in,' he agreed, 'and the tax from traders. And all those clerks sat at all those benches over there along the wall, weighing the gems and bars, counting the cash.'

We looked at the benches, which were of marble. There were also marble stands and flat upright desks, and curious balances of stone weights.

'The carving is complicated,' I said.

It monopolized every surface. Curls and tendrils (leaves? hair?), out of which squinted disturbing faces again, that were not quite human, not quite anything else, like the figure in the fountain. They had, the faces, no necks, but little paw-like hands. The sparkle winked slowly over their marble eyes, polished by age and the rubbing quality of pure vacance.

There was an uneasy melancholy about the carved faces, but this did not dispel the sense I had of something more ominous. Like the cry we had heard, I thought, misery coupled here with some dreadful other thing, a sort of evil so unlike anything that mankind knows or makes – as to be utterly beyond hope.

'I don't like this room, Hassent.'

'Retie your boots,' he said. 'Lick your finger and rub it on the wall,' he mocked. 'Pee in the comer. Say a *Pleasetosaveme* nine times –' Hassent juggled his eyebrows. 'You're right,' he said. 'It stinks of something foul in here. Like a dead rat the size of a kronarch's palace. Only, it isn't a smell.'

'No.'

He reached out and took, my hand, squeezed it, let go.

'What do you want to do, Aira? Go back?'

I considered. I am contrasuggestive, evidently, because now he had come round to my own view so suddenly, I began to decide we were being crazy. Greed, no doubt.

'We've got this far,' I said. 'Let's –'

And then, oh then, out there *It* cried out again.

Hassent too made a small noise. The Arrival Room went black as he slammed off the sparkle like a blow.

When the awful, *awful* threnody had finally died – from the air, from our inner ears – I heard us start to breathe again.

'That was,' he said, 'nearer. Wasn't it?'

'I think so.'

'What the Bear's Best Bits *is* it?'

'Something … very big.'

'And lonesome.'

'And malign –'

'– beyond our worst-ever nightmares. Why,' he added, with virtuous indignation, 'did no one tell us about this?'

'Do you think it saw your light?'

'Don't ask me,' he said.

'Well I'm not about to call out and ask it.'

We poised, in soundlessness. The Cry now was not repeated. I said, at last, 'What time is it, Hass?'

He cupped his hand, shielding his time-piece dial, and read the lighted sign. 'Thirty-first hour plus nine. Only half an hour till the second sun comes up.'

We thought about this, both of us. The Great Lantern, which some had claimed to have read about, circled round the City, going back to sink again in the mountains where it rose, a brief space before real dawn. It gave a vivid illumination very like the Earth's Sun. Or so it was said. Would it then give enough light therefore to frighten anything off – or alternatively, give anything enough light – to hunt by?

'Downstairs,' said Hassent presently, 'inside this building's core, the treasure – there may be catches, but it's a vault. Do you see?'

Vaults might be closed off, be defensible. I nodded in the dark as if he could see me. 'Yes.'

There were about seventeen flights of stairs, some short and some of fifty steps – or so I judged; I was hardly counting very exactly. We employed both glow-worms, and even when the stairs became wet and slippery from something – rain, or a watercourse that had broken through somewhere – we did not put on the sparkles. Despite being enough underground by then, it might be safe, and despite our not having heard anything – *unusual* for ages.

Below the seventeenth (if it was) staircase, there lay stretched a bizarre and awesome thing. It was a guardian, sure enough. Mages, and royalty occasionally, have access to such creatures. Perhaps not stupidly, I had anticipated several of them scattered about the City. But this one was still as the stone, and even when we came right up to it, it never raised its head, or blinked an eye.

'It's dead,' said Hassent.

'More than that. It's fossilized. Ancient.'

We spent a while walking around it, touching it, marvelling. It was very big, the size of an elephant, or mammatoth. From the large head, the curved tusks extended, black as jet, but the great eyes were shut by crenelated lids. Apparently it had died peacefully, maybe of old age and in its sleep. It was not this which had made those sounds.

Beyond the guardian was a closed door of iron, patterned all over by what looked like magical inscriptions.

'This is it.'

Our Source had been precise about this door, the one recognisable entry to the treasure chamber. So we stood and chanted in unison the formula we had learnt by heart, and repeated over and over for a year, for practice. And then Hass struck the door seven ringing clouts against the to-us-unsecret secret lock.

For a moment, nothing. I thought, *Everyone's deranged. This won't work –*

And then, like the strangest animated cluster of vines, the door began to unfurl and untwine from itself, until all the unroped skeins of patterned iron had drawn away into the walls either side.

We moved into the treasure chamber, Hassent and I.

'Oh, Aira –' he exclaimed, 'just *look* –'

Never in my life had I ever seen anything like it. And I had seen inside quite a few treasure-stores in the past.

The granite-clad hall rose up and up, about five stories of it, tunnelled right through the middle of the Thesaury Building, windowless, yet lit by the dullest yellow lights that were blearing into awakeness on every ledge, roused presumably by someone's coming in.

By this vague illumination, still we saw the substance of the tales.

Zi-rubies, mostly of absurd enormity, stacked up from floor to distant ceiling, like columns of fiery blood, emeralds green as the sea that lay packed tight as figs in clear glass boxes, pink sapphires heaped more carelessly in low pens, over which they had sometimes coyly spilled ... Electris was ranked along, row on row; in bundles, like spears, as we had been told. Next to the pale gleam of it burned the matured glow of gold, in bricks, rings, rods, and hot-white jidel silver, one good piece of which sells for a year's luxury, in cups and shields, body mail and beast-armour, or formed into books, where every page was of thin leaf-silver set with thick lines of golden qualium. Qualium was there in balls too, and milky galvanic schist in globes, which were only less in girth than the breathtaking globes of the rose-white pearls ... Against the walls, marshalled behind the rest, were banks of jade, green and purple, and man-high sheets of aromaticor, with useful perforations so strips could be torn off – And there were other things one barely glanced at, faced with such riches – showers of polished diamonds, crusts of scintillant coppery tope –

We forgot everything, even ourselves. It was almost a religious experience, standing there in the Thesaury, gazing at all this unbelievable but *actual* and proximitous wealth, and thinking of the splendid cities of Yot and Belu and Charinth, in which we might, now, be going to reside like kings –

But then. The thought came too, riding in over the others, and *because* of them, the thought which asked, Why have so few benefited from this place?

For there are thieves everywhere, and mostly they are trained professionals.. And even though the maps are scarce, several are reckoned to exist and look, *we* had one. And provided you had too the two or three necessary charms, and some stamina, and a head for heights – crags or stairs – what was the problem?

As often happens in the end, Hassent and I were having this thought together. Though we are as unlike in most ways as chosh and cheese, we know each other's minds, since, at root, they are about the same.

'Well,' he said.

'Yes,' I said.

And then a *voice* said something, clear and mild, out of the walls.

We jumped like grasshoppers.

Even though all it said was a statement of the obvious:

YOU STAND IN THE THESAURY OF THE CITY.

After that there was a pause, presumably for us to collect ourselves. And then:

WE ARE GONE. THEREFORE YOU ARE WELCOME TO OUR WEALTH. IF YOU HAVE COME SO FAR, TAKE WHAT YOU WISH AND ARE ABLE. WE GRUDGE YOU NOTHING, FOR WE HAVE NOW NO USE FOR IT.

This is where our similarity of minds, Hassent and mine, diverges. He began to relax, he began to look glad and approving of this ancient wisdom which had generously made him its heir.

I, however, braced myself tensely for the rest.

Which presently came.

KNOW ALSO THAT YOUR ACQUISITION IS TO BE BRIEF. NOR LUCKY.

Hassent, already scrabbling at one of the shorter hills of rubies, slid noisily back to the floor.

'*Ssh!*'

But even over the rush, rattle, thump and plink of disturbed gems and Hassent landing on the marble, I heard every, word. And so did he.

I had been wondering, as I said, about them, where they had gone, and why. I even pondered why exactly the City had been attacked, and by whom? Magicians collect animosity, of course. That was what everybody who spoke of it had apparently concluded. Jealous or afraid, the enemies had come over the mountains in their war-balloons, and meted out electric bombardment.

The voice in the Thesaury was mechanical. I have heard such voices in other spots, in theatres, or religious auditoriums. Our entry or activity seemed to have triggered it, just like the magically automatic lamps.

Now the voice explained, in its calm and genderless tones, how the City of magicians had in fact bombed *itself*. They had been attempting, it transpired, to wipe out a dread menace which had grown in their midst. But the menace, as they had feared, proved elusive and invulnerable, and eventually only much fruitless destruction was achieved.

After that, seeing resistance was not to be made to their adversary, the mages, regardless of their powers, surrendered to fate. They put away their armament and their sorcery, and waited without remonstrance, until the menacing horror they had been unable to destroy killed each and every one of them.

ASK THEN WHERE WE ARE GONE? IT IS THERE WE HAVE GONE, announced the voice, INTO THE MAW OF IT. THE FAULT WAS OURS, FOR WE OURSELVES CREATED IT, ALTHOUGH IN IGNORANCE, UNMEANING TO, AND SUPPOSING WHAT WE CREATED WAS ITS VERY OPPOSITE. REGARD THE RUIN OF THIS CITY WITH COMPASSION, FOR YOU ALSO, SINCE YOU HAVE VENTURED HERE, MUST NOW BECOME THE PREY OF THAT WHICH MURDERED US. BE ADVISED, THIS THING IS INESCAPABLE. WASTE NO FUTILE STRUGGLE UPON EVASION. SUBMIT WITH GRACE. SOON YOU WILL JOIN US IN ETERNAL SILENCE. THUS FAREWELL – AND *GREETINGS*.

We stood strainingly alert for some further while, but the voice rendered nothing more.

It's always like this in these historic dumps,' said Hass. 'Bloody old dog-in-the-trough curses everywhere, *We* can't have it anymore, so neither can you. Touch the cash and it's unavoidable doom.'

'That isn't what it said,' I protested.

'All right, it smugly told us: Take everything, but we conjured up an inescapable demon anyway by accident, and it'll get you, so cheers!'

We had recovered enough to choose some of the glorious stuff that was additionally portable, and pile it up in two neat heaps near the open door. But our hearts were not in it, really.

We both kept looking *toward* the open door, as well. And out over the hump of the fossilised guardian they had been-so powerful they had not bothered to replace, along the last stairway, into the dark. Where lay that which the powerful ones had been forced to submit to.

Neither of us had discussed the notion that the thing which made those noises was the very self same.

But besides, nothing stirred. And we had heard no further sound, no other – *cries*.

'I can't *concentrate*.' Hassent growled suddenly, kicking into a miniature stack of faultless emeralds, so they spun in all directions. 'All *this* – and I can't *appreciate* it.'

'No. It's the pits.'

We sat down by the loot we had accumulated. 'We have enough here,' I said, 'anyway, probably, to ensure we can live individually to three hundred, in relative comfort.'

'That's not the *point*.'

'No, Hass.'

'This is like – like a wonderful gallery of artefacts and *art* – it should be savoured. It should be *searched*, carefully, for days, for the most perfect and unique items –'

'Well, we could,' I suggested doubtfully.

'It's been *spoiled*,' he petulantly grieved.

Later he said, 'It's the thirty-third hour. The second sun's up by now, though not high yet. I have a theory about their Great Lantern, Aira. I think they put it up to counteract this *thing*, this monster menace they so sloppily *inadvertently* created. It must be at its best in the night. Only the extra sun didn't work either,' he gloomily finished.

No wonder nothing came in here – no animals, no birds – not even a nocturnal lizard, bat, or moth.

'I've got a theory too, Hass. I think the only people who turn up here – adventurers, thieves, whatever – get sent here by the ones who've got too much sense to try it themselves. Like our beloved Source, who gave us the charms and such a choice map. He wasn't that old, he could have done it. I believe we've been used like experimental beasts. We've been sent in to see what happens to us – if the City is safe yet for a general stealing spree.'

'And when we don't come back,' appended Hass grimly, 'they'll know it still isn't.'

Again later, I said, 'I wonder if just waiting it out down here until full sunrise might work. Perhaps it – goes to its lair –'

'No,' he said, '*think*. Those magicians – they all died. Hiding didn't work. Although – well, have you even seen any skeletons – any remains? Only that guardian over there, and that's been deceased for centuries from the look. As for people of our sort, have we met anyone *ever* who claimed to have been here? Even if nobody would boast, word gets round. No, no one ever got back, Aira. And neither will we.'

Because I am contrasuggestive, as I said before, or over-optimistic – or, more likely, too scared to be pessimistic, I began quietly to try to reason us out of this mood. I produced many clichés, perhaps even one stating the magicians had been spineless to give in.

And then something extraordinary happened and shocked us both to our feet.

A flaring orange light began to slant straight in at us from nowhere, yet somehow above, igniting as it did so the guts of the treasure chamber and a million jewellery eyes.

Inexplicable – then it was obvious. The roof of this chamber, which had seemed to be stone, was another example of that sombre metal-glass. And over it the Great Lantern now took its way. Second dawn poured in.

If things had been different, I might have been impressed by this underground view of the magic sun. It looked, through the glazing, precisely like a sun, rather smaller, though hardly less brilliant than the real one. I had heard the magicians produced it out of some alchientistic combustible previously unknown, firing it from a vast gun, which also struck it alight like flint-and-tinder, straight into the sky. Even at its apex, it hung lower than the true sun, of course, or the moon, inside the atmosphere of the world – but seen like this from the Thesaury, you would never guess.

As we gaped at it, Terror, which perhaps we had both mislaid again a second, burst shrieking from the City above and dropped down on us.

I thought it was a cloud – something passing between us and the blinding amber of the second sun. Something falling ... weightless, *harmless* – But once through, that cry came with it, from silence, booming, like a wind of steel needles –

We two tumbled, rolled, crashed against arcades of rubies that only rocked, throwing off a few bloody drops.

Terror landed, still screaming, there in the Thesaury. It had come, not from the stair, but *right through the metal-glass roof.* For it could come right through *anything.*

There was no time to demand idiotically, What is it? Though the mechanical voice had been ambiguous and everyone else had lied. There was also no room for speech in the noise-punctured air.

I had rolled all the way back against a sheet of the priceless purple jade beloved of tyrants. The jade obligingly tipped down all round me, cracking, then breaking in shards on the floor – but that was nothing.

The creature crouched now in the middle of the vault, not needing to position itself, passing *through* and *over* everything that was there. It was shadow-black – everything that it covered passed within it, and disappeared – and formless. It was like those things they say are in the ocean deeps, and swim without limbs and see without eyes. This was all that, nor did it have any mouth to make its crying, nor any maw to take us in and keep us, as it did *not* keep the other things it swarmed upon and through and over. And it was Fear Incarnate. My bones had turned to jelly and my blood to talc. Though I am strong, then I had no strength. I lay among the broken fire-conducting jade, and became an abject victim, as the mages had done. Just as Hassent was doing. As anyone would.

The core of it was fathomless yet void. I stared. That was where we would be going. Like them. Into that blackness that was a Nothingness, into that silence aeons beyond its own aching scream. All-blackness it was, black night without moon or stars – yet it was unrepelled by the light of the second sun, which boiled around it. Indeed it seemed to have been the second sunrise which had brought it –

Bewildered, I saw Hassent abruptly roll again, and leap back to his feet. He was running to where the huge rods of electris stood in ranks, and the bails of qualium and schist. Sprawled there, I watched, and observed him heft one of the enormous spear-like bolts. I thought, *Panic has sent him off his head* – he was going to attempt to lance the creature of darkness – which somehow could swallow nothing save one thing – *anything* which *lived* – but a spear would pass through it, useless, for It was made only of black, only of nothing, only of utter night –

As the first electris rod smote against the metal-glass ceiling five stories up, I too was on my feet. I seized the nearest object, a lesser zi-ruby dislodged and still of substantial size, and flung it too. From that, and Hass's rain of spears, the metal-glass had begun to fracture. Spider webbing flashed over the scald of the sun.

We kept at this, slinging, casting anything we could manage. During the activity, neither of us looked – over *there*, where death was moving without haste, savouring or only sluggish after the hunger of such a long wait for food like us.

Not looking … throwing missiles, yet I began to lose hope. This seemed the proper moment to do so. And then, the miracle. In one spasm, all the roof glass fissured together, the metal bonding preventing its breaking open or dropping through, keeping the outer skin whole, but letting it shatter internally. For a second there was a kaleidoscope of spattering lights, then a freckled darkness, and then full dark came back.

When the dull lamps winked on again, the only dark in there *was* the dark. The other Dark – that had vanished.

I knelt on the floor, shaking. Shaking too, I imagine, Hassent leant on a pen of sapphires.

'We had the same thought again,' he said.

'That's generous. You had it first.'

'Well, let's not debate our genius potency. We have whatever time is left before either 1) the whole ceiling collapses and we go back to the first chess-square, or 2) the ceiling collapses after the Great Lantern has passed but while the *real* sun is coming up. The only safe time was dusk. But we daren't wait.'

'We can't stay here,' I agreed.

'And meanwhile, up there, what chance do we have?'

'We've discovered now what it is.'

'*They* learned that, the mighty magicians, but they couldn't do a thing.'

I said flatly, 'They were altruistic, perhaps, or guilty. It was their fault. We're innocent professional robbers.'

'You have a plan?'

I nodded, ridiculously glad to be the one ahead this time.

Yes, they had felt guilty. (A glance at those carvings of theirs showed what they believed loitered in the wretched soul of anyone with their sort of power – nasty little pawing squinting imps, only partly concealed by the foliage or curlicues of gracious living.)

Yet when they made their sun, they were high as balloons on the joy of their talents, and what they could do. Possibly they built it on a whim, because they wanted long summer evenings that went on till dawn. But maybe they were afraid of the dark in their souls.

And perhaps *that* facilitated the thing which happened. Their own ever-present self-distrust.

They launched the Great Lantern and outlawed night from their City forever. More, they *killed* the night there. Then there could only be twilight, a sunrise, and another sunrise.

If this were a story, you might say the night became angry. Out of rage at this bit of itself having been slaughtered in the City, it raised up its dead and let it loose for vengeance. But night has never harboured resentment, that I ever heard. It was only that, from every bright light there proceeds a shadow. That is one of the Laws of Balance which especially mages know very well. And their invented sun's shadow took on their fear of themselves. The stronger any light, too, the blacker the shade it generates. The Great Lantern was incandescent and convincing – and false. So the shadow it started was deadly, ominous, negative – and *alive*.

Animate things straying into the City, beasts, birds, people, stirred it up. Very likely it would lie almost quiescent when no one was about. Yet despite its birth from an unreal sun, in the violent light of any sun – therefore, the *true* sun – it must also be active. It was a *shadow*.

Not anything that gave light energized it; some things were too weak. Although I thought the sparkle had, a little, at least attracted its attention. *Solar* light was its catalyst and inspirator. But frankly I would have taken no chances on a fully visible and lushly lit window, let alone the moon. Moonless dusk, as earlier, was the only lucky time. Which meant that even if we had been able to stall until the following night, we would have stood not a chance. Tonight had been moonless. Tomorrow the moon was new.

Getting everything up the seventeen or eighteen staircases was quite a haul. We did it again in total darkness. That was the only way to be safe.

And at the top waited blasting fake daylight. And daylight's Shadow.

When we reached the area behind the outer Arrival Room, we kept well back, because through the windows the sun was boring, shining it all up to gold. The Great Lantern gives a radiance resembling that kind of ripe, syrupy desert sunset people remark on and praise. I hate that sort of sunset now.

'Ready?' he asked me.

'No. Let's do it.'

Jade is always valuable. The black, white, and green jades for jewellery and statues. The purple jade is also beautiful but has other properties worth a lot more.

There in the dark behind the light, a scratching began like giant mice. It was Hassent and me, maniacally working with the two flint-and-tinders, setting the ends of endless shards of purple jade alight. Brittle and easily broken, the material catches very quickly. The jade grows red-hot in seconds, so one must be quick in spinning it away. There is no *flame*, only a thick magenta smoke. It has been used for approximately two centuries in the most unprincipled ways, during warfare, or to control popular riots when kings become aggrieved. The jade bums for hours, the smoke thickens and spreads. It smells nice, and chokes you, you can see nothing in it; conversely, the damage to property is minimal, as no fire ever results. It is worth a fortune. We flung it back down the stairs, out over the Arrival Room, and, when the voluminous swirling miasma began to expand, advancing with the cloud, with our shirts tied over half our faces, we dropped it also clear of the balcony into the sunlit street.

I have heard them say, in the places they have used fire-conducting jade, called also so playfully, Plum-Breath, that it turned day to night, and put out the sun.

We put out the sun too, that sunny dead night in the City, Hass and I. Coughing and crowing, eyes streaming, and thinking we would probably anyway soon strangle and expire, we moved up the steps, over the plazas, along the boulevards, until we reached an outer wall. I can only guess how we climbed it, clinging retching and weeping on the ropes. But I said, I believe, he and I are strong. And the terror of certain death is always a wonderful incentive.

We got down the mountain wall too, only falling parts of the way, well-roped from practice, accumulating cuts, gashes, bruises, a cracked rib and chipped bone or two – nothing worth mentioning, really. Or I feel it is unworthy of mention, in the light – the *dark* – of the alternative.

We were not attacked. Nothing came near.

When we had got down in the valley, it was dawn. The sun rising was the actual sun. Staring back up, even if we could barely see with our tortured eyes, we beheld how the City of the magicians now perched under a chain of tiny umbrellas of Plum-Breath, which marked our escape route. The Great Lantern itself was invisible, then visible, coming and going as it sank. But we heard something somewhere, crying. They were etiolate cries of anguish and excruciation beyond human comprehending, endurance, or pity.

We lay around in the valley for a few days. We took turns vomiting, complaining, drinking the local streams dry. Gradually full sight returned, and some sanity. (By then we had crawled on at least far enough not to have to see the City above, or its sun.) Hassent and I told each other that we were on the mend, although we found out, the hard way, that it would be another month before all the poison of the jade had been voided. Before we left the area entirely, the smoke had mostly faded overhead, though it was obvious how far it had drifted. And the lamentation of the thing which haunted the City, that had faded at last too, though now and then, in the stillness – just now and then, even a hundred miles off as we then were – Unless maybe, it was an aural hallucination.

From the treasure city we had brought out not a single valuable. All we had carried was as much purple jade as we could, and we had spent all that to save our lives. What is life worth, after all? To most of us, everything we have.

In the after days, trekking back, urt-less, over the desert toward civilization, we planned a dainty retribution on our helpful Source, who had experimentally sent us to die. We did not ever talk about the City. We never discussed either one ultimate thing – which was the reason no one had ever attempted to destroy the Great Lantern, the sun which had caused the creature of dead night. I will put this down, nevertheless, in case anyone ever thinks they would be doing us all a service (and incidentally enabling themselves to become incredibly rich) by smashing that unreal, second sun. *Leave it alone!* Why? Because the second sun is what keeps the creature in the City, If ever that disc goes out – all It will have left is the moon and the stars and the sun, and any other great lights of all this world *outside*. And then everywhere will be open to it, everywhere – and everyone of us.

Beware!

Jedella Ghost

That fall morning, Luke Baynes had been staying a night with his grandmother up on the ridge, and he was tramping back to town through the woods. It was about an hour after sun-up, and the soft level light was caught broadcast in all the trees, molasses-red and honey-yellow. The birds sang, and squirrels played across the tracks. As he stepped on to the road above the river, Luke looked down into the valley. There was an ebbing mist, sun-touched like a bridal veil, and out of this he saw her come walking, up from the river, like a ghost. He knew at once she was a stranger, and she was young, pale and slight, in an old-fashioned long dark dress. Her hair was dark, too, hanging down her back like a child's. As she got closer he saw she was about eighteen, a young woman. She had, he said, not a pretty face, but serene, pleasing; he liked to look at her. And she, as she came up to him, looked straight at him, not boldly or rudely, but with an open interest. Luke took off his hat, and said, 'Good morning.'

And the girl nodded. She said, 'Is there a house near here?'

Luke said there was, several houses, the town was just, along the way.

She nodded again, and thanked him. It was, he said, a lovely voice, all musical and lilting upward, like a smile. But then she went and sat at the roadside, where a tree had been cut and left a stump. She looked away from him now, up into the branches. It was as if there was nothing more to say. He did ask if he could assist her. She answered at once, 'No, thank you.' And so, after a moment, he left her there, though he was not sure he should do. But she did not appear concerned or worried.

'She had the strangest shoes,' he said.

'Her shoes?' I asked. Luke had never seemed a man for noting the footwear of women, or of anyone.

'They were the colours of the woods,' he said, 'crimson and gold and green. And – they seemed to me like they were made of glass.'

'Cinderella,' I said, 'run off from the ball.'

'But she had on both,' he said, and grinned.

After this we went for coffee and cake at Millie's.

I had no doubt he had seen this woman, but I thought perhaps he had made more of her than there was. Because I am a writer people sometimes try to work spells on me – Oh, John Cross, this will interest you. You can *write* about this. It does them credit really, to make their imaginations work. But they should take up the pen, not I. Usually, I have enough ideas of my own.

About ten, I went back to my room to work, and did not come out again until three. And then I too saw Luke's lady of the mist. She was standing in the square, under the old cobweb trees, looking up at the white tower of the church, on which the clock was striking the hour.

People going about were glancing at her curiously, and even the old-timers on the bench outside the stables were eying her. She was a stranger, and graceful as a lily. And sure enough, she seemed to have on sparkling stained-glass shoes.

When the clock stopped, she turned and looked around her. Do any of us look about that way? Human things are cautious, circumspect – or conversely arrogant. And she was none of these. She looked the way a child does, openly, perhaps not quite at ease, but not on guard. And then she saw – evidently she saw – the old men on the bench, Will Marks and Homer Avory and Nut Warren. She became very stilly gazing at *them,* until they in turn grew uneasy. They did not know what to do, I could see, and Nut, who was coming on for ninety years, he turned belligerent.

I stepped out and crossed the square, and came right up to her, standing between her and the old boys.

'Welcome to our town. My name's John Cross.'

'I'm Jedella,' she said at once.

'I'm glad to meet you. Can I help?'

'I'm lost,' she said. I could not think at once what to say. Those that are lost do not speak in this way.

I knew it even then. Jedella said presently, 'You see, I've lived all my life in one place, and now – here I am.'

'Do you have kin here?'

'Kin?' she said. 'I have no kin.'

'I'm sorry. But is there someone –?'

'No,' she said. 'Oh, I'm tired. I'd like a drink of water. To sit down.'

I said, and I thought myself even then hard and cruel, 'Your shoes.'

'Oh. That was my fault. I should have chosen something else.'

'Are they glass?'

'I don't know,' she said.

I took her straight across to Millie's, and in the big room sat her at a table, and when the coffee came, she drank it down. She seemed comfortable with coffee, and I was surprised. I had already realised, maybe, that the things of civilised life were not quite familiar to her.

Hannah returned and refilled our cups – Jedella had refused my offer of food. But as Hannah went away, Jedella looked after her. The look was deep and sombre. She had eyes, Jedella, like the rivers of the Greek Hell – melancholy, and so dark.

'What's wrong with her?'

'With –?'

'With that woman who brought the coffee.'

Hannah was a robust creature, about forty. She was the wife of Abel Sorrensen, and had five children, all bright and sound – a happy woman, a nice woman. I had never seen her sick or languishing.

'Hannah Sorrensen is just fine.'

'But –' *said Jedella.* She *stared at* me, then the stare became a gaze. 'Oh, those men outside …'

'The old men on the bench,' I said.

Jedella said, 'I'm sorry, I don't mean to be impertinent.'

I said, squaring my shoulders, 'I think you should see Doc McIvor. He's bound to have some plan of how to go on.'

I had formed the impression she was a little mad. And I confess, I wondered how she would react to the notion of a doctor.

But Jedella smiled at me, and then I saw what Luke had only heard in her voice. Her smile made her beautiful.

For a moment I saw her as my muse. I wondered if I would fall in love with her, and feed upon her mystery. The writer can be selfish. But, in my own defence, I knew that here was something rare, precious – rich and strange.

'Of course I'll see him,' she said. 'I have no one, and nowhere to go. How kind you are.'

What happens when the doctor is sick? An old adage to be sure, But Doc McIvor had gone to visit his niece in the city, who was expecting her first baby. Everyone knew but me. But then, I had only lived in the town for five years.

I did not want, I admit, to give Jedella, with her Lethe eyes and Cinderella shoes and heavenly smile, over to the law, so I took her to my rooming-house, and there Abigail Anchor came sweeping forth in her purple dress.

'I can give her that little room on the west side,' said Abigail. 'This girl has run away. I know it.'

'Do you think so?' I asked.

'Oh, to be sure. Her daddy is some harsh man. Perhaps forcing her to marry. I won't sit in judgement, Mr Cross. Indeed, Mr Cross, you may know more than you say. But I won't ask it.'

'I don't know anything, Mrs Anchor.'

'That's as you say, Mr Cross.'

I met Luke Baynes that night in the Tavern. We had a beer. He grinned at me again.

'They're talking. Your sweetheart's stashed away at Ma Anchor's.'

'Yours and mine. You saw her first.'

'Then it *is* the girl with glass shoes.'

'A strange one,' I said. 'She keeps to herself. But when I came out tonight, she was at her window and the blind was raised. She was looking along the street.'

Luke said,' Don't you know anything?'

'Not a thing. Abigail has sheltered her from the goodness of her heart. Her name's Jedella.'

'I don't believe,' said Luke, 'she's real. She's a ghost. '

'I took her arm,' I said. 'She's real as you or I.'

'What is it then?' he said.

'I think she's crazy. A little crazy. Probably someone will come after her. She can't have come far.'

'But,' he said, 'she's – wonderful.'

'Yes,' I said. 'A fascinating woman. The woman you can't have is always fascinating.'

'You're too clever,' he said. 'I fancy going courting.'

'Don't,' I said. I frowned into my drink. 'Don't.'

Two weeks passed, and Jedella lived in the room on the west side of the Anchor house. She gave no trouble, and I had had a word with Abigail about the rent. I believe Abigail helped with any female things that Jedella might have needed and certainly, I was presented with a bill before too long. My trade had brought me moderate success, and I did not flinch.

Otherwise, I saw no reason to interfere. I gathered from Abigail that Jedella did not much wish to go out, yet seemed quite well. She ate her meals in private, and enjoyed the services of the house. Now and then I noted Jedella at her window, gazing along the street. Once I lifted my hand, but she did not respond. I let it go at that.

Of course, word had got around about the unknown young woman. I was sometimes pestered, but knowing next to nothing myself, could be of little assistance.

Did I want to draw Jedella out? Rather, I was inclined to avoid her. Real life that takes the form of a story, or appears to, is so often disappointing. Or, if one learns some gem, must one become a traitor who can no longer be trusted with anything? I prefer to invent, and that keeps me busy enough.

Luke did try to introduce himself to the woman on the west side. He took her flowers one afternoon, and a box of sweets in a green bow another. But Jedella apparently seemed only amazed. She did not respond as a woman should, hopefully a flirtatious, willing woman. He was baffled, and retreated, to the relief of the two or three young ladies of the town who had such hopes of him, some day.

On the last Friday of that second week, just as I had finished a long story for the *Post*, I heard at Millie's that Homer Avory had died in his bed. He was nearly eighty, which for the town is quite a youngster, and his daughter was in a rage, it seemed, for she had always loved him and had been planning a birthday dinner.

Everyone went to a funeral then, and presently I heard it was fixed for Tuesday. I looked out my black suit with a sensation of the droll and the sad. My father had once warned me, 'You don't feel a death, John, not truly, till you start to feel your own.' He was fifty when he said this, and he died two years after, so I may not argue. But I felt it was a shame about Homer, and about his daughter, who was sixty herself, and had lost her husband ten months before to a fever.

On Monday evening I was reading some books that had come in the mail, when a light knock sounded on my door.

It was not Abigail, evidently, who thundered, nor Luke, who burst in. I went to see, and there stood the apparition called Jedella, still in her dark dress, but with a new pair of simple shoes. Her hair was done up on her head.

'Good evening, Miss Jedella. Can I help you?'

'Mr Cross,' she said, 'something is happening tomorrow.'

'Tomorrow? Oh, do you mean poor old Homer's funeral?'

'That,' she said, 'is what Abigail Anchor called it.'

'Abigail? Well, what else. A burial, a funeral.'

She stared straight at me. She said, still and low, 'But what is that?'

Abigail had her rules, but it was just light. I drew Jedella into the room and left the door an inch ajar.

I made her sit down in my comfortable chair, and moved the books.

'How do you mean, Miss Jedella?'

She seemed for a moment disturbed. Then she composed her pale face and said, 'They say the – old man – has died.'

'He has.'

'Was he one of the three men I saw in the square that day?'

'Yes, just so.'

'He has some terrible illness,' she said. She looked about distractedly. 'Am I right?'

This unnerved me. I could not put it together. I recalled, I had thought her slightly insane. I said, quietly, 'Unfortunately, he was old, and so he died. But, please believe, he had no ailment. He passed away peacefully in his sleep, I gather.'

'But what do you mean?' she said.

'He's dead,' I answered. 'I'm afraid, it happens.'

I had intended irony, but she gazed at me with such pathos, I felt myself colour, as if I had insulted her. I did not know what to say next. She spoke first.

'This funeral, what is it?'

'Jedella,' I said firmly, 'do you say you don't know what a funeral is?'

'No,' said Jedella, 'I have no idea.'

If I had been three years younger, I suspect I would have thought myself the victim of some game. But peculiar things happen. Oddities, differences.

I sat down in the other chair.

'When a man dies, we put him in the earth. If you are religious, you reckon he waits there for the last trumpet, which summons him up to God.'

'In the earth,' she said. 'But how can he stand it – is it some punishment?'

'He's dead,' I replied, like stone. 'He won't know.'

'How can he not know?'

In the window, the light of day was going out. And it came to me, as sometimes it did when a child, that perhaps this was the end, and the sun would never return.

In ten minutes or so, Abigail's boy would sound the bell for dinner. Jedella did not join the communal table.

'Jedella,' I said, 'I can't help you. It's too profound a question for me. Can I ask the minister to call on you?'

She said, 'Why?'

'He may be able to assist you.'

She said, looking at me, her countenance bewildered and yet serene even now, as if *she* had seen that I and all the world were mad –

'This is a terrible place. I wish that I could help you, but I don't know how. How can you bear it, Mr Cross, when you witness such suffering?'

I smiled. 'I agree, it can be difficult. But then, it could have been worse. We all come to it.'

She said, 'To what?'

The bell rang. Perhaps it was early, or I had misjudged. I said, 'Well, you're very young, Jedella.' Some phantom of my father's words, perhaps.

But Jedella went on looking at me with her Lethe eyes. She said, flatly, 'What does that mean?'

'Now this is silly. You keep asking me that. I mean that you're young. About sixteen, maybe.'

I confess, I tried to flatter, making her a little less than she appeared to be. One should always be careful with a woman's age, one way or the other. In those days Sixteen was the dividing line; now it is more twenty.

But Jedella; who Luke had thought a ghost, stared into my face. She was not flattered.

She said, 'Sixteen years do you mean? Of course not.'

'Sixteen, eighteen, whatever it may be.'

Outside; my fellow boarders were going down the stairs; they would hear us talking and realize that John Cross had the woman in his room.

Jedella stood up. The last glimmer of light was behind her; and played about her slender shape, making her seem suddenly thin and despoiled. Abigail must have persuaded her to put up her hair. She was a shadow, and all at once, the shadow of someone else, as if I had seen through her – but to what?

'I am,' she said, 'sixty-five years of age.'

I laughed. But it was a laugh of fright. For I could see her there like a little old lady, five years on from Homer's daughter.

'I'm going down to my meal, Jedella. Are you willing to come?'

'No,' she said.

She turned, moved; the new lamplight from beyond the door caught her. She was eighteen. She went out on to the landing, and away up the house.

What we ate that night I have no notion. Someone – Clark, I think – regaled us with jokes, and everyone guffawed, but for Miss Pirn, and Abigail, who did not approve. I chuckled too – but God knows why. Did I even hear what was said?

In the end we remembered. Homer was to *go* into the ground tomorrow, and a silence fell. I recall how Abigail lighted a candle in the window, a touching gesture, old superstition, but kind and sweet, to guide a soul home.

I had mentioned nothing of what Jedella had said to me, and no one had ventured to ask what she and I had had to converse on.

In my room, I walked about. I lit the lamp and picked up my books, and put them down.

Over in the west end of the house, she was, that girl with dark hair, who had come up from the morning mist, like a ghost.

In God's name, what had she been talking of? What did she suggest? What did she want?

I have said, if I had been a few years younger, I would have thought it a game. And, forty years older, as now I am, I might have deemed it quite proper, to go across the house and knock on the door. Times change, and customs with them. It was not possible then.

At length I went to bed, and lay in the dark, with all the gentle quiet of that place about me, my haven from the city. But I could not rest. She said she did not know what a funeral was, she inquired how he could bear it, Homer, going into the ground. She told me she was sixty-five years old.

She was mad. She had come from the river in stained glass shoes, and she was crazy.

I dreamed I was at my father's burial, which once I had been, but no one else was there, save for Jedella. And she looked down into the pit of black earth, and she said to me, 'Will you leave him here?'

I woke with tears on my face. I had not wanted to leave him there. Not my father, that lovely and good man, who had given me so much. But surely it had not been my father any more, down there in the dark?

The first light was coming, and I got up and sat by the window. The town was calm and the birds sang. Far off beyond the woods and the forests of pines, I could see, it was so clear, the transparent aurora of the mountains.

I knocked on Jedella's door about nine-thirty in the morning, and when she opened it, I said, 'Will you walk with me?' I wanted no more clandestine meetings in the rooms.

The funeral was at two. Outside there was nothing out of the ordinary going on. The trees had their scalding full colour. The stores were open, and a dog or two were nosing down the street. Jedella looked at all this, in a sad, silent way. She reminded me of a widow.

We went into the square, and sat on the vacant bench under the cobweb trees.

'I want you to tell me, Jedella, where you come from. If you will.'

She said, 'Beyond the woods. Up in the pines. A house there.'

'How far away?' I said. I was baffled.

'I don't know. It took me a day to reach this town. A day, and the night before.'

'Why did you come here?'

'I didn't know what else to do. I didn't mean to come. I was only walking.'

'Why then did you leave the house – the house in the pines?'

'They had all gone,' she said. For a moment she looked the way I have only seen human things look after some great disaster, the wreck of a train, the random horror of a war. I did not know it then. What she spoke of was a terror beyond her grasp. It had hurt her, but it had no logic, like the acts of God.

'Who had gone?'

'The people who were there with me. Often they did, of course, but not all at once. The house was empty. I looked.'

'Tell me about the house.'

Then she smiled. It was the lovely, lilting smile.

This memory made her happy.

'It was where I was, always.'

'Where you were born?' I asked.

As if from far off, she smiled on at me. 'The first thing I remember,' she said.

She sat on the bench, and I realized absently that, in her old-fashioned dress, she was clad as an old lady, like Homer's daughter, or Elsie Baynes, or some other elder woman of our town. The air was sweet and crisp and summer had died.

I said, 'I'd like to hear.'

'It's a big white house,' she said, 'and there are lots of rooms. I was usually in the upper house, though sometimes I went down. All around was a high wall, but I could see the tops of the trees. There were trees inside the garden too., and I walked there every day. except in winter. Then it was too cold, when the snow was down.'

'Who was in the house with you?'

'Many people. Oh, lots of people, Mr Cross. They looked after me.'

Curiously I said, as if encouraging a child. 'Who did you like the best?'

'I liked them all – but you see, they didn't stay for long. No one ever stayed.' She was sad once more, but in a deeper, softer way. She was indeed like a child, that was what I finally saw then, a child in an old lady's dress, which fitted. 'When I was a girl,' she said, oddly mimicking my thought, 'I used to be upset by it, the going away. But in the end, I knew that it had to be.'

'Why did it have to be?' I asked, blindly.

'That was their lives. But I remained. That was mine,

'Tell me more about the house,' I said.

'Oh, it was only a house. It was where I lived. Some of the rooms were large, and some, my bedroom, for example quite small.'

'What did you do there?'

'I read the books, and I painted on paper. And I played the piano. There was always something to do.'

'Your father and mother,' I said.

Jedella glanced at me. 'What do you mean?'

The sun was warm on my face and hands, and yet the air was cool. A blue shadow descended from the tower of the church. Something had hold of me now, it held me back. I said, 'Well, tell me about something that you enjoyed especially.'

She laughed. Her laugh was so pretty, so truthful and young. 'There were a great many things. I used to imagine places, places I'd never been – cities of towers from the books I'd read, and rivers and seas. And animals too. There are lions and tigers and bears, aren't there?'

'So I believe.'

'Yes, I believe it too. Have you ever seen them?'

'In cages,' I said.

She looked startled a moment. But then she brushed that away from her like a fallen leaf. 'I longed to see them, and they said, one day.'

I said, 'Did they tell you when?'

'No. I suppose it was meant to be now. After I left the house.'

'Then they told you you must leave?'

'Oh no. But when they were gone, the doors were all open. And the big door in the wall, that too.'

I was trying now, quite hard, to follow along with her, not to delay or confuse by protestations. I thought how, when I had spoken of her being born, she had had that look of the polite guest at the party, when you say something he does not understand, but is too nice to debate on.

'The door had never been open before?'

'No, never.'

'Did – they – say why not?'

'I never asked, because, you see, it was the way I lived. I didn't need anything else.'

She was young – or was she young? – yet surely there had been some yearning, like her wish to see the animals from the books. The young feel they are prisoners even when they are not, or not decidedly. Something came to me. I said, 'Did you see pictures in your books of lion cubs?'

'Oh yes,' she said.

I said, 'And once, you were a child.'

'Of course.'

Above us the clock struck – it must have done so before. Now it was noon.

Jedella looked about her. She said, 'Something's very wrong here. Can't you tell me what it is?'

'It's the way we are, the way we live,' I said.

She sighed. She said, and there was that in her voice that filled me with a sort of primeval fear, 'Is it like this everywhere?'

I said, intuitively, 'Yes, Jedella.'

Then she said, 'Abigail Anchor brought some books up to me. It was a kindness. I didn't understand them.'

'In what way?'

'Things happen in those books – that don't happen.'

I could have said this might be true of much poor fiction. But clearly she did not imply this.

'You had books in your house,' I said. 'What about those books?'

'Parts had been cut away,' she said. I said nothing, but as if I had, she added, 'I used to ask, where those pieces wore. But they said the books had been there a long time, that was all.'

I said, blindly, as before, 'For example, the lion cubs were there, and they grew up into lions. But you didn't know how they had arrived there.' She was silent. I said, 'And how long did the lions live, Jedella? Did the books say?'

Jedella, the ghost, turned her dark eyes on me. She was no longer a temptation, not my muse. She said, 'Always, of course. To live – is to live.'

'Forever?'

She said and she did nothing. I felt my heart beat in a wild random crescendo, and all at once that peaceful square, that town where I had come to be quiet, was rushing all apart, like a jigsaw, broken. Then it settled. My heart settled.

'Will you come,' I said, 'to Homer's funeral?'

'If you think so,' she said.

I got up and offered her my arm. 'We'll take some lunch in Millie's. Then we'll go on.'

Her hand was light on me, as a leaf of the fall.

She was quiet and nearly motionless all through the ceremony, and though she looked down at his old, creased, vacant face, before the coffin was closed, she made no fuss about it.

But when everything was done, and we stood alone on the path, she said, 'I used to watch the squirrels playing, in the trees and along the tops of the wall. They were black squirrels. I used to throw them little bits of cake. One day, John Cross, I saw a squirrel lying there on the grass in the garden. It didn't move. It was so still I was able to stroke its side. Then someone came from the house, I think it was a man called Orlen. And he picked up the squirrel. He said to me, 'Poor thing, it's fallen and stunned itself. Sometimes they do. Don't fret, Jedella. I'll take it back to its tree, and it will get better.'

Over the lawn, Homer's daughter walked, leaning on the arm of her son. She was rubbing at her face angrily, muttering about the meat dishes and the sweet pie she had been going to make for the birthday. Her son held his hat across his middle, head bowed, troubled the way we often are at grief we cannot share.

'So the squirrel was stunned,' I said.

'Yes. And later he pointed it out to me, running along the wall.'

'That same squirrel.'

'He told me that it was.'

'And you think now that Homer is only stunned, and we've thrown him down into the ground, and now they'll cover him with earth, so he can't get out.'

We stood, two respectful and well-behaved figures. Her life had been an acceptance, and she was coming to accept even now the unacceptable.

'Jedella, will you describe for me very carefully the way you came here, from your house in the pines?'

'If you want.'

'It would be a great help to me,' I said. 'You see, I mean to go there.'

'I can't go back,' she said.

I thought she was like Eve, cast out of Eden because she had failed to eat the forbidden fruit.

'No, I won't make you. But I think I must. There may be some clue to all of this.'

She did not argue with me. She had begun to accept also her utter difference, and that she was outnumbered. She guessed something had been done to her, as I did. She had ceased to debate, and would never resist.

When I first took up my life here, I went frequently to walk or ride in the wooded country. Then I got down to my work and adventured less. To ride out on this cold bright morning was no penance, though I had grown a little stiff, and guessed I should feel it later, which I did. The horse was a pretty mare by the name of May.

We went with care along the route Jedella had outlined, even drawing – she had a fair hand with a pencil – landmarks I might look for. Beyond the road we climbed into the woods and so up the hill called Candy Crag, and over into the pines.

I was high up by nightfall, and I could feel the cold blowing down from the distant snow-lined mountains. I thought as I made my camp, I might hear a wolf call up on the heights, but there was only stillness and the swarm of the stars. Such great calm is in those places and the sense of Infinity. Some men can only live there, but for me, I should be lost. I like the little things. This was enough, a night or two, a day or two, up so close to the sky. At dawn I went on.

A couple of times I saw my fellow humans. A trapper with his gun, a man far down on the river. Both glimpsed me, and hailed me, and I them. For the rest, the wild things of the woods came and went, a porcupine, a deer, the birds, the insects. May stepped mildly through their landscape, her skin shining like a flame. I spoke to her now and then, and sang her a few songs.

I found the house with no trouble in the afternoon of that second day. Jedella had travelled more quickly than I, unless she had lost track of time.

You could see the mountains from there very well, a vast white battlement rising from the pelt of the pines. But near at hand, the forest was thick, so dense we had to pick our way. The house was in a clearing, as Jedella had told me shut round with its tall white wall. It had a strange look as if it had no proper architecture, no style of anywhere at all. Like boxes put together, and roofs put on, and windows set in. Something a child had made, but a child without fantasies.

The gate was open, and the sunlight slanted down through the trees and showed me a man standing there, on the path. He wore a white suit, and was smoking a cigarette. I had become used to the pipes and chewing-tobacco of my town. And somehow I had anticipated – God knows what. He was a very old man, too, but spare and upright, with a mane of thick, whitish hair, and eyebrows dark as bands of iron.

He lifted his hand, as he saw me. And this was not the lonely greeting of the trapper or the river man. I could see, he had expected me, or someone. Had he come there to wait for me?

I am not given to drama, except sometimes when I write, and can have it there on my own terms. But I eased myself off the horse and undid my saddlebag and took out the two brightly-coloured shoes that looked as if they were made of glass, and holding these out, I walked up to him.

'Jedella's slippers,' he said. 'Did she get so far in them?'

'Quite far.'

'They're not glass,' he said, 'something I fashioned, when I was younger. A sort of resin.'

'I'd hoped,' I said, 'you would come and fetch her.'

'No, I can't do that. I haven't time now. It had to end, and she has to go on as best she can. She wouldn't know me now, in any case. She saw me for five or six years, when she was a child, and I was in my twenties.'

'That would make her old,' I said.

'Sixty-five is her age.'

'So she said.'

'And of course,' he said, 'it can't be, for she is eighteen or nineteen, a girl.'

Behind me, May shook her amber head, as if in warning, and a bird hammered a moment on the trunk of a tree.

'I came here,' I said, 'hoping to find out.'

'Yes, I know it. And I shall tell you. I am Jedidiah Goëste, and for now this house is mine. Will you step inside?'

I went with him up the path, leading May, who I settled in a sunny place. The trees were all around inside the wall, the trees where the black squirrels played. I had been struck by his name – Scandinavian, perhaps, and its affinity of sound to what Luke and I had come to call her: Miss Ghost. *Jedidiah*, too, the father's name, and the daughter taking a feminised version, Jedella. Was it so simple? For yes, if he had been in his twenties, he would be near his nineties now, and she would be sixty-five.

Inside the door was an open room, white-walled, quite pleasant, with ornaments and pictures, and with a large fireplace where some logs and cones were burning. Hot coffee stood on a table. Had he known the hour of my coming? No, that was too fanciful. It seemed to me I had better be as careful as I had been when riding through the denseness of the pines. Something strange there was, but not all of it could or need be.

A wide staircase ran up from the room and above was a sort of gallery. I noticed another man standing there, and Jedidiah Goëste gestured to him quietly, and the man went away.

'My servant. He won't disturb us.'

'Is that Orlen?' I said.

'Oh, no. Orlen is long gone. But Orlen was a favourite of Jedella's, I believe, when she was still a child. It was a pity they all had to leave her. She used to cry in the beginning. She cried when I left her. But later, they told me, she was philosophical. She had grown accustomed.'

I had given him in turn my name, and he had taken the privilege of the old to call me at once John. We sat down in two large velvet armchairs, and I drank some of the coffee, hot and sweet and good.

'I have come back here,' he said, 'to die. It's comfortable for me here, and I have all I want. A few months, no more.'

I said, 'Then shouldn't you have kept her here?'

'She was given, implicitly, the choice. She might have remained, although I didn't think she would. If she had been here when I returned, I would, I think, have had to pretend to be someone else. And even then, the shock –'

'Your age. But it's your death that was the reason for letting her go.'

'Yes. I can't anymore manage things, you see. The experiment is over.'

'Experiment,' I said.

'Come now,' he said, 'I believe you grasp it, John. I truly believe you do.'

'I've read rather widely,' I said. 'Years ago, I came across the legend of the Buddha.' Goëste folded his hands. He smiled his old strong teeth. 'Buddha was originally a prince,' I said, 'and they resolved to keep all ugly things from him – poverty, disease, old age and death. He saw only beauty. Until one day something went wrong, and he found out the truth.'

Jedidiah Goëste said, 'You see, John, I began to think of it even when I was quite young. From the start, everything comes our way. Even when they tell us lies, the facts are still before us. There is a moment when we must work it out. The old lady in the mauve dress with her hands crippled by rheumatics. The dead dog the cart ran over. The bird shot for the table. In Europe in the Middle Ages they fixed a skull over the church door. Under that skull was written, *Remember thou shall be as me.*' He leaned back. His eyes were black, like hers, but paler with the watery encroachment of old age. 'How does the infant learn?' he said. 'He copies. The sounds from the mouths that become language. The gestures that become manners. The opinions that he will, either adopt or rebel against. And he learns that the sun rises and sets, and as the days and the years go by, he grows, he changes. All around, the lesson is. We grow to our fullness. But after that, we decline. From the summit of that hill, the path leads downwards. Down to weakness and sickness, down to the first lines and wrinkles, the stiffening and the lessening. Down to the bowed spine and the loss of teeth and sight and hearing. Down into the grave that awaits us all. *Remember thou shall be as me.* We are taught from the commencement, and reminded over and over.'

He pointed at the rug before the fire, where I had laid the glass shoes that were not.

'I made those, to show it could be done. I've done many things like that. I had money, John, and time, and a brain. And, I confess, here and there I have experimented with living things – not to hurt them, never that. But to see. Always, to see.'

'Jedella,' I said, 'was never told about old age, or death. Illness was for some reason mentioned, but as something that no longer existed. Pages were cut from books. The people of the house were always young and fit, and when it became likely they would cease to be, they were sent away. And when a squirrel died under her window, Orlen told her it was stunned, and took it back to its tree, and later he showed her the squirrel running on the wall.'

'A girl came to me in the city,' said Jedidiah Goëste, 'it was shocking, I had given her a child. She didn't want it. So she was paid, and I took the child to myself. That was Jedella. She was a baby – younger than Buddha, who I believe was twelve – too young to have learned anything at all. It was so perfect, John, and I had the means. I brought her here, and for those first years, I was her friend. And after, of necessity, I had gone, those who came after me carried on my work. They were well-recompensed, and clever. There were no mistakes. She grew up in a world where no one sickened or aged or died. Where nothing died, and no death was seen, not even the dead animals for her food. Not even the leaves of the trees.'

It was true. She had seen only the pines, renewal but not obvious slough – and then she had come from the open door and down into the woods of fall, where ruby and yellow and wine, the death descends from every tree.

'Now she sees it,' I said. 'She saw it as sickness to begin with. Or something that made no sense. But she's turning towards the terrible fact, Mr Goëste, that all things perish.'

'Recollect,' he said, 'that she is sixty-five years old. She's like a girl. So many lessons, all the same. Can they be unlearned?'

I stood up. I was not angry, I have no word for what I was. But I could no longer sit in the chair before the fire, nor drink the fragrant coffee, nor look in that old man's face that was so strong and sure.

'You've acted God, Mr Goëste.'

'Have I? How can we presume to know how God has acted, or would act?'

'You think you've made her eternally young. You think you've made her immortal.'

'I may have done,' he said.

I answered him, 'In a world where all things come to an end – what will become of her?'

'You will take care of her now,' he said, so easily, so gently. 'Your quiet little town. Good people. Kind people. '

'But her pain,' I said, 'her *pain*. '

Jedidiah Goëste looked at me with her look. He was innocent, in her way. There was no chance against such innocence. 'Pain, I think, is after all in the unfathomable jurisdiction of God. I've never been able to believe that mankind, for all its faults, could devise so horrible and so complex a thing.'

'She never questioned?' I asked.

'Questions spring from doubt. Now she questions, I imagine?'

A log cracked in the fire. There was a small ache in my back I would not have had a year ago.

'If you wish, I should be happy for you to be my guest tonight, John.'

I thanked him and made some excuse. Even then, even there, the etiquette of my father stayed with me. Those first lessons.

As I reached the door, Jedidiah Goëste said one final thing to me: 'I'm glad that she found her way to you.'

But she had not found her way to me, nor to anyone, how could she? She had not found her way.

The years have passed in the town, and it has been faithful to Jedella. She has been protected as best we might. She has her little house behind the church, and her piano that we sent for from the city, her paints, her books – all kinds of books now. She reads for days on end, with her clear dark eyes. Sometimes she will read something out for me when even my glasses fail to help with the small print.

More people have come to the town with time, and for them she is a mystery that, largely, they are indifferent to. The new creatures of the world are very self-involved, and this has taken away some of the curiosity, the prying, that came to us so naturally. But then, the avalanches of war, and fear of war, the wonderful inventions that cause so much harm and confusion and noise, all these things change us, the children of this other world, much more so.

Luke died in a war. I have said elsewhere, and will not, here, what I did there. Many were lost, or lost themselves. But others take those places. I was even famous for a year, and travelled in the cities and on other continents, and grew tired and came home. And there the town was in its misty morning silence, that the new cacophony cannot quite break.

That was a morning like this one, a fall morning, with the colours on the trees, and the new restaurant, where Millie's used to be, was having its windows washed.

But today the restaurant is old and familiar, and instead I passed Jedella's house, and she came out and I knew I should go in, just for an hour, maybe, and drink coffee, and eat chocolate cake which she vaunts, and rightly so.

I went with caution over the road, for now there are sometimes motor-bikes upon it, and as I did, I saw her waiting, pale and slender, a girl, with her hair cut short and permed, a touch of lipstick on her mouth.

She touched my arm at her door.

'Look, John,' she said.

My eyes are not so good as I would like, but there in the pure, sheer sunlight, I did my best to see. She pointed at her cheek, and then, she put one finger to her hair.

'Is it your powder, Jedella? Yes, your hair looks grand.'

And then I did see, as she stood smiling up at me, her eyes full of the morning, of the new beginning of all things, I did see what she had found to show me with such pride. The little crease that had grown in her cheek. The single bright silver hair.

Kiss Kiss

You see, I was only eleven when it began. I'm twenty-three years of age now. Just over twice that lifetime. But did I know more when I was younger? Was I wiser then than now?

The estate was small, and although my father was a prince, we were by no means rich. That is, we had fires in winter, and furs heaped on the beds. There was plenty of game in the forests for my father and his fifteen men to hunt and bring home as dinner. We had wine and beer. And in the spring the blossom was beautiful. And all summer there was the wheat, and afterwards the fruit from the orchards. But I had holes in all but my best dress, as my mother did.

One day, I would have to have something fine, because I would need to be married. I didn't question this, the only use I was, being a girl: the princess. Sixteen was the normal age. My mother said I was pretty, and would do. It was all right. And on my eleventh birthday, he gave me, my father, this incredible present. Since we didn't have so very much, seeing it, I knew, despite appearances, he must think I had a proper value. My mother gasped. I stood speechless. I really didn't need him to say, 'It's gold. Gold over bronze. Be careful with it.'

I said nothing. My mother said, 'But, dearest –'

He cut her short, as usual. 'It can be part of her dowry. They're popular in the city. They're lucky, apparently. You may,' he said, 'throw it up and catch it. Don't roll it along. It would get scratched.'

'Thank you, Papa.'

I held the golden ball in utter awe. It was very heavy. It was, I think, for strong young lordlings to throw about. My slender wrists ached from its weight.

But I took it out through the neglected garden, and walked with it down the overgrown paths, to the lake among the pine trees where, in the worst winters, the wolves came, blue as smoke, and howled.

I've heard it said that sometimes when a man stands near the brink of a cliff, he may think, What if I step over? Just such an awful thought came to me as I stood by the lake, which was muddy and rushy in the summer evening. Suppose I let go the golden ball, and let it roll, scratching itself, over into the deeper water?

No sooner had I thought it, than a bird screeched in the trees of the forest on the lake's far side. And I started, and the ball dropped from my tired hands.

It rolled, flush, through the grass, in through the reeds with their dry, brown-purple flowers. I ran after it all the way, calling to it, stupidly crying, No, no –

And then it slid over the water's edge, straight in and down. Under the surface I saw it glimmer for one whole second, like a drowned sun. And then I saw it no more.

What could I do? I didn't do anything. I stood staring after the lucky golden ball, lost in the brown mirror of water, sobbing.

My father hadn't ever beaten me, at least, not with his hands. He had a hard tongue. I dreaded what he would say. I dreaded what I'd done. To be such a fool.

Gnats whined in the air. One stung me, and I scratched my neck, still crying. The scratching made a noise in my ear that suddenly said, 'Little girl, little princess, why are you weeping?'

I stopped in amazement. Had I imagined it? The voice came again, 'Can I help you, little princess?'

No one was there. Only the gnats furled over the dry flowers. At the edge of the water, in the shallows, something was stirring.

The sun was among the pines now, flashing. It caught the edges of the ripples in brassy rings. And two round eyes.

'Have you lost something precious?'

What was it? A frog … no, it was too big. The round the eyes, coloured like the duller flashes of the sun.

'Yes – I've lost – my golden ball.'

'I saw it go down. I know where it is.'

I thought, blankly, I've gone mad. It's the fright. Like the girl last year when the wild horse ran through the wedding party. She went mad. She was locked away. They'll lock me away.

I turned, to rush off up the sloping ground, towards my father's dishevelled towers.

The voice called again. 'Here I am. Look. You'll see, I'm well able to go after your precious ball.'

Then I stopped and I did look. And it came out of the water part of the way, and I saw it.

I gave a squeal.

It said, 'Don't be afraid. I'm gentle.'

It *was* like a frog. A sort of little, almost-man thing that was a frog. Scaled, a pale yet a dark green, with round, brownish glowing frog's eyes. It had webbed fore-feet that might be hands. It held them up. They had no claws. And in its open mouth seemed nothing, but a long dark tongue.

I was terrified. It was a sprite, a lake-spirit, the sort the old women put out cakes for in the village, to stop their mischief.

It said, plaintively, 'Don't you want your golden ball, then?'

My first adult decision, perhaps, was between these two evils. My angry father, and the uncanny creature from the lake.

'I want the ball.'

'If I fetch it,' said the frog-demon, 'I must have a favour in return.'

'What do you want?'

'To be yours.'

It was so unequivocal – and yet, as I found out soon enough, so subtle. 'Mine? How?'

'To belong to you, princess.'

Was it pride or avarice, a desire for some power in my powerless existence? To have a spirit as my slave. No. I think I only knew I had to get back the ball. And because it hadn't said to me, I must have your virtue, or, I must have your first-born child, as in the stories they do, I was just relieved to say, 'All right. You can be mine. Please fetch it me!'

After it had gone down, with one treacly little *plop*, I stood there thinking I'd been dreaming. I even started to search about for the golden ball, in case that too was a dream, a bad one.

The sun went into the blacker lower third of the forest, and the sky above grew coppery. Crickets started across the fields. An owl called early for the shadows.

Then the water parted again, and up came the necessary golden ball, real and actual and there. It was clasped by two scaley frog hands.

I went gingerly down and took the ball, snatched it. I held it to my breast with all my fingers.

Then the frog-thing's face broke the water. Even then, I could see how sad its face was, the way certain animal faces are. Its eyes might have been made of tawny tears.

'Remember your promise.'

'Yes.'

As I hurried back towards the pile of the house, I heard it coming, hopping, after me. Not looking, I said, '*Go away!*'

'If I belong to you,' it said, 'I must be with you. Every minute. Day and night.'

Then I saw, the way the maiden does, always too late, in the tale, what she has agreed to.

'You can't. You *can't.*'

'You promised me.'

I started to pray then to God, in whom I believed, but from whom I expected nothing, ever. He'd never answered any of my youthful prayers. And didn't do so now.

But the frog-thing came to me, quite near. It stood as high as my knee. It had frog legs, huge webbed feet, without claws. Sunset gleamed on its scales. In its scratch of a voice it said, 'I won't speak to them. I won't tell them you lost the ball. I can do things they'll like. Find things. It will be all right.'

But I ran away. Of course. Of course, it ran after.

In the garden, by the broken statue of a god, an old god even more deaf than God, I had to stop for breath. The golden ball had weighed me down. I hated it. I hated it worse than the frog-demon. In that moment I knew too, how much I hated my father.

The frog had reached me without trouble. It hopped high, right up on the stone god's arm. And out of its mouth it pulled a most beautiful flower. Perhaps it had brought it from the lake. Creamy pink, with a faint perfume, thinner and more fresh than roses.

The demon leaned, and before I could flinch away, it had put the flower in my hair.

I thought, out of my new hatred for my father, Anyway, he'll kill this thing as soon as he sees it.

I tossed my head, and the flower filled the air with scent. I hated everyone by now, and all things. Let them all kill each other.

'Come on, then,' I said, and went towards the house, and the frog-thing hopped along at my side.

They called it Froggy. That was their way. They used to throw it scraps from the table. It wouldn't ever touch meat. It had a little fish, and it liked green things, and fruit, but I don't know how it ate for it seemed to have no teeth.

And this I never learned.

In the beginning, they were more circumspect with it – after, that is, the first outburst.

When I came into the hall, the women were at the hearth, and the boy was turning the smaller spit for the dead hares my father had taken in the forest. The house had a kitchen, but it was only used when there were guests. Half the time the bread was baked here too.

The owl-shadows were gathering, red from the fire, and one of the men was lighting the candles. In all this flicker of red and dark, no one saw the frog for some while.

I got up to my mother, who was wearing her better hall-dress that had only one darn in it. She took hold of me at once, and called her maid to comb my hair.

It was the maid who saw the frog first. She screamed out loud and pulled out a clump of my hair.

'Uh – mistress – ah! What is it?'

I was too ashamed to speak. My mother naturally didn't know. She peered at the thing.

It stood there patiently, looking up at her with its sad face. It had vowed not to speak to anyone but me.

The maid was crossing herself, spitting at the corner to avoid bad luck.

At the fire they had turned and were gawping. And just then my father stormed in with his men, and three of the hunting dogs, stinking of blood and unwashed masculinity. One of the dogs, the biggest, saw the frog at once. He came leaping for it, straight up the hall. As this happened, the frog gave a jump. It was up a tree of lit candles, wrapped there about one of the iron spikes, and the wax splashed its scales, but it didn't make a sound.

The dog growled and drooled, pressed against the candle-tree, its eyes red, its hair on end.

My father strode over at once.

He said to me, as I might have known he would, 'Where's your golden ball, girl?'

'Here, Father.'

He looked at that. Then up the candle-tree. My father frowned.

'By Christ,' said my father.

Although I hated him, hate can't always drive out fear, as love can't. In terror I blurted, 'It came out of the lake. It followed me home. I couldn't stop it. It wants to be with me.'

My mother put her hand over her mouth, a gesture she often resorts to, as if she knows she might as well not cry out or talk, since no one will bother.

My father said, 'I've heard of them. Water demons. Why did it come out? What were you doing?' He glared at me. This must be my fault. And it was.

'Nothing, Papa.'

He folded his arms, and lowered at the frog. The frog eased itself a little on the stand. Leaning over from the waist, it bowed, like a courtly gentleman, to my father.

Who gave a bark of laughter. Turning, he kicked the dog away. 'It's lucky. They bring good luck. We must be careful of it.'

He ordered them to carve some of the half-raw hare, and offered it to the frog, which wouldn't have it. Then one of the women crept up with a cup of milk. The frog took this in a webbed paw, and had a few sips. Despite its frog mouth, it didn't slurp.

Once they had driven the dogs off, the men stood about laughing and cursing, and the frog jumped on to the table.

It got up on its hands and ran about, and the men laughed more, and even the women slunk close to see. When it reached the unlit candles at the table's centre, it blew on them. They flowered into pale yellow flame.

This drew applause. They said to each other, See, it's *good* magic. It's funny. And when it scuttled over to me and jumped out and caught my girdle, hanging on there at my waist so I shrank and almost shrieked, they cheered. I was favoured. They'd heard of such things. It would be a *good* year, now.

It was. It was a good year. The harvest was wonderful, and some gambling my father did brought in a few golden coins. Also, the frog found a ruby ring that had been lost – or hidden – by an ancestor in the house. All this was excellent. And they said, when they saw me coming, the demon at my side, 'Here's the princess, with her frog.'

But that was after. It took them a little while to be so at home with it. And that first night, after my father encouraged me to feed it from my plate, let it share my cup of watered wine, when it started to follow me up the stone stair, where the torches smuttily burned, he stood up. 'Put it outside your door,' he said. 'We don't know it's clean in its habits.' This, from one who had, more than once, thrown up from drink in my mother's bed. Who defecated in a pot, who occasionally pissed against indoor walls. The servant women being expected to see to it all.

When we reached my room, I tried to shut the frog-demon outside in the passage. But it slipped past.

'I must be with you,' it said, the first time it had spoken since we came in. 'Day and night. Every minute.'

'Why?' I wailed.

'Because I must.'

'Horrible slimy thing!'

I tried to kick it aside. Did I say I was a nice girl? I hadn't learnt at all to be nice, and was almost as careless and cruel to servants and animals as the rest of them.

But it eluded my foot, which anyway was only in a threadbare shoe, not booted like the feet of the always-dog-kicking men.

It wasn't slimy. I'd felt it. It was dry and smooth, its scales like thin plates of polished dull metal. When it sprang lightly on my bed, I took off my so far useless shoe, and flung it. But the frog-demon caught my shoe, and put it on its head like a hat.

At that, finally, I too laughed.

I didn't want it on my pillow. But on to my pillow it came. Its breath was cool and smelled of green leaves. In the dark, its eyes were two small lamps.

It sang to me. A sort of story. At last I lay and listened. The story was the accustomed kind my nurse had told me, but I was not yet too old for it. A maiden rescued from her brutal father by a handsome prince. Even then, even liking the tale, I didn't believe such men existed. I knew already what men were, and, without understanding, what they did to women, having seen it here and there, my father's men and the kitchen girls. It had looked and sounded violent, and both of them, each time, seemed to be in pain, scratching and shaking each other in distress.

Even so. No one had sat with me and told me a story, not for years.

In the night, I woke once, and it was curled up against my head. It smelled so green, so clean. I touched its cool back with my finger. It was mine, after all. Now I too owned something. And it would only talk to me.

Already when I look back, my childhood seems far away, my girlhood even farther. Old women speak of themselves in youth as if of other women. I am so old, then?

During the time they all came quite round to it, and called it Froggy, and the Princess's Frog, I must have been growing up with wild rapidity, the way the young do, every day a little more.

While it performed tricks for them, found for them things that had been lost, seemed to improve the hunting, the harvests and the luck, I became, bit by bit, a woman.

You *see*, I don't remember so much of it, because so much was always the same. It's all, in memory, one long day, one long night. The incidents are jumbled together like old clothes in a chest.

I recollect my bleeding starting, and the fuss, and how I hated it – I do so still but the alternative state of pregnancy appeals less. I recall the bear in the forest winter who mauled one of the men, and he died. I remember the priest coming on holy days, and blessing us, and that he too liked to touch the buttocks of the maids, and once of the kitchen boy, who later ran away.

The priest looked askance at Froggy. He asked was it some deformed thing from a travelling freak show, and my father prudently said he had bought it for me, since it was clever and made me laugh. Also, he said, it was fiercer than the dogs and would protect me. That was a lie, too. The frog was only gentle. Although, in the end, the dogs respected it and gave up trying to catch it. The biggest dog would let Froggy ride him, and all the while Froggy would murmur in the dog's ear. This was after the big dog was bitten by a snake in the forest, and ran home yelping, with terror in his eyes, knowing he would die of snake-bite, or the men would cut his throat.

But Froggy, when the dog fell down exhausted, scuttled over and latched its wide mouth on the bite. Froggy sucked out the poison, and dribbled it on the floor with the blood. Everyone stood back in astonishment, one of the men muttering, stupidly, if the dog died it would be Froggy's fault. But the dog recovered, and never forgot.

The women took to tempting Froggy to lick cuts on their hands to make them better. Froggy never refused. They said it was because they rubbed on honey first. They called this a 'frog's kiss'.

It never spoke to anyone but me.

And I remember one afternoon, when I had the by-now familiar black pain of menstruation in my belly, and I was lying in the spring grass, and Froggy was sitting quietly on my stomach, where the pain was, kneading me gently, until I was soothed and slept and the pain died.

The sun was in the orchard trees, that were just then losing their blossom, and all this yellow-white-green shone behind my frog, all puffed with light. The frog sang or chanted. Some old tale again. What was it? A knight who rescued a maiden. I saw for the first time how beautiful it was, this creature.

Its amber eyes like jewels, the smooth pear shape of its body, like burnished, carven, pale, dark jade. The paws that were webbed hands and feet, and had no claws. The sculpted mouth, with its rim of paler green, toothless and fragrant. The healing tongue.

I smiled at the frog, not from amusement, but from love. I loved it. It was my friend.

After this, I seemed to learn things. The meanings of birdsong. The ways of animals, and of weather. I was more gentle, too. Who had I learned that from but Froggy? There was no one else.

My mother pulled me to her about this time. She was, despite the luck, still unchilded, and my always-displeased father had slapped her. There was a bruise under her eye where one of his rings had cut her skin. She seemed proud of the bruise, often touching at it in the hall, as if to show off that her husband still paid her attentions.

'Look at you, such a big girl. You must have more binding for your bosoms. And you mustn't run about so much.' Sometimes I would receive these lessons, no one else took any notice of her. Finally neither did I. But now she added, playfully tweaking my ear, 'You must have earrings. He'll want to find you a husband soon. He's mentioned it. A man with land and soldiers. You're a pretty girl, if only you'd leave off these sluttish ways. Do you ever comb your hair? I'll send you the girl to brush it every night with rose oil.'

I thought of my father, planning to marry me to some large, uncouth and appalling landowner, someone like himself. From my thirteenth birthday, until now, I'd tried never to think about it. But I was fifteen. The awful appointment approached.

I ran off as soon as I could, the frog bouncing after me like a jade ball – the golden one had long ago been put into a coffer.

In fact, I don't remember I ever spoke of my troubles to Froggy. He was always there. Every minute. Night and day. He knew. And when my stomach hurt he kneaded it, or when I woke crying from a nightmare he comforted me, or made me laugh. I'll say He, now. I might as well.

I sat on the old stone horse statue at the foot of the garden, which now I was tall and agile enough to climb, and Froggy sat in my lap, plaiting for me, web-fingered, a crown of red daisies. Butterflies danced, and the willows by the lake looked very bright. Later there would be a summer storm.

Froggy told me a story. It was new. A prince was cast into a dungeon. His lady came to find him and rescued him by putting magic on the bars.

At first I didn't know why the story was so strange.

Then I said, 'But it's the man who rescues the maiden. She's weak and helpless. She can't do anything. He's strong and clever. It has to be him.'

'Oh, no,' said Froggy. 'Not always. A man may be made weak, and overthrown. And do you think men are so clever, then?'

I shook my head. I gabbled, in sudden horror and fear, 'I'll have to marry one of them. He'll take me away.'

And then I said, 'He may be unkind to you as well.'

'But I shan't be with you,' said Froggy softly. 'If you marry this man.'

Astounded I stared. He raised his wonderful topaz-amber eyes. 'Not be with me – but you're always there.'

'Then, it would be impossible. He'd kill me, you see. Or I'd die.'

I put my arms round Froggy and held him. He never struggled, as an animal, a puppy or a cat, would do. I laid my cheek against the crown of his head, the scales of smoky jade. 'You're my only friend. Don't leave me.'

'It must be. If you marry the man your father finds you.'

My tears will have streamed over him. But I said, at last, 'It won't happen. I'll stay here. I won't be married. Never.'

I might as well have said. Night won't fall, or the sun won't rise tomorrow. Before when I first bled, and ran about screaming, thinking I was dying – no one had bothered to prepare me – Froggy had calmed me instead – before I bled, I'd never have thought such a filthy thing was possible. And with marriage, the threat had always been there, as long as I could recall.

My husband-to-be visited us just before Christmas that winter.

He was like the bear they said had killed my father's man, and clad in a black bearskin cloak, with clasps of gold. He had a gold stud in his ear, too. His boots were leather, his shirt embroidered. His men were well-turned-out and armed to the teeth. He stank of everything. I can't begin to itemize his smells. He was about forty, and I nearly sixteen.

I, contrarily, had been bathed in the porcelain chair-bath, and my hair had been washed and brushed with rose oil. I had on my best, newest dress, without darns, and earrings of grey-white pearl, and a ring of gold.

When he saw me, he struck a pose, my intended husband; he bowed and fawned, as if I were some great lord, or a bishop, or a king. Everyone laughed heartily, and he straightened up all good nature.

'You see, I like her. I'll take her.' Then he kissed me. He had shaved, but already his skin was rough and he scraped my mouth. But that would be nothing.

The dinner was lavish. My frog did wonderful tricks, lighting the candles, cutting a fruit with a tap of his hand, finding things people had hidden, and juggling the bones of some poor little birds we had eaten.

In the end, we were able to go, the women and Froggy, to leave the men to get spectacularly drunk. My mother took me to her bower, the shabby room that led from the bedchamber. She sat me by the fire to pat my flushed face and feed me sugared walnuts.

'What a good girl. He liked you so. Oh it will be a lovely wedding. The church all hung with flowers. The day after your birthday. And you must have three new gowns, your father says. He's a generous man. And your husband will shower you with things in your first months. He's rich. Be careful to please him and you may even see yourself in silk.'

'How do I please him?' I asked, sullen with terror.

'It's simple, child. Never ever say no. God said women must be obedient. Do whatever your lord wants. And – well, I'll speak of that later, your wedding night. But you must always pretend that you like what he does. Recollect always, he's your superior. You owe everything to him.'

I couldn't say that he made me sick, that I wished to throw up from his kiss. I knew about sex, although she had tried to hide it from me, as she had successfully hidden menstruation. The thought of that struggling and grappling and the obvious pain, with him, repelled me so greatly I couldn't even think about it.

I said, 'I see, Mama.' And at my feet, the frog ate a little sugar, staring into the fire that made his eyes look, also, green.

When she sent me to bed – I must be at my best to see the monstrous husband off tomorrow: in fact she knew my delighted, drunken father would want intercourse with her tonight – I ran. Froggy in my arms, and shouted at the woman with the rose oil to go away.

Then, rocking Froggy, I wept, until needles seemed to be drawn through my eyes.

My own fire was out by then. It was growing stealthily and awesomely cold. I said, 'Let's go into the forest. The wolves may kill us or we'll freeze. Let's do it. Anything. Anything instead of *him*.'

There was a long silence. I heard the stars crackling like icy knives in the black sky. Then the frog spoke back to me.

'There's another way.'

'No. No other way. Nothing.'

'Yes. Do you remember the maiden who was rescued?'

'Oh, that story –'

'Do you remember the prince that the maiden saved with her love?'

'Shush,' I said. I would say today, But this is true life. This is real, and inescapable. Here, there are no miracles or magic. Then I said, 'Don't talk about those silly things. They can't help me.'

'Yes. I'll tell you how.'

I held him in my arms and he spoke and I listened. His voice – the very voice he used to charm the dog, to charm *them* – scratchy and little, mesmerizing in the silence.

'A spell can be broken so simply, princess. Do you love me by now?'

'*Yes.*'

'Then all you need do is kiss me. On my frog's mouth. Is that unthinkable?'

'I had to kiss *him*.'

'I'm not like that.'

I looked down at him, my slumberous, umbrous jewel. His holy frog face. My friend. 'I'd have done it – I just thought you might not like me to –'

'I?' He couldn't smile. His eyes smiled, half closing, like a cat's. 'Do it now,' he said.

I never in my life did anything more easily. I lifted him up, and kissed him. His mouth was like a summer leaf, cool, a little moist, smelling of fresh salad, and with a crumb of sugar from the walnuts – *sweet*.

When I opened my eyes it was because my hands and my arms were empty.

'Who are you?' I said. I was so afraid, I was numb.

He said, 'My God, it hurt so much. Worse than before. Oh God.'

He leaned on my wooden chair, and then dropped into it. His shining golden hair fell long over his pale face.

I had never seen a man who was so beautiful. He wasn't like a man. An angel, perhaps. I heard him breathing. Presently; in his musical voice, he said to me, 'Little princess, my enemies worked against me. They changed me to the form – of what you saw. But your loving kiss – has brought me back. Now I'm yours for ever, and you're mine.'

His eyes, as he looked at me, were not amber or green. They were very dark, the colour of night, just as his hair was the colour of day. His garments too. Fur, gold, steel, gems.

What did I feel? I was excited. I tingled all over. The fairy story had come true.

I didn't need to hear the sound of hoofs below, galloping, bells ringing from the village, to know his men were coming, all glorious as he was, washed, perfumed and brave, armed to the teeth. Spell broken, he could drive the unwanted husband away. And my father – he would never cease to be grateful to me for the alliance I had brought him instead, this other husband, a prince who had been a frog.

And yet, I only went back to him slowly. He was now far larger than I. My head, when he stood up, reached just below his shoulder. The enormous rings on his fingers were icy. He had a smell like fire not water. But it was very cold.

My arms were empty, but he took me into his instead. What was wrong? What did I miss?

Oh, I missed my friend.

There was never such a wedding. They still talk about it, seven years after. Of course, I left my father's house. A bride does. She belongs to her husband. But he owns a princedom. My father cried large tears of greed as he bade me farewell.

There's everything here. A bed all my own, with a canopy shaped like a firmament and stitched with diamond stars, a different bath for every day of the week, marble, rose-quartz, cinnabar, and so on. There are foods, and drinks, I'd never heard of. He has a menagerie, with lions. His people, now he has come back, worship him like a god.

It was almost a year before he began to eat meat again. This was advised, to make him strong, and it worked, because soon after I conceived a child and it was a son. I've given him three sons now, and my body has changed shape a little. This happens. A woman's lot. Sex remains a mystery to me. But yes, it does hurt.

In our third year together, he struck me for the first time. It was over some small quarrel – I'd forgotten my mother's rule of obedience. I mean, God's rule. My husband was gracious afterwards, said he was sorry, and sent me a rose made of rubies, just the colour my blood had been from the broken tooth.

Despite the baths, he's just a little understandably lax that way. He smells of health and meat and wine, sweat, lust, sometimes of other women. From politeness, he says, he shuns me during menstruation. He never sings to me, or tells me stories, being very busy. He kicks the dogs.

I don't know why he changed so much, changed spiritual shape as pregnancy and birth physically have altered me. Was he always this way, when human? Yes, naturally. A fine, noble virile man. A prince. He doesn't juggle, never lights candles himself. Evidently, he's mislaid all the magic.

Every night, when I'm alone, as increasingly now, thank God, I am, in my heavenly bed, I say a prayer for the one I had. He taught me so much. He was my friend, my frog.

He never left me. I loved him. Not like a baby, or a pet, not like a man. A unique and crystal love, all shattered now in pieces. I didn't know what was happening, and he must have suffered, being that other one. And so we wasted it, that perfect time. Now, it's forbidden to all of us to speak of it, the period of his life when he was enchanted. When he was a frog.

Nevertheless, I dream of it still. Sometimes. All that we did, when I was slender, young and free, and how I loved him so. And how I lost him forever to that hateful betrayal of a kiss.

Lost in the World

Magnanimous Despair alone
Could show me so divine a thing,
Where feeble hope could ne'er have flown
But vainly flapt its tinsel wing.

Andrew Marvell

1

On the last day of every month, at the same hour, the same visitor would mount the steps of the narrow house on the west edge of Clock Tower Hill. In summer it would be sunset, and all the normal phantasmagoria of dragons, galleons, and burning towers would be on display in the sky. In winter the dark was well set, the stars above the hill dimmer than the street lamps, perhaps a light snow falling. In autumn, there was the magical dusk as now, when Monsieur Mercile, immaculate and apparently stern, would stand on the top step and ring the bell. And it would be evident that the dusk's magic was quite lost on Monsieur Mercile, that he felt no pang, just as he rarely noted the stars, the dragons, and towers, of winter and summer. This was custom, his visit to the narrow house, not unmixed with duty. He was a man of the world, understood its rules, had kept them, and prospered. But the one he visited, he was different.

In answer to the bell, a servant woman came, compact and elderly, a being from an earlier era, where she had completely stayed in all but body.

Monsieur Mercile acknowledged her, and passed into the house.

The rooms of the visit were on the floor above. The first was a sort of pleasant alcove, lined with books, a kind of library, having padded easy chairs by the fire, and on a highly polished stand a globe in ebony. Through the open doors of the alcove was a dining room, an oval table perched with candles, and a sideboard of sparkling decanters; here too a fire burned gently, cheerfully.

The comfortable rooms showed nothing of a woman's touch: Beyond the meticulous servant and one careful girl, no woman ever had access to them. They were graced with bachelor things, and Monsieur Mercile might have felt happiness and security in them, but he was never quite able to do so, here; here there was always a demand on him. The demand was implicit in his friend, Oberand, who now stood up before the library fire.

The two men greeted each other as if they had not met for a year, and yet with the sort of offhand sidelong glances of the eye that evidence usualness. They asked each other how they went on and mentioned the weather, and a certain cognac was produced, which they both settled to like pigeons to a familiar roof.

Oberand, like Mercile, was slim and upright, and in his fifties, but where Mercile's waist had slightly thickened, Oberand was only a little stooped at the shoulders. Oberand's hair receded, where Mercile's had retreated altogether. Oberand's eyes were larger, brighter, lacking glasses, and fraught with thin lines of pain, perhaps physical, but perhaps of something older, deeper, more difficult to bear. Mercile had no mark like this. His hands had stiffened with a trace of rheumatism, but his heart was light. What of Oberand's heart?

After their brandy, and their introductory conversation, they went into the dining room, and here soon appeared an extremely tasty, ordinary dinner. There were too a trio of excellent wines. It was all very good, orderly, and pleasing, redolent of the male satisfactions and luxuries often used in literature as the preface to a ghost story.

And Monsieur Mercile warmed like wax, lost a certain hardness of contour he had had, seemed to be thinking, *Now this isn't so bad. You see, there's nothing to dread.*

Then they took their cigarettes and wine to the fire in the library, and Oberand paused to lay one finger on the ebony globe.

Here it comes! thought Mercile, and braced himself.

The stroking of the globe was an omen as constant and unfortuitous as a comet.

'I took out the small map again,' said Oberand softly, as if they were conspirators, as if they had waited only for this moment to begin – and probably this was true of Oberand; Mercile thought so. 'I mean Eshlo's map. I sat up over it until three this morning. After a time, I began to seem to connect a particular ridge with a description in the geographia. I took out the two other maps of Klein's. There is one distinct formation, to the south. Eshlo marks this as the Mountains of the White Moon – I love that name, so evocative, so unhelpful, and yet … so alluring.'

'Yes,' said Mercile, 'it is a marvellous name.'

'It's possible to pinpoint this geography. The first of Klein's maps relates it to the Charda region, as you know. But then, I wonder with Klein if there isn't some game involved, if some of his assertions aren't meant to be misleading.'

'That might be likely.'

'And does he offer any reward for struggle? But my struggling attention seems to bear fruit.'

Mercile could not quite bring himself to answer, but naturally Oberand did not take this gap for disapproval. Oberand trusted Mercile, had done so for more than ten years. It was incumbent upon Mercile, now, to be trusted.

As always happened, every month, the floodgate of Oberand's obsession had opened as it did before no other one, since no other *could* be trusted save only Mercile. The waters roared and poured forth, as vehement and strong as they had been a decade ago, stronger probably. And Mercile listened, as he always did, every month, with a great patience blunted even as it had been honed, threadbare even as it was perfected. Every visit to Oberand concluded in this way, in two or three hours of Oberand's obsession (until Mercile escaped) – Oberand's maps, his notions, discoveries, dismissals, the throbbing violence, only just held in, of what he believed and *knew* and could not prove, and for which he had been mocked and laughed from eminence, squashed into the gutter, discarded by everyone.

For Oberand had been reckoned a genius, at the start. He was not merely a literary figure of reckoned worth, a bright star elevated at an age supposed precociously early, but also a scholar. Among the countries of manuscript he was thought an explorer. For Oberand had translated screeds previously declared inaccessible, he had unearthed, paying terrifying prices for them, obscure treatises and scripts – of the Romans, from Egypt, and further back and farther off. He had dealt in a murky underworld of the esoteric as other men had trafficked in bodies. And by that he made of himself a creature fabulous, permitted only in the glaring light of its own cleverness. And then it happened that Oberand, thirty-eight years of age and coruscating brightly, came on the work of Eshlo, an explorer out of the countries of landscape. And, too (doubtless), a liar and romancer.

But Oberand believed the words of Eshlo; they caught his fancy and fascinated him.

There had never been in the life of Oberand anything but his work, the pen and the page. He had never, except perhaps briefly in adolescence, felt anything special for a woman, he had not itched, let alone ached through love. The pursuit, the conquest, the culmination were intellectual, and he knew them regularly.

Now, as with a mighty philanderer, for whom love had been always too easy, there must come an elusive quarry, one that did not consent, succumb. In a space of weeks Oberand left everything he had in hand to search after that which Eshlo proffered, to hunt down the clues and keys of which there were hundreds, spurious though they might be, *ridiculous* though they might be. In doing this, Oberand uncovered Klein, a scholar so obscure he was almost invisible, but Oberand lifted him up on high, to the very pedestal where he had placed Eshlo, and lit before them a flaming torch for all to see. From the hilltop Oberand bellowed. He had been given an unlicensed and uncensored voice, he had been made a darling of that most dangerous fraternity, the mature, wise, cunning, erudite, and cruel. They will worship heroes, then at a stumble tear them to pieces in their teeth. And Oberand had stumbled. What a distance he had to fall.

Eshlo had travelled widely, in the Indies, and in Africa. His accounts were exotic, combining the information of facts with flights of elaboration having a logical wildness resembling the development of inspired symphonies. Was it the logic that had misled Oberand? If so, only at a single juncture. Many of Eshlo's claims he had amusedly sloughed. But one story, the very wildest, he had defended as if he had been present at its inception.

For Eshlo claimed to have come upon a pocket of incredible land, a freak valley locked inside a mountain wall unscalable, and penetrated by him via a secret entry that, even in his documents, he had omitted to describe, referring to it only as the Hidden Door, and marking it only in this way on his maps.

The valley, when reached, was of an appalling beauty. It was a land from the prehistoric dawn, a place of giant plants, carbon swamps, and a sea like sweat, and inhabited by monsters, huge beasts and flying things that stormed and raged and *were,* in defiance of time.

Like an echo, Klein backed up this wonder, claiming himself not to have witnessed such a place but from innumerable sources to have heard legends of it. The natives of that area, Klein posited with imaginative flirtatiousness, avoided the mountain slopes for fear accidentally of being precipitated to their doom in the valley of monsters. (Eshlo, who had refused the secret of his entry, also denied readers the means of his exit.) Several of the indigenous populace of hutments and villages had been lost in this manner, Klein avowed, stipulating a cave or hole through which they descended. A god was propitiated in the region, a god said to be white, and of abnormal size, a giant like the plants and beasts of the valley.

Klein quoted many passages, both in their original language and in adequate translation, but the oddity of sections of syntax pre-translated instantly led a critic to deduce that Klein had himself invented these paragraphs of Latin, Greek, Graeco-Persian, and the Egyptian hieroglyphs with which his essays on the subject were scattered – for the Egyptians also had heard of the monsters of the valley, which they had at first named in terms of a coffin of the day's fall, a land of shadow through which Ra the sun must pass each night, overcoming what rampaged there in order to return into the world.

The maps of Klein related to Africa as he had known it from travellers' tales and the official reports of colonial officers. Everything was second or third hand, but he too, though never having met with Eshlo, never having himself gone farther than the hills above the City of Paradys, had caught the fantasy that Eshlo exhaled, had been poisoned by it. As, in turn, was Oberand.

To make matters worse (perhaps), both Eshlo and Klein were long dead by the hour of Oberand's first discovery of the Valley of God, as Eshlo, next Klein, had called it. Oberand could not, no one could, question the perpetrators of this nightmare- dream. Alone, he impaled himself on the hook, and presently was nailed up, crucified, by those who until then had sung his paean and encouraged him in everything.

Possibly his eccentricity alone would not have alienated them. If he had kept a measure of lightness, and so of light. If he could have chuckled, smiled at his own enthrallment, if he could have said: *Well, I may be wrong.* But Oberand was accustomed by then to be right. And such was his passion that he shouted, argued, insulted, twice came to blows.

No one would believe in his belief. His brilliance and innocence went bitter and rotted on the boughs of his mind.

Inside three years he had shut himself away. He reformed his life to an insistent search, a scientific chiselling and scalpelling, of the truth as he had found it. He amassed further material, he dissected and quantified that material he had.

Sometimes he wrote a little. But always, in some however subtle way, it was tainted with his obsession. He was published as a curiosity, and then he was not published. The lecture halls and palaces of books did not any more clamour for him. He was cut. He was forgotten. It was as if a solid figure of iron had faded into mist.

And yet, this stooped man, fifty-two years of age, seared with a hot-cold life, had a dreadful fire that could not be put out. And it was this Mercile confronted, this intolerable and pointless, relentlessly gouging fire, howling on inside the unobliterated shell. Confronted tonight again, also, for the thousandth time, or maybe the thousandth-and-tenth. For Oberand could not keep it down. Mercile was the only one left to him, the only one who had never scorned, never ridiculed, always apparently tacitly accepting the veracity of Eshlo's valley, listening to the facts of it over and over, never quibbling, offering only sympathetic assent, the occasional partial challenge by which Oberand might fuel himself further for his burning. Mercile had never let him down, not once, not in fourteen years. This, of course, pre-supposes Mercile had, originally, met Oberand more often – or the thousand and ten times would be in arrears.

And to Oberand this had been because Mercile credited the truth of the Valley of God. But it was not that. It was only the valiant loyalty of friendship. Something as deep, and as shallow – as useless – as that.

An hour passed. Mercile knew this for he had begun to glance surreptitiously at the clock on the mantelpiece. It was terrible, the slow passage of time now, for decently he could not yet absent himself. Calm and unequivocal, Mercile felt building within him, as always, an unspecified urge to flight, or worse, to choke Oberand to silence.

The maps were now spread on the table, the geographia had been brought. Animated, like a boy, Oberand went about the display. He discoursed on the potential of Klein's frivolity, of Eshlo's secretiveness. 'No one is meant to find this place. Yet we are invited to it. Irresistibly we are seduced.'

He dreamed of the valley. Mercile knew this, for Oberand had told him, now and then. Oberand already had gone there, had wandered the jungle forests, stared into the pools of salt, and heard the trampling of the vast feet of things that elsewhere had left only bones under the rocks of centuries.

'I feel the moment has come to collate these disparate works, to publish my own conclusions,' said Oberand suddenly. The clock ticked. Oberand said, 'Don't you agree, some reorganization of the treatise is in order?'

'But,' said Mercile, slowly, 'your publishers –'

'No, I must approach others. Perhaps I'll need to put up the money myself. I realize perfectly the low esteem in which I'm held, as if by tongs.'

'But,' said Mercile, 'further efforts with this work – What else can be said of it?'

'Very much,' said Oberand. 'I can speak volumes.'

'You should not,' said Mercile.

'Oh, my friend, don't worry on my behalf. What else can they do to me or say of me?'

Mercile felt the knife rise in him, its handle toward his hand. He had never understood it was a knife that had been forged by the years of patience and listening, the *boredom*. He tried to evade. He said, 'But why expose yourself to more of the vicious attacks that –'

'Why?' Oberand cried, his eyes giving off a flash from the flames of the hearth and the spirit. 'Because the truth must be spoken at whatever cost.'

'You must face it,' said Mercile abruptly, 'this truth is doubtful. For God's sake, give it up.'

And now the clock ticked more loudly, and the fire cracked like gunshot. Little sounds in the street, a whisper of wind, a distant song, came up and filled the room, thickening its air until it was nearly unbreathable.

'But I thought,' said Oberand, 'that you, of all of them –' He stopped, and Mercile hung his head. Inside him was an awesome sadness, as if Oberand had just told him he, Oberand, was near death.

'Pardon me,' said Mercile humbly, at last. 'I've tried very hard.'

'No, I don't pardon you,' said Oberand. 'You should not have tried. Or you should have tried much harder. Did you only wait all these years to make a fool out of me tonight?'

'Oberand, my faith in you is unimpaired. Only I believe that your trust in this thing – is preposterous, ill-founded. I should have said so long before.'

'You must leave my house,' said Oberand. 'You must go at once. There's nothing to say.'

Mercile was shocked, yet not surprised. The knife had glittered in his hand, he had used it. What did he expect now? With an exhausted relief strongly enhanced by automatic regret, he rose, shaking his head in an effort at normalcy.

'Then I shall leave, at once. I'm very sorry.'

Oberand said nothing. His face was blank, wiped of everything. He had been stabbed in the back, of course, what else?

Mercile went down, donned his greatcoat, stepped into the street. Below, he glanced at the house, wondering if he would enter it again, aware he would not, then turned into the night of lamps and leaves. He felt a satisfaction. It was terrible. He nearly laughed as he walked homeward; certainly he could not keep back a smile.

2

The great mountain range filled the sky, and was the sky. Pitted and scarred, fissured and cracked, it was not white but dark. It had earned Eshlo's name for it not through its tints, but because it seemed to belong to the surface of a dead satellite circling the earth. Anything might lie inside the wall of it. It was impenetrable.

The man who sat in the camp half a mile from the mountains' foot was tall, thinned, and sunburnt by the lion orb of summer. He was thirty-eight. So much he knew, feeling these things sit on him, the frame within which his soul balanced. He looked from his own clear eyes, scanning the dusty plain and the first clawed slopes that pushed out of it. In the etheric sky a pair of vultures dawdled. They had been there about an hour, interested by something on the middle heights, something not yet dead enough to warrant their descent. He had noticed, no bird ever flew toward the summit of the mountains. Nothing came up over them, except rounded drifts of cloud toward sunset, like steam.

He had been here, at the foot, a month, thirty-one days. Before that was the journey, a period not of time but of time's dissolution, an unravelling of dates and seasons, flowing sidelong, nearly backward. There had been sea, a crust of land, a wide river with a belching steamer, at length the long sinuous tributary of the Charda, with its curtains of banks dropped to the water, the masks of its reflected islands. Lions passed, or lay in the sky. A herd of zebra galloped, an alligator raised its artefact of head – such images pinned themselves upon his brain. The man thought he should and must remember such things distinctly. But then he saw that visually they did not matter, that he might let them go from him if they wished; thus they stayed.

At first he had been fearful. So much so that seasickness and mal de terre had almost disabled him. Then, as he began to accept that he was quite adrift, lost and companionless, without hope of assistance, he relaxed, grew stronger, left behind the stomach cramps and blinding migraines, and emerged from his five decades into the newer younger body, which had wasted no years, which had sprung here immediately after Eshlo's song and Klein's echo. Somewhere on the river of the Charda, while the two black men rowed and the black white stared about, his rifle ready, Oberand caught up his younger self, who all that while had been there ahead of him, waiting.

They moved through the land as Eshlo had, as if nothing had altered, save in the villages they could now barter for cigarettes. It was all quite familiar to him, the people coloured like coal and the beasts of the plain, and the towering sky and the river, and the mountains finally rising into view. Eshlo had been here, and told him. More, he had himself been here, often.

They made the camp under the Mountains of the White Moon. None of them had before approached the place, apart from Oberand. The man who cooked was superstitious; he had heard something of the region. He made a shrine by his improvised cook house and sank into it a collection of bones and teeth, for the god, the giant. Oberand had tried to question this man. The man then became heated, hysterical. Sweat flew off him and he gesticulated, refusing to look at the mountains or to say anything that was of use. Froth sprayed out of his mouth and Andre, the black white, touched Oberand's arm, glancing at him from his odd eyes, one black and one pale gray. 'He knows nothing. Best to leave him, monsieur.' Oberand obeyed, and Andre ordered the cook back to his rice with sharp staccato words.

Oberand explored the base of the mountains with Andre. They climbed a little, Andre the guide and adviser. He would never fully meet the eyes of the white man, he had been taught not to.

They found caves, and chasms where smouldering chains of water fell, they found the carcasses of things, one with hyenas feasting on it, the nests of birds abandoned, a defile with old painting on a wall, but these symbols gave no revelation. Every cave had a back. Each access ended against the gut wall of the rock. From boulders they looked down at the tiny camp, and saw the blacks lazing or quarrelling over a game, and the river far away like a varnished seam in the ground.

'There is no way through,' said Andre.

'Yes,' said Oberand, 'of course. There is.'

Andre was the first man Oberand had had any prolonged conversation with since Mercile. For this reason Oberand did not trust Andre. Andre was not like Mercile. He was young, and could have been a prince if his blood had not been mixed. His white drunkard of a father had taught him books, mathematics, and two languages. Andre had grown up aware he had been ruined for everything, accepting, wise, and mostly silent. Of the Valley of God he had heard, distantly, now and then. It was one of the dim wandering wisps of myth that go about any continent. It was a white man's myth of the darkness, and as such he gave it a defined and cordoned pen. The white portion of Andre's mind suggested to him that only white men would evolve a legend of black men worshiping a white god. But the giantism was not alien. There were stone cities of the jungles, and the size of these cities did not belong with the six-foot men of present days but, like certain temples of Egypt, suggested bigger beings nearer to the sun.

Eshlo's maps, and Klein's maps, brought into the realm of the actual, were a travesty. Though the mountains had been recognisable, they were also altered by reality. Small vital geological clues, essential in locating Eshlo's Hidden Door, were changed or unrevealed, or else had only existed in the imagination of the writer.

It was the splitting off from Mercile, the betrayal by Mercile, which had brought Oberand to the Mountains of the White Moon, more than Eshlo or Klein, more than fourteen years of waste, and fermenting humiliation.

Oberand did not miss Mercile. At first there had been no time, for within a week of their dinner, Oberand had been making arrangements to travel out from Paradys into the wide world. Presently, looking back, there was only a slight disgust that such a man as Mercile had been permitted to deceive him. At last, and very soon, Mercile was a shadow. Beneath the Mountains of the White Moon, however, it was Eshlo that Oberand began to miss, and Klein, although Klein less painfully and clearly.

The sun was setting on the rim of the plain, and the mountains flared up, then turned suddenly to ash, lit only at their tips. There came a curious half-heard whirring note, perhaps the sunset wind passing through some hole or crevice higher up, sound carrying in the glassy air. Transparently the night came to Africa, without subterfuge, bearing the bone moon from which the mountains had been transposed. If the sun was a lion, the moon was a white-faced buck. It peered, vulnerable and savage, above the plain, lighting it as bright as day. The mountains glowed. The fire of the cook house became the centre of the earth, marking, like a cross on Eshlo's map, their place in things.

'I am here,' Oberand said aloud. *'Here.'* But that was not enough. Yet the excitement stirred in him, properly, the first occasion. It had taken so long, for he had been so long coming to it, he had kept it waiting, like his younger self.

Andre stood smoking, looking at the mountains, thin and still in his European clothes. The blacks squatted at the fire, where the pot hung, full of

God knew what jumble.

Speak to Andre, Oberand thought. Why was that important? Andre knew nothing, less than the cook, who feared.

Oberand watched the camp from his tent, the pale dust and the moonlight, patches of sand between the mountains' claws, shining. The strange sound had died out from the mountains, and the reflection from their tops. Miles off a lion roared. The stars were liquid, like mercury, in the bulb of sky.

Here I am.

'My father taught me that men have no souls,' said Andre, 'that this life is all we can expect, and that it will probably be unpleasant.'

The moon had set; it was darker, and somewhere hyenas were busy. The night was not the same, and Andre had begun to talk at the fire. He had started by saying he thought the two blacks might run away tonight. He said they were not so much afraid as anxious, a kind of anxiety attack that, because they did not see it as nervous in origin, they attributed to bad spirits of the plain and mountains. Oberand said that if this happened, it must be accepted, but would the two men steal very much? Only enough, said Andre, to support them on their journey back down river. Let them go, then, said Oberand, they would manage, but what of Andre? Andre had said he would remain. He was not afraid, since he did not believe that anything lay over the mountains, even if a way to it were to be found. A dry crater perhaps, an extinct volcano, poisonous and dead. Oberand was not offended by Andre's pragmatism. His truthfulness, coming in a straight line after Mercile's years of deception, was nearly appealing. Because he had wanted to, Oberand indulged himself, beginning to attempt the drawing out of Andre, whom he had judged as clever, and almost in his way as educated as anyone met with in the vanished metropolis. Andre had alarming potential that, since he was black, could never be realized – Andre was not strong enough, evidently, to evolve solely for himself, as so many were not.

In the background the hyenas had commenced, and then the two blacks initiated a vague annoying chanting from a stand of trees a hundred feet off. Andre opened a little like a crumpled paper. He spoke of the ancient cities of giants, the legends of white gods. He explained he could not believe in anything like that, although its metaphysic intrigued him.

'But why, Andre, is it necessary for men to have souls, in order that there be gods? Can't this be something of a different order?'

'Man tries,' said Andre, 'to find something greater than himself, promising himself he will one day become such a thing. Is that not the basis of the religion of Christ?'

'I think that the religion of Christ offers a chance that we are already such a thing, and have only lost the way.'

'Without a soul,' said Andre, 'where is the need for a god?'

'But this is a god with a valley like the Garden of Eden, the Garden before the Fall. This is a god so large that he could cover the bodies of thirty men with his palm, and crush them. What are men to such a god?'

Andre did not reply. He smoked his cigarette. Then he said, 'What would you give to find this secret valley?'

'Everything,' said Oberand. He said, 'Already, I've given most of it. From the first, the idea possessed me. I sacrificed all I had, and followed it.'

'Be wary, perhaps something listens.'

'But,' said Oberand, 'what could that be, if there are no gods?'

'I don't know, monsieur. But I sense it. The way a man whose hand has been cut off will feel the hand at the end of his arm, itching him. Like that. It isn't real, but it affects him. What listens may not be real either, yet it may hear.'

Oberand felt a sudden emotional liking for Andre. Why in God's name had this man not been given him to argue with, to wrestle with, this black angel in the night, over the body of Eshlo, on the ladder of light? But it was too late now.

'Let it hear me,' said Oberand, 'please God.'

After a while longer, Andre put his cigarette into the fire. 'If we go to sleep, monsieur, the men will have their chance to run away. I will take the sugar and hide it, or they may have that too, for barter.'

Oberand got up, half tranced. His muscles ached as if a heavy wine were swirling through his system. He held out his hand. Andre shook it solemnly. They parted without further words, the black man to his shelter, Oberand to his tent.

He lay on his back for half an hour, and the chanting ceased. The night was silent as an open bowl of space upturned upon the land.

In the night's middle darkness, sound awakened Oberand. It was as if he had been expecting it, had been prepared by a lesser sound of the evening, the huge silence that had domed in the plain as he slept.

What he heard was a sort of low rumbling, and at first he took it for lion in the distance, then for the movement of a herd of animals, shaking the plain. Then, thinking of some tremor of the earth, he sat up suddenly, but although there was the faint sense of vibration, it was not that of an earthquake. Nothing moved, rattled, or fell. After a moment, Oberand got up and went out of the tent, to see what Andre made of this.

Outside, the night was incredible. It had changed itself yet again, the way no night of the north ever did, or so it seemed to him. The clarity of the darkness was wonderful, like crystal, the sky miles high, drawn back like a blind to reveal the world. On the horizon something vaguely shifted about, probably deer feeding. The other way, the wall of the mountains, lunar, frozen.

Nothing stirred in the camp. Perhaps the runaways were already off. But neither had Andre emerged. And the sound – it was real and definite – could not be ignored.

Oberand took a step, meaning to wake Andre, then instantly checked.

Andre had not woken, or had not come out. The sound was not a summons to Andre, who did not believe. And the men who were afraid had already run away.

Oberand's heart gave a great leap, catching him like a spear in the breast.

He ducked back into the tent, and picked up the knife and the pistol he had not yet used, some ammunition, water. It was not a careful readying for any vast expedition, it was a token. The token of the traveller. It was ritual, as if before an altar of the night.

When Oberand emerged again, he stood, staring up at the Mountains of the White Moon. They were charcoal gray now, with pale frills of silver from the stars. To climb without ropes would be impossible. Even roped, with the expert advice of Andre, to reach the crest had been thought out of the question.

The rumble of sound went on, becoming part of hearing. It emanated from within the mountains, borne upward on a column of stillness, opened like an umbrella into the bowl of the sky.

Oberand walked away from the camp, crossing through the shrub and boulders, to the foot of the rock. He came among the patches of sand. He began to climb diagonally, going along the base of the wall, moving south to north, circling. He did not investigate the upright slopes of the wall, as he had been doing, he climbed up and over, and down, and up again. The starlight sliced out swaths of rock, and made pits of luminous blackness between them. He got down into these, and each time, without words he thought, *It will be this one*, but it was not. He did not know what he anticipated, some crack in the rock, something so
evident as an avenue with pillars of stone … The camp disappeared around the curve of the mountains.

As he was climbing down, the sound stopped. He felt a moment of deafness, almost disorientation. As if the sign had been taken from him, the promise. He hesitated, and after a moment, the sand on which he stood tipped and settled, lurched and lay flat again. And then gave way completely.

There was no time for Oberand to think. He was falling as the earth caved in. He knew what this was. It was a quicksand. It sucked him under and he caught at the land, but it slipped sideways and nothing would stay put or firm, nothing would hold him. He knew instantly reasonless mad terror and cried out, but his cries hit the void of space, and the gleaming stars swallowed them. Terror and despair, without thoughts. Screaming, he was sucked into turmoil. The sand filled his nostrils and mouth, and he struggled, choked, his eyes were put out, his ears were full of miasma, and panic began to recede into a ringing emptiness. But something struck his heels a blow like a mace. His whole spasming, suffocating body was jolted and spun. In a rush of mass he seemed catapulted down into the stars. He saw them, burning and mocking him. This was death.

He lay in the belly of death and vomited out the sand, and as he did so, the grains of other sand sprayed down on him in the dark. He could breathe, he heard the noise he made, but the thing which had smote his heels struck him across the skull. He slid with the darkness closing. Thought had not yet returned.

He thought nothing, and nothing. Nothing.

3

'Like a pearl, softly the morning was, and rained … He could not remember the line. He saw the soft pearl light and tried to recall, '… and rained … like …' But this did not matter. The poem was not important now. It was the light that was relevant to him. The light–Oberand pushed up from the cloud and discovered himself, bruised and sore-headed in the tunnel of darkness with the fresh light, so pearly, raining at the tunnel's end a long way off. He should go that way. And he must go on his knees for there was not the room in this cave to stand up. He was in the mountain, in the wall. He had fallen in there through a place of sand, and somehow under it was the cave and the air; he had lived, and there the light was, he had only to crawl. In the light he could see the plain. He crawled, hurting and breathing, forward. After five minutes the oudine of the cave mouth grew concrete and exact, and beyond it a dripping pre-dawn mist, and out of the mist a fern cast its tendrils like a dagger, a fern so large it surprised him. But he crawled on, and drew level with it, and from there he beheld the place outside the cave, which was not the plain.

First, perfect stasis, dim reflection of water polished under smoke, tricklings and susurrus unseen, and the nets of things flung over, and the pylon of a tree where flowers clung that were the size of flowers in a dream. Next, motion: Birds lifted from the shallows, while their pale shadows sank away from them like ghosts. They were very big, with the heads of anvils, and the leather slap of their wings tore water drops from the air. Then through the mist the creature came, quite slowly, gracefully, like a vehicle of armour, wet like silk. It was a giant lizard. Reaching the water, it glided through the colossal reeds, which bent from it in the action of courtiers. It dipped its slender and enormous head, and drank. It was beautiful as a thing fashioned, with the life blown into it by magic, and at its delicate step, the ground had moved.

Oberand watched the lizard drinking. It armour made towers upon its back. He did not know its name. Its eye was like a jewel. Ripples spread in a muscular glittering from the firm licking of its tongue that was the length of his body.

He had reached the Valley of God.

There was no exit from the valley. Inside four weeks he knew this. He had become, again, a new and different man; he did not care, he had resigned himself to death or madness, and to life. He had met Eshlo in the dark, and the *true* truth of Eshlo. Which was romancer and liar. For somehow Eshlo had guessed the existence of the valley, perhaps even found the clues to the valley, but he had never entered it. For if he had, demonstrably, he could never have come back to write his account. The genius of perceptive imagination was Eshlo's gift, what he had handed over to Klein, and to Oberand. No more.

Oberand had searched systematically along the inner rim of the mountains. He was more thorough and more experimental than in his outer searching of a way in. There was nothing, of course. There was no route from Eden, save God made it, and ushered out there with a flaming sword.

Once this problem of escape had been dealt with, all vestige of rules or ethics was sloughed from Oberand, and he was free.

Perhaps because Eshlo's dream adventure had been charted, Oberand had ceased to calendar events. On the journey to the mountains, and in the camp, he had kept a journal. But that had been left behind. He made and attended to no device for the recording of time. The season did not alter, and he had no constant but for the recurrence of day and night. Dawn was not as he had ever seen it, neither sunset. The dream had been made leaf and flesh and feather.

He lived (the mere necessity) through lessons already learned. He set traps in which small rats and lizards, once or twice a tiny type of pig, enmeshed themselves, and these he killed with the pistol, as at other times he shot things that ran before him. He rationed these meals, knowing that with the end of his ammunition he must resort to other more brutal methods. He did not like to kill, but hunger made him able. And at last he would have to do it with a stone. Among the plethora of growing stuff he found roots and pods and berries, which he ate. He had no means of judging them, and some caused him violent sickness. One species laid him up for two days with a fever. He considered if he might die, yet did not believe it. And always he recovered. The fruit of the garden was mostly to be eaten, he had not yet come on the Forbidden Tree.

At first he sheltered in the cave tunnel from which he had first emerged. Nothing troubled him there save for inquisitive rodents (food) and once a fly with wings of jewellery gauze, larger than he from shoulder to shoulder. It startled him, but did not haunt him long.

During his search around the inner base of the mountains, the valley was hidden from him by the fern forest, which began between ten and twenty feet from the rockside, with here and there a break or glade such as that where he had seen the great lizard. Swampy places and dips of silver water lined these glades, but nothing else came to drink there that he saw, except for infrequent, peculiar birds. Others he beheld in the air, birds like a sort of enormous swan, and again arrowings of the bat-winged anvil-heads, which seemed to emanate from a distant smooth height that emerged only in the clearness of midday far above the cycad forest. His search of the mountains for an exit point was instinctive and foolish and actually alien to the person he had become. While it took his days and his thoughts, he understood it was futile, unimportant. Although he saw no further lizards or mammals of the valley at that time, apart from those little ones that supplied his traps, he heard them. Their voices were various, thin and sweet, or trumpeting and terrible. They could not be compared with anything. He sensed there would be huge beasts that fluted and sang, and smaller more fearful things that roared, ate organs and muscle, and drank blood.

When he gave up the search and his freedom came, Oberand took the few items he had constructed, the pillow of rolled dried fern and the best traps, and went down into the forest. So far he had come across several shoots of pure and drinkable water splashing from the rocks, although the pools were consistently full of salts and slimes.

Initially the cycads detained and distracted him. He must cut a way with the knife. He moved by a chain of pools where the giant spangled insects were swarming. He did not know what they were at, perhaps mating like dragonflies above a fountain in a park of Paradys.

The cycads harboured groves of magnolia and laurel. Conifer trees rose in dark pagodas. The scent of these mingled through the heavy, curious air. The sunlight began to stream in shifting smoky shafts, between embroidered eyelets in the canopy.

Oberand watched in wonder. This world was imbuing him, its smells, the lens of its mist where sunrise and sunset dissolved their fires, from which mountains came and went like ships lost at sea.

Oak trees appeared, around which lianas roped and spiralled, and flowers like faces looked at him. Water droplets, the warm dews of the forest, sprinkled from bough to bough, so the atmosphere was filled always by this sound and sense of gentle rain.

He went slowly, and found in the mud the footprint of a mighty creature, perfect as if sculpted for him, although already the moss was growing in it.

Then the forest parted. He saw across the valley.

It was rimmed by mist, was a lake of mist, from which its shapes rose, a map of jungle forest, and silken troughs of open land. The great mountain cone ascended from it, and today a twisted skein of white extended from a vent. It was a volcano, sinisterly sleeping. Even as he stared, a flight of birds went upward. Beyond, a steel-shining water. And on the curve of the misty skyline were twenty waterfalls (he counted), descending in pristine lines like frayed thread.

A bird passed overhead and its shadow enveloped him. It was enormous. He felt no fear in the presence of something so extraordinary. He was in the country of the god. And did the god live on the volcano-mountain? A new goal now. Oberand had reached the unreachable, was here in the unreality he had always known to exist. The god, then, also existed. Did he walk through the Garden in the cool of the day? Which of the cries of the valley heralded his passage?

He had been alone for years. He had learned that each man is alone, even in company. He missed nothing of civilization in the valley, not even books, for his books had all *been* the valley, had something of the valley, and here the valley had become his book at last, open and to be read. He did not mind the random and ill-cooked food, it interested him. His body, which had hardened and improved on his journey, had now reached a peak of fitness and energy that delighted him. His eyes were never tired, his eyesight had sharpened. Noises he had sometimes heard in his head had vanished in the constant natural sound of the valley. Everything was better.

It took almost a week of angling descent for Oberand to reach the valley floor. There, he had only the volcanic cone for his guide. A herd of cattle, huge and black with devilish horns, burst out of the mist and over his path on the morning he came down. They were the size of elephant, and filled him with joy. One hour later he saw three lizards, upright and grazing on the trees, with long serpentine necks, tiled with plates like burnished iron. Their bodies moved very little, their heads were busy with the leafage. Once one of them spoke. Its voice was of the sweet bell-like sort he had heard from above.

That night, in his shelter of reeds and steams, Oberand dreamed of the god walking through the valley. The great lizards lifted their heads to see him pass, and he rested his hand briefly upon them in blessing. To him they were tiny, like squirrels in a shrubbery. The earth did not quiver at the footsteps of God, it was his constant movement that caused a ceaseless, now unnoticeable tremor, which turned the world.

Oberand worked toward the cone of the volcano. Cycads grew again on its slopes. The water beyond he judged for the inner land-locked sea of Eshlo's descriptions. For Eshlo, who had never entered the valley, had yet somehow been here, so much remained obvious.

Oberand was by now mad. It was a fact. Much of his freedom came from it. It was sanity that had caused unhappiness, as so often it does.

Time, then, in the valley, unspecified. The beauty of the days of travelling toward the mountain cone, the sights and wonders, the giant snakes, the feeding vegetarian towers of lizards, a fish in a lake like a fearsome sword, the snows of the birds, the cattle that roamed the valley like soft thunder. The sun coming up in tempest, going down in such colours the sky was another country, with other mountain ranges, other seas, other airs. And the nights of stars.

He missed Andre just a little. He would have liked Andre to have seen certain of the wonders. Andre would have respected them, Andre who had not believed, would have accepted the magic instantly. But Andre had not fallen through the sand into the mountain wall, Andre was not there.

Oberand had begun to see something white, dully gleaming on the lower slope of the volcano, where the cycads grew.

The way up the volcano was a zigzag of lush and grassy tracts. Among the cycads, it had absurdly the charm of a wild orchard, and miniature reptiles darted from the path like rabbits. The sea lay beyond the body of the mountain, a sheet of light at the edges of vision. Oberand climbed, eating the fruit of the vines, which he recognized from below. And in a dusky grove he found a headlong pillar. It was gigantic, and broken in many pieces lying with gaps only of a foot or so between them, ribbed and veined, yet freshly white. He guessed the length of the pillar covered half a mile, and not far behind, between the cycads and the vines, were four others.

Standing at a break in the trees, Oberand saw other evidence stretching away, parallel to the places through which he had climbed. A tier or sloping plateau of the mountain cone ran out, with a white line on it like the base of a toppled barricade, and further below was something similar, hidden until now in the patches of forest. Above, as he moved onward, a vast gate reared up, parting the sky. Oberand did not stop, he went to the gate, and under it, and trod across a fissured bridge that in places raised him perhaps twenty feet from the ground, and came into a hall. Nothing remained of it but the arched struts which once had held its masonry. Their whiteness burned and turned the sky between to darkness. The height was limitless. That was of no consequence. He knew what he had found. It was a temple, of colossal bigness, erected to the god of the valley. He sat down on the grassy floor, and gazed at the arches of pure whiteness, where the moss grew and the lianas festooned themselves. Again, he wished that Andre had seen this. Presently Oberand lay on his back and watched the darkened sky between the arching ribs.

The temple had collapsed, and the forest moved over it like a slowly turning wheel. Everything was eaten away but for this marvellous fretwork, its bones.

Oberand felt emotions that had no name.

After an interval, the light altered, and the sun was setting. He made a fire there in the grass on a flat white scale of the temple. He ate some of the meat he had cooked the night before, and drank water from the bottle.

'I have found a temple to the white god of the legends. I do not pace it out in cubits or miles. It is of exceptional size and surely that is all one needs to know. Besides, I have no one to show it to, no means of sketching it, no means even to write of it. And so I simply write this in my mind. And perhaps, by going over these phrases again and again, as doubtless I shall come to do, I will memorize them.

'There is the remains of a walled avenue leading to the temple, and about two-thirds of the way along it I found the fallen pillars. Probably other pillars have weathered or been absorbed entirely by the forest, for surely others there must have been. Everywhere are great plates and chippings, everything so white, and oddly crenulated, and often split by the ravenous plants of the region. The gateway and the bridge puzzle me. I can find no steps, and only a crumbling of the material of which the temple is made–I do not know what that is – enables me to get up and down. The hall is awe-inspiring and staggering, like a glimpse into outer space. Even if it could be measured exactly, its circumference could only baffle, it is so huge, and yet so perfectly constructed. What walls hung from those alabaster struts? What windows pierced them? And what creatures moved about here, to worship?

'Beyond the arch-vaulted hall is a white mass at some distance, over a ravine in the mountain. Here, too, there must have been a linking bridge … smoke from the volcano sometimes rises in the ravine. I cannot so far reach the farther building, which is very overgrown. I think it must be a shrine, some holy of holies. This is frustrating. But possibly, approaching from another direction of the cone, I may find a route over.

'I am very excited. I do not begin to grasp what may happen now. Sometimes the mountain rumbles faintly. Perhaps it will erupt. I feel so well, so fulfilled and gratified, so optimistic, I do not believe it can go on. But my traps continue to feed me, although now I have resorted to the method of the stone – my bullets are all gone. There is water from a rill just above the temple hall.

'When I remember the City I do not credit it. It does not exist for me anymore. The world has gone and there is only this.

'Tomorrow I will go down to the lower slopes again and try to find a way across the ravine, to reach the shrine.'

As the sun was rising, Oberand was woken by a disturbance from the forest. Something too large had entered one of the traps, and was destroying it.

Oberand went out of the temple hall and beheld a tusked pig wrenching itself out from the trap in a shower of wood and broken vines. It rolled hot eyes at him, then bolted away, the creepers unweaving over its back.

At that moment an ink black shadow fell on Oberand, covered him and all the ground, cold and depthless as sudden water.

He looked up – and saw a whirlwind.

Out of the whirlwind flashed a wing beat, the writhing and whipping of a snakelike tail, also eyes like fire, a scimitar beak open to reveal the little pointed endless teeth, and claws of steel that gripped. They had him. The pain of them was numbing and unrealistic, and even as he tried to pry himself away, to fight this demon of the upper air, it soared and bore him with it, up between the railings of the cycads, into a vortex of sky.

Oberand heard himself shouting. He flailed and beat at the demon. It was a bird from the volcanic cone, massive, and feathered as if with wire. Its talons held him more tightly than any trap. It peered at him with its soulless mechanical eyes, seeing only his meat, not caring that he fought it.

Already he was fifty feet above the earth. It was hopeless. Oberand ceased to shout. He found he had voided himself in utter terror. Tears of pain and fear ran down his face. The bird dived upward, obliterating gravity, bearing him to some nest high on the cone, where it would kill and feed on him.

The calm of death smothered Oberand. It was as if every sensation and every thought were extinguished together.

He looked down and saw the shape of the world of the valley under him. From the claws of the bird he was granted a vision of the mountain, laid sideways and flat, combered with its forest, wreathed by its smokes and steams, and there the sidelong plateau where the temple stretched downward against the sea. And Oberand, in the claws of murder, saw what the temple was. It was the skeleton of an enormous man, a giant to whom the giant beasts of the valley were small things, like fowl and squirrels. A giant fallen, the tibias and fibulas of the legs an approaching avenue, the pelvis a mighty gate, and the smashed metacarpals of one hand, five toppled pillars. The rib cage made the hall of arches, and over the smouldering ravine was the detached head of the shrine, its two eyes forever wide, its teeth choked by the reclaiming vines. The god lay on the mountain, the god of white bone. Held high in the air in the claws of murder Oberand looked and saw, and an irresistible smiling lifted his face against its bones. Carried toward his horrible death, he could not keep back a terrifying laughter.

A Madonna of the Machine

Industrial canticles
Sing the steel,
A secret language,
Pain.

John Kaiine

Touch touch touch the dial, and the dial turns. Now to the left, and now to the right. Grey light flickers down the coil: Half a mile below the platform, where the spiral ends, a lever raises its leviathan head. *Ting* says a bell. And the process is accomplished.

Peter sits on his bench, He watches the figures moving noiselessly long the panel. After one seventy second unit, a soft flare glows in the panel, Peter reaches out again and touch touch touches the dial, and the dial turns, left and right, and the grey light flickers away down the snake-bowel coil, down down into the dusk below, and there the leviathan raises its head, and *ting* says the bell.

And the process is accomplished.

And Peter sits on his bench, watching the figures move until another seventy second unit passes and the flare glows, and he reaches out and touch and turn and left and right and flicker and down and raise and *ting*. Sometimes, as he sits, or periodically stands for a unit or two, when the passing mechanical overseer reminds him, Peter thinks. He thinks about whether he is hungry now or not, and if he is, he takes a fibre bar from his overall and eats it. Or if he is thirsty he presses a tube in the grey-silver wall beside the bench, and the tube issues him a vitamin drink. Or he thinks of the talkto in his home, which tells him things or answers questions, if he has any, or murmurs him to sleep. Or he notices the other persons who sit or stand before their own sections on the platform; lines of people six or seven metres apart. He has been among them all his adult life. They are the same people he has always been with, here. And in the start of the diurnal, after the mechanical lark trills him awake, he has heard, for twenty-five years, the other mechanical larks in main building of D district going off one by one, to wake these others. Then they, like him, enter their hygiene cubicles, rid themselves of waste matter, are cleansed and dried, go to their food counters and are fed, expel themselves into the two-thousand metre long corridor, for the twice daily walk necessary for their health. And in the cage-lift they go down into the street, where the pale grey verticals and horizontals stretch away and away, and the air-bus comes and sucks them in and bears them off and sets them down here, together, in the heart of the Machine.

Peter knows the names *of* some *of* his neighbours. But they have never really spoken. There is no point. What is there to discuss? Each has a talkto in his or her home. The talkto adapts entirely to each individual personality. It knows, by mechanical instinct, what to say, and even when to speak and when to keep silent. It knows the proper sounds and encouragements to aid occasional vague masturbations or to sooth the aftermath *of* some unremembered yet disquieting dream.

There is no need for human conversation, awkward and effortful.

The flare glows, and Peter touches touches touches, and the dial turns. The harmony of the activity and its result are satisfying. It is a dim yet pleasing thought that throughout the Machine, hour by hour, unceasing for its duration, so many millions of men and women carry out, endlessly and faultlessly, similar or complementary actions. The Machine serves and is served. The empathy is perfect.

The light reaches the lever which raises itself. *Ting* goes the bell.

There is a meal-break, and Peter leaves his section for the moving ramp which goes down under the platform. On the ramp with him, Peter recognizes Yori and Marion, Ted and Malwe and Jane. They reach the lower level and step off, into the canteen. Everything has a mild gloss of cleanness. The clean walls, in reply to the pressure of his fingers, give Peter a slice of protein and some vegetable cubes, and a caffeine drink, Peter sits at a table to eat. The table is shared by Yori, Jane and Ted. They do not speak to each other. Everyone thinks their own thoughts and slowly consumes the food.

It is as Peter is finishing his drink that there comes to him the first Intimation.

He does not know it for an Intimation.

It is *a* feeling he has never felt before, it has no name.

It startles him, and wondering if he has not chewed his food properly and so has caused some gastric imbalance, he half rises to approach the canteen health dispenser. But then the feeling without a name ebbs away. It goes so softly, (not as it came, sheer and hard, like a glass sliver), that Peter is reassured, He does not, however, finish his drink, *subconsciously* blaming it.

On the ramp back to the platform, Ted speaks.

He says: 'There was a pinkness over my screen, before meal-break.'

No one answers. Jane glances at him, then politely averts her eyes.

Ted says nothing else.

They return to their positions, Peter touches. The dial turns.

Just before the next meal-break, Peter feels the second Intimation. It is unlike the first, coming insidiously, sweetly, like the gentle libido which sometimes wakes him in the twilight of sleep prior to the trilling of the mechanical lark. This is not a bodily feeling, nevertheless, even though it invades his body. What is wrong with him?

Peter is struck by a sort of paralysis. He stares inward at the feeling, trying to determine its shape.

It is a type of wave, with an upcurling head, pliant, mutable, yet formed. Running in.

It strikes him, somewhere in the region of the heart.

He is ill. There is something medically wrong. His heart is beating strongly and very fast, Peter looks up from his panel to the emergency button in the wall. And there, above his section, he sees a gleam of light that is pink, the colour of a rose, a special colour that perhaps his genes recall, although he has never seen a flower of any type. Peter looks at the rose light, and gradually, it unfolds itself, and it too, like the wave-shape within him beating on his beating heart, takes on a form.

He thinks it is like a woman. Yes, it is like a woman. She is clothed in a flowing, pleated garment, all the rose-colour, and on her head is a drift of scarf, the palest yellow, also rose-like. Her flesh is pale, luminous and white, not like skin. She has eyes, although the rest of her features seem to him blurred. The eyes of the woman fix on Peter. He tries to look away. It is not possible. Something terrible is in her eyes, something he has never, in all his twenty-five years, seen in a human face and expression.

Peter opens his mouth and makes a sound, and something happens to him. His chest is heaving, and the air is coming out of him in gasps and liquid is rushing down his cheeks, as if he bled, but it is only water pouring out of his eyes.

And then, the rose light fades from the wall above the panel.

Peter comprehends, as he struggles helplessly with the paroxysm of the body once known as weeping, and which he does not understand, that the figures have reached the seventy unit interval and the soft flare has gone off and he has not touched –

Then he sees that the dial is turning left and right. The flickering energy is running down the coil to the lever below which lifts, and the bell goes *ting*.

Peter has not touched the dial, the three immaculate touches. Absorbed by the dreadful vision above the panel. Peter has failed the Machine. But despite this lapse, the dial had turned, the coil has been activated. The process has been accomplished.

Peter stops crying. His chest and throat are raw, and his eyes sting. He wipes his nose on the sleeve of his overall without thinking, and as the light flares again, he touch touch touches –

He does not know what else to do.

He hopes what has happened will fade, as the first Intimation faded.

In a way, it does.

The talkto comes on as Peter enters his home.

'Peter,' says the talkto. Peter smiles. The smile is involuntary, not precisely automatic. When he hears the low mechanical voice, he is always pleased. A kind of happiness envelopes him. It is hour seventeen, and now he is here in the room that is his home, to relax and to sleep, for ten hours.

Home is rather bare, like every home, (with variations) in main building, and in d district, and in all districts and buildings about the heart of the Machine. The walls of home are concave and dust-resistant, although every diurnal they are mechanically wiped. The cushioned floor supports a low sleeping couch. On one wall is the food counter, and through a sliding door the box of the hygiene cubicle, with its water-tap, lavatory bowl and shower. There are no windows in Peter's home. Air is constantly breathed in and out via hidden orifices. It is the clean, dry, odourless air, common throughout the Machine.

In one corner, near the convex ceiling, the talkto perches, a small grey bulb that faintly shines when peter is at home. Nearby, the mechanical lark waits above the bed. The light, like the air, is constant, never-changing, muted yet clarified.

There is, too, a languid, unmodulated hum, which is the eternal music of the machine.

The Machine is outside, and all about, and home is merely a tiny microcosm of the Machine. Home needs no textures and no patterns, as Peter himself needs no decoration or individual markers. He, all humanity, are the pattern within the Machine, the jewellery of its vistas that stretch in every pale grey direction upwards, downwards, and in parallels towards an infinity which Is.

Peter knows this and is consoled by this. He speaks to the talkto. He speaks a sort of meaningless, friendly jargon, which the talkto answers in the same vein.

Going to the counter, Peter is given a light supper, and a mineral drink. He and the talkto exchange banter throughout the meal. When Peter falls silent, the talkto falls silent, only continuing to shine.

Peter takes off his overall and drops it into the shute. Tomorrow a fresh garment will be ready for him, complete with a fibre bar snack in the pocket. He goes into the hygiene cubicle, where his teeth are cleaned, and his body sluiced with warm water.

He urinates at the lavatory bowl, and finally comes back into the room.

'Today,' he says, 'today.'

The talkto waits, ready to take up his phrase.

'Today,' says Peter, 'I saw a woman above the panel. How can that be?'

The talkto pauses, then it says, 'A woman. Yes, Peter.'

'How could she be there? She was in the wall of the Machine.'

'Machine, Peter,' says the talkto.

'And I missed touching the dial. But the dial turned. As if I touched the dial. As if –' Peter fumbles for his own meaning. He says: 'As if I needn't touch the dial.'

The talkto says, 'Bedtime, Peter.' And it begins a sort *of* song it *murmurs* before he sleeps.

Normally, he finds the song very soothing. Now, an unaccountable tension runs through him, and sensing it, infallibly, the talkto becomes utterly silent, only shining there above him as he lies down.

Presently he loses consciousness.

Peter dreams he is walking up the pure surfaceless wall of the Machine above his section. A woman in a pink garment and silver-yellow veil is walking before him. Her feet are white as roses, and they leave, in the steel endurance of the wall, delicate indentations that vanish in a few moments, as if she walked over the film of a lake – the memory of which his genes recall, although he has never seen water save from a faucet or in a lavatory bowl.

As Peter follows the woman, he is aware of a powerful brimming bursting within himself. This is like the feeling he has experienced in his penis, sometimes, in the seconds before his hands and the murmurs of the talkto have caused him to climax. But the feeling is not sexual, actually, although it is orgasmic, far more so than the jetting irritation of random lust.

The woman walks up the never-altering face of the Machine.

Peter comes to wonder what he is doing, following her.

Then his feet slip. There is no purchase. He falls.

'Hush, you're here,' says the talkto. 'Here you are. You're safe.'

Peter realizes he has cried out.

He listens to the talkto as it comforts him, then sinks back into sleep.

Anna arrives at the heart of the Machine, as she always does, in the one-seater air-car. It sets her down before D two, and she enters the round office where, with three others, she overlooks the D levels of the machine. As usual Vaslav and Rita are already at their panels. Anna crosses to her seat and allows it to form itself about her before giving it her weight. This diurnal she is wearing a pale grey one-piece suit. In her two room home, she is always offered a choice of clothing in off-white pale or dark grey, Rita is clad in dark grey, Anna notes.

Sometimes at meal-breaks Anna and Rita exchange a little conversation. They talk about the Machine, the abstract comeliness of its lines in some new area they have, on a free walk, discovered. Or they speak contemptuously of the workers who man the D levels. These do not seem as efficient as workers of other levels, Q, for example or Y. But since all workers are efficient in deed if not in essence, nothing can be done. It is the aesthetic of the workforce that troubles Anna, Rita. Both Anna and Rita have, at prescribed times, met with Vaslav for sexual union. However, they do not speak very much to him, nor he to them. At meal-breaks he tends to sit with Han or Olif from D top three.

As Anna sits into the chair, her panel shows her a portion of the D levels. After a minute, it shows her another portion. The panel continually shows Anna portions of the D levels, as the panels of Rita and Vaslav show them, also, portions of the D levels.

The coils and pipes are flickering with energies, the wheels turn, the levers lift and engage.

Anna is rested by these images. Only now and them, she has a wish to move the human figures a little, put their bodies into slightly more effective angles, or simply to make them stand when they are sitting, sit when standing up.

Sometimes she thinks *of* what she will order from the tops canteen at the meal-break, *or* sometimes of the poetry which her talkto *has made for her. Although she discusses* the Machine and the workers with Rita, and intermittently meets with Vaslav, for sex, Anna prefers – as Rita and Vaslav do themselves – reticence, and the solitude of a home.

At the end of the diurnal, Anna's talkto had recited:

Grey is the line forever
Forever is as the grey line

And this fragment has become locked into the memory of Anna, and as the panel shows her the parts of the levels where the workers touch and touch, the coils sparkle and the wheels turn, the poem weaves together with every view, contenting her in a deep and tender fashion.

So that when an alarm goes off, like a tiny white firework somewhere in the screen, Anna is horribly jolted.

In the thirty years during which Anna has watched the D levels, no incident has ever occurred. Nothing has occurred at all.

Now she feels personally slighted. Threatened.

She stands on the bridgeway, and looks down to where a mechanical medical is attending to one of the workers. Because something has happened to him while working, she will have to speak to him. Anna knows this is the procedure, although such an event is unprecedented.

Anna waits until the medical is finished. Then the worker is taken by an overseer to the ramp which connects with the bridge. He gets on to the ramp reluctantly. As he rises towards her, Anna looks away. She sees that none of the other workers has paid any attention. They regard their sections, and at the proper intervals their hands go out to touch the transmitters of the Machine.

Despite the fact Anna has sometimes walked these levels on a free walk, when the Machinery is quiescent and the workers in their homes, to be so near the manned levels makes her uneasy.

The male worker is deposited ten metres away. He stares at his hands, which he holds out slightly in front of him. All workers resemble one another, Anna accepts that her own class of watchers is not exempt from familial resemblance – but the worker is alien. He is a worker.

The overseer approaches Anna and she is glad to have it between her and the worker. The overseer says: 'The worker, Peter, climbed up on to the panel housing of his section. He then attempted to climb up the wall surface above the panel. He then fell. Injuries are superficial and have been corrected.'

Anna is forced to look at the worker, Peter.

She speaks clearly. 'Why did you do this?'

The worker Peter opens his mouth. Then he closes it.

'You must tell me why you climbed up on to the housing,' says Anna. 'Such a thing is unheard of.'

'There was a light over the panel,' says the worker Peter.

Abruptly water pours out of his eyes. He drops on his knees and Anna beholds a man weeping, which she has never been shown before. She knows the idea of weeping. She knows what tears are, although she has never grasped the notion, and does not really grasp it now. She sees the man is shaking from head to foot. She is amazed. She can think of nothing to say. And so she says, 'This must never happen again. Do you understand? Now go back to your section.'

The overseer takes hold of the man and helps him up and the man says distinctly, 'A woman walks over the Machine. Her eyes – her eyes –' Then he stops and the overseer puts him on the ramp and he is carried back down into the levels.

Anna watches from the bridge and sees Peter return to his section where, standing before the dial, after a moment, and at the correct instant, he touches, once, twice, three times.

She lets out her breath and finds her ribcage is aching from holding the sigh pent within herself. Her nails have dug into her palms.

She peers down at the housing over Peter's section, where the shimmering grey wall runs up and up and up and away and away.

The wall of course is empty.

'Anna,' says the talkto in her two room home. 'Grey is grey. The Machine is the Machine is the Machine is the Machine …

The concave walls are done in grey and off-white.

The bed has a pillow in a dark grey case. There is a window, that reveals the horizontals, verticals, parallels of the streets of the limitless complex that is the Machine.

'… is the Machine is the Machine …' Anna summons a soporific from her dispenser.

She drinks it, lies down with her head on her pillow, and closes her eyes.

'The Machine.'

Anna sleeps. She dreams. The worker Peter is walking up the wall above his section. His face is full of a wild joy. Anna approximates the look to that of successful sexual climax, which she has seen on the face of Vaslav. Anna herself finds coitus debilitating. When she experiences pleasure, for several diurnals after she cannot bear the sight of Vaslav.

No, the look of rapture on the face of Peter is more profound than anything she has ever seen, Anna stares beyond Peter, and there is *a glimmering incoherent pinkish light wavering on the surface of the wall. Anna thinks of roses, of which* somehow she has been informed, which she has never been shown. A ghost of a rose glides over the Machine.

Anna wakes up. Her face is wet and this frightens her. She has been crying in her sleep.

At six hours, the levels of D are empty, and as she walks along them absently, Anna can hear only the faint tympanic hum of the Machine. The walls slide up, and the coils descend down and down. When she looks from the bridges, Anna sees eternity stretching away below and above, and on all sides. Caught in this web, she searches after the accustomed peace such vistas have always brought her. But there is a slight vertigo, too. Perhaps there always was.

She is drawn towards the section of the worker Peter. She reaches it, and stands there, where Peter habitually stands, or sits. Anna can see nothing unusual. She finds she is straining her eyes. To see – something. What? A woman. But what kind of woman? A worker? A watcher? Intuitively Anna knows that she will never see, or learn, by looking.

At twenty-one hours that evening, Anna arrives for her quarterly meeting with Vaslav, at a cell in tops building. She had almost forgotten the appointment, and her talkto had had to remind her twice. Anna is always perturbed when she goes to have sex, although sometimes she is also uncomfortably eager. She has come to dislike such eagerness. It generally means she will be disappointed, but that in turn ensures more cordial after relations with Vaslav.

In the cell, beside the couch which can be adjusted to complement a number of positions outlined in diagrams on the walls, a beaker of alcohol is served to Anna. She drinks it as Vaslav, tonight rather impatient, begins to touch her in the ordained manner.

Anna tries to respond, and succeeds to a certain extent, Vaslav wishes her to mount him, a position she finds awkward and in which, never, has she been able to climax. As she moves obediently to Vaslav's rhythm, she feels a warm contempt for him, quite friendly and acceptable. He climaxes and she pretends to be satisfied.

As they are putting on their clothes, Anna says, 'Do you know the word *vision*.'

'That is a sight; to see,' says Vaslav. He too, after pleasure, is morose, not wanting further bodily contact.

'No, I mean in the sense of an image conjured or witnessed. An hallucination, possibly.'

Vaslav orders a second glass of alcohol.

'Workers in D have seen –' Anna breaks off.

'The worker Peter,' says Vaslav. 'Probably there's something wrong with the brain. He will have to have a medical check.'

This reassures Anna. She feels a bright flash of gratitude, and turns to Vaslav impulsively.

'You're awkward in that position, Anna,' says Vaslav. 'Rita is better.'

Anna does not know what she is doing. She reached out and pushes Vaslav's glass so that the alcohol spills over him.

In the air-car on the way home, Anna begins to cry again. She runs into her two rooms and the talkto shines and says to her: 'Here *you* are, Anna. You're safe.' But for several terrible moments, Anna does not feel safe *in* the least.

With its trilling the mechanical lark signals Peter. He gets up from the sleeping place before he is quite awake. He has responded to a mechanical lark since his first year. His body knows exactly what to do. It walks him to the hygiene cubicle. It relieves itself of waste matter and is cleansed. As it stands beneath the shower, Peter, carried by this body, wakens in fact.

Peter leaves the shower, before it can dry him. He goes to his bed and lies down, on his back. He looks at the ceiling, and presently the talkto says, 'Peter, get up, Peter.' Peter takes no notice. He blinks sometimes but makes no other movement.

'Peter,' says the talkto, 'you will be late, Peter.'

After an hour, the talkto falls silent. It continues to shine, but Peter does not notice.

On the platform, at his section in D level, Ted looks round, quite suddenly. He has become aware that Peter is not working near him. Ted has not defined the absence until now because, as ever, the dial at Peter's section has turned regularly and the energy has gone flickering down the coil to the lever below.

Ted gazes at Peter's empty place. He assumes at last that Peter is ill, which is uncommon among the workers.

Ted looks back at his own section, in proper time to touch touch touch the button under his panel.

There is a pink light over the panel, Ted has a jumbled notion he has seen it before. The colour, however, is so novel. He stares at it. The pink unfolds like paper, or a flower. Ted sees a woman walking up the wall of the Machine.

In the cage-lift to upper top two, Anna avoids glancing at the levels of D. The vista makes her dizzy, the long, pure lines slipping effortlessly down, like the striations in an ancient rock she has never seen, perhaps never been told of, perhaps does not even genetically recall.

Anna vacillates mentally between annoyance and nervousness. What she is about to do it seems no one can ever have done. The choice has always been open to her, but has gone unconsidered. Now, sometimes, in a rush of strength, anger braces her. But it fails to last out the long smooth journey in the lift.

What will she say? How phrase it, to throw the maximum of blame upon the other? Simple. Her very request will see to that.

The lift reaches upper top and Anna gets out.

Before her is office corridor P nine. Anna walks along the corridor briskly, ignoring the side ramp. Watchers like exercise. She begins to feel virtuous, strong again.

A door opens. The robot assistant speaks, inquiring who she is and whom she wishes to contact.

'Co-ordinator Shashir.'

The assistant assures her that her request is being delivered, and she will soon know whether or not co-ordinator Shashir is available to attend to her.

Anna stands biting her lip. She becomes aware she has been gnawing it since leaving her home early today. Should she not have come here? Will the co-ordinator be able to give her an appointment? Will he question her thoroughly? What will he say?

Anna has an uncomfortable burned feeling in her stomach. She swallows and finds she needs to swallow again.

On the wall of the office cubicle she supposes there is something pink

… it must be a trick of the eyes – she did not sleep very well. The murmurs of her talkto, and the soporifics her dispenser offered her, have rendered her up to the diurnal cloudy but not rested.

A screen in the wall comes on and shines, putting out the pinkness which she had imagined was there a moment before.

With tension and relief, Anna beholds the face of Co-ordinator Shashir.

'Anna. What is it that you wish to discuss?'

'I –' Anna swallows again. She drags in a breath and says tightly, 'I want to discontinue my sexual meetings with watcher Vaslav.'

The face of Shashir does not alter. Perfect and whole, he hangs there. What is this like? The word *icon* enters Anna's mind. She is not sure what an *icon* is. With slight difficulty she realigns her brain with the image of the co-ordinator. He has started to speak.

'… to your liking?'

Anna guesses. She does not desire an interrogation. She says swiftly, 'My pleasure in sex isn't great, and Vaslav has told me he's unhappy with my performance. Watcher Rita suits him better. He won't be sorry, I'm sure, if we don't meet again.'

'But for yourself, Anna? You understand that you are highly sexed, and that these meetings are, for you, preferable to other more solitary methods?'

Anna does not know what reply to give. She feels her face grow very hot.

Finally co-ordinator Shashir says, 'Your view has been filed, Anna. I suggest that now you return to top two. At the next period for sex, if you still decline to meet with watcher Vaslav, you may omit the visit.'

Anna turns. She is cold and sluggish now. She takes the ramp back to the lift.

Along the platform, Marion turns to see why Ted has cried out. She glimpses a female figure which seems to float about Ted's panel, but glancing quickly away, Marion finds the figure is actually poised directly before her, looking down, into Marion's face. Marion tries to avoid contact with the eyes of the figure, for they seem to contain a dreadful depth, or electric fire …

Marion is not able to avoid the contact of these eyes.

She falls to her knees.

Ted has done the same.

All along the line of the platform, the workers of the D levels are sinking down, as if it is some new procedure of their service to the Machine.

As Anna reaches the round office, she discovers an event is in progress. Both Rita and Vaslav are on their feet, and Vaslav is busily pressing the emergency button in the wall.

On the levels, small mechanics of maintenance and overseeing and medicine are whirling to and fro.

The workers have adopted strange attitudes.

The Machine contrives to function flawlessly, although no one, anymore, appears to be engaged with or upon it.

The mechanical lark has fallen from the ceiling and landed on an area of floor, where it made a Weird noise hinting damage, and then became silent.

Peter has no notion why this should have happened, but then he does not really care. He is not even disturbed that the light has gone out of his talkto, as if, indeed, he were not presently at home.

He lies on his back, on the bed, his half-closed eyes fixed without focus on the convex ceiling.

He has been lying here, in this way, for hours. He does not analyse how many. Time has ceased to matter. His body, which once or twice has itched, or disconnectedly wished to urinate, he ignores. All feeling seems to have left it now.

On the ceiling, she comes and goes. Whenever she comes back, at each appearance, she is clearer, better defined.

Day young, in her robe of roses, and dawn-veiled in yellow, under which fair fountains of hair flow out. On her feet are painted little silver flowers, and there is a golden flower between her brows. Her eyes are summer blue, or green, it is difficult to be sure which, but the colour is less urgent than the intensity of the eyes. This terrible wild emotion that is in them – Peter does not recognise it, even now, but it no longer frightens him. He has surrendered. He has drowned himself in her eyes.

All bodily needs, all thought, all senses – these are unimportant. Only the vision, the icon, adrift there as if in the pale space of sleep or death, has power. And silver and golden flowers sift from her hands, and he believes they brush his face, and there is a perfume in the room he has never smelled until these *moments*.

And then at eighteen hours a wall opens and a tube comes snouting through, with a mechanical eye gleaming at its tip. Peter shifts, not intending to, and his body returns about him with a pang of nauseating heaviness. He is very stiff, cannot roll away from the pursuing serpent, which probes him with its chill eye and with a poreless tasting tongue.

'No –' cries Peter.

'Everything will be quite all right,' whispers the tube from somewhere in its unessential being. 'Lie still, Peter. Let me examine you, Peter.'

Peter lets out a scream. As he plunges to his feet, (like a crashing upward fall) the icon of the woman breaks into stars upon the ceiling and scatters like soft snow which – even as he runs from home – he tries to catch with hands and mouth and eyes.

Shashir partly sits and partly reclines in his globe in upper top, and permits his mind to wander through the labyrinth of its own self, after the shade of Anna, whose recording he has just replayed.

Once before in the seven decades of his service to the Machine, one of the watchers came to Shashir with a request to end sexual meetings with a woman of his class. The request was naturally granted, but a year later, the watcher, a man Shashir dimly believes was called Millo, developed health problems. He was reassociated with the woman, and their meetings were resumed. Millo's health improved, but for some while, from time to time, he would still try to terminate the sexual meetings. His later requests were listened to but otherwise ignored.

By this juncture, Millo has ceased petitioning.

It is as if Anna has come to fill the gap.

Shashir loses interest in the fundamentals of the problem. He allows himself to sink down through two or three of the upper sleep layers into the half trance he mostly cultivates, and in which he is most comfortable. Some of Shashir's most profound insights are achieved in this state. It is now he feels closest to the Machine.

The supportive globe cushioning Shashir's body, carries out for him all necessary bodily functions, by means of a series of concealed pipes and synapses. Shashir, who has grown, over the thirty years of his englobement, into a sort of balloon, itself resembling a globe, has only to meditate and to think.

Shashir thinks.

He thinks of Anna, but Anna has ceased to be either watcher or woman. She has become a rosy feather that floats across the inner screen of Shashir's eyes.

The image is very peaceful, Shashir swims through the serenity of the trance. A beautiful yellow thought surfaces like a fish of crystal and he has just the time to see and wonder at it, before the thought submerges and he forgets –

The music of the Machine plays, and Shashir hears it in rapt quietude. He senses filaments of himself which stretch out along the hollows of the Machine, which coil and combine with the Machine's intricacies. He makes medullary love with the Machine, and sleeps, wrapped in the cushion of his brain.

Robot overseers have herded away all the workers from the D levels. There has never before been such an emergency. Gradually, once the levels had been emptied, and the tops vacated by the alarmed watchers, the Machine has concluded its function in this area, closing down with muted sighs and pale flickering.

There is never darkness in the Machine, never any night as there is never any day, only the diurnal, and the obsolete words left behind – today, *tomorrow*.

At twenty-four hours, forgotten midnight, Anna steals along the walkways, creeping from transparent shadow to opalescent illumination, avoiding generally looking down or up. Reaching the platform, she comes to Peter's section, and Peter is standing there.

Anna stops, twelve metres away from Peter. She says: 'Tell me what you saw. What you *see*.'

Peter turns and stares at her. His eyes are large and dark, of a dense blue colour she has never noticed before, of perhaps which, before, they have not been. He says nothing.

Anna tries to be impatient. 'You must tell me,' she says, officiously.

Then Peter laughs.

'The lark broke on the floor,' he says, 'the talkto doesn't function. A tube came after me. I got away. What will happen next?'

'You must go to a medical cubicle,' says Anna.

'Why? It isn't necessary. I want to see her again. I want to see her beauty,' he says. He stares into Anna's eyes and out the back of them at infinity. And all of Anna's blood, which she knows she has though she has never seen a drop of it, spins inside her.

'I'm going away now,' says Peter.

'Where? Where is there to go?'

'Everywhere. Nowhere. Out of –' he struggles for a phrase and manages at last, 'this. *Here*.'

Anna trembles. She leans on a bank of dials and buttons which, quiescent, makes no response to erroneous pressures.

'There is no other place.'

'You'll be safe,' suddenly he points to his own skull, 'In there.' And then he points away into the endlessness of the Machine. 'In there, too.'

Anna stands and suitably watches as Peter trots along the platform, metre after metre, and off the bridge and on to a ramp, loping ahead of its rhythm, springing off on to another bridge, along a walkway, growing smaller and smaller, vanishing into the horizon of the Machine.

Anna sits down on the platform and rests her head on some part of the section. She has an abrupt sensation that everything is trembling, as she is, coming unjoined, disunited, that all of the entity about her may unravel, and float away, leaving behind something else, which it had hidden, naked there, burning bright, with colours that do not exist.

Inside the walls of steel and sound, the sheer total silence inside the deepest wall of used and percolated time, the Machine ticks soundlessly, a pulse current solely with, known only to, itself. And the Machine Is. And the Machine Thinks. In one form the Machine is Thought. Composed of Thought, a cerebral capability made flesh in metal, fissions, clockworks, and therefore in endless powers, as if in arch-angels.

The Machine, if it can be said to have any purpose left, has become the purpose of Thought. Once, the purpose may have been different. Once the Machine was a mighty servant, which in turn was served. (But service also has become a mere capability, made flesh in flesh.) All service is now redundant. Anything that was ever essential to the service and servitude of, or to, the Machine, continues through a math of infallible mechanical habit. For centuries the Machine has been free to do nothing, and indeed the *human* infestation of the Machine, (like ants in a hollow mound) has been freed. To this freedom humanity, but not the Machine, is blind.

So the Machine Thinks, It has been thinking almost but not quite forever. The thought Process is very slow, but extremely deliberate. (It is unlike the thinking dream of such as Shashir, the co-ordinator.) Nothing is squandered. Every strand and fibre, artery and node of the Machine is involved.

Thinking.

Thought drips, like water, and like mercury.

Like rain upon the face of a flower.

The rose lies in the heart of the Machine's heart, as the rain of mercurial thought drips upon it, curving its petals wide, its radar-bowls of sugar-tint receptors, pulled on tines of lustre, a rose that spills into sentience, wider than the core of the Machine, that softly explodes, passing by a savage osmosis, and leaking like wet fire, getting out by every link, interstice, and microscopic vent.

The levels of D are a desert. Nothing moves there save, now and then, a slender worm of some galvanic passing up or down, or there is the faintest rustle, a vibration, some piece of the whole engaging accurately with another.

A pink bead, part of the overspill of the inner rose, hangs like a butterfly on a panel.

Anna has left the platform. She is not there to see the butterfly spread wings, become the angel of the rose, the goddess in a veiling of forgotten dawns.

In the levels, however, of B and K and I and S, the rose-angel-goddess poises like a young summer of the world ill-lost. She is waiting, for the workers and the watchers to return and find her. And Peter, as he lopes beneath the arching bridgeways of I, not glancing, does not see her there. And

Shashir, in his globe, his *sleep*-mind *wandering accidentally to the* levels of H, moves aside, finding a horned rose in the labyrinth. He is not ready yet for roses.

So it is after all Anna, lying on her grey pillow, who sees her insomnia take on, like stained glass in the wall, the Madonna which the Machine has obliquely created.

Anna knows at once what there is to fear.

The terrible eyes of the Madonna are full of love.

The terrible eyes of the Madonna are full of *life*.

Peter has come to a wall which does not appear to have any aperture in it, or ending. He moves along it, sometimes climbing up the bridgeways that in parts run beside it, or descending again into the lower levels. There are no apparatuses issuing from this piece of wall. It is a blank.

After a long while, several hours, Peter stops moving along beside the wall. He sits down on a walkway, his back against a girder, and looks about. There is a great sameness. He has absorbed the idea of it, as he ran. How he examines the blank wall. This is surely cessation. It is a barrier of the Machine. Presumably, the wall is impassable.

Peter is conscious of hunger and thirst, but nowhere that he can see are there any dispensers or recognizable buttons.

Eventually, with a foul emotion which is shame, he is forced to urinate behind the girder.

He is tired out, and elation and terror have left him together.

He sits down again and dozes on the walkway, missing the talkto, missing the shape of his home. The way back is lost to him, and although the Machine hums here, as everywhere, no mechanical activity of any sort appears to go on. He has achieved an outer boundary before he was prepared for it.

He wonders if he will see her again, the Madonna he has not put a name to. But there is nothing, no motion, no colour, no image but the wall, and behind and about, grey horizontals contracting away.

Detecting the disturbance of a life-reading, a rubber snake breaks into Anna's home and locates her trying to drown herself in the hygiene cubicle. Somewhere she has grasped the notions of suicide, and drowning, but she has found the act difficult, forcing her head to remain beneath the spout of the shower, choking and swallowing, sightless through water, half-conscious, but nowhere near dead.

The medical snake eases her into the outer room and resuscitates her.

No one dies. Dying is long over. Workers finally become watchers, after a supine interval during which the brain is modified. At length watchers become co-ordinators, after a period during which both the brain and the complete physical ecology are reorganised and adapted. In the normal course, Marions and Teds and Peters change to Annas, Vaslavs and Ritas; Annas, Vaslavs and Ritas to Shashirs. Shashirs endure neverendingly, until, conceivably, amalgamated into the very nature of the Machine, its very Soul, becoming flawlessly integrated fragments of the godhead itself ...

(Anna, maybe not in any form aware of this, screams and gags, fighting off life like a tiger her genes may recall.)

Later, lying in a medical cubicle, wired up to life, its claws deeply embedded, unable to escape, Anna dreams poetry, and is a blonde goddess rising on a shell from a pink dawn sea.

But if *it* is certain that humanity is itself *at last* compounded with the Machine, *becomes* the Machine, they are the ancient most dreams of humanity, too, not merely the great Thought Of the Machine, which are now causing an upheaval in the levels of B, K, I and S.

Anna dreams only Vaslav lies over her on the shell, in the water. They are drowning, their hands sliding over each others' bodies in a frenzy of panic and joy.

Peter sits before the blank wall for nine diurnals of tearing hunger, sickness, bemusement, calm, until a small mechanical apparatus approaches him, fluttering out of the parallel miles of the Machine, homing unerringly in on him.

When he turns to see, he beholds the small machine is a white bird, with pleated glimmering wings, and in its beak it bears a fibre bar to feed him, and a sealed container of drink.

As the dove settles on his shoulder, Peter realises that, in a space of time, long or short, interminable or simply futile, the impassable wall will melt, metamorphose, give way, and he will see the vision, whatever it is to be, the truth, (or the secondary dream) which lies beyond it.

There is no barrier which is ultimately infinite. There is noticing anywhere that cannot change.

The Nightmare's Tale

The Devil beats his drum,
Casting out his spell,
Dragging all his own Down into Hell.

David Sylvian

1

Of the many thousands who had died in the murderous blood tides of Revolutionary times, there had been a young poet and his innocent wife. Their names and lives may be found elsewhere, he a dark and clamorous man, she pale as a swan, following her husband to the scaffold in the white dress of a bride. They left behind a child, then only two years old. This offspring was brought up by a surviving sister of the mother's – although in those days, it was not unusual, when one member of the family was confiscated for the gallows, for the rest soon enough to be dragged in tow.

The woman, who shall be called Andromede, raised the little boy in the best fashion she could, and at the proper age saw to it that he was educated to the highest and nicest degree she could afford. Along with the nourishment of his body, clothing of his person, and tutoring of his mind, she also saw to it that her sister's son was fed, garbed, and schooled in most incredible amounts of pure bitterness. It may have been that she herself was once in love with Jean de St Jean's father, the poet, or that she had loved her sister excessively. Or it may have been simply the fact of the terrible shock she had undergone when all her familial world was swept away in the space of two or three horrible months: Something made of Andromede a powerful and insidious instructor in the lessons of enduring hate.

How she did it can only be guessed. One half imagines that instead of grace before a meal, some other words were spoken, rather in the way of the antique toast 'Death to my enemies'. Or that over the beds were hung samplers that read 'You shall seek out the wicked and destroy them'. And 'An eye for an eye'.

Probably, when she knelt down like gray marble in the church at the end of the street, and the child asked what she prayed, Andromede may well have replied: 'For *justice!*' And probably also she indoctrinated the little Jean with anecdotes of his parents, their vivid talents and virtues, their fairy-tale love, and their death.

For eighteen years, until the age of twenty, Jean de St Jean grew to manhood in that shadowy City of aftermath, the wreckage of a revolution, going about between a grim stony school with turrets and cobbled yards, reeking stoves, mealy books, and a maze of crooked, crowded, dirty streets that led up into an apartment with windows that peered across a joiners' court at a high wall, three rooms that were thick with dust in summer and wet with cold in winter, and whose stove smouldered and reeked worse, and if there was generally sufficient to eat, it came at the cost of something, some gnawing, obscure pride to do with a state pension, a recompense for the unspeakable that could never be enough. And as he grew up, then, forcing his way toward the light like a plant in flinty ground, Jean de St Jean, the poet's son, breathed up, with the damp and dust and the church bells from the street's end and the invisible samplers of hatred, an exquisite yearning for he knew not what. But it was not ambition or carnality or fame or happiness. And one day, one morning, by accident, he discovered its being and what it was. It was revenge. And like a luscious berry, God had put it in his hand.

He rushed home to the mean apartment of his aunt, along the knotted streets, his heart in his mouth, bounded up the stairs, and flung wide the door.

'Anny!' he exclaimed, which was his pet name for Andromede the hateress. 'Anny, you won't credit –'

Andromede came through from her bedroom, where she had been pinning up her hair tightly. For the first time in eighteen years she felt the full spasm of fear. She stared into her nephew's face and saw him for what he was, as if, until this moment, he had been partly hidden from her. He was a man, with the hair of her sister in a sun-caught cloud around his face, and his eyes dark and clamouring.

'Whatever –' she began.

He held up his hand to silence her.

'I have seen,' said Jean, in a wild cold voice awful to hear, 'a *thing*, a *monster*, walking in the garden of the Martyr Church.'

'I don't understand you, Jean,' said Andromede. She did. She shook from head to foot and her bowels had turned to water, exactly as had happened eighteen years ago on the night the Citizen Police hammered at the door.

'It was Dargue,' said Jean. '*Dargue*,' he repeated.

Then he fell silent and stood looking at her. It would have been difficult to say which of them had gone the whiter.

Dargue was the man who had been directly responsible for the execution of the poet and his wife. It was he who denounced them, and later, by adding his signature to the warrant, he that ensured there would be no escape. He had supposedly been drinking wine as he wrote his name, and a spot of the drink fell beside it like a drop of thin blood. The document had since been displayed, with others of its kind, and perhaps Jean had even seen it. Of course he knew the six letters that composed the monster D A R G U E. And, too, he knew the man by inner sight, having had his appearance and mannerisms described uncountable times over. That Dargue had, as Jean, aged eighteen years, did not prove a deterrent. He had been away all this while, like a fiend in Hell, revelling in the illicit riches the Revolution had given over to him when, in the last days of its madness, he fled.

'He has been living in the Colonies,' said Jean, referring to these far – flung possessions of the City as to another planet. 'An island … Black Haïsa. He has a house there. They jokingly say he has three wives. Negré women.'

'*I don't want to hear!*' screamed Andromede abruptly, clasping her hands over her ears.

'You must, you must,' pleaded Jean. And going to her, he put his arms around her and held on to her just as he had when a child. For her various reasons, Andromede had never been a caressive or physical woman. Her returns to an embrace, especially an importunate one, were awkward and laboured. Now she did nothing at all, but stood there in her gray marble mode, waiting perhaps for all this to end. 'Anny,' said Jean, 'listen carefully. I'm not a boy now. You know, I'm well educated thanks to you, but have no prospects in this rotten, corrupt City. I've had it said to me already, my best chance … would be to try my luck – in the Colonies.' He paused, and when she did not respond, hurried on with 'There are fortunes to be made in the islands.'

'Yes,' she said stupidly, sounding almost asleep. Her hands had fallen back to rest on his arms as he held her.

'There's the money you put by for me. Let me have it, Anny.'

'So you can take yourself to the Colonies?'

She stole a glance at him. Her eyes were stunned rather than bleak. Was he going to leave her?'

'Yes, so I can go there. Don't you see. Where *he* is.'

'Why?' said Andromede.

It was astonishing, after all her work upon him. After eighteen years of a single lesson perfectly repeated and learned by heart. Now, when he replied, solving the mathematical formula in its preordained and only way, now she could not make head or tail of it.

'To kill him,' said Jean de St Jean. 'What else?'

Andromede had the correctness of soul at least to bow her head and not to protest again.

'He's to return to the Island shortly. Out there,' said Jean, 'in that *lawlessness*, it will be easy.'

'Yes, it's easy to kill.'

'Anny, it's what we wanted in our dreams, and here's my chance.'

'Yes.'

'You'll let me have the money, then?'

'Very well. I saved it for you, Jean.'

'For *us*. For *them* – my father. *Her*.'

'Yes.'

'You mustn't grieve. In a year I could be home. We might be rich. You'll have a carriage, and beautiful clothes – velvet for church.'

'Silly,' she said, brokenly.

She tried to smile. Maybe she even tried to take on again her serpent's craning, the fore movement of its venomous strike, the attitude of her insatiable hunger for justice, retribution, the getting of eyes for eyes. If so, she failed in that too. The smile was meaningless and unconvincing, but she pressed it on her face from that morning to the dawn, ten days later, when Jean caught the boat from the old Quay of the Angel, and was borne out limblessly toward the jaws of the sea.

Andromede, standing on the quayside, amid the plumes of hats and tears of others come to wave someone away, was dry and upright, like a thin blasted tree. It was her pride not to weep until she was at home, alone there amid the dust and cold and shadows, listening helplessly for the sound of his footsteps on the stair, for the snatch of a song he might now and then sing, the dropped book, the rustle of his coat, his *Anny, here I am*, his *Goodnight, God bless you, Anny*. She told herself she would never see him again, and in this she was quite right.

The journey was a lifetime. It passed across seasons, geographical barriers, climates, and spatial zones. Months were consumed by it. You could not embark on such a journey, and complete it, unaltered. And yet, with all its doings and happenings, its events of seasickness, storm, calm, boredom, the visitations that were foreign ports (and progressively more and more foreign as one advanced, moving tableaux that swam up from the depths of the ocean and slid away again behind like the white wake of the moon by night), the fishes that leapt, the stars that revolved, and the whole reasonless, rocking environ of the sea itself – such things eventually classified themselves into mere living, ordinary existence. For Jean experienced them and survived them all, and to some extent they were lost on him in any case, for he was already in pursuit. His hunt had begun at the Angel Quay indeed, when he learned which boat, and which ship, were to carry Dargue a week before him.

It was, however, as though the entire passage comprised and was framed within an afterimage: that of sailing through a sort of bottle of pale skies and water holding rain, and coming gradually out of the bottleneck into a violent sunset burning in heaven like stained glass.

Although the conflagration died as quickly as it blew up, going down beneath a curious cloud.

'There,' said Jean de St Jean to one of the less disreputable of the crew, 'what is that?'

'Haïsa,' the man replied. He added that they had anchored eight miles out, and would not be going in until sunrise.

Jean was left to observe the cloud darken in a sheet of drained fire, and then to darken and harden on, blacker than the star – sprayed sky.

There were mountains on Haïsa. Haïsa was, in fact, it seemed, made of mountains. There was something in the Island he had not expected, the young man intent upon his quest and his vengeance. The Island itself had importance. It possessed some kind of sentience, dimly discernible across the rhinestone rollers, the reefs, and the night.

As he stood at the ship's rail, Jean became aware of another being on the deck.

It is almost impossible to describe the way in which the awareness stole over him, especially in view of what will follow. The sensation grew rather in the manner in which a man may come to feel he has some illness, amorphous at first, the faintest disinclination, ebb of the spirits. Yet presently depression is reinforced by a score of other slight intrusive signals. At last he must acknowledge the onset of the fever that will lay him low.

Jean bore the feeling, which was not exactly of being watched, more of being waited upon, for a count of five or six minutes. They would have seemed interminable, except that all the while he was trying to argue himself from his certainty. Frankly, he did not for a moment think anything human or explicable was with him on the deck. He knew, from the evening's previous sounds, and a by now general familiarity with the noises of the vessel, crew, and passengers, the position of all men and objects. Even the ship's dog had become detectable to him during the voyage, as it lightly padded its rounds. *This* presence was of one who had not, until that hour, inhabited the ship.

Finally, Jean turned, and scanned the area about him. The moon was rising, the heavy lush moon of these regions, which on its nights of waxing seems full of sweet juice. The deck glowed and was laid bare, the masts and bundled sails, the cabins and hatches, the station of the great wheel. No one was there in all that stretched instant of moonlight. The vessel was like a floating coffin on the ocean. Only Jean remained at the rail. And nearby, somewhere, invisible and untenable and nonexistent – the other.

Jean crossed himself. It was an involuntary action, a reflex of boyhood. But when he did it, he thought he heard a soft, long, low laugh go pulsing around the deck. This laugh, if it even occurred, was suddenly in all places at once, and gone as suddenly and utterly. Jean had grown very cold, but he was not afraid. He said, under his breath, 'I know you. What have you come to tell me?' But that too was only his instinct, for he did not know, either what was there with him, or what he had said to it.

Nevertheless, there came a swift flash, like a star falling or a light quenched somewhere between himself and the next item of solid material, which happened to be one of the masts. What it was he did not see, although it seemed afterward that it might have been the reflection of a face, glimpsed as if in a mirror. It was a peculiar face, too, more a mask, that was at one and the same time black and white, but whether the black was laid over the white or the white on the black, Jean could not make out.

And then he found he could move, the air had soaked back to its usual tepid warmth, and he started to hear real sounds from the ship, and to behold some sailors over by one of the hatches smoking their pipes, and the watch motionless aloft. The other thing was gone.

The young man went down to the saloon to take his supper, trying to put off a vague sense of shame, which apparently naturally replaced the supernatural sensation that preceded it. Below, he drank more than he was used to with his meal, and went to bed amused at himself and engorged by notions of his arrival at the Island in the morning, where his search would commence at once for Dargue.

The ship entered port an hour after dawn. For whatever other reason, it was likely Haïsa had earned the epithet 'Black' in one way from her looks. Behind the harbour the Town straddled a vast swooping slope that expended itself abruptly, miles off, against enormous uplands cumbered in jungles or forests that showed jet black against the vibrancy of the sky. Beyond these nearer heights yet more gigantic cliffs scaled up, thick with vegetation and trees, until distance reduced the panorama to transparency. In two or three spots a solitary waterfall shone like a straight white smoke. The Town itself was by contrast pastel and tawdry, the ripe smell of it drifting out across the harbour with the stink of fish and fruit. Parrots, in cages on peeling balconies that overhung the water, screamed. Although he had seen black men as he neared the Island, Jean had never gazed on such a quantity. Their species was so different he could not fit them into any comfortable niche. It was easier to detail them as some form of higher and less tractable animal. The brilliance of their teeth shocked him, and their women, walking barefoot on the sharp stones and broken shards above the shipping, with metal necklets and coloured scarves circling their waists and brows. The women of Jean's landscape had figures made of laced bone and hair like ravelled silk. These had pelt or fleece upon their heads. Their breasts swayed with the rhythm of their steps as they walked like cats.

Had he not been imbued by his purpose, the young man, alone and mostly penniless in this alien world, might have given way to preliminary panic. But he was armoured, was Jean. And in his armour he went ashore, and carrying his bag himself, went up the first curving street from the port, between the balconies and bird cages, across a square of big-limbed trees pendulous with gourds, under the stucco and the palms and over the steps, clung with orchids, that led to the upper Town of Black Haïsa.

And the cat-women passed him in their skins of velure, and higher up he saw the ones who were half cat and half human, swarthy near-white, driving in their carriages with fans of feathers in their carved, ringed hands. And he saw the gentlemen too, lounging by the barbers and the hotels, in striped waistcoats, and some of these were black and some not quite black. But the whites had gone to the very surface-top of the Town like froth to the top of coffee, and there were to be noticed, like pieces of mosaic among the plantains and palm trees, their froth-white mansions with faded names, and colossal gardens gone to seed, passionflowers and flowers that ate flies, snakes in the dry fountains, and giant spiders hung among vines, weaving with their legs.

But the visor of his armour was down across the eyes of Jean de St Jean the poet's son. He knew the word 'Dargue.' That was what he had come for. He climbed up because that was the way the streets and steps led him, and the hanging parks of Haïsa Town. Dargue was a man of substance in this place, and should be simple to find.

And Jean knew an aching urge to see him again. It was nearly poignant. As if, in looking at this man, he could perceive, lifted miraculously out of time and decay, his two parents, whose faces he knew only from some little paintings kept in Andromede's apartment.

Jean had of course conceived a plan, partly conceived it in his home City in the days after sighting Dargue. Aboard ship, during the ocean months, he shaped the plan or was shaped by it, perhaps. The fuss that some of his fellow passengers made of him – as a young hopeful setting forth to try his fortune (naturally the true purpose was not revealed to them) – and the general talk of the way of getting on in the islands, moulded the plan further. It became outrageous and possible. It appealed to Jean by its audacity, its very terribleness. For what he eventually proposed to do was to approach Dargue directly, rendering him the false identity which he, Jean, had already adopted for the voyage out – it was one of the few provisions the poet's son had taken to protect himself. And having so engaged his enemy, Jean would stand before him and beg for an occupation, flaunting the good City education, making of himself a charming and valuable prospect. That Dargue should take him on, employ him, as a secretary or assistant of some sort, was so balefully ironic, Jean did not believe it could not come to be.

Installed in Dargue's very household, privy to his secrets, which rumour suggested were often dark, debauched, dangerous, Jean foresaw a hundred opportunities both to ruin and, ultimately, to commit murder.

How the murder was to be accomplished – this he did not know, and had never truly visualised. It was a shadow act performed in dream. *That valid.* He trusted that the hour and the means would be given him.

Jean made his inquiries at Haïsa Town after Dargue in the manner of the young hopeful off the ship, a fellow citizen, speaking a common tongue, clever, and prepared to be industrious. Quite quickly he had his directions to a mansion out along Oleander Road. It was a two-hour ride, which to Jean, on foot and with his bag in hand, would furnish an afternoon's walk.

Oleander Road was not a road in any sense of a city street. It was a broad avenue of earth that rambled out of the edges of the Town and curled itself away for miles through the hills. It was barricaded by banana trees, and continually encroached upon by the forest, a swollen, lubricious wall of leaves and trunks that bulged inward with incredible potency, alight with sun, with bird noises, and the quiver of insects. The air was warm, it seemed to run down in rivulets, so that everything to be seen wavered. Along Oleander Road, at considerable distances from one another, the old houses lay off the track, behind spilled paths, rough-haired lawns, and plantings of cocoa and tobacco. In one place there was even a milestone, but it indicated the leagues back to Haïsa Town.

Shade was thrown all over the road, and shots of sun. The shambling route went always higher and higher, and began at length to show, through windowpane openings, sky and sea below.

Drenched in sweat, Jean walked the road. His bag came to weigh like the weight of the sins of the one he sought.

There was nothing else he could do. It was out of the question to turn back, and he never debated that he should. He went on, sometimes turning his head to catch the weird bird cries of the forest, or slapping at some bloodsucking thing that had bitten him. It was a type of hell, this walk. He had not foretold the punishment, but neither did he resist its infliction.

The shade pool on the road deepened, and spread, and a breeze started that shook the huge hammered-iron leaves of the plantains. It was evening, and abruptly, on his left hand, Jean saw the notice that indicated the estate of Monsieur Dargue.

He felt a start of the pulses, as though he had encountered a lover unexpectedly.

The garden of Dargue's house was positively enormous and dense with the coming of darkness. The overhanging shrubs and trees seemed hung with heavy coils of snakes. A scent began of strange pale-coloured flowers. The stars were piercing the sky like drops of silver sweat or blood bursting out upon a thin black skin.

Jean wandered through this tangle of night, and behind the little fires of flowers the house had suddenly appeared, two stories of masonry in a cage of verandas, lighted by oil lamps that hung on it like ripe fruit.

A dog commenced to bark and howl drearily. Jean stood beside a fountain and saw the mansion of his enemy before him, and everything became for a moment unreal. It was as if he did not even know who he himself was, or his own name. As if he had forgotten the name of his father, and why he had come here. And the word 'Dargue' was meaningless.

The moment was frightful to Jean. It actually frightened him, but more than that, it caused him to struggle with some faceless adversary, and to win.

After that the house was Dargue's house, and he must get to it at once.

Perhaps he became aware as he drew nearer that there was a hush on the building. The dog had left off its dirge and the crickets were very loud. One lighted window burned in the second story, nothing else. The lanterns around the veranda seemed to grin. Beyond the house stretched the fields of the estate, but no lamp moved there – it might have been a primeval swamp.

Jean rang the bell, which was quite ordinary. He had to wait some while, and was reaching out again for the bell pull when he heard a kind of dragging step coming toward him through the house.

Jean was conscious then that something had gone wrong.

The door opened. An elderly black man was craning out, peering up at him. He had the face of a beautiful marmoset, which themselves resemble the princes of another world. But he was so old and bent, and maybe had had to bend his inner self also; he looked at Jean with a timorous indifference, saying nothing.

'Dargue. I am here – to see Monsieur Dargue,' said Jean stridently, his voice too noisy, like something that escaped him.

The old man continued peering up at him.

'I've come a long way,' said Jean, and suddenly realised that he had. He trembled.

'Monsieur Dargue,' said the black man, softly.

'Yes. Tell him –'

'No, monsieur,' said the black man, 'I can't tell him. Monsieur Dargue is dead.'

The whole night caved in upon Jean, shadows, trees, darkness, stars, all came rushing down, pouring in through the top of his skull. He dropped his bag somewhere in the maelstrom. Then found himself leaning against the wall.

The servant man still watched him, still indifferent, but saying now in a craven way, 'He take ill on the day he come back. He take to his bed. Then the doctor come. Then the priest come. Then Monsieur Dargue, he dies. He dies last night.'

In the silence that followed the servant's recital, Jean heard himself say, equally softly, 'But I've come such a long way. I came to find him.'

'He dead, monsieur.'

Jean said, 'Yes'

And then the servant seemed to try to reward him for his compliance.

'He is lying out on the bed. You want come in, monsieur, have look at him?'

A rush of nausea. 'No,' Jean said. 'In God's name –'

When he recovered a little, the servant had closed the door, and was audibly making his dragging progress off again through the house.

For a few seconds Jean leaned on the wall and wept. It was the ghastly disappointment of the passionate child, whose desired gift has been snatched away at the last instant, literally out of his hand.

Worst of all, he did not know in the least what to do next. He had been almost four months tending to this, more, his entire life had in some sort latched on it. But the dream act was already performed. Even as he had stood on the ship's deck, scenting the odour of Haïsa across the night, even then. Death himself had pre-empted the frail revenge of Jean de St Jean. Face to face with his own mortal inconsequence, the young man turned from the house of his enemy, a shell as meaningless as if gutted by fire. He trudged away, not quite knowing what he did, through the serpentine garden.

2

On Oleander Road, near midnight, Jean beheld a strange procession.

He supposed he had sat down at the road's edge, as he might have done in some country lane of the north, above his City. Here there were snakes and poisonous toads, hairy lianas, vampire insects – but he was past considering them. He did not sleep but sank into a stupor, in which he was aware of moisture, the dew of old rains dripping down, and things that hastened over his hands. The moon crossed the road, and when it was gone, through the dark a throbbing seemed to come, like the pulse of blood along an artery.

Jean gazed with dull eyes. Presently the curtains of night were parted, and from some obscure avenue among the trees of the forest, a troop of men and women emerged onto the road. They looked themselves black as the night, and would not have been easy to see but for the fact many of them wore light-coloured garments that shone in a skull-faced flicker of lanterns. Jean noticed that several of the women carried bunches of some plant. It was not unfamiliar, perhaps he had seen it growing wild here and there, an ugly shrub, stringy, like an uncombed horse's tail.

The leader of these people was a tall man dressed in white. He stalked ahead as if alone, staring directly before him. He held a whip with a bone handle. There was also a girl who lugged in a wicker cage two or three black birds that jumped and flapped, but their outcry was lost in the drums and a deep, ceaseless murmuring that went with them up the road.

Jean was aware, incoherently, that he looked on something that maybe it would have been better he had not seen. There was an overt secrecy to the procession, which seemed to make no attempt to hide itself simply because, by an inexorable law, it must not be witnessed.

When the vision had disappeared into the tunnel of the road going in the direction perhaps of Dargue's estate, Jean stayed motionless, listening after the fading drumbeat, until it mingled with the beating of his own heart in his ears.

When he moved again, it was with a stupefied caution. He was not afraid, but he suspected he should be.

He stumbled on, and with no further encounter, came eventually back to the brink of the Town. Here, earlier, he had found a possible lodging. Having climbed the wall, he slept in the garden of this place, for he would not rouse them at that hour, the prohibitions of his upbringing forbade such a thing.

It was almost dawn in any case. The sky's membrane palpitated. Beneath a mango tree with savage leaves he fell, and using his bag for a pillow, began to tell himself mindlessly over and over what he must do. That all there *was* to do now was to seek labour, as a clerk, or even at a meaner occupation, earning his return passage to the City. What else could he attempt? For he was like a somnambulist roughly wakened. The dream had misled; he had lost his way.

Although he could not sleep, every now and then the image of the procession on Oleander Road went swaying through his thoughts, scattering them.

Had the procession been going to the house of Dargue? But they had told him on the ship, the black race of the islands hated the white race. The last wave of the Revolution, breaking there, had freed the slaves of Haïsa, but made of them instead mostly serfs. And those that had become black masters, in their turn, hated too, in a more perilous, educated manner, anything that was pale, even where darkness ran just visibly under the skin.

This was a land of nightmares, this country he had woken up in. He must get home. Anything else was futile. He was broken.

It is probable Jean went mad that night. Of course he had been tinged by insanity for years, for all his life. But like a deadly flower it burst open in him then, in the hours on the road, going back, cheated. Beneath the mango in the garden of the lodging house.

That is not to say his madness was incurable.

When day arrived, he heard persons stirring in the house and went and claimed his room there. Next, having washed himself and shaved, he went into the Town to look for employment. He did all this very correctly, and like a man with no soul. There is a name for this condition in the islands, and he was to hear it quite soon.

In the afternoon, when a bruised light hung over the Town, the outrider of the storm that usually occurred daily at that season, Jean de St Jean was sitting in the dusty little office of someone who might be willing to give him some work. He had been waiting an interminable time, which was in reality only a few minutes, and his nerves were urging him sluggishly but repeatedly to get up and leave, for this could be no use to him. Then the door opened, and a black man entered.

He was dressed as a labourer, and his personal scent was strong, like the musk of the panther. He looked directly at Jean and, without a word, jerked his feline head toward the street.

Jean saw this, and said, 'What do you want?'

He had not achieved the proper purblind arrogance of the white in Haïsa, or the proper uneasiness either. He reacted as he would have done to something unreal yet fundamentally inimical. To a threatening and *superior* thing.

The man did not answer him, but poised there, plainly expecting Jean to get up and go out with him.

Jean was so exhausted, so demoralised and unhinged, that in a moment this was exactly what he did.

When they were on the street, Jean said, 'But –'

That was all.

They went down and down, through a kind of corkscrew of streets, where vines and palms poured over walls, and the houses came to be built of planks and tin. Finally there was a space, and a rickety hut with a tin roof, and the black man pointed at its door.

'Who are you?' said Jean.

The black man laughed. He looked like a god when he did so, lawless and all-wise. Then he spat on the ground and walked off another way, and Jean was left there, at the bottom of the corkscrew, with only the door in front of him. So he pushed the door wide.

Inside was the dusk again, redolent with such stuff as cooked rice, blood, spice, tobacco, washing, and rum. He could make out no furniture, but some black beings were seated on the earth floor in an open circle, and before them was a scatter of objects lit by one window. Jean saw dried beans and cards, a shawl, a fruit, and the bones of a dog brightly painted.

'Shut our door,' said a voice.

Jean drew the door in against him, and the shack became more solid and less visible, and the bones glowed, and the white eyes in the faces like ebony, like beautiful alien masks, and like nothing human.

'Sit down with us,' someone said. And someone else gave a cruel laugh.

Jean remained in the shut door. They were figments of a new dream.

Finally, a man said from the circle, 'M'sir Dargue is dead. Are you sorry he dead?'

Jean choked back a confused reply. He felt compelled to respond, unbearably excited, could not speak.

'Why you would want him alive?' said the voice.

There was a great attention then. They focused it upon Jean. He did not know how many of them there were, but the eyes fastened on him like claws.

'Alive – so I –' said Jean.

'He not loved, Monsieur Dargue,' said the voice. The others purred in the dark. 'No one is sorry.'

Jean covered his face with one hand. He longed, as though to vomit, to evict the cry: *My father's murderer!* It would not come.

'You not sorry,' said the voice, soothingly.

The illness flooded from Jean, the words released him. He said hoarsely, 'Yes, I came to kill him. Too late.'

'Not so. We give him you, for killing.'

And the others purred.

They were smiling at him. In every night of a face a sickle moon.

But Dargue was dead.

'We invite you to come our God-Place,' said the first voice. A black hand reached out and took up one of the bones from the ground. The bone moved as if still alive, and animal. 'We invite M'sir Dargue. We fetch him. You be surprised. But we give you have M'sir Dargue, because you want him so.'

Jean thought they must have pursued him back along Oleander Road on the previous night, and read his mind. They were sorcerers, so much was apparent. He had always half believed in sorcery.

But what were they saying? That Dargue was not dead, but in some way their prisoner?'

'You pay the price,' said the voice.

Jean said, 'I haven't any money –'

They purred again. The shack reverberated. Jean thought, Not money. It isn't that. Something they want and I want, but I must pay and then they need not.

He thought, very clearly: What am I doing? Where am I? What is happening to me? And someone else said, *'This is the Religion of the Night'*

Then he was sitting close by them on the earth floor, cooking hot as if above a volcano, with his back to the wall and the tin ceiling above, from which feathers and paper blossoms and bells hung on threads. A mirror floated in space, like a tear, a small lizard clinging to its cracked, uneven rim. A black woman was giving him drink out of a calabash gourd. It was rum with something sweet. Jean drank, and thanked the woman, and she laughed, and touched his brow with her finger. Her touch was like a star, it burned.

Rain was drilling on the tin roof. They had given him a direction, where he must go tonight, not too late …

'No,' said Jean.

'Good day.'

Jean returned to his lodging and dozed feverishly on the bed. He dreamed his Aunt Andromede was standing over him, wringing her hands, saying, 'Let me advise you, Jean, you mustn't go anywhere with such people.' But there were feathers pinned into her tight hair.

The storm flew toward the sea, and the evening descended clear, as stars rose up through it.

He went out and moved toward a market at a crossroads known as Horse Tail. He had already asked the way. He received solemn looks and vague replies, until a wizened black woman had shown him the route, drawing a diagram in the dust. Still, he meant to be late. He did not guess why he was going. They might set on him, though there was surely no motive. He was destitute; he had done nothing to annoy them, except that being alive might be enough. He concluded they meant to play some trick. But he was drawn as if by a magnet. It allowed him to dawdle, but not to resist.

It was dark when he reached the crossroads. There were some carts and awnings, and fires burning on the ground, and candles in gourds strung up. Commerce of a desultory type was in progress, scrawny chickens changing hands, some barter over beans and pots of jelly.

The market ignored Jean, as if he were invisible. Then a man came walking straight between the carts, the refuse, and the market seemed to make way for him. He wore a black robe, black on black, but in his hand was a whip with a white bone handle.

When he reached Jean, there were all at once five or six other men at this man's back.

The man said to Jean, 'Come, now. We invite you.'

And turning away, he strode off again, toward the forest and the hills. The other men went with him and, pulled as though by tough cord, Jean walked after them.

The God-Place crouched in a sombre clearing. Water ran close by, snarled in the roots of an enormous tree, making a weird tearing sound. The roof of the temple was thatched, with an open court beneath, enclosing the sanctum, and full of the night people of Haïsa. As the man with the whip had ascended the forest path among his guard, and Jean followed, he heard the subterranean notes of conch shells blowing in the woods above. When the temple came in sight, and they approached it, these shells were blown again, a dubious, threatening greeting.

The man with the whip strode to a boundary of the court, which was marked by some small heaps of meal, petals, and paper. He used the whip's bone handle to point with. 'You will stand there. You say nothing. If you fear and run away, you not get what you come for.' He did not look at Jean, had never really looked into Jean's face or eyes.

Jean did not protest. He went to the indicated spot at the perimeter of the court. Five women who had been grouped inside the boundary, near where he must stand, ebbed away, turning their shadow masks from him.

The man with the whip passed into the temple. They had brought a chair and set it by the entry to the inner shrine. The chair had an abnormally high and upright back resembling a coffin. The whip man seated himself, and the crowd in the court deferred to him. Evidently he was their priest, and their magician.

The skull lamps of the calabash gourds burned from the thatch, and here and there glimmered wicks in cups of oil. The light only made one with the darkness. And the smell of the God-Place was intense and disturbing.

A girl in white came flaunting over the court. She carried a lighted candle and ajar of clear rum, from which she poured a libation under the central post of the thatch roof. Another white-clad girl came after her, an echo, a smoke-ghost. She poured flour or meal on to the ground in a pattern. A third girl came with a snake's rattle in each hand, and she whirled like a top until her white and her black merged into a vortex, out of which all three girls seemed to vanish away.

Then the three drums of the spirits began, and Jean saw the Dance of the Religion of the Night, a forbidden thing, both prayer and invocation, during which power descends, along the temple's very spine, and rays out among those who call themselves the Night Beasts, the black lynxes of the hills, whose true hills are older yet and whose rites began in cities of stone and bone when white men only whimpered at their cave mouths, afraid of all things and the dark especially, with some continuing cause.

Jean saw how the people formed into a black serpent of flesh, a body of many parts linked by a communal soul. And they passed about the spine post of the temple in the ancient benign positive right-to-right motion known in the Craft of Europe as God's Flowing, and commemorated by artisans in the action of clocks and watches. The steps of the Dance were a rapid stamping and tossing, and the drums formed these steps out of the muscle and skeleton of every dancer, lifting them, setting them down. The names of the three drums, which were later told to Jean, were the little cat's drum, and the drum of the second, and the mother Drum, which roars like a she-bull under the ground, the earthquake birth, the summoner.

As he watched, Jean felt his own body beginning to move with the rhythm of the Dance, although, too, he was rooted to the spot. A crazy exhilaration rose with the sweat and perfume of the God-Place. Naturally, educated and refined as he had been, Jean was instinctively resistant to it. He could not and would not give himself to the surge of power. He stayed outside, his breathing rapid and shallow and his eyes on fire, steeled, aroused, dismayed, in chains.

After a while, out of the dancing serpent, a young woman broke away. She raised her arms and screamed aloud. The dancers gave her room. She was the mare-horse, and one would come to ride her.

She was the mare among the Night Beasts and the horseman would possess her, riding in her skin, a god mounting her, and she would lose herself, gaining him.

The woman who was possessed was now in an open space against the central post. Her eyes were like blind windows, yet something flashed behind them. A girl in a pale robe came to the woman and handed her a black hen. Its terrible fluttering exploded in blood and feathers as the possessed tore off its head and wings with her teeth.

The woman flung the hen down, and drawing a pin from her dress, she thrust it through her arm, once, twice, three, four, five times. Jean beheld the bright point going in and coming out of her, but there was no blood now, no pain. She danced on the carcass of the dead bird, twirling and shouting.

The magician-priest had risen from his coffin-chair. He pointed at the woman, and all at once the blood-beat of the drumming fell away, leaving behind an extraordinary absence, as though part of the very ground had dropped into space. He spoke in the patois, which Jean did not truly understand. It was evidently a welcome.

The possessed ceased her whirling. She stood before the priest, laughing with tiger's teeth. Then she cried out in a deep man's voice; Jean caught the idea that she was now a lord and would be obeyed.

The priest nodded and bowed. Clearly he said, 'Lead us.'

And then the woman, or whatever she had become, went springing out of the court, and bounded away through the clearing, and the dancers broke and raced after her.

Jean stood still, not knowing what to do, until fingers brushed on his arm and someone said to him, 'We go to the graveyard now.'

He did not see who spoke, and the hand was gone from him like the flick of a paw.

He turned and half staggered into the rear of the swirling wave. It accepted him and rolled with him away across the clearing and up into the matted forest darkness sprinkled with wild stars.

Afterward – that is, one month later – Jean conjectured that some drug might have been pressed on him. Though he ate and drank nothing throughout the ceremony of the Night, yet there were certain poisons he had heard the Night Beasts used, and these, rubbed into the skin, worked very swiftly on the blood and brain.

As he ran through the forest, Jean had only the sensation of forward motion, and that his eyes were strangely enlarged, like those of some nocturnal animal. It occurred to him he saw, in glimpses, creatures that normally a man does not easily see – birds upon branches, lizards and frogs, etched in fine silver … There were other things, too, of which only the vaguest impression was left – of a huge man, naked but for a cloak, of a species of demon that grew in the trees like leaves, of a woman anointing herself in a glade. None of them were real, yet he saw, and acknowledged, each of them, as he ran by.

The graveyard must have been some way up behind Oleander Road. It was presumably respectable, but to the Beasts of Night, open as a door. They made an invocation at the gate, and again it seemed something went prancing along the wall, but it was gone before Jean could identify it.

His next formed impression – which was abnormally apparent, in fact – was of a woman he took for a priestess standing out before the others at a place where the ground was freshly dug. All around were Christian crosses and ornate monuments on which the lianas fed in a still gray moonlight. There was a headstone, too, naked and unfinished, and here the woman's snakelike shadow fell. She wore white, like the others, but it was a gown that might have come from Jean's City, ivory satin, sashed, and sewn with brilliants, leaving her shoulders bare as smooth black lacquer. She wore a plumed hat also, and a white domino with scintillants stitched about the eyes. He did not know where she had come from. He thought she carried a fan, then he saw it was a bunch of the ugly horsetail plants. She smiled as she stood over the new grave. Jean could make out no name on the headstone, but there was no need.

The priestess straddled the grave in her satin gown. She frisked the horsetail in the air and shook her head of plumes. From everywhere there came then the clacking together of rocks and stones.

Jean held his breath, could not catch it, had surrendered. He believed in anything at this moment, and accordingly, liberated night did not fail him.

'Monsieur Dargue!' cried the night, in all its voices, over and over again.

Jean found that he had called out, too.

And the stones clacked.

And something pranced along the wall, and there went the possessed woman whirling with a burning branch in her hands, and a man's face, and the black masks all turned one way and the moon that was like a quartered fruit –

And the earth on the grave shook. It shook and shattered and a piece of wood shot up out of it, and the satin priestess screamed down into the grave, 'Come out, come out, come out!' And then half a wooden coffin lid burst up and stood on end and a colourless white man's hand came creeping out of the soil like a blind crab.

The priestess stayed as she was. She never moved. The strength that seared from her was hot and palpable as the smell of living bodies and decay.

Then the ground fissured, and Dargue came up out of it.

Instantly the noise of the rocks and the shouting ended in a dense ringing silence.

Dargue stood in the bell glass of it, or what had been Dargue, a sort of man, clad in a nightshirt, and a crucifix on his breast pushed sideways. His nails were torn and dirty where he had used them to thrust off the coffin, a feat of great strength, which, alive, he might have been incapable of. His face was a dead man's face. He had lost his good angel, they said, *soul-gone.*

The dead eyes did not look around, the head did not turn, having got up from his bed he did not stir.

'Ha!' said the priestess. And she spat a stream of something that glowed into his face; it might only have been the white rum. Then she moved aside.

Some men ran forward. They carried the horsetails in their hands, and with these they slashed Dargue across the head and body. The spiky plants made wounds in his flesh, but Dargue did not bleed. He did not attempt to protect himself, and when, quite suddenly, he fell to his knees, the gesture evoked neither pity nor satisfaction, it was plainly only that the tendons of his legs had relaxed.

Jean stared at what he was witnessing, and now he tried desperately hard to feel something in response. Perhaps he did not even know that this was what he did. He was not afraid, no longer exhilarated. If anything, he felt very tired, for he had not slept properly or eaten much, and everything was alien, and therefore somehow all strangeness had abruptly become mundane.

What he tried most to feel was his anger, hatred of Dargue. It was there within him, but he could not get hold of it. It had faded to a memory.

The priestess moved up in front of Jean. She looked as though she were laughing at him, her wonderful dreadful teeth glittering. Her hands were gloved as if for the opera, and she was balancing on them, before him, a sword.

She nodded, and the plumes in the hat fluttered, while the sword was motionless.

'What do you want me to do?' said Jean. He used the stupidity as an amulet, but of course it was ineffectual.

'Take the sword,' said the black priestess. And she put it gently into his hands, which had somehow risen to grasp it.

The Beasts of the Night waited, and the moon waited, and the graveyard, and the Island, and Dargue who was dead, he waited too.

Jean went across the silent ground, toward Dargue, who kneeled there with his head sunk on his breast.

In all his least lawful, most incoherent dreams, Jean had never deployed his vengeance in this fashion.

He used both hands and all his strength to swing the sword backward and forward again, ramming it in through the wall of Dargue's chest, through the linen, and through the flesh, which crumbled like biscuit. A trickle of murky stuff oozed out. A rib snapped and came pointing from the cavity. The body of Dargue crumpled over and took the sword with it out of Jean's grip.

Jean stood there like a fool, feeling nothing except a faint disgust, until someone should tell him what to do now.

Shortly someone did come up, and murmured – was it courteously? – that he might go, his portion was finished, out of the gate, and follow the path, and he would soon come to the edges of the Town, with the moon to watch over him.

So he stepped off the grave and walked away.

He kept repeating to himself as he went, *My father's murderer.*

This did not help.

Then, when the graveyard had been left behind and he was on a rambling track through the forest, with the moon glimpsing out like a girl's face among the balconies of the trees, he saw what he had done, that he had cheated death in an odd, insulting manner, and this was why he had been allowed to perform the act with the sword, since death was probably venerated here, and to cheat him was such a bit of cheek it must require payment.

But all Jean wanted, actually, by this stage, was to find his lodging and go to sleep. He no longer cared about anything else. He shook everything off him as he went on, like dust from his coat. And like dust, some of it was already in his system, he had swallowed it, it was a part of him.

When he reached the lodging house he no longer had scruples about waking them up. He knocked and banged on the shutters. When they let him in, he crawled through the house and dropped on the mattress in his clothes, with the dust of night in his belly, mind, and spirit. And without a single dream that he knew of he slept, like the dead.

3

As it happened, at any rate as it was told, the story of Jean de St Jean has here a break or interval. Real life, and its experiences, are seldom completely serial. Yet the space of a year may be recounted quickly, the method indeed of my informant.

Jean's recovery – or lapse – from the hour of his murder of a dead man seems to have been immediate. His impulse was to ignore what had happened, then boldly to question it. Though he kept his reasons private, by asking casually here and there in knowledgeable, biased circles, for facts concerning Haïsa's Religion of the Night – that is, among the sceptical white community – Jean learned to behold himself as a victim of drug or fantasy. Perhaps the shock of Dargue's death had unhinged him temporarily, perhaps he had the voyager's malaise, a kind of earth-sickness, induced by stepping ashore after months on the ocean. Whatever it had been, any slight fears he may have had that some further pursuit might be made of him, threats or pleas offered, based upon his participation in the ceremony, were allayed by the passage of time. No one approached him to accuse or mock or coerce. He even grew used to the black beings of the Island, and came to think of them as inferior men, or sometimes as men, so that they lost for him their appearances of shadows and panthers, lynxes, and night personified. He was even briefly tempted by their women, but some moral code he had always tried to obey precluded such adventures. He had been brought up on a diet not solely of hate but ironically of an ideal of true love.

The previous votive of working to obtain his passage home he quickly sought and achieved. His City education and person assisted Jean, and he gained the secretary's job formerly mooted. Presently, along with the accumulation of bank notes, he was absorbed into the social context of white Haïsa. Class was held, since the Revolution, to be immaterial, but was still insidiously observed. Jean's manners were of sufficient quality, however, and his looks of enough attraction, that insidiously observed class did not much hinder him. He rose, and he bloomed, and even as conditions bore the harvest of money to return him across the sea, they drew in about his roots and began to secure him to the Island earth.

It must be wondered, in this time, if he wrote at all to his Aunt Andromede, and if so, what he told her. His reports could, soon enough, be of the nicest, full of good prospects and nostalgias. How he put it to her that

Dargue had perished is conjecture. He could not have made of it the grim joke it was, nor, certainly, even in the most unsolid terms, could he have hinted at the scene in the graveyard. Letters took so long, in any case, going back and forth. It is possible that they were mislaid, or unsent. One senses she did not receive any, but that may be false. One knows at least she never heard the facts in their naked form.

Presently, along with the rest, Jean became accustomed to the climate. He came to look for the seasonal afternoon rains, the thunder, the moon-drenched nights in which, by then, he would stroll or ride without glancing over his shoulder. He liked the friends he had made. Though assiduously he saved his fare, it had turned into a sham.

He did not exactly know this until one morning, going to his office along a street above the bay, a carriage slowly passed him. Looking into it inadvertently, he saw a young woman in a dove-coloured frock and pearl earrings. Her name was Gentilissa Ferrier – he identified her from the carriage, which he had seen about before. Monsieur Ferrier was a little known to Jean, and had mentioned that his daughter was to come home from one of the other islands, where family connections had for months concealed her. The sight of the girl startled Jean. For some minutes, when the carriage had gone on, he did not know why. Then he recalled the features of a Madonna from a painting he had seen as a boy. The Venus of Haïsa was also a Madonna, both carnal and immaculate, having two aspects, a flower virgin and a black virgin. Jean had in his researches heard the name of this goddess, who is wedded to all men and to none. He did not, naturally, for a second associate her with Gentilissa Ferrier, but by the time he had reached his office, Jean sensed an immanence. His father and mother had fallen in love at sight. In his efforts to recreate them, possibly Jean had yearned to do the same. Now the opportunity was before him. He took it.

Once he had convinced himself of what had happened to him there came about one of those coincidences that, to a person obsessed, indicate the hand of Destiny. Jean found he had been invited to a dinner party at the Ferrier house. This had already happened twice. There had been no reason not to invite him again; he had behaved very charmingly before.

It is curious, maybe, through this sliding frame of a year, to see Jean now, earlier an incarnation of Hamlet, currently Romeo. But the passion is constant, merely the object has been changed.

With the same headlong zeal that sent him aboard the ship, that goaded him along Oleander Road toward the estate of Dargue, in just that way he prepared himself for his first meeting with the girl Gentilissa. His eyes blazed, he was excited, fiercely determined. He had been disappointed then, by those appalling words: *He is dead.* But he put all that behind him, and could not credit a disappointment now. Gentilissa was there to be won. A year of success proved that he was able to win things. He had a half vision of her in the City on his arm, when his fortune had been made. Or they were driving through the forest roads above Haïsa Town in a taper of brief dusk, and she leaned her head upon his shoulder.

The Ferrier family was quite wealthy. This pleased Jean only because it meant Gentilissa would have been elegantly reared, though she would not, he understood, be as sophisticated as a girl of his City. What impediment could there be? He had prospects, and it was up to him to make her love him. If only he could do that.

He said a prayer to the Virgin. It was not the Virgin of the two faces, but the albino Madonna in the church. But he had already noted, if he had thought of it, that the shacks of Night Beasts often had their crosses, their icons of Christ. The gods had many names and were everywhere.

When he rode up to the house, it had a certain look of some houses in the Island. He knew it, anyway. Set off the road among large mango trees, ferns, and thickets of bamboo, constructed of apparently crumbling sugar, with orchids, and a tame parrot in a cage on the veranda, that called out in the tongue of the City: 'Who goes there?'

A black servant ran to see to Jean's horse. Jean climbed the steps and went up into the big dining room, lit like the church with candles. Once the sun set, the moths would come in droves to die, and the sun was setting now. The guests were for going down to the classical pavilion, to see it.

Jean, with his glass of white wine in his hand, was lightheaded and anxious. He had not found her yet among the women. He wondered if he had been mistaken in her, if she would look the same.

Below the veranda on the other side, screened by a towering plantain, the kitchen fumed and two black women were poised there to be ignored as Jean had learned to ignore them.

The pavilion stood against a break in the trees, and beyond, far down, the sea was lying, with the sun going into it like a bubble into glass.

Jean wandered off a short way. He had seen the sun set before. He was instinctively searching for Gentilissa. And suddenly there she was.

It was perfect. Against a dusky, mossy wall, she was sitting on a bench, in her party gown, which was white and left bare her throat and shoulders. Her dark hair was done in ringlets, with a rose.

This he observed, and that she was lovely. But he noticed too she cast a shadow, and the shadow was a house woman, who sat with her on the bench. And by the bench there was a plant growing that Jean remembered.

It was true, he had seen it since about the forest tracks and the cemeteries of the Town. He had even garnered its title: the Queen-Mare's

Tail. They said it flourished where there had been a death. A graveyard bloom. He had never quite come to like it, or be comfortable in its vicinity – that was the residue of the night he had once spent in the hills.

Now the sight of it struck him a glancing blow, that it should be growing there, against Gentilissa's skirt. And all at once the shadow figure beside her assumed an unnamed identity. For a moment Jean even thought he knew her. But she was only an old black woman, a house servant.

Just then Gentilissa got to her feet, and looking up she saw Jean gazing at her. She must have taken his apprehension for interest, for she lowered her lashes, and hid her face behind a little fan she carried, in the coquettish mannerism of young white women of the islands. It was a silly gesture, and it reassured him.

He followed her with his eyes as she went away behind the wall, the black woman slipping after.

The sun had gone down and night smouldered in the Ferrier garden and on the veranda the parrot called. There was nothing to discompose. The family and guests and Jean went in to dinner.

Gentilissa Ferrier was beautiful and adorable; she flamed like the candles, she was serene as a nun. Her moods were variable but not hectic. Jean was fascinated. She was all he had surmised. And in addition she had the power of speech, and thoughts, she could play the piano, had a thin sweet voice that sang. When they asked her about books she had read some, and she had a dream of going to the City.

When Jean attended her, she did not seem to mind it. As he turned the pages of her music, once or twice her eyes rested upon him.

When the dinner came to its end, he was sure, and going up to her candidly, with the mantle of the City she dreamed of nonchalantly over his shoulders, he asked if he might have the rose from her hair.

She was prettily flustered. For what could he want it?

'It has been close to you, Mademoiselle Ferrier,' said Jean. He was a poet's son. He had the taint if not the gift.

His final sight of her that night was upon the veranda, the whole sugar house caught in a splash of stars. The lamp that twinkled upon her put the stars at her ears and in her eyes to the very last twist of the path. The black woman was her childhood companion, a sort of nurse resembling Juliet's. She dressed neatly and had a bracelet. Jean had been polite to her on the veranda, and the woman bowed. They called her Tibelle.

In the weeks that followed, Jean often found occasion to be passing the Ferrier house. They were never unwelcoming. Monsieur spoke of the City, and of business, Madame was earnest to have cards. Then Gentilissa would come and serve juices in crystal jugs. She would take Jean away to show him birds and butterflies in the garden, and Tibelle would be their chaperone, gliding some distance behind them. And sometimes they would sit in an arbor while Gentilissa coaxed tunes from a mandolin, and Tibelle would sit far off, a black shape still as the iron owl on the gate. The woman had a pipe and now and then would smoke it, and the smoke moved in rising, but not Tibelle. The jewellery birds darted through the foliage. Jean began to court Gentilissa.

It was pleasant, there was no hurry. Everything acquiesced. Time seemed to stretch forever. If he was impatient, it was only through physical desire. He had not kissed her. These things, this temperance, were inborn. The climate, which could incite, could also calm with its false assurance, Go slowly. Lazily, a man and woman drew together. No one denied.

Then one evening, as Tibelle the black volcano sat smoking on the horizon, Gentilissa leaned to Jean and brushed his cheek with her warm lips.

It was as if a barrier fell down. He turned upon her and pulled her to him, but before his hunger found any expression, she moved away.

'No, Jean,' said Gentilissa, as sweetly as she sang and out of her nun's face. 'You mustn't.'

'But why?'

'Because Papa would be horribly angry.'

Jean was reckless at last. 'But he'll have to be told. I shall ask him for you. You know I will.'

'No,' said Gentilissa. She looked neither sad nor unnerved. She was entirely at peace.

'You feel nothing for me,' said Jean. It was a boastful demand. Despite her look, he was certain by now that she loved him.

'Oh Jean,' she said.

'Then I'll ask him tonight.'

'He will refuse you.'

Jean hesitated. He had not made his intentions obvious, but neither had they been opaque. Would Gentilissa's father not have sounded some warning previously, if he were vehemently opposed?

'Allow me the attempt,' said Jean.

'I can't. How can I? Papa has no objection to my holding court … that I should have admirers. But he expects me to marry a man of substance. Already there is someone in view.' 'That's barbarous.'

'It's how it is done here.'

'Nonsense. I –'

'Jean, you will grieve me.'

It was so shocking, this development, he could not credit it. He sought to take her hand. Gentilissa would not permit this. 'I love you,' he said. 'I think you care for me.'

'I may not answer.'

'Your eyes answer.' This was a lie. Her eyes were blank. She said nothing, either. But he had all the evidence of several weeks, when every sigh and tremor and sideways look had concocted meaning. 'Gentilissa, in a year or so I might be a rich man. It's been said to me, promised.'

'Dearest Jean,' said Gentilissa. Her breast rose with delirious softness as she drew in her breath. 'I can't go against Papa. He means me to marry a man from another island. There's nothing I can do. I never guessed the strength of your feeling. I thought you amused yourself with me.'

Jean swore by God. Gentilissa averted her head. She said, very low, 'You must leave me now. We must never see each other again, until after I am married.'

Jean sprang to his feet, but already Gentilissa was moving lightly away, like a piece of white cotton down. And summoned uncannily without a cry, the servant woman, Tibelle, was slinking toward them.

In a rage of powerlessness and disbelief, Jean stood in the Ferrier garden until the black woman and the white had disappeared together beyond the mango trees.

There is another name for the Religion of the Night among the islands. They term it Nightmare Magic. Once you have ever been touched by it, there is no getting free. To the devotee that is no problem. To the outsider, whom the gods, however obliquely and remotely, have ridden, the Religion is fever. It may lie dormant ten years. But it is not to be escaped from, in the end. They tell you, have nothing to do with it. But sometimes wanting is enough to bring it down, like a cloud from the mountain. No sooner did Jean run into the apartment of his aunt with the branch of their hate in blossom, no sooner did he set sail, than he called the Devil, and the Devil started forth. Before he left the ship, the first night, the entity had shown itself. It was too late. Death brought Jean de St Jean to the Island, and cheated him and bargained with him and claimed him. There is not a boulder or a leaf there without some life in it, or something of death in it. It was not only the forests or the human skin of Haïsa that earned it the adjective *Black*.

For a month, Jean dwelled in a condition of misery and fury that was almost lunatic. Initially, he did his best to go about his affairs of business and existence otherwise as before. But that was impossible. His heart had been cut out. He was in constant agony and barely alive. Sometimes he would lose himself in awful daydreams, riding to the house and confronting Monsieur Ferrier, bursting in upon her wedding and shooting down the groom. At other, worse times, he visualised his own life stretching to infinity bereft of Gentilissa. It seemed to him his pain would never cease. If he got drunk it might abate for half an hour, only to return with redoubled ferocity. Sober, he was like a man beneath a ton weight, he could hardly raise his head.

He was thought to be ill. He was treated with sympathy, next with concern, ultimately with impatience. This was not the obliging, efficient Jean they knew.

At night he would sit in his rooms and look at his money saved for the homeward voyage. It was like the coinage of oblivion. To go away was out of the question. To remain was not to be endured.

That he also thought of killing himself is conceivable, but it was a symptom rather than an intent.

Then one afternoon there came to his office, where he was sitting in rapt dejection, a letter. He knew at once that it was from her. Tearing it open he read: *I can bear our separation no longer. If you still love me and will dare the consequences, be here this evening just after sunset by the statue of the slave. Tibelle will bring you to me.*

The effect upon Jean, after his unhappiness, was galvanic, almost injurious. He shook, went white, laughed aloud once or twice, and generally furthered the prevailing opinion among his colleagues that he was not long to be among them.

The letter he did not let go of, and leaving his post early, he rushed to his rooms to prepare himself for this clandestine and romantic assignation. He had not a single qualm, although he did think her a trifle foolish, and very endearing, to trust him so much. Surely she loved him, and through the blessing of that, everything else could be made to come right.

The statue of the slave, a rough and ready work attempted in the classical mode, stood near a crossroad and a market. They were unfamiliar to Jean, although he found the statue easily enough. He had arrived before time, and watched the sun go down behind the towers of a pair of churches, and then the darkness came, and he beheld the fires burning in the market, and the ragged awnings, and the chicken corpses along the carts, and smelled the over ripeness of the gourds, and heard the chattering of the black men and women who idled there. An unpleasant memory wakened in Jean. Before he had satisfactorily thrust it off, he saw the woman Tibelle coming across the street. Her hair was tied up in a cream kerchief as always, and on her ebony stick of wrist the bracelet dripped like water. She walked right up to him, and scrutinised his face. *To be sure of me, for her mistress' sake,* Jean thought to himself, but he was not easy with her look for all that.

'Now you come with Tibelle.'

'Where?'

'Tibelle take you.'

'Where are we going?'

'You come, you see.'

Jean shrugged. He no longer felt as he had done, elated, slightly drunk, a little afraid. Now there was something heavy again, something pressing down on him. As he went after the servant woman, his entrails were cold and his heart beat in hard leaden strokes. His father might have told him, these are the sensations of a man en route to the gallows.

Up behind the market the streets rose and then there began to be the wide avenues where the fine old houses had been built, the houses of broken sugar under the poured molasses of the vines.

And then they were on a stretch that could have been Oleander Road, or Mango Tree Ride, or one of those other flowery, fruiting tracks that led into the forest and the hills. And then they came over a stony slope showing the sea in a net of trees, and there was a cemetery before them, a graveyard.

Jean stopped, and in front of him his guide halted and turned to look at him again.

'Where you think she can meet with you?' said Tibelle contemptuously, 'in the hotel?'

'But here –'

'Here is safe,' said Tibelle. 'What you got to worry?'

And she went on again, in at the gate with a sort of stumble that might have been an obeisance, and between the graves.

Jean followed her. There was perhaps no going back. The night was all around, and the hills of Haïsa. It was too late to fly.

He noticed as he got down the ridged path behind her that things were hanging out on many of the headstones, like curious washing. There were bunches of feathers, and beads, and garlands of paper flowers, with here and there a rosary, a mask on a string with staring eyeless eyes, bones and bells that clinked and rang sometimes as the night breeze twisted at them. There was a feeling of immensity and congestion, everything too close and the night outside vast as all space where hung the bells and bones and stars inaudibly clinking and fluttering in the breath of the gods.

Jean began to cough a little, something that had not happened since he was a child, it was a sign of nerves.

Tibelle said, 'Hush, hush, here you are.'

And there was a shack or hut before them under a stunted palm, in the middle of the death-place.

Tibelle went aside, as she had been used to before, as if to smoke her pipe, and Jean was left by the hut in the darkness. He knew quite well that all there was to do was to push the door. He knew, and it no longer mattered. The interval of a year had evaporated, and its pleasures and agonies with it. Therefore, without hesitation finally, he opened the door and walked into the hut.

He was half surprised. For Gentilissa was sitting there before him, on a small chair, with her hands folded in her lap.

'Jean,' she said.

Her eyes were large and luminous. He had always been struck by some quality in them, an effect he had taken for purity or innocence. But it was a sort of vacuity really, he could see as much now, a sort of vacancy, and when she had been with him and seemed to shine, it was because her eyes reflected him, he filled up the emptiness. It had made her attractive, like a flattering mirror.

'Jean?' she said again, now in a questioning tone.

She was wearing black. That was arresting, for Tibelle the black woman had worn white. Gentilissa in black was changed, her face was like a moon, a mask.

'Oh, Jean,' she said.

And outside, the drums started, as he had heard them countless times from the hills, throbbing and rattling, for some festivity or dance, the little drum and the drum of the second and the mother Drum who roared in the earth.

Gentilissa came to her feet. She stamped lightly and tossed her head and her hair flew out, the heavy ringlets. Her eyes were flat as windowpanes. Then he began to see that something moved behind them.

Gentilissa laughed and gave herself. Her face slackened and became an idiot's. Her eyes rolled. She seemed about to fall. But something caught her and held her. Her head turned on her neck and moved around again to confront him. Behind the mask of her face, another was there, that Jean recalled. It was at the same time black and white. Whether the black lay under the white or the black was fleshed out upon the white he could not be sure. But in the eyes there was no mistaking it, the night being, the lord who had come to ride his mare, and to claim the bargain price.

Gentilissa's mouth gaped open. Out of it boomed the note of a deep bass bell. 'I *here*. You *know* me,' she said, in the voice of a giant man taller than the treetops, older than the Island, with the sea for blood and the bones of all the Island's dead in a necklace at his throat. 'Know *me*' said Death. And Jean knew him, knew him. Knew *him*.

They said he died of a fever in Haïsa Town, having been sick for some while. The Island is noted for its seasonal fevers. They said it was a shame he died so young, the same age as his father, indeed, and far from home. You may come across the grave in a shady corner of the Christian Cemetery near Oleander Road. There is no inscription beyond his name, *Jean de St Jean*. Though sometimes flowers may be left there, by girls in coloured scarves who walk like cats and smile, blackened by the sun to the darkness of night, Negré girls, who cannot, probably, have known him.

The Sixth Night travels forward, some distance beyond tomorrow, and concerns the magic element known as celluloid. Watch carefully the flutter of the glowing screen reflected a million avid eyes ...

Oh, Shining Star

I

Up there, floating on darkness, the goddess widens her eyes, and two gleaming tears fall out of them. Many times larger than life, the eyes of the goddess need to be perfect and perfect they are, white onyx and black; her skin seems poreless as a leaf. And down the poreless skin the tears so beautifully fall. She sings sadly as a bird at sunset. It is the love song again, which is going to be so popular.

'I have your monitor-record in front of me,' said Mhal. 'It shows me you hadn't been out of your apartment until you were called here. That is for three consecutive days, four consecutive nights.'

'I was exhausted. The last picture –'

'Yes, that's all very well. But you know what it says in your contract.'

'Of course I know!' Indu rose to her feet angrily. 'If I didn't, you tell me often enough. No more than two days in one's apartment at a time, per month. It's inhuman, Mhal. It's monstrous!'

'No, it is not. It's just.'

Indu stalked up and down the main chamber of Mhal's office suite. It was spacious and comely as were all places and things in the Taja. As she moved, the solid gold anklets clashed above her four-inch high heels on which, for two and a half years, she had known exactly how to walk and stand and dance most gracefully. '*How* can it be just? I'm so tired. Do you want them to see me with bags under my eyes?'

'They would find that romantic. Touching. Yes, I want them to see you like that.'

'Oh, I can't listen to such –'

'Hush, Indu. This is no good. You've always been a model of our values. Why be different now?'

Indu paused. She was fair, the palest colour of cloves, framed in black hair that grew long and thick as grass to her slender, pliant waist-hair it was illegal for her to cut or style without the Taja's permission.

'In the beginning it was exciting. Everything I wanted, and always to be admired. Now I'm worn out. I work very hard. And they – they're always watching. I can *feel* it. When I rehearse. What I eat. Where I turn my head. If grit blows into my eye, they know about it. It's vile, Mhal.'

'It's the price of fame,' said Mhal. 'Pay it.'

'I *do* pay.'

'And, "they" you said. You were one of them, once. Can't you be a little compassionate?'

Indu widened her eyes, as she had done in the picture, and therefore now did many times over every day and night all across the State, in several thousand luminous screens. No tears came, however, and no sad song. Nothing came. Very slowly, she relapsed, sitting down in the chair that reformed itself to assure her total comfort.

'Good,' said Mhal. 'You're starting to think again. So I can go on to more important matters.' Indu did not reply. Mhal said, 'With the success of the Prince and Slave-Girl picture, the Taja will be promoting you to the *Sundah-Sona*. Your fee automatically trebles once you are in the Gold. Are you quite happy with your apartment? There's a new twenty-room roof accommodation in Rose Dawn. You might like to look it over.'

'Yes,' said Indu. Her voice was flat.

'And Vashari will be your leading man for the next five pictures.'

'Yes, I see.'

'Do you? I'd have thought you would be more excited than that. Most of our actresses in the Gold are on their knees to work with Vashari. No non-Gold, of course, ever has the chance. While the women outside tear their hair out by the roots as they watch him. And three years ago, when you came here, you –'

'When I came here I was lovesick for Vashari like all the rest. Yes, yes. But I never met him.'

'You'll meet him this evening.' Mhal got up. The vista of suite doors, anticipating his wishes, began to melt open. 'Now, go and stroll in the park. Look at the new apartment. Swim. Ride.'

'While they watch me.'

'While they watch you. Oh, and Indu, no more meals for a while in your rooms, please. Breakfast on the balcony or the terrace. Lunch – wherever you please, outside. Remember, I'm not asking you to leave the Taja. At some point there will be an interview about your entry to Sona. And your feelings at the prospect of working with Vashari.' The doors stood wide, ready for Indu's departure. 'Be more enthusiastic at the interview than you have been with me, just now.'

'Yes,' she said. She walked out, and down the glowing corridor.

The Taja rose at the centre of a low brown plain, its colossal towers white as snow from the Himalayas, against a day sky that was always cobalt blue.

It was the dream, the Taja, almost as soon as you could see and reason. One of Indu's earliest memories, a little child sitting in the village dust, was of her mother's hand upon her neck and the words, whispered from superstition, 'She is so pretty, perhaps pretty enough to try for the Taja.' And that explained why, as she grew up, Indu was spared certain of the hard chores. She was the one who would walk to the well with the red pot balanced on her head, and she was the one who prepared *bajara* and stirred the rice, coaxed to sing as she did so. But never the one who worked bent double in the fields or out on the new highway with the pans of cement. And the family went regularly without food so that Indu could go twice or three times every week to the cina. She could sing all the songs. 'Sing, Indu!' And the stereophonic radio, the pride of their hut, played all day so Indu might sing with it.

When her sisters, who came to hate her, tried to vent their hate in blows, Indu's father ran up with a stick. How well she remembered that, too, the screaming girls chased in a circle all about the space of baked earth, till they fell and screamed louder, and were left weeping.

The year Indu was fifteen, it was time. The family had been starving once more, to save enough to buy two tickets on the *Hunting Hound*, the hover-train that ran the fastest of any train in Azadi Asia. Still, the journey took twenty-eight hours. As the other passengers, wedged in the fifth-class carriage, slumped and snored, Indu sat wakeful with fear beside her mother. There had been a story in the village, told from malice (though no one officially knew Indu's destiny, it had been fairly obvious). Another girl in a village to the east had been pampered and sent off to the Taja, and the Taja had not required her. Outside the Taja gates, the girl's mother had handed her a dagger and the girl obediently killed herself. Would Indu's mother also offer her a dagger?

When they arrived in the city, they bought a gap under an awning and slept in the street. The next day there was no time to stare at the height of the buildings or the swarms of traffic. In many ways, the city was like the village. Gray-white cows wandered the pavements, women gossiped at public wells or water taps, and washing hung like banners. But there were stretches of steel, concrete and glass that seemed to have nothing to do with human life. While on almost every comer there was a kind of box with a slot for coins, men and women clustered thickly around like flies on meat. Also there were beggars everywhere. Indu's mother pointed. They raised their eyes and saw the sparkling facades of the cinas dominating the city.

In the noon heat, Indu and her mother set out to walk the twelve miles across the plain. Even before they left the city outskirts, there it was, the Taja, blazing on the horizon.

There were other pilgrims on the road. Some walked praying, and some rang bells. Others went in silence. A thin crowd lined the first part of the way. Occasionally there would be a muttered curse, or blessing, or a comment on their chances. The cherished children, males and females, were sometimes taken to the roadside to be dusted, tidied, fanned, given sweets and milk purchased from vendors who wandered the crowd along with small groups of police. Mothers on the road held parasols over their sons and daughters. The maternal hands trembled with fatigue, while the children trembled with fear and craving. Some of the young girls murmured, not prayers, but the names of favourite actors, particularly that of Vashari, a litany in which the starting crowd now and then joined. But when Indu thought of golden Vashari, who for a year then had been the prince of the cinas and of the fantasies of all women, she could not believe he too had travelled this hard road with feet bare as her own. Though they said he had. His publicity announced he was the son of a snake-charmer in the north. He had run off, bluffed and begged his way south, entered the Taja gates alone, arrogant and afraid. He had been older than Indu's fifteen. Vashari had been twenty. In one year more he was the idol of the people and received into the *Sundah-Sona*, the Gold, the actors' high Caste, and attainable only by actors. The Taja must have educated him well. When the reels of film sometimes shown before a picture revealed him working or relaxing in the Taja, or elsewhere giving autographs, he did not seem to be a snake-charmer's son from the bazaar. And though Indu worshipped him like the rest, golden Vashari gave her no courage that day as she walked toward her fate.

The season of *Thundama* came every year, like the Rains, though no rain fell on the Taja, under its canopy of controlled weather. The gates, electronically guarded, were already open to the weary arrivals.

Marvelling and terrified, the shambling stream trooped in onto the gilded avenues between the fantastically sculptured snow-white towers like columns of hibiscus. Some were three hundred or four hundred stories high, making nothing of the rectangular sterile blocks of the city.

It was in one of these hibiscus towers that the choice was to be made. Ushered into and left in a wide hall with a floor like a pool of water, suddenly the jumble of applicants was broken up, hurried away in different directions. Indu found herself bereft of her mother, whisked upward in the elevator into the sky. A new room. She was given instructions by a voice out of the wall: Go there, do this. Walk, sit, kneel. Then two women came, dressed in wonderful garments. Another new room, with a waterfall for a bath and great mirrors which abashed Indu. She was washed, anointed, tinted, burnished. Her eyes were inked in by kohl and became the eyes of the antelope. She too was dressed in wonderful alien clothing. In the next room, blinding lights stabbed down at her, now this way and now that, and again she must go there, do this, walk, sit and kneel.

You see a tree in bloom, said the disembodied voice, and there was a subtle difference in it, it had particularized. *Pluck one of the blossoms, as if you think of your lover.* Indu blushed, and did as she was told, and thought of Vashari, who else?

Did she know, asked the voice, the song 'Chamakata Tara'? Of course she knew it. It was the hit of the month, sung in Vashari's latest picture by a golden goddess in a swing.

Music played. Indu grew rigid. But singing had become natural to her, pounding *bajara* under the radio. All at once her voice sprang from her throat, wild and sweet, twining the notes of the *sitar-maya*.

He is like the light to me, the sun and moon to me,
Without such light I could not see.
But he says I am the light to him, like a bright star to him,
Oh, sun and moon, my lord. Oh, shining star.

They chose two girls at that season of *Thundama*. The first acted in only one picture, which flopped. She was heard of no more. But Indu, the other, was a success. She played a dancing girl, and a demon, and a princess. She made picture after picture, more and more expeditiously as she learned more of her craft.

Inside half a year, her family had migrated to a fine apartment in the city. Each sister had a bedroom to herself. There was controlled atmosphere, a freezer, a radio that took up almost one whole wall and a viewer that took up another. They had a free pass to the best seats in any cina in the state. Indu seldom saw her family, and then only by appointment. No one expected anything else. She had become a maiden of the Taja. Men watched her every night and day on the screens, watched her and began to fall in love with her, bought radios to listen to her songs in their huts. And women envied her, tried to copy her walk and her smile, to laugh like her and cry like her.

When she met them, her father too shed tears of gratitude, and her mother reminisced about the long train journey and the burning road to the Taja. Indu's sisters fawned on her cold-eyed. By the end of the first year, Indu did not see her family anymore.

She was so busy. She had made ten films that year, and was contracted for sixteen the next. She was a star, and not only in a song. And stars must give light.

'You see,' Mhal said, early in the second year, 'how the people are responding to you. How you fulfil their need.'

They were crossing the Taja's thirty-acre parkland. A tiger rustled by through the silken bamboo. The animals of the park were kept gentle and tame by their drugged food, and this one came to eat from Indu's fingers. Mhal and Indu had paused under a giant bo-tree that rose a hundred feet high and spanned half an acre with its shade. They gazed up through the branches, and a flying peacock spread its fan over their heads. It was very flattering to Indu, a young actress not yet into the *Soria*, that an executive of

Mhal's importance had taken time to discuss her work with her.

'This is your home,' said Mhal. 'You're happy here? You have everything you want?'

'Oh yes, oh yes,' cried Indu.

A fountain flowed against the eucalyptus trees, but it never rained in heaven. Miles away, the city was hidden behind a curtain of rain. There had been floods to the north, crops lost, and lives. But that was there, not here.

'In times of hardship,' said Mhal, 'we're needed the most. Do you see that? With only a handful of beans, still they queue up outside the cina for two hours of solace. We can give them something beautiful to alleviate the misery of this life. And the hope that, in some life to come, some other turn of the Wheel, such a life as this may be their lot, too.'

He spoke of reincarnation so respectfully that Indu guessed he had no religion. The shock was sudden and brief, for the Taja was not the village; she had soon learned that.

Mhal said: 'Will you do something else to help them, Indu? Something that will be of great benefit to the masses that already adore you, and which will increase the number of your fans, and therefore your returns as a performer.'

'… If you think –'

'Yes, Indu. At this stage, I always advise it.'

It was quite simple, Mhal told her. This evening, in the seclusion of her own apartment, a small device – 'Very small, about the size, say, of a ground nutmeg' – would be painlessly inserted under the skin of her left earlobe. 'There's no discomfort, I assure you. Would we let any of you, our precious children, suffer?'

'What will it do?'

'It will make you more accessible to the people who love you and depend on you to brighten their hard lives.'

The device was a relay monitor. Once it was in place, her image and her voice could be broadcast anywhere in the State, at the selection of the proper viewing channel. Indu herself had seen, had she not, the public viewers in the city where, once a coin was put in the slot, you could watch for ten minutes, live, your favourite actor? 'Your family have a large private viewer, don't they? Just think what a delight it would be to them to see you whenever they wanted to.' And did she recall the reels of factual film the cinas often showed before a picture? Much of these was compiled from the recordings of such monitors. 'Naturally, there are areas where your monitor does not operate – the dressing rooms, the cubicles at the pools, for example. And in your own apartment, the relay is nullified.'

Indu, on the crest of all that had happened to her, recently sixteen, touched one of the silver bells on her bracelet. 'But I'd be afraid of – saying or doing –'

'Ah, no. Don't worry. The Taja monitors include a delay principle, and automatically edit anything that might – shall I say *surprise?* – your fans. An indiscretion, a bad word … the gods of the Taja are human after all, aren't they? No, no, nothing to your detriment will be seen or heard. And remember,' said Mhal, 'you can retire to your apartment when you need to. You'll still have your privacy.'

Indu thought of the staring wretched ones who hung desperately on the vision of her.

'You may have noticed,' said Mhal, 'those factuals you saw at your village cina, of Anba-Jeet, or Vashari – the faces of certain other actors were blurred and obscured by obstacles – fems, veils, the pole of a sunshade … These were the artists considered of not much interest to the public, those without monitors.'

A venomless snake danced in the grass before a painted mechanical charmer.

'Do you see, Indu,' said Mhal. 'Privileged person, you can give joy to millions, merely by being alive.'

She felt a rush of nameless emotion as she consented.

Yes, in the beginning it was exciting.

She had been taught to move and to speak beautifully, to pose, her body, tensing or relaxing, falling always into graceful lines. Before the cameras, it was commonplace. It gave her life outside an extra zest to know cameras still turned. Even when she rehearsed, much of her work
would be relayed. That moment when she had had, she thought, an exact interpretation – and the voice of the director had called her back … That moment was not, after all, lost.

She was used to it, yet still enhanced by it, when she was asked to go on a mission out of the glorious haven of the Taja. The days picked for such excursions into the city or the surrounding landscape were carefully computerized, so the season would be fine and the journey seamless. Police dotted the crowds as she drove with Anba-Jeet in the shut, air-cooled limousine. At the stops, the people plastered themselves to the car, pressing their hands against the windows, tracing her face and Anba-Jeet's face on the impenetrable glass with their fingers. Anba-Jeet was *Soria*, and little older than Indu. Her rounded arms, the shade of dark honey, were patterned by traceries of golden beads. She smiled and nodded at the crowd, showing Indu how to be enchanting yet aloof, a true goddess. There was no rivalry. Relationships in the Taja were expected to adhere to a flawless moral and ethical code.

'You do this, you see, like this?'

Indu did what Anba-Jeet suggested and demonstrated. Wave on wave of faces grinned and desperately gazed and fell away as another wave came in. Sometimes the cluster of people was so great the car could no longer move. Then the chauffeur calmly pressed a button. The outsides of the limousine began to grow very cold. Repelled, the hangers-on unpeeled and jumped away, shouting with outrage and fright, or a sort of strange mockery, it seemed.

They arrived at a multi-story shop on one of the city's main boulevards, and drove up into a private garage. Escorted by an impeccable police guard, the goddesses were elevated to the fiftieth floor. Here, the store sold radios and film-tapes for the private viewers of those who had somehow afforded private viewers. Such tapes were not very durable and were generally played to death in a month. There were also film posters for sale, nine, ten, eleven feet in length when unrolled, and exquisitely tinted photographs of the stars.

The two goddesses sat down in a cubicle scented by flowers from an aerosol. They drank iced sherbets. One by one, the people who had been queuing in the basement days and nights, passed through the electric guard and laid the article they had bought, the radio, poster, photograph or tape, uneasily on the table. The goddesses marked each item, not with a signature, which would have taken too long, but with the personal seal the Taja provided and by which each artist was known. Anba-Jeet's mark was a hummingbird, Indu's a bell.

Thousands had waited. The session, roboticised by the police and the guards and the changeless cubicle smelling of flowers, dragged on and on. To smile too often became uncomfortable.

A young man flung himself down before Anba-Jeet. Police lifted him up. 'I love you,' he said. Anba-Jeet smiled at him wistfully: 'It is such love that gives me life.' He began to cry, and was taken out, his tape unsigned after all. There was no need for Indu to feel envious. A little later, a youth fell also at her feet with similar words.

'You look pale,' said Anba-Jeet presently. 'And I'm tired.' She added to the police, 'How many more in the vestibule? Six? Very well, that's enough.'

Indu was startled. 'But –'

'Oh, dear child, there are hundreds more. When you've undergone as many sealings as I have, you'll know it's impossible to cope with all of them. The Taja asks that no session be less than three hours. The three hours are done.'

Although their monitors were relaying the sealing session, they would edit out, of course, what Anba-Jeet had just said.

After the six last fortunate fans were gone, the goddesses went back to their car. The unlucky ones, Anba-Jeet told Indu, would riot in the basement for about a quarter of an hour, then give up and disperse apathetically.

Indu was drained. The mob pressing again at the windows began to frighten her. 'There, there,' said Anba-Jeet, patting her gently, as the editing monitors erased. (One heard that when a prolonged sequence must be removed, a 'fault' appeared on the viewers. Was each watcher's coin wasted then, that money which could have bought essentials – clothing, food?)

Returned to the Taja, for the first time Indu felt guilty and unnerved. It was a month before she had broken free of these feelings. Three months before the Taja asked her to perform the task again.

She did so, since it was an edict of the Taja, and because she still loved to be loved.

Her friendly acquaintances, the actresses who were her peers, were of one mind with her. It was a heavy burden, this consolation of the people. No one ever refused. It would be unthinkable.

One day, after a sealing, Indu burst into tears of nerves on the set. The director, who could be harsh, did not chide her. He merely sent her to her dressing room, where the monitor did not operate.

In a short while Mhal appeared, and Indu's dressers went away. Mhal told her those watchers who had seen her cry would be sympathetically moved. It was no bad thing. But the Taja understood that the sealings exhausted her. They should therefore be limited until she was in the *Sundah-Sona*, older, more used to her own impact; its duties.

She had still trusted Mhal, then.

Indu sat up, for she had fallen asleep in Sandalwood sun-lounge, and dreamed of millions of eyes. They were watching her now, of course, her awakening, those eyes. They had watched her as she slept. How many men, having placed money in the slot of a street viewer and selected the channel marked with her mark of the bell, had fantasized in those moments that she slept in this way in their arms and on their ragged mats?

She would not think of it. She must not. That was the advice Mhal had given her, months after the outburst of tears. She had gone to him and said, 'I'm restless. I can't concentrate. I remember how they were at the sealings, and in the streets. And now, always, I feel them – *looking* at me.' Mhal had said, 'Yes, Indu. Of course you feel it. But that will pass. Any sensitive actress has moments like these. What you must do, when the idea of your audience troubles you, is to *forget* your audience. Trust the editing monitor, and put everything from your mind. You're charming, modest, very talented, and most beautiful. There's nothing for you to fear in being observed.'

And Mhal had still seemed her friend, though she trusted him rather less.

How had things built up to this impossible pitch? Hiding in her apartment, when in the open – afraid to yawn, afraid to speak to a companion – and was the companion also afraid? No. It was a neurotic phase. Mhal, though she no longer trusted or liked him, was right. She recalled a one-armed man in the village, who had answered her childish query:

'*Dharma*. I am used to it.'

II

When Vashari arrived, some hours late, his skin seemed made of the dark gold of the candlelight. Here and there across the night terraces, other tables, lit like stages, stood as he came by to call Vashari's name and applaud him. He bowed to them as he passed, then ran up the steps, laughing.

'Forgive me. To be late – what can I say?' His hair, thick and shining, falling across his left brow, was like black water.

The couple of directors at the table laughed with him. 'As usual late, and what can he say?'

'Sit,' said a golden actress. 'Sit by me?'

But Vashari contrived to sit by all of them, and at last he sat by Indu.

'Welcome to the *Sona*.'

She thanked him, and turned her head from his handsomeness, for which she was not prepared. She had grown used to it on celluloid.

'Why do you turn away? Look at me, beautiful Indu. I saw your last three pictures.'

She had been thinking, *People are watching*. Out beyond the light, the slender pines which moved in the breeze – eyes. *Like the eyes of jackals round a hunter's fire*. But for a moment he astonished her, and she forgot.

'My pictures? Do you mean –?'

'I'm your fan,' said Vashari, the High Prince of the Taja.

'My pictures,' she repeated.

'Yours. And in – what is it? – one more day – you and I make a picture together. Your last role wasn't right for you.' (Did the monitor edit?) 'This will be better. I can help you. My one criticism, you seem too aware of the camera. By all means allure and flirt with it, but not quite so deliberately.'

She thought that, of course he knew how it must be done, and did it with ease, this moment. Aware, unaware … the only balance. But his eyes held hers. The Invisible that watched had faded.

'You will get used to it,' he said as if he had read her thoughts, now, earlier. Indu blushed, for the blush had been mounting, through the soles of her slippers, her spine, her throat, all this while, since he ran up on the terrace.

'Ah,' he said. 'Ah, Indu. And I thought you didn't like me.'

'All women like you.'

'No,' he said, 'but enough. And it's good to be liked, little Indu. Love is food to the *Sona*.'

He was modest, too; he had not said 'food to the gods.'

He spoke for a minute with the others, trivial conversation, but not leaving her. Nearby a man of the musicians' castes played the *sitar-maya*. Vashari turned Indu's head lightly with his hand, to look. 'In order to play, the fingers must bleed and form calluses, and the calluses themselves be torn on the wire, and torn again, until in the end the fingertips are hard enough to master the strings. Then, there is music.' He looked at her a long while. With his eyes on her, no other eyes mattered. She said, quietly, 'But were you a snake-charmer's son?'

'Yes. And once I was bitten by a cobra.'

Indu's eyes widened. He laughed again – it was the mannerism she had become known for.

'Walk with me,' he said. 'I'll tell you.'

They got up and left the dinner party, and the golden ones gestured them amusedly away. As they walked down the terraces, one by one the glittering tables which had called: *Vashari!* dimmed and were gone. They walked into the umbra of the pines, where crystal rivulets of water ran. The moon had risen, made misty by the weather shield. The white towers were like distant ghosts, moonlike, and far off like the moon. In the shadow, Vashari's colour altered from gold to bronze. It was simple to believe they were alone.

He told her of the cobra's bite, the travelling snake doctor and the medicines. An old woman with glorious eyes saved him, he said, by a magic song. Indu's own glorious wide eyes filled with tears. (A thousand women wept, maybe, hearing him, seeing him, tell the story. No matter). They walked a long while, talking, not talking, now laughing, now serious. She thought, *I am with Vashari. How can it be so?*

Where the great elephant of ivory stood by the lake, he helped her climb the rungs, and they sat together in the cushioned howdah, looking out across the soft water where the moon reflected. When she sighed, he said, 'Rest if you want, Indu. I'm here,' and put his arms around her. She rested her head on his breast and the world was only Vashari and Indu and the dreaming lake and the moon.

After the long stillness they had shared they climbed down from the elephant. As they returned across the park, black panthers lay along the boughs above them, birds called, and the dawn began to lift the sky. Vashari broke a flower from a bush. He marked the stem of the flower, slowly, with his white teeth, and gave it to her, unspeaking. Unspeaking, she took it.

What do poets and scriptwriters know of love? she thought. *I love Vashari.* She said the words within herself, with joy. For now it was not the love of an adolescent girl for an image floating in darkness, it was the love of a woman for a man.

His first letter to her came at noon. She read it in the privacy of her apartment in the Rose Dawn district. Yet she did not remember the question of privacy. She stood at the window, reading, and so perhaps was glimpsed. He spoke of her beauty in the first letter, a spell she had put on him. It was quite usual, almost formal, and she was disappointed. But she selected a new outfit, soft fabrics and hues. In the later afternoon, Vashari was at her door. They rode up to the high places of the Taja. They sat together, were very silent together. No one came to disturb them.

When it was dark, the palatial macrocosm of the Taja glowed like a spangled carpet below them, though still some of the towers touched the stars. Indu and her lover glanced about them. He said, 'There is only you. Nothing else. They say, the truth of all things is to be found in love.'

When the moon rose that night, they parted. Their picture began its relentless schedule the next morning.

His second letter arrived at sunrise, a moment before she left her apartment. His second letter was very brief, but Indu was not disappointed by it. There was one word only on the paper: *Karma.*

The first picture which Vashari and Indu made together was finished quickly. There seemed to be an electricity in the air. Before the camera their characters met and fell in love. And it was true. Each time they also met, they also fell in love, freshly. That the whole earth knew they loved seemed to Indu quite reasonable. And it appeared their love found favour with the Taja. Wherever they went, a kind of spontaneous good wish burst up about them with flowers, lights, songs. And there was no jealousy, of course. The code of the Taja did not permit jealousy.

The second picture followed the first, the third the second. By then the first picture was breaking records in the city and there was every reason to suppose it would do as well or better in other cities, and throughout the whole State. Undoubtedly, factual films of the lovers' meetings had spiced their audiences' hunger.

Vashari the screen prince, the idol, and the chaste, mysterious Indu ... The film posters blossomed everywhere, and the god and goddess, in their historical film garments, smiled and shone their happiness over the stained walls of the metropolis, and the squall of traffic on the highways, the yellow dust of tracks far away in the hills.

There were countless interviews, but these no longer troubled Indu. She had only to speak the truth. She loved him. And he, who might choose from so many, had chosen her.

That they would marry there was no doubt. They were of the same artistic caste. Their working partnership was spectacular. The Taja gave its sanction. It would be one of the most lavish and beautiful weddings of the cinematic calendar.

'But you must gain your family's blessing,' said Mhal.

'Oh, my family. How would they object? I've written to my mother, and she will have the letter read to her and –'

'No. Indu, Indu. You're not usually so heartless. Don't let excitement make you forget too much.'

They stood in a pavilion on the lake. A midnight party went on all around the sudden bubble of silence. Whenever Mhal approached her, now (she had obeyed all the strictures for the past two months, ever since meeting Vashari; there had been no need for her to be summoned to Mhal's offices), this little chill silence grew about them. Indu stood inside it. She looked the length of the pavilion and saw Vashari garlanded with flowers, singing, while the grinning drummer beat the time for him. Across the distance, she could not hear Vashari's voice, nor any words.

'Then, what must I do?' she asked Mhal.

'You need to ask me? You arrange to go with Vashari to your father's home. Vashari naturally knows what must be done. You have merely to be a dutiful daughter.'

She remembered, as she remembered only in vague flashes now, that the watchers watched and listened. This conversation would be edited. It would not be good promotion for Indu to be seen as lax in filial duty, if filial duty was what the Taja desired.

'And Vashari's father?' she said, to cover a dull confusion. 'Vashari's parents are dead and his relatives scattered beyond trace. The Taja is Vashari's father, and has arranged and condoned your union already.'

'Arranged … The Taja arranged –?'

'Of course, Indu. What else? You are, all of you, the Taja's children. We encourage you to meet and mingle, those of you who are suitable for each other. A flexible program, always. A long time ago, the Taja believed that you and Vashari might partner well. His magnetism, your sweetness. You were groomed for him, and he was kept for you. And how cleverly the Taja selected you both, didn't it? Look at you. A pair of lovers fit for –'

'Stop,' she said. Her breath choked her. 'I was so happy – How could you ruin my happiness? Oh, how could you do anything but ruin it.'

'You must face facts.'

'I've no choice. Does he loathe me?'

Mhal smiled. 'You know he loves and cherishes you. In confidence, the moment he saw you on the screen, he was smitten –'

'Then you've made a fool of Vashari too –'

'Not at all. Vashari understands our system. Inescapable Chance may rule the world, but not the Taja, Indu. In your village, you wouldn't have met your bridegroom until the wedding day.'

Mhal's face spun and bloated before her eyes and she covered them with her hands. When she looked again Mhal was gone, and Vashari was there in front of her.

'What's the matter, Indu? Tell me.'

She looked at him, not knowing what to say to him. If he did not love her, her life was worthless.

'Mhal is a trickster,' she said.

Vashari laughed. 'Does that matter?'

'It's not a joke. How many lies have there been?'

'Some perhaps. None mine,' he said. He took her hand. 'I can't prove anything to you, except in our future life together. Then, I can, and will, prove everything.'

They walked out onto a bridge that led from the pavilion to the shore. They stood there, suspended above the water. Was the monitor still editing? A 'fault' of this duration – how many coins lost that could not be afforded?

Her anger left her. She cried bitterly. Vashari held her. Every line of his body, the incense of his flesh, assured her he loved her. And tears could be construed as for many innocent reasons, and so would be shown.

She imagined them very clearly, the eyes that watched her weeping in Vashari's arms.

III

The car had a police escort. Even so, at the stops, the crowd surged forward. Indu smiled, her eyes sliding always away and away, never resting for more than a moment on any particular face – the gambit Anba-Jeet had taught her. During the drive she held Vashari's hand, and he smoothed her fingers. His touch said, *Hush, Indu. It's all right. I'm here,* while his own smiles dazzled the crowd like lightnings, and women swooned against the car sides. Indu thought, *If it weren't for the coldness that can be made to come on the exterior, they would clamber up onto it, on top of us.* The crowd would submerge the limousine, lying many bodies deep all over it. And then what? A boy, as the car began again to move, clung for a moment to her window, licking at the glass. She thought: *They would eat their way in.*

As they reached the block where the apartment building stood, banners had been hung in the streets, scarlet and dark red, and orange and gold. People extruded from windows and doors. The police sirens wailed, and they roared into the apartment garage where the automatic doors closed tight.

The elevator had been cleared, but a number of people had paid to wait in the lobby. They came forward quietly, bashfully, insistently, and Indu and Vashari sealed autograph pads and pieces of clothing.

The apartment was on the top story, its rooms set around a fine open court with an ornamental cistern. Washing had been brought out to dry, deliberately, for the clothing was of good quality and modem cut, and against the washing, Indu's family stood stiffly as dolls.

The greetings were formal and courteous. Indu watched the sweat rolling off her father's face, and how her sisters breathed in quick sharp pants, looking only at Vashari.

Presently the men went into the main room to drink tea. The sisters hung about in the courtyard by the open door. Indu's mother showed her a huge new freezer, crammed with provisions, capable of feeding hundreds of people for several weeks. With great pride, her mother selected frozen stuffs in brightly coloured bags, and bore them across to the kitchen on the far side of the courtyard. Here, Indu was shown the wonderful 'atomic' stove, as her mother called it, and then all the gadgets were produced and demonstrated. There was also the decor of the sisters' bedrooms, the new carpet, the new stereophonic tape machine. Indu had never been to the apartment before, since her family had formerly come to her, when they still met by appointment, in the Taja. Indu realized she was a visitor. Her mother never touched her, except once or twice by accident, apologising. Nor did Indu want to be touched. She stared about politely, working hard at her role though unsure what it was, dismayed.

Now and then a burst of laughter came from the main room, where the men were. No one came out, and at last Indu's sisters gave up and stole to the kitchen door. They came in a little way, like cats, sniffing at her perfumed body from a distance, then advancing and fingering the edges of her dress, which brought her close to panic. They kept their eyes lowered. Their eyes were full of hate, as usual. They chattered on and on about Vashari. 'How handsome he is!' 'More handsome than in the cina.' One said boldly, 'When he's my brother-in-law, will he find me a husband as good-looking as he is?'

'Shush!' cried Indu's mother, tickled and appalled. The sisters retreated sullenly into the courtyard again. An outdoor radio stood by the cistern and they turned it on loudly, and abruptly, with no warning, Indu's own clear bell-like voice came from the speakers, singing a love song from her second picture with Vashari.

'Oh,' said Indu's mother, 'do you remember when –' But compunction overcame her. She opened a cupboard and showed Indu all the modern culinary implements for the third time.

Later, as the sky bronzed, Indu's mother and sisters carried cooked sweets into the main room, token foods, and the two sexes mingled. Indu went up to Vashari, because it was expected of her, but in that place, surrounded by her family, she felt no closeness to him; she was almost in awe of him. Even so, she saw the hollows strain had made under his eyes. He was so easy and charming, eating *laddu*, talking of films, allowing the men to discuss them, as if their opinions might be helpful. He aided the others over their hills of awkwardness as Indu had failed to, and it wore him down.

They went out into the roof-courtyard, and looked out over the fume-hazed sunset city. Indu's father made a proper show of giving Indu to Vashari, but it was embarrassing to all of them. Under everything, the swarming noise the crowd made below, waiting for the film stars to come out again, blotted any other sounds from the streets.

And under everything too, the monitors, meanwhile, went on soaking up the ghastly business, editing out, probably, such things as Indu's mother's apologies for tactile contact, or the way the eldest sister had seized Vashari's arm and the father reprimanded her.

The pink sun levelled behind five apartment blocks. A flight of birds went over, and Indu knew the viewers would show them, herself, Vashari, her father shaking Vashari's hand, her mother tucking her face into nervous little wincing laughs, against the romance of the bird-flown sunset.

At last it was possible to leave. Mhal might say, 'There were too many edits, Indu. And you should have embraced your mother.' But Indu and her mother could not help it.

The betrothed pair stepped out into the lobby, smiled, sealed photographs and clothing, got into the elevator, and went down to the car.

'Vashari,' Indu said, 'why did we do it? It was so horrible.'

(Edit.) Indu thought, All our conversations could be private, if always we said things that must not be said.

'Oh, Indu,' Vashari said, his temper short, his nerves mauled. He did not sit close to her, giving love-looks to the crowds about the car, but not her. 'It wasn't my fault,' she said.

'Of course not.' He sighed harshly. 'It had to be done. It's done.'

'But why?' she said again. 'We have no peace from it. To be *seen* –'

'Forget it. When we're married, there'll be privacy –'

'In our apartment, for two days at a time, per month.'

'And all the nights.'

Furiously she said: 'How do we know?'

'Don't be absurd.'

'Very well. But supposing the policy of the Taja changes, supposing Mhal comes to us and says, Let them see you, in your apartment, man and wife, one kiss, or –'

'Indu, the Taja wouldn't ask such a thing. Don't be such a baby.'

The sea of faces surged and broke on the windows. For the twenty-third time, as the car tried to move, behind his partition the chauffeur pressed the button for coldness. Screaming and fleeing, the crowd fell away.

Indu said, 'I don't understand anything. Even you –'

'What about me?'

'Can I trust you, Vashari?'

'Yes,' he said shortly.

'Yes? But you're a part of what they want. In your second letter to me you told me you believed we were destined, by the actions of other lives, to be together. It was so wonderful to read that, Vashari. And so simple to write down.'

Vashari's calm gave way. 'Be quiet, Indu!' he shouted at her, as the crowds flowed by the moving car, shadows now, for the city was darkening, its huge neons erupting on the skyline, and above all, the neons of the cinas, where he and she stood gleaming in unsullied happiness on their poster.

Indu held her tears in check.

'Forgive me,' she said.

'Yes, Indu, of course.' They were slowing again, another stop. Darkness rushed to their windows, lit with eyes and teeth. Through the thick glass came the noises of slipping nails, like claws. 'Smile at them, Indu. They have little enough. And let's talk about something else, or our channel on the viewers will be blacked out all night.'

So they made conversation, acting, for they were used to acting. And the outskirts of the city retreated, and the crowds were thinner and thinner, like crops in a dying field.

Halfway across the plain the police escort veered and turned back toward the city. None approached too closely to the Taja without invitation. Before the god and goddess now there was only the road they had once walked barefoot to fate, as the tall sheen of that crown of towers pushed continuously higher into the sky.

'Not yet,' said Indu. Vashari looked at her. 'Tell him to drive on, into the hills. Just a short distance.'

'It's unusual.'

'I don't care.' They both laughed brightly and frivolously, still acting to avoid edit. To drive anywhere was something the children of the Taja did not do, unless requested to do so. 'Please, Vashari. The stars … I want to look at the stars from the hills.'

Vashari tapped on the chauffeur's partition, and told him to drive into the hills. The man hesitated, then acquiesced. Perhaps he had been warned over his radio-link about the multitude of cuts which the monitors had had to make, and which an argument might swell. Certainly, no one, nothing, denied them.

Presently the limousine turned smoothly aside from the road, taking an upland track into darkness.

Blackness soon surrounded the car, the lights of the Taja and of the city had ebbed away. Up in the black sky the hot stars burned, and the headlamps beat their path before them, but through the windows there was nothing, only night. And nothing came from the night to peer, to touch.

After ten minutes, the car began to slow.

'Tell him to go faster, please,' said Indu.

'I think he wants to turn back.'

'Not yet,' said Indu.

Vashari shrugged. He rapped on the glass.

'Go on and go faster.'

The chauffeur said nothing. There was a pause, and then the engine gunned. The car sprang forward, its stabilizers carrying it lightly over the bumpy rocky track.

Vashari leaned back in the cushioned seat. He did not look at her. His face was tired and empty, the profile of a magnificent stranger.

They drove for perhaps half an hour, and covered maybe seventy miles. None of them knew where they were by then, and the chauffeur insisted on a stop. He asked where they wished to go. 'I want to go on,' Indu said, and Vashari, dismissing the editing device, rounded on her suddenly like a tiger. 'You only want to escape, and there is no escape. Do you want to lose everything you have? Would you prefer to be an outcast of the Taja? No work, no money, nowhere to live? Without comfort, without –'

'Without you?' she said.

'Yes, and without me. This life is the life I chose. I want it. Oh Indu, Indu, stop this foolishness. Be my wife. Let me protect you. I love you and honour you and need you. But I can't be a beggar again for you.'

Indu opened the car door and got out. She began to walk away into the blackness under the pinpoints of the stars. The chauffeur made a noise. Vashari sat for a moment. He ran his hands over his face, through his hair. The chauffeur waited, then began to speak to him rapidly.

'Yes, it's all right. I'll go and fetch her,' said Vashari. 'Stay here with the car.'

Vashari left the car and started after her, but she had already disappeared over a hill.

Indu heard his voice calling to her, behind her in the darkness. She walked on, stumbling in her high-heeled shoes, feeling before herself with one hand as if blind, the other over her eyes to wipe away tears. But when he reached her, she said his name in a small voice, expecting his anger. He only put his arms around her, and she felt the savage drumming of his heart.

'Come back to the car,' he said at last.

'Even here,' she said, 'they watch us. Can you sense the eyes, Vashari? Even here. But not, listen to us, not while I say, "Can you sense the eyes, Vashari?" Not then.'

'Indu, Indu.'

'When we're married, alone in our apartment in the Taja, I shall feel them watching us and everything we do. They *do* see everything. They imagine it, when they can't watch us. They think of us always. They haven't got any lives. They have only *our* lives. And we have no lives either, because our lives belong to *them*.'

He held her and she buried her face in his chest, aware of the eyes, glinting and unblinking, encircling the light of their glamour and fame, the eyes of the jackals around the hunter's fire.

Then she felt him start violently. She drew away and looked, and there was a dull light somewhere nearby, then another and another, scattered around them through the darkness.

She had wandered down into a village it seemed, unlit, and so meagre and ramshackle she had not made it out from the hills. And she had mislaid the smells of the lower human commune, smoke and spice and goats, dung, flesh, gasoline. But now, as the lights came up in the huts, the oil lamps and the one or two murky electric bulbs, she saw surrealistically the scenes of her childhood returned. There, the well with a tree growing over it, and beyond, the mud-walled hovels with their cakelike doors that had seemed only caves a minute ago. And there, yes even in the midst of this poverty of all things, looming over everything at the end of the beaten earth of the street, the building that served the village as a cina, with the pale posters glimmering on its sides.

Indu giggled. 'Look, Vashari.' She pointed. Just discernible in the light, the perfect faces of the god and goddess, themselves, shone down upon the wretched huts.

But Vashari was only looking at the straggles of people who were coming out of the huts. Some brought their lamps with them. The lights glinted in their eyes, but the lights were also like eyes themselves, the lights, the eyes-which-were-lights, forming a circle of which Vashari and Indu were the centre.

None of the villagers seemed surprised, and clearly they knew who the man and woman were – as if, even now, they were images on celluloid, projected on the darkness.

At first, the circle was motionless. Then it moved a little, coming closer.

'What do they want?' Indu whispered.

'Money, perhaps,' But Vashari made no move to take out money to give them. He stood very still, and Indu, by his side, was also still.

And the circle drew in again a little more; paused, quivered, and once more drew in. Some of the people were grinning with what seemed to be pleasure yet, lit by their lamps, the expression was frightful. A hand came softly on to Indu's sleeve, her skin. Indu snatched her arm away. She was terrified. But no sooner had the hand gone from her arm than another settled gently on her hair, and uncontrollably she screamed. Wildly she looked up and saw Vashari nodding at the circle. Holding Indu against him, he began to walk forward, and responding to his apparent ease of manner – though she felt him trembling, as she was – the human barrier swayed as if about to give way. But there was a woman directly in front of them, and she would not let them through. She was gaunt and ugly, but she stretched out her hands to Vashari, and as her fingers brushed him she breathed a great *A ah!* And this cry seemed to release the vast, unnamed and unknown greed that inspired the crowd.

Vashari had ceased trying to force a way through. He held Indu tightly, as if to protect her, and she clung to him, as the endless rain of touches came down and down on them, first in the nature of a rough shy caress, but a caress which grew ever more eager and more possessive and more certain.

As the first small fragment was ripped from her dress, Indu understood, and for a lost moment her terror submerged in a frantic wish to mark indelibly, against all the odds of the turning Wheel, her love for Vashari, so that this at least should remain.

But she could only shriek his name as they were pulled apart, while his face was filled by desperation and fear, as if he had already forgotten her.

Only up on the poster over their heads did she catch a final glimpse of the real Vashari, and the real Indu, invulnerable and beautiful, smiling down on the village through the dark.

The cremation, performed inside the Taja but relayed to all the operating screens in the State, filmed and played over and over in the cinas, was spectacular. A structure of wood a hundred and eighty feet high, painted, gilded, carved, scented, draped with coloured flags of costly materials, went up in a rush of smoke and flames, forming a lurid cloud above the towers that was visible far across the plain, and, in the case of some high buildings, from the city itself. In the midst of the wooden architecture, the bodies of Vashari and Indu were consumed. It had not been possible for these bodies to be displayed. The car accident which killed them had inflicted mutilating injuries.

The dual tragedy had been widely reported throughout the State. The radios carried little other news for thirty-six hours. What had happened was still unsure. As those who had been watching the Indu-and-Vashari channels of the viewers were aware, the couple had driven up into the hills. Faults on the viewers became pronounced shortly after, and soon the screens went blank. It was thought there had been some mechanical failure in the vehicle. The driver, flung clear, sustained head wounds and was amnesiac. The Taja had not required him to give any interviews.

Following the first death bulletin, fans of the two stars had spilled from the city to stand or sit all across the plain, in abject mourning. By dawn the next day visiting mourners were pouring into the area by train or on foot. Police patrolled the crowds in great numbers. But, enclosed by its walls and electronic guards, the Taja remained impervious and calm.

On the day of the cremation there were scenes of hysteria on the plain. As the wooden sarcophagus went up, a colossal firework on the deepening sky of evening, countless women and a number of men chose to immolate themselves, frequently by means of petrol and matches.

The second and third of the pictures Indu and Vashari had made together, released posthumously three days after the cremation, commenced to break all previous records at the box office.

In Mhal's suite, this data was noted and filed as all, or almost all, data was noted and filed. From the core of this suite, too, had come the fiction of the accident and the details to uphold it, and the authorization for the use of a minor amnesiac process on a member of the transport caste of the Taja. While, locked away in the suite prior to being destroyed was the monitor-record which only a select few of the Taja's internal viewers had been able to receive, and to record, unedited.

Those hired by the Taja for the work found the village docile and mindless, persisting at subsistence level. The anticipated famine or outbreak of disease would wipe it from the face of the earth before much longer. What certain documents called The Remains, had been flung into a ravine, from which the Taja's officers retrieved them.

There was not much left of the bodies. As the reels of film, soon to be dissolved in acid, revealed, they had been torn apart, wrenched into pieces, just as their clothing and hanks of their hair had been ripped from them in the preliminary. As the film had shown, too, the act had not been truly frenzied, not even actually bestial. It had appeared less like hunger than love.

Up there, floating in the darkness, the lovely goddess widens her eyes, and the handsome god takes her hand and leads her through the shadow of a forest where birds fly upwards. Though they are ashes they can still be seen, these lovers, still be looked at, up there on the celluloid, in the darkness, flawless and beautiful and bright. For, like all stars, their light continues to shine down on the world, long after they are dead and cold.

The Pandora Heart

I was born the daughter of a king, and my nurse told me early that a princess carries her head high, and is proud. But when you learn early too that you are only the child of a palace woman, who anyway has died, that you are plain of face, that your sisters are full-royal, (all but one) fierce and fiery, and wear red-gold necklets to match their hair, (and that anyway, to be a woman is to be an afterthought of the gods) there comes a little droop to the neck, and any pride is very humble. Or so it was with me.

But then this story naturally, is not really about myself, but about the strange and mystical fruit so many do not even believe in. I had heard the tale long before Akris, my brother, brought his trophy home. I remember it as one of the first tales, told in the warm light of the brazier, one winter, in my small room. The slave girl sat weaving a dress length for me by the cold shine of the darkening window, and the lamps were not yet lit because, being who I was, we were careful with our allowance of oil. I must have been about four. I had wanted to look into my nurse's private chest, which stood in a corner. I do not know why – maybe only a child's curiosity about all things adult. Or perhaps she had promised me a surprise. She told me it was not always wise to look into a chest, or to open up a sealed jar. I, of course, asked why.

'Araegne,' said my nurse, 'I'll tell you the story of Pandora.'

My nurse looked old to me, with grey in her long fair hair, but also oldness did not matter. To a child the grown ones are difficult, godlike, and so tall, with carved faces.

'Pandora was not born, but made by the gods. She was given every gift – beauty, wit, grace – and guile. She never had a childhood, because she was fashioned as a woman. And so there was always something childlike to her – which seemed at first very charming.'

I saw from the corner of my eye, the slave was listening too, her fingers slowing. She liked the tales of my nurse as much as I.

My nurse told us then how fire had been stolen from the gods to assist mankind, and Zeus, the king god, was angry. He meant Pandora to work out a punishment on men. And so he gave her in marriage to the brother of the hero who stole the fire. This man – who was partly mortal and partly divine – wanted Pandora from the second he set eyes on her, and was overjoyed.

But Pandora brought with her a dowry from the gods, a black jar sealed fast. Cunning tricky Hermes, the god of messengers, thieves and whores, told Pandora she must on no account allow it ever to be opened, since what was inside was so precious.

Her husband had no interest in the jar – he would have taken the gorgeous Pandora gladly without any dowry. He forgot it. But Pandora – curious and always asking Why? – like all children, could not rest. And one day when no one else was in the house, she broke the seal and opened the jar.

I held my breath – so did the slave, although surely she at least had heard the history of Pandora before. Even old Ebony, my Cat Owl's mother, seemed to be listening. And they say cats know all stories.

'Every evil of the world was in the jar,' said the nurse, 'and they escaped to plague mankind. Illness and sadness, bad luck and old age. But, too, the very best things were in the jar as well, true love, glory, genius. And they also escaped, and now men only come on them by chance, or the will of the gods.'

'What did Pandora do then?' I asked. Always a question.

'She wept,' said the nurse. 'But soon she dried her eyes. When her husband came home she was all smiles. She said she had cleaned the house and wiped out the old jar – which had nothing in it. She hoped he didn't mind she had peeped inside.'

After this, Pandora and her husband lived together a long while, but in the end he died, for now there was death on the earth. Pandora, being a creature created rather than born, existed for longer. But in the end even her perfect mechanisms wore out. She too fell into the sleep of death, and was buried. It was her children who survived the Great Flood.

By now it was so dark in my room, the slave left her loom, and dipping a taper to the brazier, touched two lamps alight.

'A tree grew from Pandora's tomb,' said my nurse, 'out of the side of it. It was nourished by her beauty even in death. Such a tree had never been seen in the world. The leaves were so deep a green they were almost the black of her hair, and in spring there were amber flowers, the colour of her peachy skin. Last, in the fall of the year, came fruits, a deep, glowing red – her uncanny blood, Out of awe, no one harvested these fruits, and one by one they fell to the earth. Here, they never rotted, but remained like smooth rubies, lying round the tomb of Pandora.'

'After the Flood, however,' my nurse went on to say, 'the nature of the tree was forgotten. Long, long after the waters receded, a new race of men came upon it and found it still blooming and fruiting. Then they tried the fruits, but so terrible and impossible was their effect, if eaten, that in the end humanity was mostly afraid to touch them. The gods at last sent a great serpent with orichalc scales to guard the tree, so few would be tempted. And finally, after the earth had changed her shape two or three more times, the situation of the tree was lost.'

I asked for a more detailed description of the fruit.

My nurse said that they were roughly heart-shaped. I shuddered. I had seen the hot, still-vibrating hearts of oxen and rams offered to the gods by priests. My nurse guessed, and said, 'No no, not like that. The poetic shape seen only in jewels – look.' And she drew with a charcoaled stick on the floor the shape we associate, wrongly, with the form of the human heart.

'What did the fruit *taste* like, then,' I asked, 'was it *meat?*'

My nurse and the slave both laughed. My nurse said, 'No one knows except those who tasted it. But they say the fruits had a lovely smell, and inside there were seeds, as there are in pomegranates.'

I asked what happened to those who ate the fruits, something which she had seemed to gloss over.

She frowned and said, 'Fate dealt them what was theirs.'

I could get nothing more helpful from her.

When I was older, then, I heard the other story of the fruit, which was that still, even in our age, it might be found. For, after all, a scatter of heroes had, by drugging or distracting or fighting the serpent, robbed the tree. Some of the fruits were then eaten, but others, since they never decayed, even when cut in two, had passed into various lands, as curiosities and treasures. They were known as Pandora Hearts and worth a king's ransom. I had heard a harper sing, too, a tale of one of them, one night when I was old enough to sit in the women's place in my father's hall. I was twelve years old then, but did not ever forget the song. It was of a hero who tricked the Serpent which guarded the tree, and took a fruit away, and cutting it open, ate one half with all its rosy seeds.

'Then came on him such madness,' the harper sang,
'That the very rocks made themselves small.
'But he ran up the hills, and baying like a dog,
'He raised his sword against the sun,
'Shouting and crying out.
'Till merciful and merciless,
'The sun god struck him down.'

Curious yet, I asked my sister Pyrrha, so called for her fiery gold-red hair, (but the name was also that of Pandora's daughter) what the song meant. Did the flesh and seeds of the fruit drive a man insane?

Pyrrha struck me lightly. I should not have spoken to her directly, she told me so, and that I had been corrected. Then she said the Pandora Heart fruit brought out of men their best or their worst, depending on which was the strongest in them. I protested, 'But he was a hero.' And was slapped harder. My sister said, 'Don't do it a third time, or I shall tell the king. He will get a slave to give you three lashes from the whip. Do you want to be whipped by a slave?' Then she added, 'Only the gods know what's truly deep inside us. We may be brave and wonderful in all eyes, but have a secret flaw. Or most wretched, and have a true heart. The fruit finds it, whatever it is.'

I had the sense, nursing my slaps, not to ask her anything else. By then I no longer had my old nurse, but only my slave, who was a mere five years older than I. Therefore I told my cat, Owl – his mother had passed on the summer before.

Owl is striped and spotted in such a way that, from a short distance, he seems to have feathers not fur. His eyes are large, round and yellow, and his ears extend sideways rather than up. The nurse said, when she saw him – he was Ebony's last child – that some god, probably tricky, cranky Hermes, had taken cat form to mate with her. But I think it may have been Dionysus, who likes cats, especially spotted ones.

Owl sat quietly while I spoke of the fruit of Pandora's tree. Then he lay down on his right side, which signifies that what has been said is true. So Pyrrha had been right, even though she had made me pay for her telling me.

At that time I never, of course, thought I would see such a fruit, for my father Rhexenor's kingdom lies below the Towering Gates, and above us were the great snows. On our other side was the Green Sea. Though travellers came, they came rarely. But then there was the war.

Up the coast King Labron had his kingdom. Our people traded with his, and my father was in alliance with him. Suddenly a prince from across the Sea, staying in the Golden Palace as Labron's guest, hatched a plot to steal the Luck of the City: a famous statue of the goddess Artem-Qirri. Soon the princely thief was gone, and the statue with him. Labron sent battle galleys after him, and next was at war. Into this war, as allies of Labron, many smaller kingdoms were drawn, Rhexenor's with them.

A band of our warriors was sent, and a levy of male citizens. My full-royal brothers Pallos and Akris went as war-leaders, because my father, having no intention of fighting pointed out his grey head. Pallos and Akris were eager to go in any case. They were at the ages thought perfect for war, twenty and eighteen, the ideal of young manhood, bronzed and athletic, Pallos all golden, and Akris, the younger, with more red than gold in his hair.

The war itself was short, less than three months. The thief gave way, the statue was brought back in triumph to Labron's city. Akris said it was made of cedar, coated four inches thick all over with silver, and ornamented with gold, the robes decorated with gold crescents and silver bees, the eyes being two sapphires. But the autumn weather had set in, and some of the returning ships were lost. Pallos sailed home within two months, but there was no news of Akris. The queen, Rhetis, went into a shadow phase of grief, which angered my father. Pyrrha said it did not matter if Akris were lost, because the heir had survived. There were sacrifices in scores, the morning air thick with smokes and the stink of cooked blood.

Eventually we had news that Akris lived after all.

His vessel had foundered, and he and his men had been picked up by a captain, Udyzeus, who knew the sea route well, and the islands. But then again Fate befell them, and a storm forced the ship to put in at one island even Udyzeus, who claimed also to be a king, did not know.

Akris and his band, when they arrived home, were not the poorer for their adventures. They were burnt almost black by the sun, dressed in the finest of leathers, and with wonderful foreign jewellery. Akris claimed the island, a large one, had never been mapped. The women there went veiled, and only the lowest of them was ever seen. In the centre of the market place was a well which spoke oracles in a human voice. They worshipped Zeus, but also a mother goddess they named Herakte. The king of the city entertained them for three nights with feasts, and shows of extraordinary skill, one of which was a girl who danced with a huge gilded snake. As a parting guest-gift, the king had taken Akris to a treasure-chamber, and loaded him with presents. Then came a slave as black as night, who kneeled and held out a tray of beaten gold.

'On this tray,' said Akris, 'was a single fruit. It was a bright dark red, firm-fleshed and smooth of skin, with a deep central division, and two swelling sides. The stalk was also red. Even from where I stood, the perfume overwhelmed me.' Akris looked about the hall, where he was telling the story to everyone, evidently with Rhexenor's permission.

I recollect to this hour the hush, greater than the respectful but broken quiet in which they had heard the tale so far, now and then bursting into laughter or applause.

Behind Akris, where the two king-pillars of indigo-blue went up to hold the roof, my father sat on his carved chair, listening, his face very still. Akris turned and bowed to the king.

'At first I didn't think what it could be. So I asked the island king if this was a local refreshment. His face went pale, although he was a dark man.'

The island king had told Akris that the fruit was a treasure of the island, one of several that had been brought there long ago. All were kept hidden, and guarded by strong men and savage beasts together. But this one was to be a gift) a token of friendship between himself and Prince Akris.

The fruit was, of course, a Pandora Heart.

When Akris, thanking the king profoundly, took the Heart in his hand, it felt warm and living, like an animal.

He had put it swiftly away, and presently brought it home to his father.

One of the old lords, who were accorded special privileges, spoke straight out, 'Were you tempted, prince, to eat some of the fruit, for glory's sake?'

'Yes,' said Akris simply. His eyes blazed pale as diamonds in his sunburned face. 'But I had a warning dream. I saw Fate herself, standing with her knife, and her sisters behind her, one of whom kept her finger to her lips, and one of whom shook her head slowly at me.'

The hall sighed. My father said, 'You did very well, my son.'

The old lord spoke intransigently again. 'But will the king eat the fruit?'

My father scowled. Then he said, 'It never rots. Its perfume, I promise you, is delicious. If eaten, it's gone. Though it might make one man into a god, we are many. It is better, sir, to keep our treasure, as does the king on his island.'

At this the old lord bowed. It could not be, demonstrably, Rhexenor was afraid of some flaw in himself that might, should he eat, rather than deify him, send him mad, or otherwise destroy him. No, it was for the good of all he took thought, putting us before his own desires.

Soon, the Pandora Heart was set out where it might be seen, in an antechamber of the king's apartment. It rested on an amber dish, on a stand with claw-feet of gold.

All those of any position, however slight – even I – were permitted to go and look.

The king was there, and Akris, and my father called me up to him.

'Your hair is fine and brown, and of a good length. Araegne, is it? You may buy gold wires to have plaited in. You've not done badly, and you walk well.' He turned to my brother. 'No beauty, but tidy and meek. In a woman, two solid virtues.' Akris nodded, not even glancing at me.

I should not have been humiliated by this, perhaps pleased, relieved not to have offended. But that night I cried into my pillow. So the first view of the magical fruit, and the smell of its sweet perfume, were mixed with the salt of tears.

Of what, then, did the fruit smell? I have heard some people say it smells of Pandora herself, like a lovely woman freshly bathed and anointed with sweet unguents. But the fruit of Pandora's tree smells of fruit, as really perhaps is reasonable. Yet, though, it is no aroma we recognize. Soft yet acidulous – a grape? an apple? – but with something of flowers, the asphodel, the purple hyacinth that grew from blood. It is a clear scent, that comes and goes in waves.

In shape it is the form of my Nurse's drawn, spiritual heart, not the lump of offal pulled reeking out of carcasses to read omens.

The colour is lush, dark, ripe crimson, with that glow of a paler redder light inside. One longs to cut or bite, moisture fills your mouth. But this is so terrible, too, knowing that, if unworthy, it may ruin you, and you tremble more, the more hungry for it you become.

I turned away in fear at last, and saw others do so.

But Rhexenor ignored the fruit, chatting to his men, calling up Pyrrha to pinch her slim waist and laugh. A king must be easy with supernatural, valuable things. But the frown lines were between his eyes, the sort that came, not when he was angry, but when he had a slight difficulty, as say with a parchment he was unable to read, and tossed to his scribe with a, 'You do it. Why else are you here?'

After the Pandora Heart had been among us for some twenty days, attention turned rather from it. Akris went away hunting with his friends, and there was rumour of a marriage between Pyrrha and one of the younger sons of King Labron, a reward for work in the war. Pyrra tossed her fiery head. At fifteen, she knew, here was her chance. No man could fail to want her, and she thought she could manage men. Besides, king's heirs died, and a younger son might one day become a king after all. (This was in fact how it happened with her. There was some strange talk. I know nothing about it.) For myself, I was just then fourteen, and had sandals now with little heels, and the gold wires for my hair. It was my old nurse who taught me to walk 'well'. I only stooped and drooped when I stood or sat, and then, apparently, this was virtuous. I would besides no more think I could manage a man than call the mile distant Sea to my window. There is still only one male I would trust, Owl, my cat. Who at that time had already sired several families around the palace. His sons would tend to have one or two unusual spots or stripes about them.

On the twenty-third day after the fruit was shown, I woke to uproar. My slave came flying in to tell me that during the night, someone had struck unconscious the guard who stood in the antechamber, and stolen the Pandora Heart.

Rhexenor's palace was in pandemonium. Slaves ran in all directions with enormous staring eyes. The men stood rigid and warlike. It was as if we were about to be sacked. There was too the smell of heavy smoke in the air, an extra sacrifice and divination was taking place at the altar on the sunside terrace.

No clue was found, however. Nor did we need one for very long.

To my last days I shall carry the image of that scene.

I saw first the queen, Rhetis, staggering down the passage like one of the slaves. Her hair was coming undone from its ornate dressing, and her eye-paint had run. Against the wall, I flattened myself, but she seized me with her hand. 'This way, girl.' She had no idea who I was, and probably thought me one of the lesser handmaidens, exactly what my mother had been. But she forced me along with her, leaning on me, and after her rushed her slaves and women, all squeaking and crying out.

The king was coming from the sacrifice. His face was slightly smudged with the soot. Behind him were the three priests, and his lords and warriors.

'What is it now?' he said sharply.

Rhetis put back her head and let out a scream of terror and despair. Then she sank over in her women's arms.

It was one of these who crouched before my father.

'Oh, king – your son – your son has gone mad –'

'Akris is in the hills,' said Rhexenor.

The woman made a little mewing sound. 'Pallos,' she whispered.

It was then that Pallos, the king's heir, came.

He strode through the women, and his passage was like a hot and burning wind from some land on fire. I fell to my knees in utter horror. Because I had glimpsed his eyes, his mouth –

His face was stern, not mad, drained pale behind his bronze. His mouth was stained red, and for a moment I thought he had been drinking blood – but then I knew what he had taken.

'See me,' he said, loudly, without inflexion. 'Down on your face, my father. I am a god.'

'What is this –' said Rhexenor. He too had gone sallow.

'A god, a god,' boomed Pallos. And then he swung around at us, the women fallen at his back. And again I saw the mouth stained from eating the Pandora Heart. And again, I saw his eyes. They were *scarlet*. The white, the iris, the black centre – all blood red. His eyes were pools of ichor.

'I can see the stars through the earth,' said Pallos, almost carelessly now, 'and the Encircling Ocean. I can see the bones in your bodies. Yes, worship me.'

Rhexenor said, 'He has eaten –'

And Pallos said, 'Only seven seeds. Seven seeds of the Pandora. The taste was holy. Look now – I'm invulnerable; immortal. I will climb the White Mountain and be received among the gods. Give me your sword.'

'Pallos,' said Rhexenor, 'wait a moment –'

'Shall I take it? Don't anger me, it will rock the world.'

Pallos leaned and took the king's sword by its golden-bound hilt. This was treasonable, but no one moved.

'Now watch me, and know my power,' said Pallos, and he ran the sword straight through his belly, as if his body were made of butter. 'See, I am immortal and take no hurt,' he said. Then he crashed headlong. His appalling eyes shut, and the blood poured instead and in fact out of his mouth.

The funeral of Pallos was an awesome occasion. Maidens walked behind the bier, singing in lament. I was one of them. We rent our hair and scratched our faces, with red paint under our nails so we did not have to score the skin. A white bull, ten white sheep, were sacrificed, and a red dove. Pallos' band of warriors watched all night *about* the tomb. In the morning, piled with vessels of gold, and swords set with jewels like the one which killed him, it was closed. Rhexenor had wanted to slaughter the two hunting dogs of Pallos and send them with him, but Akris pleaded for them. Under his care they recovered from their grief.

Alone in my room, I held Owl in my arms. I told him, if I died, I would only wish him to live, faithless and happy without me.

But anyway, I made an offering to Hera, and to Persephone, to care for him above, or below, Philos, who had never spoken to me one word, and probably, like the rest, did not know I existed.

In the days which followed, the fruit of Pandora's tree, what was left – most of it – was put into a chest, and the chest sealed with the seal of the king. A slave known for his massive strength and utter stupidity, was set to guard the store room where the chest was set. Magic rituals took place also, closing the corners with blood.

It was put about that Pallos had died of a sudden fit. But I believe the story flew, how he had eaten of the Heart, and it had found the imperfection in him, and so he lost his mind and died.

There were few legends of those who had eaten the fruit and become great. Yet they existed. One heard them spoken of, behind hands, curtains. My father's house had been spoiled, for the king did not want the fruit, and even wondrous Akris had been warned from it in a dream.

Once, in his cups, my drunken father was supposed to have said, 'It's our curse. I wish we might be rid of the thing.'

Akris, they said, wept for shame at bringing it home, and the king comforted him.

When I was just turned fifteen, I was informed the queen had sent for me.

I knew at once what this meant, and I felt a shiver of distress, and, partly, fear. My slave, Onopi, was watching me with big eyes, so I told her that probably they had made a marriage for me. At once Onopi burst into tears. She dropped down and clasped my ankles and begged me not to leave her behind when I went away. I was astonished. From her cries I came to understand I was a kind mistress, that she liked me, that, in fact, we had become friends. I lifted her up and hugged her close. 'Of course I shan't leave you. I'd be lost without you. And Owl would never forgive me.'

Actually, it was unlikely they would deprive me of her, because I mattered so little, she mattered even less.

I determined, however, to ask my father, as a parting favour to me, to free her, so she might become my handmaiden, which had more kudos in it.

Warmed by the exchange, I went in to the apartment of Rhetis. There were paintings of doves and dancers on the walls, a bed of walnut with gold rings, sunlight and women everywhere. One could have fit my own room inside four or five times over.

Rhetis was sitting in her gilded chair, while her hair was dressed carefully for the day. She had recovered from her anguish at Pallos' death, yet it had left its mark. Strands of grey in her hair now were being twined with sea pearls to hide them.

I kneeled and obeised myself. Rhetis said I might get up.

'Tell me your name again.' I said my name. 'And you are fifteen?' I said I was. 'I think,' she said, 'you know, Araegne, why I've sent for you.' Then, not waiting for my irrelevant comments, she told me I was to marry one. of twelve part-royal princes in a neighbouring kingdom. The alliance was obviously helpful to Rhexenor, but not of vast importance. It plastered up the family ties between allies, but in the smallest and least costly way.

When she had given me the news, she asked if there were any questions I might have. I inquired the prince's age, and was reassured he had twenty years – sometimes, in such concoctions, the man maybe as young as eleven or twelve, or as old as fifty. There was nothing else that could be of any use to me. If he were ugly or handsome, cruel or easygoing, were things I had maybe better not know until I met him before the altar. (In fact he is a good man, not ugly, nor so good-looking my plainness can offend him unduly. Although he has many other women, he accords me always absolute respect as his wife. I am not unhappy.)

I asked Rhetis if she would speak to the king on my behalf, in the matter of freeing Onopi. She said she would, but of course forgot. I was able to have a letter written to him, and so see to it myself, later.

After all this, Rhetis had me poured a courtesy drink, sweet wine with butter and honey.

Then the tokens of my dowry were brought. I had expected very little, but the king had been quite generous to such a lesser, part-royal daughter. There were some vessels of silver, a whole tiring set, with copper paring knives and dishes of alabaster for cosmetics, and bronze tongs for the hair. And a necklace of amber, with eight silver disks and three golden sunflowers.

When the last thing was brought I was already amazed, and had thanked Rhetis, bowing low. Then I checked. Even after so many months, even though the dark smoke of the funeral sacrifice had come between, I knew at once that perfume.

My mouth fell open, and I stared, suddenly numb as if with terrible cold, at the little black, painted chest the slave was setting down on the table by the jewels.

'Yes, you're right in your thought,' said Rhetis, in a light, metallic voice. 'Your father does you very great honour.'

'But –' I gasped, 'but is it – it is – the fruit –'

'The Pandora Heart,' said Rhetis. The words slid from her lips as if she had oiled her mouth to get them out quickly and without harm. Then she said, '*Oh*, naturally you are surprised. In the general way of things, such a rarity would never fall to you. But – here, I will be honest – the king believes you were meant to have this treasure. You have had very little in this house, and now must go far away. It will remind you of his care for you.'

I collected my scattered wits, bowed again, and again thanked her. Her own slaves carried my dowry after me to my room, and put everything on a table, and left me. Onopi was elsewhere, and Owl up in his usual morning place on the sunlit roof. The scent of the Pandora Heart swiftly filled the chamber. And as I stared and stared at the painted black box, which was closed with the king's seal, I seemed to see through it to a core of gleaming crimson.

The horror on me was very great. I knew, obviously, my father had not given me the fruit out of kindness. Since the death of his eldest son he had been oppressed, and had sought an oracle from Hera's Oak, that stands just below the Towering Gates. No one else knew what the oracle had said, but perhaps it was exactly this, that the Heart had brought a curse on us, and must be given away, sent out of the kingdom.

He could have sent it with Pyrrha, in *her* dowry, when she married Labron's son. But Rhexenor loved Pyrrha, and there were rumours he had wept in private after she was gone. I did not matter much, and might take the curse with me. To the neighbouring kingdom it would seem a marvellous gift. Let them, then, deal with it.

While I was thinking all this, someone scratched on the my door. As I opened it, I found the slave of my half sister Kleia, with Kleia at her back, all ruffled and startled, saying she wanted to come and bid me goodbye, though I had otherwise spoken with her that year perhaps twice, and when we were children she had pulled my hair – she said, to make it grow.

Kleia's own hair was the colour of lemons, and shiny as water. But, despite her pretty face, she was sour.

'Oh how lucky you are to be wedded. To have a man soon, and all those *delights*. I wonder if father will ever remember me?' She was the daughter of a dancing girl, and not yet fifteen, but mature for her years.

Then she pretended to become aware of the black box.

'Can it be true? I heard it whispered – He gave you *that*. *Is* it?'

'Yes.'

'Aren't you afraid?'

'Yes.'

Kleia, who had sent her slave out and shut the door, now prowled about the box, sniffing the scented air.

'Don't you want to look at it again? I'd have to see. Oh, open it, Araegne. Let's see if it looks the same. Palos cut it in two pieces, and ate seven seeds. But it never rots. Shall I break the seal?'

'No!' I cried.

Kleia laughed. 'But the king means you to eat it. Surely even you can see that he does.'

Such a possibility had not occurred to me. Kleia was a maker of mischief, and I tried to keep my head.

'It's a present for my husband, and his father the king, through me.'

'No. Oh, Araegne, what a fool you are. Our father knows that, inside yourself, you are all the things a woman is meant to be. The Pandora Heart can harm, but also it can render wonderful. If you ate the fruit – just think – it *might* make you beautiful, and powerful as a goddess. Just *think*, Araegne.

Wouldn't you like that? Even if you ate just one seed.'

The door flew open, and there stood Onopi. 'Lady,' she said, bowing to Kleia, 'someone said the queen wants you.'

Kleia made a vast flurry and was gone without farewell.

Onopi shut the door and lowered her eyes.

I said, 'You lied.'

'Yes. But I knew she meant no good.'

I thanked Onopi. Next day, when she was doing my hair I saw a welt on her arm. Kleia had done it. I sent a message to Kleia that, if she hurt my slave again, I would ask our father to make her pay me restitution. It was the boldest thing I ever attempted, and certainly Rhexenor would have paid no attention, but Kleia was always careful where the king was concerned, and so we lived in peace.

By that next day, too, I had put my dowry into a chest and the Pandora Heart with it. The scent still hung about the room, however. Even in the passage outside it was faintly to be smelled.

Did all the palace know it had been given to me? I shrank, and made excuses to leave my room. At night I slept poorly, dreaming of gardens where the crimson Hearts hung on every tree, beating softly, exuding perfume, and all about lay the tangled skeletons of men and women who had eaten them, gone mad, slain each other, or themselves, or been struck down by the just and pitiless gods.

Indeed, along with the harper's song, which had prefigured the death of Pallos, there were the stories of how a Pandora Heart was eaten by old men, who grew young and mighty, and by crippled children who then ran fleet as deer. And there was one story of a hideous woman, so foul she dared not show her face, who was given a little sliver of the flesh of the fruit, at which her beauty became so flame-like, it burned off the veil from her face.

It was not often that I looked long into my mirror, but now I came to do so. I was young enough, and my secret dreams, kept even from myself, uneasily began to surface.

Surely I was not wicked. Surely I had done no wrong to anyone, or slighted the gods. If I were to taste the fruit, could it be that I would change – my hair into gold, my eyes into the sapphires of the lucky Artem-Qirri? And I would be not only beautiful, but have the powers the goddesses have, of healing and wisdom and love. To be a woman, even a fair woman, counted for little. But to be a goddess among men –

However much I chided myself for these thoughts, I could not help them. Who has never yearned for something they may not have? To see, even once, a handsome man gaze at me, as I had seen them do always at Pyrrha. To see them gaze, not in that way alone, but as they must at the loveliness of a goddess. To command my own destiny. To say, I will not marry here, but where I choose. To have the power to say this and not to be denied.

Over and again I wrestled with these ideas. Then would come the other notion. Pallos had not seemed flawed. And yet, eating the fruit, it had found him unworthy. I too, no doubt, was worthless, and if I risked the fruit it would kill me, perhaps even outright. And did my death matter? No, for I did not. Would it be better if I died?

Otherwise, living, I should take with me, to the new kingdom, the Pandora Heart, sealed in its box. And would they not find it irresistible? Would they not remove it from its cover, stand before it, charmed and mesmerized and full of fear, as we had done? Would there be dreams of warning such as Akris had had and heeded, and would at last some man, perhaps even the man to whom they would wed me, take up the fruit already cut for him by my brother, eat it, eat it all – and be plunged into the horror that had taken Pallos, besmirching forever the king's house, as our house had been besmirched, with the shadow of untimely death.

And how then would they look at me, my second kindred. I, the woman who had carried the misery to them all as a gift. Maybe, worse, it would bring on a war.

With all these thoughts, I, at fifteen, struggled, day by day, and night after night. Until at last I dreamed Akris' own dream.

I was in some starry place, and the three Women stood before me, Fate in her grey mist, with the knife in her pale hand that cuts the thread of life. And behind her the others, their spinning set aside. And one shook her head at me, but the other nodded solemnly. And when I woke up I wept in dismay, and only Owl, coming in at my window from his nightly hunting, where he kills like the gods, pitiless and swift, brought me any comfort.

My wedding garments were almost done, the borders of colours almost woven, when at last I gave in. I took the box from the chest, broke the seal with one of the paring knives of copper, and tipped out the fruit of life, glory and awful death, into a dish.

At once the scent of it flooded the room, making me dizzy, and from the plate seemed to rise a ruby glow, as if from a lamp.

It lay in two almost circular halves now, the flesh moist and succulent as it must have been in the moment of cutting. The seeds, like tiny drops of fire, nestled in the centre of each circle, and it was just possible to see that a few had been daintily picked out by the tip of a knife.

Apart from myself, the room was empty, and dusk powdered over the window.

I leaned to the fruit, and it was as if I hung above a great abyss. Had Pallos felt this, too? No, for he was, and thought himself, a hero. He had not hesitated.

I had meant only to look, and then to replace the fruit in its box. Or had I meant only that?

The gods know our inner minds, not we.

Breathing in the aroma of beauty, I could guess the deliciousness of the taste. It would be easy to gobble every part of it, the ever-ripe flesh and thin silky skin, the crackling little seeds with their bursts of bright juice. Could I? Would I?

Onopi was gone on a long errand that would keep her busy until late after supper in my father's hall. I had devised it with care. And if I did not go to supper, who would miss me? If I lay dead, who would mourn, save only poor gentle Onopi. But she and Owl would soon forget. She was free now, and skilled, and might even leave the palace if she wished.

And I would move between them all and Fate. Perhaps they would remember that.

Or, I would become a goddess.

Oh the scent. I smell it still. There is truly no fruit like it, and no flower. What must the gods be, if this came from them?

So near I was to the fruit that when my door was knocked upon, I started almost out of my body – or back into it, more probably.

For a moment I did not know what to do. But in my father's palace, someone like myself might not ignore a summons. I took up a light shawl that had been lying on the chair, and flung it over the dish and the fruit. Then I went to the door.

There was no one outside, but looking along the corridor I seemed to see the flit of a skirt, the flash of a bangled heel turning the corner. As I left my room, the door closed on the latch.

At the corner there was no one, but a little further on a guard stood, to keep the entrance to the women's apartments. I went up to him.

'Did some slave pass along here just now?'

'No, lady. No one passed. I'd certainly have seen.'

I wondered if it were another trick of Kleia's, and the guard had been bribed to be in on it. But I would never get it from him without a larger bribe, so I had better pretend I did not mind.

Beyond the corridor, I saw the evening on the palace courts. Doves, gold-lit by a now-invisible sun, fluttered over the roofs. It was supper-time. After all, I was here, finally. I would go and sit with the women, and eat some food, and hear the harper play or the princes strum some song of war or male cunning.

I felt lighter. I had escaped the tyranny of the fruit. And tonight I would drink a little extra wine, and when I went back to my room, I would put it away, the Pandora Heart. This was too vast a thing for Araegne to tackle. How could I ever have thought otherwise?

I had no fear, being gone, that anyone would go in to steal the Heart. They were all afraid of it. As for Onopi, she would be busy. She would not have to suffer the temptation I had done.

Yes, I felt light. As if reprieved, let off some ghastly duty to the living – or the dead.

To this hour I do not know who knocked upon the door, to save me. But Hermes is the god of messengers, and tricks …

The harper sang a long history of two lovers that the gods parted, and I was late returning, and hurried, concerned that Onopi might get back before me. Then I glimpsed her down at the Little Fountain under the torch, gossiping with a kitchen girl, and knew all was well.

When I reached my door, I opened it, and saw the one lamp burning I had wastefully left, and everything in its place, except for the shawl I had put over the Pandora Heart. And on the dish, a dark red smear, like blood, and nothing else.

My heart gave such a jolt I almost fainted. I leaned on the upright of the door, gasping, and then I saw lying under the table, my cat, Owl, on his left side, the lamp limning his stripes with gold, still as a stone.

At once I was in tears. This, of all things, I had not thought of. But he was adept at jumping, clever at finding, always hungry. The desperate beauty of the fruit must have lured even him. (I had known him lick flowers before.) And so simple it had been for him to come in at the window, jump to the table, eat the Pandora Heart, skin and flesh and seeds, till everything was gone but that one smear of juice, almost licked clean.

I ran to him and took him up, and only as I held him weeping on my breast did I feel that he was warm, and flexible as a snake. And waking up, he yawned smiling in my face.

His tongue was stained red, and his carnivore's breath had on it the faintest, most unusual, most marvellous perfume.

'Oh Owl – what have you done?'

Owl yawned again, and let out a rippling bead-string of purrs. In my arms he stretched, then rested his head, as he does, on my shoulder.

'Owl – Owl –'

It was true, he had devoured every shred. Every seed. Nothing was left but the smear of juice I wiped up now with the shawl. I then put by the shawl for burning in the morning.

He stayed all this while purring and praising me, for to Owl I am a goddess, if also an idiot, being omnipotent in some things, and otherwise not always able to do what he demands or guess what he wishes.

I puzzled over him and his deed. Until at length he desired to go out again, and I placed him at the window, and watched him run off along the roofs, a black shape glimmering on the night.

What had happened to him? Was it that the fruit could not change him, since he was already perfect, beautiful and partly a god – was it that he *had* been changed, yet I could not see it, being myself human and mortal?

His eyes had shone, their normal exquisite lamps.

His paws were fleet. He sprang like a lion. But this was as it had always been.

I could ask him nothing – how he felt, what now he could see and hear – for perhaps he saw the Ocean under the world, the bones in my body, the faces of the stars, and the goddess standing on the moon; perhaps he heard the language of the birds and the wind. Or perhaps, being a cat, he was impervious, the same, immutable as the purest metal and the purest heart.

At the hour Onopi returned, the box was shut and sealed and put away. Sealed and shut, it went with me to my new home, and sealed and shut it remains. I think they have forgotten all talk, by now, of what it might be the plain, foreign princess brought with her in the black painted little casket. (Its lingering perfume had faded and gone by the time my journey ended.) They do not credit every legend they hear, and Onopi has even told me that she once slapped a slave girl who announced that Owl had not been fathered by a god. My husband asked me only one question, 'That fruit, did your brother Pallos die of it?' I shook my head and replied as they had said I must, that he died of a sudden fit. My husband expressed no desire to see the Pandora Heart. If he had, or his father, the king, I should have had to confess. The gods know what would have happened. I suppose it may one day happen yet. But I think really they believe we are all liars, and that the box is as empty as, in fact, it is.

Owl is growing old now, but as with his race, shows little sign of it. He has sired new families about this palace in the mountains. In the winter, when the snows come, he is sometimes gone a day or a night, at his hunting. Perhaps I will find he is immortal now, but I think not. I discovered some grey hairs in his spotted coat not three evenings back.

He sleeps more than he did. And though he talks to me often, it is still in the language of cats.

My father by now has died, and Akris is king in my birthland. I wonder if he thinks of me sometimes, seeing that I took the curse away from his kingdom. Otherwise, they have forgotten my name. I do foretell that in the end they will forget other names than mine. For men go back to dust and cities crumble, and even the earth changes her shape. At last our world will be gone, and with it, its mysteries and its essential terrors. Let me say softly, I have heard that even the gods may one day die.

Queens In Crimson

We climb the steps of the castle, my husband and I. We go slowly, for I am soon out of breath. Sometimes he will forget, and hurry up the steep stone treads two at a time, leaving me to come on at my own pace. Then, courteously, he hesitates. In his face, as he watches me approach him, is the familiar mingling of contempt and pleasure. Ten years older than I, he still finds me very beautiful, or so he says.

The castle is, of course, magnificent. Its enormous walls and towers, barbaric, impenetrable, dominate the border. Below the rocky slopes fall into the valley and the city, whose roofs shine pale copper and paler green in the slanted afternoon sun. To the south, the mountains rise with combs of snow. And above, the sky. The castle is almost like a natural thing but inside the stone rooms are more recent modernisations of the fifteenth and sixteenth centuries, carved furniture and stands of huge candles, carpets from the East, windows of crystal, and opaque glass, coloured like blue flowers, blood, and treacle. Within, the castle is clearly an artifice. But what else could it be, for it was formerly the house of a king.

Ahead of us, the guide moves, pointing out many things, which the scatter of tourists, and my husband, understand, for they speak the language of this country, as I do not. I have often wished and tried to learn various languages, but have never been able to master more than a few standard phrases, all of which I can only speak with a stutter, although normally I do not stutter at all. Curiously, my accent is often quite good; good enough that, here, once or twice, when I have been forced to utter one of my phrases, (at my husband's insistence) the person addressed has assumed that either I am indigenous or fluent, and broken into a torrent of words incomprehensible to me. I have then stood, shaking my head, smiling and blushing a redhead's blush, moving my hands helplessly as if searching out some support in mid-air. I am locked, it seems, inside my own language, which, to some extent, I can bend to my will. It is as if I am afraid to learn another tongue, in case, then, I lose my ability with the original. My husband thinks that I am lazy and do not apply myself. He thinks this of me also in other areas, even in the area of my failure to conceive a child. Indeed, I have not tried to become pregnant, except by the basic formula of entering into the sexual act with him. Nor have I tried to prevent pregnancy. However, I have never wanted to be pregnant, never wanted to give birth to another human being. The notion fills me with surprised alarm. But to my husband, a child, or rather children, preferably one of each gender, have been a goal of his since his twenties. When our marriage had been decided and we had begun to make love, he told me that we would have children, and I had not argued. On some level I think I knew I would not, and perhaps deceived myself that he might come to be philosophical. Did I love him madly, promising him by my silence or acquiescence that I would do whatever he desired? Did I mislead him because I in turn desired him so much? No, I could not say that. He was handsome and rich, clever, an intellectual man of forty, with a wide experience of the world. I found him interesting, fascinating, physically very attractive. He admired me and was kind to me. He said he loved me. Probably, confronted by such perfection of person and luck, I had felt I could not refuse. In the middle of the South Tower of the castle, we reach the suite of rooms that once belonged to the king's wife.

Below had already been seen the splendour of the armoury with all its extraordinary weapons, mail and banners, the banquet hall, the king's own apartments – strangely – inconveniently? – far off from those of his spouse. In the king's rooms were services of gold and cups of glass, Bibles with covers of silver, intricate tapestries, musical instruments of bewildering variety, also swords and bows, complex obscure games, the least of which was chess, even a canvas that purportedly the king himself had painted. For he had been, I already knew, a man of stature and genius. Elsewhere, but not here, I had been shown his portrait. Although in his middle years, he was a tall, muscular man, with a gorgeous leonine face framed in tassels of ripe gold hair. His eyes were narrow with vision, and his lips sensual. Behind him in the picture poised an angel, a unicorn, a stag, a lion, an eagle. The sun and moon stood in the sky together as, sometimes at evening, they do. He was good at everything. His skill in war and diplomacy, in sword-play and dance, gaming and wise talk were unrivalled. Not a single report of him could praise him enough. Besides, he painted beautifully, profoundly, and composed exquisite music. One of the loveliest airs of any era or time was his, and even now recordings are made of it. It is called: *The Red Gown*.

In the suite of the queen everything is quite different. The furniture is light and delicate; the walls hung with pastel things, the bed dressed in silk and gauze. There is a table based on a classical design; and with a mirror of sub-aqueous greenish glass. By a stool leans only a little guitar of wheat-coloured wood.

The guide speaks *to* us, and, as always, I find myself stupidly nodding, although I have not recognized a syllable.

My husband cranes over and whispers loudly in my ear. 'He says that the lute belonged to the second wife.'

'Oh, yes.'

'But the bed was arranged like this for the third.'

I want to ask what evidence remains of the first wife, but my husband does not tell me; possibly the guide has not said.

The tourists turn to glance at me disparagingly. This had happened below.

I am a foreigner who; arrogantly; has not bothered to learn the language.

From the queen's suite, a door gives on an oddly contemporary creation, a roof garden, laid out, (my husband says) for the third wife. Trees rise in terra cotta pots, their heads each round as a globe. They cannot be the trees that were here then. A balustrade cuts off the massive descent to the courtyard below.

In a bird-cage sits a stuffed yellow bird, representing the pet of the third queen. It, the guide – my husband – says, died on the morning of her execution.

As everyone clusters about the marble bench that had been carved with maenads for the queen, I wander to the balustrade and look over. Down there, all of seventy, eighty feet – I am bad at judging such things – she had come out into the white winter snow, and placing her forehead into the scoop of that small stone block, had had her neck sheered through by a honed steel sword.

My husband taps me impatiently on the shoulder. 'What are you doing?'

'Looking at the block.'

'That isn't the block, of course.'

'I see.'

'If only,' he says, 'you had tried to grasp the language. But then, I knew I'd have to take charge of you.'

If it is not the block, what is it? A mounting stone perhaps, used by the knights of the king in bounding on to their horses. Some had done this to get away, the three who had made love to the three wives of the king.

My husband draws me back towards the guide, who shoots at me a look of aversion. But I have also, from time to time, intercepted such looks from my husband. Whenever, in fact, I remonstrate at his wishes, which, naturally, I seldom do. If I had always crossed him, would he have grown accustomed and forbearing?

I had been poor when we met, and for a short time after. He had come into the place of business where I worked, to see one of the directors. In passing, by error, through that long and dismal chamber, he had glimpsed me, noticing me first, no doubt, because of the astonishingly red shade of my hair. He said nothing, but later one of the women of the upper offices came down, and handed me a note. I was invited to call a particular number. Bemused, I did so. I thought I had been selected for some secretarial duty, and did not relish it, since I was not especially competent. Instead I heard the voice of an educated man, my future husband, who inquired if I would meet him that evening for a cocktail. I agreed. I had never resisted the sexual advances of important men in my working life, for I had seen the trouble resistance could lead to. When I entered the shadowy lounge of the hotel, where white death lilies stood like phantoms, I was expecting nothing but something mildly unpleasant, like a visit to the dentist for a routine filling. But I was greeted by someone elegant and beautiful, who handed me into a little gilded chair, plied me with red Champagne, and later took me away in a silver car to a dinner of tiny delicious endless courses. He did not then sleep with me. He told me that I must learn his life and he would help me. He thought it would become me, and we should both see. In parting he kissed my cheek, and handed me an orchid so transparent that in the morning it was dead, killed simply by being alive.

There were many dinners after this. And many other things. I was removed from my job to a wonderful flat that overlooked the great park with its birches, planes and fountains. I was fitted for clothes. My red hair was re-styled, though left as long as ever. He wished to give me a dog, but I begged him not to. I was afraid for it, after the orchid. Living things should not be awarded between us – for that reason, perhaps, I was sure I would never conceive his child.

But somehow he took my refusal of a dog as a need to have instead him, and now that I had been creamed and smoothed and shaped to receive him, he told me we would marry, and led me to his bed. He informed me there I could never leave him after that. I had known as much.

He knew nothing of me. I do not mean that he had not had me investigated, obviously he had done that and maybe still does. But of me, nothing. I was for him a dream he had had, in his youth. He would cherish me. He would make me his own. He would change me. I should benefit.

Half a decade has passed since our wedding, in a Byzantine church at the foot of a mountain. I have failed him. I am not clever. I do not like the books of music he values or the food he prefers. I am ordinary in sensual matters I fail to arouse him now by anything other than my looks, and indeed, for me, I have not experienced interest, let alone orgasm with him, for five years. Evidently, I pretend. I think that he believes in my response, but reckons it limited, uncouth, possibly tasteless. And I have not become pregnant. He knows he is not at fault. He underwent some tests and learned that he is potent and fertile. I too am supposed to be fertile, but then I bribed the doctor to tell my husband this, not wanting to undergo the medical examination.

Suddenly the guide says something which, startlingly, because I know most of the words, I can understand.

'A lover reached this garden, using a rope.'

I suck in my breath, but no one else does. Have I misinterpreted? Surely I have. How could the queen's lover have scaled this terrible tower on a rope? He would have been seen, certainly. Or fallen.

I think of the three queens of the king who composed *The Red Gown*, a melody which has lasted five centuries.

In the past, and again before we came here, (my husband has always insisted that I read books on all the countries to which we travel) I have found the history of the three queens. Each was a redhead – the king, it seems, was partial to this fiery colouring – all redheads, but all different. The first was voluptuous, heavy, with a skin like milk and golden eyes. Her hair was the dark red of mahogany, and, unbound, it hung to her hips. She could sing, and singing one of the king's songs, she won his heart. He married her, and for a few years they lived happily. But she gave him no heir, and finally he concluded that she had born a premature child in secret, by another man. He ordered her tried, and she was found guilty. Her body showed the marks of pregnancy and birth. On the morning of her execution, she was dressed in crimson, as the custom was, not to show any blood. Her long hair was bound up into a tower of gold. She went to the block with her hands on a prayer book. She did not speak a word, and when her head fell, flowers sprang from the spots of gore that scattered on the yard.

The second queen was a slender princess of another land. She was given to the king and he loved her at once. Her skin was pink, her hair was the red of Eastern amber, so fine that it was like rosy golden rain, and her eyes green. For a few years he adored her, but she did not conceive his heir, and then she too took a lover, in order to have from him what she could not get from the king. She was tried and found guilty. She was dragged to the block screaming and puking with terror, and all her hair came loose over the crimson gown, so that they had to cut her locks in the courtyard, before they could successfully decapitate her.

The third queen was a plump and olive-skinned slattern of the kitchen. The king was older then, and not so discriminating. She had black eyes, and her hair was ginger like the spice, and curled, and was so long it reached her knees. She would wrap the king's member in it and he would lose control. For a few years she kept him happy, but her belly stayed flat as a plate. He came to be told she was a witch who practised against him, had several lovers, including the Devil, and could not get with child since her womb had been neutralised by sorcerous intercourse. She was tried, found guilty, and sent to the block. She had already cut off her hair herself, and burned it on the fire, when she glided out upon the white snow in her crimson dress, and lay down on the block, smiling. It took four strokes of the honed sword to sever her neck. After she was dead, the executioner threw himself off the castle wall, ashamed at having botched the job or nervous of demons.

'See, up there,' says my husband, 'that is the window from which the king watched the beheading of his wives. He contrived to have an exact image, the glass is magnified.' He smirks strangely. Something in all this pleases him. I have never thought he liked women, only the way they look, the feel and scent of them, the fruit of their bodies. His total power upon and over them.

The window is extremely high, set with seemingly plain, cloudy glass. It reminds me of the windows in the street of shops where once I tried to buy him a present. It was something I was sure he would care for, a rare old book, and although I purchased it with money which he himself paid into my allowance, even so that money was supposed by then to be mine. However, my husband was not impressed by the book. He explained to me that he already had a copy of it in his library, a copy far older and more valuable, and that this any way might be a fake. Someone returned the book and I was given a cheque for the money I had spent.

It was in this same street, a month later, that I met a young man with wild dark hair. I forget his name, but I remember his white thin body very well. He was the first of my three lovers. I have only had three, and each only for one afternoon.

The guide is saying something about the view now. I recognise the word *view*.

We stare out across the valley and the city, with its pretty roofs, out at the mountains. Beyond them is another country, to which my husband says he wishes to go tomorrow. He turns now to look at me and I feel his eyes on my face, but make believe I do not know. I can picture his gaze. It is half evaluating. He says the new country is lawless and dangerous. This seems to inspire him. Last night he gave me a necklace of rubies, such crimson stones, and requested that I wear it as he performed the act of sex with me.

The guide has finished. The tourists are pressing tips into his hand, but my husband does not do so, he does not believe in tipping. Instead he graciously bows to the guide, and we return into the suite, and next begin to descend the stairs of the tower.

'How lovely you are,' he says to me, quite loudly, the way he translated what the guide said, when he thought I should know it. 'I could never let you go.' His hand presses on the back of my neck like a blunt blade which may be sharpened.

We come down and out at last, into the awful courtyard. Some of them are staring at the block which my husband says is not the block of the executions. But it is sunny, and birds are calling over the castle tops.

'Wouldn't it be bizarre,' he says, more quietly now, 'if you had finally consented to become pregnant while we were here? That is in the hotel,' he adds, in case in my foolishness I might think he means it had happened without penetration, by magic, at the castle.

'Yes,' I say. Recently, I never argue.

But I have not become pregnant and I never will by my husband. Last night I dissolved, in his brandy and soda, the undetectable capsule my third lover, the doctor, told me how to obtain. I saw my husband drink it down. It takes twenty-four hours to work. After midnight, in his sleep most likely my husband will suffer a fatal heart attack. I will find him dead beside me in the morning. Most of his wealth will presently be mine – if I want it, which I am not sure that I do.

A fresh wind blows the yellow flowers on the rocky slopes under the castle. Tendrils of my hair flutter across my eyes and I brush them back. Behind us someone shuts a door with a colossal clang.

Rherlotte

They fell in love – and lay stunned, and staring at each other, their bodies and hearts already broken, from the hardness of love's floor and the height from which they had crashed down.

Various Philosophies
Anna Garber

1

This is the story of how I died.

2

Because I don't remember my father, all men have a look of him, for me. Even young men, since he was once also young. Old men, too, although he was never very old. Little boys in sailor suits – once he may have been a little boy in a little sailor suit, his mother wiping an orange ice from his chin. Babies in perambulators. Therefore, Armand looks like my father. He is thirty-three years old (Christ's death age), and handsome. A dark brown head of hair and darker moustache, bright, shoe-polish eyes, tawny, rosy complexion. He has the build of someone who played cricket at an English school, and who rides horses in the chestnut woods at Petignot, which he did and does. He is well-dressed, too, his top hat like a black mirror. A silk tie in claret red, a rose in the buttonhole. The elegant gloves tossed aside the way he tosses things aside. Armand Blos.

'Drink your Champagne,' he says to me.

I smile, and raise my glass. Sip.

'We'll have those little birds, with the sauce. Do you like those?'

I smile once more. I hate them, actually, or would rather have them twittering on the trees, than have their bones crunching between my teeth. But I intend to please Armand Blos. A lovely pliable, admiring supper companion, which is what he expects.

'Your eyes are quite green,' he says to me.

'Yes?'

'Quite, quite green. Like young gooseberries. That's strange. When we met, I thought they were blue. But through that veil … How provocative.' He laughs, having liked being provoked, as I meant him to.

'What about this fish? Do we fancy it? Perhaps the dish of chops. But you women, you always must have the sweet things, mustn't you? Eat nothing, and only want the sugary trifle or the strawberries in chocolate.'

I smile. Armand knows everything about women, and he has good reason to. He's studied them such a lot.

I say, lowering my gooseberry eyes – Lilas compared them to jade, the last time they were compared to anything – 'Perhaps to kiss is the sweetest.'

His heat comes all across the table, across the embroidered cloth; white on white, from Sevres, where we only thought they made china.

'My little darling. You know I can't wait. But we'll eat first. You must eat. There is nothing of you. I could snap that little waist with my hands.'

I flutter. Briefly. Fluttering isn't really what I am best at. Even an Armand might just see through it.

He refills my glass. It's so lucky I have my grandmother's head for alcohol. Maybe more of her than that. More than she'll ever know.

The private room is perfect, and I'm aware he'll have used it often before. He is known at this discreet and expensive restaurant.

Long ago, revolutionaries dined here, he says, Danton, perhaps, Robespierre. The decor has changed somewhat. The red velvet swags and the thick lace curtains, the gas-lamps above the cheerful fireplace with its heap of coals. The candles on the table, that don't smell as good as candles at my grandmother's, but then she has beeswax put into them. She's a bitch. A queen bee.

I'm bored with the room, its good taste just slightly, accommodatingly garish, the almost but not exactly naughty classical painting of Leda, twined with a puffed-out, ugly and penial swan. I'm bored, oddly, with Armand, as if I really had come to dine with him, and afterwards let him screw me, probably on that velvet couch over there, just behind the Chinese screen.

How peculiar.

I find my mind slipping away already to my own flat on the street that I will call rue Bucher. To my own fireplace and the monstrous electric kettle, my cup and saucer, the Russian tea caddy, my slippers, my cigarettes in their box, the bowl of apples. I don't think there's a sweet thing to eat in my flat. Even the apples are sharp and acid, as I like them to be. I refused from the age of five to have sugar in my coffee.

When the waiter comes in, despite my wandering mind, I turn my face away, under the heavy sweep of reddish hair I have arranged just so. Perhaps I have a husband I'm betraying. Maybe he simply thinks, poor, lowly waiter-worm that he is, that I disdain him utterly. Only an Armand Blos is good enough for me.

Outside it's raining, silver beads heavy on the panes behind the lace. Carriages in the street. The throaty sound of the city, and the mumbled swish of wheels stumbling weightless through the water.

Autumn dissolves in tears. New, fluid, clean and gleaming in the rain. I, in my pale blue silk, my hat with violets, and veil of blue lace. In my wig of red hair that Lilas loaned me. She said, 'Don't tell me. *Dorit*. Hush. Not a word.' Of course, I'm still dressed for the afternoon, discreetly obscured. This evening I was caught in the rain – my fiction. I went innocently into that notorious cafe to save myself from a wetting. But seeing Armand – who could resist Armand?

The waiter's gone. The dishes are all set out under their covers. There's more Champagne. The man opened it and was sent packing with a robust tip.

Armand puts one finger on my right hand.

'Won't you take off your hat?'

Oh, he likes my hair!

I look into his eyes. It's safe, he only sees shiny gooseberries. 'Soon.'

Where I was first brought up, they fetched the milk warm to the door every morning, and the gossip with it.

Constance, my rich grandmother, had made herself such a niche that, in front of her, they pretended she was gentry.

Of course, when I say brought up, I was only there off and on, when my mother was too engaged or dismayed to have me.

The plain fact was, my grandmother, and my mother, both of them, were whores. Mind you, whores of a valuable sort. The *cared-for* sort. Courtesans, perhaps. My grandmother being very adept, and my mother a complete fool, who fell in love with her protectors, or with young servant men. I remember her always in tears, always in the rainy autumn of an affair, or the winter following its death. I despised her, and feared Constance. I suppose I have something of them both. Well, yes. I have to say I have, although, then, I would not have seen it.

Anne Blos wrote to me on a piece of palest mauve paper, in a deep blue ink. She didn't use my name, addressed me only as *Mademoiselle*. She said she had been a friend of Lilas Dule, and that she wished very much to get my advice.

When I received this letter, assuming at once it was what it turned out to be, I didn't know quite what I felt. I'd been living the life of a sloth, or a wealthy old woman's life, almost. My flat had everything I wanted. The meals, when I desired, were sent up from the restaurant across the way. Strolls I took in the park among the statues, or up the Bois, in the green summer sunshine. I needed only a small dog on a leash, but – not needing one at all – had none. I rose when I wished. Slept when I wanted. Sometimes I paid a visit, here or there. Was I happy? God knows. Contented, smug, I think. How well I ran my life. Everything in its place.

I took a carriage to the address Anne Blos had sent me, knowing it would be her very own house, and so it was. I mean to say, not her house, *his*, Armand's, where she lived and had her being as his wife.

'Who shall I say?' asked the fussy maid.

'A friend of Mademoiselle Dule.'

The room was big and polished, with lace on the chairs. It led into a conservatory, a glassy indoor city garden. A palm dominated the vista, crowding up to the crystal roof, and all the pots of flowers crouched in its shade, turning pale.

Anne Blos got up to greet me. She was herself extremely white. She looked as if someone had died that morning, which was curious or not, depending on one's taste. After she'd sent the maid for coffee, she offered me a chair. I passed a mirror on the wall, and in between the gilt cupids, glimpsed myself. But then I knew myself very well. I didn't merit a second glance.

She however went directly to the mirror, as if to check up on me by means of some sorcerous left-over of my reflection remaining there. In fact she was seeing to herself, patting her hair, pinching her cheeks for colour – no one, apparently, had told her about rouge.

She settled on another chair, folding the wings of her dress. Sat staring at me.

She said, 'Lucette will be back in a moment. We'd better wait.'

I looked at her coolly, and thought, *She sounds like a lover*. But I could never have been tempted. Anne was a big-boned woman, her hair dark and piled high with some help from a bad hairdresser. Her face was that of a bug – large popping eyes, small features but for the long, thin mouth. He had married her for her money, and so got her money, but she had not got him in exchange.

It wasn't really what I'd anticipated. But then, it had only happened once, almost twice, before. In the other instances there had been beauty and motives of passion. Yet wasn't this also passion, bubbling under her anaemic skin?

The coffee came in an incised silver pot, with wafers that had cherry paste, and a dish of chocolate creams. Women liked sweet things, didn't they? Did she want them, or think I would? Neither of us touched a mouthful, and the coffee mostly went cold.

She was one of those women who are foolish over their children, trying to turn a boy into a tiny, nearly sexless husband, or a girl into an adventurous version of themselves. But I understood Anne had no children. Nor any pets to console her. She had had to face up to destiny unbuffered by anything but wealth. And banknotes make poor cushions in the end. Money does bring happiness, but it can't send away certain miseries: illness, death, unrequited love. And anyway, the money was now all his.

She explained to me about the money, hesitantly. The small income she had now, and what he did with the rest. Of course, he treated his friends, went deeply into ridiculous business ventures and failed, gambled and lost. But mostly he spent on women. Other women.

'May I – may I call you Phèdre?' She misinterpreted my gaze. 'Not if you don't wish.'

'Please.'

'It's such – a classical name.'

'My mother was fascinated by the theatre.'

In her true life, Anne Blos would never have stopped to speak to me, let alone speak about my whore-courtesan of a mother who had died of a broken heart when an Italian pastry cook, fifteen years her junior, had told her they were done. Promises of love are like pie-crusts, and so, seemingly, are hearts.

When my mother died, I was about fourteen. I had had a random schooling, strange country schools, and tutors in Paris, one a thick-bearded German, who, rather than teach me his execrable language, liked to sing me mournful German songs, hammering the while on my mother's piano.

After the funeral, Constance, a corseted stone stem in black, topped by a cartwheel hat that had more plumes than the horses, took me aside. She told me I was to go to another school, farther south. She said I could learn the things I required, music, etiquette, other tongues, how to draw. Probably she was instinctively training me to be the perfect expensive whore, or gentleman's companion.

I stayed at the school for years, doing very little. You paid for your daughters or granddaughters or nieces to do little, there. I never mastered anything, except how to play pieces of music from memory, even one piece of Liszt – my show-piece, as they said. I would never acquire the ability to read music. I was eventually the oldest pupil left abandoned there.

Constance had married before my mother died. At forty-five, she had borne two more daughters. These girls, my aunts, were younger than I by some eight years, while the husband was dead of apoplexy.

She allowed me to come to her house at O—, for a visit of a few weeks, then sent me to find an apartment with the help of an agent. The flat was found, and the agent swore he was in love with me. I was nineteen. When I told him, standing there amid those bare rooms, to go away, he said he would drown himself in the river. But I think he didn't.

Constance, at her country house, had given me one last lesson, which rendered mirrors, thereafter, mainly redundant. Standing me naked, but for my chemise, before the long cheval glass, Constance told me what I was.

'You're very beautiful, Phèdre. You can even carry the silly name she gave you. You have quite a calm air of piquance, the mysterious. What do you want from life?'

'I don't know, Grandmother.'

'How strange that sounds. Well, there's no need for you to do anything at all. I've settled an income on you, as you know. I don't expect thanks.'

'Thank you, Grandmother.'

'Use rose-vinegar to bring out the highlights in this black hair. Bathe your eyes at least once a week. Shed a few tears every day, if you're able, it clears the ducts. Use no cheap eye-black. I'll give you the address of the ones who make my charcoal powder. A touch of rouge for the lips. Never corset too tightly. You have a small waist, but may need to do it when you're older. Believe me, it isn't to be wished for.' She drew back. 'Have you had a man?'

'No, Grandmother.'

'Have you ever wanted a man?'

'I don't know.'

'That means, of course, you haven't. They're filthy brutes. But you're not a nun. When the time comes you want to, be careful. Do all the things I told you. I fell pregnant only twice, and that in itself is a miracle. I think those two demon girls lay in wait for years inside me. My penalty for all those escapes.'

She leaned forward and laid her lined dry face against mine. Her features had broadened, but she had good bones, and her complexion, though powdered and papery, is unblemished, and once like petals, or so they were said to have said. Her eyes – are like vipers.

'Youth and Age,' said Constance, my grandmother. 'What colour are your eyes?'

Outside, in the garden of O—, I could hear the demon daughters shrieking as they climbed trees after birds.

'Grey.'

'No, quite wrong. They're hazel. Wet the charcoal and apply it to your lashes with the brush I shall give you. Don't blink until it dries.'

Armand eats heartily, now I've taken off my hat. I had to take off the wig too. Lilas got it for me through her theatrical connections, and although it would look convincing on the stage, close to, without the hat, there can be no doubt it's false. My black hair cascaded, down my back, over my shoulders. He watched in delight. 'But *why* – dear girl – when you have such hair?'

'My secret,' I said. 'I'll tell you … later.' I've had a few mouthfuls of things, and when he presses me, I say I'm a little nervous. And he concludes I am waiting for the crystallized fruits and ginger tarts.

Anne Blos had smoked cigarette after cigarette. She explained to me that Armand hated to see women smoke, and she whitened her fingers with lemon juice and egg-white to hide the stains.

'I suppose you think I've been an utter fool,' she said. I said nothing. She said, 'I don't know Mademoiselle Dule very well. But one day she came here – some sort of charity she does, or pretends to do, for the families of dead actors. I burst into tears. She'd seen a mark on my face, you see. Oh, he hadn't hit me, but it was what she thought. Of course, after her own – I told her that I truly had cut my cheek on the edge of the dressing-table.

But it was because I was so upset that it happened. I was stupid, too, with something I'd had to take. My head hurt so much.'

I finished my cigarette. Hers were not so good as my own, or at least, I preferred my own.

'Yes?'

'It was what he said to me. From the very first, he's taken everything from me that he can. He even took my mother's rubies – he said, Can I take them, dear? I need some money quickly. I was so scared of his disapproval, the way he looked whenever I said no to anything. So I said, Oh, yes. If you have to have them. And he kissed my cheek, and took them. And now some Jew woman is wearing them all over the Champs Elarnes. Well, there you are. But so long as I've let him have his way, and never said anything about his women, he's been kind to me.'

Poor pathetic creature. She put down her lids over her locust eyes. Her lashes were pale. She'd never heard, either, of charcoal powder.

'The women,' she repeated. 'I can't begin …'

'There's really no need.'

'Well,' she said, 'I have to tell you this. There are always women, but also, there's one. *One* woman. He thinks of *her*, I believe, as he would a wife. Not me, *oh*, no. But her. She's supposed to be lovely, but she remains faithful to him and winks at all the others, and he goes back to her. She has a house he bought her on the Boulevard Strauss. Maybe he helped pay for it with my mother's rubies.' She looked up and straight at me suddenly. 'If Papa had lived, he'd have shot Armand.'

'Yes, perhaps.'

'He would. I've had no one to guide me.'

And obviously had not been able to guide herself.

She said, 'It was – I made the mistake – of mentioning this woman. His *mistress*. A Mademoiselle de Gillan. He'd been extraordinarily extravagant; he wanted me to get some money from a particular trust, all I have left. I flashed out, If you're so desperate, couldn't she do something? Eh, he said, who d'you mean? I mean, I said, Mademoiselle de Gillan. At that he ruffled up. He looked furious, as if I'd insulted, yes, his *wife*. I. I who am his wife.'

'Most trying,' I said. She expected something, the way the hungry seal in the Zoological Gardens expects a fish at feeding time. She received it the same way, snapping her jaws.

'He said I wasn't to mention *her*. There was nothing immodest. She was only his friend. The only woman friend he'd ever had, since women were generally so ignorant and foolish. I said, And so am I, I believe, for putting up with all this. Oh, I'd never said anything like that to him before. You should have seen him. He swelled up. He strode up to me. I thought he would strike me. He shouted into my face. I can't repeat what he said. I'll never forget it. It goes round and round and round in my brain. That I was slow-witted. That I was – I was so hideous I made him physically sick. He told me – oh, he told me even the smell of me made him – vomit – I can't, oh, I can't …'

'It's all right, madame, there's no need to say any more.'

'Never has anyone been so cruel. Oh, I *know* God never blessed me with any looks. But I've done my best. I've tried to make up for it. And this, my reward.'

'Please don't upset yourself.'

'Upset – I've wept every night until my pillows are wringing wet. It isn't my fault I'm ugly! How could he – how could he – he's had everything. There's no one to protect me. He went straight out and left me there, he went to *her*, this *bitch* de Gillan.'

Anne Blos stood up, flaming, rouged now with rage and pain. It did not improve her and her eyes and nose were red, too. It showed the measure of her desperate grief, that word she'd used, which a woman of her 'refinement' should not have let past her lips. That word, and sending for me.

With Lilas, it had been quite the other way.

I had seen her act, I think it was Racine. She had a very small part. But she was achingly pretty. Then, a year later, I met her in the street.

I met her because she was standing in the street, holding on to a blossoming almond tree with her gloved hand. Properly dressed, immaculate, she was fainting, and no one had noticed.

It seemed I was drawn to her on runners, something pulled me right up to her. I said, 'Excuse me, mademoiselle, are you quite all right?'

She turned up two swimming azure eyes, and instantly leaned against me, her head on my shoulder. I held her up, she was very light. She said, 'Oh God.' And presently, 'Is anyone looking at me?'

'Not at all.'

Of course, a few people were, but she hadn't fallen down. I'd opened my parasol too. We might have been sharing a joke, under the almond blossom, two elegant women friends, fashion-plates, with our lace jabots and shady hats.

After a moment I said, 'My flat is just across the courtyard. Can you walk a few steps?'

'Yes, if you don't let me go.'

Rather odd. Lucky, or not.

By then, at twenty, I'd had a few encounters. Indeed, there had been at the eccentric school, with its Swiss and Italian mistresses, a pair of girls with whom I had sat, on the old swing, up in the green woods. I remember so well the slender leg of Marie-E in its black stocking, the neat shoe rustling the fallen papers of another year's leaves. Putting my hand upon the ankle. *Oh, you feel just like a snake! And* my snake tongue in her wild raspberry flavoured mouth. Later the stockings were peach-coloured, with embroidery. Her garters had roses. There were also small roses on her breasts that I liked particularly, gently, to bite. Sweets, after all.

I helped Lilas into my apartment, let her into the armchair with carved arms, and started up the kettle. The flat has electricity, a wonder to some. (Constance frowns upon it. She quotes the novel *Frankenstein*; galvanics create monsters.)

'How idiotic. I've never fainted.'

'You didn't quite faint.'

'If you hadn't rescued me, mademoiselle, I would have done.' She sighed. 'What a lovely sitting room. Do you live alone? I thought so. There's nothing masculine. How very restful.'

Her pale colour was coming back. I gave her a brandy made at O—. She stretched in the dark green chair, and unpinned her hat. She had a fine mass of light brown hair, some of it tumbling down.

'It was the pain,' she said.

'Are you ill?' I think I may have been alarmed. It wasn't in me much, to become involved with such things. My mother perhaps made me fearful of and impatient with illness and tears.

'No, no. But – someone – no, I mustn't burden you, mademoiselle.'

I told her my name. She exclaimed at Phèdre. 'But I played Phèdre once! Oh, not in the city, not here. No, it was a little seaside town. But I was very *good*.'

I told her I'd seen her act, forgotten which play, but remembered her. She blushed. I think she can, as some can, blush at a wish. She did it to thank me for the compliment, and thanked I was.

We drank Russian tea and ate slices of orange. We smoked my cigarettes, for which she used an ivory holder. Finally she told me, very fast, very simply, 'I'm the property of a man, a jealous man who beats me. He gave me such a blow on the side this morning – the bruise is black. My maid put on a poultice and bound me up. I felt better, and came out – but suddenly, I thought I'd be sick, and then all the trees turned into a big pink cloud.'

She smiled at me with blue, cat's eyes. 'You came out of the cloud and held me up. It was very kind.'

During the afternoon we talked about her life. Her stage career which ended when The Man – she called him at first only Jean – took a fancy to her. He didn't like her to act. He said it was a whore's profession.

Gradually, as the evening shadows gathered, his shadow gathered too over the room. She had no one to talk to but her maid, and a couple of feckless friends who were envious of her 'luck'. 'Being kept,' they called it, and didn't want to hear anything serious.

Jean Viktor Pascet had some money. He worked in an office of banking.

He was, she said, tall and grotesque but very strong, hirsute – exciting, she had initially found him. But with his primal appearance came the primitive lusts of a cave man. He was rough in bed and vicious out of it. Although he refused to marry her, which at first, she said, she might have liked, he wanted her to be 'loyal'.

'I mean,' said Lilas indignantly, 'I've had only two tiny affairs since I've known him. He never guessed. It's such crazy things he takes against.' He accused her of bedding the butcher's boy because she had said he had nice curly hair. The first beating came after a party among the actors, to which she'd gone, and taken him at his urging. He'd flirted with all the girls, but since she kissed her former manager on the lips, Jean Viktor Pascet, once home, knocked her across the room. 'My head caught something, the fender, I think, and bled. He got upset and picked me up, promising he'd never hit me again if only I was *good!*'

But Jean Viktor had moods, just, said Lilas, like a woman before her courses or in the middle years. He was unreasonable.

Only once she tried to leave him. He indefatigably followed her as far as Versailles and there, in a grove of the famous gardens, blacked her eyes and loosened one of her teeth.

Early on, when she guessed he had another woman, she begged him to leave *her*. Then he beat her worse. The latest assault had been because she had said she wished to visit her actress friend, Minou. Jean Viktor accused Minou of poncing for the manager again. When Lilas explained this manager had died, Jean Viktor grew violent. Probably, I thought, he had cracked one of her ribs, and urged her to see a doctor. 'Oh, I did see someone. He said that a corset was the best thing for it. And then, you see, if *he* finds I've gone to a doctor, Jean will say I'm interested in him, though he's a man of sixty.'

Finally it was late, and she went home. She said he wouldn't be there. There was a prostitute he now sometimes attended on the rue Bac, especially after they had, as he put it, had a tiff. He would be gone for two or three nights in a row, to show his displeasure.

She wrote to me the following day.

All is well. But already I miss you. May I come and bring you a little present for your kindness?

The little present was a pearl pin. She said it had been her mother's, but it was modern, and quite valuable. She was already wooing and deceiving me. Days passed, and in her eyes there was a look I had seen in the eyes of all my Maries. Presently she stumbled upon some invisible thing – her bruise was quite gone by then – we fell together and I kissed her. It turned out she too had had her 'little pleasures', as she called them, among the actress dressing-rooms, two or three excited women crowded together in a small space, damp with scented sweat, chalkily powdered, dressing and undressing. Lilas had painted toenails and a smooth interior, which, plumbing it with two of my fingers, I found made her into a maenad. Her hair tossed, full of feathers from a punctured cushion, she was holding up her breasts in her hands like lovely ripe fruits, giving high screams, kicking, until she fell back dazed and laughing.

She liked deceiving the cave man too, so safely. He was convinced, she said, women could do nothing for each other. If they said they could, it was a ploy to get a man 'at the job'.

'You know,' he says, 'I'd like to discover a bit about you. Won't you tell me anything?'

The third bottle of Champagne is open. He wanted to send for more, but I said, No, no, wait a little. He guessed correctly, I don't want the waiters to see me without hat and wig.

'So little to tell,' I say. I take his hand, large, well-manicured, male, a blush of hair at the bases of the fingers. What is obviously a marriage ring. 'And you?'

'Let's both be secret then,' he says.

I drop my gaze. 'I've been – am being – very indiscreet.'

'I'm glad. I'll take care of you, my pretty little girl.'

It's strange to me, the way men see me. Always the little, the pretty, this fragile, snappable, slender wisp. Strengthless and yielding. Whatever do I do to them, or do they do it to themselves, to cover their eyes with the lenses that make me, if not the world, into a rosy rose. There are thorns, of course, but all women are untrustworthy.

'Do you think you can give a little of yourself to me, my dear?' asks Armand, '*you*, if not your history.'

'Yes.'

He beckons me. I get up and go and sit down beside him. He puts his hand around my waist, another to my chin. He leans to me and kisses me. The eating kiss. He tastes of tobacco and wine. Smells of some cologne. I clutch him, and as I do so, clutch with my hand at his glass, as if not knowing what I do, careful not to upset a drop.

'What is it? Do you want a drink? Here, here's my glass …'

'No, no more. I can't. I haven't a good head for wine.'

'One sip …' coaxing. But to this he won't coax me.

'I feel rather dizzy. I must …' I stand up.

Alarmed, perhaps even annoyed – will I puke or swoon and spoil his fun – he swigs off his Champagne and pours himself some more.

I go back to my own side of the table, to get the furniture between us.

'Dearest monsieur, I want to give myself to you. So much. But you see …'

'What?' Yes, he's impatient. He'd thought my going over to him, kissing him, that was it. It was, obviously. Not what he expects, however.

And now he mustn't, whatever happens, *kiss me again.*

My grandmother, Constance, gave me a great many useful things. The charcoal powder, a special rouge, a bottle of scent made uniquely for her when she was young, called *Palis-sandre*, which was no longer quite fresh enough to be put on, but which smelled wonderful sprinkled on my fire. Also, things came to me from my mother's enormous hoard of clutter, in her dark apartment that looked towards the river. I spent hours in that sombre yellow light, the blinds down at the windows for death.

Sorting through the drawers and closets. She seemed to have kept everything. Old letters about nothing, and a few that were improper, empty powder boxes, blouses crumpled into heaps because they were no longer fashionable, or were impossible to clean, two or three of Indian silk, or lace. She kept cards of invitation, dead dry roses given by admirers, slips from the theatre, tokens of the railway, bits of wool, ancient novels, combs, broken earrings, stockings with holes, and worn out coins, unknown keys, a lucky rabbit's foot that hadn't worked.

There was very little from her childhood, however. She'd left: her toys, and part of her soul, at O—, in Constance's mansion that was called locally the Chateau, despite being a mere house. It dominated the top of the village street, its garden tumbling behind it down and up, to the woods and fields, and to a carriageway down which quite a few aristocrats had scrambled for the coast in order to avoid the guillotine. In my mother's day, sometimes sheep fell into Constance's garden from the one particular field that stood above the terraces. They were never hurt, but their bleating would fetch an old woman and a boy from the kitchen, beating pans, to drive them back up the sloping returning way they had been too sheep-like to notice for themselves.

The house had come to Constance from a powerful man, when she was in her thirties. She later took her apoplectic husband there in her forties, and killed him off with my shrieking, insane child-aunts, the local cream and butter, the ghosts of my mother and the sheep and all her illustrious previous men.

She had thought herself past the age for children, she boldly told me. When she fell for Sophie and Susie, she hadn't had her courses for a year. What was God playing at? But Constance didn't believe in God, and never set foot in the village church. Her absence, as she said, sat there for her.

'Grandmother, what's this?'

'That? It was among your mother's things?'

'Yes. I thought it was scent, but it doesn't smell.'

'Let me see.'

This conversation occurred just before she packed me off south, at fourteen, to that school with swings and Marie E.

She took the small bottle, uncorked it, sniffed.

Then she stared at the bottle.

'Where was this?'

'In the drawer by her bed.'

'Oh, my God,' coldly said Constance, who did not believe in God. 'But no. Surely not. The stupid little simpleton. And I gave her this!'

My mother had, after the Italian cook-boy, sobbed herself into a dreadful cold, and taken to her bed. There she seemed to grow smaller and smaller, shrinking away. On the very evening the letter I had written to Constance reached the Chateau, I walked into her blind-yellow bedroom and found my mother had crumpled in like a dead flower. She'd wanted to die. Said it over and over. And there she was, her goal accomplished.

Broken hearts would of course kill if they truly broke. Ah, but they do break, they do.

At fourteen, Constance took the mysterious bottle away from me, but about five years later, she gave it back.

After Anne had told me about Armand's ill-treatment of her, she wept for a long time. Her big, spare body, that the corseting hadn't quite made to look like a woman's, shook. I waited. Eventually, she said, 'Do I presume Mademoiselle Dule – Lilas … She said you helped her.'

'Did she?'

'Yes.'

'In what way?'

Anne Blos blew her nose yet again into the lace handkerchief. What joy all the laundresses have.

'I'll give you anything I can. There is a little money left, although it won't last much longer. I could sell this house – I hate it now. I don't need so many rooms. Whatever you want. Not to have to look at him. Not to have to know it's there, that mouth, that said those things to me.'

That day I call, in retrospect, The Day I Stole My Servant's Hat. It has the sound of a modern play. Something frivolous and smart, perhaps by Foline. Or, I suppose, maybe a short story by Chekhov.

The sequence began with Lilas coming to see me for a luncheon of grapes, pears, and new bread with Normandy butter. She'd powdered the bruise on her cheek and arranged a curl over it. I said nothing. I never did say anything, she would always tell me. Generally now, too, he beat her on the body, although never, through some curious code, on the breasts. 'He'll say, Turn around you slut, I don't want to hit you there. He likes me to thank him after, for being so careful with me.' *That* was on the day her back was black from one shoulder to the slim, almost-not-there buttocks.

We sipped Muscat, and she said, not how he'd hit her, but, 'I can't stand any more, Phèdre. I'm going to run away again.'

'But you always say, he'll catch up to you and beat you worse.'

'I know. But – oh Phèdre, will you help me?'

'What can I do?' Did I mean, I would do anything, only tell me what? Or did I mean: Don't involve me in this, please?

Lilas wept and drank her Muscat. Tears and wine and the dew on the pears. Charming, like a painting. *Weeping Girl with Fruity* an illustration from The Day I Stole My Servant's Hat.

'I don't know. I won't ask. No. I'll think of something.'

We drank more. She cheered up. About three, she delved into her handbag, and brought out a package.

'It's a present. But for both of us. Oh, you'll never guess. Maybe you'll be shocked.'

She said Minou had been given it by an admirer who purchased it at Karikal in India. Minou had been too afraid to use it. Just looking at it, Minou said, made her skin prickle and blush. But Lilas said she had used it, now and then, alone. Alone? I didn't believe her. But there are always taps with water and wash bowls, even bathrooms, now, in Paris.

The thing was almost shaped like a flattened crescent moon. Not quite. It was ivory, she said, and whitish, very smooth, like silk to the touch. In the middle was a little bulge that might be anything, rather like a slender napkin ring. From this, the two smooth, round-topped horns went up. They were only the width around I could make between finger and thumb. A toy, not for virgins, but for young girls, or those who wished always to be surprised by well-made men.

Having sloughed all her outer garments, the frilly knickers and petticoat and corset, and lying there on my sofa in her ribboned, transparent chemise, she slipped one of the horns into herself, to show me. Then she wriggled a little, giggling.

I wasn't a virgin. It was a woman who had taken that, with her strong pianist's hands, two years before.

'Let me do it,' Lilas said as I kneeled astride her.

She pierced me with great care, but having seen so much of her, I was already trembling and prepared.

Lilas sat up against me. I grasped her under the arms, the little fawn hairs there like rough tinsel. Her breasts swam up and down from the chemise-top. She put her arms around my neck. As we kissed, trying to suck out each other's tongues, the two little ivory phalluses worked away busily against the itching inner mound of Venus which is called the womb, and the dear little napkin ring rubbed us.

Lilas pulled her head aside. She gasped she could feel my tongue deep inside her, tickling her vagina, although she used words both coarser and more euphemistic.

My crisis came like claps of thunder. Lilas shrieked, dying in my arms, her arched back offering her breasts as I died on them in turn.

'Isn't it a lovely present?' whispered Lilas. She insisted that we mustn't move, but lie there, myself burying her beneath me. She said she wished everyone were as light in weight. Of course, quite soon, we began to itch again, the clever ivory moving about at every breath. She screamed so loudly this time I was glad some of the other tenants in the building were deaf.

Because the cave man would be off at the rue Bac, or, as Lilas said, picking up some harlot from the alleys at St Germain, Lilas stayed with me until nine o'clock. She went home in a carriage, sore and smiling.

I was woken in the morning by my cleaning woman, who seemed to have no name, but whom my grandmother had christened Brunhilde.

She regarded me, in my dressing-gown. Then came in as if by right. I suppose she had one.

The concierge had arranged for Brunhilde to do my cleaning when she learned I hadn't a proper servant. Brunhilde 'did' for two others in the building. She cleaned very well, and, once every month, dusted all my books in the five bookcases in my study. Everything, but for three things, was always replaced in perfect order. The three things were: a stone egg that lay on my blotter, which she put on the windowsill, a picture in the sitting room of a meadow with poppies, which she always tilted to the left. And a dictionary, which she put back once a month upside down.

In winter, Brunhilde had sometimes made me, over my fire, a garlicky, thick cabbage soup, bringing all the ingredients, ready cut up, herself. It was served with sour cream and was good. She refused payment for this additional task.

As she cleaned the sitting room and study, I sat in my bedroom brushing my hair. The door was ajar, and outside, on the table beneath the hall mirror, lay Brunhilde's dark hat, quite small and unfashionable, with one cabbage-like red rose. Roses weren't suited to Brunhilde. She was big and brown, with a bush of grey hair held fast by a thousand pins. Her wedding ring was sunk so far into the flesh of her finger she boasted a thief would need to cut off the finger entire to get it. Although she seldom spoke, it was often in startlements. I had gathered too that her husband was long dead, killed by a train at Paisse-sur-mer.

Perhaps the hat had been young then.

Now I studied it, and saw for the first time that it was the hat of a prostitute of several years ago. Only its dinginess disguised it.

Brunhilde had made coffee, but before I went to drink it, I picked up the hat of my slave and put it into the bottom of an ornate wardrobe from O—, under a pile of old dresses meant one day for charity.

Did I know what I did, and why? Yes, surely. I can't remember, but they tell us now, that the mind does things, and causes us to do things, that we don't always understand, but which have a true meaning in our inner awareness.

When Anne had cried herself to a standstill, she apologised to me. She added, 'But you see how it is, Mademoiselle Phèdre. You see what's been done to me.'

I stood up.

She too jumped to her feet. 'Don't go …'

'It's better that I do. I want you to write to me and tell me where I can meet him, where he goes to find these better-class women you speak of, that you say he likes.'

'To incriminate me,' she said. She squared her square shoulders. 'Why not. Very well. But do you mean – you will?'

'We haven't spoken, madame. Do what? We're friends of Lilas Dule, and have been speaking of the actors' benefit.'

He's becoming elated. I mean, Armand. He has stood up, and he's telling me all about the things he wants and intends for his future. He keeps veering away from talking of one particular woman, because he still wishes to possess me, and she's a favourite, probably that one Anne Blos made a special mention of: Mademoiselle de Gillan. Even so, his enthusiasm sparkles. And rain like harsh gravel is flung at the window.

Yes, he's sweating, too. I'm careful, smiling, agreeing, keeping my distance. Sometimes he takes a turn around the table, needing to move about now, his heart beating fast with energy and decision. He tried to snatch a kiss, but I turned my head. 'Just give me a moment, dear monsieur. Let me look at you. How I love the sound of your voice.'

Far gone enough now, he accepts this. Flaunts himself. His colour is red and his eyes brilliant. I can see he would be thought handsome.

He's thirsty, but I left him all the Champagne.

Then his heart flutters, apparently. He touches his breast, looks surprised. Laughs it off. Continues to harangue me, now with a Greek poem, which he rightly thinks I can't translate.

Brunhilde went hunting about.

'What is it?'

'I can't find my hat.'

'Oh, but I thought – how strange.'

We hunted together, and obviously didn't find it. 'Look, there's one of mine. Why don't you take it? The hat will turn up somewhere. Perhaps I moved it without realizing.'

'I can't take your hat, mademoiselle.'

'Yes. Look. This is plain and respectable. And see, it has a red rose.'

She took my once fashionable hat, examined it. She knew she would not look her best – that *is*, her worst, her most dowdy and sensible, her most iron and clay self, in it. But needs must.

'It's kind of you. I'll bring it back. Perhaps, if you find my hat, you'd send it on. To the Post Office on rue St Michel.'

'Of course. I'll look thoroughly this afternoon.' (She would never see it again.)

'My uncle used to say,' said Brunhilde, 'things vanish away. Goblins take them. He vanished just like that. He walked into a shop that sold cigars, and never came out. They never saw him in the shop, either.'

With this, a tale told often in different forms, but one I'd never heard from her before, she left me. Her uncle was my omen, in his way.

That evening, clad in one of the charity dresses, and in my cleaning lady's hat, I went out and took the omnibus to the rue Bac that lies some twisted way behind the church of St Germain. I had powdered *my* face very much, rouged my cheeks. I kept my eyes down, and the better women shrank away from me.

Demonstrably, I might have missed him. But I knew he'd probably be going there, and how he went first to drink, and then came swaggering through the streets about this hour.

It was dusk. A lamp stood on the corner, sickly near-green as a bad duck's egg. Jean Viktor Pascet came from the shadows of non-existence, the wings of life, out on to the stage.

I couldn't miss him. He was just as she'd described. They always have seen. Women who are so terrified and angry, remember well and paint vividly. If she says to you, And he has one leg one inch shorter than the other, or one hair that grows awry in his moustache, you can be sure it's so. It is love that's blind.

When he was close, I accosted him.

'Pardon me, monsieur. I was looking for the church.'

He looked right at me. Although the lamp was behind him, I saw his face was squashed and dark and sodden. He had terrible small eyes that never stretched the skin around them. His eyebrows met. An unlined face, that of an evil child. For certain, a cave man.

'Church, eh? Sure of that, are you?'

I gave the low coarse laugh Lilas had long ago taught me, her own in unguarded moments. 'Well, it's church, if there's nothing better.'

'Like a drink would you, lovely?'

'I've got my own. Do you like brandy, monsieur?'

'Oh, yes, I'm partial to a brandy. What'll it all cost?' I told him a low whore's price. He nodded approvingly. 'That's a bit high.'

I put my arm through his. 'Maybe I'll take a little less, monsieur. I think you can please me. I like your kind of gentleman.' And where, you ask, did I learn these nauseous acting skills? Oh, but women always act. And I'd been to the theatre, hadn't I.

And the school where they told you, incidentally, how to behave with a man. What a lady does. And that means, by the way, what any woman does. Constance once said, 'Almost any man will believe you want him. The ones who don't – beware of them.' But Jean Viktor believed. He saw the twinkle in my eye.

We walked, and he asked if I had anywhere to go. I said there might be a room we could have at a hotel I knew. By then we were in the darkness of the alleys, and he was drinking the brandy fast. He felt me as he did so, with his hairy hands, my breast, and my central parts, through my skirts. 'Or we could do it here,' he said. I said, No, I wasn't used to that, primly. He said that was good. He liked to see I didn't expect him to lean me on a wall, although a moment before, he would have done exactly that.

I wasn't sure, of course, how long I'd have to spin all this out. I didn't know precisely how it would work. But I could see he was getting very excited, and sweating, and he was drinking now for thirst. When he offered me the brandy I turned my head away with it, pretending to drink, all prim again. And when he tried to kiss me, I said, Not here, not here. It wasn't safe. Some ruffian might try to take advantage of us. And he approved of my common sense.

He started to tell me I was a lovely girl, and better than his regular girl in the rue Bac. He might just set me up, if I suited him. And I clung to his arm, so when he staggered, I was pulled about, and I laughed as if it was such a joke. Which it was, naturally.

I had no second of fear. I never have, in those situations. And I wasn't afraid with Armand Blos, not even when he lurched away from the fireplace and clutched the table, glaring at me, the sweat thick as syrup on his forehead, his brown hair black with it.

'What the deuce is the matter with me?'

Did they both say that? Probably the first one, Jean Viktor, spoke more coarsely. *What the fuck's up with me?*

I moved away from the table, and Armand crashed down on his chair. He pulled at his silk tie and sprung his collar open.

'Can't breathe. Open the window –'

I didn't bother with it. Next minute a gush of saliva came out of his mouth.

Jean Viktor's eyes were bulging. He reeled away from me, hit the wall and slipped down. The brandy went with a smash. He clutched his throat, belly.

'What have you done to me?'

Did either of them say that? Probably neither. What was I, after all, an easy, willing woman, found in one case on the street, in the other fluttering her lashes from a momentarily raised blue veil, in a cafe where plenty of bored or loose women went to display themselves.

Armand did give a choked cry of pain. But the rain on the windows was loud by now, and a carriage galloping by. Then his throat closed. He collapsed across the table.

I didn't watch, with either, the death spasms. Jean Viktor lost control of his bowels, but Armand, for some reason, did not. The mixture in Constance's bottle, which she gave my mother for her protection, a compound perhaps of opium and strychnine and some other tincture, unnamed, has variable effects. If my mother took it, she died quietly, for example, and no one save Constance suspected a thing.

When Jean settled into the muck and night on the alley's floor, I walked briskly away. I went up by the old Odeon, and came out at last against the river, which holds this city together like the hooked-up seam of a gown.

No one had seen me then. And, with Armand, they saw only what they had seen so often, a slender, well-enough dressed female creature, red-haired, and veiled to protect herself.

I put on again my disguise. There was a useful mirror above the hearth, and a back stair from the restaurant, of course. I took the stair, leaving Anne's husband also, dead as a doornail, all over the tablecloth from Sevre.

3

There is a passage in a Greek play – Euripides, possibly, I'm not definite. The hero laments that, on the morning he inadvertently committed a terrible sin against nature and the gods, Apollo had 'Dressed the land in gold, set crowns upon the mountain tops.' Surely they might instead have warned him to be careful, by an influx of ominous darkness, tempests, lightning.

This day was overcast and crystallized by a cold like white sugar. The chestnut trees were already dropping dead black leaves, and the almonds in the street were dusted white, as if by a thin snow.

The letter was white with black ink, simple. It said:

> *Dear Mademoiselle,*
> *May I trouble you to meet me at the cemetery of St Luc, about three this afternoon? I think that we should speak.*
> *I remain, in appreciation of your acceptance,*
> *Mme R de G.*

My first thought was, the great network of women's whispers, sighs, hisses, screams, had caught in my name yet another one who needed me. But I was reluctant. Even though I didn't know, not having bothered to inquire, that le Jardin de St Luc had been the place of Armand Blos' burial, not eight days before.

Whether to go? What should I do?

I ate my warm roll with white butter, and drank my bitter coffee.

Gradually the sugariness faded from the almonds, and the street bustled.

She knew my address, after all, Madame R de G. If I failed her, might she seek me here? Would that be any better? I found her name irritating. Its secrecy. Also some notion it evoked of awkwardness.

In the early afternoon I found myself dressing to go out. I put on a dark green tailored costume. I was elegant. I would after all arrive at the place, look for her, spy, slip away if unimpressed or uneasy.

Mme R de G.

The lid of the sky hung low, lined with silver towards the river and the cathedral. The carriage jolted me. Were there bones lying on the ground?

Near Les Invalides, a dead carriage horse lay in the road, with two cabmen shouting above it.

Indeed, I had my omens; I won't complain.

So many gravel paths lead to a small chapel. Dark trees bend over the gravestones. Here and there are the monuments. A Virgin with stone roses gathered in her veil. Such things.

I walked slowly. I was ready to pretend to be interested in some particular grave. It was, by the big old clock, fifteen minutes past the hour of three.

Some false note of weather had drawn out a clump of pale yellow narcissi. Looking across from them, I saw a woman standing alone, quite near the chapel. She wore black. Mourning, obviously. If this were she, and she wanted my skills as an assassin, did she have vengeance in mind?

But this might not, after all, be the one.

I went up slowly, stealthily, as if only searching out a special marker. During this, I studied the woman covertly. She was quite tall, slender, curved at the bosom. The dark hat tilted, allowing a glimpse of hair that looked now quite deep in tone, now lighter. Was it red?

Pausing. I gazed down raptly and read the words: *You are taken from me to God.* Death, the arch-lover, snatching away. Betrayals of all sorts.

'Mademoiselle … pardon me,' her voice was soft, yet it carried. When I heard her voice, it was as if a hand had passed over me, or some shadow. I've heard them say: *A step on my grave.* But there were graves everywhere, and none was mine.

I straightened, as if vague, my mind elsewhere.

'Can it be, mademoiselle, that, like myself, you came searching for Armand Blos? He's here.'

I straightened and looked directly at her.

'Blos?' I asked. 'No, not at all.'

'But you're the one they call Phèdre,' she said.

I stared at her coldly, and hard. My grandmother has perfected this look, and I'd learnt it long ago. It quells servants, women. I'd never dare it with a man, who must always seem the superior. But this one might have been a man, for all the giving way it produced in her. She stared me down, and I stared her down. At last, as if merely exasperated, she shrugged one shoulder, turned a little, pliant in her black clothes. She pointed to the mound at her feet with the ferule of an umbrella. 'He died recently. He was found dead. In a private room of a restaurant, but then you know, don't you, Mademoiselle Phèdre.'

I said, as remotely as I could, 'If you want me for something, you'd better explain. Are you the one who wrote to me, *R de G?*'

She turned abruptly back to me. 'My name, mademoiselle, is Rherlotte de Gillan. I've heard you called only Phèdre. I believe some families do lack a second name.'

'And who told you all this about me?'

'Why, mademoiselle, women hear these things murmured, and murmur to others. You're common property, with some.'

My heart was hammering. I was flustered, perhaps frightened. At the grave I didn't glance. It might not be his. And her strange name, which might not even be real.

'I ask again, *Madame* – so you styled yourself, I believe – do you want something from me?'

'Yes,' she said. 'I know what you did to him. Ah, don't be alarmed. The police are utterly in ignorance, as so often in these cases. And of course, I have no proof. But mademoiselle, I wish you to know, not all the world rejoiced at Armand Blos' death.'

She was the mistress Anne had ranted against. Of course, *de Gillan*. I'd been told. She didn't care what she did; loved him. And he had treated this one as a wife.

'I regret your loss,' I said. 'It seems to have upset your mind a little.'

Her face *flamed* white. Her eyes – *burned*. For a moment, she couldn't speak. Then she said, 'Don't talk this rubbish. I know you killed him. Was it poison? Yes, the woman's weapon. I'll tell you now, I'll bring you down. I'll make you pay for what you've done. Consider me mad, if you like, if it helps you. You won't escape me.'

I said. 'Madame, I might in my turn go to the police. I haven't done a thing, and your unhinged threats make me think you'd be better taken care of.'

She left his grave. She strode in her straight skirt up to me. She stood tall almost against me.

'Do what you want,' she said, *'think* what you want. You'll never be free of me. I'll make you give it back in your blood, your heart's blood. You've spilt mine.'

'You loved him,' I said. I was, I thought, trembling, but I didn't show it. My voice – trained in the theatre of the world – was firm. 'But from the very little I ever heard, he was a poor specimen. He's dead then. Well, well.'

She was so near, her breath met my lips, pure but alien.

'Some of us,' she said, 'do love. I don't care what he was, never cared. I loved him, you're correct. He was all my life was worth. But now, I have another purpose. Now I have you to hunt down, Phèdre.'

I smiled. I thought she would lift her gloved hand to hit me and I would catch it.

But she was already walking away, she was on one of the gravel paths. The shadow of a black tree fell on her blackness, and as she came out from it, her fiery hair gleamed in the paleness of the afternoon, like something in a famous, recent, clever painting.

I watched until she reached the gate, and went out. A carriage came up. She was gone. Then I did look at the grave, and there it was, this new mound, the marker not even set there yet. But someone had laid violets – How? It was autumn ... oh, some florist's hothouse.

This had never happened before. If there had been any mourners for Jean

Viktor I never learned. For the other girl, she had recanted and called me off.

I had been the hunter.

What had I better do? I went over to a seat, and sat on it. Countless women no doubt had done exactly that, shaking and not quite able to catch their breath.

She might try to kill me in turn. Had she been promising that? But if so, why not here, a sop for the dead, just as in the Greek and Roman myth. A dagger, a glass of vitriol – what a fool I'd been to chance this meeting.

I walked down from the cemetery, and lost my way in a maze of streets, and finally found a cab. But I gave the address of Lilas' apartment, then changed it to the apartment of Elise. Did I think Rherlotte de Gillan was following me? Why should she? She had already got hold of my address.

After I killed Jean Viktor, Lilas became afraid to be my lover. Was she afraid of him – or of me? Although I didn't tell her what I'd done, she knew, of course. He had been found dead, and in a strange morgue she had had to see him, and when she fainted, it was reckoned quite proper. They had said they thought a woman had poisoned him, some jealous whore of St Germain.

I could see her afterwards, not avoiding my eyes, but staring straight through them. As if to find the true Phèdre at their backs. She would make excuses. Then, if we coupled, either reach a tremendous crisis, or writhe uneasily, incapable of pleasing herself or me.

Once she began to avoid me, I soon found others. One meets women so easily in this city. It's all so innocent, at first. There was a little waitress who would put her pink feet on my shoulders and say in rapture, 'Oh, as good as chocolate!' Or the financier's wife I met once in the park, who turned very passionate in the carriage, urging me on, until, by the time we had reached the rue Bucher, she was violently gaspingly finished, worn out, had a headache, and wanted to go home at once. I had only seen an inch of thigh, and touched her breast through all the ruffles. A week later, she wrote me a pitiable letter, begging me never to tell a soul about our *misunderstanding.* I sensed there had been many of these, both letters and misunderstandings.

I liked especially the girl I found in a bookshop. She was just seventeen, and had been in love with all the heroines in all the books, and made me into each in turn. Now a cold priestess, now a hot-blooded princess riding astride a horse, now a great singer. Even sometimes she wanted a little game, where she would lie in her chemise on the bed, her hands clasped on her bosom, eyes closed and lids flickering, and I would have to 'wake' her, which I always did with great interest.

But I'm listing here my triumphs. They're redundant in the face of what I have to tell. Let me desist.

Elise had been available to me some while. She was a slimly plump, ash-blonde young woman of nineteen, who lived with her mother near the church of St Sulpice, whose bells we heard sometimes at odd moments. The mother was a milliner, and absent from seven in the morning until seven or eight at night. Elise, who painted, and sold her pictures, stayed at home. She did the housework, and in the evening prepared their supper. I had met the exhausted mother only once, when she had come home most unusually a little early. Elise and I had been saying our goodbyes, and were utterly decorous. I paid my dues by purchasing on the spot a small picture of a spaniel, which, at my flat, lay in a drawer, except on those rare occasional days when Elise came over the river to visit me.

Although Lilas and I remained 'on friendly terms' we had seldom had possession of each other for more than a year. Besides, she had passed on to others her secret, of which she refused to talk, ever, with me. She saw sometimes too, a handsome lawyer, who, she said, often threatened to make her his wife. She was useful in the matter of loaning me the red theatrical wig – I'd wished to inculpate her, under the circumstances. I had even returned the wig to her. She had thrust the box away at once.

Despite or because of these things, now it seemed more sensible to have come to the apartment of Elise.

Elise was my slave. I think she liked to be. Her mother, from the position of her own servitude, had somehow instilled in her the wish to wait on others.

From her startled 'Phèdre – oh is it really you? How pale you look. Your hands are ice. Oh, come in,' to the goblet of cognac, kept only for medicinal aid – 'I'll tell Mama I had one of my headaches –' she fluttered warmly over me. At another time, I would have been stirred by her attentions, her scent of lavender, charcoal, painted paper. Not now.

Was I at all clear? I suspect I wasn't. I immediately said to her, 'Will you do me a favour, Elise?'

'Anything – anything at all, darling.'

'A man's been pestering me.'

'Wretched brute.'

'Here's some money. Would you take the cab outside and go over to my flat? Make sure no one's loitering.'

Elise sprang up at once. Seldom going out, except for slow tired walks with her mother on Sundays, she yearned for action. She had on her hat and wrap and was gone in five minutes.

But how stupid of me. She would be looking out for some hulking male figure. Not for the terrible svelte figure of 'Madame' de Gillan.

Patently, I made Elise go so that, under cover and in a different room, I could consider alone what had befallen me.

And what was it? Did I even know?

De Gillan had no proof, she said so. She could do nothing, because she had wanted to do something and not found what it was she would do. Although she'd had the opportunity to murder or disfigure me, these things she was too fastidious perhaps to attempt.

The threat was all she had, her declared vow of revenge on me. Revenge she would never get. She was beneath my contempt. To have loved such a creature as an *Armand*. To parade her distress at the loss of an *Armand*. What a dunce she must be.

I drank the cognac down. I sat back in the battered, comfortable chair where Mama sunk her creaking bones and weary stitch-pricked fingers every night.

Shutting my eyes, I felt myself fall a thousand feet into something that wasn't sleep – for I was conscious. A kind of trance. Beset by moments of dreams, knit together by apparently rational thoughts.

I was back at the gate of the Jardin de St Luc. I was going in. It seemed I had to play over again that scene. As if, playing it for the first time, I'd missed so much. But what had I missed? An encounter with this ordinary, well-dressed, bourgeois, cool – yet obviously hysterical – woman, who had loved Armand Blos.

There she is on the path up near the little chapel. Why not turn back, now; avoid her. I should have done so then. Yes, I was as much a fool as she, risking the interview.

But on I go. Along the graves, to meet again, yet properly for the first, Rherlotte de Gillan …

She's wearing black – mourning for whom? (It was Armand. I know it, now.) Yes, she had vengeance in mind. Upon Phèdre.

Something at that moment seems to check me, but I take no notice. I move up slowly, stealthily. During this, covertly, I study her. Tall, almost my height, surely. Slender, but curved at the bosom, blossoming there. The dark hat tilted, allowing a glimpse of hair. It's red.

Pausing. I gaze down. Words on a grave … *gone from me to God*. I've never thought of death that way. The taker, the taken. My mother all crumpled up in that bed. Meaning nothing. One more object to be tidied.

'Mademoiselle. I beg your pardon.' Her voice, this woman's voice, is sweet, soft, yet carries. A hand passes over me, a shadow.

I straighten, vague, and interrupted.

She says, 'Can it be you are also searching for the grave of Armand Blos? It is here.'

She has, now I look at it, the face of a statue. Not the white Virgin near the gate, with her veil of roses. Rather something classical. The antiquity of Rome, the proud daughter of some noble house, the Flavians, the Caesars. But in the white and classical Roman face, these two eyes, somewhere between jewel-blue and jewel-green, level, unblinking, flashing light like steel, under the graceful, hand-carved brows.

'Blos? No, not at all.'

'But you're Phèdre,' she says.

My name in her mouth. My name sounds changed and new.

I stare at her, with my grandmother's cold, hard look, but she, this one, gives it back. Not jewels then, the eyes, but turquoise mirrors. She stares me down. I stare her down. Do I give way first? I think … I may have. And she shrugs, and turns her shoulder. Tiny waist. But the shoulders quite wide, very straight, not tired by supporting the sumptuous breasts. Flame runs over the coils of hair under the hat. She points her sword – for a moment, a sword it is – but now – an umbrella – at the mound before her feet.

One can just see Armand lying inside it. He laughs. And is gone. She says, 'He died only recently. Was found in a restaurant. But you know.'

I say, 'You'd better explain. Are you this woman, *R de* G?' With the movement of a fencer, she spins back at me. Her chin is up. A rounded chin, such as a statue would have. The eyes flash again. So cool, so brilliant, adamantine – only soft with, flooded with, *colour*.

'*I* am Rherlotte de Gillan.'

I stare. This name. Have I heard it ever? I must have heard it. I know it. Anne must have said. She did. But not the first name. *Rherlotte.*

She insults me, without raising her voice. She never has.

'Your family, I believe, has no second name.'

Who told her this?

'Women murmur about you,' she says. What's she saying now? Not only am I a bastard, but also an 'unnatural' woman. A woman who prefers women to men. *Is* she saying this?

My heart, hammering. Flustered and shaky, frightened perhaps. Her strange familiar name. It might not be real. It's outlandish.

'What do you want?'

Her skin is white as the marble statue she was before some magic – the kiss of Armand? – brought her alive. Her lips are perfectly shaped, the upper arched, the bottom lip rounded as if for biting. The tint of rosy amber. Is it rouge? They look, her lips, her mouth, warm to touch. She says, 'I know what you did to him. Don't be alarmed. The police are as usual in ignorance. And of course I have no proof. But I want you to know, Phèdre, not all the world rejoiced at his death.'

He had treated her as his wife. Not Anne, who was, but this one.

I say to her face that she's unhinged.

Her *face flames* white. Her eyes – *burn.*

That red, shaped mouth says to me, 'Rubbish. I know you killed him. I'll bring you down. I'll make you pay for what you've done. You won't escape me.'

I say I will go to the police, and tell them I've been threatened by a madwoman.

She leaves his grave and strides to me. She stands so close, almost against me. Is she an inch shorter than I am? But the power of her fills up the space, and she towers. Her eyes belong to the caracal, the lynx, set in the luminous marble face. Her lashes are the colour of shavings of bronze. The arched brows like long, combed, tawny feathers. The lids of her eyes are, seemingly artlessly, a little dark, and burnished. I can smell the faint ambrous musk of her hair. She's cleaner than the inside of an apple.

I imagine her eating apples, biting them. Drinking white milk, so her throat ripples, the wonderful mechanism under the drum of smooth skin. Her teeth are *white* as milk. I see their biting edges.

She says: 'Do and think what you want. You'll never be free of me. I'll make you give it back in your hearts blood. You've spilt mine.'

A shudder passes up my back. Every bone of my spine quivers. What has she said? Is it some spell?

I won't show her that I tremble. That would be most unwise. The years of controlling my voice before my harsh grandmother, my weak mother. To men who came into my mother's apartment in Paris. That makes me able to say, flat and firm, 'You loved a poor specimen, from what I've heard.'

She turns her head then, as if she can no longer breathe the same air that Phèdre breathes. Her profile – yes, the goddess Diane on an ancient silver coin. The straight nose, rounded chin, the huge, moulded eyes, the lips that are pure and forbiddingly chaste, yet sexually cruel, voluptuous with saying No. Did she tease him to her feet? Did he lie helpless under her strength? He's there now, on his back in the ground, but why does he laugh at me? I killed you, Armand. It was I who won.

The face of the moon goddess Diane strikes back at me.

'He was all my life was worth. But I have you now.'

She is the huntress, not I. She rides them down, the fleet deer in the forest, even the tigress she rides down, and casts into them her moonlit spears.

If she raises her hand, I'll catch it. I'll crush the bones until blueness appears about her lips, until she screams and falls against me.

But she's also too fastidious to strike me with more than the angle of her face, her eyes. Her spears.

In any other place or world – she *would* have killed me. A dagger through my heart.

She's walking away. Her hair, flames, fades, flames.

She's left him violets. Shall I tread on them, mash them? There had been violets on the hat that I wore for Armand, as I wore Brunhilde's roses for Jean.

In the cab – is she following me? Or has she gone the other way, to wait at my door.

Rherlotte de Gillan. Diane of the marble flaming moon.

Let me run to earth.

But the last net of dreams shows me death standing in the road, above a fallen carriage horse. Under the hood, Death has a red mouth. Is it myself I see, or her?

When I extricated myself from Elise, reminding her that her mother would be coming home – it was almost six – I returned to my flat. No one, according to Elise, was anywhere about. She had even, as I'd found at the door, inquired of my concierge if anyone had left a message. No one had.

But when I entered the building, I saw the envelope addressed to me.

A pang went through my side. An actual pain.

I took up the envelope. It was pale mauve, with blue ink. Inside was an instruction, where I might receive quite a large sum of money.

Anne Blos added, in her prim way, *I am so grateful to have had your help in this enterprise.* She had incriminated herself with idiotic honourableness. The night of his death, playing Bezique with friends. Only I could bring her down.

I didn't need the money. Would write to tell her so. Instead I must pack my bag. The night train was not so pleasant, but I would take it. And tomorrow be at O—.

4

The house at the top of the street is large enough, I had no thought Constance would be put out by my unannounced manifestation. She has countless servants. All in terror of her. The only drawback was my aunts.

At the gate, *they* were both waiting, as if they knew.

Perhaps they did.

'Why are you here?' said Sophie at once.

'To visit you,' I said.

Susie, also staring at me, said, 'We don't need you.'

They have such big, unblinking eyes, which sometimes they narrow, a sort of yellowish blue. White, small, sharp teeth, in small, soft *shut* mouths. Cascades of hair, which in Susie is quite dark, more tortoiseshell in Sophie. Sophie is plumper, too. Otherwise, almost identical.

These, the demon children who lay in wait in Constance's womb, for her to be careless in her forties.

They were thirteen. An unlucky number.

With little polished nails, Sophie pawed at my two bags. Georges-of-the-Station had got down from the trap, and was preparing to carry my luggage to the house door. I thanked him, tipped him, and took the bags. They weren't heavy.

Susie's white dress was stained with garden things, fallen leaves, bark, moss. Sophie had a spot of something pink on her blue blouse.

'Are you coming in?'

'Of course, what else.'

'It's very early,' said Susie.

'We've been up since dawn.'

'We always are.'

With difficulty I got by them, as they plucked my tailored jacket, wove around me, and up to the door, which stood open.

In the flagged stone passage, a maid was hurrying towards me.

'Oh, mademoiselle. Mistress isn't waked yet. Shall I tell her – I don't like to –'

'It's perfectly all right. I'll see her after breakfast. Would a cup of coffee be possible?'

Constance anyway called me in to breakfast with her. My aunts came too, but she sent them out.

When they loitered in the doorway, she threw a slipper at them, and they vanished.

'They'll listen at the door.'

'Perhaps. But they're soon bored. Then they'll go away.'

I said, boldly, because Constance hadn't been, herself, very polite to me ('Good God, isn't there enough for you to do in Paris?'), 'Are they mad?'

'I expect they are. Children of old age. He was almost sixty-five, and I, as you recall, was not young.'

She had a country breakfast, two eggs in their shells, a plate of bread, dishes of butter, jams, apples, a bowl of cream. She drank strong tea, and tossed back an inch of some white spirit, maybe the local brandy.

To me she offered only bread and butter.

'I know you don't eat.'

'I'm tired. I was travelling all night. A maniac with an accordion or hurdy-gurdy, I'm not sure which, went on and on in the carriage. It snowed at Petignot.' I had been troubled by that at the time. The train jerking over the crossing with its little house of one yellow window, the flakes drifting on the wind to mingle with our cinders. Armand Blos had ridden his horses in the woods there. Anne had had a farm in the neighbourhood. She had it again now, and the horses wouldn't feel his impatient and perhaps inhumane hands ever again.

'Snow. There's no snow until November. Don't you remember? You always hated it as a child.'

'Yes. I hate snow. I don't know why.'

'A gypsy told me snow was your enemy. Or ice. That was a long time ago. Another said men would be the enemies of your mother. Is that why you're here?'

'I don't understand.'

'You do. Because of a man.'

I'd have to tell her something. I had made something up on the train, altered it, fiddled with it, as the hurdy-gurdy churned round and round in the back of my nose and ears.

'In a way. A woman of my acquaintance became envious. She thinks her husband has an interest in me.'

'Does he?'

'Nothing less likely.'

'I thought not.' She began on her second egg. 'By which I mean, Phèdre, you wouldn't be interested at all in him.'

'He wasn't appealing, no.'

'No, I'm sure.' She ate, swallowed. She drank her tea. 'Your mother put you off, didn't she? What you saw. So much sobbing and wringing of the hands.'

'She had an unhappy time.'

'You despised her.' I said nothing. Constance said, 'So did I. You, I. We're not fashioned from the same clay as your mother. Then again, you're not like me. We'll say no more. How long will you stay?'

'I don't know. A few days, if you'll allow me to.'

'And then this matter will have blown over?'

Would it? I was without thought, the hurdy-gurdy had eaten my cunning. I must wait for it to grow back.

'I expect it will.'

'She's so very angry.'

'Mortally so.' It was out before I could stop it. I visualised myself and Rherlotte de Gillan fighting over the favours of Armand. This made me laugh.

My grandmother frowned. 'Is it a law suit?'

'It – might be. I don't think she'll bring herself to that. She's very … abstemious, I think'

'Was he worth it?'

'I said, I had nothing to do with him.'

'Very well.' She peeled an apple. Belatedly offered the bowl to me. I took one of the fruits. It was russet, red, the smooth colour of a mouth. I held it in my hands as she dismissed me to the upper room that had always, in this house, been mine.

Little blue checks on the curtains and brown flowers. The wallpaper sallow damask, patched with a hint of damp near the ceiling. Ivy grows over the window. Sometimes they cut it back, but this time they had let it alone for some while.

There's a memory always of lying sidelong to this window, on the pillows of goose-feathers, with the dark mahogany posts and back of the bed all gathered into shadow, and that window, green as jade outside from the ivy leaves, and inside from the old fern that grew in a pot.

What was I, as a child? It doesn't matter now. Someone else.

I couldn't sleep, tossing and turning, too cold at first despite the stone bottle filled with hot water, then too hot, throwing off the old fashioned quilt that smelled of dried roses.

Then I dozed. Rherlotte stood on a huge monument above the tomb of Armand. She was made of marble, all but eyes and hair. She drew back her marble arm and hurled the spear at me.

I woke up with it in my breast.

What had happened?

Sophie and Susie were at the bed's foot.

'Will you take us to Paris?'

'No.'

'We want to go.'

'Tell Constance.'

'Constance says no.'

'Run away. Hide on a train.'

They looked at me scathingly. They had thought of it perhaps, realised that it wouldn't work.

Why weren't they at school? Would a school refuse to have them?

They stood in the window now, and their shadows crossed the bed like two bars. I should have locked the door, but had forgotten.

'Go away, I want to sleep.'

'You had a nasty dream.'

'Yes.'

'What was it?'

'I dreamed I woke up and you were in my room.'

One of the maids knocked, came in and told my aunts that my grandmother wanted them for their lessons, so explaining the mystery of their presence in the house. They went quite eagerly, but only, I was sure, to do some mischief.

For a while I did sleep then. I dreamed of the usual inane things one does. And then a dream of making love to Lilas, she screaming with joy, but not myself experiencing anything at all. As if those parts of me had turned to stone.

In the afternoon, after our huge country midday dinner of roasted chicken pieces, rice and vegetables, the house lay torpid. In my grandmother's room, the old stove chugged. She often said it was a wonder she'd never been asphyxiated, but then, there were so many cracks and tiny holes in the house, and the windows rattled loosely at the softest breath of wind.

Sophie and Susie slept curled together on their blue eiderdown. They shared a double bed. I had once considered if they did anything surprising together, but they seemed sexless to me, probably not. They'd rather catch butterflies and eat them alive, which I had seen. Or sit on the highest front wall, throwing small stones at passers-by on the street. There had been many complaints to Constance. But such was the spurious power the village had given her; she was able to dismiss them all with little presents.

Once the house slept, I went up to the attic. The ceiling was low enough it touched my head, although Constance could walk upright. Had she shrunk?

I found at once the enormous trunk with the broken lock. Reaching far down inside it, among old mothy clothes and ribbon-bound masses of crumbling paper, I inserted the poison bottle. She had given it back to me when I took the flat in Paris. She said it was for my protection. I'd said, But my mother had had it, and maybe used it in on herself. Constance said briskly, 'Then the more fool she. But she didn't. That was a silly woman's fancy I had.'

I accepted the bottle from curiosity. Sometimes I would take it out, uncork it, sniff. It had the same dead aroma of nothing, as before.

Still, it had had a taste of life – or death – with me. Jean had sampled it. And, of course, Armand.

As I let it go among the contents of the trunk, I felt no relief, no lightening of my burden. But really, I hadn't expected to.

When I left the trunk, standing up, I looked a moment around me. The attic was full of terrible things. A stuffed snake from India that perhaps belonged to Constance's husband. A set of antlers from a stag, and a whole box of bones and fossils out of the hills around. In a chest lay embroidered, spangled clothes falling to pieces; some might have come from the eighteenth century. There were paintings of men on horses, and women with faces like masks, so tight-lipped and empty eyed. Everything was being spun together into a thick dough of cobwebs. One shouldn't come in here at all to disturb it.

Below in my room again, I gazed through the jade plates of the ivy. A light rain was sprinkling down. The elderly fig tree looked as if made of metals, iron, copper. They had already stripped the figs, which ripened early here. Up on the slopes the fields blew with tasselled stalks. Elsewhere you saw them, men and women walking with their scythes. Cutting everything down. It might have been the Middle Ages. They'd moved the sheep, Constance had said.

I picked up the apple from breakfast. Although I'd only played with the hearty lunch, I was unable to bite at this fruit that was the colour of the mouth of Rherlotte.

What was she doing? Evolving some plan? Or had she stormed and wept herself out at last, now in the grey limbo which is called healing, but is only the realisation that one can do nothing, nothing will ever improve.

How had she loved him so? *She.* I had only been able to look at her properly in memory, but then I saw what she was. I couldn't understand it. I pictured Constance saying sternly to me, 'How would you ever know what was attractive or not, in a *man?*' Very true. Very true.

Days passed. Nights passed.

There seemed to be too many meals and not enough of anything else.

I went for walks about the village, where ancient villagers, brown as the autumn leaves, took off hats, or sometimes bowed to me. Once a woman came to her door leading her two fat, smiling children. The girl ran up and handed me a posy of crocuses already fading. Another time, a crone came and put a huge egg, honey-coloured and still warm, into my hand. 'To make your cheeks bloom.'

Laughable and embarrassing though it all was, I found something also sinister. I had been a child here. Had they then pitied or mocked me? I was in some sense their prisoner even now, because they had watched stages of my early life, seen me after my mother's death, and when I returned from the southern school.

At night, I heard the wind grind and whine round the house. There was a full moon, and the dogs for miles about bayed at it for hours. Owls yelled as they swooped across the fields. So much noise. So much life.

Although I locked my door, my aunts had found a way to pick the lock. Twice I came back to find all my few clothes, my hair brush, pins, powder box, scattered on the floor or bed. Why twice? I'd added nothing. Perhaps they'd forgotten their first foray. Both had a poor memory, except for slights or particular pleasures. The woman who brought the milk, the postman, were *bad* – they'd both once shouted at the sisters, one could guess a hundred reasons why. That jam was *good*, this one *nasty.*

Constance seemed to make no attempt to control them. Although she had conceived, carried and borne them, she never thought of them as being hers. They were two tricks played on her. And in just this way they went on. However, they'd never crossed her. She was the only one.

I asked what lessons she taught them. She said, very little, they wouldn't sit still, or if they did they fell asleep. She had brought them tutors, but the tutors ran away.

One day Constance would die, and would I then inherit my aunts? Perhaps I should have retained the poison bottle.

After six days, I was desperate to leave. Rain fell heavily and glutinously now as glycerine. The trees were almost bare. It was very cold. Constance accused me of bringing this forward winter from Paris.

'Then I'd better go back.'

'High time,' she said.

When I packed my bags again, Constance sent a boy for Georges-of-the-Station, and the trap. It would be a morning train now. I would reach the city by night.

My grandmother sat in her drawing room, upright in a carved black chair. She had put on her rings, for my departure.

Do I have any actual appearance of Constance? Her hair is lavish, worn folded in a snood behind her skull, a style at odds with everything. Deliberately, I expect. Long jet earrings. She keeps to touches of black, a proper wealthy country widow, this well-heeled whore.

I can see nothing of me in her, or her in me. But she's there.

'Take this,' she said.

'What is it?'

Had she given me some memento?

'Unwrap it, if you like.'

I undid the plain; and withered paper. Inside, the bottle of poison.

What could I do? I stood there holding it. She said not a word, and so finally neither did I.

I got wet in the trap despite the large umbrella Georges put up over me. He and his brown horse steamed in the rain, sometimes shaking their heads.

I fell asleep at last in the train, and had no dreams I recollect. I might have been dead, unless the dead do dream. One hopes not. In death one hopes to escape from everything.

5

Paris by night, dry with gas lamps and dull, warm windows. Above, the web of stars. The sound of the city, which grumbles.

I seemed to have been away a year. It had been a mistake. I had no one to assist me, no one who loved or wished to protect me. (I could hardly count servile little Elise, who would probably run errands for a street porter.)

Who, anyway did I need? What had I to fear? Some maddened lover, a fool who had loved a fool. By now she doubtless wished she had never accosted me.

Even so, stepping into the building, a catch at my heart. But no one had left anything for me. And if anyone had come, they'd left no trace.

I'd thrown the softening apple away on my journey. There was nothing to eat. I didn't want a thing. There had been too much food. Some wine, one narrow glass. A water biscuit dipped into it. Then my bathroom – there were no such luxuries at O—. And my harsh, horrible, amazing electric light. My Frankenstein kettle to make a cup of tea.

I lay in bed, warmed from the bath, drinking the black tea.

It seemed I'd fall back into the nourishing dreamless sleep of the train.

At first I did. At three or thereabouts, I woke again. Wide, wide awake, as if I'd been shaken.

In the darkness, I *smelled* her. Was it in fact a dream? That amber musk, her fresh skin and breath. She might have been bending over me, the dagger poised.

I jumped up and put on my light,

No one was there. I searched to be sure. Outside the outer door only city silence made a noise like the sea.

Damn the bitch, she'd been waiting all the time, here in my own refuge, to smother me. Or was I going quite mad. It might only be that.

They were small but elegant, these houses. This one was washed with palest oyster pink, and had dark green shutters, like something from the far south. Behind the railings prickled along a box hedge. A tall linden grew in the courtyard, stripped of leaves and already in the grip of early winter. A giant child of bones.

The ride hadn't been long. Across the city in the afternoon. The river shone with its different, winter light.

The Boulevard Strauss was perfectly easy to find, and alighting from the cab, at once, as if it were meant, a maid came down a path with a letter in her hand.

I'd thought anyway I should be able to make out the house. It would be a house of mourning, its blinds down, even black crepe hung about. Of course, it was nothing of the sort.

The maid looked at me as I stood before her, waiting, my predestined messenger. 'A Madame de Gillan lives in this street, I believe?'

'Oh, yes, mademoiselle. That house down there.' She had pointed it out carefully, so I couldn't go wrong at all.

Armand, according to his wife, had bought his mistress this house. Had it already been in these colours, or had some celebratory mode in her caused her to repaint it? To celebrate him, even. I could just see him arriving; quite drunk, very late, beholding the lamp left burning for him in the hallway, and the one seductive rosy upper window of her bedroom. I hesitated by the gate. Then pushed it open and walked around the tub that held only green shrubbery. Up the steps to her door. It was not a modern street. No electricity at all. The knocker was of well-polished brass, a fine hand from the seventeenth century holding a slender scroll.

Without any choice, I took a deep, uneven breath. I felt very cold. I rapped the knocker decisively.

The maid came, dainty and neat, not a hair out of place.

'Good day madame.'

'Is Madame de Gillan at home?'

'Yes, madame.' No preamble. No feinting, to make sure I was welcome. Did the bitch *expect* me? Or some other woman – 'Who may I say?'

'Say *Phèdre*.'

Not one flicker of query.

'Very well, madame. If you would follow me.'

She led me straight upstairs. The treads were polished with a rich olive runner. The banister post was a woman like a caryatid. This seemed compatible. De Gillan was just such a being.

An upper room opened before me, with glass doors, shut. Irises of stained glass framed in clasps of purple: the image of her, already there, before me, and I wasn't ready, so half turned myself away. I gazed back down the stair, holding to the caryatid at the top.

But the neat maid had trotted to the doors, opened them, then gone through. An iris-coloured curtain drawn aside. A Persian rug across the floor. Everything immaculate, burnished, wiped, dusted, kept faithful to its most lovely hue. And there. Herself. She. *Rherlotte.*

She was standing now, by the desk where she had been sitting writing.

I must look at her.

I turned back, lazy, as if I had only been more interested in something else.

My God. Oh my God.

What is this feeling, of falling, of panic, of heat, of ice? Am I truly so utterly terrified of her? All the way here, my hands trembling, shivering, a sickness lying under my breastbone.

The light was behind her from a long window. She seemed to float, her feet not quite on the floor. She wore not black, but the darkest grey. Her hair was loosely done, drooping in heavy, silken loops and ropes. The colour of her hair. There never was such a colour. It wasn't *red*. How could I have thought it was red? It was the colour of marigolds that are almost pink.

I hated her face. I'd slap it. I'd walk up to her and strike her as she'd have liked to do, but was too bourgeois to attempt, with me.

'Thank you, Marthe.'

The maid went by me. Left us, closing us both up in a glass cage between the crystal window and the glassy iris doors.

Could I speak? It seemed I had to. Or she'd smother me, like the half-dream when her ghostly soul leaned over me the night before.

'I hope you're well, madame,' I said. No one would know, would they? Did she know I couldn't breathe?

She said, remotely, idly, 'Quite well, thank you. Yourself?'

What an exchange.

'No, madame,' I said. Inspiration appeared. 'I'm vexed. It's been very trying for me. So I've come to see you.'

'What's vexed you, then?' she said. Her bizarre politeness hadn't extended to inviting me to sit. I paced up and down, once, twice. I'd had to move. Everything else seemed moving. But when I stopped, all things stopped. My heart had been thudding wildly, now it too was stilled. I couldn't feel my flesh at all. I hung in the air, as she did, feet off the floor.

'Your accusations, Madame de Gillan, upset me very much. Another woman would have sought a lawyer. I've come to confront you, as you saw fit to confront me.'

'Oh,' she said. She seemed nearly listless. She went drifting off down the room towards her fireplace. A cosy fire burned there. On the mantelpiece was a Louis XVI clock, or what looked as if it were. 'There wasn't any need to come here,' she said. 'I told you the facts. There's nothing more to say.'

I shouted then, stagily throwing my voice as Lilas taught me by doing it herself. 'How dare you, madame. How *dare* you. To accuse me of a crime. To threaten me. Your very actions prove you know me to be innocent.'

She half turned. She had a little sad, humorous smile just creasing her cheek. 'And how is that?' she asked.

'For God's sake, if I was such a villain – a murderess – didn't you fear for your own life in accosting me?'

'That,' she said. She sighed. The world was leaden on her today. She looked into the fire that made her hair pale and ordinary. 'I must explain, Phèdre, I don't care about my life. Not anymore. Once he was dead, my concern in living left me. To go on – is just a show.'

'You said to get vengeance on me gave you a purpose.' There were tears in my eyes. How astonishing. As if she actually had distressed me by her false verdict. She'd spoken my name. I could still hear it ringing round and round, making my head spin.

In my handbag, the bottle. Yes, brought with me. I could go to her, force open her mouth, force in the edge of the bottle. One sip, one choked swallow. If she resisted, I could throw her down. Though she was tall, she was less strong than I, this I could sense.

She remarked, 'I said many things to you. Yes, if I'm able to destroy you, I shall. But you see how it is with me. How weary I am.' Again she sighed. She leaned her arm on the mantelpiece, rested her head upon her hand. Her back was to me. How easily I could attack her.

But she didn't care. No longer the huntress. Or, if she was, she was lost in the great wood of the world. As I now felt myself to be.

I sat in a chair unasked. About her eyes I'd seen fine lines. She was older than I.

She straightened up suddenly and turned around and looked at me. When she did it, my blood seemed to drain out of me, straight into the floor.

'You're in a bad way,' she said. 'Have I scared you?

'I told you you had, by your lies.' (She had seen.)

She was brighter. Her eyes, sparkling.

'Yes, you do me good,' she said. 'I like it, to dismay you. After what you did to me.'

I would need to get up. She was moving towards me now, along the carpet. Before she reached me, I should be on my feet. Too late.

She leaned right over me. Everything swirled, my sight occluded. The ceiling seemed to swim down. She had put her hand on my face. It was a gentle hand, warm after all, not marble.

'How satisfying to find you're only made of flesh,' she startlingly said. 'So vulnerable.'

I wrenched my head away, and rose against her. For a second my body brushed over hers. It was like an electric shock. It threw us both back from each other.

Then again I saw her warrior's face. She showed her teeth at me. Her eyes were blades. So much for having no fear of death at my hands.

'You're insane,' I said. I had to speak her name. I got it out as if it were made of rocks and briars. '*Rherlotte de Gillan.*'

She raised her chin at the battle-note of her title. We were still close enough, I could feel the warmth that came from her, the scent of her, some perfume, brought out by the fire.

'Are you going?' She seemed genuinely amused now. She gave a little light laugh. 'I should like to see you from time to time.'

'Should you? You fucking bitch, you can rot.'

Her eyes widened at the words. Her lips pressed together. She was affronted, not by my violence, but by my uncouth phrases. Worse than Anne Blos. Little bourgeoisie. Had she ever known a moment's pain, until her buffoon of a lover was shovelled into the ground?

I said, 'Never come near me again. If you do anything, I'll have you put away. You swore your own oath to me. I swear this to you. Damn you to hell.'

Turning to go, I lost her. I couldn't see her. Then, she came towards me again, her refection, in the iris doors. She stood immobile. Her red mouth lay upon a petal of an iris. I could have smashed the glass with my hand, but before I did it, I saw the blood, the shards, the mess on her neat and pretty room. And I didn't want to, didn't want to.

I opened the doors and went out. Down to the street, I suppose. Into the street. Away.

6

We went to the funeral in a carriage, my mother and I, Is it only a memory again, the yellow blinds, half down at the carriage windows. Death, then, always dressed for me in yellow. It was my father who had died. Was I about four? One of my earliest recollections. I believe he was in his late thirties. Perhaps a little older. My mother must have been something like twenty-four years old. She sat crying under her veil. She kept saying, I'm sure she did, 'What shall I do without him?' although I never recall he had been there. And, 'He was so fond of you, Phèdre.' But did I ever see him for more than a few seconds? He's absent from my mind except in the words of others.

He must have been wealthy. He left her something. But we shouldn't have been at the burial, that was most improper. And she went in a spirit of utter abnegation. It wasn't any passionate protest or display. It was, in an awful way, her total *respectability*.

The cemetery was full – with the dead, but also with the living. Where was it? I can't think at all. The day was overcast, or was that only the mood of death and my mother's continual weeping? She stifled this as we stood at the back of the crowd, where actual sightseers, a charwoman, a road-sweeper, two gallants on their way home from an all-night binge, had accumulated to stare, cross themselves, or mock.

I kept waiting for us to do something, go forward, look at the grave, as, even then, I'd been told people did. I didn't relish it, but couldn't grasp why we didn't have to. There must have been a priest, at least. He too, a casualty of my memory.

Then I wanted it to be all over. I was tired and very bored.

One of the gallants came up to us. He started to play with my long black hair, and I pulled away.

'What a pretty little girl, madame.'

My mother raised her tear-soaked face. 'The dead man was her father,' atrociously she said.

The gallant sussed her at once. Not so difficult. She was well-dressed, yet stood at the back of the crowd, had no place in it. He said, 'If you'd allow me, I could take your child for a little walk. This must be very sad for her.'

But then his friend came up and hoisted him away. 'For Christ's sake, Philippe. Not that young, you stinker.'

If my mother knew what went on, if she'd have let him have me for an hour, to feel over and probably worse, God knows. She only went on crying. And finally the funeral concluded, and then, when all the other mourners had gone, she went and stood over his grave, that they were waiting to fill in.

The first flung clod was on the coffin, which was a handsome one of mahogany, with silver handles. Some flowers were there too. Incense still spiced the air.

'What shall we do?' said my mother.

No one answered, and we went home.

The current maid – we were always losing and replacing them – gave me blancmange and cake. But I wasn't upset. For my mother, the maid had, naturally, only the most resentful contempt. She muttered something about her sister, whose husband had been taken from a brawl, not of his making, dying, with his arm pulled off. 'Ten kids to feed and clothe, and never a tear in public. It's them with the time to grieve as mourns.'

The sound of my mother sobbing was so constant in my ears, I sometimes still hear it. This isn't quite madness. Little noises of the street, the wind under a latch, rain that drips down, these can be mistaken. Do I feel sorry for her now? I feel sorry for no one, not even myself. I have few tears and none for loss, even my own. What does that make me? What do I care?

A day or so after my visit to the Boulevard Strauss, Lilas came unexpectedly to see me.

I say unexpectedly, because no longer did she ever call on me. When I went to her, it was in order to get hold of some necessity – the address of a bookseller. A red theatrical wig …

'Oh, Phèdre, darling love. I never see you now. You do neglect me so.'

She acted as if we were women friends in the conventional way. But I knew her. There was a certain light in her eyes. As I poured out the tea she'd requested, she kept touching my hand with little, fluttering pecks. At last she said, 'Are you quite all right, Phèdre?'

'Yes, quite.'

'You look so beautiful – almost not *here*. Transparent. *Glacial*.' On the bureau behind me lay the letter she'd handed me on her way in: 'It was in the birdcage.'

This is where the letters were left below. On the round table at the common entrance, stood an empty birdcage, courtesy of the concierge. In this cage the letters lay, sleeping birds. Dead birds. This bird was white with fine black writing.

I'd put it aside. Lilas said, 'Won't you open it?' Nosy and pained at once. She would always rush to receive her post. 'No, it's nothing. Perhaps the glove woman's bill.'

Now the letter sat behind me. Crouched there. If it were a bird, would it fly up, and settle suddenly on my neck, tearing with its claws and red beak?

Yet there were others in the city who wrote with black ink on white paper.

I couldn't recognize the writing so soon. The writing of Rherlotte.

But Lilas said, 'Can't I sit beside you?'

'Why not.'

'Are you putting me off? Oh dear. You know, my sweet, I think I'll have to marry that young man. My lawyer. He's so insistent. And he's two years younger than me. But his old father – bless him – well, I charmed the old man. At first he was dead against it all. But now he says nothing matters, I have a *goodness* in nature. Of course, there's only supposed to have been one indiscretion.

That was – that was *Jean*. I said I'd been frightened of him, which I was. They know he came to a bad end.'

I said nothing. Lilas said, slowly, 'I know I'm quite safe in your hands.'

'Yes, you know.'

'The other one. Oh – Phèdre, Phèdre –' suddenly she flung her arms about me, laid her head, with its floss of fawn hair, on my breasts. 'How are you so brave? You're like a knight. The knight who fights the dragon. And rescues us.'

'Am I?'

'You hate me now,' she said. She played with a false button on my blouse, as if knowing this one couldn't come undone. 'Ever since – you've put me off. Did I revolt you, poor weak Lilas, unable to help herself.'

'I think you've been the one who stayed away.'

'Let's change that. Oh, it will be lovely. I'll have a beautiful apartment near the Louvre, looking out to the Tuileries. The old man's promised. And dearest Edouard will be away such a lot, sometimes all night, on his cases. And he just isn't the sort of man who'd suspect a thing, even if he found us in bed together. And if he did,' she looked up at me laughing, her breath fragrant with a cachou she was sucking, 'do you know, I think he'd leap in beside us.'

'And I should leap out.'

'Oh, Phèdre. Haven't you ever felt anything for a man? I can't believe you haven't.'

'Where are you going with this?' I asked her. 'Do you want him to marry both of us, in case I testify against you, or blackmail you in some way. Rest assured, Lilas. All that's forgotten. I'd never trouble you with it. You're the one who speaks about it in drawing rooms. And doubtless receives a tip.'

'*I*? What are you saying?'

'Anne Blos,' I said, 'approached me. How else do you think – You'd told, her, she said, how I helped you. I expect that was worth a few sous.'

'I only said that you'd been kind when I was desperately unhappy. She jumped to a conclusion because she wanted to.'

Lilas pretended to be affronted. I wished to slap her pretty face, put her out, kick her down the stairs.

'Let's say no more about it,' I said.

'You hate me. And I still love you, Phèdre. I've had my little pleasures with women. But oh Phèdre, Phèdre. With you – I thought I'd die of it sometimes. I don't mean *that*! I mean needing you. And you so cold. You only wanted me for that. You felt nothing.'

'All right.'

She got up. She picked up my cup – not hers, mine – of white porcelain painted with little flowers, and deliberately threw it into the fireplace, where it smashed.

Calmly, disgusted, I compared this petty, mean upheaval with my session at the house of Rherlotte.

'Perhaps you should go, Lilas.'

She was in tears. Had she really never learned tears don't move me, or only the tears and weeping sounds of lust.

I stood up, and she backed away. She said my name. Then snatching up her hat rammed it hard on her head, sticking in the pin as if to skewer her brain.

She ran for the door and was gone.

As I gathered up the bits of the cup, I smelled her perfume over everything. The oriental scent her betrothed had found her: *Frankincense*, it was called. The heady aromatic of churches, funerals –

I spent some time putting the pieces of the cup into a linen napkin. I don't know why. A souvenir?

Then I tidied up the tea things.

Then I went and took hold of the white and black letter.

I walked about the room with it. Adjusted a picture, straightened a cushion. Into my study I went. I poised at my desk, running my eye over this and that. The sinister egg on the blotter. Books.

Eventually I sat down, tore open the envelope. Spread the letter before me.

No idea remains to me of how long I sat there, reading the letter over and over again. It grew dark. Then I rose and drew the curtains.

In my sitting room the fire was low, I stirred it and put on some more coal. My hands were nearly numb, and the letter somehow still stuck to one or the other of them.

Dear Mademoiselle Phèdre – so Rherlotte addressed me. Then – *I said I should like to see you. I can't resist seeing you. It's quite frantic with me. Perhaps you'd meet me in the White Room at Les Epices for one of their lunches. With so many honesty mundane people all about us, we should be safe enough from each other, do you think? I wonder if you will come again to meet me. Shall we say noon, tomorrow?*

Inevitably now, I considered her quite mad. I lay awake two thirds of the night, thinking this. In the morning I bathed, used a powder with the scent of crushed honeysuckle. I dressed myself in a blue silk dress. The dress I'd worn

– that night. (The night I'd poisoned her lover.) Demonstrably I should have burnt it. Long ago, I'd disposed of Brunhilde's hat, first the dress, in bits, on my fire. It took me some while, scissors, sparks careering dangerously up the chimney. The hat from the dinner with Armand, even that, I'd seen to, snipping it to pieces and feeding it away into the flames.

I had another hat, more suitable, a pastel sky of silk, with one long green feather.

I chose green gloves.

Blue and green. Her eyes?

The White Room, like Les Epices itself, was once an English experiment that dared to open in the city. Now it was in the hands of the French, but faded, not very popular.

The door was opened for me by a lackey in black and red.

What could be more ordinary, two bored, well-to-do women of the smart, but not extravagant order, taking a little lunch, while they discussed fashion, children, men. What else do real women discuss or do? Real women, the kind men have invented.

What did I feel, all that time. What does one suppose? I had had to take a brandy before leaving the flat. I dropped my key. In the carriage, I was giddy, longing to make it turn about and take me back.

When I got out, again that sensation of having no feet, floating. Everyone was a puppet, a ghost. Nobody had any solidity at all, least of all myself.

I wouldn't have been surprised if she'd got hold of a pistol and shot me dead as I crossed the threshold. What worth did her words have – the honest, mundane about us. They didn't have any part in this. It was only she and I.

I saw her at once. She was already there. Sitting at a white table in the room that was like a sculpted confection of meringue. The unlit chandelier wafted in space behind her, lit to lights by the windows shining in its prisms. She wore a mauve costume, still the colour of mourning, of course. In her hat was a spray of feathers, cinnamon in colour, like the combed feathers of her brows.

She was just the same. All things change with memory but not Rherlotte. She was identical to her recollected image. Was she beautiful? Something. She was something that had no logical adjective to describe it. One might say, fire sat there, or sun in winter ice.

I was at the table before I knew what I was doing. She watched me all the way, and the ground seemed to tumble off under my feet which didn't touch it.

'How nice that you could come,' she said. The waiter was at her shoulder.

'It was kind of you to ask me to meet you.'

'Oh, not at all. We're such old friends.'

Laughter danced behind her eyes. She was all amber, white-amber, amber-amber. Her eyes were blue amber with green amber stars.

I sat down.

The waiter was decorous. Two such charming young women. And wealthy. (Had she forgotten my coarse language to her previously? But I hadn't smashed the door.)

She was choosing things. She was asking me if I would like this, or this. Like a clockwork toy, Phèdre was saying, yes, that would be just right. She could have offered me a dish of woodchips in arsenic. Perhaps she had. What, after all, had I given *him?*

When the waiter went away, she looked at me. Her eyes held mine. She drew in a little breath and said, 'I wondered.'

'What?'

'If you would come here. After so much rage.'

'Yes,' I said, stupidly.

Rherlotte drew off her kidskin gloves. Her hands were pale, with tapering fingers. Her nails had been polished into sea pearls. She wore no rings, despite her masquerade as 'Madame'.

'We have both,' she said, 'been brave. And here's some wine for us to drink to each other's courage.'

The waiter saw to us protectively and patronisingly. We were women. But she had chosen something luminous from the north, with a golden look and faint taste of strawberries. I can't remember what it was. Sometimes, even now, I lie awake again, trying to recall such details. I saw it, drank it, heard it spoken of. But no, it's gone forever. As they say, forever and a day.

We drank.

'Don't be frightened,' she said to me. 'I haven't forgiven you.'

'Do you want to talk of all that again?' I said. The wine, after the cold ride, perhaps the brandy, had gone to my head more than I was used to.

'No, I don't want to talk about the past. Not now. I'll say only this, Phèdre. You're all I have left of Armand. All I have left.'

Blood or wine thundered in my brain.

They were putting a dish of something before me. What was *that?* I can't, I can't remember. But, you see, I was looking only at her. Devouring her. That meal tastes of her, is scented by her. I ate her flesh and sipped her soul. Rherlotte.

Well, you knew. Why must I lie? I didn't know it then. No, I was simply curiously happy, there in the middle of this madness, breaking bread with my enemy. I almost laughed, and she, she did laugh. She stretched across and put a delicate leaf of some herb on to my plate. 'Eat this, then drink the wine. Yes, like that.'

I did so. I recollect a flavour of strange elements. Pleasing. I said, 'Did you put something on it?'

'Ah, no,' she said. 'No, Phèdre. I couldn't do that to another, even to you.'

The last course was a lemon water-ice. We toyed with it with tiny silver spoons.

All around, the honest and mundane, most of them of the male species, eating, rumbling at each other. There had been many eyes for us. She'd say, 'Look at that one,' or, 'He wishes we weren't quite so proper.'

The luncheon had only been her. She said, 'You eat very little. Were you kept hungry as a child?'

'Yes. But not for food.'

And then she said, 'How beautiful you are, Phèdre.' Almost what Lilas, what others, had said.

When I looked into her eyes now, I dropped again, miles down. Struggling I put up my head out of these oceans.

'Why do you say such a thing?'

'I'm puzzled. How could you *do* such a thing?'

Was I drunk? I'd never been so. A couple – three – glasses of this unusual wine. A brandy. Some liqueur that was bitter. 'But I haven't done anything,' I said, 'I'm under your spell.'

'Are you?' she said softly. 'Then you would have to tell the truth.'

'I'd tell you what you wanted to hear. If you want me to say I killed your lover, then I'll say it. I didn't, of course.'

'Of course you did.' Then she said, 'I seem to have known you since I was a girl. Is this what happens? The murder has made us intimates.'

I began to see her throat, the white column with the moving wonder behind it that throbbed as she spoke. Her lips were a moment moist with liqueur, then matt. The lobes of her ears were translucent, and from each hung a tiny raindrop of opal.

'What shall we do about it all?' I said.

'There's nothing to be done.'

Soon after, the lunch was over. We'd finished. Didn't linger over coffee or petit fours. We got up. We walked separately together to the doors and glided through.

I said her first name. It came easily to me now. Much too easily.

She turned and looked at me, her eyes just an inch below my own. 'Goodbye, my dear,' she said. 'What a pity it all is. Never mind. Goodbye. Until we meet again.'

What had we talked about? I must have been asked about my childhood – for I'd told her something of it. The 'Chateau', my grandmother. But I diluted her strengths and said nothing about her calling. In my mother's case, too, I was reticent, or think I was. I seem to recall I presented her only as an indolent and rather unhappy woman. I tried not to show my irritation (but must have done?). Did I want to make a favourable impression – *on Rherlotte*?

The lunch had been a craziness. For hours after, despite what she'd said, I thought she must have poisoned me. I awaited a burning sensation, nausea, death. And all the while I sat or moved about in the blue silk dress.

Why hadn't I offered her, instead of those tamed vignettes of my life, the knowledge that this was the dress I wore when I killed Armand Blos, and watched him die in front of me?

Had she guessed?

Had she told me *anything* about herself, beyond only the unutterable yet uttered fact of her lover's murder? I seemed to remember a sentence here or there, lilies floating on the surface of the phantom, fairy lunch. She was once a shop-girl – could I believe such a thing? Or that she had, like me, relatives in the country, a small house or a farm, but it had been sold. She had in childhood swung in a swing suspended from an oak tree. But then, wasn't I only confusing this with my memory of the swing at the school, where I had sat rocking with Marie-E.

Did I entirely confuse her, Rherlotte, in some peculiar and unsuitable manner – with *myself*.

I wasn't even sure really that we'd spoken to each other. Everything had been anyway a conversation. Her lifting of the glass of wine. My hand upon a spoon or knife. The herbal leaf she passed me which could have been deadly aconite.

I took off the dress at last and laid it on the bed with the hat and gloves. I looked at the things. They were my witnesses, but couldn't speak. None of them carried a mark. I sniffed them. They smelled only of Phèdre and her scent. Had I imagined everything?

Before, I had sworn I'd never go near her again. Told her so. But I'd gone without a thought, or only thinking she was insane and it didn't matter.

Did I sleep that night? I don't know. This begins a time when there's nothing of me, except when I'm with her. I think there was a dream. Of her, obviously. She was bending over a pool and feeding white creatures, perhaps swans. Something she may have told me from her youth, or some children's tale. The Little Goose Girl, the Swan Princess.

Her notes came. I'd find them in the birdcage, or fallen on to the table. Once the postman handed me her letter. He seemed suddenly rimmed with terrifying gold in the cold grey street. It was always the same. Would I come to lunch with her at Les Epices, or some other old-fashioned place, or take tea with her at the Cafe Flor? I wasn't invited to her house. I knew she wouldn't come to my flat. Always neutral – safe? – ground.

The second note, I remember that. And how I sat down at once and penned a reply, sternly … *Since you don't believe what I've said to you, I can't credit that you truly wish to see me.*

But she assured me that this was the very reason. I was the last of him – all she 'had left.'

I tore up my note, and hers, and the next day I met her. This was five or six days after the first lunch. In elegant gilt chairs we nibbled lettuce sandwiches and drank tea flavoured with bergamot.

From this point all conversation between us becomes one long conversation that circles about itself, always repeating the same things, altering them subtly, developing upon them, like the movement of a symphony, or variations on a theme.

I see her with the slice of lemon, held by a silver implement, like a tiny round of stained glass. She wears a grey hat, the velvet trim, something white fluttering, white lace at her throat, a little cameo brooch from the Roman, a girl with the same alabaster face as her own.

'The winter is so long. Too long. Already it's begun. Spring seems to vanish in a flash and summer soaks away. But the cold. Is it a premonition of something?'

'Death,' I say, 'do you mean?'

'Do I mean that? What do you think I mean, Phèdre?'

'I imagine you to be a good Catholic,' I say. 'What have you to fear?'

'If I were, everything. But I don't believe in God. A God would be merciful and kind to us. There'd be no pain.'

'God, allegedly invented pain, to try us.'

'I defy Him, if so,' she said. 'That wouldn't be a God, Phèdre, but the Devil.'

'You're a Cathar,' I say, and then, always pausing before I speak it, 'Rherlotte.'

'Perhaps. They believed the Devil made the world to deceive and hurt us. Oh, yes. I could think that.'

And I see her in the White Room again, mixing a drink for us–I'm sanguine now, she won't kill me here – something lucent, something like strawberry syrup.

'All these minor actions, Phèdre, with which to fill our days. We wake, we get up, we put on our clothes and go about, turning over knives and forks, swallowing tea, writing in our journals, until it's time to go to bed again and pointlessly, stupidly, dream.' 'Dreams …' is all I say.

Rherlotte says, handing me the silvery pink drink, 'I dream of Armand. But even when he takes me in his arms, I know that he's dead. There's a sound in the dream, like a low pessimistic drone. From that I know.'

Do I say to Rherlotte, I dream of you. You feed the birds, and swing on your swing, or ride on a red horse over the meadows.

I've seen you as Jehane d'Arc, and they were tying you to the pyre. Lighting the first of the wood. Your proud, cool face, your raised chin. You wore mail at the stake, but your hair was put up just as now, with these two full ropes of marigold covering the tips of your white shells of ears. You wouldn't give in. You never do.

'When I was a child,' she said once, 'I used to think one had only to be good. That it was easy.'

'I think it would be easy,' I said, 'but the mind outwits it.'

She put her hands together. 'Ah, Phèdre. You're right. How clever you are. Like an arrow, straight to the point.'

And a tight hot wave passes up through me. Is it a blush of pleasure at this inane little accolade?

Ah Phèdre, the mind. But there is the body too. All this while I hide her from myself, myself from myself, myself from her. That she fascinates me I must accept. That I would, if *everything* were different, and she inclined, like to make love to her; this I can't be so imbecilic as to refuse to see.

But when I first look at her, each time, this sensation of falling, falling down, but into an abyss which has no floor. Even when I think of her, quite often, when the image of her comes into my inner eye, and she is physically distant across the city in her pink house of green shutters, the naked linden tapping its bones in her yard, even these sightings throw me off from the precipice of falling.

If I fall, to where do I fall? Shall I reach the bottom of the chasm? Will it kill me, this fall? Or is it only flight, the sole form of flight of which I am capable?

Rherlotte …
    Rherlotte.

And now, our fifth luncheon. It was to be special, but I didn't know this. One thinks, when a pattern is established, it will continue for a while at least. Until some new thing comes to disrupt it. She and I, sitting and talking out our variations on a theme of her loss, the unadmitted development of my murder. What could change or dislodge us? I should admit the truth, or she find some other interest? We would quarrel, as at the first, the second, time of meeting. Although *quarrel*, of course, is not the proper word. Even then each of us spoke like some musical instrument, sounding across the panoply of a whispering orchestra. First this phrase, and then the responding phrase. Hers harsh, then dainty. Mine obscure – then violent.

There was still the violence. I choked it back. I saw it now as lust, which must be held away from her, since perhaps she knew, as she seemed to indicate the second time, what Phèdre is.

And yet, she must keep seeing me, it was she who wrote, it was she who asked me always, begged me, to come to her. She said, 'You saw him last alive.' I answered, 'Only in your fantasy, madame. I was nowhere near Armand Blos when he died. Wherever he was.'

I wait for her notes. I look for them, going endlessly up and down stairs. If something white is in the birdcage, I pull it out. Even if not white – perhaps she's changed her writing paper. But the notes are always the same, black upon white. Her hand is well-trained but not exactly careful. At the end of her gracefully-formed sentences, sometimes a coil or dash of the pen. Her name is signed small, yet there's a flight from the final *e*. Away, away it goes, a stroke of darkness, towards the future.

And now, here's the note speaking of lunch. Just like all the others, the seven or eight notes from Rherlotte. Tomorrow. Now there's a tomorrow.

I've burnt that dress. The blue one. Cut it up and fed it to the fire. In the depth of a drawer, the little bottle. I should throw it away, but someone might find it.

In the dusk, the frosty stars come out above the city. The street lamps shimmer in the icy air.

I dream, that night before the special lunch, that Rherlotte is in a boat on the river. She sits there quietly, trailing one hand in the green, luminous dusk water. Who steers the boat? I can't see. Perhaps, after all, I do. At the Cafe Flor, then, they set aside an area 'for ladies', and fat pigeons of waitresses attended to one. I had been there several times recently, with Rherlotte, and was greeted: 'Good day, madame.'

Rherlotte hadn't yet arrived. I sat down at the table, shook out a napkin, drank from the water glass which had now been filled.

'Such a cold day, madame. Will you have something to warm your

Rherlotte would warm me. 'No, thank you.'

Did I really admit it to myself? Perhaps not.

I looked about. The walls were painted with almost-innocent terracotta frolics, girls of the eighteenth century with stemmed waists and pushing breasts, carrying panniers of flowers and fruit, young men in culottes, with powdered hair and hunting dogs. Here and there a satyr playing a syrinx. Cherubs at the corners. After half an hour, the waitress returned.

'Madame's friend is so late today! Can I get you anything while you are waiting?'

I came out of my daze, my dream. I looked at a clock. Rherlotte had never been late. Normally she was there before me, or if I was early, she would come in on the very hour.

I picked up my glove and put it down.

Would the pigeon waitress go down and ask if any message had come round for me?

She did so. Returned again, she seemed humble. 'No message, madame.'

I waited, drinking water, playing with the napkin, the glass. Looking at the pictures on the walls, trying to explain for myself some story behind them. This young man wanted that young woman, but the satyr would have her first.

All about, the other women ate their lunch, chattering. It sounded like a nest of disturbed starlings. Rherlotte did not have this sort of voice. Hers was low, and sweet. If she sang, she would be, perhaps, a light contralto. And there was a trace of accent, wasn't there? What could it be? From Marseilles, Normandy? I'd wondered at her name, but never asked her. It was like an antique name. It didn't quite belong here.

Now it was after two. They were clearing the tables. The velvet cord was lifted away for me by a bowing waiter from the 'men's side', as I went out.

In the foyer I stood at a loss. Was she ill? Should I go to her house – no, no, surely not. Had there been some accident on the icy road, a horse slipping, wheels sliding –

Outside the windows of the Cafe Flor, the city was set in glass-grey twilight. The winter sun already westered, in a court of clouds, scorched but without colour.

Why was I being such a fool? Of course, she simply hadn't come. Hadn't wished to. Maybe even in the moment of pinning on her hat, taking up her umbrella or her handbag, she had thought distinctly, What am I doing? Go there, to *her*? But *why*?

And she hadn't come to me. She had realized at last the height of her folly. I would never see her again.

I drank a glass of white Voule, and smoked two or three cigarettes. I played English Patience at my table, and couldn't get the game ever to come out.

After sunset, the evening passed. Once I heard a sound, as it seemed, at my door. I went to see, but no one was there, and so I went down to the birdcage table. There were three letters, but none for Phèdre.

About ten o'clock I sent for some chocolate from the neighbouring restaurant, something I seldom drink. I didn't like it, had only a few sips.

I slept at first, then woke. Every time I woke I seem to have heard someone calling me, urgently. I wasn't so fanciful as to think this a communication of the mind from her to me. Near dawn, I began to sleep quite deeply. There was a sensation of dropping deeper and deeper, as though into sand. After which … oblivion.

We were in the carriage, and the yellow blinds were down. Everything was very dark. I looked at my mother sitting there, a shadow, in her black. We were going to my father's funeral.

But I wasn't a child. This seemed wrong. Surely I was too old to be here?

I glanced at my mother again. She sat very upright, her hands folded in dark kidskin gloves. Under the blackness of the hat, her red-marigold hair gleamed like metal in the sub-fuse.

She smelled fragrant. I couldn't identify the scent.

Then the carriage stopped. We got out, and there was the cemetery, miles of it, sweeping away and away between the chestnut trees that were not green but coppery. The grass was high and stiff with frost like icing sugar.

I walked behind her. There were no others there. We came to a grave. A tall white marble marker rose, with a carved satyr on top.

She stood looking down, and I stood beside her. Finally she said, 'He was of no importance, Phèdre. Now I have you.'

When she said this, a tide of warmth, of heat, went through me. I felt lifted up. I reached to take her arm, but now we were in another place, high up on the marble balcony of a chateau, with a vast darkened window at our backs, a window with many panes, and below a park with enormous trees where a full moon, pale, opaque yellow, was rising like a night flower from the ground.

Our clothes had changed. I liked these better. She wore a white dress with a tight waist, a full, swinging skirt. Her breasts, mounted upon the bodice, flushed with colour against the white silk. Her hair was loose, her marigold hair, streaming down over her shoulders. She pushed it back with a laugh.

'Well, here we are,' she said. 'Now where is your heart?'

'In the usual place, I suppose,' I said.

'Oh, there?'

She put out her left hand and laid it over my left breast. I wore the same sort of old-fashioned gown, mine a yellow like the moon's, and my hair loose as it was in childhood, and on that other night.

'But I can't feel your heart,' she said, 'haven't you got one, Phèdre?' I said nothing. She said, 'Or have I taken it?'

We walked down a long, curving stair, the kind one might see at Versailles, some palace. The lawns were clipped and plush, and the moon stood now on the turrets of the chateau, which hadn't one light, garlanded below by the huge green trees. There was a lake, stepping stones. I ventured out only on these, but Rherlotte slipped into the water like a swan, in her white dress, and swam a little way.

The moonlight was warm as a fine spring day. It shone down through the water. At the bottom were strange bony plants without leaves. But then Rherlotte swam back to me. She raised her head. Her hair was like amber now, but wet over her shoulders, darker, like water weeds.

'There's a fish in the lake,' she said. 'Look down. There it is.'

I looked and saw there was a golden fish swimming about. It had the wings of a dragon-fly which beat slowly, glittering, under the water.

'Come with me,' she said. 'Come with me, my dear.'

She came up out of the water and left her dress in the lake. She was naked, and white as snow. On her round breasts the buds of her nipples were a rosy fawn. The rose of hair between her legs, the gossamer in her armpits, these were rosy gold.

Her hair now looked gold too, until it reached her shoulders, and, wet, seemed dark as my own.

She took my hand. We were under the trees.

The grass was warm, so real, so real. Did I know I was dreaming?

I kissed her body. I began at her eyelids, her mouth, her chin. Her neck I kissed. Her arms, her palms. Her breasts and belly. Her rosy fleece. All down her legs, her bare white feet with little polished toenails shaped exactly like ten gems for a necklace. The smell of her dry hair was like fresh narcissus. Where it was wet from the lake with winged fish, it had the aroma of marzipan.

So much, I wanted to bring her to pleasure. She lay smiling, calm, relaxed. Not repulsing me, not averse to me. I kissed her mouth again, delving into the velvet heat between her lips. I suckled her breasts until the nipples rose firm and hard. I kissed her lower mouth, the crisp silk of her sunset hair. The valley of her loins received me, rich with her secret perfume, like cinnamon, pepper, myrrh. She spread herself for me. She made no sound. Her heart, which I felt beating in her womb, was regular and not last.

All at once she had sat up. She held my face in her hands. Her eyes in the moonlight were grey. 'Lie back, Phèdre.'

I had lain back. I too was naked. I felt the grass shiver under me, so real. She was pressing me down. She bent over me. Her hair fell round us like a tent of amber silk with the moon caught like a lily. The wet tips of hair shivered over me like water snakes. Her eyes wouldn't let go. I hung from her eyes, helpless. I saw the edges of her white teeth.

A long roller, almost the crisis of sex itself, coursed through me. She said, 'Now I will subdue you.'

In terror I gave way beneath her. All of me opening. I felt her fire on every surface. I gave myself up and screamed in agony, torture and delight. Until my screams brought down the moon, which fell into the chateau, lighting it from attics to cellars.

7

'Why, Phèdre – darling – oh what a strange thing you should call just now.' Elise stared at me as if I were something very odd, a dog in a frock, a talking armadillo.

'Then this isn't the time for me to visit you? I'm sorry.'

'Don't be offended, dear Phèdre. There's no reason at all you shouldn't be here. Mama knows you are my friend. I've told her you bought three of my pictures. Of course, I sold them to others,' she added, disapprovingly. 'I know your flat's too small, and one of *my* silly little works was more than enough.'

She was wearing a pale pink, unsuitable springtime chiffon dress, with a ribboned sash, that, because it had never been in fashion, never could be. Elise prided herself on being, as an artist, beyond such things. She was.

'But you see, dearest, before they come – and they'll be here at any moment – I'll have to confess to you.'

'Confess?' I asked idly.

Outside an icy wind funnelled down the narrow streets. The church of St Sulpice had seemed to crouch, dowdy with stone snow already.

Why I'd come here was out of a sort of habit, possibly. I'd expected my accustomed welcome, an Elise with the grey overall over her blouse, rushing to make me tea.

'Well, you see, Phèdre, I'm –' it burst out in an excited rush –'to be engaged, yes, I truly am. Oh, it's all been so sudden. But he's quite a forceful man. He came to buy a picture, one evening when Mama was at home, because he said it was more proper. He'd heard of my work, and then he spent ages looking at everything I'd done. He was very complimentary and made a few criticisms which were most astute. Actually, he didn't buy a picture. But then there was a little note. Would Mama and I take tea with him. Finally, he most decorously asked if he could see me alone. I should have told you before. It's been a whirlwind. Are you glad for me, dearest?'

'If it's what you want.'

'Isn't it what all women want? A husband. A little home. Eventually a family.

I felt my eyebrows lift. I should have known from the romping kittens and tender spaniels. Her slavishness. I said, before I meant to, 'And what about our affair, Elise. Have you told him about that?'

Elise blushed, her colour at odds with the pink of her dress. 'Phèdre, *no*. Of *course* not. *That* doesn't matter. I mean, it was a little game we played, wasn't it? And you're very precious to me. But in the end, we settle down, don't we.

And here's my chance. We'll still be the *best* of friends.'

Obviously, I should have left at once, but then the engagement party arrived, in a ringing of doorbell, with mountains of cake, sweeping through like a tidal wave, carrying all before it.

The cakes came from the patisserie across the way, and were very, very lush, full of creams, decorated with alcoholic fruits. And there was a lot of a sweet Italian wine the shade of urine, which I declined, along with the cakes.

Elise, radiant, took me presently to meet her intended betrothed. The mother, also radiant, perhaps seeing now a life for herself free of millinery, although I doubted it, spoke his name to me in a reverent voice,, and all the other guests – about twenty of them crushed into two small rooms – applauded, as if a prize had been announced.

'Monsieur Leprince!'

Moliere couldn't have done it better, with such a name. The prince was a few inches taller than Elise, and portly, the shape of an egg that finally divided in two legs. If he had a neck it was carefully hidden, and his hair was plastered staunchly sideways, oiled, and not thick. He had a small moustache with some contrasting ginger in it. His little oval eyes were dark, and also oiled, and so, very bright. He took my hand and shook it in a way that a man shakes a woman's hand who knows women are fragile, incomprehensible, marvellous, expendable creatures. The handshake said it all. Also the putting of the necklace head to the right side, the *twinkle.* 'I've heard your name with awe, mademoiselle. What a bold stroke!'

Elise said, 'It's from the theatre. From the play.'

'Of course it is, my dove. I've read the play, in the original Greek. But oh, that was some years ago. I'd stumble with it now, I fear. Mustn't stumble with the name!'

He smiled, always he smiled. His teeth leaned a little. He wasn't quite young enough, and yet you couldn't take exception. A young woman may marry an older man. The reverse – God forbid!

He patted and pinched Elise, liking her flesh, apparently. He pressed cake upon me, which again I refused.

'But Phèdre must have a glass of wine! So passionate a name, and so abstemious!'

They said he was a wit, and recounted many funny things he had done and uttered, as for example when the carriage had run over a dog and he said the bump was like riding on a camel. (I thought Elise's sentiment might struggle with this, but she only laughed.) Or when he described his superior in some firm or other, as the Great Conundrum, with a mixture, I could hear at once, of grovelling respect, and what he himself saw as dashing, daring cheek.

He stood smiling and smiling by, tickling Elise's elbows. The guests fluttered round like moths. Old women of the mother's acquaintance, an admiring old aunt of his, a couple of comrades from his office, the concierge and some neighbours.

Whenever I spoke of going, it was Monsieur Leprince who would stop me, calling them up in battalions to block off my escape. 'Now, I've only just met her, this charming friend of my dear Elise. Just think what the Great Conundrum will say, when I tell him I have met an actual *Phèdre*.'

In the end I drank a few mouthfuls of the wine, and was immediately dizzy from the horrible stuff. I thought I was in hell, where I belonged. Everything had become a punishment, if not here, then somewhere else. And so I stayed.

How long had it been since the special luncheon to which Rherlotte did not come, since the dream by which I knew I had given myself over to her? Do others find love such a terrible state? No. All the world loves a lover and loves to love. But for me – it was like illness. More so, I must think, because I was alone in it. And alone indeed.

After one week, I needed to corset less in order that my clothes, growing too large, should fit me. My wrists seemed transparent. My eyes. Did I even know what I did?

As with this, now, this awful thing in which I had been caught up. Elise's friend. Her 'best of friends', and Monsieur Leprince now *paddling* my hand, as Shakespeare puts it, perhaps eager to make another bonus conquest.

Oh *God*. We walked along the road against the winter wind, with Elise on one of his arms, I on the other. Her mother, slightly put out, waddled behind, her corns stuffed into small blue shoes.

The restaurant was just a street or two away, to take a carriage wasn't necessary – so the generous Monsieur Leprince informed us.

And then these awful long, white tables, with their dire festive flowers from the hothouse, looking now like the dreadful 'Immortal' flowers that have been burnt and dried, mummified and dead, with injections of unlikely colour. And he must have Elise on his right, and he must have *Phèdre*, the passionate, dramatic woman, on his left. (The poor mother's face fell like a bad dough.)

And this I allowed, having no reason left to me.

Elise seemed very glad. She told me clever male things he had done, and told him lovely feminine things I'd done. That she'd had toothache, for example, and I'd brought her a tincture of cloves, which cured it. And he basked between us, and, when he had had some of the cheap Champagne, called us his Two Beauties. (Presumably not knowing the slang.)

The aunt was displeased. Mama was displeased. Yet recklessly I remained. I thought of standing up and calling for a toast. 'I've had the virginity of your wife, Monsieur Leprince, which doubtless she thinks to conceal from you by squealing and being arid from disgust. And now she hopes she and I, behind your egg-shaped back, will carry on just the same. Do you know, Monsieur, there's a certain place at the side of her neck, and on the inside of her thigh, and if you play there with your tongue, she dissolves. No, you'll never learn. I can imagine you. Up like the lark, but lacking all song. Down like a shutter.'

I ached. What tincture of cloves for this toothache of the heart?

Damn them, let the meal be poison.

'I hope,' says Monsieur aside to me, sportively, licentiously, 'when you are married, dear Phèdre, your husband won't have a son!

'Ah, monsieur,' I say. 'Good husbands are rare.'

He takes it as a compliment.

If I had that *bottle* would I tip it in his wine? Rid the world of this nincompoop.

What have I drunk? I've eaten nothing.

Why am I here.

Where should I be?

Musicians come. Were they hired? Zigeuner music, hot and full of malice. Their eyes blaze on us. We, idiotic, full of drink.

It's dark now in the street.

When I get up, Monsieur catches my arm. 'But *Phèdre!*'

'You must excuse me for just a moment, Monsieur.'

But he won't. At last, Elise and I. Oh. A room with mirrors. Elise powdering her face and neck, touching her lips with red.

'Isn't he a fine man, Phèdre? You won't be angry. You *like* him.'

'Oh, enormously. Yes. You were made in heaven for each other.'

'And you'll come to the theatre? It's only us, and Mama, and his Aunt Claude. You said you would. It's a very clever play. And I shan't understand it. But *you* will.'

A play now? I've said I'll go too? Someone must have dropped out. When will this evil end?

The play. I see it in snatches. I've drunk their foul wines. I'm drunk. Drink doesn't do any of this to me. But I'm poisoned. Poisoned.

Oh, won't you come, my love, won't you lead me away. Let me lie down beside you. I won't touch. Your warmth. Your cool, kind hand upon my head.

Rherlotte.

What am I thinking of?

I don't know what the play was, but it was interminable. And then, there came in it, a masked ball.

Columns soared, flimsy plaster that probably shook a little as dancers cavorted over the stage. Orange lamps hung down in the garden of a chateau.

Huge trees on the backdrop …

There are baboons, and maidens from the seventeen hundreds. There was an elephant, and a soldier. And then Death came down the steps, in a black cloak, Death whose face was not to be seen.

Elise gasped, and put her hand to her throat. Monsieur Leprince patted her. Why do I remember that?

The footlights shone on them, the revellers caught out by Death. But now Death comes again, another Death.

There are two of them.

Each clad in black. Their faces hidden.

The lights drop low.

Which is myself? Which death am I? And which is she? Which is *Rherlotte*.

I wait for the two deaths to fling off their cloaks. One a young woman with black hair, one a naked woman with hair of pink marigolds.

But they don't throw away their cloaks and the scene relapses into a muddy twilight as the curtains close.

8

Wandering along by the river, an old man came up to me and took my arm.

I said instantly, 'You're mistaken, monsieur. I'm not for sale.'

'Dear child, I didn't think you were. But it's such a cold night. And the river. How horribly cold that must be. Just look at it. So cold and black and heavy, and do you know how dirty it is? Someone caught a fish there, ate the fish and died. You wouldn't like it, mademoiselle. Trust me, no.'

I realised he thought I'd been meaning to throw myself into the Seine, as have countless others. It hadn't occurred to me, but at his instigation, it did. Then I considered it. It was a fact, the water looked very black, thick yet empty. To go down would be easy. The shock of the cold, stunning at once. But then, how could one be sure. There might be a mistake, a rescue, or worse, death be an actual place, where one would have to go on, with no escape at all.

'I was only walking, monsieur.'

'Very well. But let me take you home.'

I glanced at him. He was tall but stooped, with a fine, grey beard. His clothes were flawless. On his head, the top hat of the Opera, the theatre.

I'd been at the theatre, hadn't I. And afterwards, Monsieur Leprince had promised us all oysters, but at such a cheap restaurant, I was certain, by then, they'd all die of intestinal inflammations.

I said I must go. He pressed my hand. Elise, drunk on pure stupidity, clung to his arm.

'No, no, our Phèdre. Phèdre must have oysters.'

'Ah, monsieur. They make me sick.'

Aggrieved, frowning, such a little thing; I had at length so simply put him off. I went away. I walked into the city.

A woman mustn't walk city streets unaccompanied, by night. I knew as much. And yet, there was about me some circle of protection. As on the night I courted Jean Viktor Pascet. The evening when I put myself in the path of Armand Blos. None else came to me.

There were trees in a dance of bare branches about the lamps. A fine rain falling. Will there be another spring? Perhaps not.

I, the huntress. But I walk in fear. Any man might cage me. One has. But not through himself.

And in the end, the shining river, and the old gentleman come from some play, that was I'm certain far more erudite than the drama Elise's amour had chosen for us.

The old man turned to me mildly, and indicated his carriage.

'I know it isn't quite right, mademoiselle. But you seem, at a loss. Will you allow me the honour of taking you to your home? You've nothing to fear. Alas. Twenty years ago, I would have offered you some danger. But not tonight. An old man, dear girl. If you won't, I'll fret, and it isn't good for me. I'll lie awake, wondering what became of you.'

What did I care? This man. His kindness some further act of the play, which he was now performing for himself.

'I haven't far to go.'

'Nevertheless.'

The carriage stood black on the black night, wet with the rain. The horses, sleek with water, looked like a funeral team for the chariot of the hearse. Perhaps he was lying.

He guided me towards the vehicle.

'Come now. Get in.'

Probably hanging about like this would give him rheumatism. It served the old fool right.

I thought of her suddenly. Rherlotte. That she would flirt with him just a little, reminding him of his youth, showing that she, at least, was not unaware that beneath his crocodile skin and cobweb beard, once he had been young. She would put her hand warmly on his arm, thank him, and mount into the carriage.

I found I had done so.

We sat. He a decorous length from me.

The carriage started.

It came to me, I'd given him, as my address, the house on the Boulevard Strauss.

Now why was that?

'Yes, I know it. A pretty street.'

Am I Rherlotte, then? Is this *my* theatre? Playing her part, since she has vanished in the wings.

Well, he'll drop me there, and I'll wait until he's gone. No lights will be in her windows. There's no Armand for her to be awaiting. It's late. As the chateau was in the dream, every pane will be black.

As we turn into the street, an asphyxiating pain roams through me. I know what it will be like to die, alone or among strangers.

But he says, 'See, there you are. And the light is burning for you.

I look. It *is* her house. It positively exists. Grey by night, the shutters black. The bare tall tree. But in the pane above the door, a globe of palest reddish blue. And above, up there, that rosy window. The window of her watch-lamp, left burning for her beloved. For him. For Armand.

'Now, what is it? Shall I come to the door with you?' says the old man.

I brush away two lines of tears that aren't mine. I stare at him. He blinks and gazes into space, astonished by my look. My grandmother's look. After all used on a man.

'Thank you, monsieur.'

When I'm out of the carriage it goes off at once. Can it be he finally saw he had taken a serpent into his bosom?

Standing on the street, and looking up. I expect the light of the upper window to go out.

Did Armand stand here? No, he strode straight to the door. No doubt he had the key. No doubt he entered and she came out, standing on the stair, her face lit by the lamp in the hall, her hair gilded by the lamp above.

What's she done to me? The night is so cold, and I'm outside. That horrible betrothal party. Am I drunk still? No, sober as if rinsed in a river. I'm quite sure of this.

When I find myself rapping at the knocker, the hand with the scroll, I can't think what I've done. What will become of me? Who am I? I don't know who I am, to have done such a thing. I hang by a thread from the stars of the rain. And as they fall, they let me go.

was midnight, thereabouts. The maid, Marthe, came) to answer my knock in a bundled dressing-gown.

'Mademoiselle –'

'Tell her, Phèdre.'

'But mademoiselle.'

From above, the voice. Her voice.

'Yes. Very well, Marthe.'

Her voice pulled me up the stairs. They were in a half-dark, and the caryatids, standing like wardresses, blank-eyed and wooden.

Where am I going? The iris doors stand open, and inside is the room. It's here the lamp burns, after all. I can see it. An oil lamp with a white bowl painted with roses. The curtain drawn a little back from the thick lace.

The other lamps are low, and the whole room itself a smoky rose, lit by glints of firelight.

Near the fire, a small table with an old-fashioned chestnut-coloured cloth of frilled chenille. Two chairs upholstered in pale lemon silk. There are candles on the table, not lit. Two places set, with two light green flutes for drinking bubbly wine.

The Louis clock says six minutes to twelve.

There's a kettle on a hook over the fire, a contrivance like the one I have at my flat. The kettle makes a faint buzzing, like a contented bee. Two tea cups and a pot stand on a lacquer tray by the hearth. The caddy, the sugar bowl.

All these things mesmerize me, Rherlotte appears from the room's farthest end, out of the rose shadows. Everything dims, retreats from her flaming centre.

She wasn't wearing mourning. Not tonight. She was dressed for a dinner, in a gown of darkest green velvet, cut low at the bosom, and leaving her arms and shoulders almost bare. Her hair was piled up high, with a comb in it. She had two silver ear-drops, and on her wrist a silver bracelet from which hung a little silver heart.

I said, 'I'm sorry. You won't want me here. I'll go in a moment.'

She said, 'It's all right. Come to the fire.'

There was a chair, and she indicated I should sit in it. I did so.

Thoughtlessly I unpinned my hat. I took it off and put it by, and then, for a reason unknown to me, I undid my hair.

She was bending to the kettle by then, but she turned. She smiled. 'What wonderful hair, Phèdre.'

I closed my eyes, but there was movement in the room, swinging and turning. I opened them again.

She was pouring the hot water into the pot. From the tea came a smell of fruit.

'But you've had guests,' I said.

'Oh, no. Not at all. I always do this in the evenings. I've done it for so long.'

I remembered the table set for two. I said, 'In case Armand should be free to come here.'

'Yes.'

'Every night.'

'Not every night, of course. But I put things ready. There'd be some cold supper. Some wine. In case he might come.'

'And when he didn't come?'

'Why then,' she glanced at me seriously, quietly, explaining. 'I'd go to bed.'

'Alone.'

She looked away from me into the fire.

'When Armand visited me, Phèdre, it wasn't always for my bed. You must recall, he was married. Generally he went home between one and two or three, to his wife. Often we'd sit and talk. We'd known each other some years.'

I said, 'Was he worth it? All this? Your waiting. Your dressing for him. The cold supper. You remind me – of Penelope waiting for Odysseus. And she promised she'd remarry when her husband's shroud was finished, and unpicked the weaving every night, so no one else could have her. While he whored with all the sorceresses and goddesses and nymphs of the islands.'

Rherlotte smiled at me again. 'How lovely, Phèdre. I never thought of that. That I might resemble Penelope. I like the image very much.'

'You were as blindly faithful and he as licentiously profligate.'

'I don't see Armand as an Odysseus. No. Now and then, there was a woman. He was easily fired.'

'You forgave him,' I said harshly. 'Over and over.'

'Forgave him for what? It wasn't a sin. He didn't do it from a desire to hurt or harm. It was natural to Armand. Why would I mind it? He came back to me.'

I spoke a curse of the streets. On this occasion she had no reaction to it. She poured the tea into one of the cups, the cup left waiting for the remembrance of Armand, and gave it to me, with the sugar bowl.

'How curious you should come tonight,' she said. Almost what Elise had said.

'I've intruded on you.'

'No, Phèdre. No. I was lonely tonight.'

Without adding sugar, I sipped the tea. It had a taste of smoke, and something acidulous, like oranges.

'But you must often have been lonely.'

'Sometimes, perhaps. That is, since his death.'

I stared at her. She looked into the fire. Her skin was flushed from its clustered light.

'Yet I killed him, you say. How can you want me here?'

She looked at me, only for a moment. She still knelt by the fire. Her fleeting eyes, starred with the flames.

'Oh, Phèdre. But you weren't what I expected. A girl. What had I imagined you'd be before I met you? A Gorgon. A monster.'

'You remembered that. On the day you were to meet me at the Cafe Flor. You remembered I was a monster, and so you didn't come.'

She said slowly, thoughtfully, still not looking at me, 'I had indulged myself too much. That was what I remembered.'

'Indulged – with what?'

'Indulged myself with you, Phèdre. And it was time to stop. High time.'

There were some white flowers in a vase. The candles were held by one of Odysseus' nymphs in yellow enamel. The wicks were blackened. Perhaps they had last burned when Armand was here.

'Shall I go at once?' I blurted.

She said, 'Yes, my dear. Soon you must.'

'And after that –'

She said, 'After that, then what, Phèdre?'

'I must avoid you.'

She sighed. She turned her head and looked up at me. Her face – was the sweetest, most living thing I ever saw. I wanted to frame it in my hands, as she did with me in my dream. I wanted only to hold her, look at her. Surely nothing else …

'It would be best, wouldn't it,' she said. 'If we avoid each other.'

'You hate me so.'

'Do I? Yes, but I must hate you, mustn't I?'

'Because I killed the man you loved. That ridiculous, crude, posturing boor. Oh, yes. How he was with me – would you have recognised him? Strutting, bragging. Stuffing me with food and Champagne so that he could push me over on my back. He was as hot as a furnace. He wanted to feel me, crush me.

He was as ready as any lecher. And that room, they knew him so well there. How many had he taken in there, got drunk, and screwed? God knows. It reeked of him, that room. His cologne. His *need*.'

I stopped. I realized what I had told her. A cold rushing went through me, then a singing heat.

'You see, I'm confessing to you – Rherlotte – if I mustn't ever see you again, better get it done with now. Yes, yes. I murdered him. I did it. There was no difficulty. It was poison. Quite quick. I don't think he suffered greatly. Except for the last few seconds.'

She too, standing up now. She was, in that rose room, white. Deathly marble white as I'd first seen her.

'Do you know what you're saying?' she said. 'That finally you've let it out?'

'Of course I know. What do you think? Did he teach you, your lover, to be as stupid as he was? I *know*. I *know*. And now you know. What will you do? Run to the police. Do it, Rherlotte. Give me to them. I'll go with you. Or do you want to kill me yourself? Look, here's a sharp knife on the table you laid for his ghost.'

She shuddered.

'I couldn't put violent hands on you.'

This definitive statement infuriated me. 'Not even to finish me off? But wouldn't it be worth it? You loved him so much.'

'Oh yes,' she said, 'I loved him.' Her head went back. Her eyes were black. 'You don't understand me, do you? Let me tell you. My life ended when you killed him, but I didn't even know he was dead. How could I? To whom could I go, to ask, when all at once he didn't ever come to me?'

'You might have thought he'd tired of you,' I said. I wanted so much to hurt her. Why? All I wanted was to hold her.

'No, I didn't think that,' she said. She drew in a long breath, and her beautiful breasts moved above the scoop of the velvet bodice. I could see her heart beating, not so fast, but in hard, hard strokes. 'In the end, Marthe went for me. She found out from the Blos' maid. That he'd been discovered in a restaurant.' The fire flashed in her eyes. 'Don't you see? Don't you *see*, Phèdre? I didn't even see him, dead. She buried him, his wife. How could I? And so he isn't dead for me, physically, and he should be. But how can he be? Had I been his wife, I'd have said some sort of farewell. But he was alive – and then there was that mound of turf in the cemetery of St Luc. Sometimes, when I'm half mad, I think perhaps everyone has lied to me. Even about you, this plot. That he isn't dead but was taken away a prisoner. Doubtless you find that bizarre. I do, myself. But you have no idea, Phèdre, what love will do. What it puts on me.'

'Yes,' I said. 'I know. Of course I know.'

'How can you *know*?' she said bitterly. 'Look at you. Phèdre, made of this cold, cold snow, with her black hair. Phèdre, impervious to all. How could you know anything about love?'

'I love *you*' I said it without any heat, and all at once all of myself seemed poured out of me. I was a shell and felt nothing at all. I saw her face from a long way off, a beautiful thing that I didn't recognize. Either she wasn't human, or I was no longer human, or never had been. Who – *what* – was she? She could be nothing to me, or I to her. And I said again, mechanically, 'I love you.'

'Oh, Phèdre.' She turned away from me.

I said, 'They told you what I was. That I've no use for men.' She said nothing. I said, 'I didn't have any use for anyone. Until you. I told you once, I'm under your spell.'

She said again, softly, 'Phèdre.'

Her back was straight, and the nape of her neck, her shoulders, so glowing, like alabaster, the white porcelain of the rose lamp, with the flame inside.

I said, 'I'm glad I killed him. What did I care before? He was nothing. But now. I robbed him of you. He didn't deserve you, Rherlotte. But you gave yourself. You gave yourself to him like any little lady's maid or girl from the dingy shops at St Germain or Montmartre. And I don't deserve you. No one could in two centuries. Perhaps after that they'll be better. But you'll be dead by then.'

I was moving towards her. By turning her back to me, somehow she enabled me to come close.

Now I could smell her hair, the scent of her supple body; so cool, so warm. Smell the velvet of her dress.

Around her body I slid my arms, crossing them, taking her breasts in my hands. I put my face down into her neck. Her pulse was against my mouth. I held her tight, trying to choke her, stop her breathing. Her neck was like silk. I wanted to bite through it and get at the flame in her lamp of alabaster, her red blood.

She was twisting. Coming around towards me. I saw the blur of her beauty, like an exquisite painting smeared, and had her mouth. For a moment I tasted her, the full lower lip and the sculpted upper one, the tongues tip, and the edges of her animal teeth. And then she pulled back and slapped my face, stinging and hard, and her nails raked my cheek.

Then, like any Armand, baulked, not being able to accept, *believe*, I struggled to subdue her. Trying to hold her off, but also to tear her gown and spill her breasts, to have her skin in my mouth, to stop her clawing out my eyes.

She beat against me with a lioness's hands. Her hair came down in a hot waterfall, full of little, hooked pins.

I was crying her name. There were tears on my face and on her face. She struck me again and the force of her blow separated us. The wall met my back, struck my skull. She ran to the table and snatched up after all the sharp knife.

I laughed at her drunkenly. 'But isn't this how *he* was? Stinking of wine, burning with his *ardour*. Don't you like me, Rherlotte? Am I too like him, that thing you say you loved?'

'Go away,' she said. Her voice was hoarse, husky and quite low. The knife shone clear, the shade the rain had been. 'Leave this house at once.'

'And never return here? Of course not. An unnatural woman. A damned woman. How could you bear me?'

'Out, I said.' She stood taller. Her face was that of a young king who can command ten legions.

Ridiculous, I knew I couldn't say another word. But I said, 'Come here. Stick the knife in me. You want to. Why not? I won't resist.

At that she flung down the knife with a clatter. 'I'll ring for Marthe,' she said, 'shall I? Will you like that? The *maid* to see you as you are?'

'What do I care. I wasn't brought up to tell lies to the servants, as you were, little bourgeois.'

And so she crossed to the bell-pull and saw to it.

And then we stood there. She and I. Still and silent in the room which now fluttered with agitated wings of light and dark. Perhaps the fire was only going out. Or else our rage had affected it.

Marthe came after a long time. She was plainly unused to being summoned so late. She looked bemused, half asleep, astonished. Seeing me, she looked afraid.

'Take Mademoiselle down and unlock the door for her,' said Rherlotte.

I said to her, from the room's edge, 'Goodnight, *Madame.*'

But that was all.

Marthe rustled hurriedly down the stairs. I followed her like a woman going to her own execution.

She undid the door with some difficulty, all thumbs. And let me out on to the street.

When the door had been shut, I stood below and looked up.

The lamp did not go out. Not for some while. Was she weeping? Let her. But Oh God, what had I done? Her pretty room I hadn't wanted to spoil. Her beauty, which I shouldn't have touched.

Do I fall still? Haven't I yet struck the bottom of the black abyss? No, for the street feels as if made of feathers. How close the sky is. And so cold, so cold.

I walked some way. Once a cab passed me. When I saluted it, the cabman leered at my dishevelled, hatless hair, the scratches on my face.

The wheels ground over the streets like those of a tumbrel. But, fool that I was, I thought myself already dead.

9

When I reached my flat, I sat in an armchair, and dropped into a tindery, feverish doze. Sometimes I woke for a few moments, and saw the sky in the windows begin to lighten. Then I heard traffic strangely echoing in the street. The moans of the wind. At last I woke to a horrible cold that seemed to be miles inside my burning body. The window through the undrawn curtain was locked in a frigid whiteness.

I got up and, going to see, saw the almond trees were in blossom, solid white, with snow.

At that moment a carriage came with difficulty along the street. I paid it no attention. I went into my bedroom, and stood looking at myself in the pier-glass.

My face was pale, the eyes had half-moons of shadow. The scratches on my right cheek had bled. My clothes were creased and my hair tangled. I appeared like a beast that had escaped from the circus. I recognized this aspect of myself at once.

How long I stood, watching this creature that was me, I don't know. Presently there came a very loud knocking on my door.

I drifted into the hall. I opened the door, not concealing myself, for nothing was real. Indeed, it couldn't be, for there in her nets and robe stood my aggrieved concierge, and behind her, my aunts, Sophie and Susie, staring at me blindly with round blue, pebble eyes.

They were dressed identically in dark blue apparel, with round hats and unseasonal white gloves. Sophie had a muff of civet and Susie one of grey fox. These were the differences, aside from Susie's darker hair. They had no bags, nothing with them but for identical small antique reticules, sewn with faded sequins.

Outlandish, they looked. As much so as I?

Between us humped the concierge, gesturing with her arms, her small eyes taking in everything with alarm.

'They said they'd come from the country to see you, mademoiselle. They say they're your – aunts.'

'They are.'

'Your face – mademoiselle, did you meet with an accident?'

'Thank you,' I said.

Sophie said to me, 'We should like chocolate now.'

Susie said, 'The train took a long time.'

'There's no chocolate,' I said. 'When the restaurant opens.'

Suddenly I laughed, and stood aside to let them in. Two demons, they passed me, bringing in the smells of girl-children who have been travelling on a train, cinders, old honey, tobacco, and the woody, vernal, mothball scents of O—.

I asked the concierge for things from the restaurant as soon as possible. It was all I had to deflect them. I closed the door in the woman's face.

'So you travelled on the train,' I said.

'You said to.'

'No I didn't. How did you manage it?' I think I was half interested. It was as if my outer skin, the part of me that was so cold, were interested. Inside, I smouldered, fumbling about, oblivious.

'It's not warm enough,' said Susie. 'When will you light the fire?'

'Oh, now, of course.'

I made up the fire, but couldn't bring myself to perform the actions of making tea. My mouth was dry, but I wouldn't drink. I sat in the armchair, while Sophie and Susie prowled about, and when I heard them in my study and bedroom, pulling open drawers, I took no notice.

About eight or nine, the breakfast arrived. A child's breakfast of bread and butter, jam and chocolate.

They ate greedily, splashing the drink and smearing butter on their clothes.

Lying back in the chair, I watched them.

'Are you ill?' said Susie 'You look quite ill,' said Sophie.

'Yes, I'm very ill, and you're liable to catch it.'

'We stole money from mother,' said Sophie, prudishly. 'She doesn't know where we are.'

'Paris is just all streets and walls,' said Susie.

'And it's snowed,' said Sophie.

'We like more chocolate,' said Susie. She opened the pot to see where the fresh supply was.

I thought drearily, I should send Constance a telegram. But I hadn't the energy. Not yet.

'Who scratched your cheek?'

'A lioness at the zoological gardens.'

'You could die of that,' they said, almost smiling.

Just then, the door again. Sophie went at once, unbidden, to open it. 'Who are you?' they asked Brunhilde, my cleaning woman, from whom I had stolen a hat when I went to poison Jean Viktor Pascet.

'An old witch,' said Brunhilde.

She came stamping in. At the sight of them, the mess, of me, she said, 'Christ on His cross, mademoiselle.'

I'd brought her a new hat, all that time ago. She hadn't liked mine. I told her how I had searched and searched but couldn't find the original. In a street market, to which she had insisted we go for the purpose, she chose a black squashed thing with a knot of little, red, unsucculent cherries. She wore it even now.

Quite calmly I told her an hysterical friend had attacked me. She imagined her fiancé paid me too much attention, which might well have been true. As I thought nothing of him, I hadn't noticed until it was too late. I told her that I wasn't well. Meanwhile these children were a relative's daughters who had come here without her (Brunhilde had never met Constance, who christened her), lacking her knowledge or consent. I asked Brunhilde to send the telegram, posting her out again into the bitter streets. But she went at once.

Sophie and Susie lay down before the fire. They fell asleep. By day at O— they often slept. At night, for all I knew, they climbed on the roofs and used their catapults against the owls.

In the end I went to bathe my face. I washed, and put on my robe. I brushed my hair. Some came out on the bristles. Rherlotte must have torn it loose.

Rherlotte. Her name sounded at intervals in my head, meaningless and far away as some unacknowledged station on my aunts' route from O—.

Brunhilde stood over me.

'It's all to be arranged like you said, mademoiselle. They're to go back on the evening train. And serve them right, the naughty things. But you do look done in. Shall I take them off your hands for the day?'

Inside myself I struggled to understand what Brunhilde had said. From my lips, a stranger speaking for me, came the words, 'Oh yes. That would be a relief. Please take some money from –'

'No, no, mademoiselle. We'll sort all that out another time. It's no trouble. My cousin's got two girls. I'll take them there first.' My mind now struggled to grasp this notion, the two demons in some ordinary house. Probably they would murder the whole family. But perhaps not Brunhilde. 'Put on your hats,' she said to Sophie and Susie, as if they were only children. 'Your coats aren't warm enough, but you'll do on the omnibus. Have you been on one before?'

'No,' said my aunts.

'Time you did then. Now I'll take you to the pastry shop first. You can each choose a cake. The one you like best.' Their avaricious eyes brightened. She held out her brown workwoman's hands to them, standing there in her battered cherry hat and split- seamed coat. 'Come along now. I don't want to lose you.'

To my outer self's amazement, Sophie and Susie came and took her hands. In the doorway I saw them look up at her. She was chattering out questions to them, which they answered. Their faces were blushed by the fire, which Brunhilde had assisted. She said, 'You came to see the city. Well, you can see a bit of it. But it's a big city, this one, and old. Do you know why the river is called the Seine?'

When I went to the window, I saw them in the snowy street. She was pointing things out, still holding their hands, moving their arms like those of puppets. And they were still staring up at her, as if they'd never seen anyone like her, or anything, either, and conceivably they hadn't.

After they disappeared, so it seemed did I.

My mother once took me walking at O—, in the winter, when the snow was down. I was little, and the snow frightened me, it was so cold, and so tall – the trees enmeshed in it, and banks of it going up so high. Now and then as I trod, my feet sank deeply. Or I slid. I'd heard a story of a local boy, skating on the ice of a pool, which broke, so that he died in the freezing water, in two minutes, they said. My mother's admonitions to look at this view, or that bird bravely (bravely – what choice did it have?) pecking the buried berries, were lost on me.

She grew melancholy of course, she sat down on a fallen trunk in the woods, that was like a pole of iced iron. She held me by the hand and said that, if we sat here long enough, the cold would feel warm and we'd go to sleep.

I was frightened worse, not knowing why. I said nothing. I waited by her side until, sighing as if foregoing a great pleasure for my sake, she got up and led me home to Constance's Chateau.

In the afternoon, a mauve gloaming settled on the city. In every window burned the fatigued yellow lights that had had to be kept going all day.

Coming back to awareness, not knowing why, I recollect I glanced at the clock. It was just after three.

In a while, Brunhilde would return with her charges, if nothing had happened, if they hadn't done some great wickedness that brought Paris to a standstill.

By seven they must board the train. A faint, awful thought occurred to me. That the snow might delay their departure. And then I thought I might go back with them. Go back to my grandmother's house. I tried to find my reason for thinking this. I didn't wish to, but then, I wished to go nowhere. And yet – and yet I had the strangest urge, as on the other day, to flight.

But I couldn't run away – from her. Even there, *she* would pursue me. And if truly she had summoned the police, which I doubted, I was hardly at this moment concerned. I could deny what she would say I had said. I had no connection to Armand Blos. And Anne must keep silent. It was Rherlotte who would be unbalanced, liable to murder.

Or I could confess to them, as to her. If I died, that might be the only perfect method of eluding Rherlotte.

But then again, as with the black river, suppose it were not the perfect method? Suppose that in death, still, I should be haunted?

I'd tried to rape her. It *was* rape. To that I'd been reduced. No wonder she flung me off.

She had seemed, before, so full of candour, so soft, melting in the light. She'd said, 'Your wonderful hair.' She had said, 'I indulged myself with you.' She had said, 'My *dear*.'

Wasn't there, or hadn't there been, in her, against all odds, some tenderness for me? I'd felt it lying lightly over her, like an extra colour, a quivering, wild scent. It was as if she claimed me, when I spoke of loving her.

Couldn't there be some chance, however slight –

But no. No. No chance at all.

Even so, all at once, just then, mentally, I saw her. At her desk in her room, behind the iris glass, writing to me, one of her notes, black on white. The gracious writing with its sudden little dashes, its ripples of something savage and lawless no longer allowing itself to be held in.

Was it possible? Did I somehow see her, penning me a letter. What could such a letter say – what *could* it say? *I was mistaken to send you away. What you offered me is something that, after all, I want.*

For she *had* wanted my love. She had. I saw it in her face, a smothered little flicker of fire, quickly hidden. Even after I confessed what I'd done to *him*. Even then. When I said, *I love you*. Now, in memory, I saw her, and the glimmer of some acknowledgement deep down in her eyes. Before she turned her back.

She had wanted my love. How then, not me? She was afraid.

But with Rherlotte, her fear might be itself distasteful to her. That alone might be enough.

What was she writing? Was it written, now? Was she folding the page? Was she sealing the letter?

I went to my bedroom in disgust, and taking up my traveller's bags, began to put into them some things for O—. On the train, perhaps marooned in the snow with the demon aunts, I might go mad. But that madness must be away from her. Out of this city which was hers. No longer close enough that I might run, stumbling and sliding, through the dangerous snow, to reach her door.

When Brunhilde returned, she brought with her by the hand, two little girls. Their eyes and cheeks were bright. They had pockets full of sweets, and were talking, jabbering. About this one and that, who they'd met. And how many stairs there were. And a cathedral, and a river, and a toyshop, and a market. They were prancing about. Susie had gained a red scarf and Sophie a white muffler. Brunhilde smiled. I had come back enough myself to be startled. She said, 'They weren't any trouble. Full of curiosity. And my cousin's cat, they loved it so.' I thought privately they might, if left alone, have tried to skin it. Perhaps not, perhaps they had only needed to be treated as children magically to become children.

'There was a man at the steps gave me this for you, mademoiselle.'

All at once, the world stopped still. I took the letter and waited, staring at it. A white letter, with black ink. The handwriting of Rherlotte.

Brunhilde and the strange children drew far, far away. I went into the bedroom, pushed to the door. Then again, I stood with the letter closed fast in my hand.

Should I open it? Wasn't it better to let this moment remain alive? For, if opened, mightn't it say to me some message of revulsion, some added thrust of pain, and a lasting silence.

I tore it. The white leaf fluttered to the carpet. Not touching it, I bent to look. Something metallic had fallen with it. That didn't matter. It was the words, these black patterns, dancing and jostling.

Phèdre – Here is the front door key to my house on the Bld Strauss.

You must know, I've tried so hard to make you mine, to make you fall in love with me. It seems, does it not, that I was most skilful?

Don't come to me today. Come tomorrow. Come at two o'clock in the afternoon. I shall dismiss my servants. Even Marthe. No one will be in the house, but for myself.

And I shall be, Phèdre, defenceless before you.

Brunhilde tapped at the door.

'Oh, was it bad news, mademoiselle?'

'No. I'll go to the station now.'

To the station with Sophie and Susie. Putting them on the train to O—. Not seeing them. Seeing always the image: her hands seizing me, her face, her mouth crushed to mine, her fingers strong as cords about my neck –

I wouldn't be, myself, going to O—.

How many years would pass, before tomorrow? Let me revel in them all. Let me press them near and suck out from them their very essence.

10

My impulse is to make a long preamble. How I bathed and dressed. How I powdered over the scratch on my face, as if ashamed. And that I didn't sleep the night before. Of course I slept. Exhaustion, delirium. Miles deep. There were no dreams that I remember.

Did I say, I stood before the mirror once again. Naked. I looked, trying not to see myself – but Rherlotte.

That I wrote on the mirror, in rouge, *de Gillan* and *Diane*, which was almost anagrammatical. Save for this G, these two *Ls*.

But such things, these twitters of the bride before her wedding … I must go straight on. Let me speak, instead, of the marriage night.

At a little before two o'clock, the slow careful carriage left me in the Boulevard Strauss.

What a change there had been. The houses were now in Switzerland. How festive they looked, like cakes, with their toppings of cream.

When I came to her house, her tree was clad in white. The urn with the shrub. The railings. The pink of the walls, the dark green shutters, these looked scathed, almost desolate. The house seemed lean, as if snow had wounded it. Also, it was like a tower. In a fairy tale. I had to scale it, to come to her. But really, only go up the icy, slippery steps. And then the gift of the key in the lock.

The door opened, and for a moment, I was warm.

I glanced about. I had only seen her hall, the stair, that one room.

It was so inevitable to climb that stair, that for a minute, I held off. Had she heard me walk in? She wouldn't come out. She'd wait for me, behind iris doors. As before.

I was terrified as I went up. A band of steel encircled my ribs. Twice I had to stop, simply to breathe. My ears sang. Was I happy? To suffer so much – is this happiness? And I was anxious. When I saw her, would she be the one I remembered? Or another woman. Or the same, but less beautiful. Or more? I didn't mind it. She could be lying on the floor in a dirty shift, kicking her heels, drinking absinthe and laughing in the raucous way someone – Lilas? – had sometimes done.

It didn't, didn't matter at all. She would be Rherlotte. She might say to me, Both my breasts have been cut off. My left knee is made of wood.

Rherlotte.

As I came up the last two or three stairs I met an enormous wall of colossal cold. A window had been left open, most likely by some departing domestic. I must remember, and warn her. We'd go to close it, maybe laughing.

Then the doors were in front of me. She'd hung them with a light pale gauze. Perhaps these curtains had been drawn back before.

As I touched them, the doors, a piece of white curtain trembled, and fell down inside the room.

Entering another, a new, world, do you expect all things to be as you know them?

Even so, I gazed down the stair again, as if to ask someone what this peculiar phenomenon might mean.

But the house was silent. It was a fact, she had sent them all away, to be alone with me.

Turning back, I pushed one leaf of the doors with the iris glass. For a moment it resisted. And then, swung open wide.

This room – I don't know it. No, I've never been in this room.

Inside a glacier, fringes of frost and ice hang down. So they do, here. And the same grey-blue light.

On the mantelpiece, the Louis XVI clock is broken, its glass cracked away. And there, on the table laid for two, the nymph of yellow enamel in a crumble of pieces. And half one of the green glasses is detached, and bits like angelica scattered.

What's happened? Was she angry? Did she smash these things?

But it's the long window, wide open as a door. A blank of white sky, which must have houses outlined in it, and the garden trees under snow. And round the window-frame, icicles. Long and beautiful, pure crystal, pointing in all directions.

In the middle of this room of ice, Rherlotte sits, looking at me.

Much later, when I find the second letter, I still don't see what has been done. Perhaps I never will see. For although I've learnt your lesson, Rherlotte, I learnt it as a child learns speech. Before ever I could understand.

Her eyes, fixed on me, are now unearthly blue. Her face also, bluish. She's old. An old woman, her cheeks sunk in. Her parted lips are brown. Withered like leaves that are dead. Only her hair has any absolute colour, but it looks dry and – false. A wig.

Her white dress, yes she put on white for me as she did in my dream, her white dress is stained with russet marks. From her left wrist, a ruby bracelet, those pinkish rubies called *Amaranthe*, come undone. Dripping, yet quite still. A pond of this on the floor near her feet. And by that, a man's razor – his? Armand's? Probably. Something he left here for convenience. The razor she's used, in the Roman fashion, to slash her wrist so thoroughly that the left hand is almost severed.

She sat this way. Her window wide, the cold making her warm so she could go to sleep.

After some hours, I wanted to put my arms around her, put my head on her bosom. But she would be hard and stiff as a dead tree by now. Since three or four o'clock yesterday, perhaps.

Besides, she'd never wanted me to touch her. She'd fought me away. How could I do it, now?

The page with her writing, on the table, says only, *I don't want my life. I know this damns me. I know it is a sin. Only a sin is ever so easy.* And her signature: *Rherlotte de Gillan.*

This letter was for all the world, and not for me. Perhaps even to make sure I had no blame. For she wants me to be free. She made quite sure of me. When she was sure, she ended. I don't need her letter. *She* is her letter. This body.

She made me love her. When she knew I did, and when I told her that I'd killed him, then – this. She taught me her own lesson. To live without her, as she had been made to live without him.

I didn't need a letter.

The cold was like a jewel around her, and I only thought, going away, that they wouldn't see her beauty, and now, I'd never properly remember it. This frozen thing, drained of its blood, would get in the way.

What does one do? As with any injury, some foolish hope. Presently it will be better. In an hour I'll feel it less, or a week, a year, a decade.

And then at last, It never will be better. All days, all nights like this one, always.

And then. And then.

When I knew I loved her, when she was sure that I'd suffer, as she did. His razor was like her friend. Anything of his. After she lost him she didn't want her life, let alone me. She promised me she would have her revenge on me. She has. Rherlotte.

Snow-Drop

Cristena's husband left her after a month of marriage, and went away on business to a distant country. She had known, when she married him, that this would be the arrangement, that she would frequently be alone. Her function was to live in the handsome house above the lake, like the blue centre of a clockwork eye. The house cleaned and scented itself, cooked meals to order from the groceries which were delivered twice a week, did the laundry, even kept the sweep of garden, pruning the trees, digging the earth and planting, and offering up cut irises and denim roses to match with Cristena's bright blue clothes. Cristena, her blonde hair wound about her head, was a physically lazy, mentally active woman. She liked to read, watch television, listen to music, and sometimes she would write a slim wild novel without any effort, which would sell well for a year or two, and then slip from view. The house suited her ideally. She had always wanted such a house, and such a life. Even the long absences of her husband were actually perfect. They left her time for herself, and would give every homecoming excitement, every leave-taking the drama of high romance.

However.

Before he had married Cristena, her husband had lived with another woman, in the house. This woman, some years his senior, had been dark, passionate, and energetically creative, an artist. She had died alone in the house, under rather dubious circumstances of wine and pills. She left behind no trace of her being, for the house had fastidiously washed and redecorated itself after the funeral, and given her clothes and treasures to charities. All that remained were some small water-colour paintings, very graceful and fine, and in fact worth quite an amount of money, for the artist had been highly esteemed. These paintings were to be found in every room, along every corridor. The subject was virtually the same in each of them. It was a young girl, about fourteen years of age.

She was slender and eloquent, sometimes depicted sitting, and sometimes standing, often in an expanse of pure snow. Her skin was white as that snow, and her long smooth hair was black as wood. She had a pale red mouth.

At first Cristena barely noticed the paintings.

They did not interest her very much – she preferred landscapes – and besides were all so alike that it seemed if you had looked at one you need never look at any of the others.

As the summer days passed, though, the lake darkened and the birches in the garden turned mellow, the coldness of the pictures, like little oblongs of winter brought indoors, began to annoy Cristena. They ached at the edge of her eyes, distracting her at her books and her Shostakovich. In the roomy passageways, they went by like white sentinels. They reflected in mirrors, duplicating themselves. They were even in the bedroom. Cristena removed them from there and hung instead two warm violet prints of hills.

The initial homecoming of Cristena's husband was not so astonishing as she had thought it would be.

He brought her a sapphire ring, which was very nice, although it did not quite fit, but rather than ardent he was tired and irascible. He spoke of business throughout their candlelit dinner. In bed, he kissed her, turned away and fell unconscious. He snored. Cristena found she could not sleep. At last, near morning, when she had managed to doze, her husband woke her up with insistent lasciviousness. He made love to her in a sort of drunken somnambulism, and while he did not hurt or distress her, he gave her no pleasure either. He fell asleep again on her breast, and she almost smothered until eventually she had prized herself out from under him. She achieved an hour's slumber on the brink of the mattress, where his bulk had gradually pushed her, for he too, apparently, was more used to sleeping alone.

At breakfast, a very ornate and sparkling one she had arranged for the house to prepare, Cristena's husband read papers and documents and made verbal notes on his pocket recorder.

Finally he looked up.

'Where are her paintings from the bedroom?'

'Oh, I didn't think you'd seen … I took them down. The prints are much more in keeping with the colours of the room.'

'Maybe, but not a hundredth the value. She was famous, you know.'

It was only in this way that he ever referred to his previous liaison, her fame. He did not like to discuss her as a person.

'Well, if you want,' said Cristena, 'I can put them back. Personally –'

'Yes, I'd prefer that.'

Irritated, Cristena said, to irk him in turn, 'They're all the same, aren't they. That girl. Self-portraits?'

Her husband grunted. 'She wanted children,' he said.

'You mean it's the fantasy portrait of a daughter she couldn't have?'

He frowned and did not reply.

He was quite ugly in the morning, Cristena thought, and he had put on weight which did not suit him.

She took the two pictures of the artist's unborn daughter out of the house storage, and set them back on the bedroom wall. Now she stared at them a long time. They had assumed a macabre importance, expressions of barren desire. No wonder they were capable of projecting such a horrid animation of their own.

That night Cristena wore her hair loose and a low-necked dress of midnight blue. Her husband seemed bemused, but nevertheless he made love -to her on the rug before the fire, knocking over a brandy glass in the process, which the following day the house would have to clean with an odourless acid preparation. Cristena found after all she was not going to enjoy this sexual union any more than the first. In contempt, she pretended, and her husband floundered into a relieved climax. In bed they both swallowed sleeping capsules. Cristena woke at dawn with the white pictures shining above her head like two slices of ice, and all the covers pulled off her, leaving her peculiarly vulnerable in the draughtless room.

Cristena's husband only spent ten days at the house, before he had to leave the country again. On the afternoon of his departure Cristena did indeed weep. They were tears of nervous thankfulness. But he was enraged by the scene, shouting that he did not want a clinging vine. He would be gone five months.

In the weeks which followed, winter came. The garden and the landscape, the road which led to the city, and up which the delivery vehicle still beat its way on heated runners, turned snow white. The lake froze to a silver tray. The daylight shrank, and by night the sky flickered with luminescent coils of phantom hair.

The house was of a faultless temperature, airy and bright, all its mechanisms performing helpfully. But Cristena began to feel threatened. She was anxious, and found it difficult. for the first time in her life, to concentrate on her books and music. A novel she had begun grew sluggish and contrived, and she left it.

She tried not to look at the pictures of the artist's unborn child, but they glowed on the walls and in the mirrors. A snow girl, nivea skin and ebony tresses and red water-ice mouth. As Cristena sat in the rooms of the house, she felt the pictures watching her, and when she walked through the corridors, the pictures blinked past like eyes.

Cristena removed the two pictures from the bedroom again, and the larger picture from her bathroom, and all the pictures from the living room. She put them into the house storage and ordered other pictures from a catalogue, and hung up those.

But now it seemed to be too late. The artist's paintings had left an imprint on the atmosphere of the rooms where they had hung, and in the places where they hung still they seemed to have amassed a greater strength.

The winter light too, which shone in penetratingly through all the clear windows, left drops of whiteness as if fresh water-colours depended there.

There was nobody to talk to. This had never before mattered.

Cristena took down all the paintings, every one, and put them into the storage. The blank marks on the walls where they had been glimmered like candles.

Cristina kept the blinds lowered and the curtains drawn and the lights burned day and night, and television fluttered and sang in every space. She had to be stern with herself, as she went along the passageways.

On the morning that it happened, Cristena was making up in her dressing room.

She had decided to travel to the city in an automatic hire car, to shop, eat her lunch in a restaurant, visit the theatre. The idea of going among people nearly frightened her, she had been alone so long, but also she was exhilarated, and she had poured a little vodka into her tea. The dressing room was very attractive to Cristena.

It was hyacinth with accents of gold. In the tall cupboards hung elegant dresses her husband had bought her, and in the drawers, folded among perfumes, undergarments of bones and lace, stockings embroidered with flowers, erotic items that once she had put on eagerly to please him, when he had been her lover. Cristena ignored these articles, as she ignored the jewels her husband had given her, especially the sapphire ring which was too small, and so almost insulting.

She dressed her face carefully, and it was as she was applying her dark blue mascara that she glimpsed behind her – something. Something white and slim and girl-shaped, standing between the mirror and the wall, there, on the carpet, visible.

Cristena lowered the mascara with a painful slowness. She glared into the mirror through a blue hedge. The snow girl was about three metres away, over Cristena's shoulder. She was quite distinct. She wore the same white, seamless, vaguely form-fitting garment she wore in the paintings, and her snowy skin that matched it, and the long glissade of wood-black hair. Her lips were red.

Cristena screamed. She jumped up and spun around.

The room was empty of the artist's unborn child.

Only a white gown gleamed from a half open door, with a mass of dark shadow above and a transparent scarlet rose sewn on its sleeve.

Swinging sharply back, Cristena took up a steel ornament and smashed the mirror. Fragments of glass tore off and flew about the room. The house would clear it all up.

Cristena pulled the white dress off its peg and crumpled it into the disposal shoot. It was carried away with a disapproving hiss.

She was trembling but angry. She realized the anger had lain dormant in her and now it sought release.

She ran out of the dressing room, through the bedroom, along the passage and down the stairs. All the way, flashing razor glimpses, like a migraine attack, assailed her eyes; the spots where the pictures had hung of the artist's daughter.

When she reached the living room, Cristena pressed the button and the blinds flew up with the noise of furious wings.

Outside was the unearthly snow, and there in the garden under the birches stood the snow child, the dark of a pine her hair, a single red berry her mouth.

At that moment the door called tunefully.

Confused, Cristena flung up her head. There was no delivery today.

'What is it?'

'A man is at the door. He carries no weapons.'

Cristena drifted in a trance into the hall. She signalled the door to open. Beyond the security bar stood a large and powerful young man, who beamed at her. He was incredibly ordinary, and real. Cristena had no notion as to who he was, or what he was doing there, but her awareness fixed on him voraciously. He was here for a purpose: Hers.

'Lady,' he said directly, 'I'm a photo-hunter. Look at this.'

And into the hallway over the bar leapt a wolf, which stood looking at her with its beautiful eyes. It was a holostetic the young man had constructed from photographs taken in the woods the far side of the lake, so he explained. It could be hers for a reasonable sum. For a fraction extra, it could be fixed to run about the house and howl.

'I can't buy the wolf,' said Cristena. The young man looked sorry. 'But come in. There's something you can do.'

After she had plied him with alcohol, and resisted his amorous advances, which plainly were what he supposed she wanted, Cristena, lit by vodka and hot tea, had him pile up on the lawn the many water-colours of the artist's daughter. The house was programmed not to harm its own possessions, but he, with a large gardening implement, smashed these pictures and mashed them. After which, together, they burnt them all, and the yellow flames rose glamorously up into the winter sky. When it was done, not a crumb remained of the snow child, not a flake or shard. The young photo-hunter dug the snow over the black wound of the fire. Cristena gave him some money, and he went whistling away along the road, with his holostetic wolf leaping about him.

And that was the end of it. The end.

And that night, Cristena's husband called from a sky-scraping mansion countless miles off, having clinched some deal. He was a little drunk, too.

'I've destroyed them,' said Cristena. 'All of them.'

'Good. All what?'

'The icons of her bloody child that she never had.'

'What icons?'

Cristena shrieked into the phone: 'The ice maiden. Her pictures. I burnt them.'

Cristena's husband was in the wrong place to make a noisy fuss. He told her she had lost him thousands of international dollars. Cristena laughed. He should have, she said, all the royalties of her next novel.

When he had rung off, she put on a disc of Shostakovich and filled the house with it. She let the windows blaze towards the lake. She sat late working out a scenario for the house to redecorate itself again, in saffron and blue. All the furniture should be moved around, and she would buy new drapes in the city. When her husband returned, he would wonder where he was.

In two weeks the house was changed to a gas flame: azure and yellow. There were new pictures and prints in all the corridors and rooms. Cristena had spent two or three days in the city, choosing blueberry and primrose curtains. The contact with people, of whom the photohunter had been the herald, hardened and revived her. At length she was ready to withdraw again into her mental vase of music, books and television.

Outside, the world stayed obdurately white, the lake shiny black beneath its ice. Cristena had had the berries stripped off all the bushes.

Cristena had almost finished her novel, the first part of which she had limpidly and easily rewritten. She sat working on the couch she had had reupholstered, her back supported by flaxen cushions. The television fluted faintly in the corner of the room. Something about the picture summoned Cristena's attention, and she looked up.

The snow had filled the screen. It was utterly white. Cristena frowned. She was about to press the adjustment control when the whiteness opened out into a petal, and so into a single flower, and then the camera sprang back and there was a girl dressed in white and holding the white flower. She bowed low, and her long black hair, smooth as poured ink, fell forward to the ground. Cristena sat bolt upright, and her writing smacked on the carpet. Without knowing what she did, she turned up the volume.

'And here is Snow-Drop,' said the voice of the television, 'one of the stars of the circus.'

The girl wore a short white costume and white tights that covered her from neck to toe to wrist, but described every inch of her young pliancy. The whiteness was coruscated by spangles. When she sprang suddenly over in a somersault, she glittered like a firework, and her hair sprayed out in a fantastic smoke.

Seven small figures ran across the space, which seemed to be that of a large arena. They wore red and black. Cristena thought they were children, but their thick dark hair, muscular faces and forearms, enlightened her.

They were dwarfs. They formed a pyramid and tumbled down, rolling expertly to the white satin feet of the girl called Snow-Drop. She then arched over backward, making a hoop, and they trotted in a train under her. Next they lifted her up high and raced along carrying her, in the way ants carry a leaf.

There was a familial resemblance. Cristena wondered if Snow-Drop was related to the dwarfs. Although perfectly proportioned, she was very slight and petite. She looked about fourteen years old.

The dwarfs set Snow-Drop down. She coiled herself up into a cross-legged snake, while her seven companions bounced into position about her. In tableau, the dwarfs grinned. They had poised, good-looking faces, and seemed quite composed and happy with their lot. The girl also smiled.

This image was replaced by a garish sign, the fiery neon of the circus, which was performing in the city. Snow-Drop and the dwarfs were to be seen every night.

The television reverted to a rather sedentary play.

Cristena switched it off.

She walked uneasily about the room. She felt a strange excited dread. For it was as if she herself had conjured up Snow-Drop in the mirror of the television.

As if, by breaking and burning Snow-Drop's image, she, Cristena, who had never wanted children, had given Snow-Drop life. For Snow-Drop was the artist's unborn daughter, correct in each detail, even to her pale red mouth.

Every evening, for several nights, the same advertisement came on the television, and Cristena watched it. Sometimes other circus acts were shown as well, a man who swallowed clocks, a woman who danced extravagantly on the head of a pole. But Snow-Drop was always there, bowing, somersaulting, making herself into an arch, carried by the ant-like dwarfs, sitting in their midst. Beyond her name, which was probably any way false, no information was given.

It seemed to Cristena that a net had been cast for her and that slowly she was being pulled in to a snowy shore. It was useless to dissemble. She knew she would eventually go to the city, to the circus. There was even a vague fear that if she delayed too long, the circus might have moved on, and she would have missed it. At last this fear got the better of her.

An automatic hire car drove her along the frozen road, back into the icicled city, and delivered her at the entrance of the theatre where the circus was resident.

Cristena took a gilded seat at the front of the auditorium. She was nervous, and as the spangled performers swung or pirouetted or leapt past, she imagined they stared recognisingly into her face with eyes as cruel as knives.

When the moment came for Snow-Drop's act with the seven dwarfs, Cristena was trembling, and she took some large gulps from a golden flask.

The dwarfs came springing out like seven sable cats. Snow-Drop appeared ethereally, wafted down on wires from the roof of the stage. She was dressed like a princess, in a long alabaster gown and diamante tiara. But she peeled off the dress and wires, to reveal her sequined second skin, and turned a series of cartwheels. At each revolution she went by one of the dwarfs, who in turn began to cartwheel. The eight forms twirled about each other until Cristena was giddy and shut her eyes.

When she opened them again the dwarfs were busy raising a body mountain up which Snow-Drop walked, and next they became a body sea on which she swam.

The dwarfs made Snow-Drop the axis of every pattern. They were landscapes over which she travelled and buildings into which she went and from whose windows she looked out.

By prancing off each other's shoulders, they made her seem to juggle them – the audience laughed and clapped – and at one point they became an animal, a dwarf for each leg and three dwarfs composing a body, head and waving tail. Snow-Drop sat on its back and it cantered to and fro, at last rearing up and catapulting her away into a scintillant triple spin.

Unlike all the other acts, neither the dwarfs nor Snow-Drop seemed ever to glance into Cristena's face. As they went through their plasticene antics, their eyes were fixed wide and brilliant and far away.

Cristena's nervousness gradually left her. She observed the acrobats with condescending interest. She began to want them to notice her. She wanted beautiful Snow-Drop, white and black and red, to look at her, to *know* her. It was not possible; realisation should be only on one side. It occurred to Cristena they were actually ignoring her, cutt*ing her*, but that of course was absurd.

Finally there was a *danse macabre*, during which three of the dwarfs stood on each other to fashion a tall man, with whom Snow-Drop waltzed. But Snow-Drop grew dizzy and fell down and died. The dwarfs bore her to the centre of the stage, where they described a funeral, and buried her in their dark bodies. Then a spot-light sun shone on the mound, and a white shoot pierced up through the earth of dwarfs. Snow-Drop dived in graceful slow-motion up into the air and was reborn like her name flower, to great applause.

As they bowed, Cristena stared at them, the seven handsome dwarfs and Snow-Drop. But their faces were like enamel masks. When they darted off the stage, anger flushed through Cristena, hotter than the vodka in her flask.

Soon after she was outside the theatre, standing back among some bare trees below the Stage Door, while across the street, the hire car waited like an obedient ghost.

A group of other people had also gathered here, and a number of children with autograph books. Artists emerged and were beaming and gracious. Presently the dwarfs came out all together in wonderful fake fur coats.

They were jolly, and teased the patrons and scared the children. In the street-lamps their eyes were now wicked and wise. Long after they had gone, when the autograph hunters had become impatient and many drifted away, Snow-Drop emerged. Unlike the dwarfs, she wore a skimpy black jacket and ankle boots. Her hair was done in a long plait. She spoke to her admirers solemnly and signed their books quickly, like a thief. Cristena watched, and wondered what she would do. But when Snow-Drop's fans had melted away, she walked directly down towards the trees. Cristena stepped out as if on cue.

'Hallo, how are you. Perhaps you remember me?'

Snow-Drop did not seen startled although she had halted at once. In fact an immediate slyness was apparent, a vixenish glaze of evaluation passing over her eyes. Then she smiled without opening her mouth and shook her head.

'Your mother ...' said Cristena. She added patronisingly, 'You would have been too young to recall.'

'I'm older than I look,' said Snow-Drop primly.

Her voice was flat and unpolished, and the statement offered its own obscure meaning, redolent of something murky.

'Well, would you like to see the house?' said Cristena boldly. She had planned nothing, but the words came as simply as in one of her novels.

'The house? Your house?'

'Yes, naturally mine. And we can have some wine, and perhaps dinner. The kitchen's fully automated.'

'That would be nice,' said Snow-Drop, in her cheap little voice. Only the under-pavement heating must have kept her slim legs from the cold in that short skirt and those unsuitable boots.

Cristena walked across the road, and Snow-Drop followed her neatly, docile. Under the lamps her face was just the face of the paintings, and her mouth had been lipsticked an even redder red.

There was no one left by the Stage Door, the street was empty, and Cristena did not think anyone had seen Snow-Drop come with her to the car. She was glad, for after all Snow-Drop was a little embarrassing. Yet, as the car drove them away into the countryside, Snow-Drop's awful loveliness filled the atmosphere like a low buzzing. Cristena felt the need to talk. She lied sumptuously.

'Your mother was so fond of you. I haven't seen her for so long.'

Without protest or overt cunning, Snow-Drop announced, 'I never knew my mother. I was brought up by the troop.'

'Are you close to them, the seven –'

'Oh, they don't like me,' said Snow-Drop, reasonably.

The house glowed at them from across the lake, and when the car brought them to the door, extra lights flamed on in welcome. Cristena could see Snow-Drop was impressed.

A nasty complacency had thinned her lips.

They went into the living room. Here, where the water-colours had hung in such abundance, Snow-Drop made a living sculpture. Cristena tensed for the house to respond in some way. But, when it did not, no poltergeist activity took place of any sort, she decided that she had already exorcised the architecture.

They drank a fresh yellow wine.

Cristena asked Snow-Drop questions about her life, and rather to her surprise Snow-Drop responded without either reticence or verbosity. She laid out events in bleak rows before Cristena. It was a sordid unjoyful existence which the Snow-Drop led, out of all keeping with her looks. And it had made her mean and ordinary in spite of herself.

She had not ascended to tragedy or grotesqueness, but plummeted to the mealy-mouthed and the dull. Only glints of acquisitiveness distinguished her, and it was obvious she reckoned she would get, was getting, something out of Cristena. Otherwise she dwelt in the shadow of the circus and especially of the dwarfs. She was their slave, seeing to their laundry by hand, shopping for and cooking their meals on those occasions they demanded it. Cristena suspected that Snow-Drop was also their sexual toy. For that matter, almost anyone's, maybe. There was a metallic fragrance of willingness, which grew stronger as the wine left the decanter and filled instead their bodies.

'Off-stage, do you always plait your hair?' asked Cristena.

'Shall I undo it?' asked Snow-Drop.

'Yes, why not? I've got a marvellous comb that perfumes the hair. We can go up. I'll show you my dresses. You might like to choose some. They'd be too big for you, but we can always have them re-tailored.'

They went up the stair and along a passage where the artist's paintings had hung, and into Cristena's dressing room.

Cristena threw open doors.

'Look, that crimson silk would suit you. My husband bought it. I never wear red. And this black one with sparkles.'

With a studied unselfconsciousness, Snow-Drop slipped off her tawdry skirt and top, and stood in faded under-things: dim pants and tights, and, since she did not wear a brassier, only a thin little cotton bodice to conceal her bosom. Her acrobat's body was perfect, firm slim muscle lightly padded by white satin, and the symmetrical rounded young breasts bobbing in their vest. She tried on the dresses greedily. Cristena pinched in material to show how well they would suit Snow-Drop once they had been altered.

From its case she brought the magic comb and switched it on. When it had heated up, she combed Snow-Drop's amazingly long tendrilly hair. A scent of warm roses, jasmine and cinnamon throbbed in the room. They drank more wine.

'There are some gorgeous underclothes too,' said Cristena. 'I never use them.'

She opened the drawers, and let fall a shower of black and white silk corsets, black stockings sewn with orchids, garters of crow lace with silver buckles.

With no apparent modesty or reluctance, the Snow-Drop pulled off her drab tights and pants, and up over her delicate head in a whirlwind of hair went the inadequate bosom-bodice. She sat on a chair and drew the embroidered stockings along her dainty legs, and fixed on the garters. She flexed her thighs and her firm, curved stomach moved, and her breasts quivered like smooth white birds. Cristena assisted her into the black corset shot with ivory silk. She fitted it round the swaying stem of body and tilted into the bone cups the birds of the breasts, so the candy pink tip of a nipple rose just above each frill. Cristena laced up the corset severely. 'You must wear it tight.'

Snow-Drop posed before the mirror. She raised her arms artlessly, and the pink sweets rose further from their black froth containers. Between the silky limbs, under the corset's ribboned border, Snow-Drop's private hair, dark and thick like the fur of a cat, seemed the blackest thing in the room.

'That's very pretty,' said Cristena.

She felt heavy, languid, tingling, mad. She put her hands around Snow-Drop's body and made a small adjustment to the corset top. Her fingers brushed an icing-sugar nipple. Snow-Drop giggled.

'Now, you mustn't be ticklish,' said Cristena. She tried the nipple again.

Snow-Drop squirmed, pressing back against her.

In the mirror, Cristena saw, the beautiful doll with its bosom popping from the frills, its hands-span waist, and its naked lower limbs, wriggling. Snow-Drop's eyes were shut and her red lips parted.

Cristena pulled the girl backwards against her body. She caressed her breasts, sought the V of coal-black fur. She watched in the mirror. Snow-Drop writhed. She parted her legs and thrust her buttocks into Cristena's belly.

She uttered tiny shrill squeaks.

Fire engulfed Cristena. She pinioned Snow-Drop, rubbing, tickling, squeezing, choked by the perfume of roses and cinnamon, hair and skin, drunken and furious, and the girl was screaming, in the glass a demon of black and white and red.

Cristena felt the climax roll up between her thighs turning her inner life, her soul, over and over in blind ecstasy, as Snow-Drop wailed in her grip and the room exploded.

When Cristena came to herself, Snow-Drop was sitting cross-legged on the floor. She sucked her thumb and played with the ribbons of the corset, like a spoilt child which knows it has been naughty, but that this will not matter.

Cristena told herself it would *not* matter, over and again, as she assisted the kitchen in the preparation of a lavish supper. Never in her life had she experienced such alarm. It was not shame, more terror. For Snow-Drop came of a dangerous, scurrilous race. Who knew now what she might do? For the moment she sat on the couch, still in the corset and still half nude, drinking wine and looking at the television, in whose speculative lens she had first appeared. Later it was possible she might be persuaded to go back to the city. But then again she might want to spend the night here. And after tonight, how many other nights? What payment would she exact, in emotion or hard cash? How luminous her eyes as she glanced about her at the furnishings of Cristena's husband's house.

Cristena put the last touches to the food and drink. Her hands were shaking, but she pulled herself together and made herself survey what she had done.

It was a meal of red, white and black, although she doubted the Snow-Drop would take this in, let alone appreciate it. White soft rolls and creamy cheeses, slices of palest chicken in an almond sauce, caviar, fat grapes as black as agate, pomegranate seeds, burgundy apples whose crisp hearts were the shade of virgin ice. In the decanter now a rich ruby wine.

As she followed the service trolley into the living room, Cristena wished there had been someone to pray to.

But there was not, she must deal with this herself.

'I hope you're hungry.'

'Oh yes. I like my food,' said the Snow-Drop, who had looked as if she lived on honey-dew. She began to eat at once; alcohol and orgasm had evidently stimulated her appetite.

Cristena observed. She was prepared to say, if pressed, 'No, I had dinner earlier. You have it all.'

But Snow-Drop, gobbling up everything in a prissy yet vulture-like way, did not bother with Cristena, did not seem to notice that her hostess ate nothing.

As more and more of the food and wine was consumed, Cristena's shaking increased. When Snow-Drop plucked up one of the gleaming red apples, Cristena flinched. Of all of the feast, she was afraid she had taken a chance with the apples.

Snow-Drop put the apple to her mouth and bit into it. Then, quite slowly, her jaw dropped. Cristena saw inside her mouth, to the piece of white and red apple lying on Snow-Drop's tongue. Snow-Drop turned to her. Snow-Drop looked madly inquiring. 'Mmm,' she said. Then her eyes turned up in their sockets and she slid down the couch on to the carpet.

She lay there half an hour, motionless. Then there was a small spasm, which did not wake her. Crystal urine flowed out and wet the rug. A thread of scarlet slipped between Snow-Drop's lips. That was all. She was dead. She could not be anything else. Cristena had crushed twenty tasteless soluble sleeping capsules in the wine, and in the sauces, meat, fish, cheese and fruit, had gone the odourless soft corrosive cleaning acids of the house, the unsmelling garden pesticides. She had burnished the apples with a vitriolic substance employed to polish the mirrors.

The house buried Snow-Drop's body without any difficulty in the garden. After the job had been done, the digger took up deep snow from the lawn and packed it in above the grave. But in any case that night new snow came down and covered everything.

If there were reports on the television of Snow-Drop's disappearance, Cristena, who studied the screen closely, did not see them.

Presumably no one knew where Snow-Drop had gone on the night of her vanishment, and perhaps ultimately nobody cared. The seven dwarfs had not liked her and would probably find it challenging to locate and train up another beautiful lost child as their helpmeet and victim.

Cristena felt no compunction. She had had to protect herself. She settled down and completed her novel, then put it into the machine to be typed. By the time her husband returned to the house, the book would be in the hands of her publishers, and she could present him with the advance, which would humiliate him.

He came home some weeks early, when the snow was still down across the landscape. Calling her from the airport, he told her that he was bringing two of his business associates, and in the background she heard their hearty, stupid and inebriated voices. Cristena was not pleased, but she made believe she did not mind, sure he would bring the men to upset her and she could ruin his trick by seeming unconcerned.

She went about the house behind the automatic dusters. For months she had thought of it mostly as hers. She did not suppose he would like the new colour scheme, and he was capable of having it changed. Cristena braced herself to be merry and careless.

The men arrived in the afternoon and came swaggering up to the house. Her husband was in the lead. He had put on yet more weight and she had never seen him look so ugly, as if he had done it on purpose.

For an hour or so the male colleagues sprawled in the living room, eating things the kitchen prepared, and drinking beer. Cristena's husband had greeted her with affectionate uninterest, and now largely ignored her, but neither did he remark adversely on the redecoration. Indeed, he abruptly praised it. 'The house is looking good. But wait until you see what I've brought for the garden.' And somehow he made it obvious he had deliberately not brought a present for Cristena, who did not deserve one, but for the house.

They went outside, into the freezing twilit day.

With the help of the house porter, Cristena's husband trundled a large lamp-like structure into the garden, and set it up among the birch trees. He threw a switch and the lamp began softly to hum. From its bowl a yellow light streamed out and bathed the slope. It became warm. Strange scents shot from the ground, the trees.

They were the smells of spring.

'The snow will be gone in minutes,' said Cristena's husband. 'The plants start coming up in half an hour. You can have a spring and summer garden in the middle of winter. Expensive, I'll admit, this sun-lamp, but wait till you see.'

They waited, and they saw. And presently, after they had been splashed with snow and mud from the broiling, roiling earth, they retreated into the living room again, and looked on from there.

The garden was in flux, in tumult. Snow rushed in avalanches from the trees and along the ground. A kind of seismic activity thrust up huge tumuli, which seemed to boil. And on these peculiar black mounds, the porcelain flowers of spring bubbled through.

'You see?' asked Cristena's husband excitedly.

Cristena did. It was only a case of time, and already she was leaden and self-possessed.

Finally, after only twenty minutes, sabotaged by the sun-lamp, the lid of dense snow had melted off and the sides of the grave gave way. The upheaval in the earth pushed from below, and the Snow-Drop came out once more from the dark.

The cryogenic cold had preserved her flawlessly. The pressure on her spine made her sit slowly up in the grave to the astonished wonder of the three gaping men. And she was as ever white as snow, black as wood, and her pale red mouth opened and the bit of apple, also exactly preserved, fell out. And so she sat there exquisitely, with her lips parted and her eyes closed, dead as a door-nail, until the men turned to Cristena with their questions.

These Beasts

From an Idea by John Kaiine

He was a tomb robber. Well. When you were dead, you were dead.

All came to it. The mighty in their gold and gems, the impoverished unknown, wrapped in rags, their legs broken to fit the grave. And even he, Carem, would one day die. He did not mind if someone robbed him, after death. Welcome, my friend.

It was this life that counted.

Oh, he had been born as no one in the splendid city among the pink rocks. Noom Dargh, once the seat of kings, but no longer. He had been a whore's son, sold at three months to another whore. At ten, evading the man who was his owner – spuriously charming, as Carem had learned to be, they all trusted him – he made off with traders. He was quick as fire. Handsome too.

Among the traders he learned his profession.

The caravan routes went all ways. And in the yellow deserts, stood up the strange bulbous stones, caught forever in mid-topple. 'What is that place?' 'Ah, we will show him.' It was a place of tombs.

They went by night. No moon. Things howled in the desert, but he was not afraid. No, not until they breached the stinking hotness of the rock and the bats, which laired there, poured outward – Then the man who liked Carem, consoled him. 'There's nothing here to hurt you. But look – what's that which shines?' What shone was gold, contrary to so many proverbs.

By the time he was a man, Carem had gained much knowledge, and some wealth. Let it be said, the wealth came from others and the knowledge was all to do with thievery. But Carem did not harm the living. No, he was kind to them. He gave to beggars in the street, and was generous with the girls he dated.

By his twenty-eighth year, he had a house on the edge of Noom Dargh, a house with gardens and channels of water, a house with courtyards and dove-cotes, and awnings embroidered by gold.

He had also two wives, Bisint, who was rich, and Zulmia, who was beautiful.

In the city they spoke of him with respect. No one publicly remembered any more what he did. Indeed, he did not do it, for now other men worked on his behalf, and brought him treasures by night through a secret walk in the starry garden.

Lucky Carem. A life from death.

One sunset as, half a mile away below his mansion, the city turned blood-red and the desert scarlet, someone came seeking Carem; would speak only to him.

They met on a shady terrace and drank fig wine.

'I hurried straight to you, sir,' said the visitor, a traveller from antique lands. 'You alone could do it. '

'Do what?'

'Get in, get out. It needs skill and wisdom. It needs *knowledge* of such things.'

'What things are they?'

The traveller smiled. 'They call yours a bestial career, but I say one does what one is good at.'

'You mean my shares in merchant enterprise.'

'No. Your tomb-robbery.'

Carem said, smiling too, 'Have I been insulted?'

'Not at all. You're known as a master. And this, believe me, who would not dare it, needs a master's touch.'

'You may explain. For purposes of amusement. If I laugh enough, you shall have gold to fill one hand, and sufficient silver to fill two.'

'Treble that. You will find you'll laugh your head off, Lord Carem.'

Then the traveller spoke of an ancient country, once astride the world, and now come down to ruination. Its great obsession, this land, had been the burial of its kings and princes – of whom there were many – in the most sumptuous and enduring manner. And, too, in deepest secret. Now and then one of these burial spots would be thought to have been discovered. Then everyone went mad. And, often as not, since they were usually also wrong, venturers came back with nothing, but sore bones and empty wallets.

'This *I* have, however,' said the traveller, 'is not only sure – and I can give you proof – it is infallible. Besides which, it is known. Spoken and dreamed of. A thin of sparkle and nightmare.'

'Is there the normal curse, then, on the tomb?' asked Carem, indolently. Had he been a fox, his ears would have stood up high enough to touch the awning overhead.

'A curse known as familiarly as the tomb. Indeed, the tomb is named for it. There in the waste beyond the pastures of the River Khenemy.'

'Oh, is it Stone-Beard's Palace? That was pillaged three years ago. So I've been led to believe.'

'Not there.'

'The Garden of Arches, then? That too. And only a wisp of gold got from it.'

'Not there.'

'More wine?' inquired Carem. 'A cake?'

'Yes, I will take more wine. The burial place I offer you is the Tomb of the Black Dog.'

Then Carem, despite the last trace of the sunset, paled. His eyes opened and closed, and opened. He said, 'Surely that is only a story.'

'Till now. Now it can be yours.'

'And your proof.'

Then the traveller took a purse out of his clothing, and out of the purse he drew a narrow gleaming snake. This he set on the terrace, where, after two or three convulsive movements, it brought up out of its jaws a small black egg.

The egg sat on the paving.

The traveller spoke a word that fell like a raw hot drop of unseasonal rain.

The egg burst, and there lay a tiny black figure of a dog at rest: its head erect, and its throat rimmed by gold.

'A copy of the image that guards the tomb?'

'Found in the sand not twenty paces from the area.'

Muttering a protective charm, Carem picked up the figurine and held it. It was unearthly cold. He put it down. It cast no shadow, turn it as he would.

'Tell me all you know,' said Carem.

The traveller did so. Presently much gold and silver was given over in handfuls.

At midnight they parted, the traveller and Carem, and Carem went prudently to sleep with his plain wife, Bisint, for in the morning he would be going away.

The journey to Khemeny took several months, longer than was ordinarily needful, since Carem undertook the end of it in disguise, as a poor lame pilgrim, seeker of the shrines of the holy River.

Many tiresome days Carem spent, smothered by dust and ringing his irritating little pilgrim's bell, at the gates of collapsed temples, until at last, moved apparently by that mystic urge which drives prophets and seers, he wandered out into the desert waste.

The desert of Khemeny was like no other.

Where the River was, emerald pastures swelled, with cows and cameloids feeding beneath palms heavy with dates, and lime green banana trees. Then there lay the strips of fields, and sacred groves, and thereafter the first of the waste, brown as an egg, where, in caves, the former inhabitants of old fallen cities lived, lighting at night their fires and lamps of horn, like yellow stars felled to the land.

After this, a place opened that was like hell.

The land was white, and blistered the soles through your boots, the sun was a ball of white matter, and the sky white, and here and there rose monuments of the race of Khemeny, which had passed away. Statue men a hundred feet tall, wielding swords of stone, towers and gateways that led nowhere, all blasted by a hot moistureless wind, the breath of something long dead.

Carem, though, had a map. Not to hand, but written accurately in his head.

So he trekked by day the burning waste, and slept by night under the suns of other indifferent worlds. And on the second evening, he reached a sort of cliff. And in the eastern front of it was a mark, that looked only natural, but not to him. It was like the face of a dog.

No time like the present.

Carem went to the cliff and stared hard, and saw how the rock was.

Then he put up his agile right 'lame' foot, and lifted himself. From the first step he discovered the second. They were set oddly, and were not safe. He negotiated them all, with only a little powdering of dust to show his passage.

Above, far up, the cliff was flat as a stone table.

Once there, it was possible to look for miles, and see nothing but the night time desert, with here and there, one of its ghastly monuments.

Instead Carem looked and saw a hag seated by a round hole in the stone.

'Stay,' said the hag. 'Let me tell you what you risk.'

'Very well,' said Carem.

'Once I was very young,' said the hag.

'That might be said of all of us.'

'I travelled here,' continued the hag, humourlessly. 'I sought to enter the Tomb of the Black Dog. Aieee! I did not know. I thought it the burial place of some great king, guarded by that fearsome guardian, Anubar, the Biter of Souls.'

Carem nodded.

The hag said, 'Know, it is the Tomb of the Black Dog Himself. So we discovered to our cost. He Himself lies buried here, that guardian invoked in so many other places.'

Carem shivered, but it was only the heat.

'Thus all of you died, granny, and you're a ghost.'

'Nay,' said granny, 'me alone He let live. But see,' and she opened her robe with her left hand to reveal horrid scars and omissions. 'He tore off my right arm and my right breast. I am His warning.'

'Thank you,' said Carem. 'Now you have warned me you may be off.'

The hag got up and walked away. She cast no shadow. That too the Black Dog had torn from her. She went down the cliff by another way, invisible to ordinary persons.

Oh, he was not alarmed. Not Carem.

He sat by the black hole in the stone and took a pipe from his garments. On this he blew. It made no noise.

It would sound however a few hours' journey away, at the spot to which he had earlier sent the men who would help him at the tomb. He had now merely to wait.

He first anointed himself from a phial, then stretched out in the hot night. The dead breath of the wind lulled him. He slept.

When the moon rose, the jingle of harness conveniently roused him again, and sitting up, he beheld the twenty men he had hired, who had gathered at the foot of the cliff.

Carem rose and poured on to the stone of the tomb some wine and oil.

'What are you doing?' demanded one of the men below among the cameloids.

'Making the first offering,' said Carem. 'Come up now, as I will direct you.'

Up they came. A mixed bag they were. Some aristocratic and anxious, others pure fresh scum. They crowded round him, and Carem pointed to the hole.

'The rope I have readied. Who will be first down into the tomb?'

No one thrilled at the chance.

Carem said, 'This gold piece, to the first.'

After this there were some offers.

Presently three men climbed down, one after the other.

'What do you see?'

'Darkness.'

'Yes, that's as it should be.'

Then Carem went down and the others followed him.

In the tomb; Carem struck a light and lit a torch.

It was very hot, as Carem was well used to, but no bats laired there. Nothing lived in that enclosure. Not even a spider or a beetle. Bones there were, however, on the floor.

The walls were brown, and painted dimly by a massive figure that had the head of a long-nosed black dog. At this the crew pointed uneasily.

Carem drew from his clothes a small dark bottle. He spilled out its contents on the stone floor. Fluid ran, and formed a pattern. It was a map, in liquid, of the tomb.

Just at that moment came a low soft growl.

The hired men, most of them, bleated with alarm.

But, 'It's only magic,' said one.

'Exactly so,' said Carem. 'You are meant to fear it and run away empty handed. Think of the treasures that lie in the inner chambers.'

The men were somewhat consoled. They rubbed their amulets and muttered.

'Do you see that door,' said Carem, consulting his liquid map, 'who will go through first?'

There was great rivalry as to who would not.

While they argued something came rushing.

It was like a wind, or five hundred hounds, packed close as fish in a shoal, running after game.

The man nearest the door was one minute there, and then his head was off. It was wrenched from his shoulders. Next the fellow beside him was disembowelled, and another split from throat to crotch. All this was done by an agency invisible.

With quick screams, and sometimes so swift there was no time for that either, the twenty men of Carem's hire landed in pieces and bits on the floor, where the bones of previous victims lay.

But Carem, who had anointed himself with a certain thing repellent to all dogs, was not touched.

When the last man had had his throat torn out, a low satisfied growl rang round the space.

'Thus I make the second offering,' said Carem.

Then he walked through the dark door without being molested, and through thirteen passages, right up to the farthest wall. There he kneeled and felt with his hands by the light of the torch.

Soon he made out a round door no higher than a child of three, and no wider than a child lying sideways.

Through that Carem crawled, and so entered the treasure vault.

There was just enough light to behold.

The room was stuffed with gold, and jewels, green and crimson, blue and white. But everything was on a little scale; even the emeralds no larger than a thumbnail, and the golden effigies of dogs and wolves, foxes and jackals were the size of acorns and peach stones.

Carem filled the bags inside his clothes, his boots, his loin-pouch. He opened the ready purses at his neck and waist. He put things into his mouth, and up his nostrils, and in his ears, and elsewhere, which shall be nameless.

Take as you find.

On the wall of this last room, which was a sort of kennel, was painted no dog, but a black eye. Carem took no obvious notice of it as he screwed a ruby into his navel. Sucking a last golden standing jackal with diamond eyes between his lips, Carem crawled back out of the inner place.

He had accrued a great amount, yet a greater was left. Let that, then, be the third offering, his temperance. For the rest, he would have reputation. That was worth a vaster amount than the store itself.

Back through the thirteen passages he waddled.

In the outer place, he stepped fastidiously over the bones.

He stood a moment to listen.

Somewhere something howled, but it was, as usual, on the desert outside.

Carem climbed the rope, awkwardly, and emerged into the boiling air, which was itself like the interior of a grave.

On the table top of the tomb, huge black paw marks were apparent in the moonlight, and overhead the mass of stars seemed to describe, for a moment, the skull of a dog.

Carem pulled up the rope, and spoke a word. The entry to the tomb, the hole, vanished.

Below the cliff most of the cameloids had run off. But a few remained, trembling and farting with fear. He would sell them at a handy village. Well, a shame to waste.

When he had got down from the cliff, Carem turned about on the sand, clanking and clinking from his weight of jewels and gold.

There on the smooth ground lay something black, pointing from him and away from the moon. He had kept his shadow. All was well.

On his return home, plain Bisint tactfully sent word that she was out of sorts, and beautiful Zulmia met Carem in the garden, plump as a white plum and garlanded with blue-black hair. Much joy he had of her, under the roses and lemon trees, while bees buzzed and the honeyed sun slowly set into the uncomplicated pink desert of Noom Dargh.

He did not tell Zulmia, or even Bisint, anything of his exploits, nor did he give them anything from his robbery. Instead he brought Zulmia a rope of pearls and sapphires to match her skin and eyes, and Bisint a rope of topaz to match her teeth.

The treasure of the tomb Carem sold carefully and meagrely. Soon nobles and lords sent word to him, and later might come the words of kings. He would be famous now. He would be feared as well as praised.

Zulmia approached her husband modestly. She told him, as if he, not she, had been clever, that she was with child.

'I am sure it's a boy, masterful husband. Only a male would spring from your loins.'

Carem was pleased, for never before, to his knowledge, had he reproduced himself.

He looked delightedly at his lovely wife, plumper than ever, her hair like silk, and at her feet her jet black shadow. All was wonderfully well.

How charmingly the days and nights passed then. Even Bisint was helpful, often ailing, and keeping to her rooms. If she should die, all her wealth would come to Carem.

He would think now, upon sunny evenings, watching the final noose of light about the towers of the city below, how he might give up for good his profession. How he might turn to other things, from which none would dare refuse him entry. His son, after all, should inherit a business, not merely an empire of robbery.

On the night of the full moon, eight months later, Bisint peacefully passed away.

In a generous spirit, Carem left her her topazes to be buried in.

It was midday, and beautiful Zulmia had gone into labour. From the arbor where Carem sat drinking pomegranate wine, the house was closely visible, and her screams of pain might now and then be heard. They were good, rounded, healthy screams. It seemed the birth was going perfectly.

Carem saw a woman approaching through his gardens.

He took her for a servant bringing roast lamb and date leaves. He smiled, and poured a little wine on the ground, an old custom, for the child to be.

Something caught Carem's eye then. It was his fine dark shadow. How bold it was. How black.

Carem studied this. He noticed, oh yes, that some curious arrangement of the awning, or the arbor trees, had caused his shadow to take on a peculiar shape. It had two upright ears. Its nose was very long.

As Carem was pondering this, the servant woman came up to him. She was not his servant, but a squat female, veiled, with the sun shining through her. Around her neck gleamed faintly a rope of yellow stones.

'I am your dead wife,' said Bisint's uncomely ghost, unnecessarily. 'I have arrived to warn you.'

'That is most kind. Of what?'

'Hark.'

Carem harkened, and heard another loud scream from the house.

'Yes,' said Carem. 'That is Zulmia.'

'Indeed,' said Bisint, 'and she does well to scream, O stupid Carem, what did you bring away from the Tomb of the Black Dog?'

It was random to lie to or upbraid a ghost. 'Some trinkets,' he replied.

'What else, O stupid Carem?'

'Nothing.'

'Yes.'

'Only I, myself.'

'Stupid, *stupid* Carem,' emphasised Bisint, and disappeared.

Carem looked down for his shadow, that had pointed ears and snout. It too had vanished.

A particularly awful scream rocked through the air.

Carem glanced at his mansion.

Zulmia's windows, which were hung with crystal clear cloth, turned suddenly violently red. More, they appeared wet.

Then came other screams, the shrieks of women and bawling of men.

A noted physician sprang suddenly out of a window. He fell down among the lemon trees.

Carem rose and went towards him.

'What, pray, goes on?'

'Your wife is delivered,' said the physician. He had broken both his legs, but paid them no heed. His robe, like the windowhangings, was soaked by blood.

'A boy or a girl?' asked Carem.

'Neither. I will tell you,' said the physician, 'since I cannot run away. Something tore itself from the womb of your wife, up out of her belly. It burst her like an orange. It was dark. It had a pointed snout.'

Carem turned from the physician and gazed at the doorway of his house.

From the golden inner walk, something black was coming. It was tall and lean and moved lightly on its hind limbs.

Nothing had he brought from the Tomb of the Black Dog, save his loot and his body, with every aperture blocked. But one. One too small indeed to fill. And the shadow had gone with him. The shadow had run out of him, there among the roses.

From Carem's doorway stepped Anubar, Biter of Souls, He was black as night, in the mid of day. His ears stood up, His snout was long. In His clawed paws lay the remains of Zulmia's womb and round His feet, like bracelets were wrapped the entrails of others. He ripped the physician's body in half, in passing. Then stared at Carem, who bowed low and waited for death.

As well he might.

Under Fog
(The Wreckers)

Oh burning God,
Each of our crimes is numbered upon
The nacre of your eternal carapace,
Like scars upon the endless sky.

'Prayer of the Damned'
(Found scratched behind the altar in the ruined church at Hampp.)

We lured them in. It was how we lived, at Hampp. After all, the means had been put into our grip, and we had never been given much else.

It is a rocky ugly place, the village, though worse now. Just above the sea behind the cliff-line, and the cliffs are dark as sharks, but eaten away beneath to a whitish-green that sometimes, in the sunlight, luridly shines. The drop is what? Three hundred feet or more. There was the old church standing there once, but as the cliff crumbled through the years, bits and then all the church fell down on the stones below, mingling with them. You can still, I should think, now and then find part of the pitted face of a rough-carved gargoyle or angel staring up at you from deep in the shale, or a bit of its broken wing. The graveyard had gone, of course, too. The graves came open as the cliff gave, and there had been bodies strewn along the shore, or what was left of them, all bones, until the sea swam in and out and washed them away. Always a place, this, for the fallen then, and the discarded dead.

By day of my boyhood, the new church was right back behind the village, uphill for safety. The new church had been there for two hundred years. But we, the folk of Hampp, we had been there since before the Doomsday Book. And sometimes I used to wonder if they did it then too, our forebears, seeing how the tide ran and the rocks and the cliff-line.

Maybe they did. It seemed to be in our blood. Until now. Until that night of the fog.

My first time, I was about nine years. It had gone on before, that goes without saying, and I had known it did, but not properly what it was or meant. My nine-year-old self had memories of sitting by our winter fire, and the storm raging outside, and then a shout from the watch, or some other man banging on our door: 'Stir up, Jom. One's there.' And father would rise with a grunt, somewhere between annoyance and strange eagerness. And when he was gone out into the wind and rain, I must have asked why and Ma would say, 'Don't you fret, Haro. It's just the Night Work they're to.'

But later, maybe even next day, useful things would have come into our house, and to all the impoverished houses up and down the cranky village street. Casks of wine or even rum, a bolt of cloth, perhaps, or a box of good china; once a sewing machine, and more than once a whole side of beef. And other stuff came that we threw on the fire, papers, and books, and a broken doll one time and another, a ripped little dress that might have been for a doll, but was not.

On the evening I was nine and a storm was brewing, I knew I might be in on the Work, but after I thought not and slept. The Work was what we all called it, you see. The Work, or the Night Work, although every so often it had happened by day, when the weather was very bad. Still, Night Work, even so.

My father said, 'Get up, Haro.' It was the middle of the night and I in bed. And behind the curtain in my parents' bed, my mother was already moving and awake. My father was dressed. 'What is it, Da?' I whispered. 'Only the usual,' said my father, 'but you're of an age now. It's time you saw and played your part.'

So I scrambled out and pulled on my outdoor clothes over the underthings I slept in. I was, like my father, between two emotions, but mine were different. With me that first time, they were excitement, and fear. Truly fear, like as when we boys played see-a-ghost in the churchyard at dusk. But in this case still not even really knowing why, or of what.

Out on the cliff the gale was blowing fit to crack the world. There were lanterns, but muffled blind, as they had to be, which I had heard of but not yet properly seen.

Leant against the wind, we stared out into the lash of the rain. 'Do you spot it, Jom?'

'Oh ah. I sees it.'

But I craned and could *not* see, only the ocean itself roughing and spurging, gushing up in great belches and tirades, like boiling milk that was mostly black. But there was something there, was there? Oh yes, could I just make it out? Something like three thin trees massed with cloud and all torn and rolling yet caught together. 'You stay put, Haro,' said my father. 'Here's a light. You shine that. You remember when and what to do? As I told you?'

'Yes, Da,' I said, afraid with a new affright I should do it wrong and fail him. But he patted my shoulder as if I were full-grown, and went away down the cliff path with the others. Soon enough I heard them, those three hundred feet below me, voices thin with distance and the unravelling of the wind, there under the curve of the crumbled white-green cheese of the cliff-face. Though I was quite near the edge, I knew not to go too far along to see, but there was a place there, a sort of notch in the crag, whereby I could see the glimmer of the lamps as they uncovered them. And I knew to do the same then, and I uncovered my lantern too.

So we brought it in. The thing with the clouded trees that was adrift on the earthquake of great waters. The thing that was a ship.

She smashed to pieces on the rocks below, where the tallest stones were, just under the surface at high tide, against rock and shale, and the faces of angels and devils, and against their broken wings.

This was our Night Work then. In tempest or fog we shone our lights to mislead, and so to guide them home, the ships, and wreck them on the fangs of our cliffs. And when they broke and sank, we took what they had had that washed in to shore. Not human cargo, naturally. That counted for nothing. It must be left, and pushed back, and in worse case pushed under. But the stores, the barrels and casks, the ironware and food and, if uncommon lucky, the gold, they were rescued. While they, the human flotsam, might fare as wind and darkness, and their gods – and we – willed for them, which was never well.

I saw a woman that night, just as the great torn creature of the vessel heaved in and struck her breast, with a scream like mortal death, to flinders on our coast. The woman wore a big fur cloak, and also clutched a child, and in the last minute, in intervals of the storm-roil, I saw her ashen face and agate eyes, and he the same, her son, younger than I, and neither moved nor called, as if they were statues. And then the ship split and the water drank them down. But there was a little dog, too. It swam. It fought the waves, and they let it go by. And when it came to land – by then I craned at the cliff's notch, over the dangerous edge – my father, Jom Abinthorpe, he scooped up the little dog.

And my reward for that first night of my Night Work was this little innocent pup, not yet full-grown as neither I was. Because, you will see, a dog can tell no tales, and so may be let live.

But the ship and her crew, and all her people, they went down to the cellars of the sea.

I was always out to the Work with the men after that. By the time I was eleven, I would be down along the shore, wading even in the high savage surf among the rocks, with breakers crashing sometimes high over my head, as I helped haul in the casks, and even the broken bits of spars that we might use, when dried and chopped, for our fires.

Hampp is a lorn and lonely place; even now that is so. And when I was a boy, let alone in my father's boyhood, remote as some legendry isle in the waste of the sea. But unlike the isles of legend, not beautiful, but bony bare. There were but a dozen trees that grew within a ten mile walk of the village, and these bent and crippled by the winter winds, in summer too there were gales and storms, and drought also. What fields were kept behind their low stone walls gave a poor return for great labour. And there was not much bounty given by the ocean, for the fish were often shy. The sea, they said, would as soon eat your boat as give you up a single herring. No, the only true bounty the sea would offer came on those nights of fog or tempest, when it drew a ship toward our coast and seemed to tell us: *Take it then, if you can.* For to do the Work, of course, was not without its perils. And to guide them in too required some skill, hiding the light, then letting out the light, and that just at the proper angle and spot. But finally the sea was our accomplice, was it not, for once drawn into that channel where the teeth of the rocks waited in the tide, and the green skull faces of the outer cliffs trod on into the water and turned their unforgiving cheek to receive another blow, the ocean itself forced and flung each vessel through. It was the water and the rocks smashed them. We did not do it. We had no such power, nor any power ever. And sometimes one of our own was harmed, or perished. Two men died in those years of my boyhood, swept off by the surge. And one young boy also? younger than I was by then, he broken in a second when half a ship's mast came down on him with all its weight of riven sail.

But ten ships gave up their goods in those years between my ninth and fourteenth birthdays, and I was myself by then a man. And the dog had grown too, my rescued puppy. I called him Iron, for his strength. He had blossomed from a little black soft glove of a thing to a tall and long-legged setter, dark as a shadow. He was well-liked in our house, being quiet and mannerly. Also I trained him to catch rabbits, which he killed cleanly and brought me for my mother's cooking. But he hated the sea. Would not go even along the cliff path, let alone to the edge with the notch, or down where the beaches ran when the tide was out. Whenever he saw me set off that way to fish, he would shift once, and stare at me with his great dark eyes that were less full of fear than of disbelief. Next he would turn his back. And here was the thing too; on those nights when the weather was bad, and the watch we posted by roster spied a ship lost and struggling, Iron would vanish entirely, as if he had gone into the very air to hide himself.

I thought after all he did not know what we were at. Certainly, he would eat a bowl of the offal of any beef or bacon or whatever that came to my family's portion out of a wreck. By then, I suppose, it had no savour of the sea.

He had not known either that we let his ship, his own first master likely on that ship, be drowned. Iron only knew, I thought, that my father, and next I, had plucked him from the water after all else was gone.

For a while I had recalled the cloaked woman and her son. I said nothing of it, and put it from me. And soon I had seen other sights like that, and many since that time. The worst was when they tried to save each other, or worse yet, comfort each other. Those poor souls. Yet, like my dog, I would stare then turn my eyes away. I could not help them. Nor would I have, if I could. We lived by what we took from them, lived by their dying. All men want and will to live. Even a dog does, swimming for the shore.

Iron is here now. He leans on my leg and the leg of the chair. Strange, for there is iron metal there also, but he does not know this. They are kind, compassionate to have let him in. Well then. Let me tell you the rest.

I had seen fogs often, and of all sorts. Sea-frets come up like a grey curtain but they melt away at Hampp and are soon gone. The other sort of fog comes in a bank, so thick you think you might carve it off in chunks with your rope-knife. And it will stay days at a time, and the nights with them.

In such a fog sometimes a ship goes by, too far out and never seen, yet such is the weird property of the fog that you will hear the ship, hear it creak and the waves slopping on the hull of it, and the stifled breathing of the sails if they are not taken in and furled. It is often worthwhile to *go* down with extra lanterns then, and range many lamps too along the cliff by the notch, for the ship's people will be looking for landfall and may see the lights, even in the depths of the cloud. But generally they do not. They pass away like ghosts. After they were gone men cursed and shrugged, wasting the lamp-oil as they had and nothing caught. But now and then a ship comes in too far, mislead already by the fog, and by the deep water that lies in so near around our fanged rocks. For surely some demon made the coast in this place to send seafarers ill, and Hampp its only luck. These ships we would see, or rather the shine of their own lanterns, and they were heard more clearly, and soon they noticed our lamps too, and sometimes we called to them, through the carrying silence, called lovingly in anxious welcome, as if wanting them safe. And so they turned and came to us and ran against the stones.

That night of the last fog I was seventeen years, and Iron my dog about eight, with a flute of grey on his muzzle.

I had been courting a girl of the village, I will not name her. But really I only wanted to lie with her and sometimes she let me, therefore I knew we would needs be wed. So I was preoccupied, sitting by the fire, and then came the knock on the door. 'Stir up, Jom Abinthorpe. Haro – waked already? That's good. There is a grey drisk on the sea like blindness, come on in the hour. And one's out there in it, seen her lamps. Well lit she is, some occasion she must have for it. But sailing near, the watch say.'

So out we went, and all the village street was full of the men, shouldering their hooks and pikes and hammers, and the lanterns in their muffle giving off only a pale slatey blue. By now I did not even look for my dog Iron, though a few of the men had their dogs with them, the low-slung local breed of Hampp, with snub noses and big shoulders, that might help too pulling the flotsam to shore.

We went along the cliff, near theedge now all of us, but for the youngest boys, three of them, that we posted up by the notch. Then the rest of us went down to the beach.

It was a curious thing. The fog that night was positioned like a fret, one that stayed only on the sea, and just the faintest tendrils and wisps of it drifted along the beach, like thin ribbons of smoke from off a fire.

The water was well in, creaming clear on the shale, the tide high enough, and not the tips of the fangs below showing even if the vessel could have made them out. But the ship was anyway held out there, inside the box of the fog, under the fog's lid, like a fly in thick grey amber.

It was a large one, too, and as our neighbour had said, very well lit. In fact crazily much-lit, as if for some festival being held on the decks. We all spoke of it, talking low in case our words might carry, as eerily they did through these fogs. The watchman came and said he reckoned at first the ship had caught fire, to be so lighted up. For she did seem to burn, a ripe, rich, flickering gold. How many lamps? A hundred? More? Or torches maybe, flaming on the rails –

A dog began barking then behind us, a loud strong bell of a bark. Some of the men swore, but my father said, 'It's good. Let them know out there land is here. Let them hear and come on. Let's show the lanterns, boys. I'll bet this slut is loaded down with cash and kickshaws – we'll live by it a year and more.'

And just then the vessel slewed, and the line of it, allshown in light, altered shape. We knew it had entered the channel and was ready to run to us.

Something came rushing from the other way though, and slammed hard against my legs, so I staggered and almost fell. And turning I saw my dog there. He was standing four-square on the shale, panting and staring full at me with eyes like green coals. Brighter than our uncovered lamps they seemed.

I said, Iron would never come to the sea, nor anywhere near it.

'Wonders don't cease,' said my father. 'The dog wants to help us with it too. Good lad. Stay close now –'

But Iron turned his eyes of green fire on my father, and barked and belled, iron notes indeed that split the skin off the darkness. And then he howled as if in agony.

'Quiet! Quiet, you devil, for the sake of Christ! Do he want to sour our luck?' And next my father shouted at me. I had never seen him afraid, but then I did. And I did not know why. Yet my whole body had fathomed it out, and my heart.

And I grabbed Iron and tried to push him back. 'Not now, boy. Go back if you don't care for it. Go home and wait. Ask Ma for a bit of crackling. She knows when you ask. She'll give it you. Go on home, Iron.'

And Iron fell silent, but now he sank his teeth in my trouser and began to tug and pull at me. He was a muscular dog, though no longer young, and tall, as I said.

The other men were surly and restless. They did not like this uncanny scene, the flaming ship that drove now full toward us and cast its flame-light on the shore, so the cliffs were shining up like gilt, and the opened lanterns paled to nothing – and the dog, possessed by some horrible fiend, gnawing and pulling, his spit pouring on the wet ground in a silver rain, as if he had the madness.

And then there came the strangest interval. I cannot properly describe how it was. It was as if time stuck fast for a moment, and the moment grew another way, swelling on and on. Even Iron, not letting go of me, stopped his tugging and slavering. And in the hell of his eyes I saw the wild reflection of the gold fire of the ship growing and moving as nothing else, for that moment, might.

'By the Lord,' said my father softly, 'it's a big one, this crate.' It was such a foolish, stupid thing to say. And the last words I ever did hear from my father.

They call them she; that is, the seafarers call each ship she. As if she were a woman. But we did not. We could not, maybe, seeing as how we killed them in the Night Work.

Just as we ignored the women who died with the ships, and the children who died.

But now I must call it she. The ship, the golden ship.

Believe this or not, as you will.

I do not believe it, and I saw it happen. I never will believe it, not till my last breath is wrung from me. And then, I think, I shall have to.

The moment which had stuck came free and fled. We felt time move, felt it one and all. It was as if the two hands of a clock had stuck, and then unstuck, and the ticking of it and the moving of it began again.

But as time moved, and we with it, it was the *ship* instead that froze. Out there at the edge of the grey slab of the fog, under it, yet visible now as if only through the flimsiest veil. She was well in on the last stretch. She could not stay her course. No vessel, even a mighty and huge one, could have stayed itself now. So far she had driven in, she must hurl on towards her finish against the rocks, and on the faces of the cliffs around, those that crowded out into the sea to meet her. Yet – she did not move. Our clock ran, hers had halted. But oh, something about her there was that moved.

I behold her still in my mind's eye. So tall, six or seven decks she seemed, and so many masts, and all full-laden with her sheets. There was not a man on her that I could see. None. Nor any lamps or torches to light her up so bright that now, almost free of the fog, half she blinded me. No, she blazed from something else, as if she had been coated, every inch of her, in foil of gold, her timbers, her ropes, her sails – coated in gold and then lit up from within by some vast and different fire that never could burn upon this world, but maybe under it – or high above. Like the sun. A sun on fire at her core, and flaming outward. Lampless. *She* was the lantern. How she burned.

Not a sound. No voice, no motion. Even the ocean, quiet as if it too had congealed – but it moved, and the waves came in and lapped our boots, and they made, the waves, no sound at all.

And then the dog, my Iron, he began to worry at me, hard, hard, and I felt his teeth go through the trouser and he fastened them in my very leg. I shouted out in pain and turned, not knowing what I did, as if to cuff him or thrust him away. And by that the spell on me was rent.

I found I was running. I ran and sobbed and called out to God, and Iron ran by me and then just ahead of me. It seemed to me he had me fast by an invisible cord. I had no choice but to fly after him. And yet, oddly, a part of me did not want to. I wanted only to go back and stand at the sea's brink and look at the ship – but Iron dragged me and I could not release myself from the phantom chain.

I was up on the cliff path when I heard them screaming behind me and some one hundred and fifty feet below. This checked me. I fell and my ankle turned and a bone snapped, but I never heard the noise it made, for there was no sound in that place but for the shrieking of the men, and one of them my father.

Of course, I could no longer stir either forward or back. I lay and twisted, feeling no pain in my foot or leg, and stared behind me.

And this is what I saw. Every man upon that shore, every lad, even the youngest of them, ten years old, and the dogs, those too, and those screaming too as if caught in a trap, all these living creatures – they were racing forward, not as I had inland, but out toward the sea, toward the fog, toward the golden glare of the ship – But they howled in terror as they did so, men and beasts, nor did they run on the earth. They ran on *water*. They ran through the air. The three children from the cliff-top – they too – off into the air they had been slung, wailing and weeping, and whirling outward like the rest, And up and up they all pelted, as if racing up a cliff, but no land was there under their feet.

Only the ship was there ahead of them, and she waited. The thin veil of the outer fog hid nothing. The light of her was too fierce for anything to be hidden. The men and the boys and the dogs ran straight up and forward, unable to stay their course until, one by one, they smashed and splintered on the cliff-face of the golden ship, on the golden fangs and cheek and rock of the ship. I saw so clear their bones break on her, and the scarlet gunshot of their blood that burst and scattered away, not staining her. As they did not either, but fell down like empty sacks into the jet black water. Till all was done.

After which, she turned aside, gently drifting, herself as if weightless and empty, and having moved all round she returned into the fog, under fog, and under night and under silence. She slid away into the darkness. Her glow went soft and melted out. The fog closed over. The night closed fast its door, and only then I heard the waves that sucked the shale, and the pain rose in my leg like molten fire.

They will be hanging me tomorrow. That is fair; it is what I came to the mainland for, and made my confession. At first I never said why I had had to. How I had crawled up the path, with my dog helping me. And in the village of Hampp all the faces, and seeing that each one knew yet would not speak of it. My mother, she like the others. How I stayed two months there, alone, until I could walk with a stick, and by then almost everyone had left the place, the empty houses like damp caves. And then I left there also. But I came here, and my dog quite willing to cross water, and I found a judge, and was judged.

Men have gone to search the waters off the coast below Hampp. They find nothing of the dead ships. We took all there was to take. As for corpses, bones, theirs and ours are all mingled, like the gargoyles and angels in the stones of the beach.

When I did tell the priest of the ship, he refused to believe me. So I have told you now and let it be written down, since I was never learned to make my letters.

You see there is an iron manacle on my ankle, but it is quite a comfort. It supports the aching bone that snapped. The rope perhaps will support my neck and then that will be crushed, or it will also break, and then I will leave this world to go into the other place, from which golden things issue out.

It is kind they let me say farewell to Iron, my dog. Yes, even though he is no longer mine. They have told me a widow woman, quite wealthy, is eager to have him, since her young son is so taken with Iron, and Iron with him likewise. I have witnessed it myself, only this morning from this window, how the dog walked with the child along the street, Iron wagging his strong old tail that is only a touch grey to one side. The child is a fair boy too, with dark sad eyes that clear when he looks at Iron. And certainly his mother is wealthy, for her cloak is of heavy fur.

That is all then. That is all I need to say.

No. I am not sorry for my village. No, I am not afraid to go to the scaffold. Or to die. No, I am not afraid of these things. It is the other place I fear. The place that comes after. The place they are in, the men of Hampp, and my father too. The place where she came from. The Ship. I cannot even tell you how afraid I am, of that.

Virgile, the Widow

What thou seest when thou dost wake,
Do it for thy true-love take …

A Midsummer Night's Dream
William Shakespeare

Act One

Laure saw the woman one rainy morning in late autumn, walking along the bank of the canal, her reflection gliding beside her in the water among the still falling yellow and brown leaves of ashes and chestnuts.

Bois-la-Diane was famous for its woods, which kings had hunted even a hundred years ago. For little else. The town was small and winding. It had one church, one rather distanced chateau, and the usual primordial shops – the chemist, the baker and patisserie, and several cranky, sly dressmakers, where women, twisted out of shape by years of sewing, attempted, spider-like, to lure young girls to dooms of drapes and flounces ten years out of fashion.

The woman on the canal bank was certainly not dressed in this way. She had a timeless look, almost (Laure thought), Grecian – but less in the manner of a classical Greek *woman* than a Grecian *vase* – tall, slim, and amphorally curved. She was all in black, the deepest mourning. Not an instant s relief of any other shade. Even her gloves – black. And the umbrella – blacker. On the canal, the white swan had dipped its head and sailed away. As Laure got closer and closer, she noted the woman had the blackest hair, and long black eyebrows, cruel-arched like scimitars. Her eyes were also black, and they had the glassy obsidian surface of most very dark or pale eyes. So Laure couldn't tell if the woman saw her at all. Then Laure had the urge to speak. But Laure was oddly as timid as she was impulsive and arrogant. What could she say –

Who are you, madame? Where are you going? Are you new to this town I have lived in almost all my twenty years?

'She wasn't a Parisian,' Laure pronounced later. 'Oh no. Perhaps not from any city. Yet not provincial either. She seemed to belong nowhere at all. Of course not to this place.'

'You could tell so much?' sneered Sophrine.

'Anyone could. Even you.'

Sophrine tossed her head like the heroine of a (badly written) racy novel. She was herself dressed very simply in white, and her strawberry-brown hair partly up and partly down in an untidy style. Laure looked at her with contempt. Usually she felt contempt for Sophrine, as for many others, including her own aunt, Madame Deschampeigne (a vague, dim figure, restrictive yet inconclusive, like a frigid larva). Sometimes, this habit of contempt worried Laure. But she was young. There was a false unspoken sense that everything had time to change, and probably for the better.

'Well, but was she as elegant as Artemise Lejay?'

'Lejay? Good God, far more. What do you think?'

Sophrine shrugged. 'To me, Artemise Lejay is the most fascinating woman we can boast at present in this town. Obviously it could have been la Reine, in her day. But now she's old. Even so, even so … One sees it sometimes. Her eyes. She's never lost them. Still so blue.'

Laure turned her back on Sophrine and walked to the lace-shrouded window of the sitting room. Sophrine's father's house, and all its fellows, gave straight onto a cobbled thoroughfare of Bois-la-Diane. The street was narrow, in spots unpaved, really a track, with puddles, and the yellow tearful trees drooping here and there along it. Such streets, unlike the houses, pleased Laure, quite. They belonged – or seemed to – to earlier eras, which she preferred. Nothing offended Laure so much, she thought, as the present day. The single advantage of modernity was that no one had forcibly married her off – but even there she had stayed exempt mainly due to the aloofness of the Aunt. Others certainly were forcibly married, or at least acquiesced to the sham. Most notably that very Artemise Lejay from Sophrine's pedestal.

Now Sophrine stole up, slipping her hand around Laure's waist. They looked from the window at the rainy street and sighed in unison. *Oh this dreary provincial life.*

'Do you think you only imagined your Grecian mystery?'

'It's possible. Or she was a phantom. The ghost of a young woman who drowned herself in the canal, perhaps. In mourning for her own death.' Laure thought, *Why am I saying this? She was as real as you are, real as the street. More real. Much.*

Every Wednesday, and sometimes Saturday, there would be a sort of unofficial Ladies Club held at the chateau of la Reine. It began around the hour of the bucolic four o'clock dinner, which la Reine had altered to a frugal luncheon. It drifted on through an evening, sometimes an ersatz dinner, with only the old Peridot to wait on them, on and on to midnight, and frequently past midnight. If the authoress of the function had been anyone other than la Reine – Sidonie Aubade-Valents – perhaps such a situation would not have been countenanced. But anyone could trace la Reine's provenance far back before the Revolution. She was one of those country aristocrats who had kept her credentials, and with them her sense of power. Besides, her marriage had been a grand one, and she had given birth to six sons, each of whom subsequently died, like the husband, of war or peace, in one way or another. To be admitted to her circle was not a favour bestowed lightly. Some that wished for it hadn't received it at all. And if the women, married or un, young, mature, middle-aged or older, wandered about her house, or the overgrown grounds in summer, their hair down, and smoking cigars, well, the town largely ignored it. What could women alone do, after all, that was so bad? They were only women. The circle admitted no male. Once only an irate husband had arrived, Monsieur Gauveille, whose wife Marguerite was just then seated at the piano in her chemise. As her agile hands struck off silver beads of Chopin, the long doors to the terrace, which stood open on the two o'clock summer morning, were filled by Maurice Gauveille, a revolver in his hand.

'There, you slut! I know what you're up to. You whore of Babylon – look at you – half naked.'

'But Maurice, it's such a hot night –'

'Undressed for high jinks. You bitch – you little cunt.'

The other women stood looking at him, Artemise Lejay, as Sophrine hinted, her breasts bare, and a clutch of cherries in her hand bleeding down her arm. And Maurice Gauveille raised the gun. But from her great chair la Reine stood up and looked levelly at him. Laure had not been there, at this time, she was only twelve, and Sophrine hadn't been there either, she got the story from others.

'Monsieur, do please come in and sit down. Shall I ring for cognac?' inquired la Reine.

Gauveille faltered, but then he barked, 'I'll start with you – I'll blast off your head, you monstrous and unnatural woman!'

La Reine, who was as always, in public, impeccably clothed, with a fabulous diamond, an heirloom, on her collar, gazed at him. ('Like a stone,' said Sophrine.)

'Monsieur, you forget yourself.'

'I have been forgotten, yes. But here I am.'

'I have no sons to defend me,' said la Reine, 'and my husband, that his regiment was used to call the King, lies in the cemetery at Pere Chasse. What is it you can fear, monsieur, in this house, save your own brutishness?'

Gauveille could not speak the words, only offer invective that in no true way approximated. He threw the gun down in the fireplace – where Artemise quickly darted to retrieve it – and fell at the feet of Marguerite, sobbing.

Told this story five years later, Laure had remained impervious to its danger. She was not shocked. Hadn't any proper sense of how close the roomful of women had come, and one day again might come, to maiming and retributory death.

Men had slight significance for Laure. Her father had been only a periphery figure, soon gone, and her mother hastened after him.

Besides, the story of the revolver might be only a legend of the tribe, the tribe that met in the chateau of Sidonie Aubade- Valents.

Sophrine first brought Laure to the house one other late summer evening. A year older than Laure, Sophrine had left the country school, and neatly set herself up typing letters and copying accounts for her father's grocer shop. He paid her little, but then she had all her board and lodging, and never went short (as she phrased it) of any small trifle she fancied. When her mother hinted at suitors or a trousseau, Sophrine would stroke her father's brow (he was now the shorter): 'I shall only marry if I can find a man as excellent as papa!' As to the afternoons and nights at the chateau, 'She is a great lady,' Monsieur Papa would declare. 'It shows she has a fine egalitarian awareness, Madame Aubade. And an honour for Sophie. Stories? What stories? What nonsense. Invented by jealous gossips. And besides, think ahead, Madame,' this to his wife, Sophrine's mama, 'the old woman may leave our girl a little something when she dies. It can't be long now. She's seventy if she's a day.'

As Sophrine led Laure up overgrown steps through an old garden, the cicadas fell suspiciously silent, then resumed once more. Laure was now fifteen or just sixteen – her birth-date unsure. She was nervous. She had only seen la Reine once or twice, driven about town in her carriage, which still carried an ancient crest on its doors. This visit tonight had arisen like smoke from a pair of afternoons' fire. Laure and Sophrine had gone into the woods, like children, gathering early mulberries, hazelnuts, and so on. 'Oh now,' exclaimed Sophrine, 'a bird's nest's dropped into my hair.' They struggled to free it, and Sophrine's hair fell down in a shining shower. They were pressed breast to breast, as Laure believed, quite pragmatically. She had become used to the sudden flashing feelings that happened at such times. Not sought to prolong or explain them to herself. An innocent.

But then Sophrine had laughingly leaned forward, her breath scented with cinnamon and fruit and her lips reddened by berries, and kissed Laure with a flicker of the tongue. 'Do you like that? Can you taste mulberries or raspberries?'

'Mulberries.'

'Let me do it again. See if you can taste the raspberries, too.' Laure forgot about the raspberries. So did Sophrine, it seemed.

There was a tree with a convenient low, wide dry lap. It was densely warm, and the forest so still but for the birds and small animals that scattered through it, none of them minding. They dallied for hours, moaning with unbearable excitement – Laure had no inkling how to resolve the glorious torture, although the sight and feel of Sophrine's breast, Sophrine's investigation of her own, sent waves, almost convulsions, through her centre. Finally Sophrine grappled her quite roughly, until Sophrine's thigh between her own, her own between Sophrine's, produced an explosion of heat, and so a heavenly fit, during which they rolled right off the low chair of the tree, among the bracken and powdery dry mulch of last year's leaves.

Nothing much was said. Only Sophrine: 'Do you love me now?' And Laure, slightly offended, 'What? Why?'

'Ungrateful little beast. After what I've shown you.' Even so, presently, the experience was repeated, in Laure's bedroom at the Aunt's house (with muffled shrieks into pillows, but the Aunt was deaf). Thereafter came the invitation to attend the chateau.

'But – you go there?'

'Of course. And so can you.'

'But why?'

'Oh, Laure. What a simpleton you are. Why do you think? Oh don't sulk. It's because you like what we do.'

Laure thought. She pivoted on one hip and stared.

'You mean *that's* what it's all about – all the women who go to the Aubade chateau?'

'Of course it is. What else?'

The walk to the chateau, half a mile from the town, had been at sunset along a lane overhung by glowing chestnut trees. The walls were high, in places unsafe. They climbed skittishly through at a break rather than use the gates or carriage drive.

In the grounds, the ancient woods had seeded new woods. Weird paths trickled off to strange little false temples, glimmering in half-light. Five feet high, an ivied Pan played the syrinx under an elm. In the old garden too, nettles, clovers and wild garlic: docks grew like tall umbrellas and a cedar tree had torn its way through a terrace, shattering the stones with its roots.

It was dusk by then, altering to night. Stars littered the sky, growing ever brighter. An owl called, then swept out over the park on impossibly wide pale prehistoric-looking wings.

They emerged from the trees and fallen urns, and there were roses bursting over a broken wall, and the scent of stocks hung heavy as a velvet curtain. There was a lawn, with another statue on it, a stone girl, nude. And suddenly two other girls, not made of stone, ran out of the bushes, and away along one of the little paths. Their hair was down and although they were fully clothed, their feet were bare. They had a Bacchante wildness to them.

Sophrine began to hum Mendelssohn's musical setting of the Lullaby from *A Midsummer Night's Dream*. Oh yes, snakes with spotted skin – thorny hedgehogs – banks of wild thyme, too and flowers of purple dye –

Generally Sophrine's responses – Laure had always known, was well able to remember even after the pair of afternoons' fire – were trite. The responses, Laure's long-lost mother might have said, one would expect from a grocer's daughter. But the Mendelssohn was not at all of that type. That it was obvious only made it more perfect. Laure felt then a rush of freeing anticipation, and too desire.

'Shall we …?'

'Not yet.'

Through the bushes, by a choked pool. Steps and one more terrace, and then the chateau rose in a ghostly shadow on the last of the twilight, pushing up and next falling away and away. It was very big. There were rounded towers with turrets which, by day, would show a steely blue, or black or green where decaying tiles had dropped out. Doves nested in eaves, but now a sparse hail of bats spun about. There were lights, here and there. Sophrine walked straight in at two long lit open windows – the very ones made infamous by Monsieur Maurice Gauveille.

It was a salon, with a grand piano resting on an Aubusson carpet. Laure also noticed paintings, mirrors and low sofas in a lemon brocade. But she noticed these things really only in retrospect, and then they were so apt, so fundamental to what she would have expected, she wondered at first if she had been mistaken, made them up. Perhaps the room was really empty No *person* was in the room. Then the old woman entered. This was not the chateaus mistress, but a creature la Reine called, scathingly, her 'Jewel.' Peridot, one of her remaining servants.

Peridot had been at the chateau apparently since her girlhood, which must have been in the eighteenth century, from her looks. She was very short and small, walnut brown, her head bound and tied by thick dark grey hair, and poked forward like a tortoises.

'One, two,' said Peridot, counting Sophrine and Laure off on the air with her right forefinger.

Sophrine only looked amused.

'Herself will see you at once,' said Peridot.

She had an accent of the south, rounded and bronzy from the weather. Sometimes she used words and expressions Laure couldn't make sense of. Perhaps no one had ever fathomed them, only come to know what they meant, like all language, by repetitious application to apparent facts.

They followed Peridot from the room, along corridors papered with silk, in places marked by the damp, and up a marble stair with a gilded handrail. Lamps burned at junctures, enough to provide sufficient light for girls brought up in the country, beyond the River Styx.

Then they went down an awful little uncarpeted wooden stair in the almost dark. Laure hated this stair. She felt cold on it, and was sure someone had been murdered there. At its foot, a door was opened, and they were in the suite of la Reine, Sidonie Aubade-Valents. ('Her name is English,' had said Sophrine earlier. 'No one knows why.')

The rooms opened one from another. They blazed and burned with scores of lit candles. She sat by a low table in a carved mahogany chair. Laure was to find there seemed to be a chair like this in every room, and it was always hers. She wore (she always would) very elegant clothes, in grey silk, buttoned high at the throat and wrist. Her gowns were always out of, but also above and beyond, the fashion. Her hands were mediaeval, long and thin and transparent, with oval translucent tawny nails. One jewelled ring on each, a dark polished ruby and a dull facetted emerald. Heavy and tarnished gold wedding rings, two of them, were worn on her right hand. Her face was less effective. She had been beautiful once (they said). Now she had, as Sophrine *always* said, lost everything but her eyes. It was a fallen face, grown shapeless, or wrongly shaped. The nose had enlarged and spread. The jaw vanished in dewlaps. Even the eyes, of course, had become diluted, like waterlogged irises, and the lashes thinned. But you had to ignore it. You had to say, in common decency, *Oh, she still has her eyes. They are still beautiful.*

La Reine gazed up at them, and Laure was startled because Sophrine at once offered a staccato little curtsy. Just like a grocer's daughter – *but I won't,* thought Laure, and did not.

'Good evening, Sophrine.'

'Good evening, dear majesty.' (Laure had been prepared for sycophancy.) 'May I present, Laure Deschampeigne, my friend.'

'You're welcome, Mademoiselle Deschampeigne.'

'Thank you, ma-madame,' stammered Laure, angering herself by flushing at the omission of the other title.

La Reine didn't seem put out. She beckoned them over, and offered them a box of cigarettes (not the cheroots of the tales). Sophrine took one, and Peridot came and lit it for her, with a match.

'You don't smoke, Laure, my dear?'

'No, madame. My Aunt suffers with her chest. No one smokes in our house.' *How provincial I sound,* had thought Laure. *How subservient and fawning even though I won't address her as a queen.*

'Do you mean then, she would otherwise allow you to smoke?'

'Oh – probably not.'

'Well, never mind. Here, you may do as you wish.'

Peridot then again came forward, now carrying a book. It was large, bound in leather, and gilded. The pages, coloured like sugar almonds, had names written all over them. The book was laid on the table, next to an inkwell and an old-fashioned pen. Sophrine at once bent forward, soused the pen in the ink, and signed her name with a silly schoolgirl flourish. Laure thought, *Is this what she does, to get us in her power!* For the names in the book were clearly evidence of their attendances. (Like school?) Laure didn't lean forward in turn to sign, and the book was left lying there. No one referred to it.

'Sophrine,' said la Reine, 'I mustn't keep you. Why don't you join the others? I *will* keep Laure, just until the dinner hour.' Laure felt almost frightened, since Sophrine instantly went out, and then the old Peridot too went out, moving rather sideways, like an old crab. And Laure was alone with la Reine. And beyond her shoulder, in the hazy blaze of candlelight, one could see right into a bedroom, to a bed canopied in tapestry.

'Please sit, Laure Deschampeigne.'

Laure sat. Disgruntled, she said, 'Thank you, madame.'

'What is it?' asked la Reine. Claws glinted in a frail bony paw: 'Do you think I'll demand *a favour* of you? In there, hmm? Well?'

Laure shrugged 'It would be beneath you.'

'Would it, indeed. But you're so young and fresh. Clear-eyed, and with such fine pretty hair. No? Are you sure I won't?'

Laure stood up.

The old woman laughed. 'Sit, sit. You shan't be harmed. I don't rub my alligator flesh against little maidens. Good God in a Blue Sky, girl. I had to put up with my husband all those years. Do you think I want to inflict any of that on my own sex?'

Laure blushed furiously and scowled at her shoes – the best ones with rosettes, put on for the occasion, damn it.

'No,' said la Reine, soothingly, lighting another cigarette for herself directly from a candle. 'I should like to converse with you, for a little while.' She had already slipped into the familiar form, the intimate rather than the formal 'you'. But she was old, seventy-eight, Sophrine had said. She looked a hundred to Laure.

Laure said, 'It was kind of you to ask me to your house, madame.'

'But you know why?'

'Not really.'

'Because – and I'm certain you do, since Sophrine will have told you – you are of my own persuasion, like the other ladies who come here. Oh, it isn't to visit me, I assure you. Sometimes I'm not even to be seen, except perhaps at dinner in the evening. But I make free my house to you all. I give you liberty, my little birds. I like it, I confess, very much, to hear or to sense those footsteps, the laughs and little cries. But more than that, to let you into a cage which makes you safe, at least for a few brief hours. Of course, when I'm gone, God in His sky knows what will become of you all. But at least you will have tasted happiness, to recognize it, or passion. Perhaps great passion, if you are very fortunate and very unlucky.'

Laure stared at la Reine's face, her attention caught. Age and ugliness became only a mask. Behind it, this being spoke to her like a bell.

'The great passion,' repeated la Reine. 'Yes, why not. I have known it, very nearly. I doubt I shall know it again. For me it was only wonderful pain. The woman wasn't of our kind, but she was accommodating. One can only stand so much of that. The glory lay all in the pain, then. Not in the rather shabby fulfilments. But for you, Laure, I wonder. Not with little Sophrine, I think.

Even if she was your tutor, for which you should always wear her like a rose in your heart and not forget.'

Laure cast down her eyes. She found she had become aroused. This old woman had the power to arouse her, solely by her words.

And in this arousal, and this nameless surge of longing and excitement – oh, not for la Reine, but for the hallucination la Reine had seemed on the verge of conjuring – Sidonie Aubade-Valents abandoned her. Cunning as an old fox.

With silence, cigarette smoke and hot summer candlelight, they sat in stasis, until Peridot poked her tortoise head inside the door. 'I have seen a repast laid. We are twenty-two tonight.'

Laure noted Peridot did not call her mistress by any title at all.

It was the first of so many evenings, dinners. All different, all familiar. Finally all quite *ordinary.* Although later ones were often more dramatic, gross even, with scenes, lovers' quarrels carried on publicly as, elsewhere, they could hardly be, recriminations or – much worse – sinking into trivia. (As, for example, seeing the nearly exquisite Lejay discussing the price of coffee and soap. Expatiating upon it, her equine beauty growing banal, like any well-off young town matron, with the keys to the family cupboard). Laure expected too much of the chateau, naturally. It *was* her nature. She had the unfortunate and self-harming habit of sometimes seeing magic in persons and things, where it didn't exist. She herself busily constructed the glamour. Then, learning the perfectly obvious truth, disliking and castigating the offending object, with a feeling of betrayal.

At least, she had not been, and never was to be, guilty of that with Sophrine. Nor did she wear the grocer's daughter in her heart like a rose. This romantic ideal had appealed to Laure, its tincture of mediaeval love-courts, secret classical nostalgias. But – *Sophrine?* Ha!

The court of la Reine was, though, partly responsible for this particular englamourment and disillusion. The first approach having been through the twilight midsummer garden, then la Reine herself, the 'conversation' (monologue) in her room, then that first dinner, at which she contrived to tell them all a story.

'This crest on the china, do you see? My own, not my husband's. Nevertheless, it belongs to the chateau. Do you see what it is? A bird? Yes. A crow – a jackdaw. Only some two hundred and fifty years old – a very immature crest. But you find him, my black bird, sometimes, worked into a corner of the tablecloths or napkins. Always the tableware. Oh, and in one picture from the 1760s, in the annex to the north tower – he's painted on a bough, holding a pomegranate in his beak. A detail of the work, but significant. It was a woman who had it painted, my husband's grandmother, the White Comtesse.'

Laure had listened intently. This was just antique enough to interest her at once. And perhaps la Reine had chosen it on purpose, flatteringly. But then it was difficult to tell if the other women had ever heard it before, this historic myth. Some listened attentively, their chins on their hands, or toying with the moist rim of a chipped crystal vessel (most of the chateau glass was chipped). Others kept eyes downcast. Some silently flirted with each other. A couple even stifled yawns. But then they might have been doing tiring things, at home, or here.

Twenty-two in number, as Peridot the tortoise-woman had said. They drifted into the meal from all over the chateau. (No rooms, as Laure would learn, were out-of-bounds, though many were vacant of furniture, or else stacked floor to ceiling with it, the haunt of mice and spiders. There were, Sophrine had assured her, priceless things everywhere, simply left lying about. You could go in and thieve the smaller ones, and who would know? La Reine never would. Laure thought perhaps *Peridot* would. Did Sophrine mean anyway that she herself had made off with items, against some parochial rainy day, and not been caught out?) Even the barefoot maenads entered the dining room with clean hands and brushed hair. None was bare-breasted, not even Artemise Lejay, although many of her blouse buttons were undone. Others, such as Clothilde Boulanger, wore rustic evening gowns. No one, though she knew most of them by sight, and had exchanged words with several, spoke to Laure during this first visit, beyond a *Good Evening* or *How do you go on?* None used her name. On her very next visit, all that changed. They addressed her familiarly, impertinently, and pulled her hair.

The table was heavily laid with silver, and incised goblets, yet everything was a little declined. The cloth, faintly stained and yellowed, the glass past its best, the silver brackish. Overhead a chandelier tinkled in the airs from the open windows. Cobwebs veiled its prisms and now and then floated down onto a bowl of apples, figs and peaches, many of which were bruised. It was a haphazard meal. Dishes of cold wood-pigeon, a cooling ragout, salad of rampion and radishes and bitter green things. Later Peridot mixed and cooked little flat sweet omelettes over a silver table-brazier. But there was a great deal of wine, blood-coloured, and liqueurs of all shades, that far outshone the story-teller's stagnant emerald and ruby.

'The story of the jackdaw is this: There were two aristocrats, an uncle and a nephew, both young, almost of an age through some vagary of the births. Don't suppose that they lived here, at the chateau. They resided some distance away, in another house twice the size. Their crimes and vices likewise, were gigantic, a marvel in an age when men of their station and wealth seldom behaved well. In short, they were a byword for depravity – worse indeed than that other, later, strange beast, known as the Marquis de Sade, who was also, it seems, a great liar. In the Revolution, these two men, the Comte de Valents-Blanches and his nephew, would no doubt have been torn to shreds by the people of their estates, long before they reached the ladder of the Guillotine. But it transpires they did not live in that mitigating era.

'One day these two were looking for a diversion. They presently hit upon something. One of them, the nephew, had chanced to see a young girl in the village, as he rode through. She was not much more than fourteen, but fully formed, as country maidens often are. She had long fair hair and a skin like damask, and lips as red as wine. What would have been usual with them, the men, was to have sent for the girl and raped her, turn by turn, until satisfied. Then, if she still lived, they would have sent her back with the normal jest, that they had prepared her for her husband. However, they'd done such a thing quite often, and by now found the experience almost enervating. It chanced they were dining as the topic was broached, and the nephew, picking up a fruit from the table, drew the uncle's attention to it. "Just so is this demoiselle, uncle. Rounded and smooth, with the bloom ripely on her. One could bite into her, one could eat her up. What a feast she would be." At this the comte narrowed his eyes. He had been handsome once, but already his methods had marked him, he was no longer so. "Then let us," said he. "No, I don't mean our usual game. Not at all." After which he outlined his plan.

'This chateau then, was in their possession, but slimly staffed – although doubtless they kept more people here than I do. All around the great woods, a wilderness of beech and chestnut, swept down, and this wonderful town of ours, Bois-la-Diane, was merely a well with two or three shacks leaning beside it. The comte ordered his preparations, and his terrified servants, whom fear had made as depraved as he, carried them out. The young girl was abducted. Brought to the chateau, she was drugged by a mixture of pink valerian and Indian opiates in brandy.

'Deep in the park, where the ancient forest then encroached, far more so than it does now, the comte's servants laid a table with the snowy moth-wing linen of Chinese looms, and falls of white lace, and over that scarves of purple so fine they were barely to be seen, only their fringes of leaden gold.'

('*The Thousand Nights*' said Sophrine of this juncture afterwards. But Laure had only considered la Reine would not carelessly have omitted the extra *And One Night*, as Sophrine had.)

'On to the table then they heaped the best of the chateau's fruit, from its orchards and hothouses. Apples and plums like garnets and yellow Carrara marble, peaches and apricots, blue grapes, and grenadines, and by that time even pineapples, cut open and leaking their saffron juice like amber resin. There were also flowers. Every flower that grew here then. The green and fine blue plumes and red spikes of herbs, the bowl-faced wax white roses, the wolf-flowers from the forest's edge, the wild hyacinths, the monstrous striped orchids, and lilies bred under slices of glass. All these cast and scattered over the cloths and veils, among the fruit. And next there were sweets, made especially, bonbons brought from Paris and Versailles, in the shape of keys covered with edible gold-and-silver-leaf, or butterflies of sugar so thin you could see your own fingers through them. Lastly they placed the decanters of old, greenish glass, or those of gold and inlaid silver, some of which had precious stones for stoppers, and goblets of filigreed gold and coloured Venetian glass that Doges had drunk from. All this, on the table. Then they carried the girl out, unconscious. She had been stripped naked and shaved carefully of every hair, but for her lashes, eyebrows, and the gilt tresses of her head. She had been bathed and sponged with essences until she too smelled only of fruit and flowers and sweets and wine. And they had draped her with strings of round white pearls.

'They laid her at the centre of the table. They spread out her long hair and scattered a few more pearls – priceless – and exotic flowers into it. They arranged, the story goes, a bunch of grapes as cool as jade over her loins. And over her eyes they let fall a long lavender ribbon. And then, they put down the plates and the table knives.'

La Reine paused here. Peridot, who hovered, refilled her mistress's glass. But la Reine did not touch it.

She said: 'Do you see? Even then they were driving there, the uncle and his nephew, driving very fast in their black carriage, towards the chateau. They were starving hungry and planning to eat her. Alive. Carve off pieces of her flesh, suck out her marrow, garnished by fruits and confectionery. The girl was to be their feast. Is that terrible enough?

'Now we come to the jackdaw.

'You can imagine, bees and wasps and flies by the swarm had been attracted to that table. Within ten minutes, every flower had a bee at its centre, while the wasps crawled over the girl's pure skin. Flies stood on the sweets, cleaning their faces like cats, with forefeet like black splinters. Perhaps he only came down for the insects, the jackdaw.

'He was ink black, with golden eyes, just as you can see him in the picture in the annex. He flew down, and maybe caught a bee or two in his beak. But then he flew up on to the girl's soft, curving breast. He stood and looked at her, lying there with the ribbon over her eyes. Right next to him, nestled in her side, was a cut pomegranate. The jackdaw pecked it, and the wine juice splashed the table-cloths. The girl slept on. When he left her, where he had stood, his claws too had made a fading pomegranate-coloured mark.

'Just then, the black carriage turned in to the lane and came rushing towards the chateau. How hungry they were, the two men, how they longed to dine.

'Then up flew the jackdaw on his inky wings. He flew over the wood, over the wall, and over the lane, straight at the heads of the horses he flew. He must have looked, don't you think, like a bolt from heaven, the thunder-bolt that brings love or death?

'The horses reared. No surprise in that. The coachman rolled from his box, and broke his legs, and walked after with a limp, but he lived, they say. Then the horses dashed on, straight at the wall, until swerving, they broke their traces and were gone. But the carriage smashed headlong against the chateau gate-post of stone. The bird had vanished.

'They died those two, the comte and his nephew. They were broken into bits inside their skins, so that picked up, they *rattled*. It was too quick for them, but if we credit Hell, perhaps not.'

La Reine took up her glass and drank.

She said, 'The girl awoke and ate the fruit. She was cared for, or she went away. She lived happily and never knew what she had been spared. But the peasants knew. In the end it was the old Comtesse Valents-Blanches who adopted the jackdaw as her crest. And now, so too do I.'

After the dinner, Sophrine took Laure through room after room, up and down stairs, along corridors of the chateau. Sophrine carried a lamp, and never, Laure thought, had she looked more like a pert little housekeeper. But also, night was there in the chateau, and Laure felt the enormity of night and of the house.

'You believed that tale, didn't you, Laure?'

'Yes.'

'Swallowed it whole. She made it up.'

'You think so.'

'Well, how could it happen?'

'Easily enough. The mere facts. The art, Sophrine, is in putting them together to create a story which seems supernatural, yet isn't.'

'Oh you. I can just see you on the table with all those melting sweets, stung all over by wasps and with grapes in your private place.'

But again, just then, Sophrine undid a door, and there was a vast room, perhaps a ballroom, with huge windows and mirrors, and moonlight shimmering like water on the floor.

'The rooms in this house,' whispered Sophrine, in awe, 'seem always to shift about. I never know where I'll find them next.'

To Laure this was a confession that Sophrine's house, and all those she knew or could imagine, and therefore all her horizons, were small. You knew where everything was. But the chateau was like a huge landscape. You could be lost in it.

She was about to make some remark, when Sophrine whispered even more softly, 'Ssh. *Look.*'

There was a low sofa stranded under one of the windows. A woman lay on it, naked, white as a statue in the moonlight. A fall of dark hair going to the floor, the narrow lines of her body, revealed her as Artemise Lejay. Her left leg was bent at the knee, resting on the sole of her left foot, opening her centre where a second darkness, not grapes but also hair, blotted off the moon-light.

Another woman, Laure was not sure who, stood over her, but not touching her with her body. Instead the unknown woman was making a painting, stroking motion, over and over, on and on, just within the smoky cleft – and her instrument was like an incredibly long and curved finger –

'A feather,' breathed Sophrine. 'A *crow's* feather.'

Over and over, and Artemise lay arched and still, tense as a bowstring, And now they heard her say harshly, 'Oh!' and then, after a few moments, 'Oh!'

But that was all.

They, and their lamp, went unseen, or unacknowledged. Outside, Sophrine pressed Laure quickly against the wall, but a sour ache had begun in Laure where pleasure had been. She did not want Sophrine at all.

'She's my ideal,' breathed Sophrine, 'that Lejay. Isn't she a marvel? I've never before seen her like that, Oh, to be in that one's shoes –'

'Leave me alone.'

'Oh, Laure, don't be a baby. Of course I like you too.'

An uncomfortable rush of heat of a different sort, and a cramp at the base of her belly, made Laure push Sophrine away. 'It's my little monthly enemy.'

'You fool,' cried Sophrine angrily, 'it won't matter. I'm not some boy –'

Laure picked up the lamp Sophrine had put down, and walked briskly away. Sophrine soon came scurrying after her, afraid to be left in the dark with only the harsh peremptory 'Oh! Oh!' to cling to.

In the salon with the piano, some of them were playing cards. La Reine had gone. Peridot had gone. Avid as chickens, the women craned forward, scrabbled and slapped down their cards with sharp clucks.

Laure's head ached, her womb ached. She presently walked along the carriage drive (past the killing gate-post), and back into the town of Bois-la-Diane, on the moonlit lane.

The chestnut trees were black as iron, with dry silver-wet edges. The trees were full of invisible rustlings, and only the town was silent, still warm, patrolled by cats.

After some four years, then, now nineteen or twenty,) Laure walked the other way up to the chateau of Sidonie Aubade-Valents, on Wednesday, in autumn. The lane was soaked and full of brown leaves, and it was only three o'clock in the afternoon.

Four years had not altered so much. One or two women no longer attended, three or four had been added. The *magic* had run out almost at once, that first night even, with the menstrual blood.

The chateau was a destination to go to. As one went on with one's life.

'They called her Madame Death, in Paris, so I'm told. And in the south –'

'How mediaeval you sound, Clothilde, Marie. Or like something at least from the seventeenth century.'

'I heard she was also in South America!'

'And she's a Jewess!'

'The *Wandering* Jew, perhaps,' remarked Violette Charpentier. 'Well I haven't seen the creature. Is she even in the town? What do you think, Laure?'

Five of the Club had gathered in the old parlour, which, like the salon, lay off a corridor from the chateau's cavernous Hall.

Violette, the scholar, would have explained, and once had, the Hall was the masculine place, the male core of the house, the hearth big enough to roast an ox, complete with rusty irons, beams that crossed like quarrels, war and duelling swords and pistols hung up, and mildewy heads of stags and bear that had once roamed the woods.

The parlour was, as its name conveyed, for talk – chatter – always a female spot.

Violette was doubtless forty, in town parlance 'an old maid'. Lack of looks had permitted her escape. But had she ever had a female lover? Perhaps. There was nothing virginal to her, thought Laure, even though she might be stoppered and sealed tight.

Now Violette looked at Laure, consideringly, along her long thin nose on which ready spectacles perched.

'Who?' said Laure. 'What are you talking about?'

But her face flamed suddenly. She knew.

'Oh look,' said annoying Marie-Louison. 'This one's seen her. Tell us, Laure.'

'I have not. That is, I did see a woman today, a stranger, probably. One knows everyone here, I suppose. So maybe it was – But what were you saying?'

'You don't know the story then?' asked Clothilde. 'Ooh! Laure, Laure – it's quite frightful. Ghoulish.'

'Really.'

'Supposedly,' said Violette, 'this woman (if she is here) is a type of prostitute.'

A chorus of admonition.

'No, no. She was *not.*'

'Any woman who marries could be called a whore,' cried married Annette Mercier.

'True, in many cases,' amended Violette. 'In this case, if the *tale* is true, definitely. She certainly marries only for gain. And does it repeatedly.'

Laure stood staring. Her heart thudded like a drum, hurting her a little as it struck the confining walls of flesh and corset. When agitated, the heart always wanted to get free.

But she had come here with some vague sense that she might hear something about the stranger glimpsed by the canal, the stranger she, Laure, had passed, unable to frame either a courtesy or a question. And yes, that face, those black eyes and black eyebrows – how truly *strange* she had been, that woman, that *stranger*.

Laure opened her mouth to interrogate them again, the silly or procrastinating women, but just then Peridots head, more tortoise-like now, four years on, poked into the room.

'Luncheon, if you will take it.'

They treated Peridot with scant politeness. This was mutual. Probably *her* attitude had come first, with all of them. The 'Jewel' stood there as the wash of women swept around her. La Reine's guests were usually hungry, or likely to be. Dishes of sweets and fruit left about were always empty by the evening's end. Spoilt children, they expected to be cared for, and were cared for.

Laure was the last to go, not hungry at all, and something in Peridot's sharp old eye delayed her further.

'What?' demanded Laure.

'What? What? The genuine country Bourgeoisie. No style.'

'I never claimed to be an aristo!' Laure flashed back. She was amazed at the exchange. Normally Peridot insulted or challenged them in subtle ways only really noted afterwards. 'What do you take me for?'

'A little girl,' said Peridot. 'Do you know what you were speaking of? No. Peridot knows. Knows it all. How not, when Peridot does the marketing and talks to the tradesmen and the laundry women.'

Laure stood stunned. 'Do you want me to tip you?'

Peridot's surface did not ripple. 'Here's my hand.'

With a most extraordinary feeling, dry mouthed, Laure took a coin from her little (bourgeois) bag and dropped it square on the tortoises palm. Tortoise-shell closed over it.

'She's called Madame Corrot. That's the name, do you see, of her last husband-gone-to-God. She's a widow. But then, apparently, she's a widow some ten or twenty times over.'

Laure pulled her lips together. They had slipped open, as if she knew she could hear better through her mouth than her ears. Her eyes, she knew, were as wide as a deer's.

'Why? *How?*'

Oh, she don't murder them, her husbands. She'd be in the jail, else, wouldn't she. Or sent to the blade.'

'Then – they die –'

'She isn't bad luck, either.' Peridot stopped speaking. *Does she want another bribe – I didn't give her enough –* But Peridot said one of her phrases, 'The cock gets up afore the pinafore, and down again he goes, too.' Then, 'It turns out, if a man knows he's on his last legs, but wants a bit of fun before he leaves, he calls for this woman, with her black hair and her white legs. She won't do a thing, unless he weds her, and makes her a settlement. Then she'll do all that'll be done under the sun. She has a reputation and is reckoned beautiful. Else she couldn't make her terms.'

Laure said, 'And then he dies, and she's free again.'

'And well-off. Which is the reason for it all. She's a professional widow, mademoiselle. And now she's called Corrot, but it used to be Duvalle, and last year, in the city, it was Lebonniere. Afore that I can't say.'

Laure didn't reply, *Why have you chosen to tell me?* One is the heroine of one's own story. And besides, Peridot had exacted payment. Maybe she had done this with everyone here, all the younger and more gullible ones at least. Maybe it was anyway a lie.

So Laure straightened her face abruptly as if to iron it; and stalked past Peridot with a 'Very well. That will do.' Just as she had seen her Aunt do in her house, with her servants, although not recently. The Aunt was softer and deafer now, more like a slightly mad nun.

In the dining room they looked up with anticipation: they predicted Laure would continue to question them, would blush again, and so on.

She didn't. And they stopped talking about the woman who was a professional widow (if she was). Wouldn't resume the chat.

Instead, Annette complained about her husband, the fat notary, and then Marie-Louison about hers (the draper's clerk). Clothilde Boulanger started on about her brothers, Rose and Honorine Eperve about their father. All classes mixed here. There was no caste system. And for now, too, they were only nagging, whining women, just the thing men joyed to despise. And Laure, glancing at them, thought proudly, I am more like a man. I despise them too. I want them only for pleasure, the tickle, rush, gasp and explosion between my legs. I don't like them at all. Do I wish I wasn't a woman, even? Perhaps not. Men repel me another way. Or, they don't matter. Am I only ashamed of these women? Their awful littleness.

La Reine wasn't at the table. Actually, Laure hadn't seen her, or at the dinners, for a month or more. Artemise Lejay too, was absent. Violette scraped up miserly portions of cheese sauce and bread, her long nose in a book. Lucide was flirting with Marie Jeanne. In a stupid, exclusive, irritating way.

Even Sophrine hadn't come, hard at work on papa's ledgers.

Rain streamed past the windows, and sometimes handfuls of leaves blew across the casements in a bad-tempered wind.

Is *she* like these women? Just the same? Oh, with some veneer of a city, maybe. Some coldness and coarseness too, because of what she's done? She looked – quite pure. Like black and white marble. Like Pygmalion's statue just come to life. They must like that in her, her *husbands*. Can it really be true? What a story. Where does she live? One of those large houses by the church, perhaps. Or a little picturesque cottage tucked behind the market? Why is she *here*? Perhaps no one will buy anymore. Fallen on hard times – *into a basket, as* that Peridot would say. A hovel then. One scruffy servant, and one meal a day. It didn't look like that. Her dress – it was silk, and fur on the jacket – but then, was it even her?

What is her name now?

Between Acts

The Aunt was seated at her own gloomy window in the large house on the rue Dalle. Yellowish light seeped through folds and pleats of lace. She had been reading one of her books (novels by men penned fifty or a hundred years before).

'Laure … I thought you had gone out.'

'I did. I have a headache. I came back.'

'I beg your pardon? Oh, your head … It's too late now for luncheon. Tell Ouelle to put you out some bread and butter. And hot coffee.'

Not to prolong the interview – the Aunt had called her in to her sitting room – Laure nodded impatiently.

But, 'You shall sit here,' added the Aunt, putting down her book absently, its satin marker trailing. She spoke as if bestowing a treat on Laure. Laure felt every hair of her head pulling tight in a rigor of dismay.

The Aunt herself rang for Ouelle, and presently the woman came in. She was plump and untidy, always straightening her apron, rearranging pins in her mass of singeing light hair – to no avail. Her anxious pink moon face swung eagerly to them.

'Fetch coffee, Ouelle. Make sure it's hot. And some of the brioches, with butter and preserves.'

'Yes, madame.'

Outside the door, Laure knew, Ouelle would sigh and raise her eyes to God at the nuisance of these two women, the old one and the chit, pestering her away from more important tasks, such as the knitting of endless caps and mittens for her herd of nephews and nieces, or her canoodling with the wood-seller, or rabbit-man, over the garden wall. With the rabbit-man especially Ouelle had had a sort of understanding for years. Now the Aunt had grown fairly vague, Ouelle invited him often to the kitchen for a quick nip of something and perhaps herself. One always knew when it had occurred. There were for days rabbit stews and pates at every meal. Ouelle's look of eager anxiety with the Aunt was merely an act, carried on for so long that now it occurred spontaneously.

'Ah, Laure, Laure,' sighed the Aunt. Then gazed into the shadows of the room. After some minutes she added, despondently, 'Soon, winter.'

'Yes, Aunt.' Laure remembered to speak loudly, making her own ears ring.

'And we, like the poor birds, our heads beneath the wing.'

She means, *thought Laure, pitilessly,* she will soon be dead. She includes me in it, too. I suppose I shall be in twenty or thirty years.

And Laure too inadvertently sighed.

'Where have you been, Laure?'

'To the chateau. It's Wednesday.'

'Ah, yes. Madame la Comtesse Valents-Blanches. The Ladies Days.' She never responded more than that to it now. In the first year, when she found out, although not from Laure (someone would always be willing to tattle), that Laure went to the chateau, the Aunt had drawn her up into the sanctum of her bedroom. At first she had seemed ready to burst out in a tirade, then deflated. 'Do you know what you are at?' was all she had said. Laure stood and waited, not knowing what to say, if the chateau was worth fighting or even deceiving for, since, in the case of Laure, already she had found means to indulge herself, on the Aunt's very premises. But the Aunt, deflating even more, had then said, 'Well, it will pass. These things. One day you'll meet someone. It will be for him to deal with.' Laure, remembering this, today raised her eyebrows.

And the Aunt now said, 'We shall be cosy together. Ouelle must light a fire.' She felt the cold, the winter breathing on her neck. Because she was well-off, and could afford it, in winter the house was always too hot, and aromatic with new tonics, and tinctures of peppermint and clove for rheumatism. *How cruel it is,* Laure thought, surprising herself a moment by her own compassion – or dread – *how we become old.*

But then the coffee came in and Ouelle lit the fire and a lamp, and the Aunt began a meandering reminiscence of her past triumphs – balls, suppers – in another town, and Laure's head began to ache in earnest.

She sat in a sort of stupor, promising herself that at four o'clock she would go up to her room. Now and then the Aunt fell asleep, and liberty seemed possible, but these sleeps lasted no more than a few seconds.

The fire, having roasted the room like a chestnut, sank low. Little golden eyes fleered among the charred sticks, spirits lurking in the grate, as Laure had believed, in childhood, they lurked in the chimney.

She had been a nervous child had she? Afraid of being left alone. Her mother had done so a great deal, only she couldn't recall any of that time. She had a horrible suspicion that, when she was nine or ten, she had wanted to stay always close to the Aunt, importunately. And that today's unwanted invitation was a resurrection of those earlier times, which only then would have comforted Laure.

She had slept with a low-burning lamp in her room, because of nightmares, until she was thirteen. What had the nightmares consisted of? She was afraid of ghosts, afraid of witches, of wolves in the woods, of things in chimneys –

'Oh, Laure,' said the Aunt. 'Laure.'

'What?' Much too sharply. More mildly, 'What is it?' Finally, mildly but also loudly: 'What is it?'

'I wish I could be young again. How I wish I could.'

Laure frowned. What could she say? The Aunts face now was that of a child. A child afraid of ghosts, winter, and a black wolf named Death.

But then, 'There now,' said the Aunt. 'You've had your tea. What a good girl. Run along, Laure. I must read a little.'

'Ouelle, come here.'

Ouelle came there. She *stood* there. Plainly interrupted.

'Ouelle, have you heard of a woman in the town, a Madame Corrot, a widow?'

Ouelle flung up her pink hands to her pink face-moon.

'There, m'mselle Laure! Fancy you should hear of *that!* Well I never.'

'It's true?'

'What a woman. Do you know, those men –' she spoke proprietary, as if all the men in the town were hers – 'they're laying bets on it. Will it be the old mayor over at St Georges-du-Marais – or that old miser Boucher – he's got something put by, and he's an old lecher, he is –'

'Ouelle,' said Laure sternly.

'Excuse me, m'mselle. But there. A woman like that. Of course,' said Ouelle flouncingly, 'it may *not* be true. A pack of lies. How could such a thing be possible here? In the city – even in Convienne – there they'll do anything. But then, it could be our Doctor St Romarin. He's an intellectual. The brainy ones are often the worst.'

Laure shook herself as if dispelling water from her pelt.

'I do think it's all a lie. You're quite right, Ouelle. It would be impossible in this town. For example, where would she live –?'

'That,' said Ouelle, 'isn't *any* mystery. She's taken rooms in the Blue House. Three day-rooms, a bedroom, and the big drawing room for visitors. Pelu told me.' (Pelu was the wood-seller. They were still on comradely terms.)

'Perhaps you're right,' repeated Laure vaguely. 'My Aunt –'

Ouelle leaned forward. 'The mistress,' said Ouelle, 'she's getting worse – can hardly hear a word unless I shout – forgets everything. Do you know, this morning she called me Susine again. Lay the fire, Susine, she says. And books in every room; she starts, then forgets and takes another one.'

'I must go out,' said Laure. She added, 'She's sent me for some thread.'

'She can't see to sew. How can she want thread? We need none – I'd know, I do the sewing.'

'Thank you, Ouelle.'

And Ouelle bobbed and sailed away, a cork afloat on others lives.

Laure's head now pounded. She ran to fetch her outdoor things. As soon as she undid the door, a white flush of rainy wind slapped her face and the leaves dazzled up in a crazy dance.

She was almost running along the street. Not quite. Etiquette and the corset she wore combined to slow her down.

Pelu said … and it might be Doctor St Romarin – or all the way to St Georges, another dreary town … And it's lies. Or it's true.

Where am I going in this fine rush?

Laure stopped. She was between two muddy, cobbled lanes passing for streets. Small houses crowded together. She had come quite a way from the grander house of the Aunt, not noticing. Only the white wind and the leaves, everything bounding with her.

The light was fading, too. Presently old Jacques would be lighting the lamps in the church square …

Here and there already a lamplit window. Two women going by, stiffly nodded to her, the Aunts niece. A black cat melted between the iron bars of a gate –

Well. But I'm going to look at the Blue House, which all this while, as ever, overlooks the canal.

Is it Laure's head which pounds, or her heart? Are her hands cold, or too hot?

She walks briskly now, her pointed little chin held up and her eyes full of something that might even look like rage.

It stood there, timbered, blue once, now only a blue superimposed by memory, peeling, the boards threadbare. It must be damp. It reflected in the water, where the woods came entirely close, it reflected like a blue sun that wasn't any longer blue, or a sun. A ghost. A ghost house mirrored in a canal.

Laure had walked as far as the gates, and now she idled, looking in through the ironwork, which wasn't at all the same gate – much larger, older, finer, rustier and less well-kept – than the gate in the town street that a black cat had melted through.

The Blue House, in its blue days, was said to have been visited by a dauphin, and by poets. Various eccentric or elderly people now rented the rooms.

The darkness was coming. The sky looked white, but everything below, but for the canal, which had turned to pewter, was filling up with shadow.

In the courtyard of the Blue House, a hawthorn tree grew. Its dying leaves were thick on the paving, sticky and slick from rain. On the gate pillars were two globes, pitted, old planets stuck there after they had dropped from the clockwork heavens.

No lights in the Blue House.

All shadows, so palpable, and the smell of damp and moss, of leaf-decay and water, of snails moving unseen, and stagnant lives, and something pleasingly sweet, like jam.

Loitering, Laure pretended to have lost a button from her glove. She searched about for it in the leaves at the threshold of the court. Now and then, as if hoping for help, she glanced up at the darkened windows.

Then, one window bloomed to gold. Laure gazed and saw, behind the now almost transparent loops of curtains, a female figure straightening from the lamp.

It was not the one, not the right figure. It was too angularly thin and bowed too low. It must be old Madame Belvard. Yes, of course. The upper floor.

And then the front door opened, and out came another figure, another woman, and it

and it

it was the Woman.

In the shadow of the fast-falling darkness, the black clothes of widowhood blended away, a charcoal drawing. Only the white face and throat were floating there a moment. One white ungloved hand, before the glove covered it. Ghosts –

Laure stepped back. She grazed against the gate-post with the dead planet on it. The Woman, the Widow, walked past her.

But now, the Woman turned and directed at her one unconditional glance.

Oh God, the face. It was like a blow.

The black rustling gown – another one, and another coat, and a hat on which sailed one ebony feather, a flicker of earrings like eyes … and the leaves, faintly disturbed by the footfall of her black boots with their slender muffs of black fur –

The face, disembodied still, hung in darkness, and the red mouth, almost as black as the eyes in darkness, parted.

'Good evening, mademoiselle.'

Laure heard herself answer, far off, reasonably, as if she were a machine, 'Good evening, madame.'

And the white face nodded, or rather gracefully inclined, and everything, every weightless atom of the phantasmal presence, slid away, through the gate.

And then, on the path outside, Laure understood a carriage was waiting, with the door held open.

From dark to dark, night to night, the being glided. She was in the carriage. The door was secured. A man sprang on to the box. The horses, evolving from the nothingness that now all things were, invisible essences of motion, poured off like running silk.

Leaning on the gate pillar, Laure looked up and saw the stars had been lit in the sky by some doddering employee of heaven – some old Jacques God kept on a pension. And she laughed. Loudly and wildly enough that above her, Madame Belvard snapped to her heavier curtains, and the oblong of gold was gone, to leave black night supreme.

Act Two

Somewhere in the woods, she was lying. Under two and a half centuries of mulch and roots, of flowers and trees. No one knew quite where, or whether to be sure.

Of course she had nourished the ground, and where the cornucopia of fruits had fallen, they had dropped their seeds, and the flowers too had left less visible flecks of propagation.

How long had it been before the suns of summer, the rains and snows of other seasons, had broken the table and its samite veilings? Even before it toppled or sank into the earth, things had been at her. Wild things from the woods – the foxes and rodents, wolves even, for there were wolves in the woods and the park then, and birds, things of the air, other crows.

The end of the story must always have been amorphous, because how could she have, that village girl scarcely more than a child, survived? She hadn't been fed poisons, or even copious amounts of opium – because, if they ate her, the comte and his nephew, they too would have to ingest these substances. But her frame, weakened by the terror of abduction, trepidation, perhaps by some inner flaw in its superficially perfect whole, had not withstood the potion and the table. Yes. She had died. Despite the helpful jackdaw, despite the miraculous accidental rescue. Died. What else could have happened?

At least it had been peaceful. Laure had thought, when Violette or Lucide or Marie-Louison, and the rest (growing ever more voluble), offered her an alternate outcome of la Reine's dinner story. The maiden hadn't died in pain, too drugged to struggle yet able to feel – their knives – their *teeth*. The creatures that ate her, did so when she was beyond feeling it, and also they did it because they had needed to eat her. She was devoured by life, not death.

'Somewhere in the woods,' had said Violette Charpentier, raising her pale greyhound's face, 'but no one can know where. Flowers and trees. Fruit trees. Bones, gold goblets, Venetian glass, pearls – sunk deep in the soil.'

'Some of the bones would have been carried off,' Laure had remarked with the asperity of fifteen.

'Oh yes. And no doubt jewels and trinkets too. Magpie's, foxes. Does it matter, Laure? An elegy resists such facts.'

And there was a secret painting. (Not the other in the annex, which Laure had seen. That one was dulled by too much varnishing and by grime, the jackdaw on the bough only just decipherable as a blot, with one half circle of gold in its eye, like a sickle.) The *secret* painting lay in the apartment of la Reine herself. Sophrine said la Reine had it commissioned, when she was a girl – which, good God, was itself more than half a century ago.

Had Laure been shown *this* painting? Obviously not. La Reine never, after the first interview, invited Laure into her rooms below the horrible murderer's stair. None of them had seen the painting. They had heard it described – by whom? None would or could say. Laure calculated they had read about it in some book.

Laure herself, hearing it described, did see the secret painting – it evolved on her inner eyes, formed itself completely. Somewhat in the elaborate, classic style of a David – but also more sensual, more merely lovely – Alma-Tadema?

Now, in the trance state which precedes sleeping or waking, within her unencumbered mind, neither a vision, nor quite a dream – Laure beheld this painting, and, for a second, entered it.

Ormolu hair, scarves, ribbons, tassels, streamlets of pearls, running everywhere, and down into the tall rough grass where poppies flamed. Fat flowers on the table, the fat, burnished fruits, the girl's succulent body. The ribbon masked all her face but for the delicacy of her nostrils and the shaped lips. Spires of precious goblets behind her head like towers of a cathedral. Insects. A bee, daintily painted, alighting now on the crimson rim of a glass.

And in the girls out flung, open right hand, braceleted by white or discoloured pearls, and chains of metal, the red coal of an apple.

Laure stood in the hot grass. She heard the drizzling choir of the cicadas, the buzz of the bees and flies that she now saw freely roving over the table. Frogs croaked from some pool, a daylight nightingale sent its mechanical chirrups and flooding trills across the woods.

She could see the girl breathing, slow, shallow breaths. The jackdaw was nowhere to be seen. Only … expected?

Laure could almost feel the hardness of the table under her own shoulder-blades.

Wake up, Laure wanted to say. But surely, she was already awake. And, if she raised her eyelids, so petal-thin (mauve-stained) some inner light shone up through them – what would she see? What first sight?

And then Laure heard the sound of wings and woke totally with a start. A blown wood-pigeon on the windowsill of her bedroom in the house on the rue Dalle, glared at her with a pink-red eye.

I am awake. I have been brought to my senses.

It was more than the surfacing from dream or sleep. What had happened? Her last thought had been of the secret painting – and her first, too – but neither was quite a dream. Between these two images, her night-long experience had gone elsewhere, into some sumptuous purple darkness she couldn't at all remember, but which must have stained her eyes.

Laure got up. With a great fuss the pigeon flew away. It was Saturday. Market day. There was familiar noise in the town. Noise in the house, Ouelle and some other servant clattering with pots and cups, and then the insubstantial voice of the Aunt calling for something piteously, like a little girl.

What have I come to?

This place has nothing to do with me at all.

Laure had no intention of going to the chateau that Saturday. She lay about on a sofa, reading a book. That was her appearance. She saw none of the words. What did she see? Every so often, a bright window lit high up in the wall of her mind. Then she saw the shadows below, and someone came out of them, also a shadow.

Ouelle accused, 'You haven't touched your dinner. This was a good dish, this rabbit pot-baked with herbs.'

The Aunt had eaten everything put before her, but it made no impression. She looked sallow and unfed, and presently, in the sitting room, asked the girl who came in with wood for the fire, 'Isn't dinner ready yet?'

'Why – madame – you just now had it!' cried the girl.

'Did I?' At once contrite. 'Oh then, I did. So I did. Oh, then.' But when the girl had gone, 'Did we have our dinner, Laure?'

'Yes, Aunt.'

The Aunt sighed.

Rain fell. In the garden behind the house, the ancient chestnut tree, the walnut and fig, were already almost bare, the wind had grown rough in the night. Clinging roses, the colour of parchment, had shed their petals everywhere. But now the wind fell away, pretending innocence.

'What are you writing, Laure?'

'A letter, Aunt.'

'To whom?'

'Oh, no one important.'

Laure, with her back to her Aunt, at a desk in the window, covered her drawing, half a tentative face. Then folded the paper over and over. 'The raspberry canes have blown down,' she reported flatly.

Darkness began to come, perhaps early. It was only four. Ouelle marched in with a tray of tea, with some fancy cakes from the patisserie. Not everyone kept this custom, but Ouelle had noticed the mistress seemed so hungry now, all the time, and indeed the Aunt started up, clapping her hands like a child.

'Did you bake these nice cakes, Ouelle?'

'Oh yes, madame.'

'And with marzipan flowers,' said Laure, 'just the same as in the shop. How clever!'

Ouelle shot Laure a look of mild hatred.

The Aunt took a cake, and holding it, forgetting it, she said, 'I'm so cold, Susine.'

Just then the doorbell jangled, too loudly and for too long, as if some stupid boy were pulling at it before running away. Sophrine always rang the bell in this manner.

'That will be Mademoiselle Merault.' Ouelle bustled out.

Laure moved swiftly to toss her drawing into the fire on the pretence of adding a piece of wood to it. (And noticed, unnoticingly, its heat; the room was quite hot enough.)

Five minutes late Sophrine and Laure had gone up to Laure's room.

'I've been all morning and afternoon again over papa's accounts. What a mess he gets them in. It's a good thing for him he has me, and not some clerk who'd cheat him.'

'Yes, Sophrine, you're quite the little housewife.'

'I am not. Why aren't you ready? Put on a proper dress. Papa offered me the pony-cart, but mama took it to visit one of her cousins. So we'll have to walk in the wet.'

'You go alone.'

'What now? Afraid of a drop of rain? You're sulking. What have I done?'

'I'm bored with that place.'

Sophrine sat down. 'How can you be bored?'

Laure cast her a withering glance. Sophrine never *was* bored. Her narrow tiny brain so quickly crammed and made busy.

But oh, the overwhelming temptation to speak –

'I went for a walk last Wednesday evening.'

'In this weather? Was it sensible?'

'Then how do you propose to return from the chateau, *in this weather*.'

'Well, you know la Reine sometimes lends us her smaller carriage –'

'Or she doesn't bother. She cares nothing for us. We used to amuse her. What did she say – little giggles and cries. It's quite disgusting. I hope,' said Laure, wondering why she was ranting all this nonsense, 'at her age, I shall be past all that.'

'Do you think you will? Men say women stay hot longer. If they have any heat to start with.'

'Men. Which men?'

'Well, I overhear talk, you know. In the shop. Or when papa entertains his friends.' Sophrine added, 'But then, do you have any heat, Laure? You haven't even given me a kiss since last spring.' 'It's what I say,' said Laure, too strongly now, 'just what I mean. What's the point of it all?'

'Pleasure,' said Sophrine simply. 'The joy of life.'

Laure looked at her warily. Perhaps Sophrine wasn't such a shrewd little fool.

Laure said, baldly, 'Would you do it with a man – enjoy it with a man?

'If I had to. I may have to, one day. Marry. Bear children. It's what they make us do, isn't it, in the end. But that doesn't have to be the end of – other things. As to enjoying it, how can I know? I shouldn't think so. Their hairiness and smells – their noises. Oh, you've been spared a great deal, not living in a house with men, your *ears* finding out at seven years old the kind of things your papa gets up to with your mama behind a closed door – ! Then again, I suppose I could dream of Artemise while it went on, the way I do when I'm – not in company. Or of you.'

'*Me?* You think of *me.*'

'Yes, yes. What do you think? You're my darling. When you bent over me just now, and I could smell that scent you wear, and see that loop of hair moving on your neck – well, look how flushed I am.'

'You're not saying you *love* me?' demanded Laure, in a sort of frightened scorn, 'I remember that, the first time. You wanted or expected that from *me.* Just like some *man.*'

Sophrine burst into merry laughter. 'Of course I love you. I love all the ones I've had.'

'You've *had* me, have you?'

'Yes. Gobbled you up like an apricot tart.'

'And like the comte in the story of the girl on the table.'

'Oh that. That's different. Oh Laure, you're always so serious. Don't you know what you're saying?'

'Pray tell me, since you're so very wise.'

'Love, for you, mustn't be easy. Isn't natural. It has to be some tremendous, colossal – collision. The thunder bolt. So I don't mean a thing. None of us does. You're waiting for love to come, *that* kind of love, that smashes you to pieces – kills you – that's what you want.'

'Rubbish. Rubbish.'

'And you may not find it. Or if you do –'

'Be quiet, Sophie. That's enough. How dare you?'

'How dare I?' Aghast, 'What have I said?'

'Leave me alone. Such impertinence.'

'Laure – are you crying?'

'Of course not. I caught a chill on Wednesday. Yes, it wasn't sensible, going out. And I shan't, now.'

Sophrine put her arm about Laure. Laure shuddered her away. Laure thought of Sophrine in the wood, the berries and kisses, and after, now and then. And Laure thought of Marie-Louison, in the chateau's summer garden, and Lucide, and Annette Mercier, who was thirty-two years old and had borne eight children, two of which had died. And of one or two, one or two others. Brief flickers of attention, culminations of greed. *Like a man, I'm like some man. I only want them for that* – these thoughts she had thought a trio of days ago. But by then, Laure had seen the Woman walking beside the canal.

The liaisons, affairs, momentary ignitions, they had faded. Laure hadn't tasted sexual pleasure, in any form, even when alone, for half a year. The riots of hunger so soon appeased, had they palled?

Did she prefer to go hungry? Did she want to *starved* But Sophrine was saying something, arch and infuriating.

'And so do come, Laure. If you don't want to walk, we could borrow the trap from your neighbour, that good –'

'I won't go, I tell you.'

'But don't you want to hear what she has to say?'

'Who?' Sophrine folded her hands and assumed a tolerant expression, making Laure long to strangle her.

It transpired that the previous Wednesday (Laure had by then left the chateau) la Reine had emerged from her seclusion at the dinner hour. 'She said that by today she would have something to tell us. And – oh, Laure, she did look so odd.'

'Really.'

'And then she drew Annette aside. She spoke to her privately, and Annette turned quite pale. And then – she curtsied.'

'You curtsy to her all the time.'

'Yes, but Annette doesn't. We asked Annette – she wouldn't say a thing. But yesterday I saw her husband riding out that way – the notary.'

'The old woman wants to sell something,' said Laure. 'You know how sometimes she does. A painting. Or those furs. And she sold her diamonds, she told us, all but that single one in the brooch, which Violette Charpentier says comes from the crown jewels of the Bourbons, and I don't believe a word of *that.*'

Laure felt fresher. She glanced at the room and wanted to leave it. She thought of the chateau. It seemed still dull – yet all at once unknown. Perhaps dangerous.

She thought of the Blue-of-memory House.

The lit window.

The shadow.

Only three days ago. How have they passed?

If I don't go to the chateau, I'll have to go there. I'll loiter about like a stray dog or some no-good.

Laure snapped: 'Very well. I'll go with you.'

Sophrine said, 'Papa told me la Reine had called Monsieur Mercier up to the big house on financial business. Papa said to me, Sophie, watch out. She's going to tell you about a little money coming your way.'

Disgusted, Laure threw off her dress, as if Sophrine had now contaminated it. She drew into her arms a garment of faded ivory yellow, the colour of the storm-wrecked roses.

'Don't pull a face, Laure. You know quite well one day you'll have everything from your Aunt (God keep her well). Below la Reine, yours is one of the best-lined families in the town. Better even than Lejay's, for all his airs. No worries for you. But papa – who can blame him if he wants a nest-egg for me.'

And all those curtsies, *thought spiteful Laure,* on account.

The great dining room was well-lighted. The chandelier, which seemed to have been dusted, glittered and spangled as it moved slightly in the chateaus eddying draughts. Also there were candles blazing, squadrons of them, on the table.

She's extravagant tonight.

Despite the borrowed vehicle, mud had splashed the hem of Laures' dress. Why should she care?

All the women were there. There were twenty-five of them at present, including herself. She knew them all by sight and to exchange words with, only a few intimately. Artemise Lejay was splendid in a dinner-gown of dark blood red. At the moment her acolytes were Honorine Eperve and Douce Rochelet. (Had the constant Sophrine ever been enlisted? Laure didn't know – or had never noticed.)

When la Reine entered, which was after they had been served a Spanish wine for warmth, Laure looked up to see her, curiously.

Well it was true. She did look most odd. She was like – an animated waxwork. And as she advanced into the room, Peridot the Jewel hovering behind her, Laures' scathing pity changed to wonder, and then an instinctive fear.

All the women were the same, or similarly affected. Their glasses catching countless bright dots or sparks from hearth or candles, their wide eyes burning. A picture of suspense.

For Sidonie Aubade-Valents had put on a brocade gown, of a green fierce enough to rival Artemise Lejay's Scarlet's. And on her neck and in her ears were emeralds, large fine ones. Her hair was piled very high, and by its pagoda effect they saw she had grown very stooped. She leaned hard on her cane. Her head poked forward, rather as the tortoise head of Peridot had always done. But the seamed and flaccid breast of la Reine, her ploughed throat and furrowed face – were powdered. And on her cheeks, not inartistically applied, but so unlikely as to seem hectic, some rouge.

Not a waxwork. No, she appeared now to be a beneficiary of the embalmer's art, made ready for the casket.

The room spun. Or in fact, not the room, but Laure herself, spun round, inside her body, which did not for a second move.

Everything, when she came back, was removed far off. And so she drifted to the table, miles away from all of them, and weightlessly stood there and waited. Not even looking now at la Reine. Not needing to look at her.

Only the terrible heartbeat, which made the candles seem massively to leap and sink, swell and diminish, and the tablecloth to pulse.

And stupid, stupid Sophrine, touching her arm an instant, seeming to think Laure's chill was after all bad, and had made her feverishly so white, and her eyes so black and rimmed with red.

She did not speak to them until the meal was mainly done. It was a substantial dinner, several courses, with small roasted fowls, glazed pheasant, a fricassee, sauces, a soup, pates, cherries in liqueur, hothouse oranges, sweets coloured like candle wax.

When she had drugged and sated them, for most of them ate heartily, maybe even desperately, and all but one of them drank the wines (Laure was the exception), la Reine began to talk. In her former way, generally, mildly, inexorably taking control of them.

At this point, in the past, she had told her stories, if she had one to tell. Legends of the house, like that of the Feast, or historical anecdotes. Or peculiar episodes of a childhood here, which seemed to be hers, although they knew she had not come to the chateau until she was a bride of eighteen.

Now she told them a story of her future.

She told it well, as she always had. Without undue involvement. And on her painted ruined face, as ever, the calm if not uninterested indifference to them and to herself, which might denote, after all, only a genuine sympathy. Ultimately, who can help themselves or anyone? The most we can give, perhaps, is our truth, and the ability to condone the truth of others.

'Well, my friends, our time together is drawing to its end. I'm going to die very shortly.' (She didn't pause for expressions of grief or protest. There were none.) 'I shall remain at the chateau for perhaps a month. Then I must go alone to Paris, to my house there. Peridot, my inexhaustible Jewel, will accompany me, to see to my needs, until it is finished. I regret, on my departure, the chateau will be shut up and presently assumed by my creditors. Like any proper aristo, I'm sadly in debt. They have waited, knowing they would get what I have quite soon, and now soon they will.

'I hope you've found some enjoyment here. I hope it's done you some good, as was my intention. I can leave you nothing. I have nothing left to leave you. I've used all I have entirely selfishly for myself, and my own wants. Peridot, of course, I've provided for; how else could I ask her service at last. A payment. But there is one other payment I shall make, a settlement, after my death, for something bought, also selfishly, to comfort my last month as a whole woman.'

The awful words – awful in every possible way – for her, for them – dropped like cool stones.

'Tonight there's to be a slight affair, not a ceremony, more an adjustment to my life. It may startle you, or dismay you. You may be angry. But, my dear friends, at the door of death, and perhaps a horrible death, I must tell you I am unconcerned by your censure or malice. Even, I'm afraid, by your kindness. Should you wish to witness the event tonight, then you may. Or you may wish to go at once. While I remain at the chateau, you may come and go as you want, although after tonight, you will never again see me, or see this carcass which is all that's left of me. And in one month, a little less or more, the gates will be shut against you by my executors. Just as, only a little after, the gates of existence will slam upon my going out.'

There was a pause, then. A silence. Perhaps the candles made their habitual soft hiss, or the fire, or rain sounded at the windows and in the chimney. Then, conceivably, they heard their own breathing. The sound of living circulating in their veins.

'During my last month, I shall entertain a companion here. She will stay, while I do. When I leave for Paris, she too will leave, although not to go with me. By then she will have done for me all that can be done, and will be free. There's always gossip in a town,' said la Reine. 'I think you'll have heard of her.'

Then someone let out a shrill yipping cry. It was Clothilde, Laure thought. But then came the voice of Artemise Lejay, haughty yet strangely common, as when she had discussed the price of soap.

'Do you mean, grande dame, this arrangement you've made – That is, do you mean it's with this woman we've been hearing of? This – what is it? Madame Corrot?'

And then, equally appalling, apt and unforgivable, Violette Charpentier inquired, 'But she serves men, does she not, that one? A *widow*, I thought.'

Not a flicker disturbed la Reine.

'Oh, she'll serve a woman too, if the money suits her. How did I know? You must allow me to be reticent on that.'

Then an outcry full of silly provincial women's' oaths. It came and went. Touched nothing.

Sidonie Aubade-Valents spoke to them once more. 'She will be arriving presently. Annette's husband, Monsieur Mercier, is conducting her in a carriage, with all the proper papers. She'll be here in – oh, twenty minutes, by that clock on the mantelpiece. Naturally, she and I have already met, last Wednesday evening to be exact. Before dinner. But you are curious, perhaps?'

Clothilde Boulanger sprang up. She looked as if she surprised only herself. 'My father wouldn't allow it – for me to be in the same room as such – Excuse me, grande dame.'

And even as she hesitated still, dithering, others jumped up. Honorine and Rose, Lucide, compressing her mouth, which was always rather too small, Marie Jeanne, five or six more. But Artemise Lejay swept to her feet, without another word, and drove from the room, taking her redness with her, and the rest who meant to or thought they meant to, swirling like leaves in her wake down the drain. The doors shut, and Violette, sitting fast, let out her thin laughter, one cruel peal.

After which they heard the clock, as if only now had it come alive and begun to tick.

Of course Peridot had known so much because she had been told. She hadn't disapproved, that wasn't her place. Yet, did she despise, the way the slave so often despised the master? Peridot, to Laure, was an enigma.

Laure though was not thinking of this. Nailed down by her hammering heart, she continued to sit motionless, and then, once or twice, took a tiny sip of wine, as if she were normally thirsty.

Then they moved to another room.

Coffee was served the remaining women, in the salon with the piano. The yellow octogenarian curtains had been drawn, and this way, their heavy swags revealed discolouration and holes. The piano even had not been dusted, nor opened. Closed, it was like a coffin.

Laure discovered she stood now nailed in one spot again, this time near the fireplace. She held a translucent cup, and sometimes took a sip, but the cup never emptied, as the glass had not.

La Reine had not come in with them.

The clock along the passage, in the dining room, struck ten. Had the clock ever struck before? Laure couldn't remember that it had.

And had a carriage driven up? It must have done. Probably it had gone round to the old stables, as on Wednesday evening. (All the women agreed to this – in one of the mad rushes of chatter that followed their eviction from the other room. Otherwise they would have heard or seen the carriage that Wednesday. But what was she like, the creature who was coming here?)

'Laure – didn't you say you saw the bitch – ?'

'*Marie?*'

'Well, what would you call her?'

'A slut, she's a true whore –'

'Laure, Laure, come to, wake up! What's wrong with you? Tell us – didn't you catch a glimpse of that woman in the town?'

Laure, turning her head, staring as if at a pack of wolves run suddenly into the salon, pawing at her skirts and slavering.

And then, Peridot was in the doorway, pushing the doors wide and standing back. And the tap-tip-tap of Madame la Reine's walking-stick on the wooden floor, tap-tip-tap. And the rustle of her gown. And a soft step, like the footfall of a cat on ice. The Queen enters the room and she is holding the arm of someone. An arm in firm black velvet. An arm that tapers to a narrow wrist, a long white hand without a ring, but a hand in a black mitten ... Widow's weeds.

In the salon, utter soundlessness.

The Queen glances round with – what is it? Complacency, nearly ennui? She longs to be rid of them all, all but the one she has chosen. In fact, was it her cranky courtesy to let them see what had come to replace them – this symbol of her death.

Death stands there.

Death, the widow.

'Let me introduce my dear companion. You may know her as Madame Corrot. But she tells me that the name is no longer hers, as other names are no longer. She prefers to be known then by her given name, Virgile.'

People move about. There is a male presence, rarely to be spotted on Club days and nights. Two lackeys in an outmoded livery, seeing to a table and chair. And then Monsieur Mercier, Annette's buffoon-like, smiling husband, bustling to lay out a document – presumably there have been others, now reduced to this single item. A contract, like a marriage contract.

La Reine crosses to the table on the arm of her dear companion, who is to be called only *Virgile*.

The Queen sits, and as she does so, let's go of the arm (the strong arm), and one of the lackeys places her cane for her.

Beaming (and sweating), Monsieur Mercier bends forward to indicate where the old comtesse must sign. And even in this extremity, Annette, about fifty paces away, is partly leaning forward too, anxious that her husband do nothing amiss.

After all, there is scarcely anything so vulgar as an aristocrat. Here in the presence of them all – this!

And by her chair, la Reine's carved chair of the salon, that one stands. Not as if to make sure of her fee, her price, her profit. Not as if, really, to do or be anything.

Laure sees her stand there.

What does Laure see?

A mask without a face behind it? A shell formed, perhaps only freakishly, in the shape of a woman about twenty-five or twenty-seven years old? Or one of those things from fairy tales of the cold north of Europe – an elf-maiden, whose back is hollow?

Laure is thinking, Oh God, shall I run out? She is thinking, Hold me up, I can't fall. She is thinking, Will she look at me, let her not look at me, I must look at her, I must look away.

But all these thoughts are only a background, like the scratching of candlewicks as they burn, or the sullen whisper of the autumn wind.

Virgile is quite tall, straight and slim, accentuated by her crow-black velvet gown, with its long sleeves, and high throat, where there are polished agate buttons. Her hair is nearly as black. It has that blued-copper sheen found on the fur of some black cats. There are quantities of it, wound and coiled, and culminating now not in a hat, but in an ebony comb, from which a bit of veiling, soft, like smoke, filters out as if to conceal the forehead and the eyes, but then skirts and only shades them. In her ears, two golden crescents, very small. Two little new moons, twinkling. Her neck is long, like her hands and waist and, it seems, her legs, under the stem of the dress. Like her white face, with its perfectly drawn nose and jaw, its cheekbones. Its effect of a shield cunningly quartered. The brows are very strongly marked. Masculine, in this face which is female. The mouth a little too large, as if infinitesimally stretched – although not in a smile. The mouth, nothing else, has been touched with artificial colour. The eyes are utterly black and totally still. Do they blink? Can she close them when either she sleeps or when she ceases to be awake – or when she pretends she is *not* awake? Lashes – like stiff fringes, the colour of tar – which makes it seem there is a black line drawn around her two long eyes.

There is to her – which could make you wonder if she has trained herself all these years, and done so because she has had to do so – this quality of complete immobility. If the autumn wind, rising again on the park and on the town, were to burst in, it would stir the folds of her dress, might dislodge her wisp of veil, might even undo the interwoven ropes of her Indian hair. But otherwise it would not move her. She is fixed. Immutable.

No sudden *other* movement in the room, no flutter or start, not even the angular jerk by which Violette Charpentier manages abruptly to drop her coffee cup with a frigid noise – *nothing* makes the black eyes look elsewhere.

But the contract has been signed. The notary has appended his signature, and Peridot, also, has made her mark.

Not one of the other women was included.

They're only the audience, at last.

Then a lackey comes in with a tray of crystal thimbles full of Armagnac, and each of them has to take one, and they do, even Laure does (and puts her full cup down on a table too, not knowing she does).

Following this bizarre marriage, there's to be a toast.

La Reine stands up. She is haggard in her slight paint.

'To our health, my friends,' says la Reine, 'yours and mine.' Sparing them nothing.

Is *Virgile* included? Is the dear companion also the friend?

What can she do, this diseased stick that must *lean* on a stick, what in God's name is possible for her, even given the skills of a *Virgile*?

They drink. Everyone drinks.

Laure drinks.

It is Marie-Louison who chokes herself. And Violette, grim as a prison wardress, who slaps her between the shoulders.

'I wish you every happiness,' says la Reine, clearly. And then she takes the arm of Virgile, flawlessly offered her at once. And Virgile at that moment finally moves her eyes, gazing round at them all. These eyes are so black they seem blind. They seem thoughtless and without either mind or soul. Laure for one second meets them as they pass. Then they are gone, and the old woman and the young woman, old age and death, the two eternal widows, stalk slowly out of the room.

Violette dropped her cup. Celine Marblon diligently smashes her glass to the ground, and breaks herself into sobs. Then Marie-Louison starts, and runs over to her. They weep and howl. Others take it up, snivelling.

Everyone is very shocked.

Peridot has gone, so have the lackeys. Monsieur Mercier, abruptly paternal, is coaxing a shaky Annette to come away, come away. 'Our little Georges is asking for you all the time. You know he never sleeps well when you're out late. He needs his mother, poor little fellow.'

Douce Rochelet steps up to Laure and seizes her arm.

'What did you think of her? She had eyes like a *snake. A serpent.*'

'Oh.'

'Oh, I suppose you'll say the old witch has the right to do it – and to throw us out. Why it's all that's kept us safe in this horrid little sty of a town. Her patronage. The chateau. The thought she might – might give us – a small remuneration – Good God, what would it have cost her, the old wretch? Less than this honey- month with that vampire! I should have left when Artemise did. *She* had the right of it. Wouldn't lower herself to be part of it. The old wretch! Any one of us could do it for her – what she wants, and be paid, and run off and leave her to die alone in Paris. What can she stand any way, at her age, in her state –' Douce was shaking Laure by the arm, like a terrier.

Sophrine stepped between them, brisk, as if to attend an irate customer in the grocer's shop.

'Now, Douce. You know we couldn't have done it.'

'What – do you think that *reptile* is more beautiful than Artemise Lejay?'

'I think this – what is she called? – Virgile – is a professional,' said Sophrine, 'and la Reine needs a professional. I shouldn't know how to begin. Should you? And Artemise is much too fine, one couldn't even consider it, for Artemise.'

'But to *pay – her –*'

'To pay to have work well done? That's only just.'

'And us? Haven't we earned something?'

'How?' asked Sophrine. 'By enjoying ourselves at the old woman's expense all these years? Come along. I don't mind it. So what.'

Douce had detached herself from Laure. She walked off. Sophrine said,

'I suppose I should get home.'

Laure said, 'You say you don't mind it. I thought you'd mind it.'

'Oh, papa will. He'll carry on. I've saved some sweets for him in a napkin. I'll feed him those and not tell him everything, just how ill she is. I'll say I don't care, not getting any money out of her. I so prefer to stay with him, so why do I need a nest-egg, and anyway I'm so proud of our own money, how he earned it so honestly through his hard work and self-sacrifice, and isn't he the hero. Well, Laure. I'll miss my times up here. But I'm grown up now. We have to put up with things, don't we?'

'I thought you would mind. I did think so.' Laure felt herself sway forward, and Sophrine drew her back, and then they stood in quite an ordinary way.

But again Laure said, 'I thought you'd mind. Yes. I did.'

'You don't know what you're saying,' said Sophrine. 'You've got a fever, I'm sure of it. I doubt we'll get a carriage now, either. Artemise's trap has gone. I'll take you home, dear. I'll take care of you, Laure. It isn't so far. The moment we get there I'll wake up that Ouelle, she must make some hot milk, and put a hot stone in the bed for you.'

Laure laughed. Languidly she touched her own forehead, which felt burning hot to her icy hands. As they walked through the park, between the overgrown hedges of box, and along the carriage drive, the wind was low and the rain had stopped. Neither looked back.

Sophrine spoke calmly. 'Such a grand place. Even now, all neglected. I can hardly believe I'll never see it again. But I don't think I'll come here anymore. I don't know if you will. Some of them may, until the house is shut up and sold. But how dreary. How awful too, poor old lady, dying. I thought she'd reach her nineties. And her Paris residence is some poky box, I've heard. We'll have to think of some other venue we can all go to. Artemise Lejay lives in that very large house, but her monsieur won't think of letting her have us visit there. Or, only her favourites, I suppose.'

On the lane, the chestnuts held out their glistening boughs, more than half empty of leaves, and rainy stars shone between.

They walked slowly, Sophrine holding Laure's arm as if to steady her.

What am I to do?

If only Sophrine would stop jabbering. It echoed in Laure's swimming head. The roadway twisted uphill, and there was a young fallen tree at its edge, brought down by the winds three nights ago, unnoticed until now. They moved aside from it, as most of humanity does, from dead things.

She's there, in the chateau.

Don't think of it now.

Not yet.

When?

An Interval

The day after the 'marriage' of la Reine and Virgile the widow, summer returned to Bois-la-Diane. There came to be a light the colour of a pale wine from Xeres. On this, the last leaves were pinned like flags of peeled bronze, and garnet scales. And the leaves which had fallen, turning to a damson mush, lit with singular orange streaks, out of which thrust the purple splash of autumn crocus. More than half unveiled, the trees showed pockets of apples, pears, left stranded like glowing lamps, or showed the fruit smashed on the ground in bitter ciders. Grapes on the vine turned gold with sweetness. A final rose the wind had overlooked, yellow-amber like the afternoons, stood upright in the garden of the house on the rue Dalle, for thirteen days, before the head fell on the path, intact, brown as a cobnut.

Warm, so warm, and hot, at noon.

The birds, misled or only driven mad, sang wildly and opened their wings to gild them like the mask of a pharaoh, and keep death out.

The town shone.

On the street Laure, fetching (strange, perhaps misguided) purchases of the Aunts from the leaning shops behind the church, met Rose and Honorine Eperve.

'How washed-out you are, Laure   is it the heat? Oh this weather! What it would have been, to be at the chateau. Do you remember the luncheons on the terrace, or when we had picnics under the great chestnut in summer?'

'And the little stream. Do you remember that scalding day we took off our dresses and bathed in the pool, and we were dry again in five minutes?'

Laure stood, quiet and solemn. Did she remember?

'Well,' she said. 'There.'

Honorine leant forward, her hat with its cornflowers of cloth tilting to cut off the sun. 'Lucide went back there. She did. With Marie-Jeanne. We were talking with them yesterday. And can you imagine, Laure. That woman. Oh! That woman.'

Laure, standing, idle. 'Whom, Honorine?'

'*That* one. *She!* You know who I mean.'

'Ah.'

'Yes, that depraved person who calls herself *Virgilie*' Almost – just able to prevent her tongue tripping out the correction – *No, no, Honorine. Not Virgilie –* 'As if *that* could be her proper given name. The effrontery. The cheek of it.'

'And,' said Rose, deceptively mild, 'it seems she takes her lunch alone. Dines with la Reine only in the evening – so her days mostly are all her own.'

'And there she sits. My goodness, queening it. Lucide said the lunch was very opulent. Better than we generally had. But then, oh yes. And in comes the woman, all in her black dress, and sits there. And there are two servants, the men, if you please, serving her. And Lucide and Marie-Jeanne, they can just serve themselves. And not a *word*, not a *word*.'

'And so,' said Rose, deceptively urbane, 'Marie-Jeanne says to the woman, "Excuse me, but what lovely weather were having." And this woman, this *Virgilette,* she just nods – graciously, Jeanne said, as if she were the comtesse herself.'

'When all the time she's from the gutters of Paris or Marseilles or the Lord knows where –'

'So, at last Lucide asks her to pass the coffee pot –'

'Seeing as how no one has bothered to put anything anywhere within their reach –'

'And Virgilette simply passes it.'

'Just passes the pot!'

'Just that.'

'And not a *word*.'

Laure, who is trembling violently, her legs weak, as often now they are, suddenly puts her hand to her mouth but can't stifle the trembling liquid laugh that breaks from her.

Honorine is affronted. Rose only bemused (deceptively?).

'What's to laugh at? She is a monster. Didn't you think her just like a lizard?'

Laure nods.

'Oh, you would laugh, wouldn't you. What do you care, Laure Deschampeigne? The old lady was nothing to you. But we – we were attached to her. She betrayed us, Laure.' And Honorine's eyes bulge, amazing Laure, with sun bright tears.

'Artemise Lejay,' says Rose quietly, 'has sunk into an indisposition. She's quite sick, Douce said.'

'No,' said Honorine brutishly, 'she's in the family way. Yes, carrying a child. All this time and she's never fallen. Her maid was up with her half the night, with Artemise crying at what it will do to her figure and her teeth. And that fiend, Monsieur Lejay, he's complaining at the expense and nuisance of her lying in, and then of the baby. As if he'd had nothing to do with it, the brute.'

'Perhaps,' muttered Rose, 'he didn't.'

'What can you mean?'

'Well, she's had lovers, you know. Not only amongst us. She's had men.'

'What do you know? That's nonsense.'

Laure said, 'I must go back. My Aunt's waiting for these things.'

She hurried up the street to get away from them, hugging the ridiculous parcels – a single short length of silk – for what? – some ribbons, the kind that would trim a young girl's hat – a packet of some cosmetic whitening the Aunt had never, to Laure's knowledge, ever used – some digestive pills the Aunt had formerly said were useless to her. And so on.

Laure thinking. Or rather, words, pictures, racing through her head, like the shadows and lights flashing between the houses and the trees.

In fact, the ancient garden, consumed by its desuetude after the storm, did not seem so beautiful, even in the sherried light of a false summer. The cedar had pulled out more of the paving, and leaned heavily towards the south-west. Mushrooms swelled, hideous frilled fungi like boils with poison. The docks had grown claws.

Was this the place where those Shakespearean lines had come to her, four years ago? The midsummer evening dreams of a fairy woman lying asleep, of the glamouring flower of love and seduction?

Over on that stone bench she had sat with Lucide, and once with Celine Marblon, kissing, fondling.

In the park, the tall statue of Pan had been overgrown sufficiently, she couldn't find him, or his guardian elm.

Jays and magpies yattered from the woods.

Laure stopped, staring up. High, high in an oak tree not yet bared of its crenulated leaves, something was caught and sparkling like a crimson star. But involuntarily, dizzy from bending back her head, she took one more step – and the star was gone. She could not find it again.

The long glass windows to the salon were shut. Laure walked about, and along the terrace. In the end she retreated among the sprawled hedges of box, and glancing round at it, seemed to view the chateau as it might soon come to be, high-roofed, curved with black balconies, deserted, a few sparrows dashing about rotted towers.

At the end of the walk, she crossed (familiar with it all), the dried bed of some antique outlet of the stream, and climbed some steps. From here, between two hazel trees, she might look across the longer diagonal face of the chateau. Out on the looped carriage drive, a red squirrel was busily foraging. And standing nearby, motionless:

On amber, ink.

But oh, so still. A lizard ? A lizard black as coal.

Laure stepped forward and walked through the high dry grass, and the squirrel, hearing her approach, fled for the trees beyond the drive. (To Virgile it had paid no attention, no more than it would to a tall dark stone.)

And she.

And:

There was something so curious. The way she stayed so still, yet turned her inky head, and then, the white face, shield-quartered with eyes and nose and lips.

Laure stumbled. Righted herself. She walked the rest of the way.

She stood.

She stood before Virgile.

Before Virgile on the carriage drive in broad sunlight.

The white face was tinted, very faintly, with daylight colours. The whites of the black eyes were nearly blue.

'Good day, madame.'

She wouldn't respond, wouldn't speak. They had said, she didn't.

Virgile's eyes blinked, once, it seemed absurdly slowly. Her lips, parting. 'And to you also, Mademoiselle Deschampeigne.'

Laure caught her breath.

'I used to come here, every Wednesday. Almost every Wednesday and Saturday, you see,' said Laure. 'And today is Thursday. But I'm here, instead. It won't matter now, will it, the regular days. I hope I don't inconvenience you.'

And at that, the face, some slight stretching of the lips, and of the eyes – already so long and wide. Mocking, of course. The idea that anyone could inconvenience a Virgile.

I want to say her – your – name.

It would be unthinkable to say it. *Though I have,* thought Laure, *been saying it.*

'I hope you're well,' said Laure.

'I'm always well.'

Again, like a blow, this voice. Like the blow of the face. I did think you'd talk to me. To *me*. Because you did before, outside the Blue House, in the dusk, the Azure Hour when all things change their shape.

Laure's own voice broke out of her. 'I saw – the most curious thing just now. Has Madame la Comtesse – has she told you the story of the Feast? No … yes …? Oh, but I'm sure she will. And the girl's supposed to lie under the park somewhere – and all the pearls and Venetian goblets – they were put with her, you see – all these things. And just now, in an oak tree – I saw a narrow red glass goblet, caught there in the branches. Or – I thought I did.' Laure couldn't breathe. She had said such a lot, but hadn't meant to say so much. Or to say more, differently. She fell silent and pressed her hand to her waist.

It might have been insulting – was it insulting – to have spoken of la Reine, to Virgile? Or had it not been?

Virgile stood, looking at her. Laure lowered her eyes. 'You make me so nervous, madame.'

Virgile looked at her. Two black questions – or only black mirrors reflecting.

Laure: 'This situation – is a strange one for me. I'm afraid, madame, of saying something to offend you. When I don't mean to do so.'

Virgile half turned, half turned away

away

Don't go in – don't go – let me stay with – stay with me –

'Have I offended you, madame?'

'No, Mademoiselle Deschampeigne.'

How does she know my name? Oh, from the old woman's book, naturally, the one in her rooms, where I wouldn't write my name like all the rest, but someone must have written it for me – Sophrine probably. Or the old woman mentioned me. 'Laure Deschampeigne, from one of those well-to-do bourgeois families, which hang on to an aristocratic name as grimly as they hid it less than a hundred years ago.'

Virgile had begun to move towards the house. She walked very smoothly, but it was just possible to see that she took steps. Yet, the image is a cobra, gliding upright on its tail.

Laure walked quickly, and caught her up. This took courage, too. Walked beside her.

'Would you prefer, oh, that I didn't come into the house?'

'Whatever you want, mademoiselle. It's of no consequence.'

Obviously not, since I am not.

'But, to take lunch there, as I've done in the past.'

'If you wish.'

What else had la Reine said to Virgile about Laure? 'She dresses well, as these families always do, quite well for a provincial. A poor education, thinks herself better-read and more modern than she is. A snappish little thing. Quick to take offence or suspicion, too cold or too frothy.'

No, why would the old woman speak of Laure at all? She would only want to talk about herself – and about …

About Virgile.

Laure said boldly, as they went in at one of the smaller doors (under a great round balcony on the floor above, hanging over like a thunder cloud), 'Is it true you come from Paris, madame?'

And Virgile didn't answer.

'I ask – because, because, because some books I had ordered just came to me from Paris, you see. How envious I am, if you came from Paris … but, well –'

In the passage, with its pale, damp-spotted silk walls, and then turning into another little parlour, which looked on to a walled rose garden.

A table was laid by a window, and sunlight fell on it and turned it to amber, as this sunlight turned everything to amber, except Virgile.

One place laid. Of course, only one. In a vase, two blowsy pink peonies – but the garden outside had no flowers. The rain had stripped them.

Virgile went directly to the carved sideboard, where a jug stood under a cover. From this she poured a glass of milk, drank it, with quick laps. She offered Laure nothing.

In a dreadful dissolution, as if she felt herself separating in small pieces, Laure stood by the table, pretending to admire the sodden wrecked flowerless garden. On their briars, rose-hips had formed, edged by the sun with blood.

A man servant entered.

Virgile spoke, distantly.

'Lay another place.' Laure s heart leapt in fire.

'Oh, thank you –' stammering. Ridiculous.

The man did as he had been told. Then went out.

Virgile crossed to the table and seated herself.

Laure sat down facing her.

How beautiful she is. How beautiful. And yet – no, I believe that she's quite ugly – the beauty is a sort of camouflage – or illusion – but I'm magnetized and pulled into it. Like tumbling into a tunnel. And her eyes. I look in her eyes and go insane.

What would it be to come close to her, that is, *physically* close?

Laure had naturally thought of this. At first stopped herself. Then, while the one yellow rose persisted in the Aunt's garden, thought of it and thought of it.

Laure felt, at her thoughts, no sexual frisson, no urgent tingling in the blood or quickening of her loins. Rather it was as if a whirlwind caught her up. She was flung through space and dashed against a stunning obduracy, and as she dropped from it, semi-conscious, it caught her and raised her, fainting, dying, to its lips.

And this ecstasy was, if anything, far more powerful than the flood of sex. Even of orgasm. It was an orgasm of another sort. Emotional, spiritual, deathly and divine. *Ceaseless.*

Then Laure had not been able to stop thinking of it. She had lain for thirteen days, mostly in chairs, imagining over and over, approaching Virgile, and Virgile, without touching her, creating the whirlwind, and being lost in the whirlwind until, at some last moment, when nothing was left of Laure, when all in her had been given over – Virgile seizing hold of her – and being dashed against Virgile, the swooning and collapse, helpless and without will, every thought extinguished.

Dying in her arms, her grip. Drowned. Smothered. Devoured?

(And today, the Aunt interrupting, staring at her own garden and killing that rose finally by exclaiming, 'Oh this wonderful July weather!')

Laure's hands now trembled so much she could hardly take up the glass the servant must have filled with wine.

Someone had brought food, too, she saw.

Laure stared at the food. She had never seen food in her life before, and definitely didn't know what to do with it.

But Virgile was eating, in hard, quick bites. Laure wished she could put her hand between those narrow white teeth. Feel them close on her flesh and pierce to the bones beneath.

She shut her eyes. Dizzily she leaned her cheek into her unbitten hand.

Virgile, it appeared, failed to notice.

Why should she have any interest in me?

Blankly, Laure said, 'How is the comtesse?'

Virgile touched her lips with a napkin.

She looked at Laure for a moment, but not long enough.

'The comtesse is, under the circumstances, quite well.'

'Shouldn't I have asked you? You see – I don't know what I may say and what I simply shouldn't mention –'

What do you do for her? I longed to ask that. Or perhaps I couldn't bear to know.

The meal was somehow over. Laure found she had peeled an apple. She bit into its nakedness, could not swallow the mouthful, managed it only with a gulp of wine.

Virgile was rising.

Blackness, the snake's stem, the spread hood of the widow's veil across a snood of hair.

Laure looked up at her now in terror.

Don't leave me. Stay with me, stay – stay – it's all I ask. Nothing else – truly – nothing –

'Good afternoon, mademoiselle.'

'I should like you – to call me by my name. My name is Laure.'

Virgile gave a little nod. But did not pronounce the name. Half turning now, turning away.

Away.

'And I – may I – address you as Virgile?'

How false the name sounded, when Laure uttered it. An unreal name, improbable. Worse than Virgilie, even.

But she said, 'If you wish.'

Laure stood up. And Virgile walked from the room. And then Laure sat down again. Trembling so much, her eyes streaming suddenly with tears, of frustration and shame.

Later, eyes dried, she walked about the gardens. She glared up into the trees, where the white doves fluttered uneasily, sensing the treachery of the sunlight. There were no ropes of pearls, no magpie nest from which a crimson glass or silver platter or red carbuncle stopper protruded.

She went to the pool, it was choked with leaves. A tawny frog, just like a leaf, sat pulsing on a stone.

The light slanted. It browned like the last rose, began like the last rose, to fall.

When she returned, shadows hung in the rooms of the chateau, and between them now and then stole one of the servants. No lamps had been lit. None of the windows, from outside, showed any colour.

Laure thought of Virgile, descending the murderer's stair.

A servant came, a girl, and Laure said, 'Does Madame Virgile take tea?'

'Oh, no, mademoiselle. She's with the comtesse now.'

Her flat face, without a trace of any simper or snigger, was somehow prurient and disgusting.

Laure knew she must at once leave the chateau and its grounds.

She must never return.

Now, as she walked, she cried again. She leaned against a bare beech tree some distance from the vast old house, and wept, sobbing. Her gloves fell on the fallen leaves. She picked them up, turning dizzy again.

Oh God, what was the point of it all?

When she reached the lane, she forgot how she had come there. But the sky was grey.

Up the lane drove an old carter behind his shambling horse, the cart piled with incomprehensible jumble, which in the gathering of dusk, might even have been bodies, plague victims shambled in there for burning.

He saluted her politely. It was old Jacques, the lamp-lighter.

She allowed him to go by, and walked slowly after him and his plodding horse, towards the town.

Act Three

'She has had a slight fall. Nothing too serious. But I'm somewhat concerned.' Doctor St Romarin stood in the Aunt's sitting room. His spectacles were grave.

'She seems,' he elaborated, 'very forgetful. I expect you've noted it, Mademoiselle Deschampeigne, perhaps put it down to the vagaries of old age. But this isn't quite normal. No indeed.'

Ouelle, with her abominable bobbing, subsequently served him the large cognac Laure had omitted to offer.

'Thank you, my good lady! Who knows when these fine evening s will turn on us, like wild beasts, eh?'

'Will I fetch another, your honour?'

'No, no, I won't impose.'

'Do, please,' said Laure.

The nasty flicker of his joviality was soon swallowed by the alcohol.

'I dislike alarming you, mademoiselle. I understand your natural tenderness towards your aunt has blinded you in this matter. But it's my duty to remind you, I fear, that madame's father, and her elder sister, both perished in this way – of a softening of the brain.'

Laure was, after all, shocked. Perhaps, it was more distaste than shock.

'There,' said the doctor, seating Laure in a chair, his duty done, 'fetch mademoiselle also a cognac, my good Ouelle.'

'No, that isn't necessary.'

'I insist, Mademoiselle Laure. Your pulse seems rather weak.'

And here was Ouelle again, with a cognac for Laure, and yet another for the doctor.

'Now, now, Ouelle, my good woman. What shall we do with you? The best course, Mademoiselle Laure, will be to confine the old lady to her bed, and to watch her. I'm afraid I must stipulate a watch both day and night, for the present. I can recommend a woman from St Georges-du-Marais, who will assist your servants and yourself. And I shall call myself, every day. I think, mademoiselle, you must prepare yourself.'

Laure said, confused by the cognac, 'But for what?'

'My dear young woman! For what do you suppose?'

'You're saying that my Aunt will soon die.'

'It's very likely. If her condition is what I fear it to be, then we must even hope so. Of course, there's the hospital at Convienne. But we won't think of that at present. However, I have a colleague there whom I think I may acquaint with madame's condition. He too may wish to visit madame, if at all possible in his busy work. Sometimes one is mistaken in these things, I should say, misled. There is always that.'

Laure went up to see her Aunt. She felt she had to, was expected to, not only by Ouelle and the girl, and the doctor, but by convention itself. Worse, by some intransigent moral code of natural ethics she had never grasped.

The Aunt lay on her bank of pillows, they, and she in her nightgown, trimmed with dull lace. No one yet was watching her. 'Laure – is that you, Laure?'

Laure was struck by an awful doubt; the Aunt might now take Laure for Laure's own mother, the Aunt's younger sister. (Laure's mother had answered to the same name, although her given name was Laurente.)

'Yes, Aunt.'

Was it callous to stress their correct relationship? If taken for her own mother, must Laure pretend to it as well?

But the Aunt didn't seem aware of any difficulty. She only beckoned Laure closer to her, and then, reaching out, gripped Laure's hand with surprising, distressing strength.

'Something I ate,' said the Aunt. 'That veal, I suspect the veal. Too rich. I never liked it. And the sauce with brandy and sorrel. It doesn't suit me. Tell the cook, he's not to serve it again.'

They had no cook but Ouelle, no man in the house.

'No, Aunt. I'll tell him.'

(There, deception.)

'Oh, dear. I've so much to do. There are those frocks ... I don't like this, having to lie up here.'

'You'll soon be well,' said Laure. (The second deception.) The voice of a deaths head, too. She wanted to tear away her hand. Death – should never come in such a guise. This creeping thief with his train of lies. In the mediaeval play he was a priestly knight on a pale horse. His sword was keen and bright.

'The mice are bad,' said the Aunt. 'Tell Susine. She must do something about the mice.'

'Yes, Aunt. Yes, I will.'

'I wish it were tomorrow,' said the Aunt. And then, quite appallingly, 'Or yesterday.'

The door opened and the girl came in. She had a basket of darning and put it down by a chair. (For the first time Laure was struck by the way they lived, so carefully, as if things might not be thrown out and new ones purchased ...) It seemed the girl was going to watch, Laure was not expected to, at least, not for the present.

But the hand still held her fast.

'Now, mistress,' said the girl, coming up with some concoction in a spoon, 'here's your medicine. That's right. Now this water with your drops in it.'

The Aunt let go of Laure's hand to take the glass.

'Isn't the summer weather lovely. I saw the first rose today.'

'Yes, mistress. That's right. Lie back and have a little sleep. It will do you good.'

Laure's mind went completely running off, trying to escape. *I read only last week, in the collected letters of Madame de Drut ...* Oh, that Laure thinks herself educated and well-read.

'I shall be in my room,' said Laure, 'if I'm needed.'

Needed. What in God's name can I do? Oh damn this awful horror.

And I'm so tired now, always. Or no, it's this savage energy which wears me out –

As she patrolled her room, she read words of Madame de Drut how death should always come in the fiftieth year, one night, after good food and wine with friends. But until then, no illness, no old age. And at the stroke, only a 'blissful tumble' as if from 'some height into a sea of cloud.'

It was dark. The lamp had not been lit.

Laure recalled her arrival at her Aunt's house. That had been more than ten years before. It was in winter, in a gloomy carriage, with snow falling. The street had looked so vast, wet and black, and the town stared at her with its narrow lighted windows.

'Poor child, she's wet through. Heat some water, she must have a hot bath, and then to bed.' Laure had felt ashamed. Why was that? None of it was her fault, her father's and next her mother's abandonment of her. But of course a child always believed it was some sin of hers that had caused everything, *her* wickedness, worthlessness.

An adult, Laure stood at the window. 'She will die.'

The Aunt would die.

Probably it would be quick. But she had heard, mostly from servants, terrible stories of the end of her grandfather, and older aunt – who had gone roaming about like Ophelia, in a ball gown, with weeds tangled in her hair. As if in search of a stream.

But the shock of the Aunt's fall, from which she was, said Ouelle, black and blue on one side, even that might see her off.

Laure stood at the window. Stood and stood, until the arches of her feet ached.

Beyond the garden of her Aunt's house, the wall and trees looked like black lace, the lit windows of Bois-la-Diane looked back at her.

Then reeled abruptly.

Then steadied.

She heard Sophrine's prim voice, 'You know quite well one day you'll have everything from your Aunt.'

Which would die first? The Aunt or the Comtesse Aubade-Valents.

Laure's heart began to pound. She turned about to evade it and saw the walls softly tumbling like a snow-bank of pillowed cloud or a balcony.

Ouelle presently found her lying on the carpet in the dark.

'There you go, m'mselle. You only fainted.'

'What are you doing in here?'

'I heard you fall. Oh you needn't think because you're such a slight little thing the ceiling didn't shake. It's an old house, M'mselle Laure. I know it well enough, that sound. Just like your aunt. Poor old lady. But she managed it on the stair. A wonder she didn't break her poor old neck. She will, next time, if were not careful.'

'Open the window, Ouelle.'

'At this time of year?'

'It's too hot. I can't breathe.'

'Yes, you are feverish, m'mselle. We must ask his honour St Romarin to look at you, when he comes tomorrow. God help the cognac.'

Laure's Aunt slept. She slept most of the time. Seven more days had passed.

'Laudanum,' said Ouelle. 'Nice that she's so peaceful.'

The woman had come from St Georges. She was big and strong and wore a white apron. (Ouelle said that she ate like a horse, both in quantity and gesture.)

Every day, about ten in the morning, the doctor appeared. He drank only one cognac on arrival, and only one on leaving. Ouelle had added water to the decanter, but he seemed not to notice.

Cursorily he glanced at Laure, who had not asked him to.

'Fainting, mademoiselle? We can't have that. No, no fever. Well. Perhaps just a little one. Your pulse is a little odd. Slow, then fast.' Then, alone with her, 'I expect you miss the patronage of the old comtesse.' Laure stared at him. She didn't like the pudgy feel of his hands, his smell of cologne, antiseptic and liquor.

He peered into her eyes at the window, telling her to look now this way and now that way, impertinently fiddling with her eyelids. Then he said, leering, 'Are your courses quite timely?'

Laure looked away. 'There's nothing wrong with me.'

'I think you may have a slight disorder of the blood, Mademoiselle Laure. You must eat more meat, and have plenty of that nourishing rabbit broth your fine Ouelle makes. And a glass of red wine, always take one with your supper. You don't smoke cigarettes? A filthy and bad habit for a woman. I know it was something of a fashion, at the chateau.'

'Not at all,' she said.

'Well, there were many stories told,' said the doctor. 'Some extraordinary things. Perhaps you'll have heard, Madame Lejay is being taken to Convienne by her husband. The anticipated death of the comtesse has upset her greatly. I've heard, by the by, the chateau might be converted into an asylum.'

What a gossip.

'Well, well. I'm not quite happy with you. Not entirely happy.' And pacing up and down before the fire, 'What do I think of you? Well, you must take care of yourself. And I must take another look at you in a day or so.' *Most unlikely,* she thought. And overhearing her thought, he added firmly, 'I may be obliged to be more thorough. The good Ouelle can chaperone you, can't she, if you're shy.'

Most unlikely.

Laure said crisply, 'Pardon me now, I have letters to write.' That night, the seventh night, they roused Laure from bed. The house of the rue Dalle was full of fretful calling. The Aunt had got up, wandering from room to room with a dipping lighted candle in her hand. 'Oh, m'mselle – she nearly set herself on fire!' When Laure came in, her Aunt clutched at her. 'Mother – where is mother?' Laure and Ouelle led her back to bed, where the girl, who had dropped asleep on watch, was now guiltily crying.

Installed in her bed, the Aunt stared at them. She said, 'They keep me prisoner here. They do.'

Laure sat until first light in the sitting room, and the darkness was very cold, not like the endless unchanging warm yellow-amber days.

Is that to be my lot when I grow old?

How selfish I am.

How selfish. Despicable. I might have sat by her bed. But I won't face it.

She heard, once, twice, a disembodied voice calling anxiously, like a lost spirit, through the house, 'Mother! Mother! Why don't you answer?'

And once a fox screamed at the edge of town.

At seven, Ouelle discovered Laure and scolded her. Laure said, 'Be quiet.' Ouelle stepped back and said, 'Yes, mademoiselle. Excuse me.'

Later, after Laure had dressed and forced down a few mouthfuls of chocolate, Sophrine came pulling on the doorbell in her rowdy way.

But her face was pale and diligent.

'No, Sophrine. No platitudes.'

'You look so drawn, Laure. Have you slept?'

'Not very well.'

'You look quite ill. Shall I come and stay with you? Papa said I might, seeing how things are – why are you laughing like that?'

'At you. I'm laughing at you. I don't want you, Sophrine. I'm sorry, but there it is. What can you do? You'll try to make me eat, or to cheer me up. You think I'm suffering because of this revolting thing which has happened to my Aunt. I'm not. I couldn't care less. I care only for myself. I hate how the house smells now, like a hospital – drugs and urine and peculiar soap. I hate this – this *indignity*. I hate life, I hate it, Sophrine, this trickery, this plot of God's to drag us all down.'

Sophrine firmly said, 'You must forget her, Laure.'

'What? Forget what?'

'You know perfectly well.'

'Oh, what are you talking about?'

'I warned you before. Don't you see, Laure, all this isn't some act worked against you. You have *connived* against yourself, and now, when everything seems to be fitting into place, forcing you to do only one thing – it's you *yourself*, Laure, who is forcing yourself to do it.'

'Gibberish.'

'Destiny – you think it's that, don't you? Your *fate*. Laure, you've sewn it together, a ball-dress, and now you only have to put it on. Do you think I'll help you?'

'Get out, Sophrine. Return to your idiotic father and your fat mama. Go and grow fat and idiotic, too. You're nothing to me.'

'Don't I know it. Any one of them was kinder to me, more appreciative, sweet. Even the Violette. Even the Lejay, although she never fancied me. But I won't let you throw yourself down into a pit of – of vipers. I knew from that night, of course I did. When you saw her in the candlelight, in that ghastly bridal ceremony that wasn't. And when we went home without a carriage, and you wouldn't let me come near this house with you. Oh, you were open as a book.'

'Be quiet, Sophrine.'

'I'll strike you if I must. I'll tie you to a chair or lock you in a cupboard. You were asleep, always sleeping. But then you woke up, that morning by the canal. And God help you, you saw that creature, all in her jackdaw black.'

'Now you're speaking perhaps of the painting, the Feast. The secret one, nobody ever saw.'

'Oh that. It was painted over. I've seen it – there's some other scene on top now. And she, that girl, she lies under layers of paint, just as her body's supposed to lie under layers of soil and roots. If she was ever there.'

Laure felt the room spin quite softly, and where Sophrine stood so prissily embattled, for a moment Laure beheld only a gleaming globe, unless it was a golden cup –

Sophrine caught her arm. 'Steady. Don't faint. You *mustn't* faint. You don't faint, Laure. You never have, as I haven't.'

'Leave me alone.'

'It isn't fate, Laure. Not yours or anyone's. You – *you* – have made it happen, and you can make it stop.'

Laure's vision cleared. She turned, slyly hiding, and said, level, resigned and slow, 'Oh, all this fuss. Stay to dinner then. Do you want to see my Aunt?'

'I'd like to pay my respects to her,' ruffled, no longer prophetic, her power lost in the natural ethics of incomprehensible morality.

'Sit down then. I'll tell Ouelle to fetch you some fresh chocolate. I suppose I must go up and see if the old lady's fit to receive you. Be prepared. She's in a sad way.'

And going out, Laure shut the door gently. Then turned, opened another door, and stepped into the street.

Her dress, somewhat disordered. Hatless, her hair coming loose. Her eyes doubtless very wide and brilliant.

Ophelia, looking for her stream.

Fireworks of golden light burst between the trees, and the walk was done in a moment, as if Laure wore the Seven-League Boots.

At the front door, the formal door, with its flight of stone steps and two statues, she wondered if anyone would come to answer her.

Twenty days – or more – had gone by, since the night of the contract. Perhaps la Reine's 'marriage' was already over, and Laure was too late.

How changed the chateau was, how changed. She had said she must never come back, and she had not, because this house was quite another one.

Someone opens the door. Some man in shirt-sleeves. And he lets her in, bored and as uninterested in her as she in him, because these demented women still have right-of-way, on the orders of the comtesse.

'Where is Madame Virgile?'

How strongly Laure speaks, although she stands there without a jacket, or a hat or gloves, and with half her hair undone – she heard pins striking the earth as she came along the lane.

The man, quite young, only points through at the great Hall, which lies across from this door.

'She's in the Hall?'

'Maybe,' he says. He's being rude to her and Laure has the urge to slap his face, but then only laughs at him, and walks on, and hears more pins spring from her hair and drop now on the polished wood of the floor.

Her hair is all down and smoking round her. She sees from her eyes' corners how the sunlight catches and fires it up. Like the mad Aunt's candle.

The great hall also is ablaze from its windows, so the moth- eaten bears' heads and rusty swords look fierce, although more scabrous than ever.

No one is in the Hall.

Laure turns, angry and imperious, but the rude servant has vanished.

Then she simply crosses the Hall and goes into the passage, and so she reaches the various rooms which open from it, and at the door of the salon (which she could have come at quite easily from its open long glass windows), she hesitates, and sees (in one of those daylit chairs done up in dying lemon brocade) black night is sitting.

Laure leant on the door. She was suddenly so faint she could not get past it. Yet she must. She must faint only inside the room.

She swung giddily, jauntily, forward into the sunlight, and exclaimed, with the license of her faintness, like a drunk, 'I should like to come in. Do you permit me to? I must.'

Virgile – Virgile. Who sat looking at her. Virgile's black skirt swept the floor. And she spoke. 'Must you?'

Laure felt the words go through her belly and her heart.

She staggered, half ran, across the room, catching pieces of furniture to help her, trying to reach the edge of the black skirt, not looking at the white face tipped, expressionless, towards her.

And Virgile interrupted. 'Do sit down, mademoiselle. Sit in that chair. What's the matter with you?' *Playfully.*

Laure did sit down. It wasn't what she wanted, and yet, to have reached the black shore over this lake of light, she would have needed to have been a far stronger swimmer than she was.

So Laure laughed, and heard the laugh like violin notes, sitting in the chair, moving her hands, which somehow fascinated her, so flexed and white, so she increased their mannerisms.

'It seems,' sang Laure, 'I'm ill.' Was it pride she detected in her own voice?

Virgile: nothing.

'You've heard of illness, of course, madame. But then, I'm forgetting, you allowed me the use of your first name. Virgile. And I – I asked you to use mine.'

Virgile: silent.

'I can explain in a few moments,' said Laure. Suddenly the wild trembling and sparkling left her. She sighed and spoke clearly and without any hurry, leaning back her head. 'You know my name. My family, therefore. My Aunt, though she hasn't the noble birth of a comtesse, has her own modest fortune. I am about to inherit this, since she'll soon die.' The faintness gathered to hold her. It was supportive and sensuous. It gave such liberty. 'And I, as you can see, am also beginning to sink. I'm prepared to die. I want to die. But you know that. You recognized it in me, the moment you saw me that morning, by the canal. Certainly that dusk outside the gate of the Blue House. That was why you spoke to me, Virgile. You spoke to my quite-costly clothes and the look of death in my face. Aren't I right?'

Virgile: still silent – and then a papery rustle, like the coils of a snake unwinding.

'And perhaps I could say,' continued Laure, 'I also recognized you. As my death. Is that too dramatic for you? Forgive me. I don't think I meant to say it. I want to make a bargain with you, Virgile. The usual one. If you made it with Sidonie Valents, why not with me?'

Laure had sounded arrogant. Why? Because this last of her independence must flash up in the face of such utter self-negation? But now she listened, heard nothing. Virgile had not spoken in return – nor moved away. Laure had closed her eyes, and did not undo them.

'When I say my Aunt has a fortune, I do mean that she has. Oh, she doesn't have much recourse to it. But once it's mine, I could be extravagant. You wouldn't tell me if you came from any city, but I promise you, I and a companion could live in a city, even in Paris. I lived there, perhaps you know that too, when I was a child. There was a big apartment near the Tuileries. My mother used to keep a little shrine in her sitting room to Marie Antoinette. But I could engage an apartment twice that size. And there'd be money for all sorts of things. Indulgences. And afterwards, a very generous settlement, for a friend. Of course, I don't know how you wish it arranged. Probably I seem very gauche. We can use Mercier again, the notary, if you like. Was he sufficient? Or send to Convienne, if you prefer.'

Virgile: has she stirred? Disappeared?

Laure says, 'Obviously, you'll conclude your other contract first, the old woman here. But that work will soon be over, I should think. She said a month – that's almost finished. Or less.'

Virgile: spoke. 'It will be over tomorrow.'

Triumph. Electric. Laure's eyes, still closed, dazzled.

The delicious luxury of giving way to this other, this shadow not even looked at –

'Then the notary must draw up a new contract,' said Laure. 'Mine. Ours. Do you agree?'

And Laure's eyes fly open, before she realizes they will. She is spent, half blind. Darkness still sits there, regarding her. She can just make it out.

'Of course I will agree, mademoiselle. Providing all this is quite real.'

Exhausted. Disbelief.

Laure says, dully now, yet with an edge of fear, 'What might not be real? What do you doubt? My proposal? My illness? My position?'

'Any of those things, mademoiselle. I shall need proof.'

'But you *know*. You knew it before I knew myself. How can you need proof? But yes, yes, whatever is necessary. Call me by name.'

'If you wish me to.'

'Now, say it now.'

But the voice did not say her name. It is a dark voice, a cello to Laure's violinish cries. And it says, 'You're very insulting to me, mademoiselle. Is it because you've heard I am bought and sold?'

Laure lies in the chair, staring, shaking now with terror, her feet and hands like ice.

'You must think of me, mademoiselle, as a woman of business, then. Would you treat your dressmaker in this way? If you did, would she not spoil your gown?'

'What have I – forgive me – Madame Virgile – I only meant –'

'Addressing me as a mercenary, mademoiselle, you have treated me to a most careless display. You have cast your old aunt into her coffin and slammed the lid in order to pull me down on it. What's this talk of death? What do you think I am, the reaper himself, tricked out in a dress?' The voice is also deadly calm. 'How dare you, mademoiselle. I have brought my clients comfort. For a fee, it's true. Most of us sell ourselves, in one way or another. Women and men both.'

'Virgile – forgive me – oh God – you won't refuse me, will you?'

'No, mademoiselle. I won't refuse you. But I repeat, I shall need proof, and sureties, as I always do. You must permit me to know best. It's how I have survived this world.'

Laure pushed herself from the chair. She kneeled on the floor. (If anyone had warned her this might occur, she would have struck them.) 'I'll do whatever you say. I can write to you today – outlining what I think must be done. My condition will be verified by a doctor. All the arrangements, as you demand, when I myself know – will that suffice, I mean all this in writing, until I can present you with something more definite? You shall have it tomorrow, before you leave. Early in the morning. Is that … enough?'

'Very well. As you say. Then we shall see.'

'Oh God – God – won't you even touch me –'

'I'll do everything you wish, if and when the time arrives.'

Laure began to cry, without a sound. And even in this extremity, what agonized bliss it was to break on her black stone like water.'

'But won't you say my name to me, just once?'

Virgile said nothing.

Then Virgile spoke Laure's name.

Golden splinterings passed through Laure.

'Say it once more – please, say my name once more.'

'Laure. And Laure. Laure, and also Laure.'

The shadow falls over her, a true shadow, cast from the amber windows and the dark figure before them.

'Get up, if you please.'

Laure gets to her feet. She only wants to fall deep into the shadow.

But even now, Virgile has not touched her.

'Well, Mademoiselle Laure,' says the Woman, 'I'll give you something, as they say, on account. To receive it, you must be obedient.'

'Yes.'

'When I leave the room, you may follow me. Do you know the wooden stair that leads to the rooms of the grande dame, the comtesse?'

'Yes.'

'There you'll stop still. You won't speak, or try to detain me.'

'Yes.'

'That's all.'

Then Virgile goes out of the salon, and next Laure follows her. This is only like a dream.

After the corridors and the upper stair, the sunlight through the windows, the turning and the stair of wood, the murderer's stair.

Laure stops, as she was told. And Virgile by then is at the stair's bottom where the light scarcely penetrates.

Standing there, Virgile is divesting herself of her garments.

As the snake sheds its skin, painfully perhaps, quite slowly. Pushing and drawing itself through the needle's eye of its former life. Just so, the black bodice, its buttons of jet rimmed with silver, undone, the black skirt which drops in one piece like an inky leaf. The white underclothes, threaded with black ribbon, stitched with black embroideries, patterns, designs half seen. Then the body emerges, the renewed snake, alabaster white. A body like a marble column, traced by the vague temporary scars of its enclosure – fabric, stays – and more in shadow than in light.

It is a fearsome body, as Laure had formally thought, like that of a statue, come to life. Nothing betrays it in those instants as remotely human.

And yet it is now out of the black carapace of Death. It is a woman's, even if the flesh is made of stone.

Virgile glances up at Laure, once only. And suddenly the faintest movement of a smile goes over the long mouth. There's no kindness in it. Not even humour. What does the smile mean?

Forbidden to speak or move, Laure stares.

She feels no erotic sensation. No arousal. Not even (now), her fear and terror.

And Virgile turns from her, gathers up her clothes, with the swift efficiency of her own servant, and enters the outer door of the apartments, without knocking. And, when the door shuts, is gone.

Leaving Laure to turn back and go away, which she does, no longer so giddy and volatile, but tired out.

There are a great many things to do. But Laure knows, as she goes through the chateau (this different chateau; even the murderer's stair is no longer that, but simply a wooden stair, unimportant beside other matters), Laure knows what she must do first.

Her first act was to come here, in the past. (Probably.) Then, the Comtesse herself acted, taking to herself the Woman, who is a serpent, and death, and yet neither, being mostly Virgile. The third act is again to be Laure's act. Her action which, indeed, will be passive. And yet, though passive, will be active.

The act of watching her Aunt die.

I am going home to do that. Her death is my classroom. So that when I too am dying, V'll know how to accomplish it.

The chateau and its morning grounds have passed over and around Laure like the folds of a dark gown. It *is* very dark. At one point Laure has had a brief hallucination, just as she did once in her adolescence, when she woke too quickly from sleep, and saw an angel, with outspread wings, and faintly flushed by rose, levitating in one corner of her bedroom.

The hallucination now occurs at the edge of the chateau woods. Laure thinks for a second she sees two wolves, tearing apart between them a purple veil fringed with gold. But then the lens of sight slips or realigns itself. She beholds two squirrels playing through a bar of sun, the mauve shadow disturbed with a brilliant flicker of long grasses catching light …

But now the sun has gone in. The dark is nothing much, only an absence of that clear mellow fluorescence which, for twenty odd days, has hung over the town and country.

And Laure spares the sky a glance. Yes, the sky is changed. No longer opulent and glazed. Now it is a discreet sky, which does not disclose all its intentions.

Beyond the park, the lane, and then the town of Bois-la-Diane, where doubtless Laure, in her dishevelment, is stared at, even pointed out. These minutes are like the turned pages of a book, papers shuffled, which bring Laure to the house of her Aunt, in through the door, and find her confronting Ouelle in the sitting-room.

'M'mselle Merault has gone home.'

'Sophrine. Oh. Yes.'

'She was most put out.'

Laure says, with a chilly authority, 'I'm going up to change my clothes. Then I shall sit with my Aunt. Bring me up some hot coffee, will you, and a little wine. Not red. A white wine, and not too sweet.'

'Yes, m'mselle.'

'I shan't dine. Perhaps something later, on a tray.'

'Yes, m'mselle.'

'Has St Romarin come?'

'Come and gone. He had a long face on him. He said he might return, later.'

'If he does, he may take a look at my Aunt. I won't see him. You may say I've decided to consult a doctor in Convienne, in my own case.'

'Well, m'mselle, that *will* put him in a proper fuss.'

'Then I hope he enjoys his proper fuss. Thank you, Ouelle.'

Having washed her face and arms and put on a dress of grey material, Laure put up her hair, and powdered her face. This last necessitated looking in her mirror. The stranger who looked back both attracted Laure and discomposed her. She hurried before the mirror, and was soon finished.

Her Aunt's room was very hot, stuffy, smelling of medicine and, despite their best efforts, of slight incontinence. It could not be helped.

The woman the doctor had sent sat there, doing her tatting, her red bony hands moving deftly. She reminded Laure, this woman, of some hag who attended the Revolutionary Guillotine, one of those women who had never really existed as such, save in fiction.

Laure sent her out with a curt expression of gratitude.

No one would argue. It was Laure's 'place' to sit here. That she had failed to take her turn, until now, had been surely frowned on. The woman only directed Laure in the intervals of medicines, and asked if she should come back to see to them.

'I shall do it.'

Alone, Laure opened one window a crack, behind its lace. Outside the daylight was now the colour of her dress. A stillness had come, like a pause. She could hear nothing, not even in the house, or in this room, beyond her own movements and the intermittent crackle of the fire.

Lastly Laure went to look at her Aunt.

Her Aunt was very frail and lay there asleep, seeming in her contours almost flat, so little there was to her. Yet she breathed, and slightly moved her head. Her face was blushed by fever or the heat.

Also in fiction, Laure would have smothered her, of course, kindly terminating the Aunt's tribulations, and hastening her own ends. For this crime she might even then have become suspect, arrested, and taken to Convienne, tried and found guilty, executed. And Virgile – what would Virgile do in such a circumstance? Nothing, obviously. Besides, it wasn't in her, in Laure, to murder this old lady. Let death take its own slow course. And she, Laure, would observe. How to place her head so and so. How to move her restless hands. But she must be decorous in her own dying, or Virgile would leave her. Virgile was not a nurse. That was not Virgile's role.

When she thought of Virgile now, Laure felt nothing. Or something so vast that, like God, it had become omnipresent, and could be ignored.

Laure seated herself at the bedside. In half an hour by the clock, she must wake her Aunt and insert into her mouth one spoonful from that bottle and two from that, and the drops in water which, the Guillotine-hag had warned, might have to be administered also by a spoon, as her Aunt had become so feeble.

She was only a doll now, the Aunt. Laure did not need to care for her, only charitably play at helping her, as custom demanded.

I remember how … when we roasted chestnuts, she would pour the syrup on them, and then put the plate into my hand. She wore a jade ring then, dark jade, like a bluish olive. That was only ten or twelve years ago, but how much younger she looked. Her hair had brown waves running through it and it curled on her forehead. And those earrings she used to wear, they intrigued me so – shaped like little kettles made of gold – and she let me wear them that time, when I was fourteen and my ears were ready. Then she gave them to me – I haven't worn them for ages –

Why do I remember that?

I remember the night-lamp in my bedroom, how she said it would be useful for me, because the house was still strange to me, as if I'd find my way about from it, and it wasn't there because of the bad dreams. Which stopped, anyway, quite soon, or happened less often.

Once I was here, in her house.

And how I didn't know which day was my birthday or if I was nine or ten, and she said nine *or* ten was perfectly good enough, and fixed my natal day for me in the spring, which she said suited me.

I remember running home here, with Sophrine, when we were children, out in the icy streets from school, when the town still looked quite large. Running into the glowing fire-lit house, and Sophrine would murmur, 'What a grand lady she is, your auntie. Always so well-dressed.'

My Aunt. She told me stories. She used to laugh.

She was pretty.

Look at her, look at her now.

Oh God, who would want to come to this. Life is the devil, not death. Doing such things to us.

Let me die young. It will be soon.

Its decided.

I have arranged it all.

And Sophrine says, 'You have connived –'

Well, and if I have. This woman will die, and I'll die. We all do, in the end.

It was midnight by the clock. After the last doses of medicine, all of which Laure had had gently to push into the fleeting mouth, some of which only ran out again and stained the pillow pink and fawn … after that last dose at – what had it been? – nine o'clock – and then a bite of the bread and cheese, and the wine, Laure had fallen asleep.

But now the next pointless dosing was specified, she had woken on cue to the clocks soft chime.

'Aunt – wake up, wake up, dear.' Laure's voice, which formerly had sounded grave and removed, now took on first an impatience, then an intimacy. This fragile debris was connected to Laure by blood. They had flowered, it and she, from one central stem. 'Aunt – wake up, dear. Just for a moment.'

And the eyes fluttered open. They were pale and cloudy, but a core of light appeared about the pupil suddenly.

'Laure … is it you?'

'Who else, Aunt? Can you try to swallow your medicine?'

'It tastes so bitter.'

'I'm sorry. Yes, it's nasty, isn't it –'

When I was a child, and sick, and she gave me the medicine on a spoon, coaxingly, and then a spoon of honey or a sip of wine to take away the taste …

'Swallow the medicine, then take a sip of this wine. That's good. And here's the wine in the spoon – is that better, dear.'

'Much nicer. Oh yes. Let me just have a spoonful more.'

And a spoonful more of the wine.

Laure had put her hand behind the old woman's neck, to support it. Her hair, all grey and no longer strong, felt soft as the fur of a cat, and warm. Close to, the old woman smelled of nothing bad, only herbs, a little camphor, and a slight dustiness. The odour in the room was separate from her.

'Thank you, Laure. How good of you. How tired you must be, sitting here with me for so long.'

Laure eased down her Aunt's thinly covered skull to the pillow. Laure sat back in her chair.

'I suppose,' said her Aunt, 'I have come to it, now.'

'To – what?'

'To death. I suppose so.'

Laure thought, *I must send for the priest. I should have done that already. And then I shall write to Virgile.*

'I'm not afraid,' said the Aunt. Her lips quivered. 'Only sad.'

'Aunt, it isn't so serious as that.'

Why am I lying? Coward, don't lie.

'Isn't it? I thought it was, I've been dreaming of it.'

'Of what? Aunt, what *were* you dreaming?'

'Of leaving the world. I cried in the dream, but I wasn't myself any more. I was in the air.'

'Don't think of it.'

'Ah, my dear,' said her Aunt, smiling, 'how can I not think of it?'

But she turned her head and her eyes closed.

Dear Madame, the letter would begin, my Aunt died in the night, and now –

And now I invite you to her funeral, your first proof. After this I will obtain a letter from the doctors at Convienne, concerning my own health. My second proof. And then we will make our legal and financial arrangement. We will go together to Paris.

Why is she sad to die? What possible pleasures has she here?

The clock ticked, and chimed the half hour.

The curtains had been drawn closed. Laure went to the windows and stared out at sleeping Bois-la-Diane. *Do I even remember Paris?* Only that awful, echoing flat, with its ghastly furniture that turned into bears at night, its draperies and bows, and the insipid shrine to that fool, Marie Antoinette. That poor brave fool …

We all die.

(I must sit down and write my letter. And send the boy with it at first light.)

And a park, trees and grass and a fountain, I recall those, and sitting crying there, because I had been left.

And then this place. And the old woman there, in the bed.

Laure turned abruptly, letting go of the curtains, the memory.

Have I really made this happen? Made her die so I can die, so I can have Virgile and languish in the arms of Virgile?

How absurd, such things don't happen. I must sit clown and write –

But if I had –

Stricken, as if by the striking clock which now tolls for one in the morning – half an hour elapsed only in a minute.

'I can't,' said Laure. 'I can't.'

The murderer's stair.

I never went down it, that second time.

I won't. How can I?

She took me in. I was a stranger to her, and she made me welcome. Poor little wizened old child, poor little lost child left behind by me in the headlong rush –

Laure was weeping. The tears spilled down.

She ran to the bed, and knelt across it, taking up her Aunt's dry narrow hands, which felt as fragile as pastry, as if they might crumble in her grasp –

'Don't die, Auntie – don't leave me – don't leave me –'

I can't let you die. I won't. What do I care for any of it, what does any of it matter? That woman in her black carapace, what can she be to me – I'll meet her in the end, not naked and white, but on a pale horse, with not one inch of skin visible, the only light the flash of the sweeping scimitar that cuts my neck in two pieces –

Virgile. Damn Virgile.

'Aunt – can you hear me? You must live. I want you so much.'

Yes, I sacrifice my death for you. My magnificent death in the arms of ebony and agate, I sacrifice my death for you.

The tears stopped, and Laure lay down beside her Aunt, holding the old woman lightly in one arm.

(So, at the beginning, she had fallen asleep beside her in this bed, a child of nine or ten.) And so now, Laure fell asleep, her head on the pillows stained with medicine and tears.

Sleeping she saw a carriage race away down a twilight avenue. Goodbye, goodbye.

I give it up. Didn't she show me anyway? Under her dark shell, she was only another woman, after all.

Dr St Romarin, when he called the next day, seemed not surprised to find Laure's Aunt so very much better. He praised his own prescribed medicines, the woman he selected from Convienne, indirectly himself. Never mentioned his gloomy diagnosis.

He found Laure, too, alert, an apron over her dress and her hair tied up in a cloth, overseeing the great tidying and cleaning of the house against her Aunt's return downstairs a week later.

'Some fever of the autumn, disturbing to the brain,' said the doctor. 'And you had a touch of it, too, I think, mademoiselle. But all gone now. A good thing you consulted me when you did.'

But Ouelle sent up clouds of dust and brought down cobwebs on his intellectual head. She had hidden the cognac.

Later, that is, many years later, Laure regretted that she had not written to Virgile. This was not for Virgile's sake, for Virgile, Laure was certain, would not be concerned much, either way. It was for her own. It would not, of course, have been the letter Laure had planned and intended. It would have been a renunciation, an apology. An honourable farewell. But Laure hadn't written. Instead she had called Ouelle to heat some broth for her Aunt, then she had gone to dress, and tied the apron round her middle. *Let her go wanting,* Laure had thought of Virgile. *She's a woman of business. I'm nothing to her. Why debase myself further.*

And in the hours and days which followed, now and then, the thought would come of that dark carriage bolting away, carrying Virgile from the chateau, from the town, away and away, to some unknown town, city or land. Virgile, now lost forever.

Virgile was not death. That was too grand. Nor was she merely a business woman, a prostitute, the professional widow – too ordinary.

Had Virgile been love? No. Oh, no. Could Laure have let her go, if Virgile had been that?

Love was banal. It was affectionate, it shared memory, bickered and had arguments, and, in the case of the sexual lover, desire, the games of delight which ended in spasms not remotely deathlike. Love, Laure decided, despite all the poets had said, was more like the mad dance of life.

A storm broke on the town in the week after her Aunt's recovery. It brought down a great many trees and tore tiles from the roofs. In the midst of the tumult, Artemise Lejay miscarried in her husband's fine house, and Clothilde Boulanger accepted a proposal of marriage from Annette Mercier's eldest nephew, he on his knees and swearing his passion out-matched the weather. (These things happened, particularly in spots like Bois-la-Diane.)

I wish I had written to her. I feel ashamed when I remember that Virgile, if ever she recalls me, thinks I was only some hysterical and spoilt young hussy, who didn't know her own mind.

I wish, how I wish I had told her, that lady of business: I have given up everything for love. I have given up *you*, the tumult and the darkness, for the banal, mundane loyalty of a provincial family bond.

But I couldn't have said such things. She wouldn't have understood. She was nothing, was she, Virgile, but the creature I made her into? Perhaps that's always how she was – or is. The invention of others, and by that she survives and makes her way.

What Laure felt for Virgile, omnipresent as God, remained with her, but only like her shadow. She did not always see it, or notice it. Sometimes, when she did, it arrested her, astonished.

The Aunt lived a further five years in good health, rather forgetful of trifles, but no worse than that. She died in her sleep one Easter, after a pleasant dinner with wine, when her table had been crowded with her friends, and Laure sat at her side.

After that, Laure let the house on the rue Dalle, having, with part of her inheritance, bought the Lejays' fine large house, orchard and gardens. The Lejays themselves had long departed, not for Convienne, but Italy.

To Laure's new establishment, the women had begun to drift, on Wednesdays and Saturdays. The Ladies Club had reformed, and was again tolerated by the town, which, as years passed, whispered that Laure Deschampeigne was a wealthy woman, who, having no husband or children, might favour this or that young girl who visited there. Although others were sure that the Deschampeigne wealth would devolve in time on the daughter of Sophrine Le Brun, the wife of a substantial man often away on business.

The old chateau passed through many hands. No one came to live there. Its walls gave way, fell down, it became a picturesque ruin. Rats ate its furnishings. Fruit was thieved from its grounds, lovers lay together in its summer woods, unchallenged, uninvited.

There was, however, a story the old Comtesse had not died, but rallied, in Paris. They said she lived still in her miser's poky house, with only one servant (the tortoise Peridot), and was reckoned to be almost a hundred.

In that case, Virgile had brought her life, not death.

I still dream of Virgile, occasionally Usually without warning or any reason at all. They are torrential throbbing dreams, from which I wake in a desolation of disappointment, and lie leadenly for several minutes, until a sort of relief brings me back.

As I become older, stouter and more stiff, no longer that Laure with lucent skin and fine bright hair, I return in my dreams to my youth, and put it on, and then she is there, Virgile. She is often standing on some pile of marble, like a plinth, but it is a stair or a hill, and she is all in black, and her face devoid of any mercy. I know I shall reach her and be dashed in fragments and she will catch me as I fall. And in a glorious agony I approach and approach this moment of complete annihilation – which I never ever reach.

Waking, I find Sophrine beside me, if she stayed the night, and it is perhaps her movements, brushing and pinning her hair, that have woken me. But even if she isn't there, or hasn't moved, never do I reach the moment, the crisis of my dream of Virgile. It is a dream of arriving, not arrival.

And Sophrine will crinkle her face at me, her face which, like mine, is showing the busy sewing and ruching of years, and she'll laugh and say, 'There you are, my sleepy-head. Were you dreaming? Here's your chocolate. Drink it up, my love, before the children start clamouring for me. What a fine day! Just look at the sun.'

White As Sin, Now

The Dwarf (The Red Queen)

The dwarf Heracty balances on the rim of a frozen fountain, drawing pictures with his nails in the ice. His handsome face is set into the frame of a great leonine head applicable to a muscular man six feet tall. Heracty's form is that of an elf. But he has, too, an elf's eyes, long, aslant, and crystal-green.

Engaged on the scales of a mermaid, Heracty pauses, listening. His hearing is so acute, his ears sometimes hear noises that do not exist. He must decide now whether this sound physically belongs in the world, is a phantom, or a memory. Presently Heracty becomes sure that two narrow feet in shoes are descending a flight of cold stones.

He turns a little, looking sideways from his slanting eyes.

Held high in an archway over the stair are towers resembling a crown of thorns, on a half-disc of twilight. Prom that point, the Upper Palace drops like a cliff into a riverbed.

And from those heights she has again come down.

It is always at this hour, just as the sun goes away. In the ghostly 'tweentime, when all pale things pulse and stare … the white beasts of the fountain, the roses of snow across the gardens.

When she comes out suddenly from the arch at the bottom of the stair, she also is glimmering as if luminous.

She only looks straight ahead, beyond the fountain and the winter lawn, to a second arch, a second falling staircase. She does not see Heracty, has never seen him there, as she passes by like a sleepwalker.

The wide eyes of the Queen are so astute, Heracty knows, she sometimes glimpses things that do not exist.

As before, he slides from the fountain's rim, and silently follows her.

They then descend twenty flights of steps one after another, and the nineteen terraces between.

The Dwarf's First Interview With His Grandmother

On a bitter morning in spring, mother and son went to visit the grandmother in her marble house.

The woman was hardly more than thirty-five years of age, but with old, terrible, unhuman, alligator eyes.

To begin with she did not upbraid Heracty's mother, but only questioned her on domestic matters. The boy sat motionless and dumb on the rugs. He was very much aware of himself and of his mother's tense and trembling awareness of him. But his grandmother, by a slight flexing of her colossal will, had shut him out, so that he was not in the chamber at all. Until finally:

'It's a curse that struck you,' announced the grandmother to her daughter. 'I don't begin to guess who you wronged, to incur it. If I had my way, such things would be smothered as soon as their nature was evident.' Every syllable referred, of course, to Heracty.

The mother whispered, as she had done on many occasions, 'His father was normal. Straight, well-made –'

'Yes, yes,' said the grandmother, 'and between you, you managed this. A monster.' Now she bent her awful glance on the boy. 'I have come to a decision,' said Heracty's grandmother. His mother waited in abjection, and he in fear. 'The Prince collects freaks. He has got into his possession, so I hear, a two-headed dog, a unicorn, a gulon. And besides, six of *this* kind, half-men – though a pair are reckoned to be females, so I'm told.'

'You mean my son is to go up into the court of the Prince?' asked Heracty's mother, astonished.

'No. Into the Prince's menagerie.'

The Hunter (The Young Girl)

While the Vampire lies sleeping, its soul, or what passes for it, roams the night, dreaming it is a wolf.

The season is winter, therefore snow covers the forests, hills and plains, and far away the mountains blackly glow upon a blacker sky where all the stars are out. Between the black and the white, the black wolf runs.

Presently there is a small stone house on the dark, with one lit pane.

The wolf runs among the fir trees. He raises himself up, something now between man and creature. His eyes of colourless mercury meet the image of a poor room, where a girl sits sewing by the hearth.

The wolf-soul does not see a girl. What it sees is a stream of living holy light far brighter than the dying wood on the fire, and an icon burning in it, as if in a cathedral window. There is a white hand containing red blood, plying the silver needle, a bending throat like the stem of a goblet of glass.

She puts her hair back from her cheek, and in that moment hears a noise outside, which is like the murmur of the trees, internalized, the rhythm of the sea in a shell.

Rising, the girl leaves her task. She has been stitching an altar-cloth For the church in the valley. But her eyes and hands, her shoulders, her very brain, are tired now. It is a relief for her to walk to the window of the room, to look out.

There is no moon. The forest stands against the door, and the wall of the dark. She beholds her own face reflected on the pane, transparent as a spirit. The strange noise comes again.

The girl lifts the latch of the door, and going out on the snow which so far is unmarked, prints it with the signature of her own bare feet. Forgotten, the door left open behind her.

She thinks she sees for an instant a tall male figure against the fir trees, but it has the head of a wolf. Then there is also a pale-faced man, and two eyes of iron.

She moves forward, leaving her last message on the snow.

And abruptly the darkness engulfs her. She vanishes. Without a cry, she is gone forever.

The Red Queen (The Lost Child)

Innocin, the Queen, has become conscious only gradually that something follows her. At first, she believes it to be a cat, then later, a child. But the presence is subtly more imminent. Crossing through the deep shadows of pillared gulleys, the Lower Palace, she realizes that what is mysteriously on her track is nothing less – or more – than one of her step-son's pet dwarfs.

She wonders if the Prince himself has sent this spy. But surmise fades. Such matters have no interest.

In the shadows, the blood-red mantle of the Queen, limned with white ermine, her hair like red-bronze surrounding an ivory face, are elements of a flame.

She enters a long corridor with a low ceiling, intricately carved. For all the hundreds of times she has traversed this thoroughfare, Innocin has never properly regarded the carving. She does not know what it represents although she has seen it over and over.

There was a day when she looked into her mirror. The light cut sharply as broken porcelain against one side of her face. She saw that she had lost her youth. It was then that she thought of a young girl, dressed in purest palest white, the sin of her husband, the dead King. Somewhere within the enormous labyrinth of the Palace, between the topmost towers and the deepest basements, the girl must have secreted herself. The afternoon had passed, and the sun gone down. But that sunset the Queen became, like a star, certain of her course.

She descended then the stairways to the terrace with the lawn and the great fountain. It had been autumn still, and sallow leaves lay adrift on the water of the basin.

Nothing disturbed the preoccupation of Innocin. She had crossed the terrace of the lawn and progressed down twenty further flights. She searched night after night, among decayed architecture, and neglected rooms, for the unmistakable, beautiful young girl.

So far, she has not found her.

Sometimes there is a glimpse or a clue – the white flicker of a skirt between two columns, a sigh that circles an upper gallery where no one seems to be and, on ascending, where no one is. Or a rose moulded from snow, poised in a hollow vase of ice.

The Hunter's Prey (The Dark Priest)

As a small child she had played about the cottage, a darling of the entire family. The truth was, the child did not belong to them at all. At midnight once, going out to make water, the man of the house had found an infant huddled in his doorway. It was late in summer, the nights not yet cold, but the child shivered and moaned. Conversely, although she could form noises, she had never apparently been taught human language. She could tell them nothing.

The woman had lost her baby some months before. This seemed the returns of heaven. Her husband was a woodcutter, quite prosperous, having three men in his employ, besides two strapping sons.

The household took in the girl-child, and gave her a village name.

Her origins she forgot instantly, except sometimes in nervous dreams. Then the woman would comfort her. 'Here is your mother,' the woman would confide, 'you're safe, my baby.' The man and the two boys brought her dolls and baubles from the town. Her childhood was happy and carefree.

However, about nine years old, by some arcane law, she had become a woman, and all was changed. She had work to do at which firstly she laboured diligently. But, as there was never respite when she grew bored or exhausted, her duties soon turned to drudgery. It did not occur to any of them, perhaps she had been born for something else.

While years sprang in flowers on the turf beyond the house, or fell in sculpted cones from the branches of the fir trees, the woodcutter's daughter also unremembered she had ever been a happy, carefree child. She was the maidservant of her father and two brothers, and her mother's nurse, for the woman waxed sickly. The evening before the girl's fourteenth birthday – that is, the night-day of her discovery in the door of the stone house – her stepmother died.

'She shan't marry now,' said neighbours, down the valley in the village street. 'She must tend her own. She's got men enough to care for.'

A new priest had taken up his office at the church not long before. He was tall and slender, with a broad low brow, and his hair – untonsured, for this was a wild place – was black as the wing of a crow.

The young girl, seeing him stand above the coffin of her stepmother's corpse, dreamed a waking dream which that night was translated. She believed she was a nun, gowned and coifed in snowy white. She served a dim altar where a tall crucifix gleamed, a man's pale body hammered on to it.

She would go to church every holy day, and often visited her step-mother's grave. She never approached the priest directly, but when he requested of his flock various attentions to the church, the young girl, though burdened by duties to home and kindred, gave her service.

The other women free to do so were mostly old, or else fat, sullen widows. The young girl felt herself shine strangely among them, a clear lily in withered reeds.

That was a terrible winter for wolves. They preyed on the sheepfolds and the byres, and several children were taken, or so it was supposed. One lean black wolf was seen frequently, but though the men scoured the forests round about, and laid snares, this animal was never trapped or killed.

The Dark Priest (The Wolfshead)

The priest elevates the Host, an offering and invitation to God. It is a moment of supreme sanctity, of supreme savagery even. Less substantially, he senses the consciousness of those persons who fill up the building, trailing from his lifted hands. A vast light, without tint or radiance, enspheres the church. And he is the arrow-head of the flight, fired out toward the celestial target of the omnipresent, awful, eternal, invisible, and actual, centre of all things. A ray of the sinking sun, unearthly and lemon-green, pierces through the window, penetrates the body of the priest – And at that instant the door of the church crashes wide.

The priest's awareness is smashed in pieces.

He turns, slowly lowering the sacred element. His black eyes give to him a scene of the sudden and the inappropriate, whatever it may be proved to be – the onslaught of a local calamity, death, plague, or war, this interruption is to him only an unforgivable sacrilege.

A body of men stands in the nave, staring from side to side, in their hands some makeshift weapons. They are the inhabitants of outlying parts. They seldom enter the village save to get their ration of beer. Now it is not beer they want. The woodcutter's second son thrusts forward. He bellows insanely into the church: 'Out! Out! Demon! Out!' And swings up his axe.

'The Devil's hiding in your flock, shepherd,' says another man roughly, to the priest. 'It went by night and murdered his sister.'

The congregation starts to its feet, becomes a beast of many limbs and eyes and voices. The church is no longer a special place. The priest does not remonstrate. He sets down the precious Host, and feels keenly how it goes back into dust. The last of the vivid sunset is perishing round the feet of trampling peasants. There is nothing to be done, or said.

Arrogantly the priest watches from his altar as the mob, not finding after all the one suspected, blunders forth on to the greenly-embered snow, bolts and plunges up an incline, collides with darkness at the entry of a hovel near the village cess-pit. Great blows shake the flimsy hut. Even from the church-door the priest hears them. He is very cold.

Shortly, a half-wit man who subsists in the hovel, the tender of the midden, is brought out on to the snow. The villagers search him, looking for marks of the Devil, tufts of feral hair, claws, certain lupine deformities of jaw, teeth and forehead. Presumably they uncover them all. While this goes on, the half-wit smiles courteously, and moves himself this way and that, in order to be helpful.

Next, still smiling and assisting them, he goes up the hill with the men, and the brother of the young girl – fifteen years of age, who, the night before, was found lying among the fir trees by her father's cottage, her throat torn open like a winter rose.

The crowd vanishes over the hill. Presently a scream sounds, shrill and sheer from the forest's edge above.

The priest does not make any gesture, except that, going back into the empty church, now closed already by shadow, he shuts and bars God's door.

Heracty's Second Interview With His Grandmother

Having reached the age of sixteen Heracty, the Prince's seventh dwarf, decided once again to visit his grandmother. This time he imagined he could do so on his own terms.

He dressed in a suit of clothes of wan green satin, a mulberry-red cloak, and wore in his ear a large pearl. He rode a most charming dappled pony, another of the Prince's gifts, and took with him for escort his little page not yet eight years old. Over the saddle of the pony, too, had been placed a couple of embroidered bags containing delicacies.

The gardens of the enormous eccentric Palace were equally vast and varied. Downhill lay the grandmother's marble box, a house given her decades before by an admirer (Heracty's unintentional grandfather), when she frequented the court. To get there first Heracty, the pony and page, must navigate an ornamental river. Then came a number of steep floral steppes. Next they entered a mock forest, densely planted with pine, fir, rhododendron and cedar trees. Even at noon it was dusk in this forest, and here and there clockwork animals prowled and howled. At the turn of the track, a grey wolf pounced out on them, and the small page had hysterics.

'Hush,' said Heracty, who had been in the forest before.

And he threw the clockwork wolf a peach from the bags, which it greedily and realistically ate, trotting off afterwards to bury the stone.

Beyond the forest lay an acre or two of modest meadows, and here the grandmother had her abode. As they got on to the path, the dwarf could see, across the shoulder of the landscape, the blurred valleys below where his mother had lived. But by this time she was dead.

The grandmother of Heracty was now not much over forty. Her complexion was nearly flawless as a girl's, her eyes had advanced from alligator to dragon.

'Well,' she said, looking her grandson over, satin, pearl, pony, page, and bags.

Heracty had the page distribute his presents. The grandmother fingered some of them and set them aside. The food and flasks of fine wine caused her short fits of harsh laughter.

'What a splendid fellow!' she jeered.

Heracty sat down, although, in her chairs, his feet hung in limbo far above the rugs.

'You did me a good turn, Granny,' said the dwarf, 'when you persuaded my mamma to send me into the Prince's service.'

'My idea was merely to get you out of the way and out of my sight.'

'Yet here I am again. What a sad nuisance.'

'Your tongue,' she said, 'has grown longer, if nothing else of you has. Or is it,' she amended, 'true? That which is said of the loins of your sort.'

The dwarf blushed, could not help it. But he had been well-seasoned at the court, and he replied, 'Those few among the Prince's eldest servants who remember you, always remark you had less manners than a pig. Naturally, I defend you, and only confess the sin of lying on holy days.'

The grandmother took one candied nut from the gifts and bit it in two. She then dropped both bites in the fireplace.

'What do you want, monster?'

'Tell me,' said Heracty immediately, 'about Innocin, the Red Queen.'

'When you hear so many remarks, how is it you never heard that?'

Heracty sat and waited. He made his face quite blank and his elf's body immobile. At last, the grandmother shifted.

'She was a slut in the kitchen, or something of that kind. He saw her, raised her, bedded her, became besotted, so married her. She's now Queen, but she was his second wife. The first died. When the King died himself, and his lechery with him, the Prince took power. It remains to be seen if he will ever get himself properly recognized, become King like his father. But for her, she's gone mad. So she wanders about, looking for a vanished daughter she had by the King.'

'A lost child?' said Heracty. He considered. 'Did it die at birth? Was the matter hidden?'

'How should I tell you?' asked the grandmother, 'what do I know?'

'Granny,' said the dwarf, 'in the basket of sugar-plums – I understood you're fond of them – is one sweet containing a potent and unpleasing purgative. Without harming you, it will cause you extreme discomfort.'

'Nasty little beast,' said his grandmother, bright-eyed. 'I'll eat none of them.'

'What a waste, and your favourites, too. The particular plum,' he added, 'is easy to identify, once I describe it.'

'Perhaps you are lying again. And perhaps any way, you'd indicate the wrong plum.'

'Perhaps. Or not.'

They sat then in silence some minutes, the dwarf a small elegant statue, she a lizard in a girl's skin.

Finally she said this:

'In the position I had at court, I learned that the Queen was to be thought of as barren. But it was not possibly the case. One infant, a girl, had certainly been born, but a portent made the Queen afraid of it, or her own shame at her low beginnings and bad blood. She sent it away into the forests, to be brought up among ignorant strangers.'

The dwarf sighed. 'Her lost child is,' he murmured, 'her own youth.'
Granny threw all the sugar-plums in the fire.

The Menagerie (The Court)

Indeed, they live close to the Prince's menagerie. On calm nights, when the music from the Upper Palace is not too lively, they may hear the gulon caterwaul and screech at the full moon, or the unicorn clicketting up and down on its gemmed hoofs, though the dog of two heads is generally reticent.

The dwarfs had been given their own town at the foot of the Palace. Each house is a doll's mansion, equipped with furnishings all the proper size, and with intelligent child servants always replaced in their tenth year. Rose gardens and knot gardens and gardens of topiary and water gardens, and so forth, make wondrous chessboard squares around the mansions. Everything is enclosed by a stout wall, whose gates are guarded at night by specially bred miniature mastiffs, who, introduced to the dwarfs as puppies, threaten to maul anyone who disturbs them. Only the Prince himself, and his selected courtiers, can invade the sanctum whenever desired. But that is not often.

Heracty quickly became accustomed to the dwarfs' estate. He grasped how they were patronised, yet simultaneously, how could he dislike anything that so suited, and that rendered him so comfortable.

The four fellow male dwarfs were comely and alert, two with high boyish voices which, in one case, flowed out into a clear alto instrument for song, seemingly much prized by the Prince. The two dwarfesses were remarkable for their charms and accomplishments, one blonde, one dusky. The latter had wed her dwarf suitor – the wedding had been a fete of the Palace; the Prince gave the bride away – and it was said the union produced a child. But as the baby evinced every sign of growing up into an ordinary woman, it too was taken off, as a potential cause of future grief to the parents.

Heracty, sent among the dwarf community when it was established, expanding it into an uneven number: Seven, though never made unwelcome, stayed an outsider. He became instead a student of men, the other species. When summoned to delight the Prince by his presence, handsomeness and wit, Heracty on his side narrowly observed everyone about him. He definitely supposed that he came of another race, human, but unadulterated – what he saw of full formed human behaviour, confirmed this opinion.

It was at a banquet that, initially, Heracty beheld the Red Queen, the dead King's widow.

She entered late, and the Prince rose graciously, and with ill-concealed boredom, to greet her. Seating herself, she stared about as if not knowing where she was, thinking it a dream. Occasionally she would take up some morsel: from her plate, or begin to lift her goblet – but sustenance never reached her mouth, for obviously she forgot its purpose half-way. She wore a gown the shade of dying autumn, not a single jewel.

The Prince, demanding antics constantly that evening from Heracty, interrupted the dwarf's study a hundred times. Courteous and wise, Heracty never once displayed his annoyance.

The Queen left the feast before midnight. Heracty was not permitted to leave until the men lay drunken in their chairs, or over the tables.

When dawn breaks, Heracty frequently goes into the menagerie. Adjacent to the dwarfs' enclosure, it is simple of access.

More often than not the unicorn falls asleep at dawn, its muzzle laid on its flank, the curving horn, more swarthy than its hide, like the sinking crescent of the moon. The two-headed dog sits sadly, one head deep in thought and the other slumbering with the tongue hanging out.

But the gulon stalks its prettified pen, disdaining the luxury of its kennel. A fox-cat, it looks now most feline, but next second mostly canine, having strong features of both types. It is the colour of Queen Innocin's banquet gown, and her hair, and Heracty has been told that combings of its long damascened fur are sometimes woven to trim her mantles.

The eyes of the gulon are rather like Heracty's own, but lack any trace either of courtly politeness or civilisation.

The gulon has been known to savage its keepers, one of whom lost an arm as the result. It is dissatisfied with its life and does not appreciate its uniqueness.

Heracty is wondering if Innocin the Queen has ever looked on the gulon.

When he witnessed her descent through the Palace, sensed the wild, inane search, it fitted her like a costly necklace. It is a perfection. She could do no other thing.

He values it in her.

The Lost Child (The Palace)

The girl Idrel wakes like an early crocus.

She lifts her head, and all about her lies the snow. Snow is her coverlet in a four-poster bed of ice. Slight wonder she dreamt she lay in a coffin, but the coffin was of glass …

The girl gets to her feet. She does not feel the cold, only a deep desire to lie down again and sleep again – and this she believes is to be resisted. She is garbed only in a shift, and not, she guesses, her own. It covers her decently from neck to foot and even drags a little behind her as she walks. But for a shield against the winter it is useless. However, she is under protection, feels it must be so. All the ways of the forest look alike to her. She consents to walk forward, in the direction she faced on waking, rising.

A stealthy umbra permeates the woods, it might be any time of day, though not of night. The snow is packed very hard and does not take an impression of the bare soles of Idrel. She expects wild animals lair among the firs and cedars, and perhaps will run out at her. Twice she catches a glimpse of some sinuous thing, the colour itself of the forest dusk – but this does not approach.

Sometimes a branch or bough cracks under the snow's weight, startling, like a whiplash. There are no other sounds but for the glacial ringing of silence itself.

How long the girl walks, in distance or time, she is unsure. But suddenly, the trees have thinned, and there ahead is a thick sky of grey nacre, and the terraces of a snow-hill cut into it.

Ghostly winds run on the hill, and blow the snow like white steam along the ground. Idrel climbs with three winds taking up her hair and throwing it to each other, and then down, clutching at her ankles, slapping her cheeks, and her eyes fill with slow tears. Then, at the summit, she discovers an odd road made all of solid ice.

Idrel steps on to the road of ice. Dimly, a reflection tapers from under her feet, and also there are objects caught there, mostly abstractions, though she begins to fancy statuary or frozen people are trapped in the glass coffin of it.

In a brief while, she perceives herself to have come in, almost unawares in the sameness of the snow, to a colossal ruin, maybe of a city. Tiles and parts of walls, doorways, roof-beams, arches, the skeletons of windows, have stolen round her, and high above a briary of knife-like cruel towers hangs abandoned in heaven.

The sight of this abnormal edifice, or what there is left of it, causes Idrel, lost and alone, to question for the first where she has come from, and who she is, and why she has travelled to such a place.

After an appreciable time, she mutters aloud, 'I shall remember, soon.'

And then she goes on, walking through the eroded architecture, down into dark avenues where pillars have collapsed and become static rollers of snow, and up stairways innumerable to her. And on her journey she passes only once something which touches her poignantly. That is an enormous flower, portionally of stone but mostly of opaque, bluish ice. The shape of the flower is a rose, but this the lost girl fails to ascertain. Perhaps she never saw a rose before, in whatever spot she has come from.

At last – the sky is stained with a more foreboding twilight – the girl Idrel reaches a wide platform against a door that seems to be of iron. Icicles drip down it, with edges that are like razors. She is afraid to put her hand to the door.

She sits before it. Night now must find her here.

The desire to sleep returns, and there in the leaden sunset she shuts her eyes and knows no more.

The King (The Queen's First Sin)

It was not true, she had not been a slut of the kitchen, not even a scullery maid, Innocin – but neither had she been called, then, Innocin.

On a day in late spring, returning from a hunt, the King had passed across the rough meadows below the Palace. A few good houses stood about, with formal small gardens, and orchards. But on the meadowland the first poppies were blooming, and a girl was there, plucking them like the strings of the day-harp, gathering armfuls of fire. Her hair was like a soft fire, also, but not much in evidence, scraped back from her yellow-white face and confined in a long rat's tail of braid.

She was dressed like a servant and doubtless that was what she was.

The King, having glanced at her – attention caught by the blot of red among the redness of the poppies – rode on. Half a mile further, he reined in. He called someone, his steward, or some aristocratic companion. 'I spied a damsel in that last field. Have her got.'

This King had whims, now and then, and his court was not unaccustomed to them. An envoy was sent – but the girl had vanished from the meadow, perhaps frightened away by her vision of loud horsemen and the carcasses of deer.

He went back behind the great iron doors of his house, the King. He brooded. He was used to getting that which he chose to want. A dark man, big and bear-like, he began to think of delicate things, waist-chains of slender gold, satin stockings, tortoise shell combs which, taken forth, let fall a light flood of hair …

Another whim came over him, and inside two days he had had made a slim dress of poppy-red velvet, and red-gold slippers with buckles printed by rubies. He had judged her measures for the footwear, if it did not fit, he supposed she would make the best of things, the shoes being what they were.

He had the garments transported around the peripheries of the Palace, and out to the marble houses on the meadows. He did not go so far as to accompany the party in disguise. His only instruction was: 'Red hair, white face. And if these bits go on to her, then you have the proper animal.'

But the hunt did not turn up anything of the right looks, let alone the correct build to fill garments and slippers.

The King began to fret. He was not used to this, to not getting his way.

They said afterwards the management of temporal affairs suffered at that time, but in fact, by now, the King was no longer necessary in the manner of a ruler. The direction of such lands as were postulated to be his was under the sway of councils, assemblies and ministers. What matter if a scatter of minor papers went unsigned, or a town or two was spared a royal progress?

Months presented themselves and were spent.

Came a morning, sportively pretending to simplicity, the King went out, on foot, with ten men and some dogs. He had almost forgotten the girl among the poppies, she was fading from him as the flowers had already had the grace to do. He would refer to how he had been cheated, occasionally, since he had stubbornly retained his dissatisfaction, the whiff of baulked romance, lose his temper then, or frown and call for music. This daybreak, it was quite out of his head.

There was a mist, mild and sweet, and in the mist suddenly he saw the girl, walking along, russet-cloaked, a basket on her arm.

She was going towards the ornamental woods out of which, further down, the King and his company had just emerged. In the mist, she seemed not to note eleven hunters and seven dogs. Perhaps her eyesight was poor, as others came later to believe.

Because she was slipping away into the shadows of the forest, the King motioned his men to silent stasis. He alone went back into the wood after her.

She had committed a kind of heresy against him. She had kept him waiting, and worse, vexed. He felt an entitlement now to do what he liked, although he would have done what he liked in any event.

The Blonde Dwarfess
(The Beast In The Wood)

Heracty has been told that the flaxen dwarfess once had an adventure in the mock forest below the Palace.

He does not know whether to credit this. She herself has never told him anything of it, though she is far from reticent.

Apparently, she had gone down the floral steppes, and wandered, astray, among the trees. She was gathering flowers, and carried a basket. But she wore courtly finery, and a scarlet snood sewn with brilliants, a gift of the Prince's. No one had warned her of the clockwork animals in the forest. Or, if they ever had, she misunderstood. She had left her maid, a canny brat of six years, behind.

When something howled, the dwarfess took the noise for that of one of the Prince's hounds, which were sometimes exercised in a large enclosure at the other side of the steppes. It was a still afternoon, and sounds might travel.

Then, as she bent towards a clump of pale hyacinths, the dwarfess saw, in the midst of a bush, two narrow, gleaming and carnivorous eyes.

Next moment, a grey wolf slunk from the thicket.

The dwarfess curtseyed to the wolf. Though she had not been informed, or had unremembered, clockwork, the etiquette of the Palace was by now ingrained in her. And at her curtsey, indeed, the wolf smiled, and prancing forward, capered all about her with expressions of amiability, so she was not in the least alarmed at it.

Presently the two walked on together. The wolf was helpful, nosing out for her absolute treasuries of flowers, aiding her in uprooting them. The dwarfess became fond of the smiling wolf, and on impulse placed her hand on his grey head.

No sooner had she done so than the wolf sprang and dashed her full-length on the ground. That done, it jumped on her, muddying her skirts and tearing them with its claws. It gave off bear-like roars, drooled and licked her, and sometimes bit her with excitement. Though these toothings were no more dangerous than the nips of an eager puppy, the lady in her terror imagined herself about to be devoured, eaten alive. She fainted.

On reviving, she found the wolf stretched heavily across her, using her pliant body and hair for a couch, fast asleep or certainly in the attitude of one grossly sleeping.

Not until the wolf awoke did she dare to stir. To her amazed relief, at her first cautious movement the beast quickly leapt away from her and darted into the forest.

The dwarfess, weeping, gathered up her slobbered skirts, and abandoning the spilled, crushed flowers, limped home.

At length, the gruesome tale was whispered to her consoeur, who pertly replied, 'Why, you should have thrown the brute an apple or a sweetmeat. That's all it wants.'

But the blonde dwarfess wished aloud, or so it was reported, that men might go and axe down the dreadful wood.

The Priest's Darkness (The Beauty)

Comfortless, the vampire dreams, while that which passes for its soul, a beast, lies snarling on the snow, pinned by hafts and staves.

The cold is like a wound, felt all through the tangled blackness of the pelt, through to the scald of the blood, and snow burns on the lashes of the fiery eyes, which are not composed of pure ferocity but of questions, and lit by bewildered distress and pain. It cannot comprehend, this thing, why it has been pursued, brought down, is tortured now, solely for being, for living as what it is.

The speech of the hunters is a blur of successful hatred and successful fear. They are recalling an idiot, tender of a midden, whom in error they did to death for these crimes. Yet here is the culprit, caught in the act, the milk-white lamb in its jaws –

'But the other shape –!' one cries out now, frantic.

'That perishes too. See – what's done here, we'll go back and search the houses to find.'

'Somewhere the devil will be weltered in his own blood.'

They laugh. It is a laugh of utter fright.

And the black wolf writhes, grinning, also afraid.

Until it beholds an axe, glinting silver in the torchlight, the rays struck upward from the fevered snow, an axe of silver iron raised over all their heads.

The axe flashes and crashes down.

He experiences the impact, the *blow*, and starts up choking, blind and maddened, calling out to God, in the turmoil of a hard thin bed.

But he is not killed, can breathe and see. And if he shouted aloud, beyond the walls his frozen village lies submissive enough, under the sterile quarter moon.

He has had this dream before, the priest. This dream, others. Once he would dream always that he led them, his flock, over the cliff of night into a valley of shadow, and there, as they entered the defile, he, the shepherd, seized them and sank his fangs into their throats.

His dark priestly robe is a black pelt. He puts it on. Beware of me, he whispers, setting the wafer between their lips, giving them their sip of God's blood, as he aches for the beauty of their wine. He stalks them and can pull them down with pitiable ease. He has had so many. Is it only hundreds?

Now he sobs, kneeling before the window, which has no glass, only a broken shutter. There are no riches here. Only the love of God and the blessing of the Devil.

What is to be done?

He looks round wildly, but there is nothing to hand. Even the razor for shaving is blunt in its dish.

Besides, it is just an evil dream. Of course, he is so tired. This terrible place, when he had once thought of lofty cathedrals, of purity, dedication, and bliss.

The priest lies down again on the bony bed. He stares with open eyes at the beams in the roof, and disciplines himself to think of … beauty.

Now he stares with open, inner eyes. He sees an altar-cloth, a white dove ascending on gold; this becomes a window in a church which touches the sky. But then it is a white girl painted against flames, and in her hands is a poisoned apple, like red flesh, which she throws to him. There is the choice, to catch the apple, to allow it to go by. If it does so, another will catch it. The apple fills his hand. He senses its fragrance. He longs to shut his inner eyes, but to do so must open again the outer ones. The moon is in the window now. His lids are wet. He is ashamed.

Beauty In The Palace (The Vampire's Dream)

Somehow, perhaps by magic, the door has been opened. Icicles lie around Idrel on her platform. Within the doorway, a stair mounts into darkness. This is not inviting, yet seemingly it is an invitation, as sure as if a dark figure, waited at the darkness' heart, calmly beckoning. Getting to her feet, the girl enters the doorway and climbs the stair.

The ruin is intent with strangeness, and the loud silence of snow and settled night.

Far beneath, in the blue ice-rose of a paralysed fountain, a mermaid had been trapped. Or, possibly, only drawn there with a dagger. And here, all at once, there are candelabra, with snow or wax heaped down their stems, but in their cups flames are beginning to burn up, like blossoms breaking too soon.

And then Idrel emerges high on the mountain of the wrecked enormous edifice, among its circlet of thorny towers. She is in a great hall, which has no roof and into which the towers seem to be gazing from huge eyes of dimly tinted glass. On the roofless walls hang lamps. As Idrel looks at them, they are being ignited, two or three at a time, by invisible tapers carried in unseen hands.

A cavern of pillared hearth has already flowered into fire. Instinctively, the young girl goes to it and stretches out her arms, flexes her fingers. The fire gives off heat. It warms her. It shows the crimson under her skin. Behind a curtain she finds a little closed chamber of some opulence, nested there in the ruin, and prepared for her, obviously for her.

A bath stands on silver feet, and from it rises scented steam, and a silver-framed table of vanities, mirrors, cosmetics, curling-tongs, and with jewellery littered about as if a princess had only just got up from it. Tall chests will offer her clothing. The unseen invisibles are pulling wide all the drawers and doors and trays, to demonstrate. While under its canopy, a bed has been aired with hot stones. It is a broad couch, the virgin notices, a marriage-bed, such as her foster parents shared. She senses, without nervousness of embarrassment, that someone may be watching her.

Idrel allows the sprites of the ruin to remove the shift of her village burial, steps into the soothing bath, and is laved so gently with unguents and water she cannot for an instant misinterpret the supernatural familiarities as anything human. She is made, and becomes, a beauty.

As she eats the dainty supper they have laid for her, the girl accepts the solution of her prior death, for this must be heaven and she is receiving her reward. As to the means of death, she cannot conjure any.

She inhabited one world, and now is here. She does not insult her condition by thinking she is dreaming. Perhaps, however, she is part of the dream of another.

That in mind, she ponders her pale hand with its new cuff of black, over both of which a coil of her hair has poured itself, in the firelight hectically coloured. A dramatic concoction for herself or any watcher: Black as ebony, red as blood, white as snow.

The Queen's Second Sin (The Dead King)

After he was done with her, the King lumbered to his feet, regarded her, and made as if to help her in turn to rise. Tumbled, her very downfall appealed to and enticed him. Provisions from her basket – she had been taking loaves and cakes to someone, somewhere – lay all over the turf. Candied cherries had bruised on her gown. Cherries, fulvous hair, maiden blood, a foam of petticoats. He was pleased by the artistic chaos he had created from her.

But she seemed to have lost her memory. He found that out when he had dragged her up. She had forgotten where she was going, where she had come from, even who she was. Her very name. He took it for a gambit, and guffawed. 'But you know who I am?' She thought and shook her fragile head. 'Your King,' he told her, hot without pride. She looked at him in complete belief and pure uninterest. He felt then he could not leave such a simpleton at large. He would have her at home a day or so more. He ate her pastries like a hearty ploughboy as they went, having summoned the abortive hunt with a yell. They had only been waiting out of sight.

'A fine quarry, eh?' said the king, jostling his lackwit doll.

In the palace, he soon grew used to her amnesia. It was rather novel. He gave her things instead, rooms, clothes. Even the dress and shoes he had bandied about. The slippers were in fact too small, and did not fit.

He had had a royal wife, once, who produced a viperish son, now being tutored, as was the vogue, elsewhere. The queen-mother next contracted a fatal plague during a pilgrimage she insisted on making, so it served her right. For himself the King did not foresee an era when he too, poisoned more slowly by various indulgences, would be gone, becoming in popular parlance 'Dead'.

What began as a clumsy snatch in a wood progressed to a merry hole-in-corner adventure, involving the game of secret passages and similar artifice.

Eventually, by accident, the King learned who it was probable he had abducted. An elderly aristocrat, living in a remote nook of the Palace grounds, which were considerable even in those days, had lost a child, a young, not quite legitimate daughter, fifteen years of age. It was suggested jealous older sisters of less beauty, the product of another union, had got rid of her. The description of the lost girl tallied sufficiently with that of the amnesiac now haunting the apartment of the King's favourite doxy.

Certain gifts were instigated. Vows of unspeaking were fashioned. The lady, garbed in her autumnal camouflage, was brought out and discovered to be, firstly, a duchess, and next, a queen. The ulcerous foot, and some other heralding ailments, had by now taken charge of the King. Virtue did not alleviate them.

Something else atrocious had meanwhile happened.

The Red Queen had ceased to be a girl, was not fifteen, not seventeen, not twenty, nor thirty, any longer. Flourished in the harsh illumination of the public court, far from her shady room and fireglims, she revealed her decay into a woman.

There was a story she had conceived but not borne to term. If one had asked this Queen, to her face, she would not have dissembled, for she did not seem to know, even now, anything valid about herself.

She could not truly be said to know, even, what she might be assumed to have realized – that she had been leapt on and vampirised, buried, dug out, thrust into the violent glare of an empty mirror which leered at, and insolently answered her, saying, Now you are old.

The King's bleared eyes, certainly, saw the etching of her bleak, icy face, as if it had been drawn on by a nail. It was unforgivable of her.

By the night of his summer death, he had, though, both forgiven and forgotten.

The son, fattened from viper to python, coming back, treated the madwoman Innocin with urbanity. He found it amusing so to do. After the amused period, it was established custom. Being very young, he thought her an antique. Such articles might keep their place, come and go as they wanted, wandering like a lost soul if no longer a lost child. Sometimes he would point her out to visitors, as another curio of his collection.

The Dwarf's Third Interview With His Grandmother

'Go away,' stridently commands Heracty's relative, as she sees him through her ice-locked window. In winter the marble houses are difficult to warm and tend to promote rheumatism. But the handsome dwarf, ignoring all temper of weather or woman, is already in, and standing by the hearth.

'What did I say to you?' snarls the grandmother.

'You welcomed me with tender cries,' says Heracty. 'And look at what I've brought you. A mantle trimmed by damascened fur combed from the Prince's gulon.'

The grandmother examines the item unkindly.

'There is no such animal as a gulon,' she remarks.

'The Red Queen,' says Heracty, musingly, 'has all her winter cloaks enhanced with gulon-fur, when not by ermine.'

'An ermine is only a weasel.'

'And what is a ghost?'

'The demon of a sickly stunted brain.'

'Wrong once more,' says Heracty. 'I'll tell you.' He seats himself by the fire, and props his boots on a stool. He notices today the grandmother looks ninety, and she that his legs seem to have grown longer. That is impossible. 'The Queen,' says Heracty, 'has visualised and hunted her lost youth so determinedly, it has taken on a shape. It has become a girl, lovely, clad in black velvet. But daylight or a lamp shine through her. She isn't substantial. And I believe, from the manner in which she gazes about, the Palace is just as unreal, in its way, to her. A ruin maybe is all she sees. Or else she exists in a previous or later time. Other dwarfs have met her. They say she lies down on their beds, with her feet and hair, both spangled, hanging over the ends. They say she wears slippers made of ice, or glass. The mastiffs fawn on her. The unicorn offers her rides. Even the two-headed dog turns one head. The gulon, naturally, spits and makes water. It's peevish. Have a honeyed almond? No? The gulon is very partial to them.'

'To hell with you, sir, your ghosts and gulons and honey and *legs*.'

'And here's a rose I found, after the phantom passed me on a stair.' Heracty extends it. 'A flower blooming in the snow.'

But, though exactly formed, the rose also is made of ice.

Grandmother burns her fingers on it, and thrown at a wall, it smashes.

The Beast (The Bride)

The sumptuous bed, entombed by its curtains on which are sewn bizarre animals and birds, has invented a separate breathing. It had, of course, not been there when she lay down to sleep – but is now so close to her that, as she wakes, she partly believes the rhythm of breath is her own. Not, however, the smooth planes of flesh, the cool hands which take her face between them, the lips which press her mouth.

She is not afraid. It was so inevitable, this. Surely she has known these caresses before. She yields without a word, with all herself. And since this place is heaven, love too is unalloyed. She is spun away as if through a starry sky. She falls to earth uninjured, but completely changed.

The man who has shared with her the bed of the act of love, invisible to her in the dark as any of the magical servants, is held in her arms. She ventures only now to question him, because now it does not matter.

'You ask me for my name,' he responds. His voice is musical and low. 'Call me Lucander. He, Lucander, will be with you here, at night. But you will never see him.'

'But will I see you?'

'At these times, he and I are the same. Never.'

'Never?'

It is a ritual. It neither frightens nor convinces her, though she is prepared to honour its outer show. In the same way, in her former life, she would have cast spilt salt across one shoulder.

'Not once, Idrel. Never. Never attempt to see my face.'

'Why not? Why?'

'Light, and my face, can't agree together. Even the moon's my enemy. Especially that. Without doubt the sun.'

'But a single candle,' she says.

'Don't try to discover me. The revelation would drive you mad .'

'But why?'

'The beast stays to be found in man. The hunter which preys on the trusting sheep.'

'A beast.'

'The bestial joke of God. Monstrous.'

In the blinded blackness, the bride describes the face of her husband. Her fingertips learn only the mask of a human male, the brows and lashes, the lips and earlobes, the jaw with its masculine roughening. And the taste of him, of the fruits of the darkness.

'But by night you will be here with me?' She employs his name, 'Lucander.'

She is already, in his second embrace, planning for his future slumber, a tinder struck and the surprising candle flame.

Innocin's Ascent
(The Queen's Last Sin)

Can it be her step-son's dwarf is continuing to follow her? No, surely, it is just her shadow compressed and thrown behind. For a new idea has occurred to Innocin. Not to descend in the twilight, but instead to seek higher, into the diadem of the Upper Palace, its tallest towers.

They are remote and neglected, and in the vast attics there perhaps a white skirt has often gone up and down, and pale feet have all this while been stepping.

As she ascends, the Queen considers the sin of her husband, a black sticky sin, or spotted red, the murder of her past amounting to an utter death. This sin it was that gave her to conceive the child clad in clement white.

The stairs are craning, spindly, thick with webs and dust. Yet far above in the air, a pastel eye beams on her, a window made encouraging by a lamp. Or only the moon in a cloud.

She crosses a passage, her cloak industriously sweeping up the dirt and old nests – once doves brooded here. The stars glint in broken bricks. The towers are very ancient. They belong to other, earlier, histories.

On a threshold, the Queen hesitates. It is now too dark for her to see anything, and the guiding light has vanished. Nevertheless, a sweet, slight voice is singing, the words indistinguishable, like a faint zephyr tingling through the bones of the tower.

Innocin sighs.

The voice she hears is like that of a child, but not a child lost and alone, bleeding or crying in the bitter cold. This is a found child, braiding her hair and playing with a rope of pearls. Roses unseasonably grow about her, a fire dances. There is food and wine. Slaves to serve, not to exact service. There is love.

Suddenly Innocin can see a cave of golden light, and a shining young woman going by through the yellow heart of it.

'Oh,' whispers the Red Queen. 'There she is.'

She smiles at the glamour and riches, all the nights and mornings, guessing the beloved is due to return. Not for the found daughter a wild beast in a forest, rending and blight.

The Queen smiles, and lets her soul go out of her.

The soul is gone.

Like an amber dove she falls from the tower-top, her mantle bearing her on its wing. She falls at Heracty's feet, where he stands in a court below.

Though her skeletal structure is dislodged at the impact, her body settles, resting her pristine on her back, her hands folded on her breast, her long lids closed, and her mouth still blossoming its flame of smile. Oh, she is yet saying, there she is. And the mirror has cracked, and set her free, at last.

The Wolf's Head (The Awakening)

There have been many nights and days. In the day, sometimes, led by the unseen slaves, Idrel explored the ruin, discovering its secret wonders. The labyrinth is full of ghosts. Frequently the girl has witnessed, tiny in the telescoped lens of distant corridors, or courtyards five flights of stairs beneath, frantic scenes of another world, which plainly do not otherwise have substance. Idrel observes impartially games and feasts, courtings and quarrellings, aristocrats and unicorns and dwarfs.

But the nights are better for exploring.

In the snow-field of white sheets, her night-husband draws her away into the forest of desire – and abruptly the darkness engulfs her.

To these delights, the lingering tension of Idrel's plan has subtly been added.

Tonight she will carry it out.

Slipping from the bed, she fetches a candle. As she does this, a sigh seems to flutter round the chamber. The ruin is crammed with phantoms, and Idrel pays no heed.

Light is absent, the fire long-smothered and all the lamps doused before her lover's arrival. Carefully returning through screens and panes of blackness to the bed, she puts the candle down, strikes the tinder, lets the fire-bud drop on to the waxen branch where, like a canary, it beats its wings. When the flame steadies, holding it high, Idrel pulls aside a fold of the bed-curtain. She stares down at what lies sleeping on the white drift of the sheet.

Shadows and sheen combine to describe. Here are the lines of a man's body, which at the shoulders culminate in the head of a black wolf.

As soon as she sees it, she remembers, everything.

In that moment, too, perhaps alerted by the light and its flickering, or solely by the intensity of the watcher, the creature wakes. It growls softly, or, the muzzle of the wolf does so. Feral, human, lupine eyes glare up at the young girl standing there, pinning it with a stave of light, and clothed herself in her white nakedness, save where the same light blushes her apple-red.

'I look and I see,' says Idrel.

Her eyes say clearly: I knew all the time it was there, your black wolf. To live is to die. I'm dead, and here with you. You made me holy, taking my blood.

And leaning down, she kisses the wolf face, over and over, with quiet still kisses. And as she does this, the candle tilts and the burning hot wax sears and seals his skin, but he does not flinch at it. When Idrel lifts her head, she finds a man, with a man's skull and features, a broad low brow, hair black as crow's feathers, black-water eyes that regard her.

'There will be another bed,' he murmurs, 'with a dead wolf in it, or a living man – but not this one.'

'But you are Lucander. You are with me, here.'

The vampire, or supernatural spirit, whatever it is, has now fully recognized the soul, or ghost, of Idrel. That is, if Idrel ever existed beyond the brain of a red-haired queen.

They contemplate each other in the melting honey of the candle gloom. When the candle finishes, who can say if they remain in the black night, or if they too have gone away.

Even the serene susurrus of their voices, which is yet to be distinguished, may not be real. Although more so, perhaps, than the stairs and galleries and towers of the preposterous Palace.

The Black Queen (The Seven Dwarfs)

Because he thinks of himself as an innovator, the Prince has had a strange new mausoleum built, on a hill three or four miles from the Palace. In the mausoleum lies the body of his step-mother, the dead Queen.

The view from the mausoleum is eloquent. Above, uncut meadows, woodland tapering to park, the mountain of the royal domicile. Below the sapphire basins of the valleys, the far-away forests which are not fakes, a thunder-cloud of trees, redolent and rowdy with every animal applicable to the clime.

The corpse of Innocin was come on at daybreak in a yard of the Upper Palace by some sozzled young nobles, who were startled but not astounded. It was decided she had toppled from a tower.

The sin of suicide was not mentioned. Nevertheless the location of the new tomb was fortuitous; it did not require sacred ground.

It could be erected as a monument. Somewhat to that end, the Prince had organised rather a peculiar funeral rite, which, repeated on and off in subsequent years, became known as the Masque of the Black Queen.

The title role was undertaken by the dusky dwarfess. Attired like midnight, with sables, and jets in her hair, she was drawn in a carriage by a team of plumed black greyhounds. The other six dwarfs, each got up allegorically, came behind, mounted or on foot as their character advised. Heracty had the part of Worldly Fame, his pony, a suit of cloth-of-gold, and the obligation of lugging on leash two ill-mannered peacocks. His brother dwarfs represented Modesty, Sloth, Rage and Joy. The blonde dwarfess, in butterfly costume, was asked to suggest Unearthly Apprehension. The dusky dwarfess, the Black Queen, was unarguably Lady Death.

Additional pets of the Prince's had work in the procession. The unicorn appeared wreathed in thorns as The Pardon Of Heaven. The gulon and dual-headed dog were excluded, however, as untrustworthy.

All this display, with the snuffling, labouring court plodding after, toiled out through heavy snow to the mausoleum, where dirges were sung, and flowers dyed black, or gilded, tossed on the ice. The mausoleum steps had gone to mirror, and the miraculous dome was topped again by a scoop of snow.

Months on, when the thaws of spring had manhandled the land and flung down the rime and snow from the slopes, the court would voluntarily visit the area, also the dwarfs. They would sit on the tomb-steps, and look pensively out into the valleys. Their reasons for doing so, particularly the reasons of the dwarfs, were banal. They liked the vista, thought it prudent to pretend respect, or relished the proof of the high brought low.

Heracty attends the tomb seldom. When giving the gulon exercise, as he now sometimes does, he will tend that way.

For its part, the fox-cat sniffs all about the mausoleum, trotting up the steps to peer with peridot eyes in at the transparent dome. Does the gulon recognize the bleached trimmings in which Innocin has been laid to rest? More likely, being fed on carrion, its interest is of that order.

The Tomb (The Spring)

The priest walks to the summit of a hill on an evening of late spring – and sees in front of him a curious monument.

The ordeal which he endured in a backward, superstitious village is over with. He has been recalled to the towns and cities of his earliest dreaming. Conversely, he has sloughed those dark nightmares that haunted his beginnings. The inner outcry for flesh, the carnal ravening, like hunger, these impediments he are surpassed. He has wrestled with the subterranean angel, and triumphed.

Birds sing in the warm avenues of sky. The westering sun flies against a dome of glass, piercing it with a brilliant nail.

Having space, and peace, the young priest makes a detour and climbs the steps, and so concludes the monument is a tomb. Marble and granite, like a fist it grips an egg of sheer transparency. And in this oval mirror a woman lies composed, robed in creamy white, coifed like a nun, a circlet of gold binding her forehead. There is not a mark on her face. She would seem to be a girl. This aspect will be eternal. The sarcophagus has shut her fast in a vacuum, where no atmosphere can enter to corrupt.

She will, therefore, never grow old. She will never decay. Always her bones will be decently clad, until the Final Judgement.

The young man gazes in at the dead, seemingly-sleeping girl. A kiss might awaken her.

It comes to him, how the Devil left him in the likeness of a black wolf, running off briskly along the roads of slumber. Of what is this dead girl dreaming, this white queen, as she lies in her shell of crystal forever?

On the other side of the tomb, a blonde dwarf lady is seated at an aesthetic angle, but she too has gone to sleep. In a basket at her side are apples and peaches, one with a chunk bitten out of it.

Above, beyond, meadows, hillside, the winking of water, a wood where rhododendrons are flowering, some hint of towers or roofs.

A nonsensical beast like a large brown cat, or possibly a tabby fox, is eating poppies in the meadow-grass.

The priest walks on, leaving the tomb of glass for the sunset and the night.

Heracty's Omission Of A Further Interview With His Grandmother

On the rim of the fountain, the seventh dwarf balances in the afterglow of summer sun fall, diving his hand into the water, making believe it is a fish. Then, removing his hand and knowing it again as the hand of an elf.

The creatures of the fountain loom over him, still tanned with pink day; great heat stays cosy in the stone. Roses have burst across the lawn.

Although she will never any more glide down the stair, cross this terrace, go by him sightlessly, sinking through the Palace, even so, sometimes he waits for her.

Heracty does not anticipate Innocin's ghost. A ghost cannot *become* a ghost.

When a ghost dies, it springs to life.

It is years now since he went to call on his grandmother, but Heracty does think of her, for that old witch is waiting for him with malicious hope, but he will never go near her again. Her vigil is accordingly as pointless as this one he keeps on the fountain terrace.

Something stirs among the roses, and shower of petals snows the dusk.

The moon is rising like a coin of breath, and the gulon, early, starts to yowl. The heart or soul of the gulon is rushing at liberty through a forest. And somewhere else, Heracty is a man with lion's hair, over six feet tall, his shoulders filling a door way. Heracty knows this other life of his goes on. It is just there, or *there* – beneath an arch, behind a door. It takes only the brush of a feather to dislodge the barrier of iron between. He believes this, and knows this, and how simple it would be to do it. Heracty is puzzled, less dismayed than nonplussed, that he had never found the way.

Xoanon[1]

It is a bleak village for sure, held there on the arm of the land, against the acres of the cold, grey sea. Stones on the beach as great as the pale seals that swim by in the summer. Hills behind, worn bare through their grass that has no colour. Not a tree to be seen, for they cannot withstand the winter gales. And the little houses, brown and white, with their little narrow windows, and the winding street where now and then some cart goes up and down, pulled by a dark and steadfast horse. And, on the slope, the white church, with its pointed roof and thick wooden door. No stained glass in its walls, but that is not what the stranger comes seeking. It is the carvings you visit.

The village lives by the fish, and has done so for three or four hundred years, and maybe longer. Along the shore the boats are drawn up, painted with their names that cannot be read, unless you speak the language of this place. But some of the boats are painted not with words but pictures. They do not all read and write here. They do not find much use for it, even now when there are books and newspapers to be had on the mainland. Nor do you find a television anywhere, and only two or three radios that give a poor reception – the sea and the sky are between them and all things, and the weather. But in the pub there is a gramophone with a horn, and three hundred records.

Crossing over is best done in the summer, or on a calm day of late spring. You arrive in a black boat painted with a girl in a long blue dress, with a wreath of shells on her yellow hair. The boat is called *The Girl in the Blue Dress*. Old Aelin hands you out, courteous and unspeaking. His face is like hard driftwood, brown and grey and torn in wrinkles, and his teeth are black. But he smells cleanly of the sea, and his eyes, where the driftwood has been opened to reveal them, are the blue of the girl's dress, clear and sane and strange and old. The eyes of a good man, or perhaps a woman, for they have here no manner of the coarse old men you will meet elsewhere, the men who think women are betrayers and fools, useful only by a crib or stove. And indeed, the women of the village are not of that sort, and the men are none of them of the coarser sort. They sing and tell stories, and in these fluid tales you will hear of the pitiful sweet mermaids who have gifted human lovers of both genders with immortal life beneath the water, of men who have died for their women and women who have died for their men, of the true love of man for

---

[1] Xoanan: Primitive usually wooden image of deity supposed to have fallen from heaven. (Concise Oxford Dictionary 1987)

man and woman for woman, of the value of daughters, and the virtues of gentleness, and how the seals have their own tongue, which may be learned, and that in the world beyond death, all are equal forever, and sometimes they call God She, and sometimes He, and sometimes They, or It. But they speak of God, as of all things, with respect, and interest. You learn, before you come, of Japanese visitors and black students, who have been unnerved that no one noticed, in the village, or so it seemed, their physical differences, in which they rightly took pride.

There was also a woman, once, who pointed out that the value the village set on animals was flawed, for they live by fishing the seas and eating the fish. But the villagers nodded politely to this woman, and since she could not speak their language, and they only a little of hers, she did not hear of their service, which is held twice a year, in which they bless the fish and ask pardon of them, as too they do when they catch them. In the service, the priest explains that the world is, in some ways, not well made, which is not the fault of God, since She, He, They and It did not construct all the world's laws, in fact only those laws which are benign, tidy and pleasing to everyone. Through their own fault, or error, man and beast must sustain themselves, and cannot always do so without meat in some form. Until a new world is made, this cannot be put right. In truth, most of what the village catches is taken to the mainland, and before the winter closes the sea, the seals are fed a catch to assist them on their journey.

Most visitors leave *The Girl in the Blue Dress* tired from the hour's crossing, which can be a discomfort even in summer, and go up the street to the public house, which has a painted sign of a strong, handsome man with the tail of a shark. This pub is called *The Guest*.

Here they serve you local drink, white whisky with the scent of turf, a thimbleful powered like any triple measure elsewhere, and milder pale yellow ale. Or there is tea to be had. On broad plates they will bring you golden loaves whose dark inner flesh tastes of nuts, pickled apples from the village orchard tucked behind the houses, trees crooked and little, that produce a sharp red fruit, cheeses like the best of Northern France, and, if asked, flakes of smoked fish with whipped fried eggs.

In winter, the fire burns in the huge fireplace of the pub, but in summer the dense stone walls keep out a blistering heat. The rafters are low enough to stun you. if you should be more than short, and they have hung about them long ribbons that check you, should you forget, and so save you a headache. Almost no one in the village is more than five and a half feet tall, it is true. But they are formed all in proportion, on a smaller scale. Aelin is probably the tallest of them, for he is five feet ten inches, and in the pub he walks bent over.

When you have dined and rested you can go through the village, and up the slope of the first hill, towards the church. On this slope, it seems you must look back, and down below, the village is, and the huge sea beyond. There comes the sense of immensity, as when you gaze up into the sky, perhaps the sky of night with all its million, billion stars. How small is the village, the land itself, and from that vast firmament of silver water, what may not come?

When you resume your climb, you may think how bare the church is, so stark and white, and inside you anticipate few ornaments, and you are correct to do this, for there is almost nothing at all. The windows are narrow and plain, and have shutters against the storms. Though there is an altar it has on it only ever a bare white cloth. There is no crucifix, though – once you have grasped their language – you will hear them speak of Jesus Christ, and as if He were well known among them, the son perhaps of some grandmother a couple of generations gone. But they speak too of others, and it may occur to you to wonder how they have heard here, cut off as they are, uninvolved as they are in television and telephone, of Mohammed and Buddha. And then again there are names they will speak you will not recognize, probably. And besides you may mistake these names for those of their forefathers, these sons of grandmothers, until maybe there is mention of what might be termed a miracle – conception without intercourse, ascents to heaven, transformations and healings, resurrection and rebirth. All these matters are apparently as normal to the villagers as the boiling of a kettle or the turning tides of the sea. The only way indeed you may be sure that they are speaking of some great one, some One who has come from God, is by the tone of pride in their voices. For they are *proud* of Mohammed and Jesus and Buddha, and all the others. They smile as they speak, as if they told you instead how rich and powerful and beautiful their ancestors have been.

On the altar, however, there is a cup made of iron, and from this they drink water during the services, a sort of communion, perhaps. The stranger too, if he or she is present and so wishes, may join in the ritual. But the services are held irregularly, you cannot be sure you will arrive at the right time.

Usually the church stands empty and unlocked, full of light, cool in summer, frozen cold in spring. You look about, and so regard the nine long pews, which are all that are ever needed here, though once, there were more. The wooden carvings are placed one at the left or south end of each pew. Finding them, it may be you are surprised that they are so small. You may need to bend close, to put on spectacles, or produce a magnifying glass.

Then you will see that the carvings are, in their own manner, very simple, although perhaps attractive to the eye. Perhaps they will seem at once mystical, imbued with all that is provoking and inexplicable. Or sinister, they might seem to be that. Or you may be disappointed. Having come so far and so uncomfortably to this pared spot, despite the good food and drink you may have taken, and the looks of the villagers, their kindness, their glowing stained glass eyes.

Yes, you may think, Well, and is this all? This little curved fish creature that has something about it of the whale, and which symbolizes the sea, for on its back it carries a tiny carven boat. And, moving forward up the aisle, to the west, there is the carving of a goblet, not unlike that which stands on the altar, but upturned, so some visitors have asked if it was not wrongly attached. Beyond the upturned cup is a carved sun, emblematic, an image seen very often and in many areas, even on the wrapping paper sold for birthdays. At the end of the fourth pew a tiny man and woman stand embracing, and a tinier child clings to the woman's long skirt. From their costume, these three, the carvings can be dated, to some mid-point of the 1700's, as the villagers do date them. At the end of the fifth pew is a skull, Spare and universal as the previous sun. And at the end of the sixth, something more complex, an angel, apparently, a winged being. Its face is so small it has no features but a suggestion of eyes, although minutely the feathers are scored into the wings. On the seventh pew is another fish, this one roaring like a lion. On the eighth pew a presentation that may defeat even the youngest eye, the strongest spectacles, and the magnifying glass. After much study, if you have the patience, you may behold an amalgam of things, cows and sheep, fish and cats, snakes, dogs, men and women, and countless other icons, most not decipherable. In the scramble of shapes it will eventually come to be seen that everything here is winged. On the ninth pew however, there is no use in study. This carving, it seems, is an abstract pattern, something not often demonstrated at that era, conceivably the invention of a broken mind. This final woodwork is disturbing, insulting to some, like a cheat. To come so far and find only these little things, and this last thing, so meaningless, therefore unimportant. Besides, have you not seen all this already in the pamphlet on the mainland, or reproduced in some glossy book that deals with the carvings of churches? Why then did you come? But, yes, there is still the ultimate bizarre object.

Out from the church then you go, an hour or five minutes after you entered it, and walking on the path that they have shown you from the village pub, you ascend the rest of the barren hill, and the white church falls behind.

In summer there will be sheep out on the hills, and three or four cows, brown cows with heavy heads bearing each the white crescent of the moon. The sheep are shaggy, and they have been described as pink. Their colour is old and washed by rain, but their faces, like those of the cows, are profound. They graze placidly, and let you by without fear or sullenness. If you should like animals and wish to touch them, they will come up to you at a call. Sometimes the horses from the carts are there also, and they gallop, but again they are careful not to alarm, or so you may think, and let you caress their rough electric manes. Under or upon the stones on the hills you might see a spotted snake, harmless. You may stroke these as easily as the cats in the village street, if you care for snakes or cats. You may have heard that the seals too will let you approach them, though only the villagers feed them by hand. It is the same with the birds, and with everything wild that lives thereabouts.

Do not be amazed that a fox trots to you out of the bushes, sniffs at your foot or knee. The rabbits that feed in the low fields between the hills never run away, unless by accident you almost tread on one.

Over the third hill, and you will be glad of your walking shoes, you find the last curiosity of your trip. To some this has more value, to others less, than the carvings attached to the pews in the church.

Much has been said of it, the ruin of the boat. Firstly, that it is a ship and not a boat at all, with the bone of her strong mast still sticking up, formed of the wood that must come from far away, where the gales do not reach formed of that wood which made the carvings. Her shell is intact, though the weather has leached it all to a grey that is almost white. But there are holes in the flanks of her and in the deck, and the cabin amidships has mostly fallen down. The metal on the wheel is red with rust bright as flowers.

Of course, reason tells you, that they brought her here, the villagers, though for what purpose? Perhaps straightforwardly to abet their peculiar story. In the story, the ship or boat fell down from the sky, fell slowly enough that many saw her, and, when she met the earth, slowly enough she did not entirely shatter to bits.

On the side no mark remains, but you will know that, like the boat of Aelin, this one was also called The *Girl in the Blue Dress*, and so painted. In those days of the eighteenth century, not one man or woman in the village could read or write.

The spar, or part of the spar, remains, and perhaps a gull or greenfinch will perch there. It will watch you as you circle round the boat, look at the places where they hauled in their nets heavy with fish, at the wreck of the planking. Before the bird flies off, probably you will be weary of the ship that is a boat, but you will sit on the warm hillside if it is summer, to rest before returning to the village. In spring even you may rest. It is a hard walk, going and coming down.

No one in the village will tell you the story of the carvings and the boat, unless you ask, and then Aelin will return and tell you. You will discover then that Aelin has a blind dog that can nevertheless somehow see, or seem to, for it knows everywhere so well. It will sit by his side, but if you wish it, it will sit by you, and you will comb its coarse silk with your fingers, should you want to, and maybe buy it a dish of the yellow ale, as you will doubtless want to buy some drink for Aelin. The prices in the pub called *The Guest* are absurdly cheap, and they employ the currency of the mainland. You may notice that the locals do not seem to pay, but maybe an account is kept. If it happened, as once it did, that you had lost your wallet or your purse, neither would you pay anything, and some money would be found in your pocket or under your glass, when you came back from the clean little pub latrine, with its cracked white enamel wash-basin, and the large cake of amber soap. Even if you had lied, they would do this. They would not care that you had lied.

Aelin will tell you, quietly and mildly, in your own language, whatever that is, the tale of the boat and the carvings, which is not in the books, but there is no reason you should not hear it twice, and he will tell it the best.

Two hundred years and more ago, the boats went out each day, the five or six or seven of them, out to reap the fishes from the sea. And sometimes it would be that a boat would not come back. The women would wait upon the shore, wrapped in their shawls, cold even in summer, looking to see if the boat their man was in would reappear at last. There were some five men to each boat, and so the lost boat meant five lost men, and five families of women, and too their children often enough, standing there at the edge of the water. They would weep, or not, but the salt sea is made of tears.

One summer the water was calm as blue silk, and the boats went out at dawn, and all came back at sun fall but one, that boat called *The Girl in the Blue Dress*.

It had been a long day, for the days are long here in the summer, but down to the beach the five women came, and with them four children, two with one woman, and one each with two of the other women, while two women walked alone. They stopped at the fringes of the sea that now was half red, as the sun burned out inland, and half the dark blue the eastern sky was going.

Who has seen beyond the shore at night, where no lamp or light can reach it, however bright, knows that it becomes finally one with the sky, and then it cannot be found, the end of one, the commencement of the other. Only the land is different from them both. But then the moon rose, and made a silver road upon the sea, yet nothing moved on that road.

And when the moon had gone over, it left again the darkness, which was void. Later came the sun, like a golden beast rising out of the water. But the sun brought nothing either, though its passing was longer.

Some days and nights the five women waited on the shore. Now and then other women brought them a little food, or took the children away to sleep. At the entering and retreat of the tides, the women moved back or forward like figures on a clock. One or two might lie to sleep an hour on the stones, while the others watched. After about seven days, the men came, and the priest, and took them softly back into the village. There they cried and railed their anger and bitterness and pain. Others comforted them who had themselves lamented in the same way, and others who understood that they too might one day so lament. Presently they got up, the five widows, from the rock of their grief, and took on their empty lives, where every moment is like every other and, as before the passage of God, there is no sundering of day from night.

A month or two passed, and it was harvest time in the few fields between the hills. As the men and women worked, they heard a strange note sounding in the sky, and in the village they heard it too, and the women that were there came out of their doors.

The sky was clear as the blue eye of a child. Nothing was in it, not a cloud, not a bird. And then there appeared a tiny dot, which began to grow bigger, and soon those that looked saw how it grew bigger since it fell towards the earth.

Slowly it fell, as if it had no weight, or very little, yet directly down. And before it reached the earth, the watchers saw plainly that it was a boat, a boat having one sail, and from her sides floated out the rent nets like a web. And those that were close enough saw too how on the curve of her side there was the painting of her name, a girl with a blue gown and shells in her yellow hair.

She settled light as a leaf over the third hill, and they went running to see, leaving their scythes in the fields, and in the village the pots to burn.

When they reached her they knew her for sure. They were afraid, how not? But going near, they started to call out the names of her crew. None answered. None were there. The boat was empty of everything, all vanished but the spoiled nets, not a bucket, not a rope, and nothing of the men, even when the villagers got up their courage and mounted the deck, and stepped into the little cabin. All was gone, even the compass, even the lamp. And of the crew not a trace.

The five widows had come up by then, and the four children. It was one of these children that remarked on the odour of the boat. It had naturally smelled of tar and of fish, and now it did not. Now they did not know what it smelled of, although the child had said that it was flowers.

The fifth widow, one of the two who had no children, saw the small wooden things that lay under the wheel. They had mostly gone back from the boat by then, but one of the men got over into her again, and took the things up and brought them out.

Sometimes the fishers would carve in wood, to pass time as they waited on a still sea, or by night at home before the fire. They recognized the carvings as their own, that is, the carving of the men who had been lost, who had disappeared. They did not know what the carvings meant, except, four of them. That is, the fish bearing the boat, which was the sea, the roaring fish, which meant a storm, the upturned cup which was the symbol of want, hunger and thirst, and the skull, which, to most of the world, has always signified death.

The other carvings, the amalgam of flying creatures, the sun, the man and woman who embraced, even the angel, these perplexed them, while the abstract pattern made them uneasy. They carried the enigmas to the village, and put them in the church, where the priest bent over them and asked God for help.

At this point in the story, Aelin will tell you that, when at last the carvings were set on the ends of the nine pews, they were placed deliberately out of order. This is because their force is so enormous, even in mere simulation, that it is considered best that it does not run in the correct sequence. So it comes about you can never properly deduce the tale merely by examining the carvings. You can only ever be told.

That night, the village slept restlessly, yet sleep it did, for the sea's sound induces sleep for those that have always lived within hearing of it, the lullaby that is heard perhaps in the womb. And the five widows and the four children slept, and they dreamed, each of them, the same dream, and waking up in the darkest hours of morning, they ran out into the street and stood there, those nine humans, as they had stood before at the edge of the sea, looking for the boat that instead dropped down from heaven.

They did not know which of their men had carved the wood, or if all of them had done it, as maybe all of them had. But; without the skill of writing, it had been their only method to reveal what had gone on. And in their dreams the women and the children had seen these men, each one her husband, or the child its father, and showing the carvings, they had explained with care the nature of events.

They had sailed, the fishermen, on a calm sea, which was the fish with the vessel on its back. But soon, they had lost sight of the other boats, as might happen. Then without warning the sky turned black, and a storm blew up – the roaring fish – worse than they had known on such a morning. They rode it out as best they could, and eventually, the wind sank, and the clouds melted, and the day was as before, blue and calm, and still now as a thing deeply asleep.

They sensed that they were far from land, and worse, most strangely, as if they had gone somewhere far from everything that they had known. The boat could not sail, there was no wind. They waited for the going of the sun at last, and for the sunset wind that almost always rises. But the day did not alter, sea did not, nor the sky, and at length they must admit the sun itself did not move from the centre of heaven.

One man had a pocket watch, and by this thereafter they timed the days and nights. They drank the ale they had brought, only a jug of it, and they had some bread to eat, but it was quickly consumed, though they tried to make it persist. Nor did any fish approach the nets. The sea was bottomless and lucid, and nothing was in it, and no bird crossed the sky. Thus then, what they foresaw, the upturned cup, and so the ultimate parting from their wives and children – that last embrace – and at the end the skull of death.

They were not afraid, more dreary, resentful, for they were all young men. They raged, they prayed, and some wept. But then they were too weak for anything, and sat on the deck, their spines against the sides of the boat, under the lovely, perfect sky. After this they forgot to measure the passage of time.

Maybe they sank into a sort of trance or faint. They woke as one, and everything was changed. Their weakness had left them, each man felt refreshed as if from a fine meal, and a sweet slumber. They stood up, and as they did so, an enormous light enveloped them, a light whiter than snow, more brilliant than the heart of the sun, a light which should have blinded and slain them, but it did not, no, it was like a balm, and they laughed aloud. In the middle of the light they presently saw a creature that they took for an angel, for it was very beautiful and had wings, yet there were no features to its face, only two most wonderful shining eyes, and even this, the form of it, its eyes and wings, they knew in those moments were more the manner of their seeing, than the reality. Nevertheless it touched them gently with its hand, and all at once, the boat was lifted up into the sky, up with the glory of the light, up and up and so to the place that now, speaking to their wives and children in the dream, they were powerless to describe, and shook their heads, smiling, and indicating the carving which had no form, was only a pattern, and that not regular, or similar to anything. An inexplicable place – but a place that was, to the world, Heaven.

In the dream then, the women had asked, and the children had asked, would they not return, these men, since they still lived. The men replied that this was not possible, now, but they had sent a sign at least, and the sign should be heeded. Not as a promise or reward, but as a certainty. Look at the final carving, which had attempted to show how everything in the world grew wings and flew upward – save that these were not wings, nor was it upward, though it might seem to be – all was not as it appeared, yet better, much, much better, as a blind man who had imagined sight, should he be able suddenly to see, or as true love is better than loneliness, or children grow up into men and women, or summer comes after winter, and there has always been a morning after night.

The village, Aelin will then say, stands where it has always stood, and the boat lies between the hills, but the carvings were attached to nine of the pews in the church, the nine pews that remain.

He will not then argue or, shamed and smirking, apologize for any foolishness, or what you might desire to call whimsy. He will not try to answer any questions to do with religion or faith, although he will be silent only in the most courteous way. If you ask him what became of the five widows, he will say that he believes, in time, they remarried. If you ask if he credits the story of the carvings and the boat, he will nod.

Then you may stay drinking, and he will stay with you if you request it, but no longer allow you to pay for his drinks; but this is done so simply and in so friendly a fashion, it will not be a rebuff, and is not a rebuff, not even if you have sneered and cackled, and said he was an imbecile. He does not mind. Why should he mind? There is nothing to mind about. Words are not always facts.

If you wish, you may sleep that night in one of the three large herbal-scented beds at *The Guest*, and tomorrow he will take you back across the sea.

Or he will do so by night even, if you crave for it.

Even he will go walking with you, back to the church, and stand by as again you observe the carvings, or he will go up the hills with you, and proceed with you about the boat. He will reply to such questions as are pertinent – the vanished painting on the side, the type of birds that fly over in the dark, singing, what he supposes might have been the thoughts of those villagers two centuries off, after the dream was revealed, how the carvings were fixed to the pews – with great ease, apparently – his age, which is almost ninety, the names of the stars above.

If you are angry he will speak softly of little things. If you are sad he will murmur that all will be well. But he has already told you that. Perhaps this is his only concession.

When, that evening or night, or that next day, he has taken you back over the water, and you get out on the mainland, hard as concrete, built high and blown loud with life, then you will be in a position of examining properly, if you mean to, what you have seen and heard. You will decide then, and possibly in a different form from your decision in the village. You may find you believe it all, or some of it, or none of it. Or next year you may. One dusk, or dawn. Or never. You may never ever believe a word.

I do.

Yellow And Red

FROM THE DIARY OF GORDON MARTYCE:

9th September 195–: 7 pm

Coming down to the old house was at first interesting, and then depressing. The train journey was tedious and slow, and after the second hour, over and again, I began to wish I had not undertaken this. But that would be foolish. The house, by the quirkiness of my Uncle's will, is now mine. One day I may even live in it, although for now my job, which I value, and my flat, which I like, keep me in London. Of course, Lucy is terribly interested in the idea of an old place in the country. I could see her eyes, lit by her second gin, gleam with visions of chintz curtains, china on the mantelpiece, an old, dark, loudly-ticking clock. But it is not that sort of house – I knew that even then, never having seen inside it in my life. As for Lucy, I am never sure. She has stuck to me for five years, and so I have not quite given up on the notion of one day having a wife, perhaps a family. Quite a pretty woman, quite vivacious in her way, which sometimes, I confess, tires me a little. Well, if it comes to that, she can do what she wants with the house. It is gloomy enough as it stands.

Beyond the train, the trees were putting on their September garments, brown and red and yellow, but soon a drizzle began which blotted up detail. It was raining more earnestly when I reached the station and got out. I had only one small bag, the essentials for a stay of a couple of nights. That was *good*, for there was no transport of any kind.

I walked to the village, and there was given a cup of tea, the keys, and a lift the last mile and a half.

Johnson, the agent, let me off on the drive. He had offered to take me round, but I said this was not necessary. There is a woman, Mrs Gold, who comes in every day, and I was told, she would have put things ready for me – I trusted this was true.

The rain eased as I walked along the last curve of the drive. Presently I saw the house, and recognized it from a photograph I had observed often enough in my father's study. A two-storey building, with green shutters. Big oaks stood around it that had done the walls some damage, and introduced damp. I supposed they could be cut down. Above, was my Grandfather's weather-vane, which I had never been able, properly, to make out in the photograph, but which my father told me was in the shape of some Oriental animal deity.

Even now, it remained a mystery to me, between the leaves of the oaks and the moving, leaden sky.

I got up the steps, and opened the front door, and stepped into the big dark hall. The trees oppress this house, that is certain, and the old stained glass of the hall windows change the light to mulberry and spinach. However, I saw through into the sitting room, and a fire had been laid, and wood put ready. A touch on a switch reassured me that the electricity still worked. On the table near the door I found Mrs Gold's rather poorly spelled note. But she had done everything one could expect, even to leaving me a cold supper of ham and salad, apple pie and cheese. She would be in tomorrow at eleven. I need have no fears.

I looked round. I am not fearful by nature. I always do my best, and am seldom in a position to dread very much. A childhood visit to the dentist, perhaps, for an especially painful filling – something of that apprehension seized me. But it was the nasty dark light in the hall. My Uncle died in this house not three months ago. Before him, he had lost his family, his wife and sister, and two sons. Before them another generation had perished. As Shakespeare points out, it is common for people to die.

Going through into the sitting room, I have put a match to the fire. This has improved things. On a sideboard stands a tray with brandy, whisky and soda. Though it is early for me, I shall pour myself a small measure. I gather the boiler is at work, and I can count on a hot bath. I do not want a chill.

10th September: 2 pm

The house is a mausoleum. Lucy be blowed, I think I shall sell it. Last night was dreadful. Creaks and groans of woodwork, an eldritch wind at the windows and down the chimneys. I read until nearly two am. Then at three I was woken by a persistent owl hooting in the garden trees. I am not a country person. I longed for my warm city flat and the vague roar of traffic.

However, this morning early I went over the place thoroughly, from attic to cellar. There are a great many rooms, more than I should ever want, and the heating would be prohibitive. It is very old fashioned, those thick, bottle-green and oxblood curtains favoured by our grandfathers – evidently by mine, and my Uncle William, too – enormous cliffs of furniture, and endless curios, some of them I expect very valuable, from the East – Egypt, India and China. I am not particularly partial to any of this sort of thing. I find the house uncomfortable, both physically – it is cold and damp – and aesthetically.

At about eleven thirty, the not very punctual Mrs Gold arrived. I was not surprised. Women are generally unreliable. I have learnt this from Lucy. Nevertheless, I commended Mrs Gold on keeping the house clean, which she has more or less done, and on the supper left for me yesterday. She is a large woman, constructed like a figurehead, with severe grey hair. She began , of course, at once to tell me all about my Uncle, and what she knows of my Grandfather before him. She is, naturally, as her class nearly always are, fascinated by details of all the deaths. It was with some difficulty that I got her to resume her work. Going into the library, I then took down some boxes of photographs, and began to go through them, more to pass the time than anything else. The agent is coming tomorrow, to discuss things, or I would have tried to get home today.

The photographs, most of which have dates and names written on the back, are generally displeasing, many the dull, antique kind where everyone stands like a waxwork, as the primitive camera performs its task. My grandfather was a formidable old boy, with bushy whiskers, in several scenes out in some foreign landscape, clutching his gun, or his spade, for he had been involved in one or two famous excavations, in the East. Here he had taken his own photographs, some of which had appeared in prominent journals of the day.

These, obviously, were not among the general portraits, nor was I especially interested to look them out. My father had been wont to tell me, at length, how Grandfather Martyce had taken the very first photograph inside some remarkable ancient tomb. I had found this, I am afraid, extremely boring, then, and scarcely less so now. I have, too, forgotten the location. Lucy has often commented that I am not a romantic. I am glad to say I am not.

Eventually Mrs Gold finished her ministrations, and I went down to learn her wages, which were modest enough. She had put into the oven for me, besides, a substantial hot-pot.

'Your Uncle was very fond of those, I must say,' she announced. 'He relied on me, once the old cook had retired. Mrs Martyce was often ill, you understand, Miss Martyce too. I had a free hand.'

I said something gallant about her cooking. She ignored this.

'It was a great worry,' she said, 'to see them waste away. First the boys, and then the sister and the wife. Your Uncle was the last to go. He was very strong, fought it off, so to speak. The doctors couldn't find anything wrong with him. But it was the same as with the ladies, and the children.'

I privately thought that no doubt a reliance on elderly country doctors was to blame here, but I nodded lugubriously, was apparently anticipated.

'Your Grandfather now,' persisted this tragic choric Mrs Gold, glowering on me in the stone kitchen, the pans partly gleaming at her back from her somewhat hard work upon them, 'he was the same, but they put it down to some foreign affliction, bad water, those dirty heathen foods. You understand, Mr Martyce – your Uncle, Mr William Martyce, was only in the house a year before he first fell ill. And before that, never a day's indisposion.' I noted that, not only did she employ words she could not, probably, spell; but that she was also able to invent them.

'It seems an unfortunate house, I said. She appeared to wish me to.

'That's as may be. The cook was never out of sorts, nor any of the maids, while they had them. And I've never had a day in bed; excepting my parturiton.' I assumed she meant childbirth; and kept a stern face. Mrs Gold was certainly most serious. She said; 'If I was you, sir, I'd put this house up for sale.'

'That might be an idea,' I said.

'Not that I want to cause you misgivings.'

'Not at all. But it will be too big for me, I'm sure.'

When she had gone, I ate the beef sandwiches she had left me, and was grateful her meals were more cheerful than her talk; although I have jotted down here her two interesting words; to make Lucy laugh.

10th September: 6 pm

I do not like this house. No, I am not being superstitious. I believe there is not a fanciful bone in my body. But it depresses me utterly. The furnishings; the darkness, the chilliness; which lighting all the fires I reasonably can – in the sitting room, dining room, my bedroom, the library – cannot dispel. And the things which so many would find intriguing – old letters in bundles, in horrible brown, ornate, indecipherable writing – caskets of incenses and peculiar amulets – such items fill me with aversion. I want my orderly room with its small fire that warms every inch, my sensible plain chairs, the newspaper, and a good, down-to-earth detective novel.

I have already taken to drink – a whisky at lunch, and now another before dinner – and even this went awry. I am not a man who spills things. I have a sound eye and a steady hand. However, sitting over the fire in the library, crouching, should I say, with pure ice at my back, I was looking again at some of the more recent photographs. These comprised a picture of my Uncle and his sons on the lawn before the house, and some oddments of him, pruning a small tree, standing with a group I took to be the local vicar and various worthies of the nearby village. In these scenes, my Uncle is about forty, and again about fifty. He looks hale enough, but I had already gathered from the delightful Gold that he was, even then, frequently laid low.

Finally I put the pictures down on the side table, and rested my whisky, half full, beside them. I then stood up to reach for my tobacco. I have often seen Lucy have little accidents like this. Women are inclined to be clumsy, I find, something to do with their physique, probably. In brief, I knocked the table, the whisky glass skidded over it, and upset its contents in four sploshes, one on each of the photographs.

I gave a curse, I regret to say, and set to mopping up with my handkerchief. The pictures seemed no worse for the libation; and so I went downstairs to refill my glass. Having looked in on the hot-pot; I decided to give it another half hour; and came back reluctantly upstairs, meaning to try to find some book I could read – my own volume was finished during the early hours this morning. There was not much doing in this line, but at last I found some essays on prominent men, and this would have to serve. Returning to the fire in haste, I there found that each of the photographs on which the alcohol had spilled was blotched with an erratic burn. I must say, I had had no notion malt whisky could inflict such a wound, but there, I am not a photographer.

This annoyed me. Although I have no interest in the photographs particularly, I know my Father would have had one, and for his sake, I would not have desecrated them. I am not a vandal. I feel foolishly ashamed of myself.

I began to think then about my father and my Uncle William, of how they had lost touch with each other, and how, oddly, we had never been on a visit to this house. One assumes there had come to be a rift between the two men. there was a marked difference in age. Even so, I recall my Father speaking of my Uncle as the former neared his end. 'Poor William,' he said. 'What could I do?' I had not wanted to press him, his heart was giving out.

Irritated, uneasy and out of sorts, I have pushed the damaged photographs together, and come down again, to eat of Mrs Gold's bounty.

10th September: 10.30 pm

Something very odd. How to put this down … Well, I had better be as scientific as I can. I had forgotten my book, and, deciding on an early bed, since I am feeling rather fatigued – the country air, no doubt – I came up to the library to collect the volume. It lay on the table, and going to pick it up, I saw again the spoiled photographs.

While I had been downstairs dining, something had gone on. The stains had changed, rather they had taken on a colour, deep swirls of raw red and sickly yellow. This was particularly unpleasant on the black and white surface of the original scenes. I examined each photograph in turn, and all four were now disfigured in this way. I had already resolved that it was no use crying over spilt milk, or whisky, to be more precise, and was about to put them down again, when something else arrested my attention.

Of course, I am aware that random arrangements or marks can take on apparently coherent forms – the 'faces' that one occasionally makes out in the trunks of old trees, for example, or the famous Rorschach inkblot test. Yes, the random may form the seemingly concrete, and mean very little, save in the realms of imagination and psychiatry.

However. However – Where the whisky had burned the photographs, a shape had been formed, now very definite, and filled in by rich, bilious colour. Not in fact a shape that I could recognize – yet, yet it was consistent, for in each of the four pictures, it was almost exactly the same. And it was – it is – a horrible shape. Most decidedly that. I do not like it. There is something repulsive, odious, about it. I suppose that is because it is like some sort of *creature* – and yet a creature that can hardly, I would think, exist.

Then, I am being rather silly. I had better describe what I see. What is the matter with me?

There, I have had another whisky – I shall certainly have a thick head in the morning! – and I will write this down with a steady hand.

The thing that the whisky has burnt out in the photographs is, in each one, identical, allowing for certain differences of – what I shall have to call – posture, and size. It has the head of a sort of frog, but this is horned, with two flat horns – or possibly ears – that slant out from its head sideways. The body is bulbous at the front, and it has two arms or forelegs, which end in paws, resembling those of a large cat. The body ends not in legs, but in a tail like that of a slug. This is all bad enough, but in the visage or head are always two red dots, that give the impression of eyes.

It is a beastly thing. I fear I cannot convey how vile, nor what a turn it has given me.

The varying size of the – what shall I call it? – apparition? – is another matter. I can only conclude the whisky fell in a smaller drop here, a larger there. Although that is not what I recollect quite. It seemed to me my drink had spread in roughly equal splashes on each photograph. But there.

In these two, where my Uncle William prunes the tree, the thing is quite small. But here, where he is in conversation with the vicar and the worthies, it is larger. And here, where William is standing with his sons, the thing is at its largest.

It is so curiously placed in this view that it seems to recline at William's very feet, spacing its paws for balance. In relation to the man and boys, it is the equivalent of a medium-sized dog. I cannot escape the illusion that it has not grown bigger, but – got nearer. That way madness lies.

If there were a telephone here, I would put a call through to Saunders, or Eric Smith, even to Lucy. But there is no telephone. Perhaps, a good thing. What would I say?

I know I am behaving in an irrational and idiotic manner. I must pull myself together.

I have put the photographs back on the table and turned them face down. I shall go up and take a couple of aspirins. Obviously, in months to come, I will reread these entries and laugh at them.

11th September: 11 am

Johnson, the agent, arrived efficiently at ten, and we perfunctorily discussed my plans. I had no hesitation in telling him that I would probably wish to put the house up for sale. I passed a restless night, mostly lying listening to the grim silence of this place. I would have been glad for the creaking of the boards I had heard on my first night, even for the boisterous owl. But both failed me. Everything seemed locked in the cupboard of the darkness, and now and then, like a child, I sighed or moved about, to make some sound.

I got a little sleep for an hour or so after dawn, and came down bleary-eyed but resolved. I had put myself into a foolish state over those confounded burns on the photographs. Perhaps this is the price for allowing myself to become a middle-aged bachelor. No matter. I am going back to London this evening. Back to traffic and fog and lights, and human company if I wish it. I must take myself in hand. I do not want to become one of those querulous neurasthenic fools one reads of. Good God, I have gone through a World War and although luck put me out of the way of most of the action I was ready enough to do my part. Is some childish horror going to undo me now?

As he was leaving, Johnson recommended that I seek out the vicar. 'If you want to know anything about your Uncle's tenancy here, that is.'

'Oh, yes. A Reverend Dale, I believe.'

'That's right. He's getting on, but pretty spry. A wise old bird.'

I said that I might not have the time, but thanked Johnson all the same. What, after all, did I want to know?

My Grandfather's forays in the East did not interest me, and all the rest seemed decline, disease, and death. Charming points of conversation – besides, the bubbling Mrs Gold had already rejoiced me with enough of all that.

'Incidentally, Johnson,' I said, as I saw him to the door, 'I suppose there is some use of photography in your business.'

'There is,' he agreed.

'I wonder if you've ever heard of – alcohol making a burn on a photograph?'

'Well, I never have,' he said. He thought deeply.

'It might, perhaps. But not anything pure, I wouldn't have thought.'

'Whisky,' I said.

'From a still, maybe. Not the stuff in a bottle. Why do you ask?'

'Oh, something a friend told me of.'

Johnson shrugged and laughed. 'A waste of a good beverage,' he said.

When he was gone, I made a decision. It was because I had begun to feel angry.

Mrs Gold was not to come today until three, but she had left me another cold plate. This I tried to eat, but did not really fancy it, although I had had no breakfast.

Eventually I took the largest soup tureen I could find from the kitchen, and the whisky decanter, and went up to the library. The quickest way to be rid of my 'monster' was to carry out an experiment. It was quite simple. I would place a selection of photographs in the tureen and pour over them enough whisky to cover them entirely. Either nothing would happen to them, or they would burn – burn all over into yellow and red. And that would be that. No random marks, no possible coincidences of shape. No doubt the pictures that I spoiled underwent some flaw in their reproduction, or there was some weakness in the material on which they were printed. I was confident, to the point of belligerence, that by this means I should be free of the horror I had unwittingly unleashed. As for ruining more photographs, if I did so, there comes a point where one must put oneself first.

I set the tureen down on the big table in the library. Outside, the birds were singing. There was a view of the lawn, and the big oaks, golden and crimson in the dying of the leaves. It is a sunny day.

I took three photographs from the box more or less at random, a scene of my Uncle and his son by the little summer-house, the two boys playing some game under the trees when they were small. To this selection I added one of the former casualties, the photograph of my Uncle pruning the tree. One thing I had made sure of, the three new scenes were of different dates, and had therefore been processed on other paper.

Dropping the four into the bowl, I poured in a generous measure of the whisky. A waste, as Johnson had said.

I have come away to write this, leaving a proper space of time, and now I am going back to look. There will be nothing, I believe, or complete obliteration. I am already beginning to feel I have made an idiot of myself. Perhaps I will tear out these pages.

11ᵗʰ September: 6 pm

The walk down to the village, just under a mile and a half, took me longer than it should have. I arrived feeling quite done up, and went into the little pub, which had some quaint name I forget, and had a brandy and soda.

Across the green was the vicarage, a picturesque building of grey stone, and behind it the Norman church, probably of interest to those with an historical concern. When I got to the vicarage door, and knocked, a homely fat woman came and let me in, all smiles, to the vicar's den. It was a nice, masculine place, redolent of pipe smoke, with a big dog lying on the hearth, who wagged his tail at me politely.

The Reverend Dale greeted me, and called for tea, which the fat nymph presently brought with a plate of her own shortbread. This tasted very good, although I am afraid I could eat no more than a bite.

The vicar let me settle myself, and we talked about ordinary things, the autumn, elements of the country round about, and of London. At last, leaning forward, the old man peered at me through his glasses.

'Are you quite well, Mr Martyce?'

'Perfectly. Just a trifle tired. I haven't slept well at the house.'

He looked long at me and said, 'I'm afraid people often don't.'

I took a deep breath. 'In what way?' I asked.

'Your family, Mr Martyce, has been inclined to insomnia there. The domestics have never complained. Indeed, I never heard a servant from there that had anything but praise for the house and the family. Mrs Allen, the former cook, retired only when she was seventy-six and could no longer manage. She was loath to go.'

'But my family – there has been a deal of illness.'

'Yes, I'm afraid that is so. Your Grandfather – he was before my time, of course. And his wife. Your father was long from home, and his brother, Mr William, was sent out into the world at twenty … before there was any – problem at the house.The two brothers did not at first choose to come back. And yourfather, I think, not at all. He lived to a good age?'

'He was nearly eighty. There was quite a gap between him and William – my Grandfather's travels.'

'Eighty – yes, that's splendid. But poor William did not do so well. He was, as you know, only sixty-two when he succumbed. His wife was a mere fifty, and your Aunt in her forties. But, in later life, she had never been well.'

I tried a laugh. It sounded hollow. 'That house doesn't seem very healthy for the Martyces.'

Reverend Dale looked grave. 'It does not.'

'And what explanation do you have for that, sir?'

'I fear that, although I am a man of God, and might be expected to incline to esoteric conclusions, I have none.'

I said, flatly, 'Do you think there is a malevolent ghost?'

'I am not supposed to believe in ghosts,' said the Reverend Dale. 'However, I can't quite rid myself of a belief in – *influences*.'

A cold tremor passed up my back. I deduce I may have gone pale, for the vicar got up and went over to his cabinet, from which he produced some brandy. A glass of this he gave me – I really must put a stop to all this profligate drinking! I confess I downed it.

'You must understand,' he said, 'I'm speaking not as a man of the cloth, but simply – as a witness. I've seen very clearly that, in the Martyce family, those who spend much or all of their time at the house, sicken. Some are more susceptible, they fail more swiftly. Some are stronger, and hold at bay or temporarily throw off the malaise, at first. Your Grandfather lived into his nineties, yet from his sixties he had hardly a day without severe illness.

Perhaps, in a man of advancing years, that is not uncommon. And yet, before this time, he was one of the fittest men on record, apparently he put the local youth, who are hardy, to shame. Again, some who aren't strong, also linger in a pathetic, sickly state – your Aunt was one of these. She succumbed only in her adult years, but then her life was a burden for her. One wondered how she bore with it. Even she, at length –' he sighed. 'Her end was a release, I am inclined to think. A satisfactory cause of death meanwhile has never been established. In your Grandfather's case, necessarily it was put down to old age. As with his wife, since she died in her sixties. In the cases of others, death must be questionable. Or unreasonable. As with your Uncle's two sons. They were fourteen and nineteen years.'

'I assumed some childish malady –'

'Not at all. Clemens was their doctor, then. I will reveal, he confided in me somewhat. He was baffled. The same symptoms – inertia, low pulse, some vertigo, headache, an inclination not to eat. But no fever, no malignancy, no defect. You will perhaps know, William's health was poor enough to keep him out of the War. He was utterly refused.'

I said, briskly, 'Well, I'm leaving tonight.'

'I am glad to hear that you are.'

'But, I had intended to put the house up for sale –'

'I think you need have no qualms, Mr Martyce. Remember, no one who has lived there, who is not a member of your family, has ever been ill. If anything, the reverse.'

'A family curse,' I said. I meant to sound humorous and ironic. I did not succeed.

The Reverend Dale looked down upon his serviceable desk.

'I shall tell you something, Mr Martyce. You are, evidently, a sensible man. I can't guarantee my words, I'm afraid. The previous incumbent of the parish passed them on to me. But he was vicar in your Grandfather's time. It seems your Grandfather, always a regular church-goer when at home, asked for an interview. This was about three years after his final return from the East. He was getting on in years, and had recently had a debilitating bout of illness, but recovered, and no one was in any apprehension for him, at that time.' The vicar paused.

'Go on,' I said.

'Your Grandfather it seems posed a question. He had heard, he said, of a belief among primitive peoples, that when a camera is used to take a photograph, the soul is caught inside the machine.'

'I've heard of this,' I said. 'There is a lack of education among savages.'

'Quite. But it appears your Grandfather asked my predecessor – if he thought that such a thing were truly possible.'

I sat in silence. I felt cold, and wanted another brandy, but instead I sipped my tepid tea.

'What did he say, your predecessor?'

'Naturally, that he did not credit such an idea.'

'To which my Grandfather said what?'

'It seems he wondered if, rather than catch a human soul, a camera might sometimes snare … something else. Something not human or corporeal. Some sort of spirit.'

Before the eye of my mind, there passed the memory of how my grandfather had photographed so many exotic things. And of the pictures taken inside the ancient and remarkable tomb. I am not given to fancies. I do not think it *was* a fancy. Like a detective, I strove to solve this puzzle.

I stood up before I had meant to, I did not mean to be rude.

The old man also rose, and the dog. Both looked at me kindly, yes, I would swear, even the dumb animal had an expression of compassion.

'Excuse me,' I said, 'I have to hurry to be sure of my train.'

'You're not returning to the house?' said the Reverend Dale .

'No. It's all locked up. The cleaning lady has been and gone. I promised her she'd be kept on until any new tenants take over. They must make their own arrangements.'

'I think you have been very wise,' said the vicar.

He himself showed me to the door of the stone house.

'It's a lovely afternoon,' he said. 'You look rather exhausted. That cottage there, with the green door. Peter will drive you to the station. Just give him something towards the petrol.'

I shook his hand, and like some callow youth, felt near to tears.

In future I must take more exercise. It is not like me to be so flabby. Thank God, Peter was amenable.

I have written all this down in the train. It has not been easy, with the jolting, and once I leaned back and fell fast asleep. I am better for that. I want to make an end of it here, and so return into London and my life, clear of it.

No, I cannot say I know what has gone on. When I put the four photographs into the tureen and poured in the whisky, I thought myself, frankly, an imbecile.

I had left them for perhaps twenty minutes, possibly a fraction longer. I approached the table with no sense of apprehension. Rather, I felt stupid.

Looking in, I saw at once, but the brain needs sometimes an interim to catch up with the quirkiness of the eye. So I experienced a numbing, ghastly dread, but even so I took out the photographs one by one, and laid them on the *newspaper* I had left ready.

The original had not altered. That is, the photograph, already damaged, of my Uncle by the tree. It had not changed, nor the mark, the yellow and red mark, that had the shape of a horned creature with forelegs and the hind body of a giant slug. There it still was, quite near to him but yet not close. There it was with its blind red dots of eyes, brilliant on the black and white surface of that simple scene.

The other three images are quickly described, and I should like to be quick. The whisky had effected them all only in one place. And in that place, always a different one, exactly similarly. The demon was there. The same. Absolute.

Where the two boys are playing as children, it is some way off, among the trees. It is coiled there, as if resting, watching them, like a pet cat.

In the photograph of William and his wife and sister – my Aunt – the thing is much nearer, lying in the grass at their feet – again, again, like some awful pet.

But it is the last picture, the most recent picture of my Uncle William's younger son, it is *that* one – They are standing by the summer house. The boy is about thirteen, and the date on the back, that the whisky has blurred, gives evidence that this is so.

They do not look so very unhappy. Only formal, straight and stone still. That is probably the very worst thing. They should be in turmoil – and the boy – the boy should be writhing, flailing, screaming –

The demon is close as can be. It has hold of the boy's leg. *It is climbing up him.* It's tail is coiled about his knee – Oh God, its head is lying on his thigh. The head has tilted. It gazes up at him. It has wrapped him in its grip.

He does not – *he does not know.*

I shall write no more now. I do not want to open this diary again. The lights of London will be coming soon, out of the autumn dusk. Smells of smoke, cooking, and unhygienic humanity. Thank God. Thank God I have got away. Thank God. Thank God.

FROM A LETTER BY LUCY WRIGHT TO HER FRIEND JB

1st November 195–:

Your letter did cheer me up a bit, though I cried a bit after. Yes, I'd love to come for a visit, and it would help to get my mind off – this. Then, I feel guilty. But what can I do? I was totally in the dark. I didn't know. He never confided in me. I don't understand.

I'd always known Gordon was a bit of an old stick-in-the-mud. But he was kind and hardworking, and I did hope he'd get round to popping the question one day. No one else has made any offers. And of course, he was well-off. Not that that was my main reason. But, well, I've never been rich, and it would be nice, not to worry all the time, where the rent's coming from, or if you can afford a new pair of nylons.

The funny thing was, when he came back from that house of his uncle's in the country, (and strangely he wouldn't discuss that at all), he couldn't see enough of me. We were out every night, like a couple of twenty-year-olds. The pictures, concerts, even dinners in a lovely little restaurant up West. And he made a real fuss of me. He even bought me roses. I thought, this is it. He's going to ask me now. And I thought, I can change him, get him to brighten up a bit. But then – well it was a funny thing that happened. It was really silly and – nasty. Peculiar.

It was my birthday – that was the time he gave me the roses – and one of my cousins, Bunty, well she sent me a really lovely present. It was a little camera. What do you expect – I wanted to use it. And one night when Gordon and I were in that nice restaurant, I was showing him the camera, and the manager, who knows Gordon, came up and said, 'Let me take a picture of you, Mr Martyce, and your young lady.' Well I was a bit giggly – we'd had some lovely wine – and I was all for it, but Gordon got really funny. No, I mean he got he really angry, sort of well – frightened, red in the face – but the manager just laughed, and he took the photograph anyway, with me very nervous and Gordon all hard and angry and scared. The manager said Gordon would have to be less camera-shy, for the wedding.

I thought, Gordon's angry because he feels he's being forced to think about that, about getting married. And he doesn't want to. And that depressed me, because things had seemed to be going so well. So it ended up a miserable evening. And he took me home. And – well. That was the last time I saw him. I mean, the last time I *saw* him. Because I don't count the funeral. How can I? They had to close the coffin. Anyway. He was dead then. I'm sorry. Look, a tear's fallen in the ink. What a silly girl. Crying over a man that didn't even want me.

Of course, I did speak to him just once more, on the telephone. He rang me up about a week after the dinner, and he said he was going to collect the photographs, you see. And I was glad he'd rung me, so I said yes. I was a bit embarrassed, because the rest of the film was all of my family, dad and mum, and Alice and the babies, and it was the first time I'd taken any photographs, and I was sure they'd be bad.

But then I didn't hear again, and the next thing was, the policeman coming round in the afternoon, just as I was trying to get money in that rotten meter that's so stiff. My washing was everywhere – it was Saturday – but he didn't look. He helped me with the meter and then he put me in a chair, and he told me. Gordon had gone out on the Northern Line and – well, you know. He'd fallen under a train. Well they said, he'd thrown himself under. People had seen him do it. But how can I believe that? I mean, Gordon. It must be a mistake. But then, where was he going? He doesn't have any relatives, and no friends out that way. Didn't have. Well.

But I was so glad to get your kind letter. You see, I went round to Gordon's flat this afternoon, they let me, because there were a few things of mine there, a couple of books I tried to get Gordon to read – I don't think he did – and some gloves I'd left, little things – oh, and a casserole dish I'd bought him. It was a nice one. I thought I'd better have it, now.

And on the table in his room, there were the photographs. The police had obviously been there, because things were a bit disturbed, not the way Gordon would have left them. But the odd thing was, these photographs were lying on a newspaper, and they'd stuck to it, so they must have got wet. And – there was a strong smell of whisky, as if he'd spilled some. Maybe he had. He'd been drinking more lately, more than I'd known him do. I remember he said something strange – something about using a spirit to show a spirit. But he was always too clever for me.

Anyway, I did look at the photographs, and I wondered if I could take them home, but I wasn't sure, so I didn't, though I can't see that they'll be any help to the police or anyone. Actually, I hadn't done too badly for a beginner. The ones of the babies are really nice, though I'd made Alice look a bit fat, and she wouldn't like that. The last one was the one the manager at the restaurant took of Gordon and me, and it was really a pity. I admit, it made me cry a bit. Because, it would have been nice to have a picture of him and me together, something to remember him by. It wasn't just that we looked really daft – me all grinning and silly, and Gordon so puffed up and upset. No, there was this horrible big red and yellowish mark on the picture – I suppose something went wrong when it was taken, perhaps some light got in, of something, that can happen, can't it?

The funny thing is, I can't explain this, but there was something – something really awful about this mark. It sounds crazy and you'll think I'm a proper dope. You know what an imagination I've got. You see, it looked to me like a funny sort of animal – a sort of snake thing, with hands – and a face. And the oddest part of all, it was in just this place that it looked as if it was sitting square on Gordon's shoulders with its tail coming down his collar, and its arm-like-things round his throat, and its face pressed close his, as if it loved him and would never let go.

Zelle's Thursday

Thursday was rather difficult. In the morning the children attacked me again, which was a pity, they'd been quite reasonable since that incident in the spring.

The trouble began because of the myrmecophaga, which had climbed up into one of the giant walnut trees on the west lawn. In the wild state, this species doesn't climb, but genetic habilitation sometimes causes sub-aspects, often feline, to establish themselves. Having climbed up into, or on to, or out of, various objects, the myrmecophaga then tends to jump. This, in a heavily-furred, long-clawed animal weighing over two hundred and ten pounds, cannot always be – ignored.

I ran down across the lawn to the tree.

Angelo was still standing under it when I arrived.

'Angelo,' I said, 'please stand away.'

'Why,' asked Angelo, 'are you calling me "Angelo"? It's Mr Vald-Conway to you.'

'Of course, if you prefer. Please do stand away, Mr Vald-Conway.'

Angelo, who is currently twelve years and three months old, will one day be handsome, but the day has not yet come. He gazed up into the tree and casually said, 'Oh, look, Higgins is up there.'

'Yes, Mr Vald-Conway. That's why I'm suggesting you should stand away.'

At that moment Higgins, (the myrmecophaga), lurched forward on his powerful furry wrists, two branches broke, and showered us with green walnuts. I was poised to pull Angelo from danger, but presently the spasms of movement ceased. Angelo said, admiringly, 'What a mess you're making, Higgins.'

(Angelo is at the age of taking pleasure in the damaging of his father's property. In the case of property of his mother's, he is more ambivalent.) Angelo stared up at the hugely draped coal-black shape of Higgins.

'Isn't he a beauty.'

'Yes,' I agreed, 'Mr Vald-Conway. Higgins is a fine example of a myrmecophaga.'

'You can stop calling *me Mr Vald-Conway*. That's what you call my father. And why do you call Higgins *that*? He's an ant-eater.'

'I shall try to remember.'

'Are you smarting me?' Angelo asked suspiciously. He is extremely sensitive. 'You just watch that.'

'I meant, Angelo – (?) – that I'll try to remember you'd rather I referred to your pet by the common term.'

'Well … Just watch it anyhow.'

Ursula, Mister and Madam's daughter, had meanwhile appeared on the lawn. She is two years and five months older than Angelo, a tall slender girl, like her brother having the black hair and black eyes of Madam Conway. She had been on the games court and had a racket in her hand.

'There's Higgins in the tree,' said Ursula, 'and there's Jelly underneath.'

'Don't call me Jelly,' snarled Angelo.

'And the Thing,' added Ursula. She sank down under the combined shade of the walnut tree and Higgins, 'Thing, go up and get me some iced lemonade. I'm dry as an old desert.'

Precisely then, Higgins jumped. It was an especially spectacular launch, and may have been occasioned by a flea, as he was due for a vacuuming.

I saw at once that the climax: of his trajectory would be Ursula. She too seemed to have deduced this, for she started a frantic roll to avoid him. I dashed forward, swept her up and deposited her on the grass three metres away. Higgins landed, and for a moment looked stunned and partly squashed.

Then he glanced about at us in slight surprise, shook himself, back into shape, and began to groom twigs and walnuts from his fur.

Angelo ran forward and clasped Higgins, who began idly to groom him also, then lost interest having refound his own tail, always a time of inspiration.

'You tried to upset him –'Angelo cried at me, nearly tearful. 'You wanted him to fall hard and get hurt.'

'If you think that falling on your sister would have made for a softer landing, I doubt it.'

Ursula screamed: 'What do you mean, I'm bony or something? You rotten *Thing*.' She slapped me in the face. Though I saw the blow coming, it obviously couldn't harm me, and I judged, perhaps wrongly, she would be relieved by delivering it.

'I meant,' I said, 'that the animal might have crushed your ribs. Only something bone-*less* could act as a break-fall for sucha large –'

'And *you* nearly dislocated my pelvis, dragging me like that. You pig! I could have got out of the way –'

'Not quickly en –'

'You just wanted to bruise me. *Look*! You're horrible. You're OBSCENE –'

And Ursula flew at me and began striking me with her racket, which all this while she had held on to.

Angelo with a wail tore over and joined in enthusiastically.

As they punched and whacked and kicked, Higgins curled up in a ball, wrapped his groomed plume of a tail around himself, and contentedly fell asleep.

I was vacuuming Higgins that afternoon when Mr de Vald came to me in deep distress.

'My God, Zelle. I don't know what to say.'

'I'm still under guarantee, Mr de Vald. There won't be any charge. Most of the damage was external and took only half an hour to put right. The internal damage is being repaired even now, as I work.'

'Yes, Zelle. But it's not that. It's the horror of it, Zelle.'

'Which horror, Mr de Vald?'

'That they could do – that such a thing – children of *mine.*'

'It's not entirely uncommon, Mr de Vald, in the first year or so.'

I had by now switched off the vacuum, and Higgins was recovering from the swoon of ecstasy into which he falls when once the vacuum catches up with him, since at first he always runs away from it. While I had watched them going round and round the pavilion on the east lawn, I removed the last of the debrasion mask from my cheek. Actually, the cosmetic renewal of my face, arms and shoulders had taken longer than I'd said, for I'd tried to relieve Mr de Vald's mind.

'You see, Zelle,' said Patrice de Vald, sitting down beside me on the steps of the pavilion, 'it's the trend to violence I abhor.'

'Please don't worry, Mr de Vald, that anything they do to me they might ever be inclined to do to a fellow human. It's quite a different syndrome.'

'Syndrome. Christ, my kids are part of a syndrome.'

He put his blond head in his lean hands.

(Higgins, annoyed at the vacuum-cleaner's sudden lack of attention, stuffed his long tube of black velvet face into the machine's similar slender black tube. It has occurred to me before that he thinks certain household appliances to be (failed, bald), myrmecophagae.)

'You see, Zelle. I want you to be happy here.'

It's useless to explain that this terminology, or outlook, can't apply to me.

'Mr de Vald, I'm perfectly happy. And in time, Angelo and Ursula will come to accept me, I'm sure.'

'Well, Zelle, I just want you to know, the house never functioned so elegantly. And my partner, Inita – she's sometimes reticent about these things … But she thinks that, too. It's so much better to have you in charge than a – just some faceless –' he broke off. He blushed. Trying to be tactful, he always came around to this point, exaggerating what he meant to avoid.

Higgins withdrew his face from the face of the vacuum cleaner.

'Here, boy,' said Mr de Vald jollily.

Higgins gave him a look from his onyx eyes, and shambled off across the lawn towards the lake. In the wild, myrmecophagae have limited sight and hearing, but the habilitation reorganises such functions. Higgins has twenty-twenty vision and can detect one synthetic ant falling into his platter at a distance of two hundred metres.

'Guess he didn't hear me,' said Mr de Vald. He looked at me, his own eyes anxious and wide. 'All I can do about the brats is to apologise. They've been punished. I've vetoed those light concerts in town they're both so keen to visit.'

It wasn't up to me to advise him, unless he asked for advice.

But now he added meekly, 'Do you think?'

'Mr de Vald, as the property of yourself and your wife, of course you could say that any damage to me must be punishable. On the other hand, half the problem arises because your children can't quite accept, as yet, that I'm no different than – say – that vacuum cleaner.'

'Oh, Zelle.'

'Technically,' I said, 'there's nothing to choose, except that I am entirely self-programming, autonomous, and, therefore, ultra efficient. That I look as I do is supposed to make me more compatible.'

'Oh and Zelle, it does. Why, our house parties – And the number of people who've said to me, who's that pretty new maid, how on earth can you afford a human servant, and so cute – just as though you were – I mean that they thought you were – weren't –' he broke off, red now to the ears. 'You think I shouldn't punish Ursula and Angelo. Just explain it over to them. That you're – not –'

'That I'm just a machine, Mr de Vald. That I'm not a threat. That if they would try to think of me more on the lines of an aesthetic, multi-purpose appliance, this fear they have of me would eventually fade.

'I guess you're right, Zelle,'

My smiling circuit activated.

He dreamily patted my no-longer-broken shoulder and went slowly away across the lawn after Higgins, who never quite allowed him to catch up.

By the drinks hour, every hit of me was repaired, outside and in. I was on the terrace, supervising the trolleys and mixers, and the ice-maker. Mr de Vald had driven over to the airport, and there was some tension, as Madam Conway, who had been away on her working schedule, was returning unexpectedly.

The children had reappeared on the east lawn, cooler at this time of day, and were sitting near the pavilion looking very subdued. Sometimes I detected – my hearing is as fine as Higgins' – Ursula's voice: 'Mother said she'd bring me the new body cosmetic. She *did*. But will she remember? I wonder how many paintings she sold? If she got het up, she'll have forgotten the body cosmetic. I don't want to look like an old immature frump all the time.' Angelo, who was being restrained, only spoke occasionally, in monosyllables, as for example 'Red light. Looking forward. *Knows* I was.' Higgins had fallen in the lake during the afternoon, and was being automatically dried in the boating-shed.

Presently the car appeared in the ravine, rounded the elms, and curved noiselessly up on to the auto-drive. Here it began to deposit Madam Conway's thirty-five pieces of luggage in the service lift.

Inita Conway came walking gracefully over the lawn with Mr de Vald, raising one hand languidly at her children. Ursula evinced excitement and rushed towards her mother. Angelo rose in a sort of accommodating slouch designed to disguise concentrated emotion.

Inita Conway wore golden sandals, and her black hair in the fashionable spike known as the *unicorn*. Ursula exclaimed over and examined this with careful admiration, 'lo, mumma. Did you sell a lot of paintings? Why are you home so soon? I'm glad you're home so soon. Did you bring my body cosmetic?'

'Yes, Ursula, I brought your body cosmetic. Your tidy's carried it up to your room.'

'Can-I-go-and –'

'Yes, Ursula,'

Ursula bolted.

Angelo approached his mother and said, 'Hi, Dad's vetoed the concerts.'

'So I have heard. And I heard why.'

Angelo lounged by the drinks table, which the organizer was now setting out. He kept putting his hands down where the organizer was trying to lay tumblers, so that it had to select somewhere else,

'You're home early, motherrr,' slurred Angelo, 'Whysat?'

'To catch your father out,' said Madam Conway, She looked at me and said, 'Zelle, I want you to come up to my suite after drinks, I have three original Sarba shirts and some things for Ursula, They need to be sorted before dinner.'

Then turning to Patrice de Vald she snatched him into a passionate embrace that embarrassed Angelo and apparently embarrassed also Mr de Vald. 'Darling. Have you *missed* me?'

'I always –'

'Yes, but in the past, you were *lonely*.'

Mr de Vald looked terribly nervous. There was no reason that I knew why he should be, but sometimes the communications between these two partners are so complex, and have so many permutations, that I can't follow them.

Their relationship seems to be a little like chess, but without the rules.

There was a dim uproar from the boating-shed.

Madam Conway disengaged herself from Mr de Vald's uneasy arms. 'I suppose that's that bloody ant-eater up to something.'

She downed her drink, a triple gin-reine, and took a triple gin-colada. She beckoned me towards the house. As we went along the terrace, she called back, 'Oh, Patrice, someone's coming to dinner. A young designer I met.'

Haying killed the automatic drier, Higgins burst from the shed and pounced along the lawn, his fringed coat now fluffed and shaking like a well-made soufflé.

'Bloody animal,' said Madam Conway. 'I'd have the damn thing put down if it weren't for the Animal Rights regulations.'

'Angelo would be distressed,' I said. 'He's very fond of his pet.'

'Yes, we're very fond of our pets, Zelle, By the way, I didn't think you offered advice unless asked.'

'I was not, Madam Conway, offering advice.'

'You mean it was just a casual human comment?'

'An observation, Madam Conway.'

'What else have you observed, Zelle?'

'In what area, Madam Conway?'

'Well, I realize you have to study us all minutely. In order to fulfil our wildest dreams correctly.'

The house door opened and we stepped on the moving stair. (As we rose past the windows, I noticed Higgins was in the lake again.)

'For example,' said Madam Conway, as we entered the elevator for her suite, 'what have you found out about Patrice's wildest dreams? Anything I ought to know?'

'I'm sorry, Madam Conway. I don't understand.'

'I'll bet.'

We entered the suite. It is white at the moment, with touches of purple, blue and gold. Inita Conway, with her slender coffee body and two metres of inky hair, dominated every room, even the bathroom, which was done in dragons.

'You see, Zelle, dear,' said Inita Conway, 'I happen to know what goes on in a house once your sort of humanoid robot is installed.'

Her luggage had arrived, and I saw that the suite tidy had already begun to unpack and service the Sarba shirts. I had not therefore really been summoned for this task.

Instead it seemed I was being attacked again. And that this was rather more serious than the assault instigated by the children.

'Well,' said Madam Conway, 'Go on, deny it,'

'What do you wish me to deny, Madam Conway?'

'That you're taking my partner to bed.'

'Exactly, Madam Conway, I deny it.'

She smiled. Throwing off her clothes she marched into the shower. A dragon hissed foam upon her. She stood in the foam, a beautiful icon of flesh, and snapped, 'Don't tell me you can't lie. I know you things can lie perfectly damn well. And *don't* tell me you're frigid. I know everyone of you comes with sex built *in* –'

'Yes, Madam Conway, it's true that my model functions to orgasm. But this is only –'

'I can just *imagine*,' she screamed, turning on another dragon, 'what erotic pleasures have been rocking the house to its core. If the bloody automatic hadn't picked up my return flight number, I'd have got here when you weren't expecting me. Caught the two of you writhing with arched backs among the blasted Sarba sheets I bought that *bastard* last trip –' A third dragon rendered her unintelligible if not inaudible. She switched off all three suddenly, and coming out before the drier could take the jewels of water from her skin, she confronted me with one hand raised like a panther's paw. 'You – you *trollop*. I know. Couldn't help it. He made you. Oh, I've heard *all* about it. Men get crazy to try you. The perfect woman, Hah!'

'I have to warn you,' I said, 'Madam Conway, that I've already had to facilitate quite extensive repairs to myself today, and although the guarantee *may* cover further wilful damage, during the same twenty-four hour unit, I'm not certain of that. If you wish, I can tap into the main bank and find out.'

'Oh go to hell you moronic plastic whore.'

'Do you mean you'd prefer me to leave your suite?'

'Yes. My God. You and that ant-eater. I'd put the pair of you –'

Although she told me, I did not grasp the syntax.

The dinner guest, Madam's designer, arrived late, in the middle of the argument over Ursula's body cosmetic. Mr de Vald insisted that his daughter had used too much of the cosmetic and looked like a fifty-year old. (In fact, Ursula looked about nineteen.) Madam Conway laughed bitterly and said that a woman needed every help she could get with all the competition around. Angelo was sulking because his mother hadn't brought him anything back from her trip; he had earlier requested her not to, on the grounds that being given presents was for girls and babies.

The fourth argument over the cosmetic was in fact a second instalment of the second argument that had taken place since the start of the meal. The first and third arguments, though having differing pivots, actually concerned Inita Conway's guest, who had seemed to fail to call.

I was stirring the dessert, (a flambeau, which Mr de Vald likes me to see to by hand), when the guest after all was shown out on to the terrace. An utter silence resulted.

Angelo glared, and Ursula gaped. Mr de Vald spilled his wine and when the tidy came forward pushed it roughly away. Madam Conway did not look up. She merely smiled into her uneaten salad.

'Oh, Jack. I thought you'd never get here. Just in time to rescue us all from the familial slog.'

Jack Tchekov was a most beautiful young man, who is sometimes featured in moving-picture zines. He has been described as having a dancer's body, a wrestler's shoulders, a pianist's hands, the legs of a marathon runner, the face of a young god and the hair of a Renascence prince. None of these descriptions seemed, to the off-hand observer, to be inaccurate.

As the guest seated himself, (by Madam Conway, glittering his eyes like those of a cabbalistic demon, (or it may have been that the analogy of a falling angel was more to the point)), some stilted conversation began, introductions and so on. I continued to whip the flambeau and, at the crucial moment, pour it into the smoking spice-pan.

'My God, that smells wonderful, I was in time for the climax of the feast,' said Jack Tchekov in the voice of a Shakespearian actor.

'Yes, timing is important, with that dish. But Zelle's timing, so I gather, is always flawless,' said Madam Conway.

When the flambeau was fumed, the service took over. Mr Tchekov was looking only at me.

'And this *is* the formidable Zelle.'

'That is she,' said Madam Conway.

'May I –' said Mr Tchekov, and hesitated dramatically. 'Might I go over and touch her?'

'For Chistssakes,' growled Patrice de Vald. 'What do you think you're doing?'

But Mr Tchekov had already come up to me with his walk like a tiger, and taken my hand with the firm gentleness always mooted as being that of the probable connoisseur. 'No,' he said, looking into my eyes with the power of ray-guns, 'I don't believe it. You're just a girl, aren't you?'

'I'm a robotic humanoid, Mr Tchekov, issue number z.e.l. one zero nine nine six.'

'Take your hands off,' shouted Mr de Vald, coming up behind Mr Tchekov angrily. 'You may have been all over Inita, but you'll show some respect to my – to Zelle.'

'Over Inita?' cried Mr Tchekov. 'Save me from the universal jealousy of the inadequate partner.'

'Come on then,' said Patrice de Vald.

'Come on?'

'You want to make something of it?'

'Don't be a Martian,' said Mr Tchekov.

'I said, make something!'

'Dad –' honked Angelo.

'Oh! Oh!' screamed Ursula, hoping Jack Tchekov would turn to see why, but he didn't.

'Oh go on, fight over her,' said Inita. 'I brought Jack,' she added, 'so that he could try Zelle out. You know, darling, the one thing she can do that you, of course, haven't *any* interest in.'

Patrice de Vald looked at me in an agony.

'Zelle – I'll throw him straight out.'

'Shit,' said Ursula.

'Don't use that *word*,' said Inita. 'My God, haven't I, for the past fifteen fucking years trained myself never to use words like that in front of her and then she goes and does it when we have people in.'

Jack Tchekov leaned close to me.

'Let's walk by the lake, Zelle. Away from all this domestic unbliss.'

Patrice de Vald took hold of Jack Tchekov's shoulder and Jack Tchekov gave a little shrug and Mr de Vald fell among the flambeau dishes.

Inita screamed now.

'Take her away! Both of you! Get on with it – get out of my sight.'

'She's given you her most gracious permission,' said Jack Tchekov. 'Will you, now?'

I could see that Mr de Vald was only winded, although several of the plates, which are antiques, had smashed. I am not, of course, a defence model, and so can do very little in this sort of situation. I am not able, for example, to separate human combatants. There was no need to carry Mr de Vald to the house or administer first aid.

Angelo was frightened and Ursula was crying openly.

I could only allow the insistent guest to steer me away along the lawn.

In the starlight by the lake, the fireflies, which like the diurnal bees and butterflies, are permitted to get inside the insect sensors, hovered about the bushes. Jack Tchekov drew me into his arms and kissed me tenderly, amorously.

'No, you *are* a girl. Some bionics maybe. But this flesh, this skin – your hair and eyes – and this wonderful smell what perfume is it you're wearing, Zelle?' (In fact it was not any perfume of mine, but Higgins. Having rolled in some honeysuckle he was now prowling the lakeside.) 'And you can't tell me you don't feel something when I touch you, like this …?'

Of course, I felt nothing at all, but my affection-display mechanism activated on cue. It had had no chance to do so in any of its modes, until now. I can report that it's most efficient. My arms coiled about Mr Tchekov.

We sank beneath a giant pine. Soon after, my orgasm mechanism was activated. My body responded, although naturally, it felt nothing, (The stimuli operate on evidence gleaned from the partner, therefore at the ideal instant.) Mr Tchekov was also as apparently ignorant about this as about the affection response, and might have been greatly satisfied. Unfortunately Higgins chose that moment to surface from the lake, into which he had again insinuated himself. He is evidently due to become a strong swimmer. His slender nose, a tube of jet on softer darkness, lifted some eleven metres from shore. He blew a crystalline water-spout that seemed to incorporate the stars.

'Go-od-wh-at *is it?*' ejaculated Mr Tchekov.

As my response subsided, the heart mechanic slowed and I was able to breathe more normally, I replied with the reassurance, 'Only the myrmecoph – the ant-eater.'

'*Dangerous?*' Jack Tchekov did not seem to relish this combat as he had the fracas at the table of his host. 'Awfully damn large.'

'They're insectivorous,' I said.

Intent on some quest known only to himself, Higgins swam powerfully and liquidly away, and left us.

'Inita says she plans to shoot that thing and say it committed suicide.' Mr Tchekov laughed, somewhat raggedly, tidying his clothes. My laugh mechanism was activated. I was more spontaneous than he. 'Frankly, to the point,' said Mr Tchekov, standing up with a slight scowl that could have been a Byronic brooding post-coital depression, or only cramp, 'I can tell Inita your seal was completely intact. I was the first.

Can't imagine why it should matter to her, that spineless dope of a partner she's got. But there you are. I better not mention to Pat what a little nymphomaniac he has under his roof, had I? Eh, little virgin?'

All devices come properly sealed to new owners. Mr Tchekov is evidently unaware too that such seals can be indefinitely renewed.

Also Inita Conway.

'I wronged you, Zelle.'

'Not at all, Madam.'

'And I wronged *Patrice.*'

All over the house the lights are on, and it is now four hours into Friday morning. Ursula is playing music and crying because she has fallen in love with Jack Tchekov who never even looked at her, and is unlikely to return. Angelo is crying because he has seen his father knocked down and his mother hasn't brought .him a present. Mr de Vald and Madam Conway are crying and shouting at each other, but there is nothing unusual in that, nor in the words they employ, which refer to painting, separation, emotional vampirism and sex.

A note addressed to me and delivered by the service informs me in contrite tones that Mr de Vald is aware of my rape, and the dreadful distress I must be suffering. He begs me to be honest with him, in the morning – presumably *later* in the morning – and not to blame Inita Conway, although she has behaved 'unforgivably'. I must marshal sympathetic explanations for Mr de Vald, to help him see that I am not harmed, and also to prevent his making the mistake of which so far he has been innocent. But probably, as with my last employer, he will not be able to resist.

Then, seal or no seal, he will confess all to his partner. Just as my last employer did. Repairing the entire cranial region after the blast of a sports rifle at close range is a job only the central bank can attempt. A fine is levied from the offending owner. Madam's paintings are not selling as well as they did, and I think both she and Mr de Vald would find payment for hasty actions inconvenient.

But, too, Madam may relent in her pursuit of vengeance. Earlier, she pursued Higgins to his ant-hill-shaped platter and poured out for him too many synthetic ants, stroking his wet fur and sobbing that he was the only clean decent thing in the house. Higgins ate all the food, and was consequently extensively ill on an antique carpet.

Altogether, Thursday was not a good day, and Friday doesn't seem set to be much better.

About The Author

Tanith Lee was born in North London (UK) in 1947. Because her parents were professional dancers (ballroom, Latin American) and had to live where the work was, she attended a number of truly terrible schools, and didn't learn to read – she was also dyslexic – until almost age 8. And then only because her father taught her. This opened the world of books to Lee, and by 9 she was writing. After much better education at a grammar school, Lee went on to work in a library. This was followed by various other jobs – shop assistant, waitress, clerk – plus a year at art college when she was 25-26. In 1974 this mosaic ended when DAW Books of America, under the leadership of Donald A Wollheim, bought and published Lee's *The Birthgrave*, and thereafter 26 of her novels and collections.

Lee went on to write around 90 books, and approaching 300 short stories. Four of her radio plays have been broadcast by the BBC; she also wrote two episodes ('Sarcophagus' and 'Sand') for the TV series *Blake's 7*. Some of her stories regularly get read on Radio 7.

Lee wrote in many styles in and across many genres, including Horror, SF and Fantasy, Historical, Detective, Contemporary-Psychological, Children and Young Adult. Her preoccupation, though, was always people.

In 1992 she married the writer-artist-photographer John Kaiine, her companion since 1987. They lived on the Sussex Weald, near the sea, in a house full of books and plants, with two black and white overlords called cats.

Tanith Lee passed away on 24 May 2015.

Copyright Information

All the Birds of Hell, First published in the USA, *The Magazine of Fantasy and Science Fiction*, Ed Gordon van Gelder, 1998

Black and White Sky, First published in the UK, *Brighton Shock!*, Ed Stephen Jones, 2010

Cain, First published in the USA, *Dying For It: More Erotic Tales of Unearthly Love*, Ed Gardner Dozois, 1997

The Devil's Rose, First published in the USA, *Women of Darkness*, Ed Kathryn Ptacek, 1988

The Eye in the Heart, First published in the USA, *The Magazine of Fantasy and Science Fiction*, Ed Gordon van Gelder, 2000

Flowers for Faces, Thorns for Feet, First published in the USA, *Twists of the Tale: Cat Horror Stories*, Ed. Ellen Datlow, 1996

God and the Pig, First published in the USA, *Tempting the Gods: The Selected Stories of Tanith Lee Volume 1*, 2009

The Hill, First published in the UK, *The Mammoth Book of Monsters*, Ed Stephen Jones, 2007

In the City of Dead Night, First published in the USA, *The Magazine of Fantasy and Science Fiction*, Ed Gordon van Gelder, 2002

Jedella Ghost, First published in the UK, *Interzone #135*, Ed David Pringle, 1998

Kiss Kiss, First published in the USA, *Silver Birch, Blood Moon*, Ed Terri Windling & Ellen Datlow, 1999

Lost in the World, First published in the USA, *The Book of the Dead*, 1991

A Madonna of the Machine, First published in the UK, *Other Edens II*, Ed Robert Holdstock & Christopher Evans, 1988

The Nightmare's Tale, First published in the USA, *Women of Darkness II: The Book of the Dead*, Ed Kathryn Ptacek, 1990

Oh, Shining Star, First published in the USA, *Tamastara: Or the Indian Nights*, 1984

The Pandora Heart, First published in the USA, *Don't Open This Book!*, Ed Marvin Kaye, 1998

Queens in Crimson, First published in the USA, *Hunting the Shadows: The Selected Stories of Tanith Lee Volume Two*, 2009

Rherlotte, First published in the UK, *Fatal Women* (As Esther Garber), 2004.

Snowdrop, First published in the USA, *Snow White, Blood Red*, Ed Ellen Datlow & Terri Windling, 1993

These Beasts, First published in the USA, *The Magazine of Fantasy and Science Fiction*, Ed Kristine Kathryn Rucsh, 1995

Under Fog (The Wreckers), First published in the USA, *The Mammoth Book of Best New Horror Vol 20*, Ed Stephen Jones, 2009

Virgile, The Widow, First published in the UK, *Fatal Women* (As Esther Garber), 2004

White As Sin, Now, First published in the UK, *Forests of the Night*, 1989

Xoanon, First published in the USA, *H P Lovecraft's Magazine of Horror #1*, Ed Marvin Kaye, 2004

Yellow and Red, First published in the UK, *The Wierd: A Compendium of Strange Stories*, Ed Jeff Vandermeer & Ann Vandermeer, 2011

Zelle's Thursday, first published in the USA, *Isaac Asimov's Science Fiction Magazine*, Ed Gardner Dozois, 1989

Other Telos Titles by Tanith Lee

<u>SAM STONE</u>

KAT LIGHTFOOT MYSTERIES
Steampunk Adventure Series
1: ZOMBIES AT TIFFANY'S
2: KAT ON A HOT TIN AIRSHIP
3: WHAT'S DEAD PUSSYKAT
4: KAT OF GREEN TENTACLES
5: KAT AND THE PENDULUM
6: TEN LITTLE DEMONS
THE COMPLETE KAT LIGHTFOOT MYSTERIES (Hardback special edition)

THE JINX CHRONICLES
Dark Science Fiction and Fantasy, dystopian future
1: JINX TOWN
2: JINX MAGIC
3: JINX BOUND

THE VAMPIRE GENE SERIES
Vampire, Historical and Time Travel Series
1: KILLING KISS
2: FUTILE FLAME
3: DEMON DANCE
4: HATEFUL HEART
5: SILENT SAND
6: JADED JEWEL

ZOMBIES IN NEW YORK AND OTHER BLOODY JOTTINGS
Horror Story Collection

THE DARKNESS WITHIN: FINAL CUT
Science Fiction Horror Novel

CTHULHU AND OTHER MONSTERS
Lovecraftian Style Stories and more

<u>SOLOMON STRANGE</u>
THE HAUNTING OF GOSPALL

<u>STEPHEN LAWS</u>
SPECTRE